W9-AJP-361

HARRIS COUNTY PUBLIC LIBRARY

J 741.597 Sta
Star wars rebels cinestory
comic. Spark
DISCARD
$14.99
ocn986237012
First Joe Books edition.

ALSO FROM JOE BOOKS

Disney • Pixar Comics Treasury
Disney Big Hero 6 Cinestory Comic
Disney Gravity Falls Cinestory Comic Volume One
Disney Gravity Falls Cinestory Comic Volume Two
Disney Gravity Falls Cinestory Comic Volume Three
Marvel Thor: Dueling with Giants
Marvel Guardians of the Galaxy: Castaways
Marvel Captain America: Sub Rosa
Marvel Sif: Even Dragons Have Their Endings
Marvel Warriors Three: Godhood's End
Marvel Guardians of the Galaxy: Space Riot
Marvel Iron Man: Mutually Assured Destruction
Marvel Spider-Man: Enemies Closer
Marvel Avengers: The Serpent Society
Disney Darkwing Duck Comics Collection: Orange Is the New Purple
Disney Darkwing Duck Comics Collection: Tales of the Duck Knight

STAR WARS REBELS™

CINESTORY COMIC

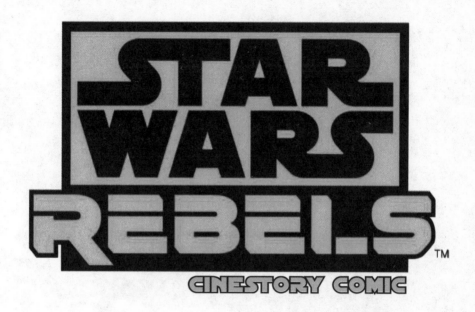

SPARK OF REBELLION

JOE BOOKS LTD

Copyright © 2017 Disney Enterprises, Inc. All rights reserved.
© & ™ 2017 LUCASFILM LTD. Used Under Authorization.

Published simultaneously in the United States and Canada by
Joe Books Ltd, 489 College Street, Toronto, ON M6G 1A5

www.joebooks.com

First Joe Books edition: August 2017

Print ISBN: 978-1-77275-340-0
ebook ISBN: 978-1-77275-484-1

No portion of this publication may be reproduced or transmitted, in any form or
by any means, without the express written permission of the copyright holders.

Names, characters, places, and incidents featured in this publication
are either the product of the author's imagination or are used fictitiously. Any
resemblance to actual persons (living or dead), events, institutions,
or locales, without satiric intent, is coincidental.

Joe Books™ is a trademark of Joe Books Ltd. Joe Books® and the Joe Books logo
are trademarks of Joe Books Ltd, registered in various categories and countries.
All rights reserved.

Library and Archives Canada Cataloguing in Publication
information is available upon request

Printed and bound in Canada
1 3 5 7 9 10 8 6 4 2

CONTENTS

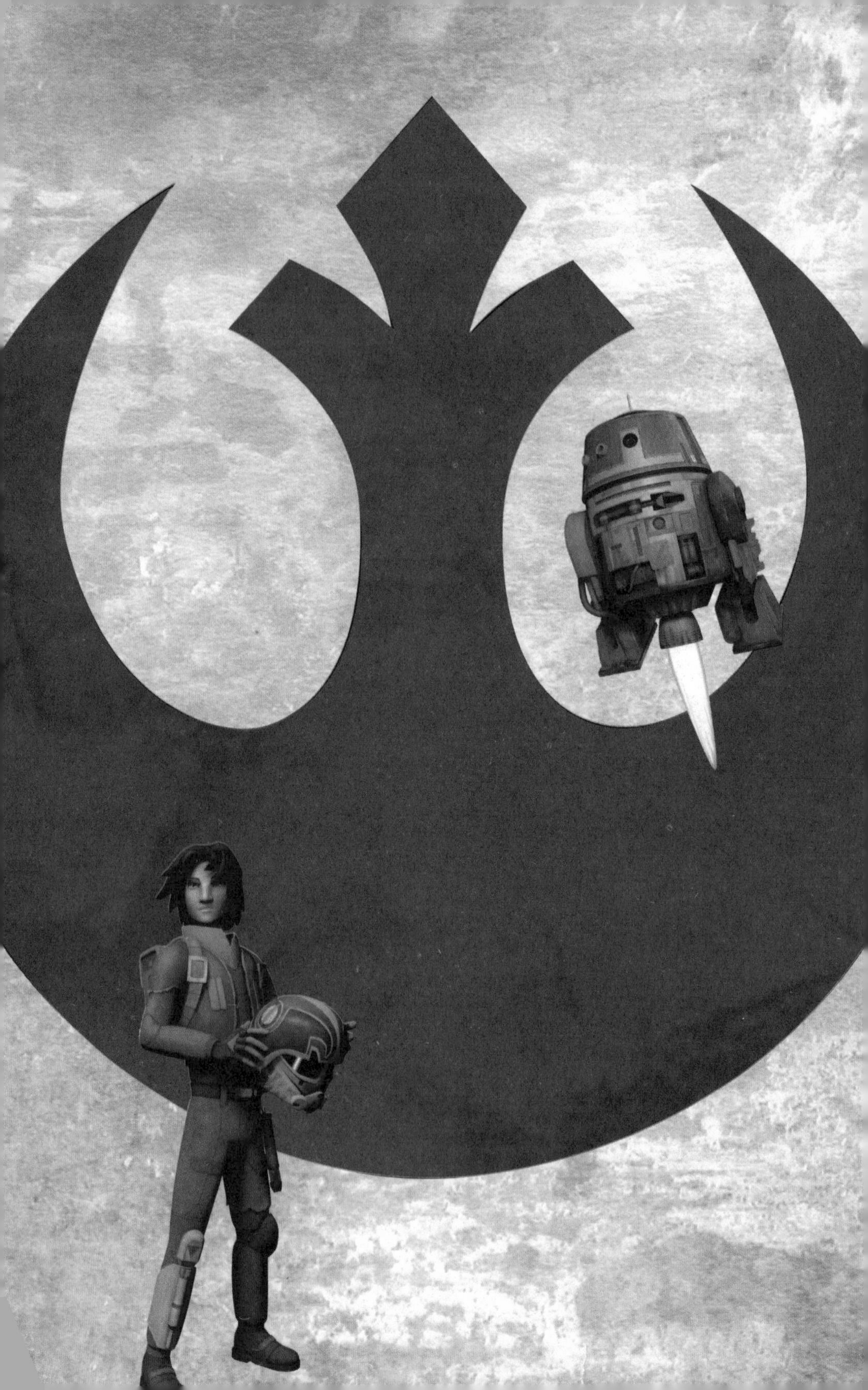

STAR WARS REBELS™

SPARK OF REBELLION

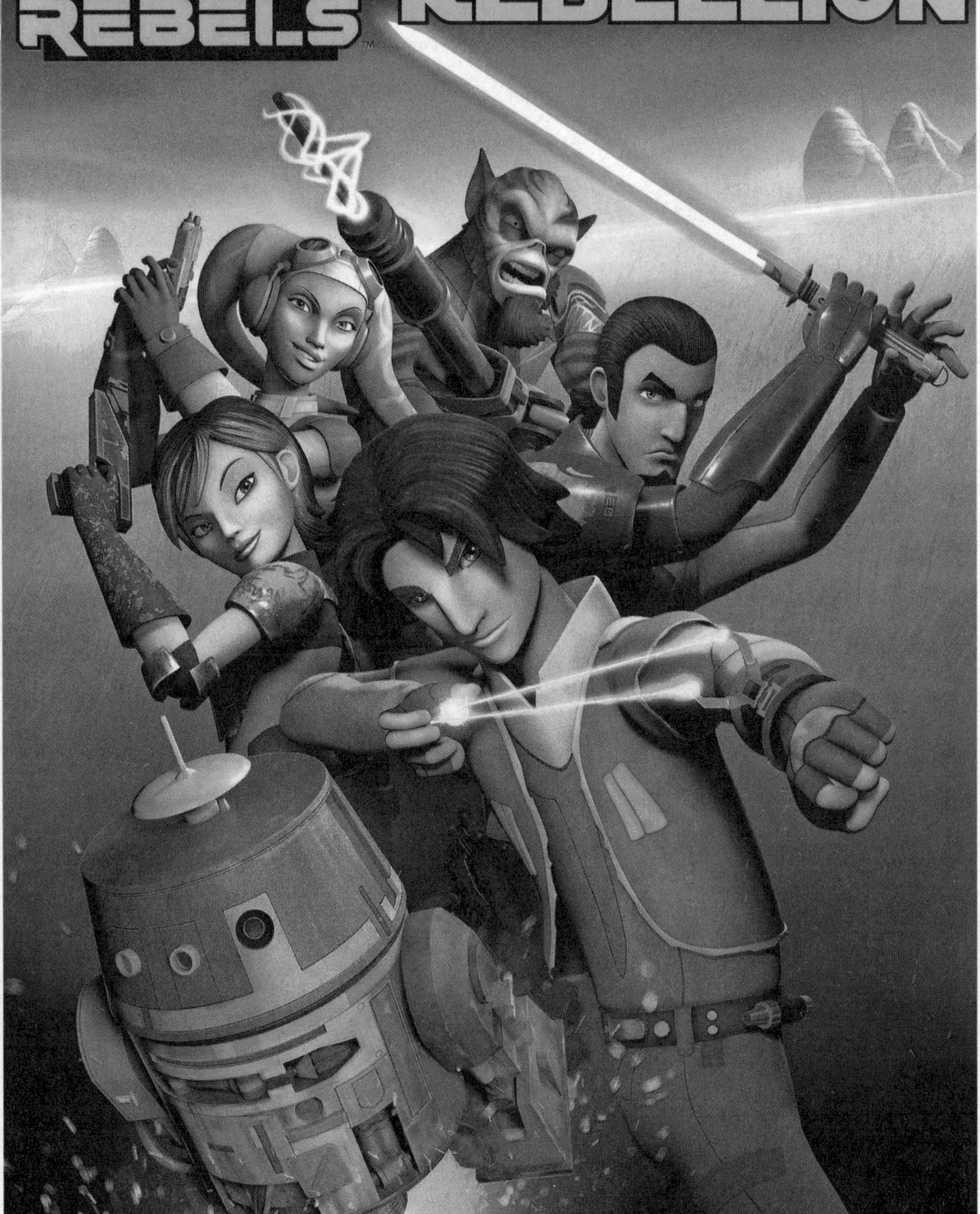

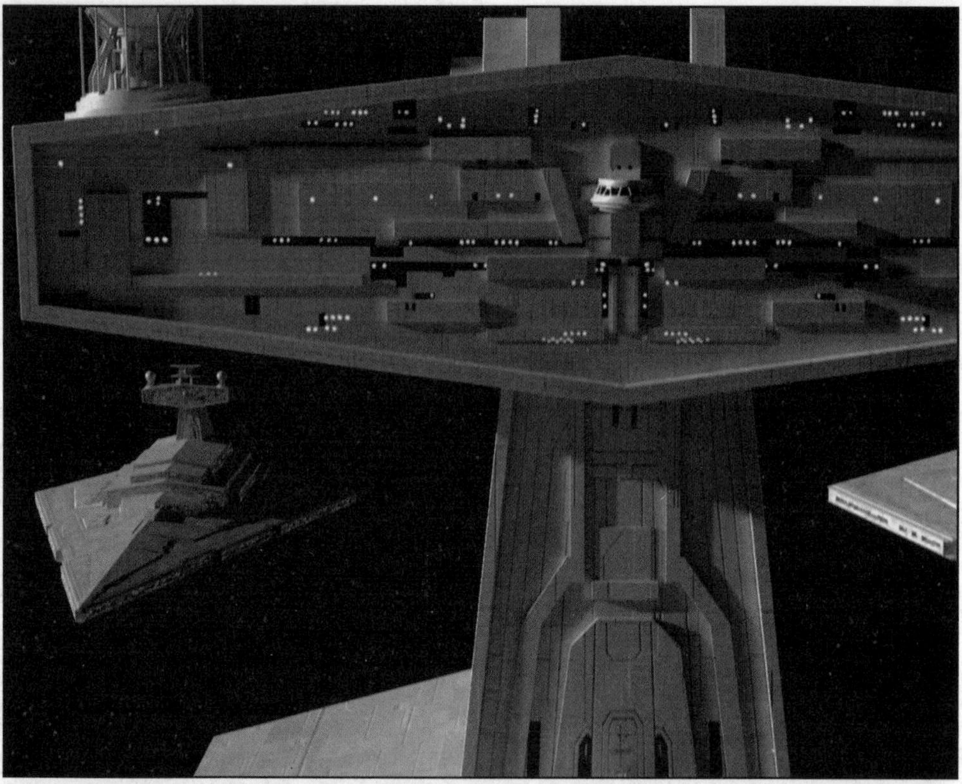

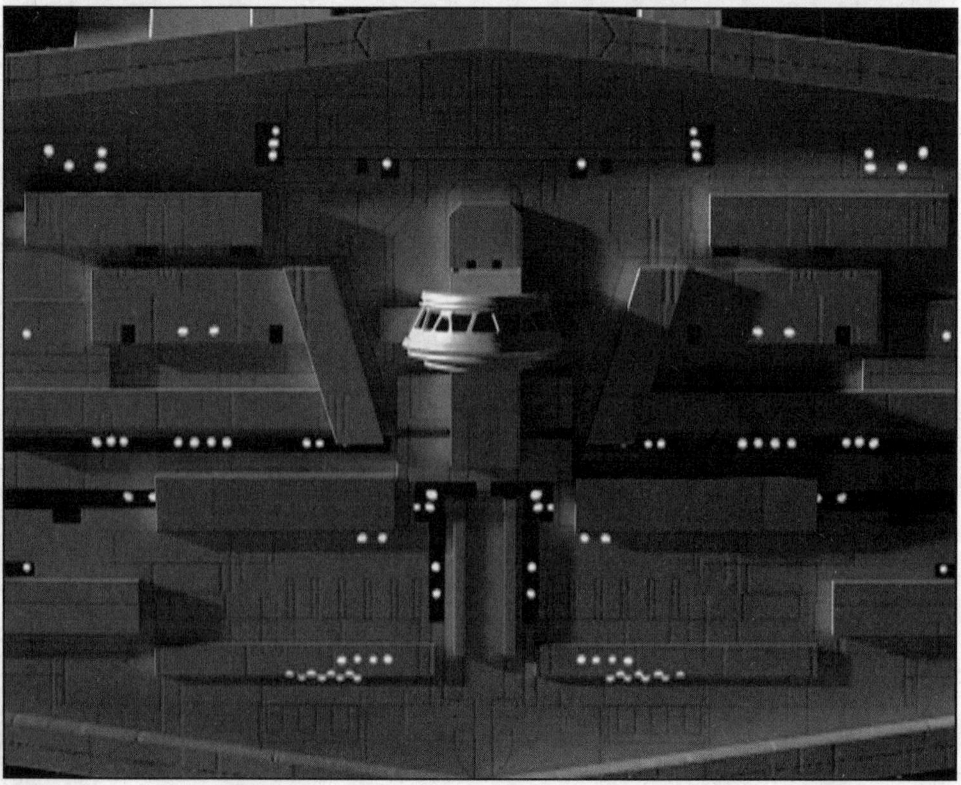

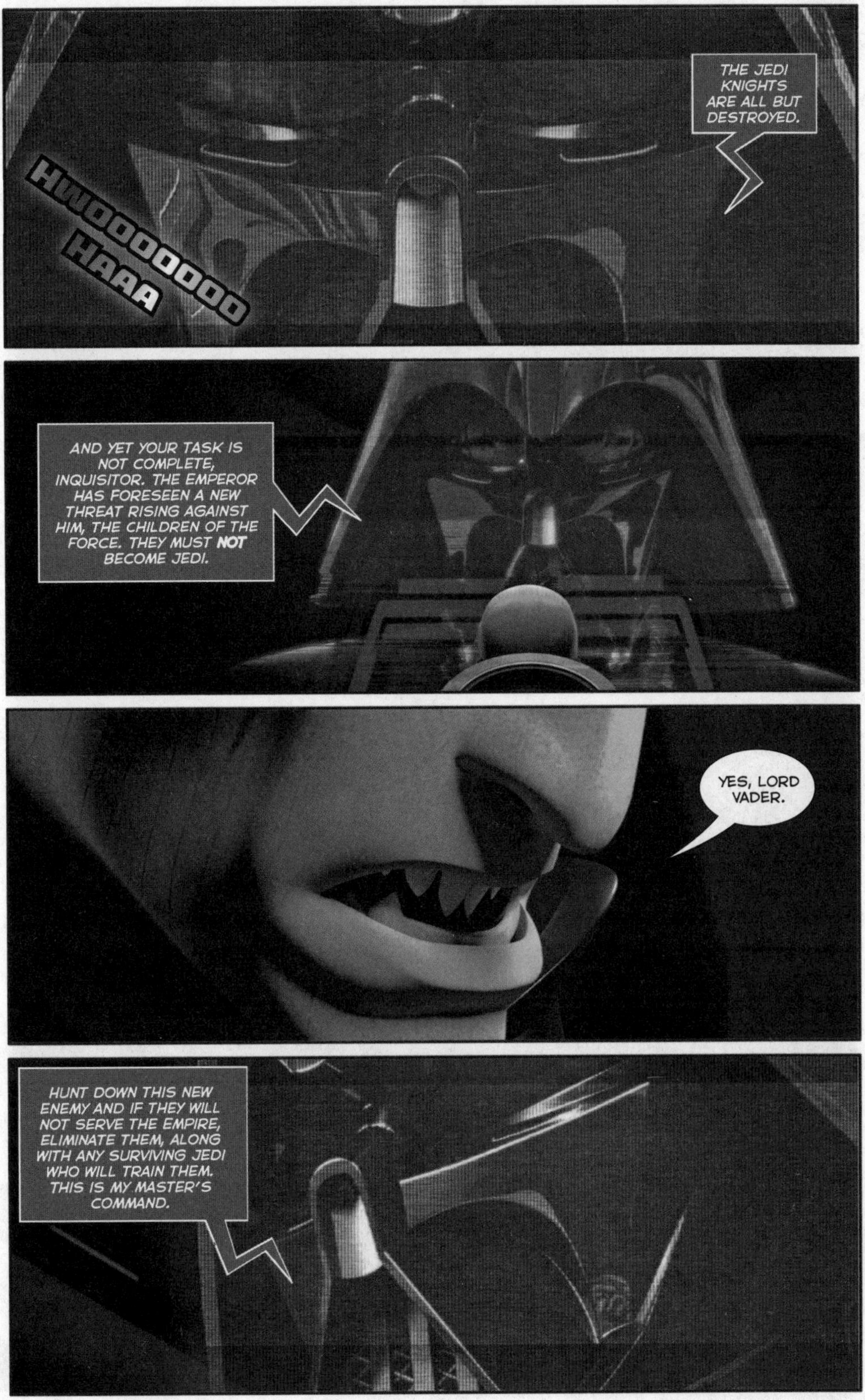
THE JEDI KNIGHTS ARE ALL BUT DESTROYED.
HWOOOOOOO HAAA
AND YET YOUR TASK IS NOT COMPLETE, INQUISITOR. THE EMPEROR HAS FORESEEN A NEW THREAT RISING AGAINST HIM, THE CHILDREN OF THE FORCE. THEY MUST **NOT** BECOME JEDI.
YES, LORD VADER.
HUNT DOWN THIS NEW ENEMY AND IF THEY WILL NOT SERVE THE EMPIRE, ELIMINATE THEM, ALONG WITH ANY SURVIVING JEDI WHO WILL TRAIN THEM. THIS IS MY MASTER'S COMMAND.

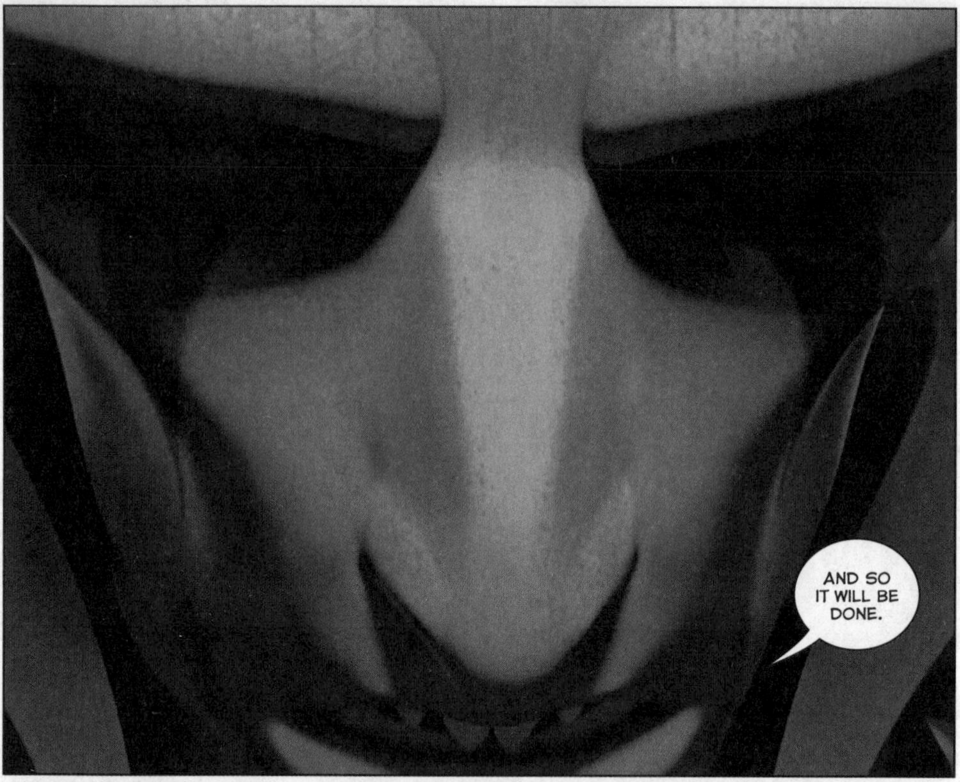
AND SO IT WILL BE DONE.

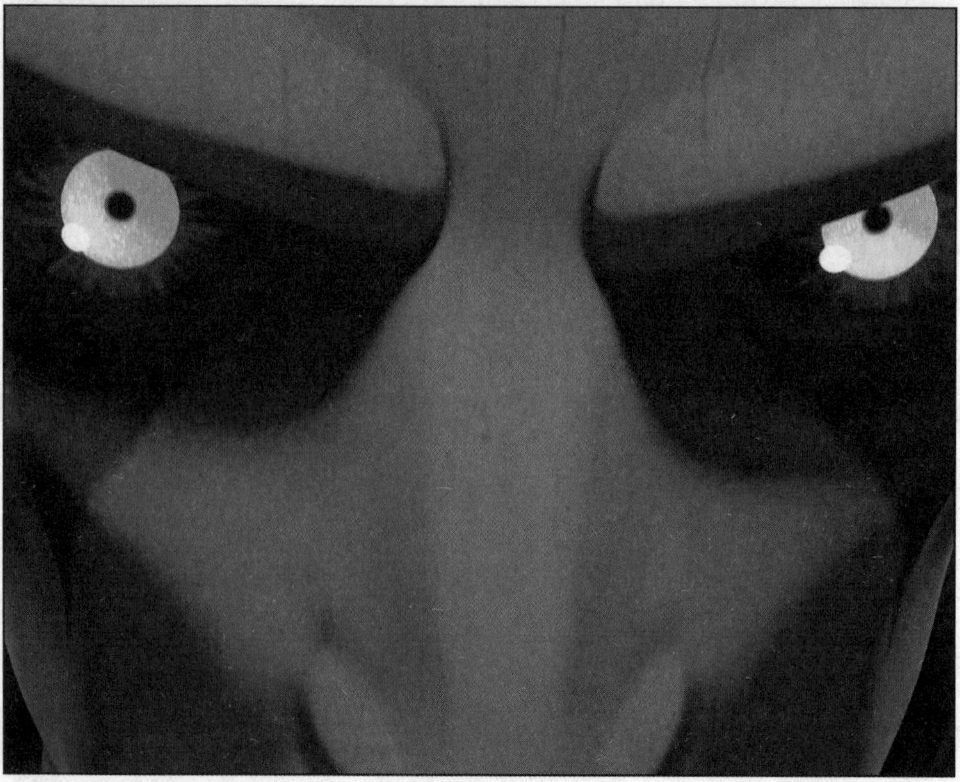

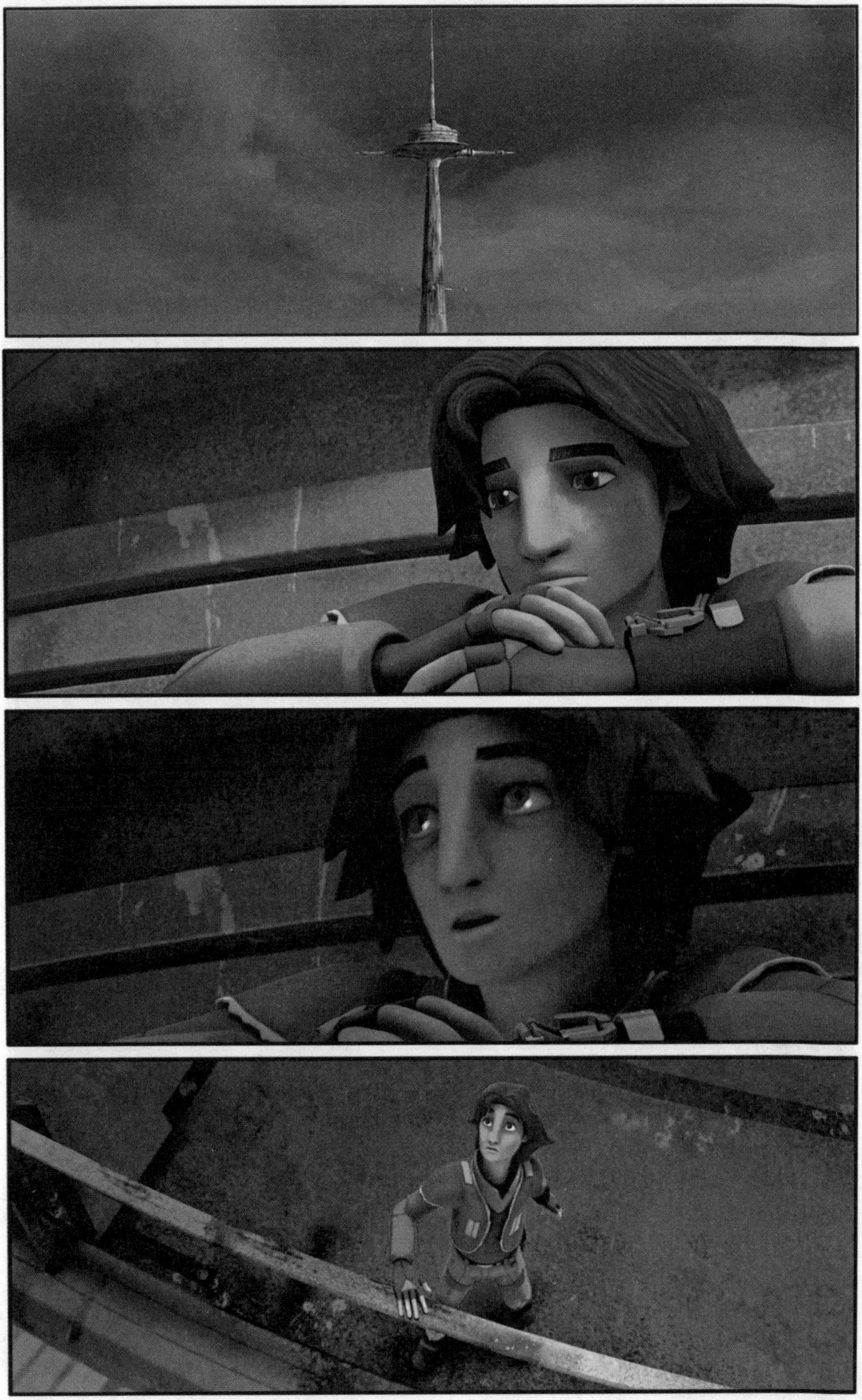

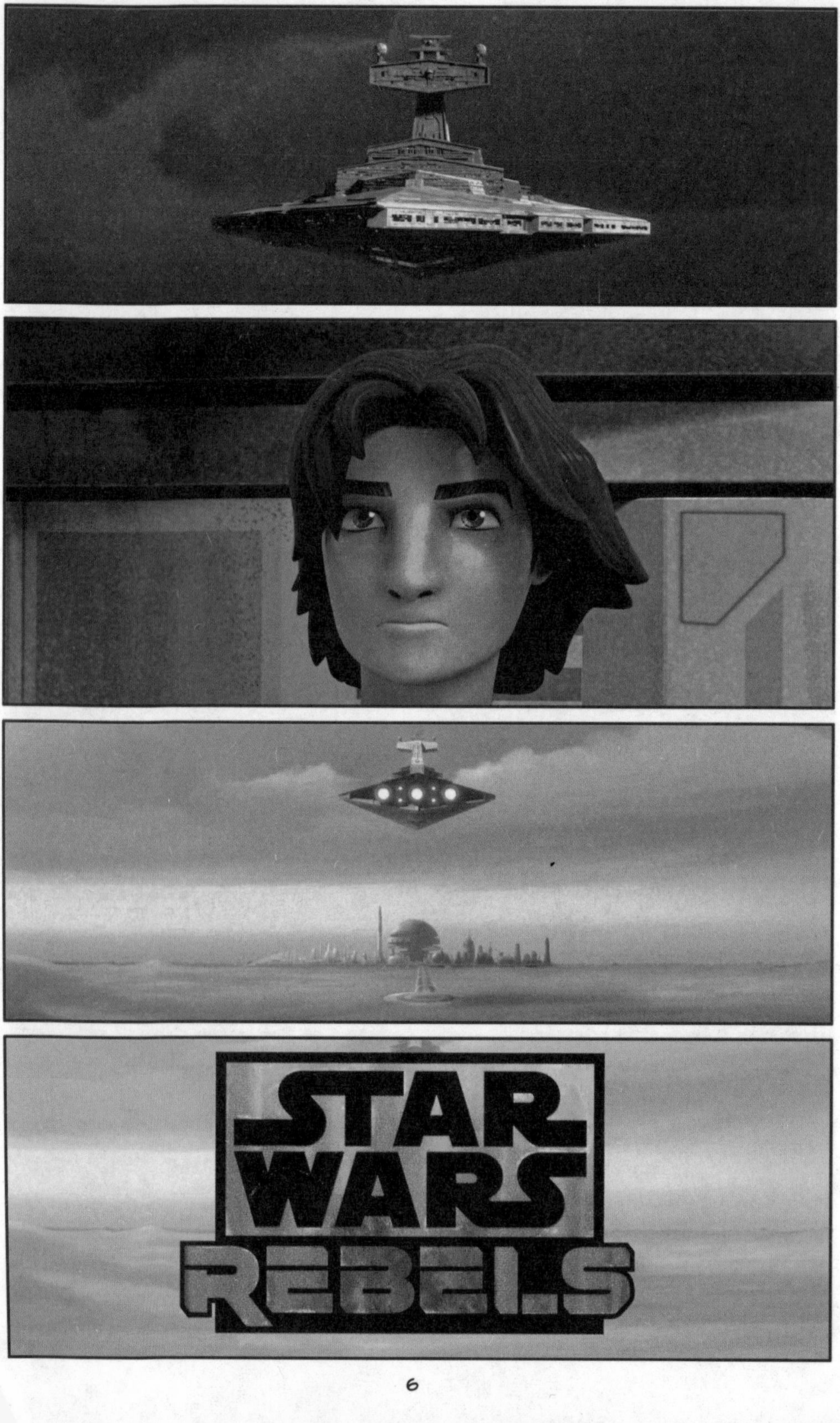
STAR WARS
REBELS

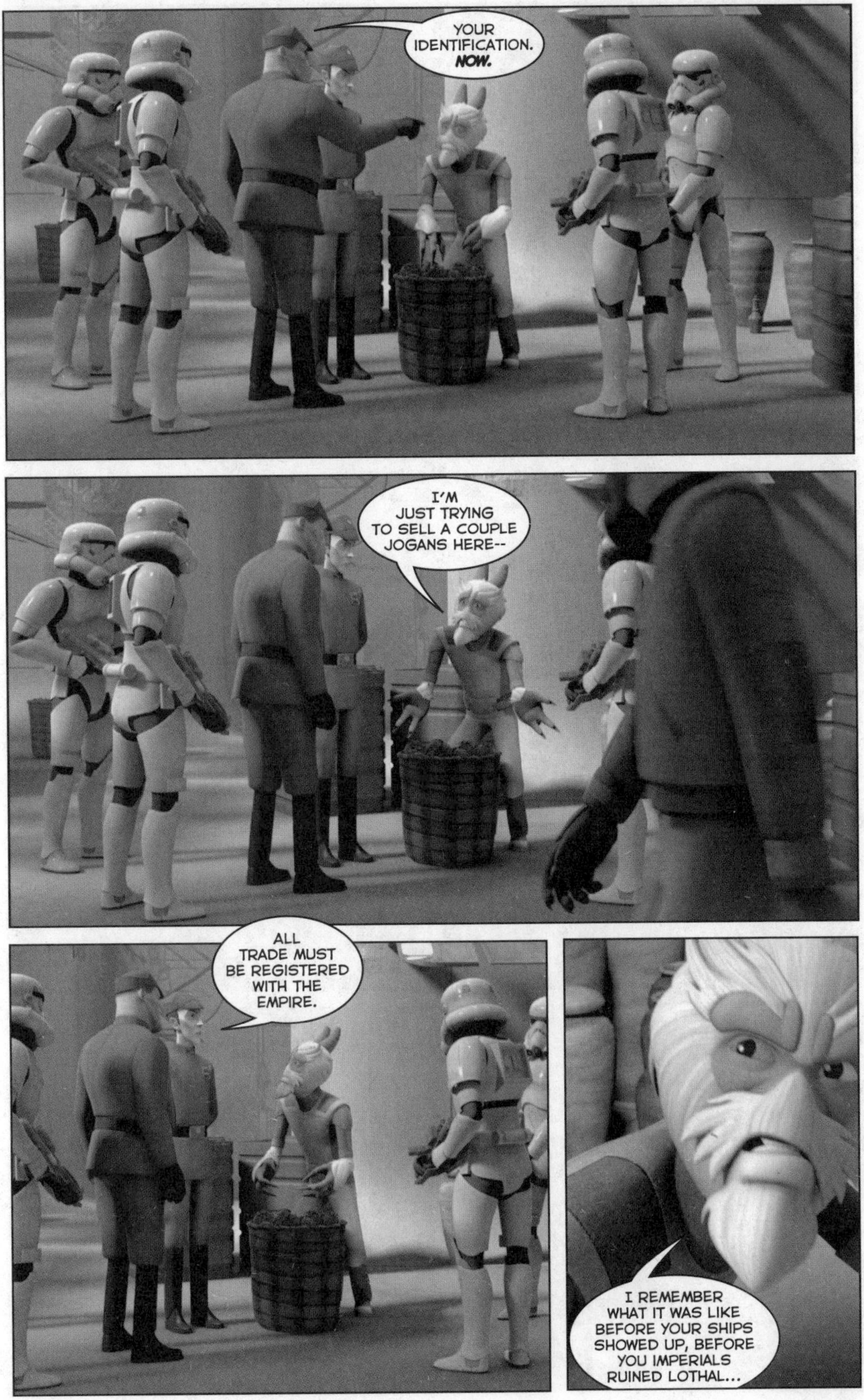

YOUR IDENTIFICATION. ***NOW.***
I'M JUST TRYING TO SELL A COUPLE JOGANS HERE--
ALL TRADE MUST BE REGISTERED WITH THE EMPIRE.
I REMEMBER WHAT IT WAS LIKE BEFORE YOUR SHIPS SHOWED UP, BEFORE YOU IMPERIALS RUINED LOTHAL...

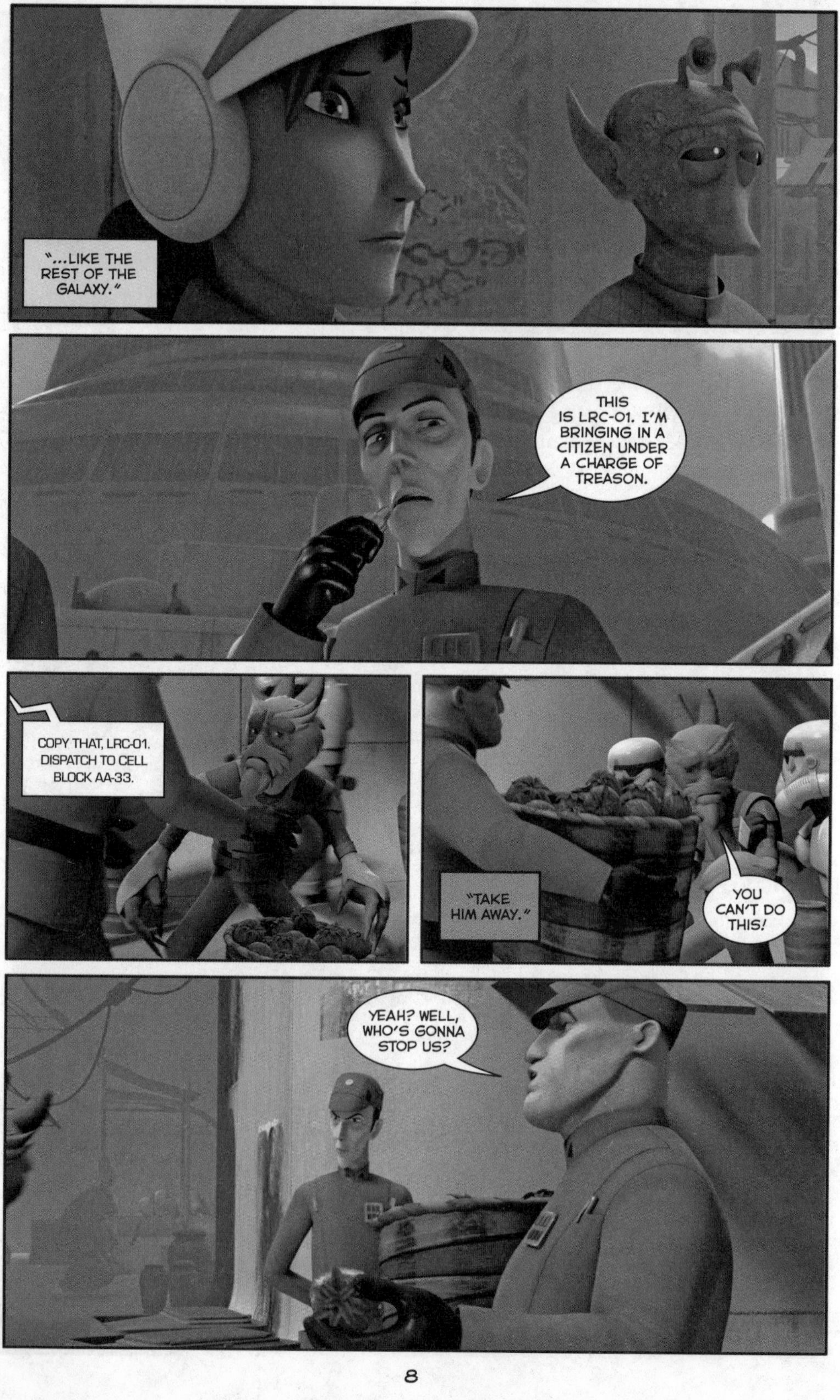
"...LIKE THE REST OF THE GALAXY."
THIS IS LRC-01. I'M BRINGING IN A CITIZEN UNDER A CHARGE OF TREASON.
COPY THAT, LRC-01. DISPATCH TO CELL BLOCK AA-33.
"TAKE HIM AWAY."
YOU CAN'T DO THIS!
YEAH? WELL, WHO'S GONNA STOP US?

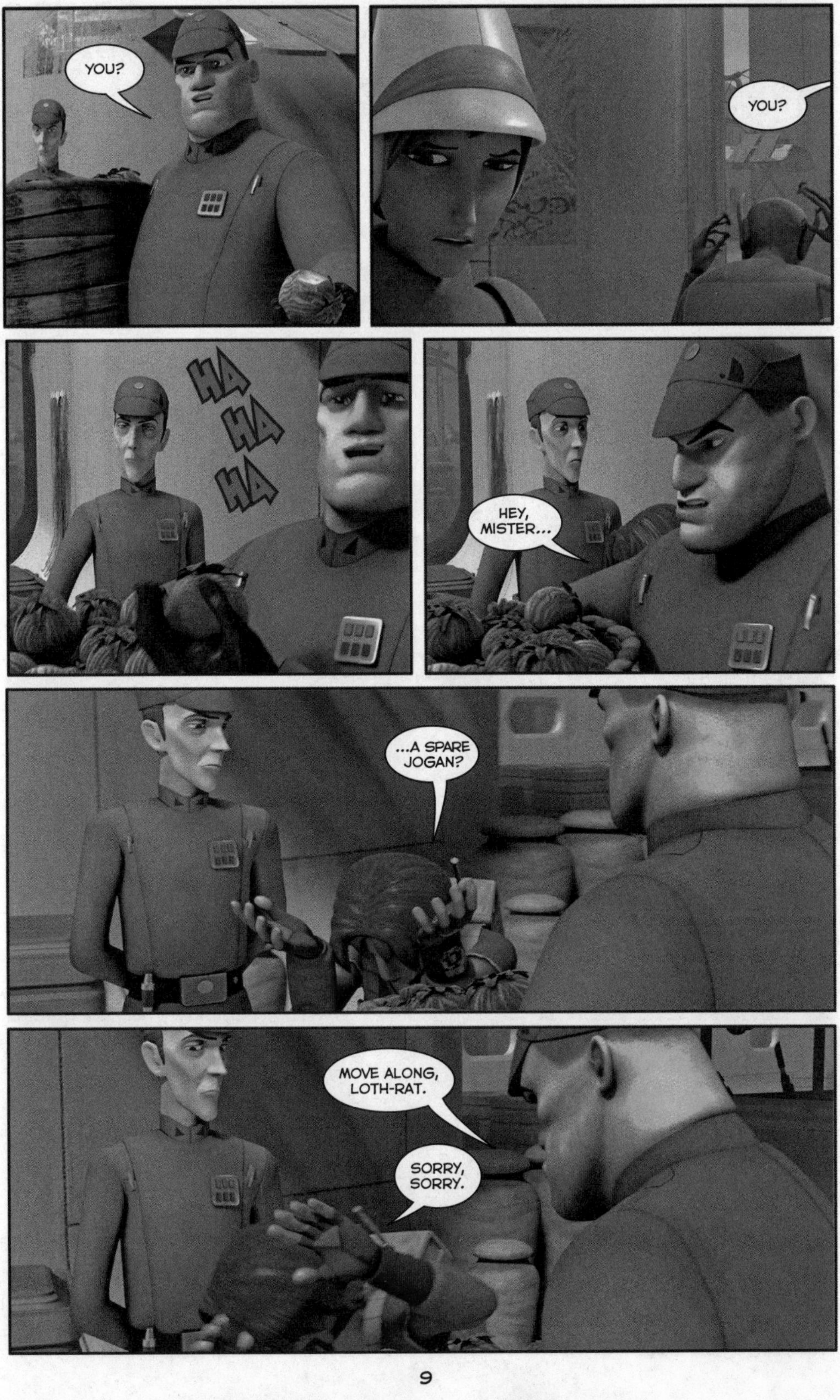
YOU?
YOU?
HA HA HA
HEY, MISTER...
...A SPARE JOGAN?
MOVE ALONG, LOTH-RAT.
SORRY, SORRY.

NOT LOOKING FOR TROUBLE...

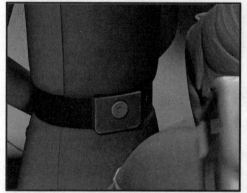

...BUT IT SURE HAS A WAY OF FINDING *ME.*

ALL OFFICERS TO THE MAIN SQUARE! THIS IS A CODE RED EMERGENCY.

IT'S YOUR LUCKY DAY, LOTHAL SCUM.

YOU TWO, COME WITH US!

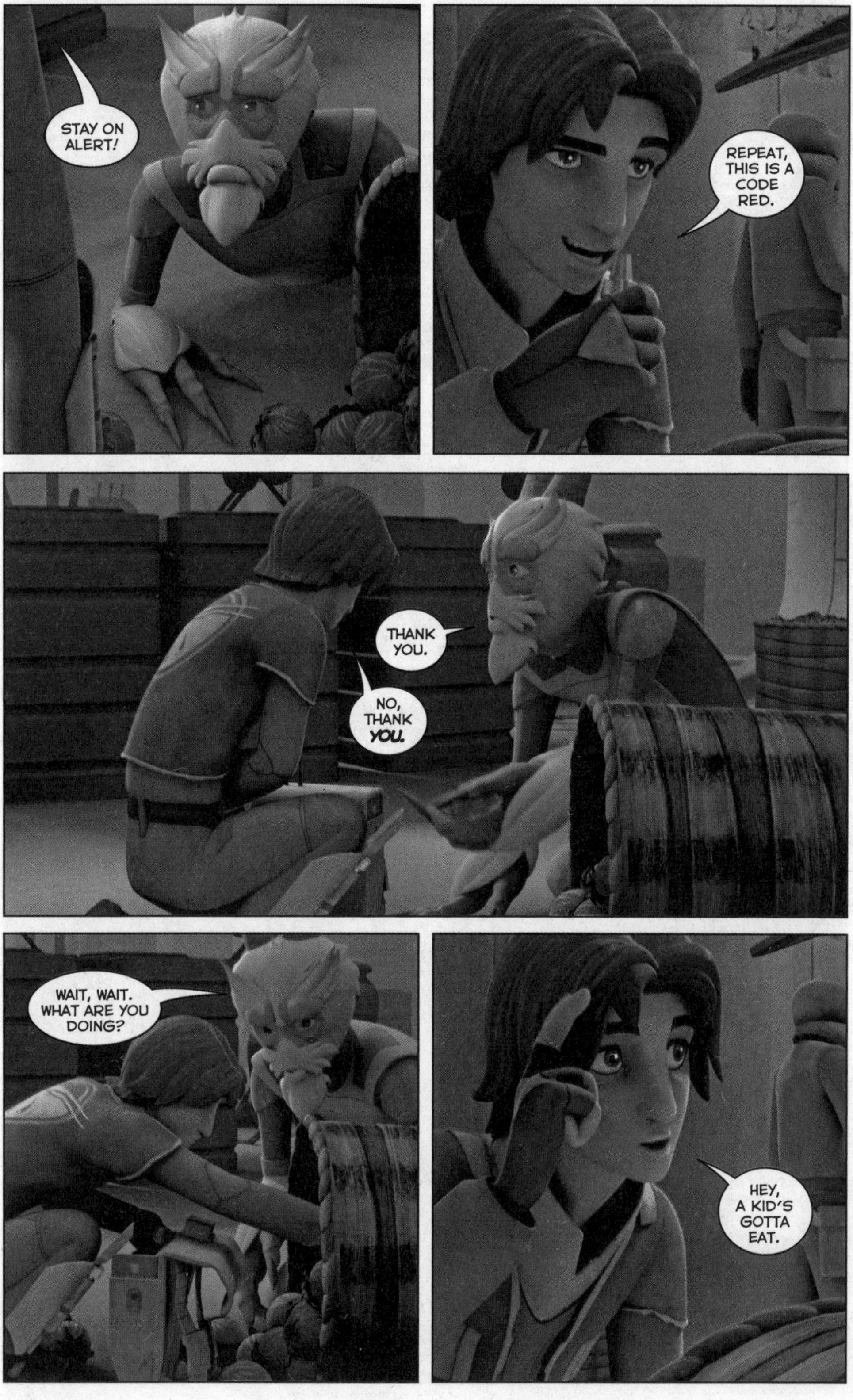
STAY ON ALERT!
REPEAT, THIS IS A CODE RED.
THANK YOU.
NO, THANK *YOU.*
WAIT, WAIT. WHAT ARE YOU DOING?
HEY, A KID'S GOTTA EAT.

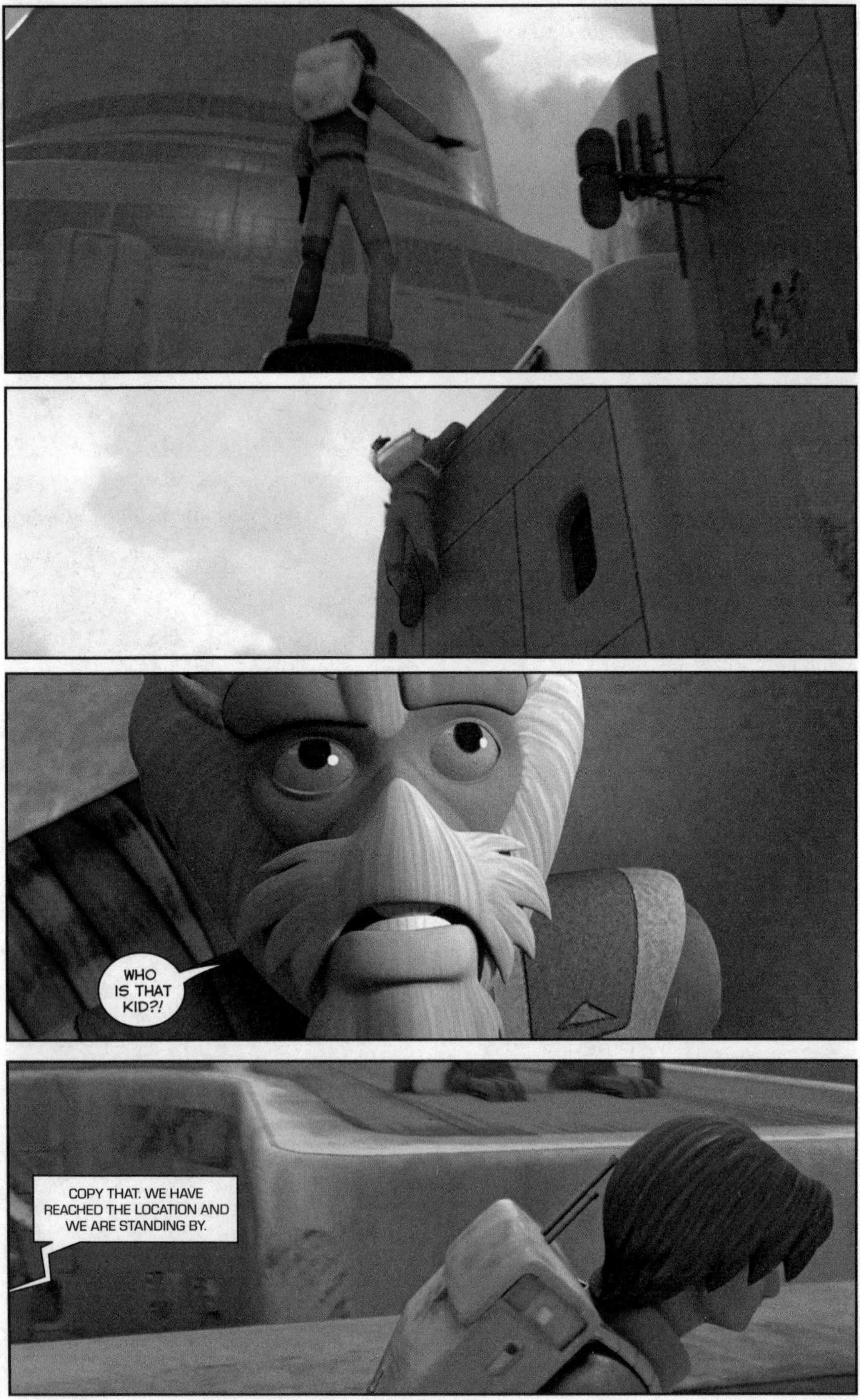
WHO IS THAT KID?!
COPY THAT. WE HAVE REACHED THE LOCATION AND WE ARE STANDING BY.

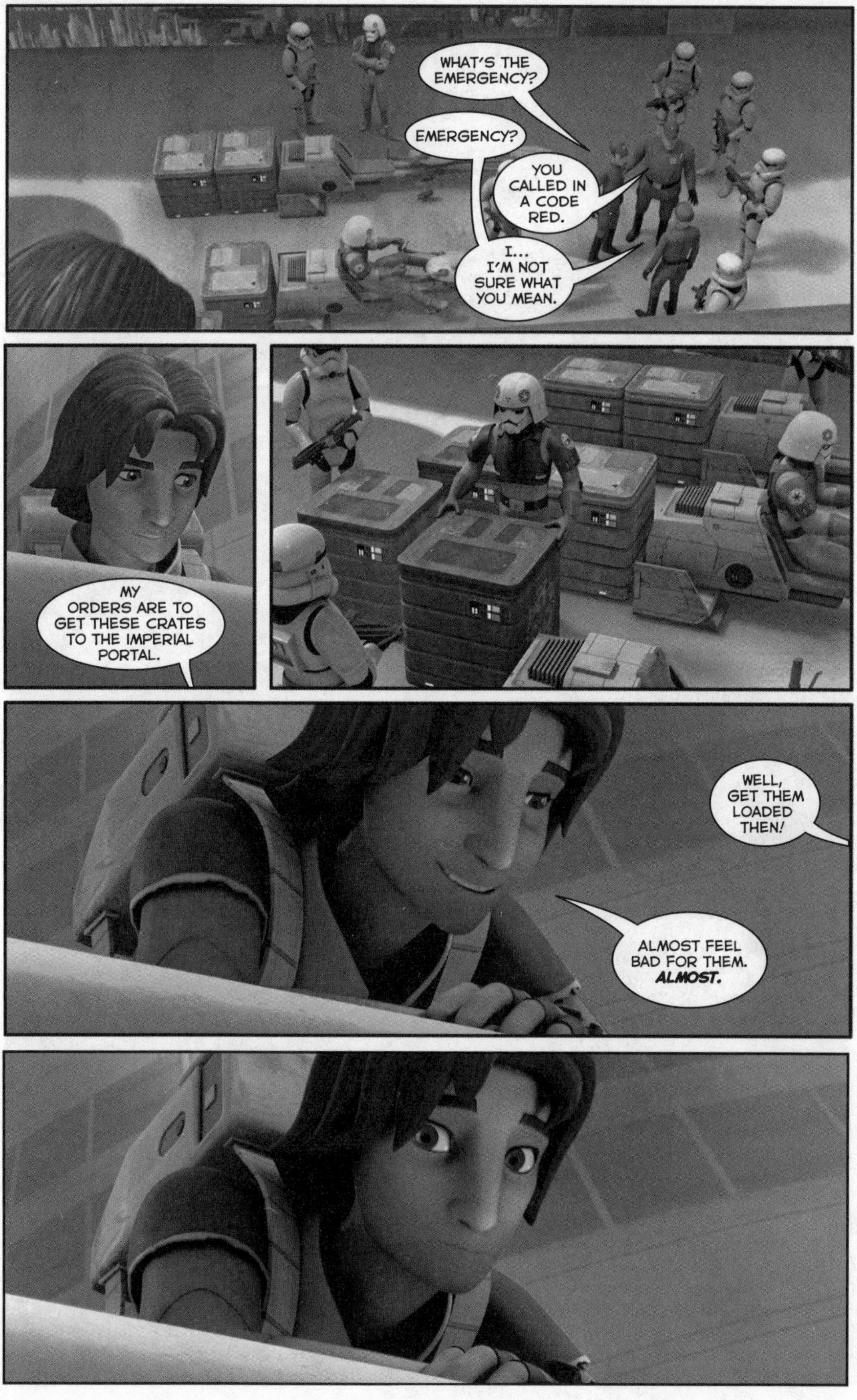
WHAT'S THE EMERGENCY?
EMERGENCY?
YOU CALLED IN A CODE RED.
I... I'M NOT SURE WHAT YOU MEAN.
MY ORDERS ARE TO GET THESE CRATES TO THE IMPERIAL PORTAL.
WELL, GET THEM LOADED THEN!
ALMOST FEEL BAD FOR THEM. ***ALMOST.***

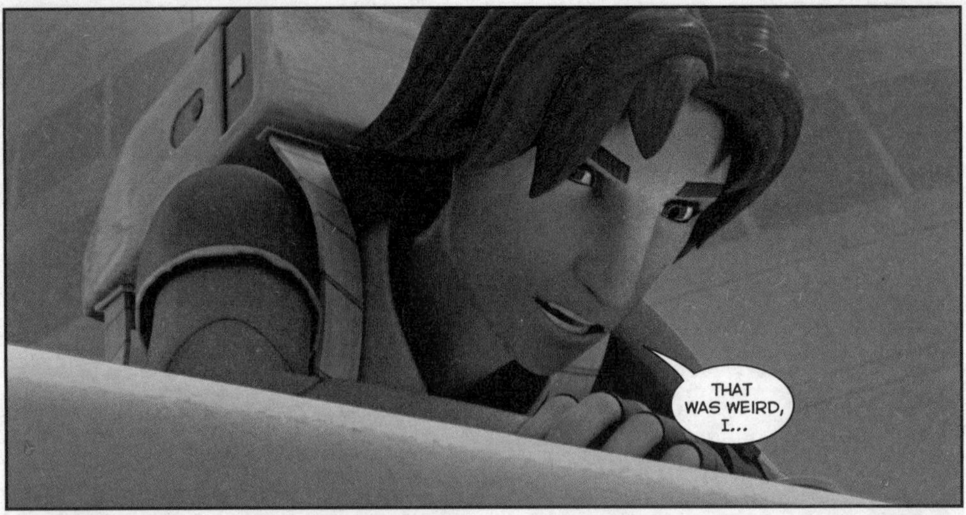
THAT WAS WEIRD, I...

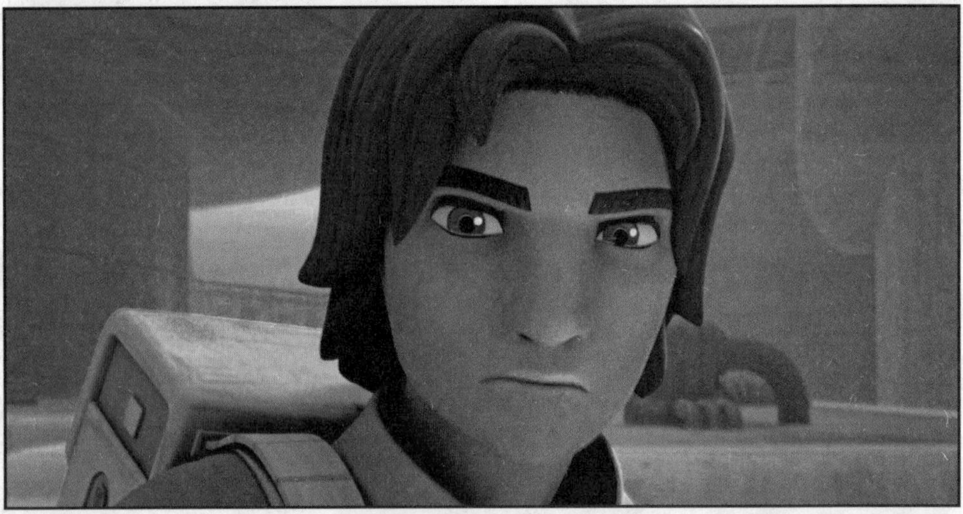

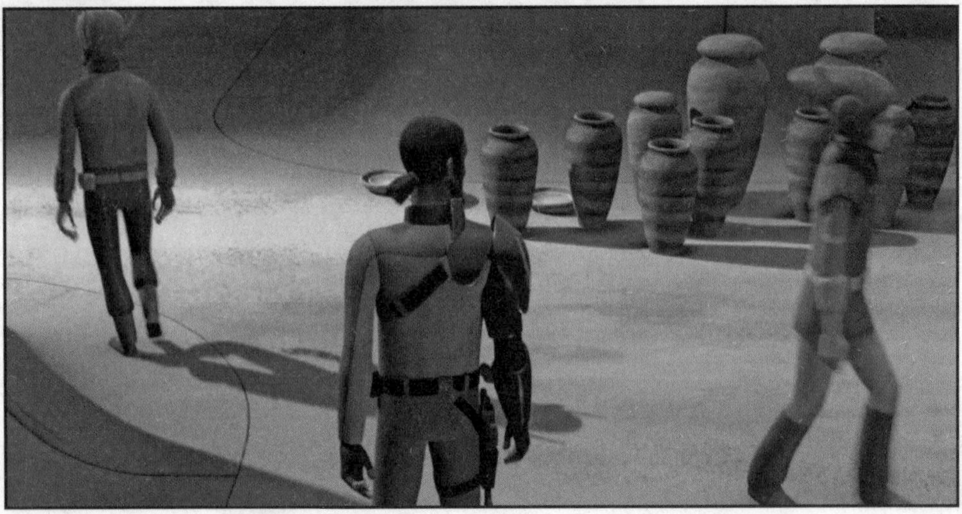

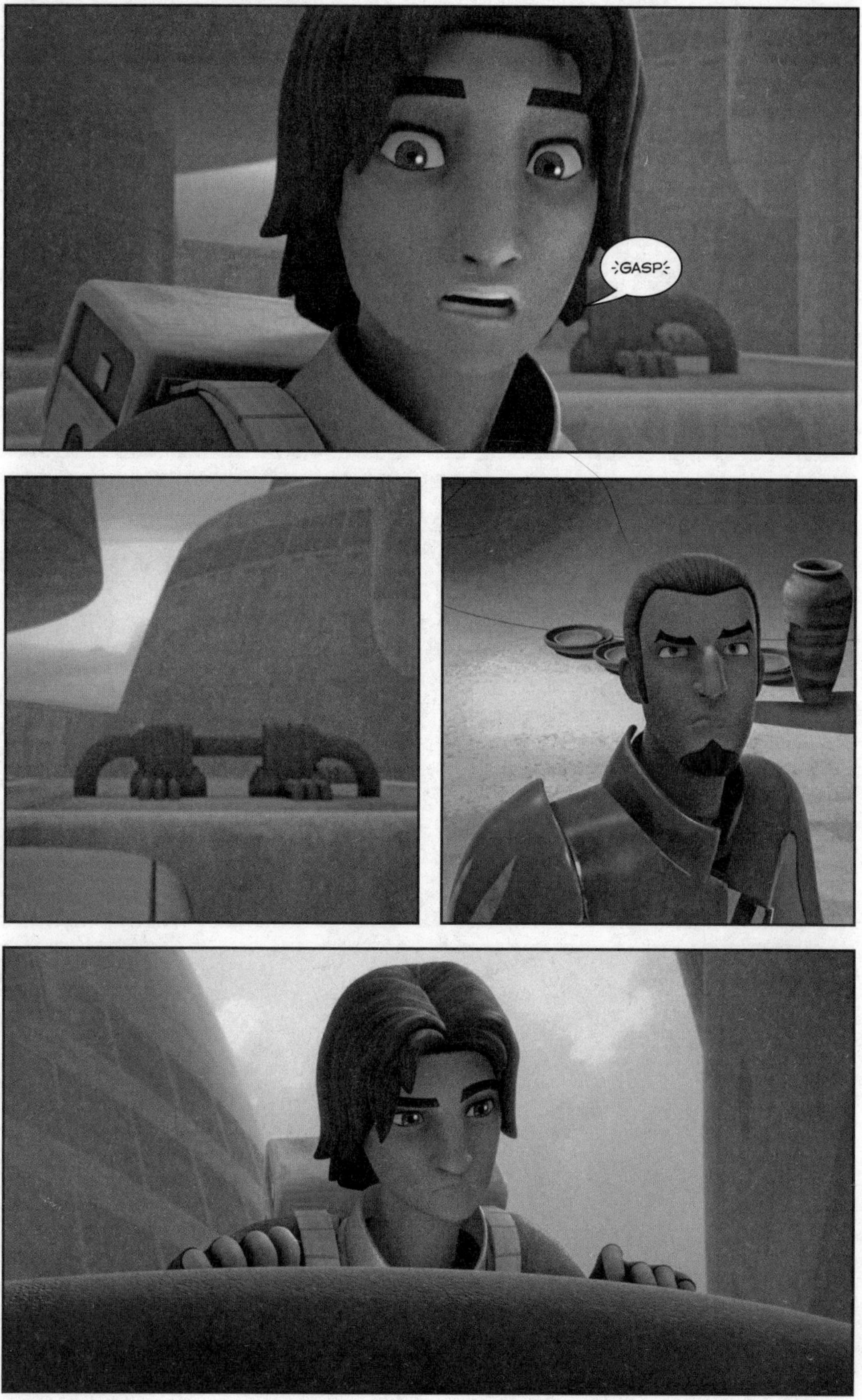
GASP

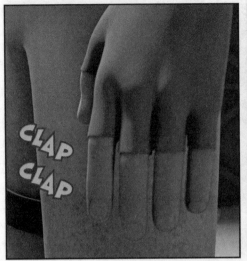

CLAP
CLAP

CLAP
CLAP
CLAP
CLAP
CLAP
INTERESTING...
WSSH
BEEEEP
BEEEEP

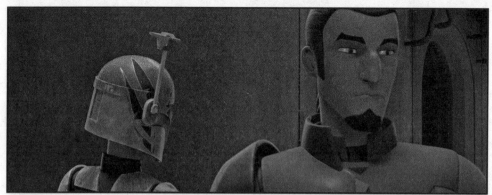

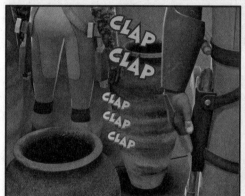

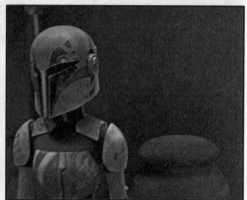

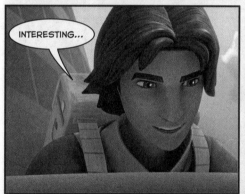

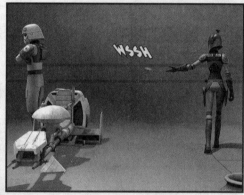

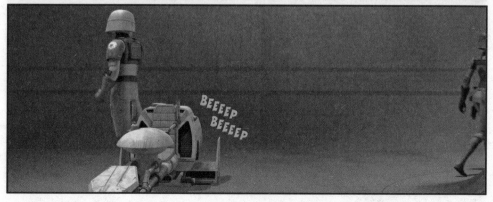

BEEEP. BEEEP. BEEEP. BEEEP

BOOM

GET THOSE CRATES OUT OF HERE! KEEP THEM SECURE AT ALL COSTS!

"ALL COSTS," HUH? I LIKE THE SOUND OF THAT.

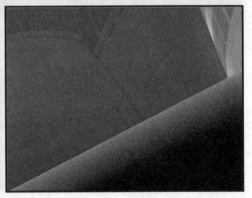

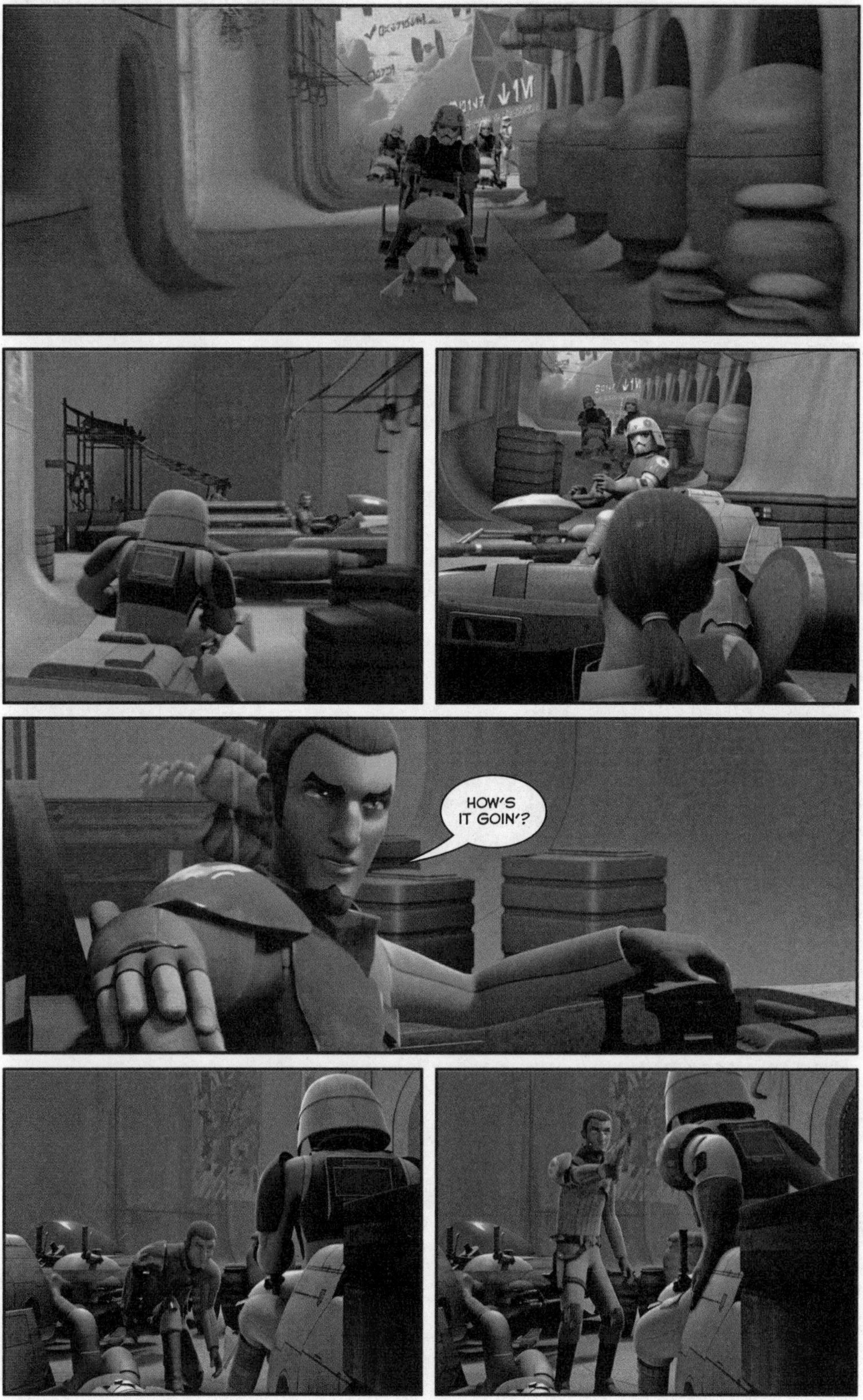
HOW'S IT GOIN'?

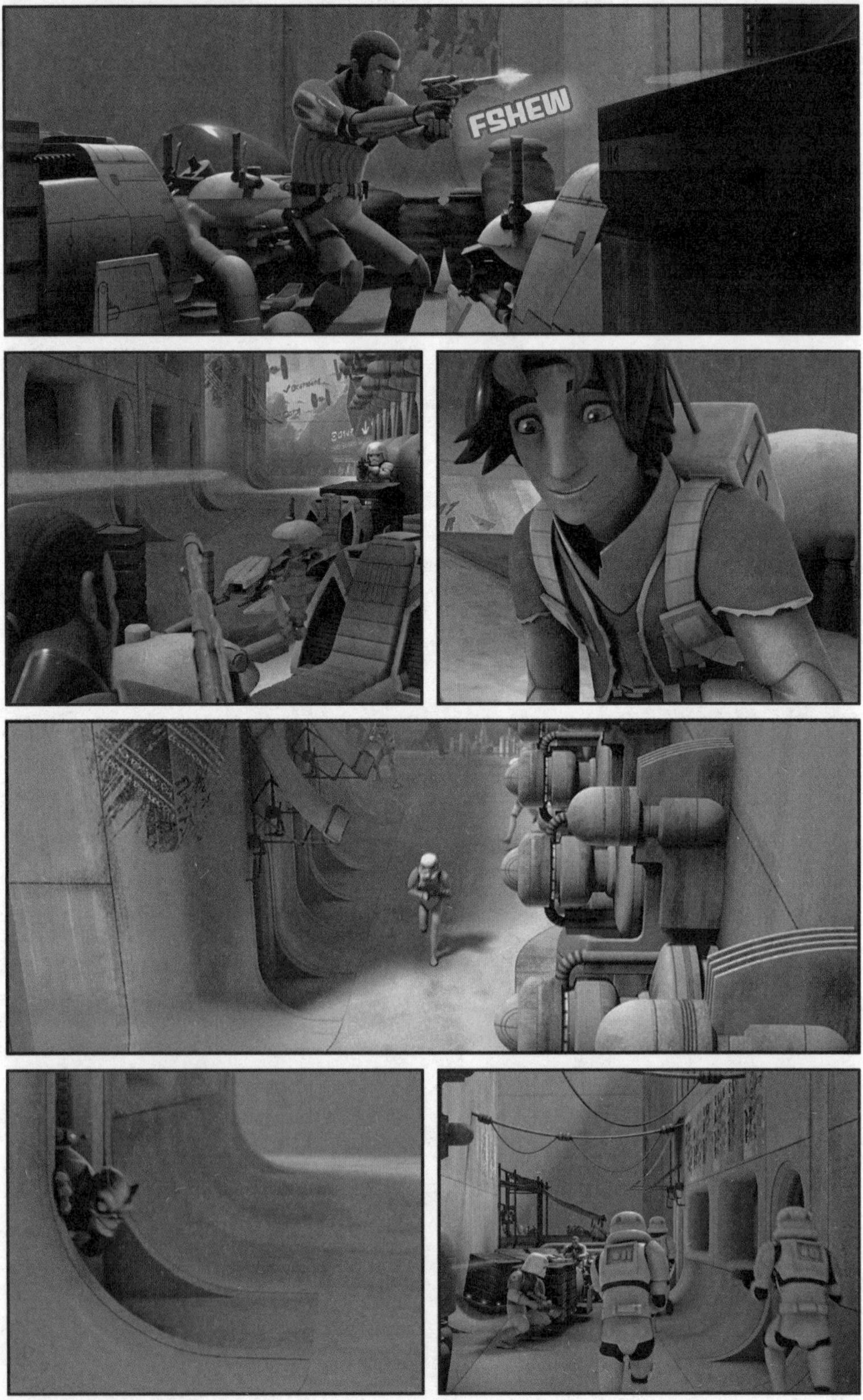
FSHEW

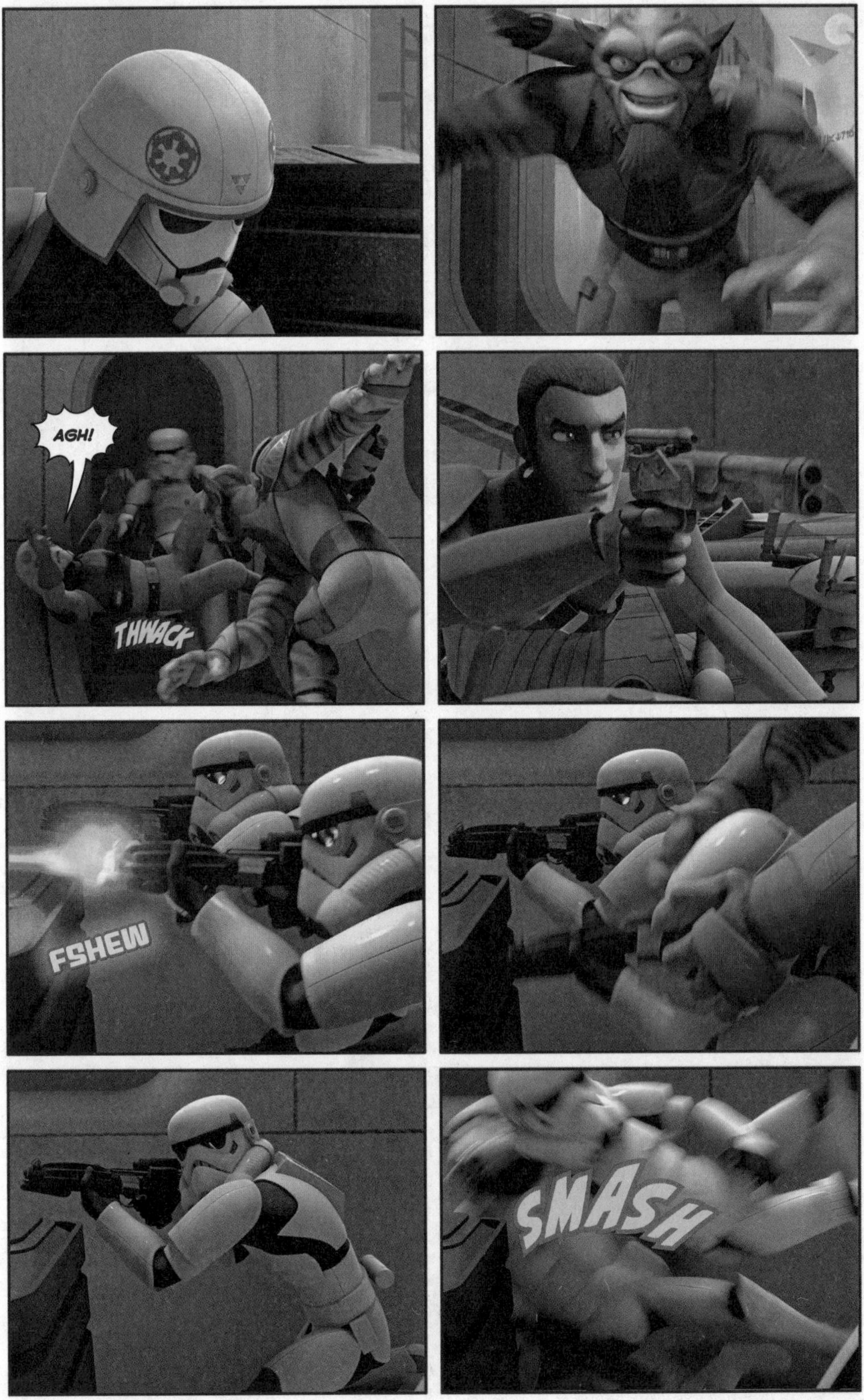
AGH!
THWACK
FSHEW
SMASH

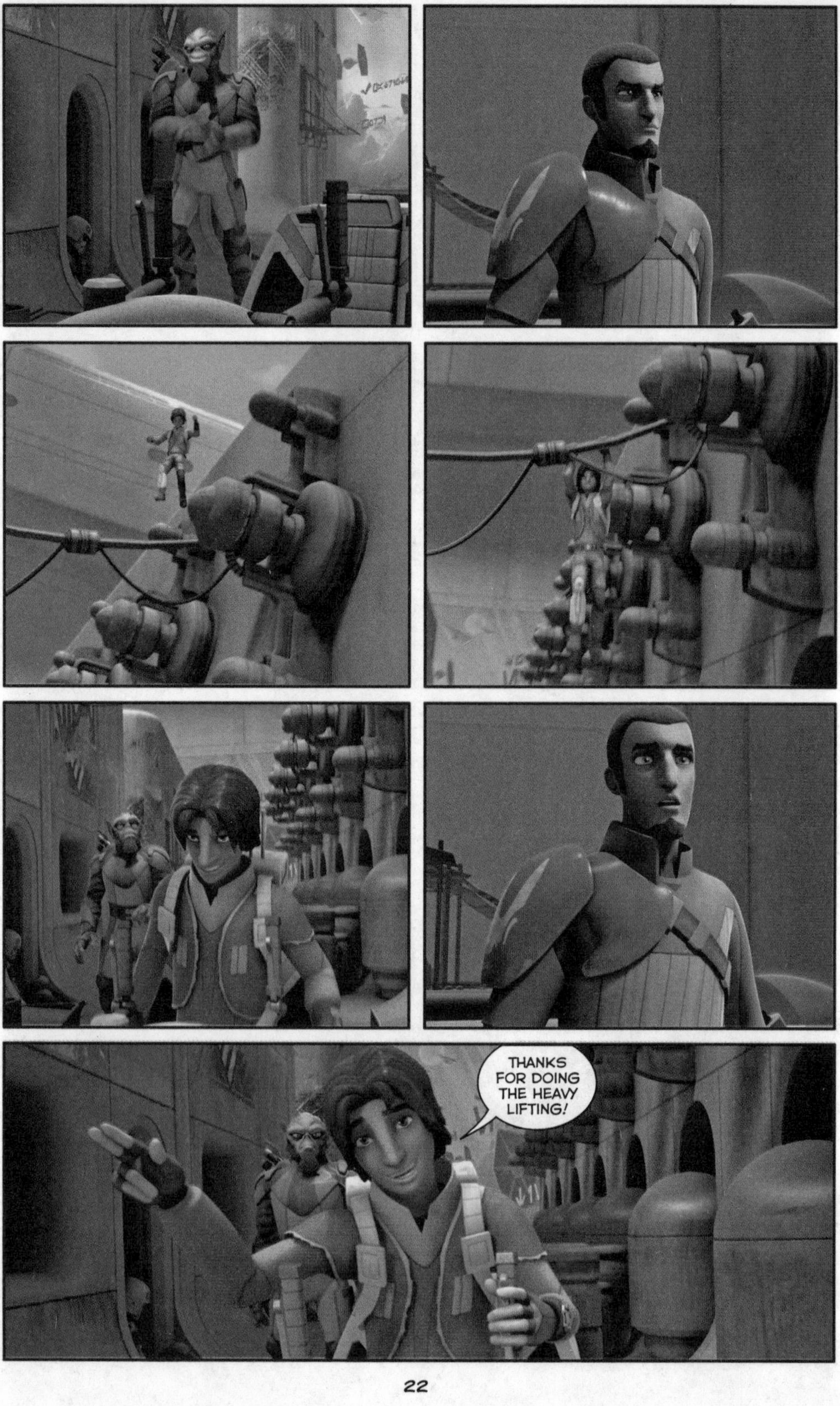
THANKS FOR DOING THE HEAVY LIFTING!

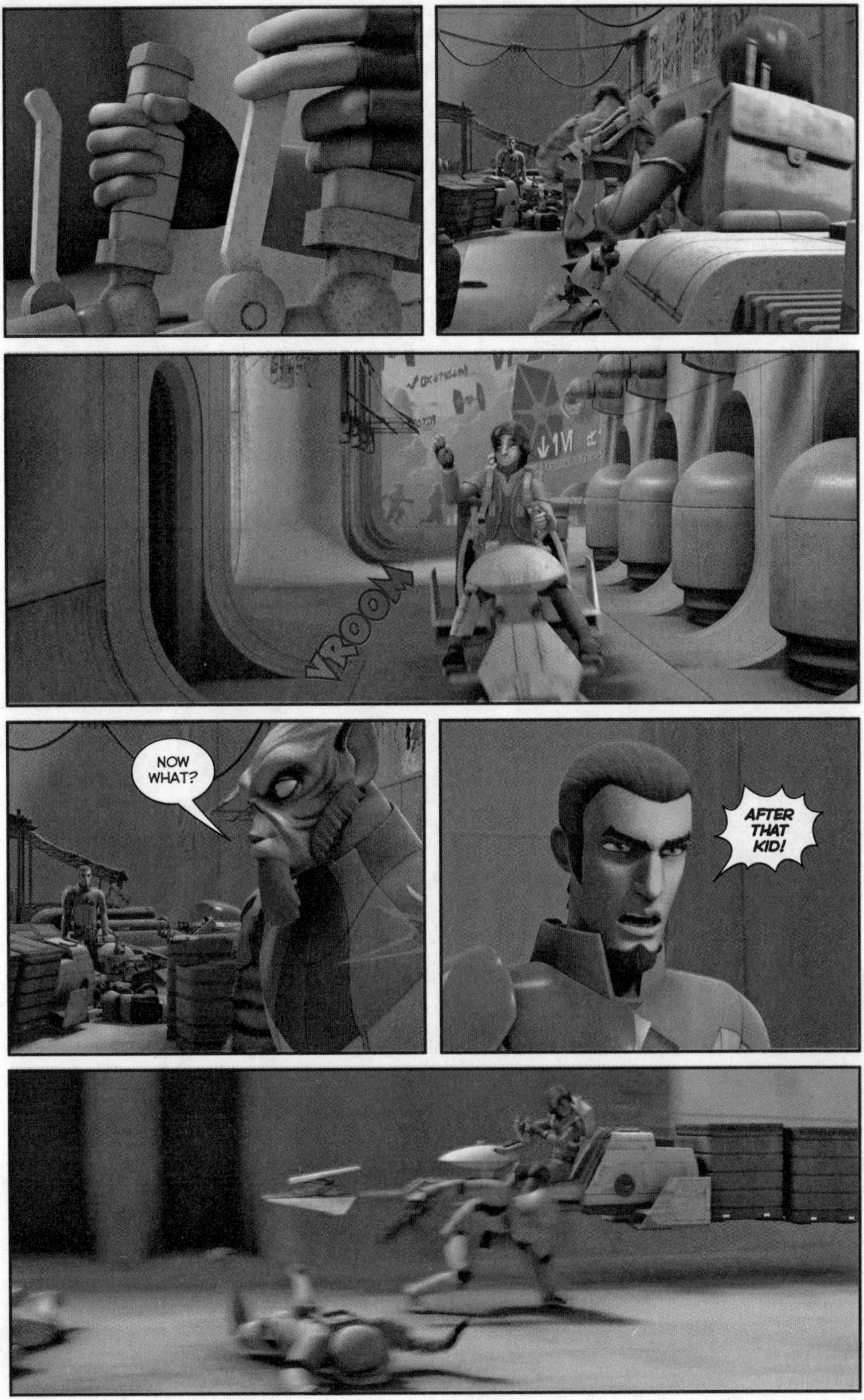
VROOM
NOW WHAT?
AFTER THAT KID!

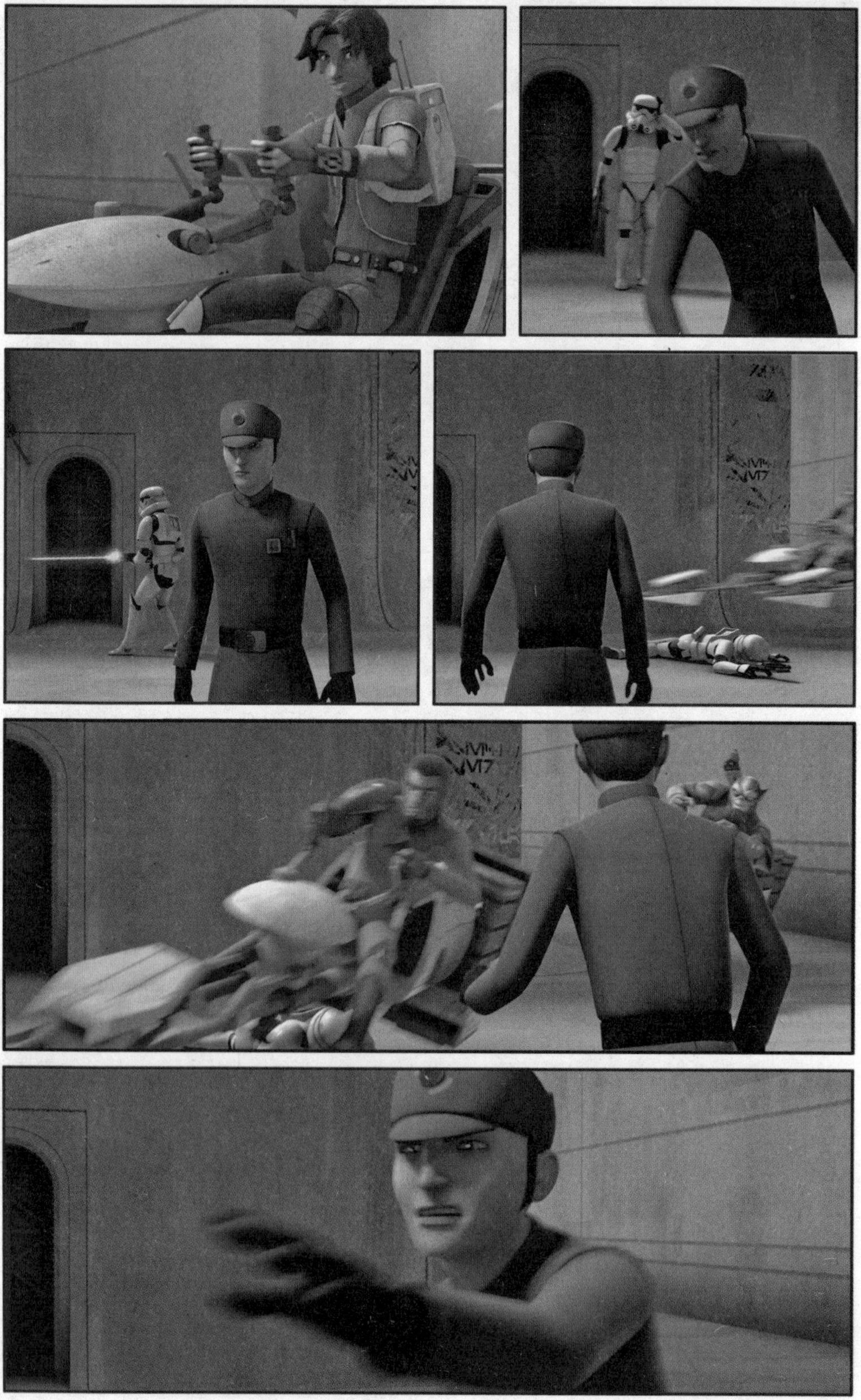

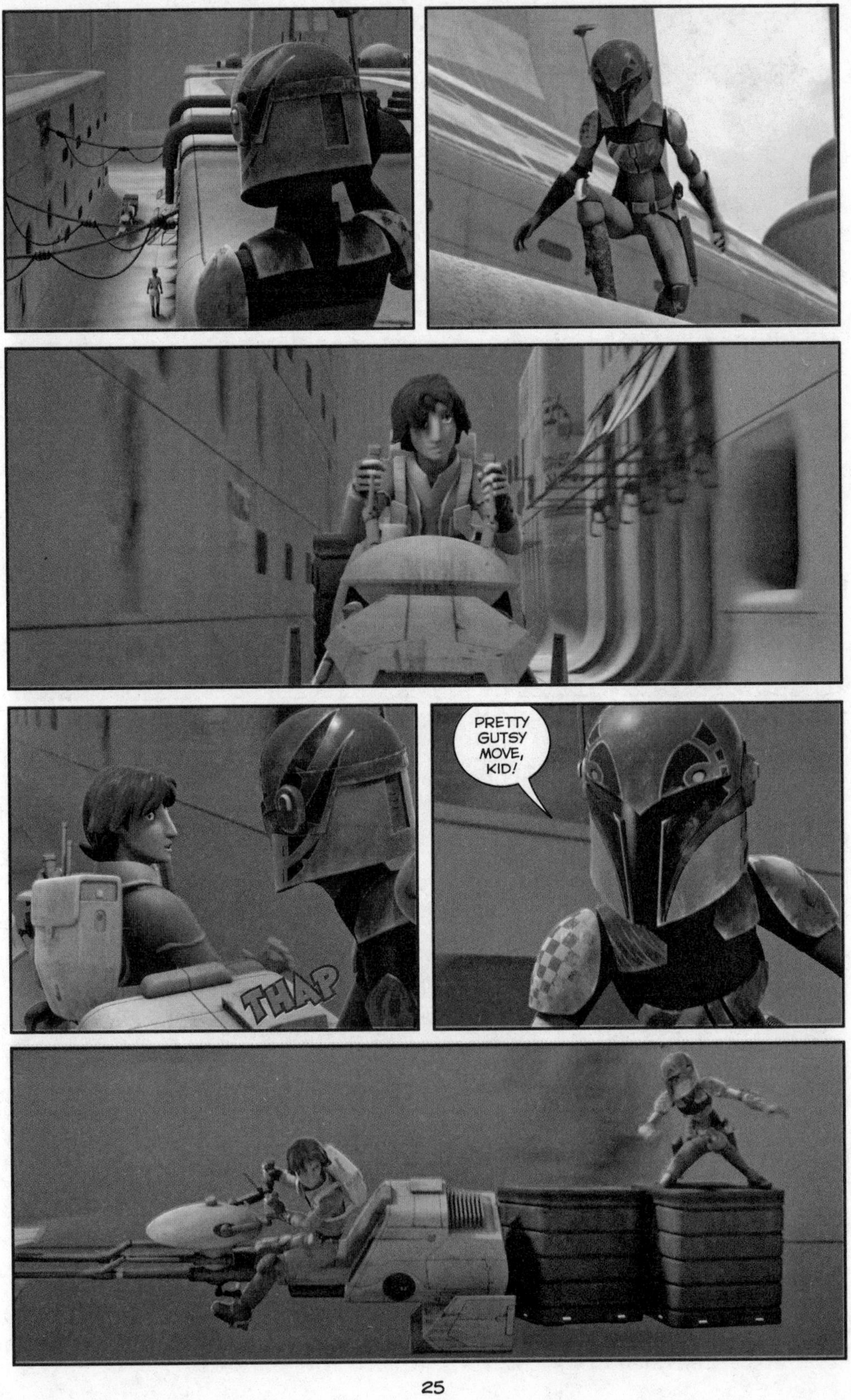
THAP
PRETTY GUTSY MOVE, KID!

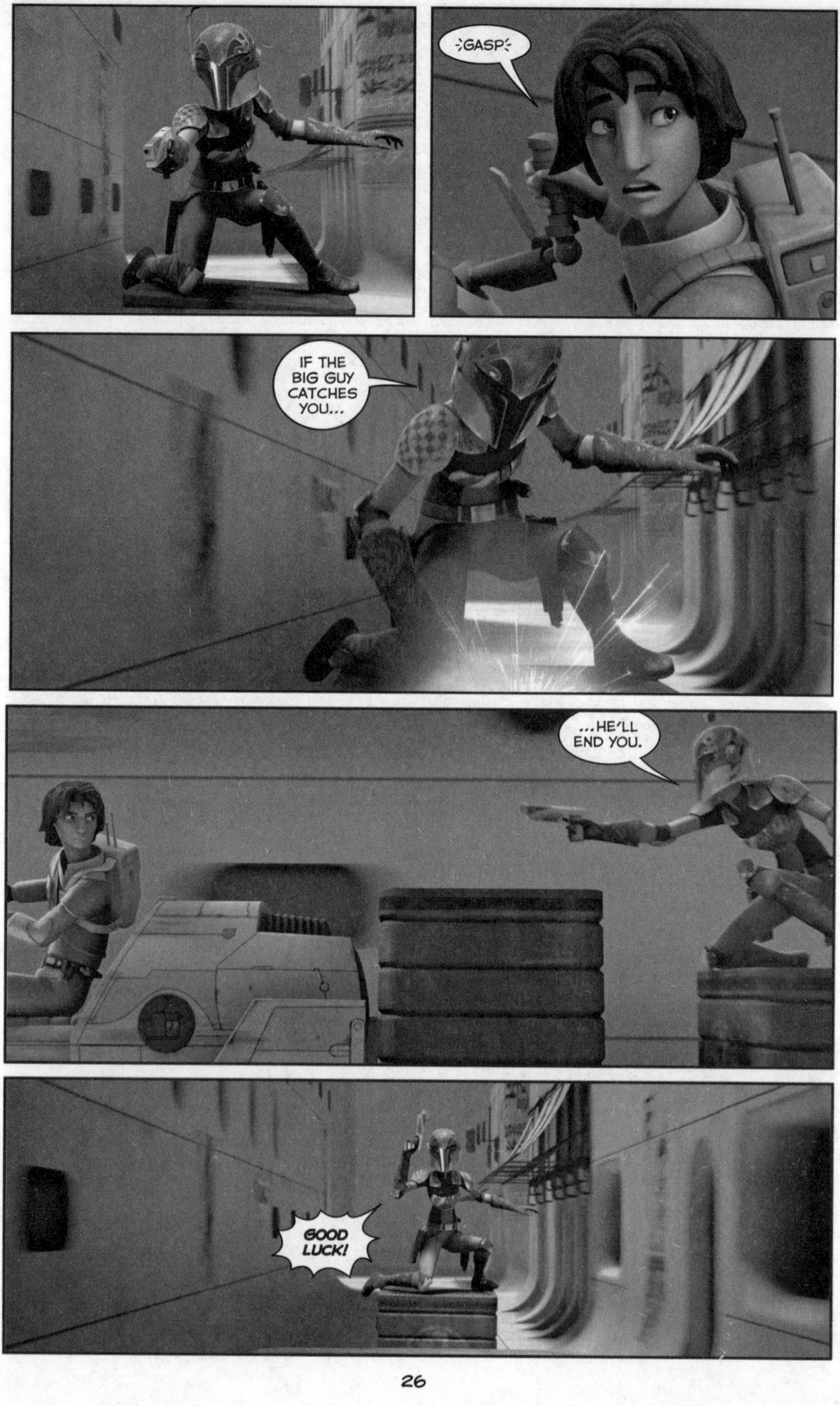
GASP
IF THE BIG GUY CATCHES YOU...
...HE'LL END YOU.
GOOD LUCK!

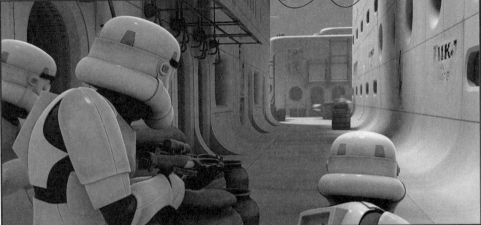

-:GASP:-

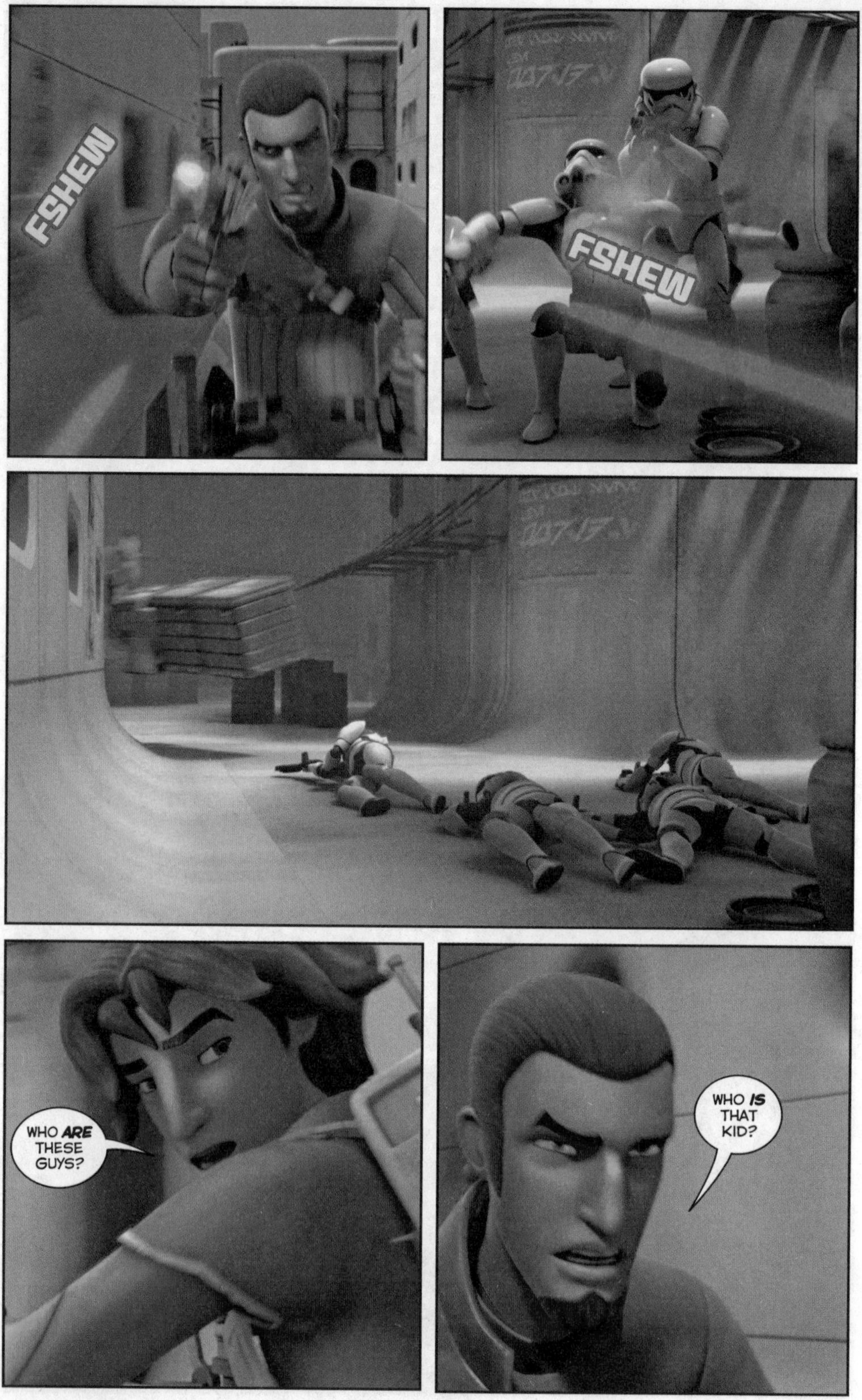
FSHEW
FSHEW
WHO **ARE** THESE GUYS?
WHO **IS** THAT KID?

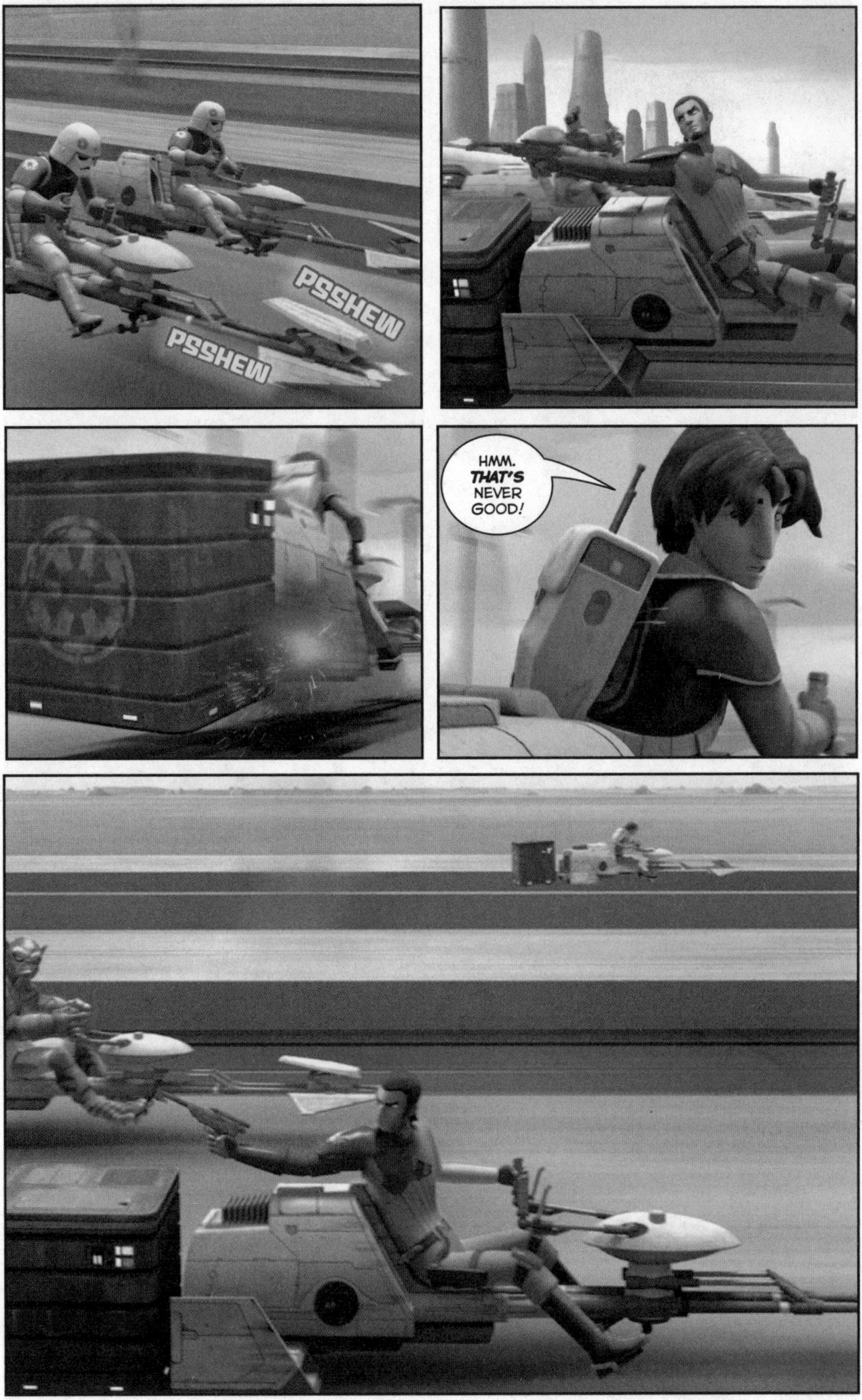
PSSHEW
PSSHEW
HMM. ***THAT'S*** NEVER GOOD!

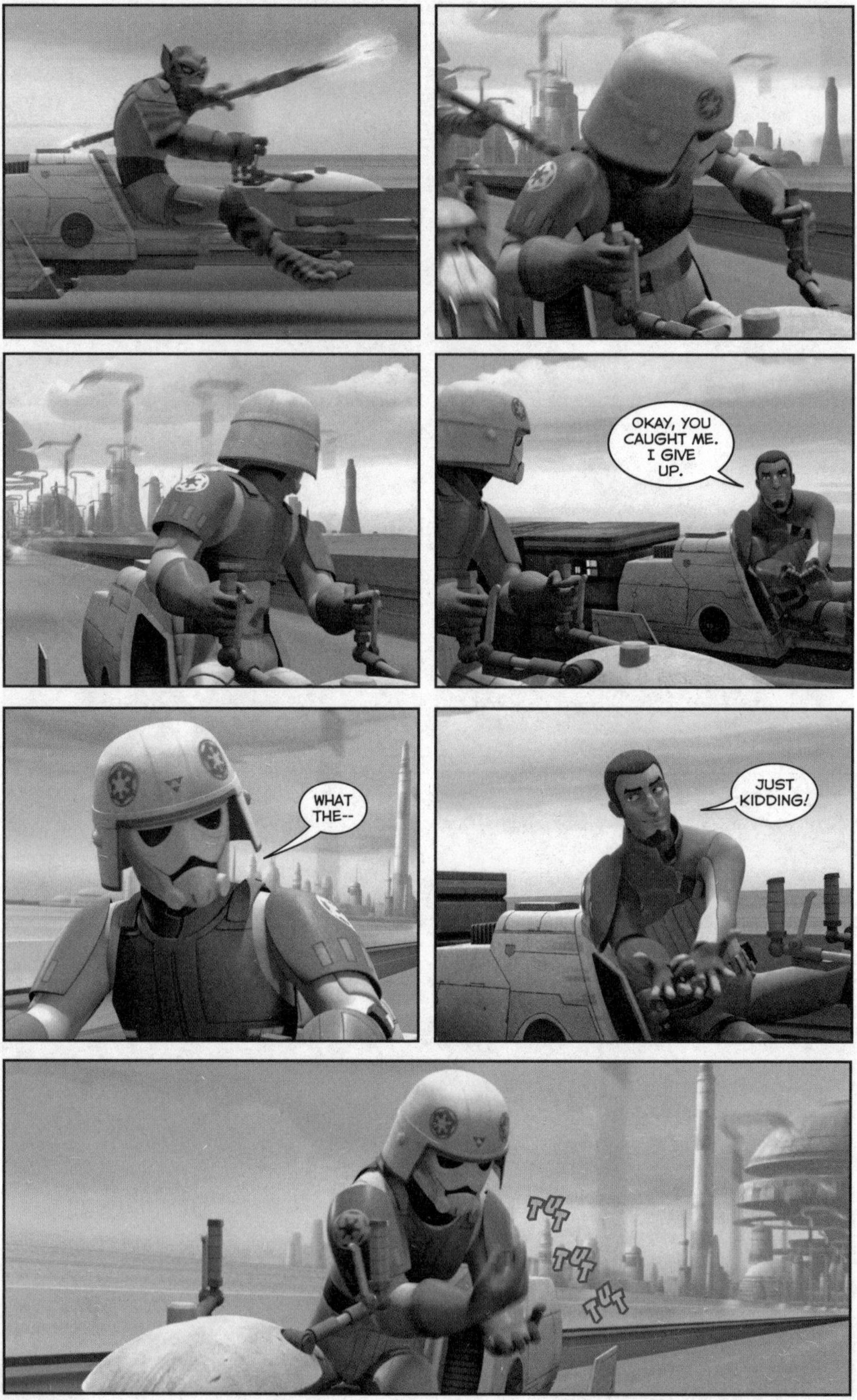
OKAY, YOU CAUGHT ME. I GIVE UP.
WHAT THE--
JUST KIDDING!
TUT
TUT
TUT

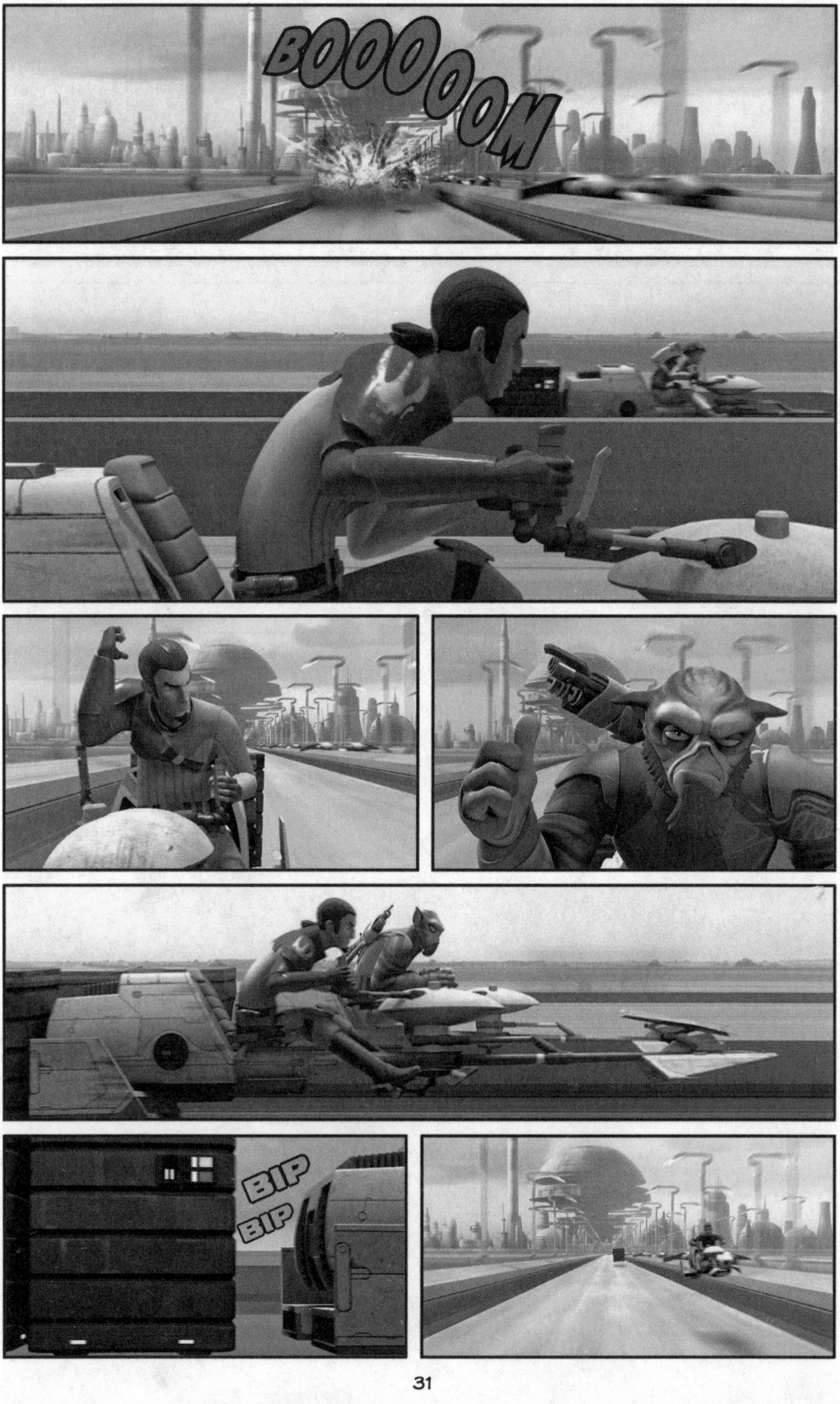
BOOOOOM
BIP
BIP

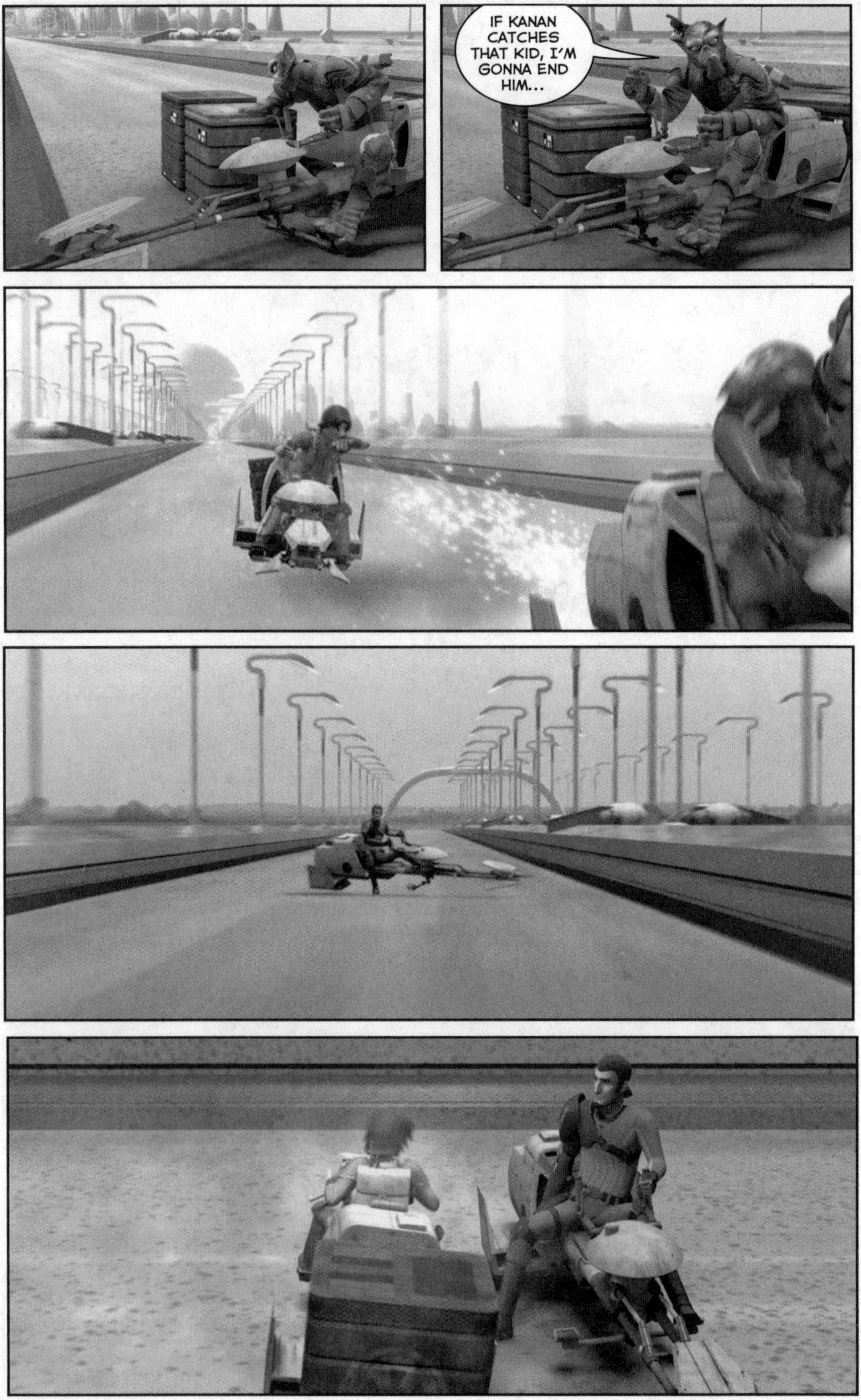
IF KANAN CATCHES THAT KID, I'M GONNA END HIM...

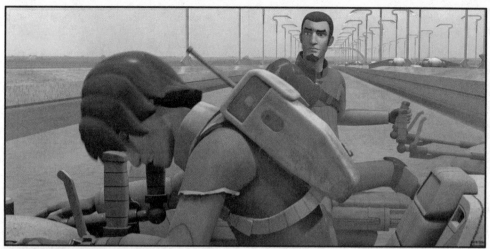

WHO **ARE** YOU?!

I'M THE GUY WHO WAS STEALING THAT CRATE.

HEY, LOOK. I STOLE THIS STUFF--

--WHATEV-WHATEVER IT IS-- FAIR AND SQUARE!

AND YOU MADE IT PRETTY FAR. BUT I'VE GOT PLANS FOR THAT CRATE...

...SO TODAY'S NOT YOUR DAY.

DAY'S NOT OVER.

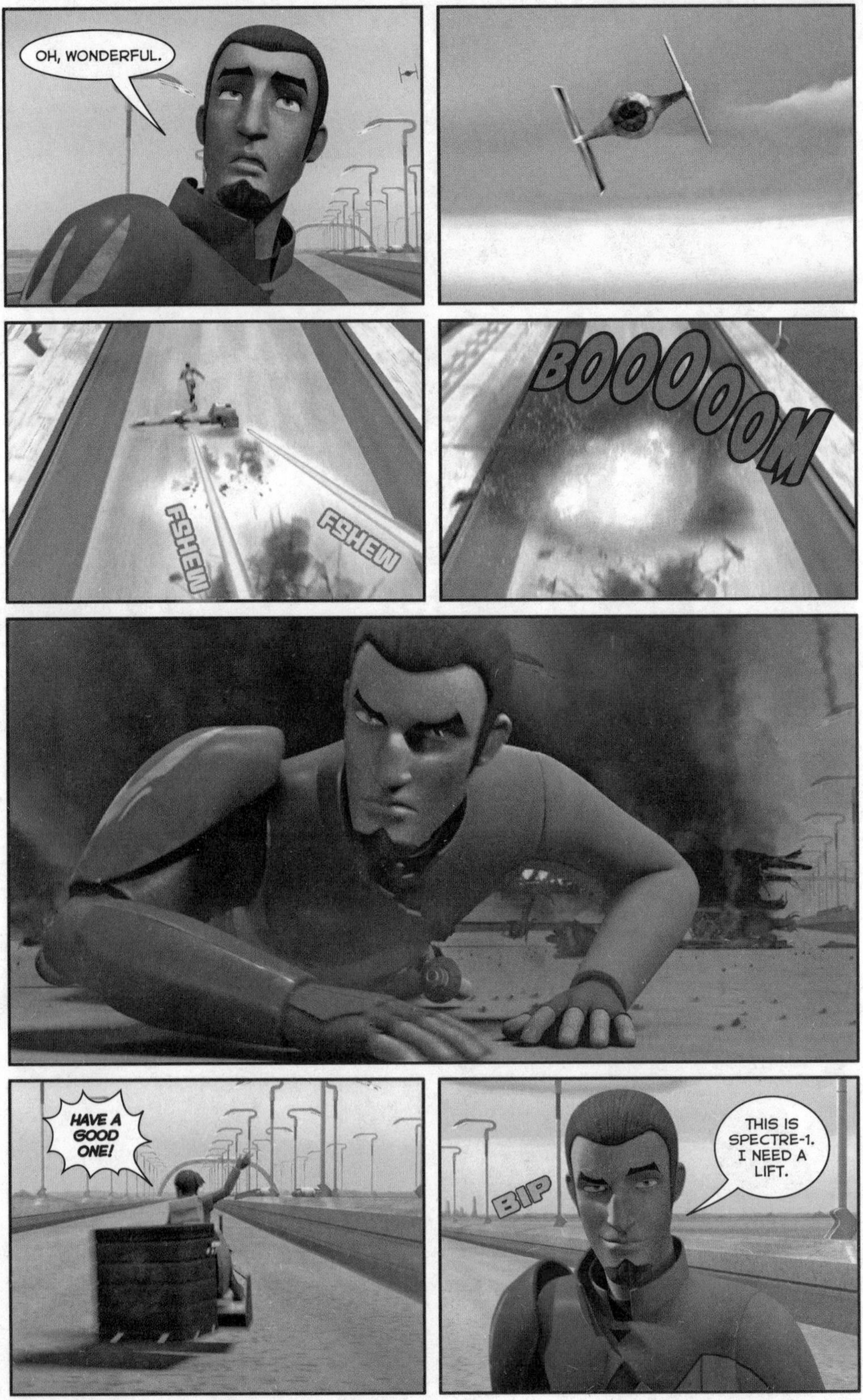
OH, WONDERFUL.
FSHEW
FSHEW
BOOOOOOM
HAVE A GOOD ONE!
BIP
THIS IS SPECTRE-1. I NEED A LIFT.

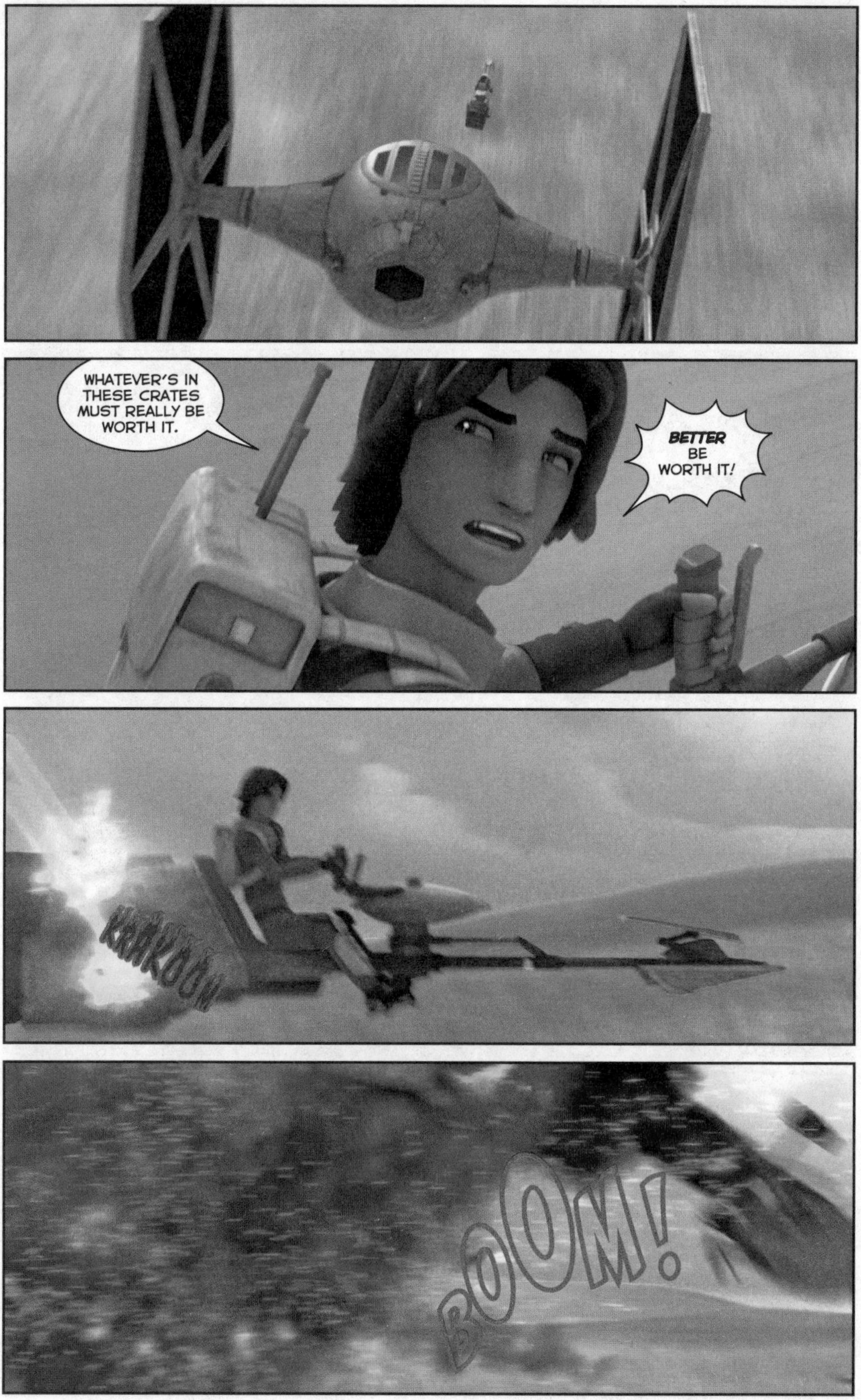
WHATEVER'S IN THESE CRATES MUST REALLY BE WORTH IT.
BETTER BE WORTH IT!
KRAKOOM
BOOOM!

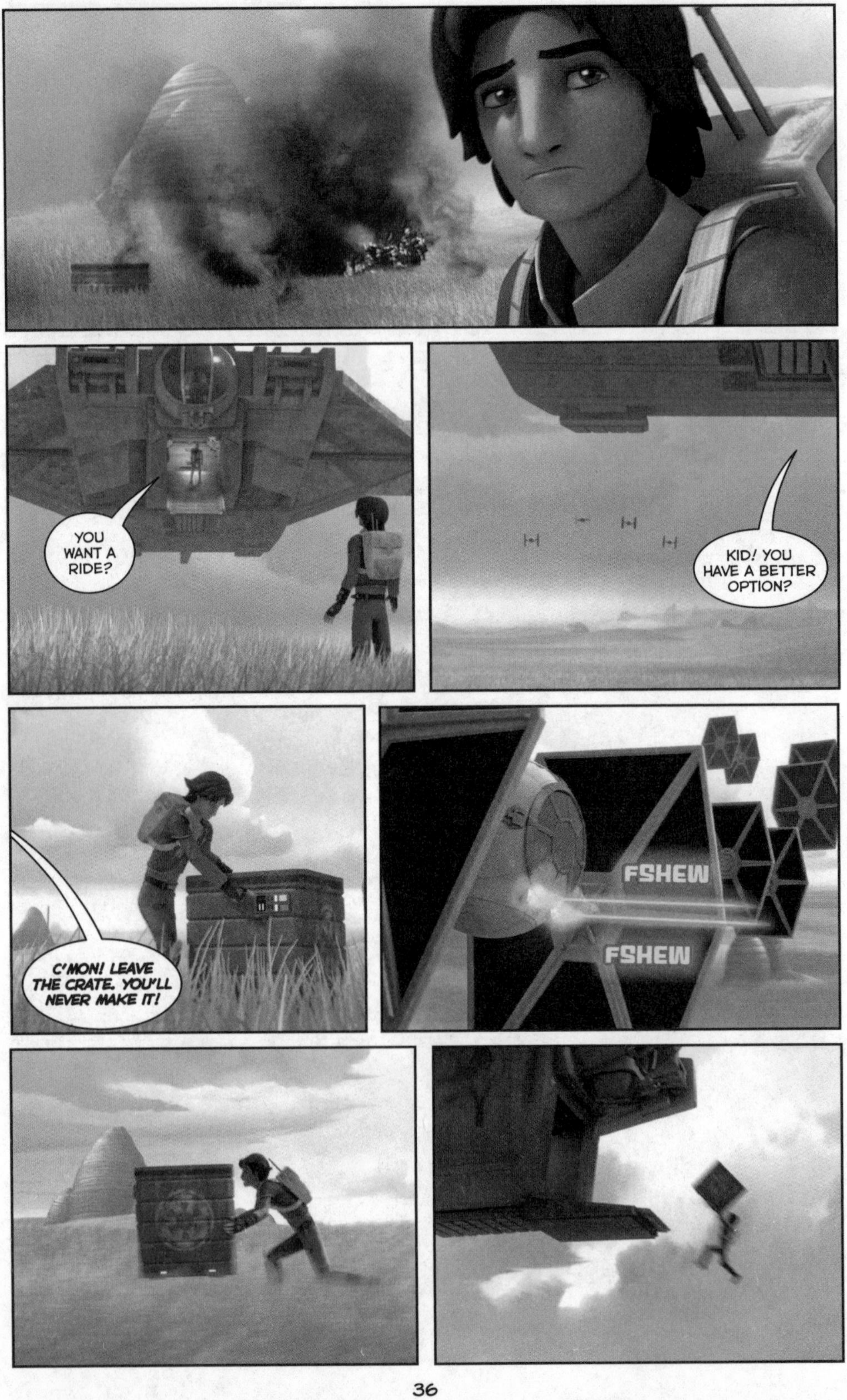
YOU WANT A RIDE?
KID! YOU HAVE A BETTER OPTION?
C'MON! LEAVE THE CRATE. YOU'LL NEVER MAKE IT!
FSHEW
FSHEW

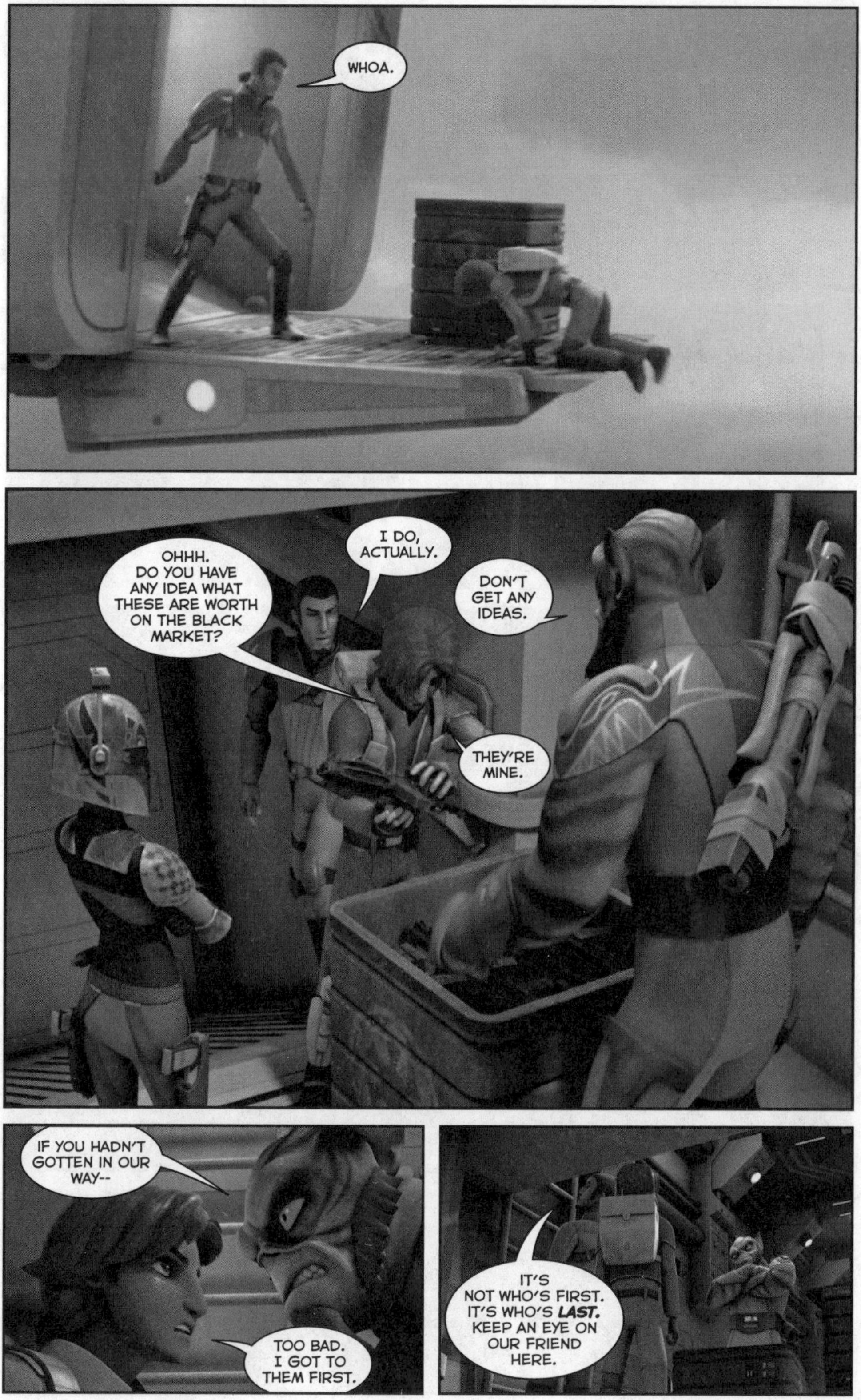
WHOA.
OHHH. DO YOU HAVE ANY IDEA WHAT THESE ARE WORTH ON THE BLACK MARKET?
I DO, ACTUALLY.
DON'T GET ANY IDEAS.
THEY'RE MINE.
IF YOU HADN'T GOTTEN IN OUR WAY--
TOO BAD. I GOT TO THEM FIRST.
IT'S NOT WHO'S FIRST. IT'S WHO'S ***LAST.*** KEEP AN EYE ON OUR FRIEND HERE.

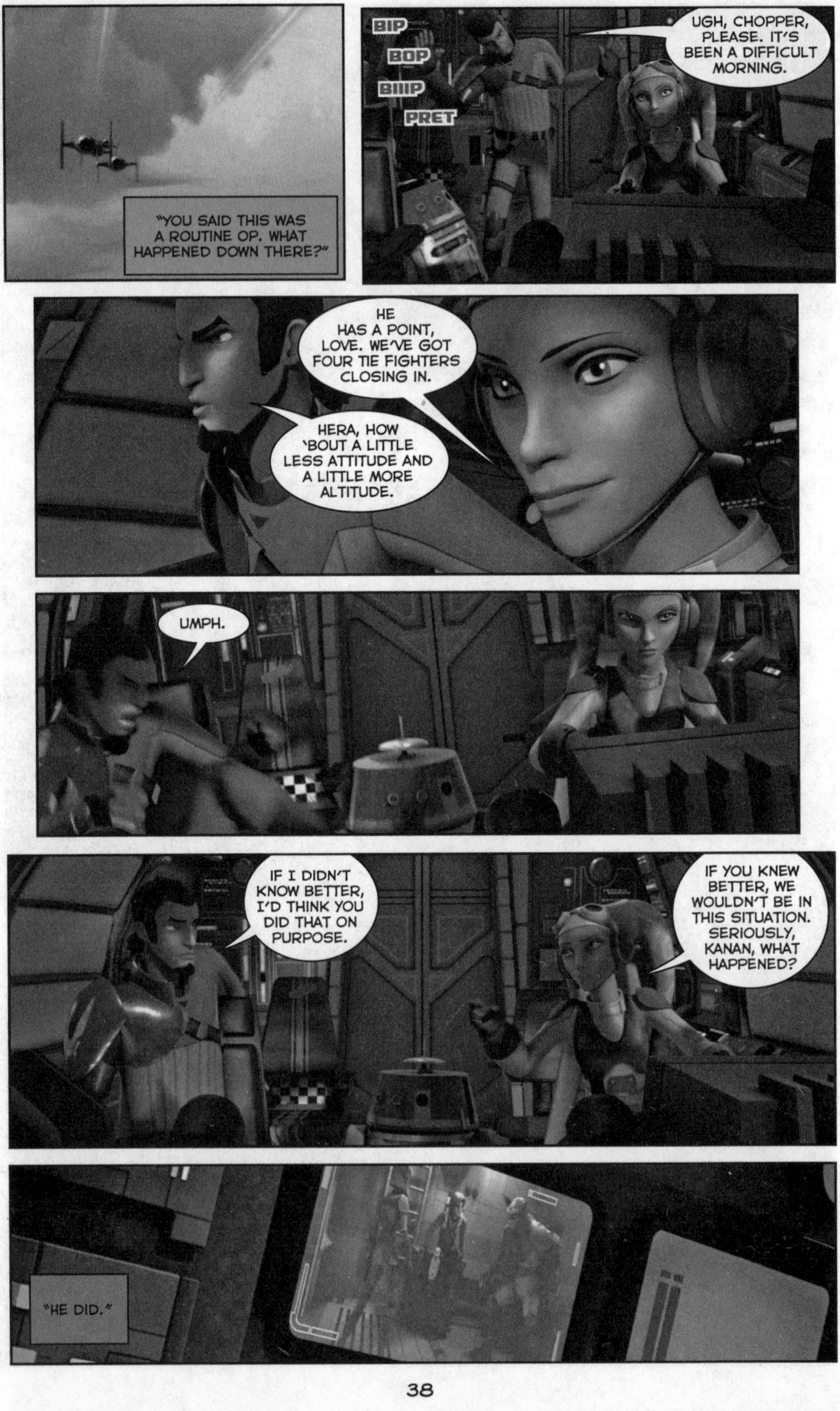
"YOU SAID THIS WAS A ROUTINE OP. WHAT HAPPENED DOWN THERE?"
BIP
BOP
BIIIP
PRET
UGH, CHOPPER, PLEASE. IT'S BEEN A DIFFICULT MORNING.
HE HAS A POINT, LOVE. WE'VE GOT FOUR TIE FIGHTERS CLOSING IN.
HERA, HOW 'BOUT A LITTLE LESS ATTITUDE AND A LITTLE MORE ALTITUDE.
UMPH.
IF I DIDN'T KNOW BETTER, I'D THINK YOU DID THAT ON PURPOSE.
IF YOU KNEW BETTER, WE WOULDN'T BE IN THIS SITUATION. SERIOUSLY, KANAN, WHAT HAPPENED?
"HE DID."

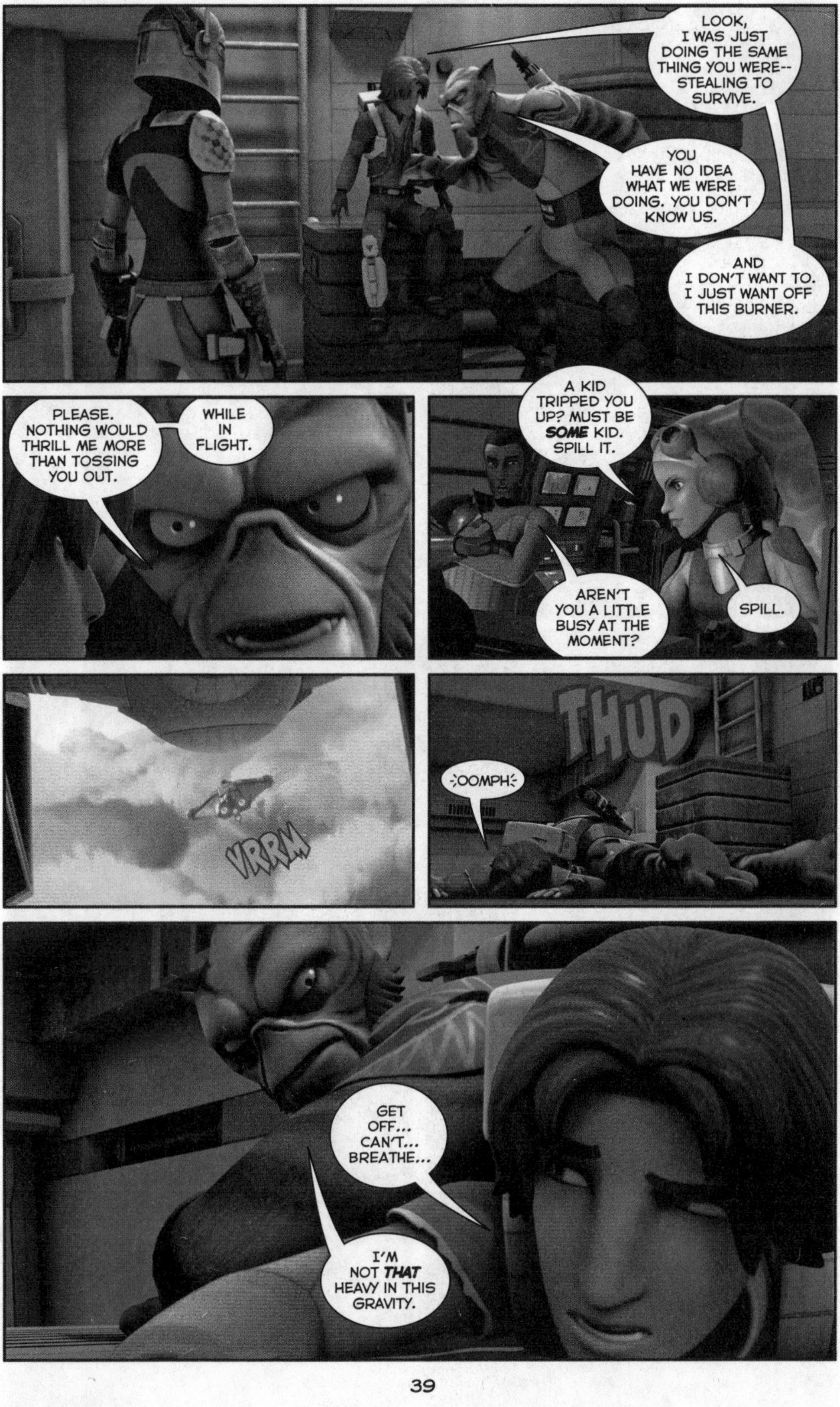
LOOK, I WAS JUST DOING THE SAME THING YOU WERE--STEALING TO SURVIVE.
YOU HAVE NO IDEA WHAT WE WERE DOING. YOU DON'T KNOW US.
AND I DON'T WANT TO. I JUST WANT OFF THIS BURNER.
PLEASE. NOTHING WOULD THRILL ME MORE THAN TOSSING YOU OUT.
WHILE IN FLIGHT.
A KID TRIPPED YOU UP? MUST BE **SOME** KID. SPILL IT.
AREN'T YOU A LITTLE BUSY AT THE MOMENT?
SPILL.
VRRM
THUD
OOMPH
GET OFF... CAN'T... BREATHE...
I'M NOT ***THAT*** HEAVY IN THIS GRAVITY.

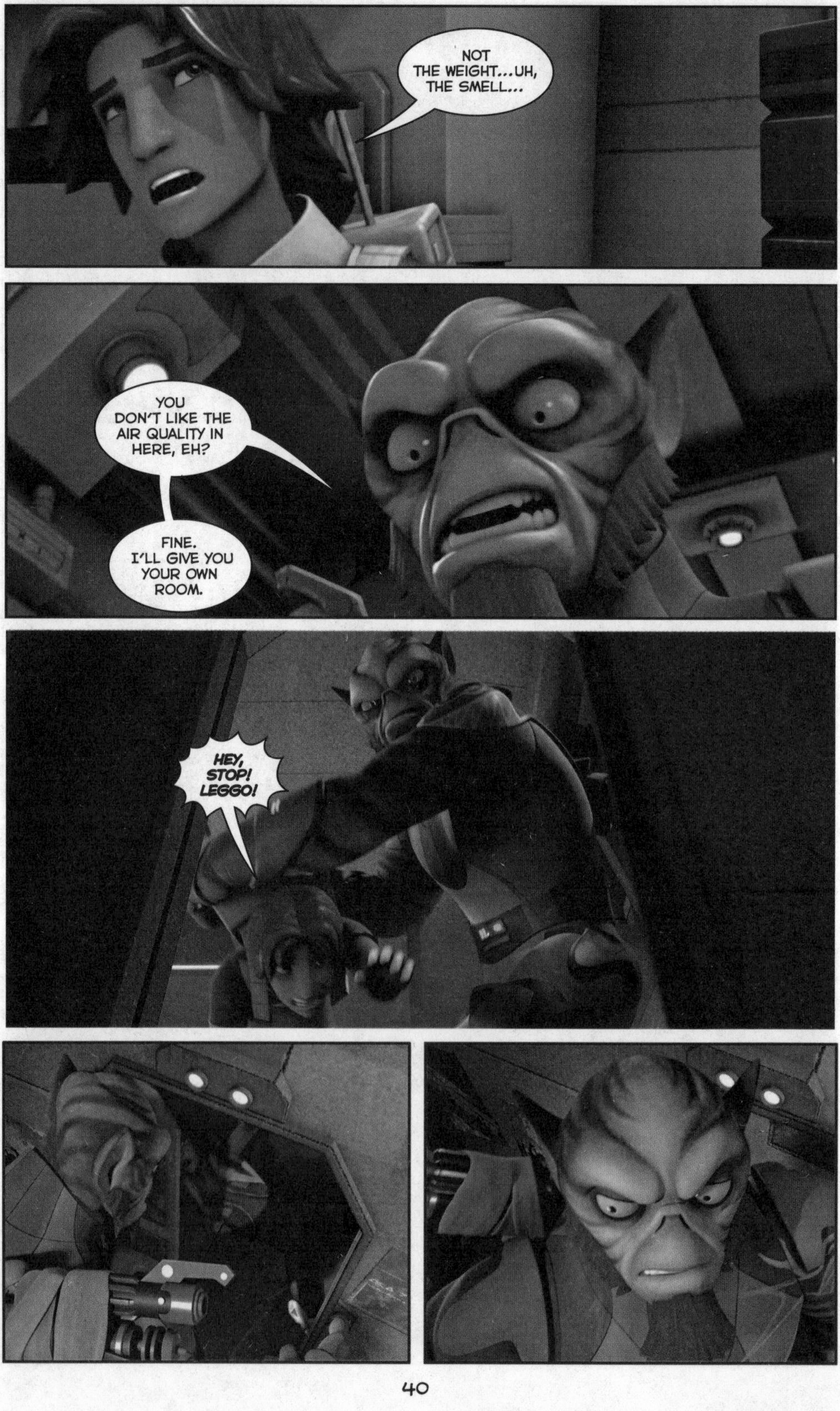
NOT THE WEIGHT...UH, THE SMELL...
YOU DON'T LIKE THE AIR QUALITY IN HERE, EH?
FINE. I'LL GIVE YOU YOUR OWN ROOM.
HEY, STOP! LEGGO!

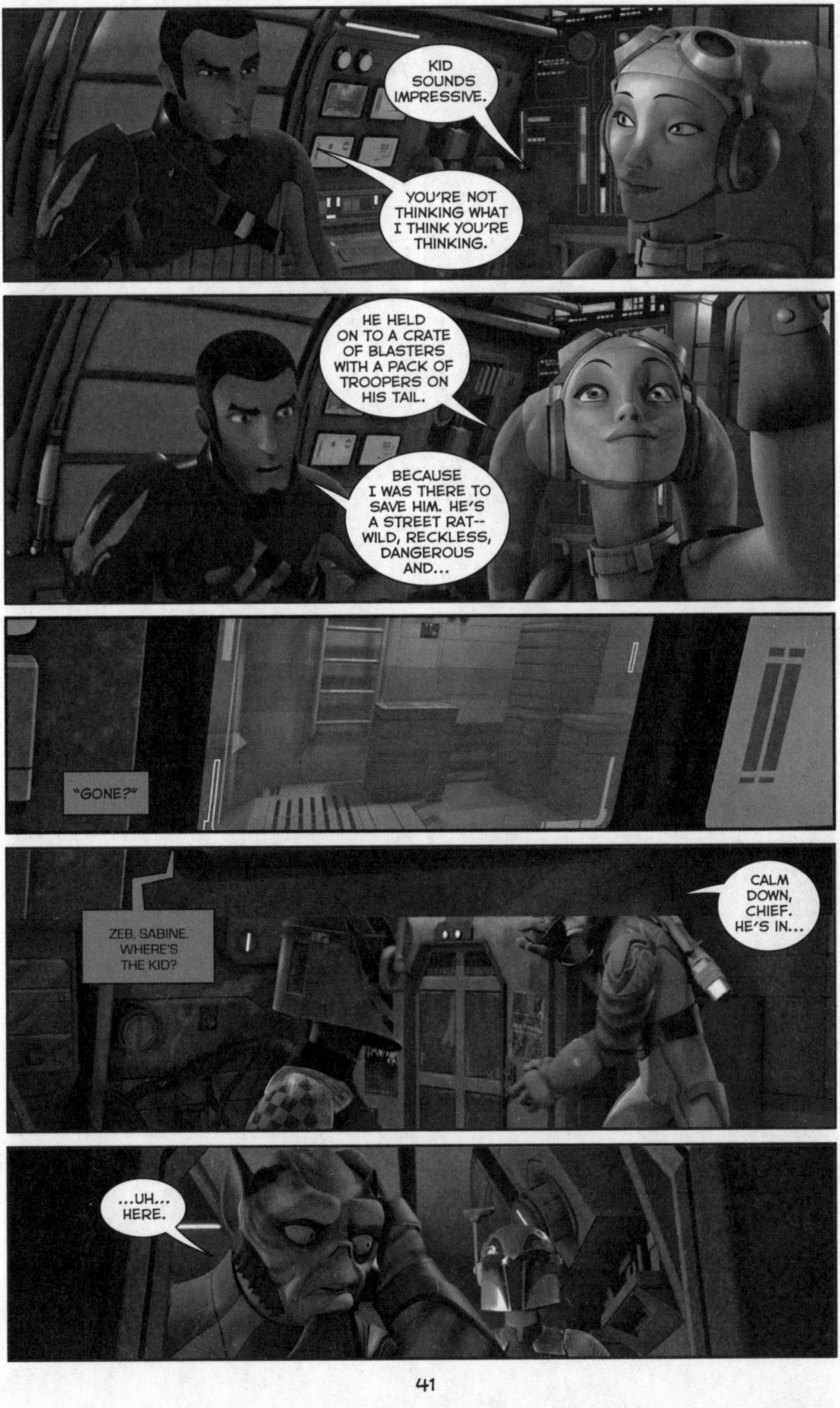
KID SOUNDS IMPRESSIVE.
YOU'RE NOT THINKING WHAT I THINK YOU'RE THINKING.
HE HELD ON TO A CRATE OF BLASTERS WITH A PACK OF TROOPERS ON HIS TAIL.
BECAUSE I WAS THERE TO SAVE HIM. HE'S A STREET RAT-- WILD, RECKLESS, DANGEROUS AND...
"GONE?"
ZEB, SABINE. WHERE'S THE KID?
CALM DOWN, CHIEF. HE'S IN...
...UH... HERE.

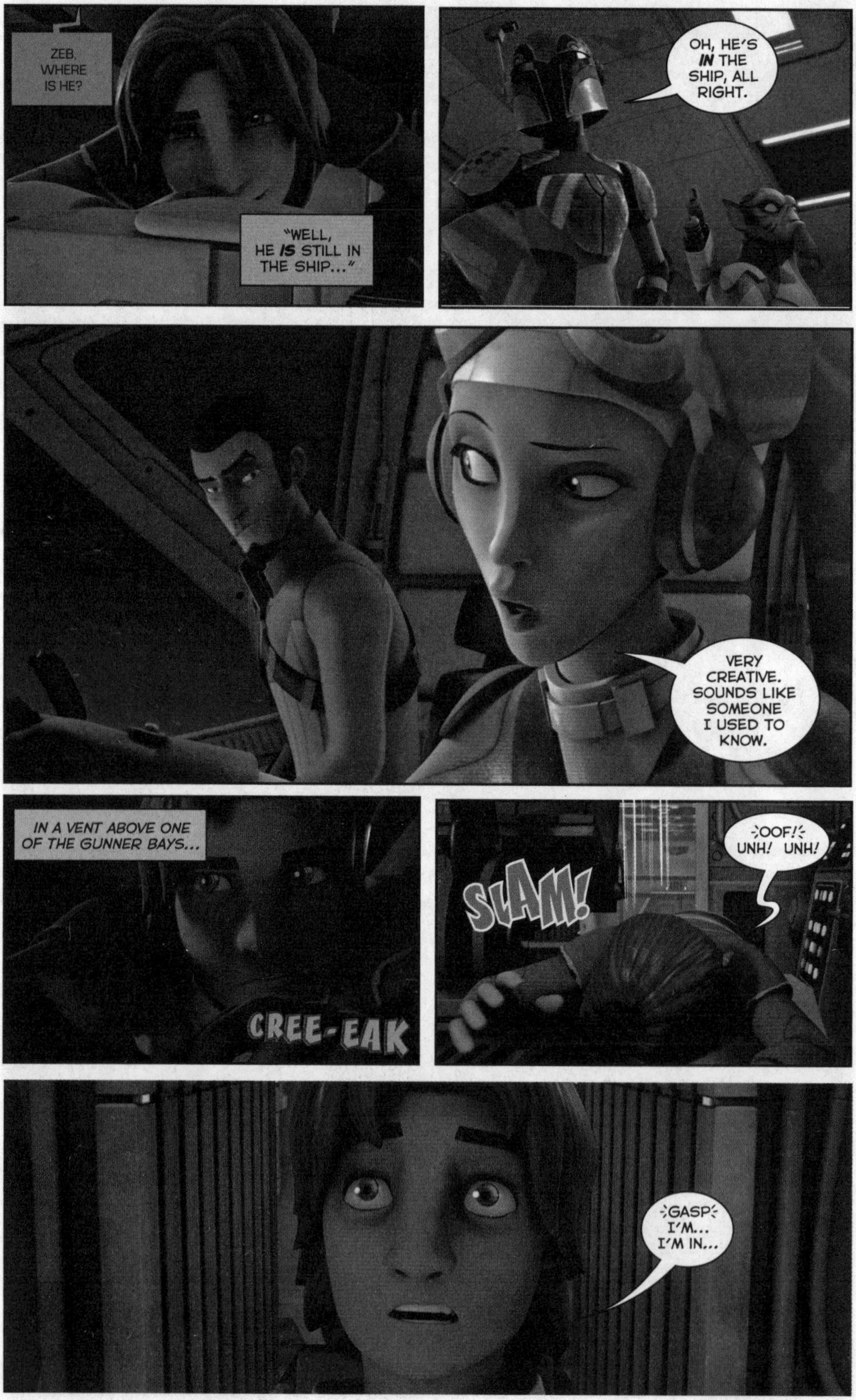
ZEB, WHERE IS HE?
"WELL, HE **IS** STILL IN THE SHIP..."
OH, HE'S ***IN*** THE SHIP, ALL RIGHT.
VERY CREATIVE. SOUNDS LIKE SOMEONE I USED TO KNOW.
IN A VENT ABOVE ONE OF THE GUNNER BAYS...
CREE-EAK
SLAM!
OOF! UNH! UNH!
GASP I'M... I'M IN...

SPACE.

FSHEW!
FSHEW!
FSHEW!

AND I'M ABOUT TO DIE!

SHIELDS ARE HOLDING--FOR NOW--BUT YOU NEED TO BUY ME TIME...

...TO CALCULATE THE JUMP TO LIGHT SPEED.

BUYING TIME... NOW!

CHOOM
CHOOM

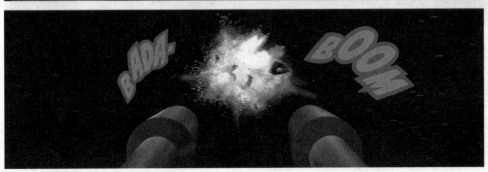

BADA-
BOOM

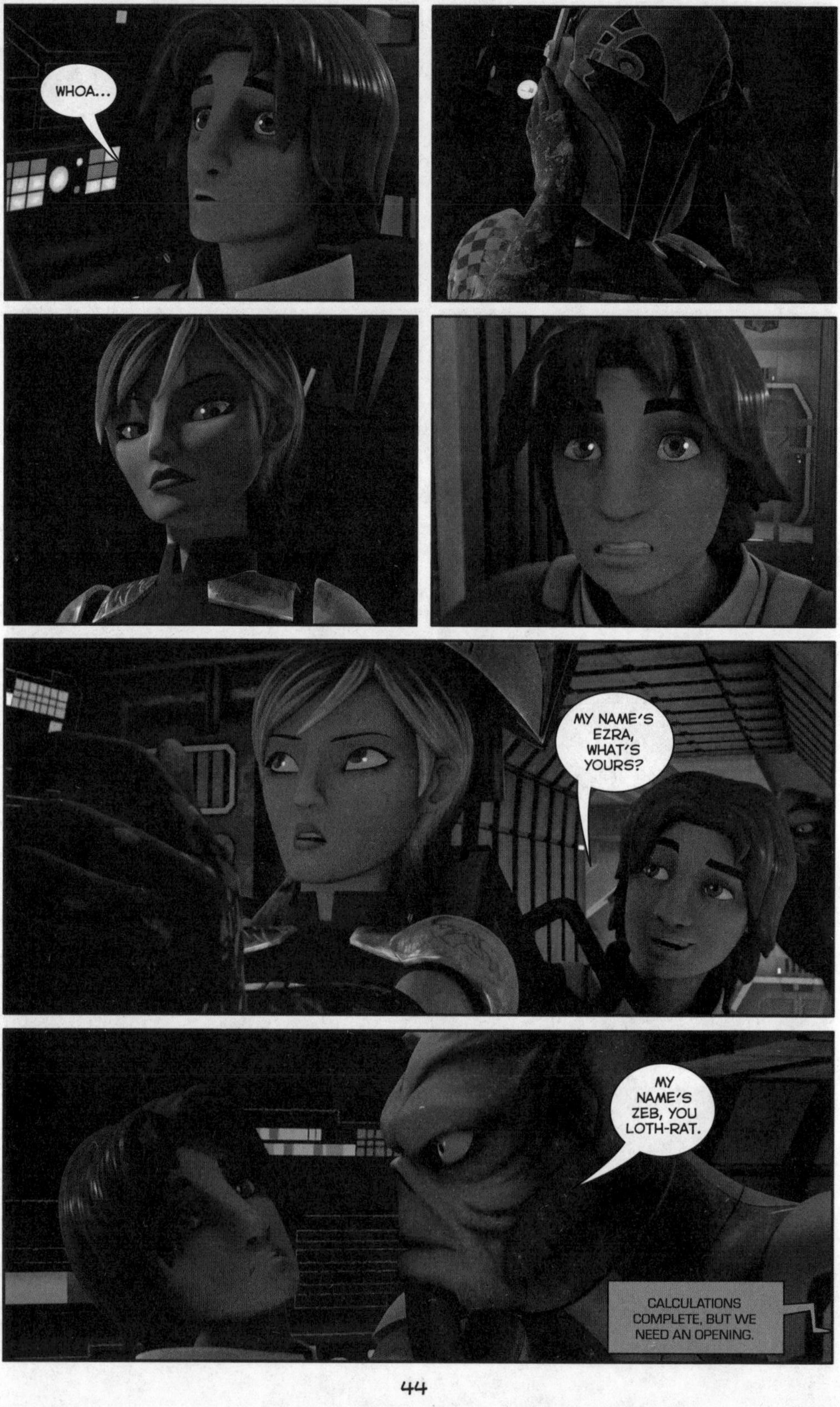
WHOA...
MY NAME'S EZRA, WHAT'S YOURS?
MY NAME'S ZEB, YOU LOTH-RAT.
CALCULATIONS COMPLETE, BUT WE NEED AN OPENING.

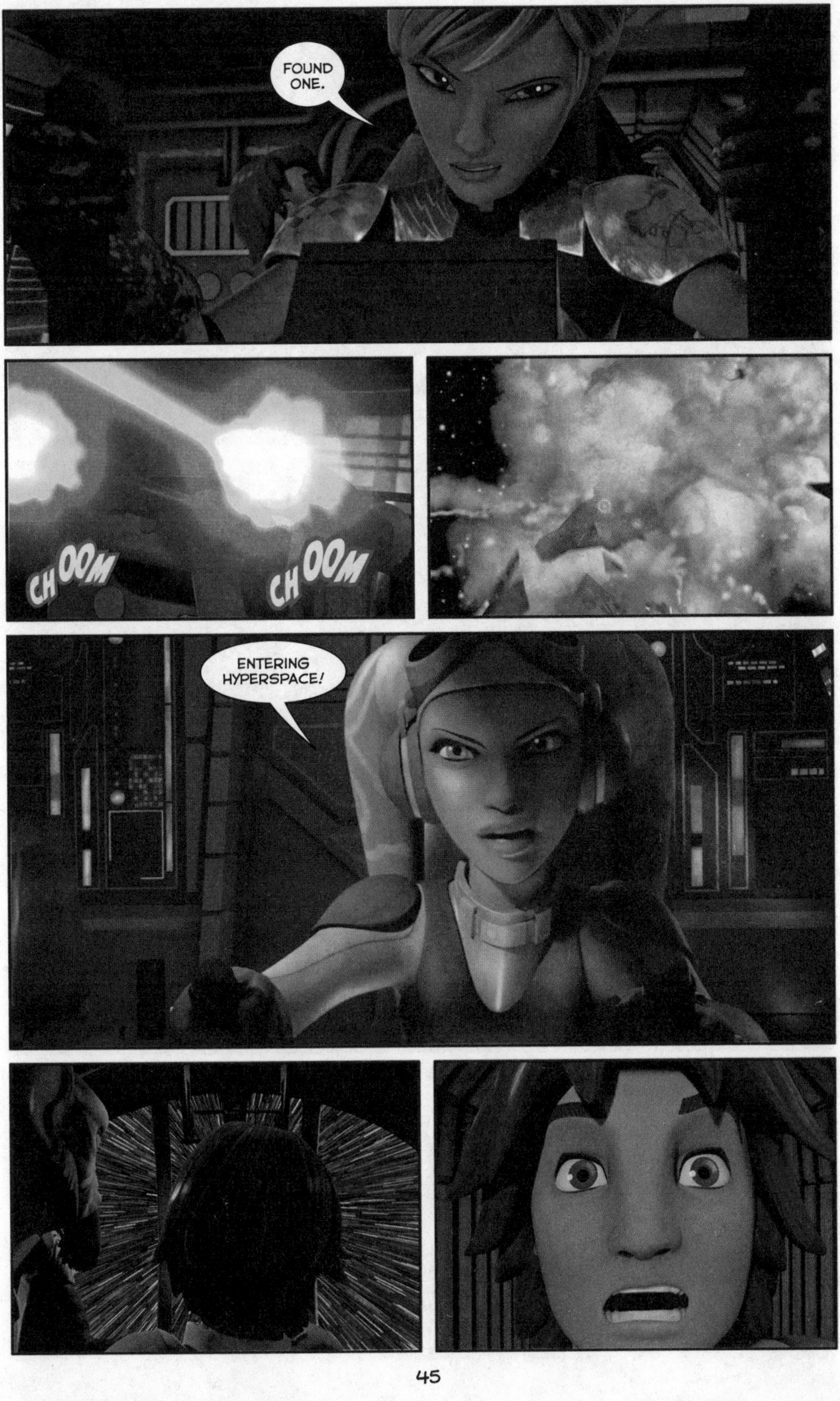
FOUND ONE.
CHOOM
CHOOM
ENTERING HYPERSPACE!

"THEY KNEW OUR PROTOCOL AND WERE WAITING IN POSITION."

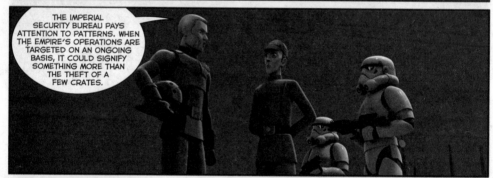

I'VE NO DOUBT. YOU'RE NOT THE FIRST ON LOTHAL HIT BY THIS CREW.

THAT'S A RELIEF.

I MEAN... I ASSUME THAT'S WHY YOU'RE HERE, AGENT KALLUS.

THE IMPERIAL SECURITY BUREAU PAYS ATTENTION TO PATTERNS. WHEN THE EMPIRE'S OPERATIONS ARE TARGETED ON AN ONGOING BASIS, IT COULD SIGNIFY SOMETHING MORE THAN THE THEFT OF A FEW CRATES.

IT COULD SIGNIFY THE SPARK OF REBELLION. NEXT TIME THEY MAKE A MOVE, WE'LL BE WAITING FOR THEM--

--TO SNUFF *OUT* THAT SPARK BEFORE IT CATCHES *FIRE.*

"LET GO! YOU CAN'T KEEP ME HERE! TAKE ME BACK TO LOTHAL!"

CALM DOWN. THAT'S EXACTLY WHAT WE'RE DOING.

WAIT... RIGHT NOW? WITH IMPERIALS CHASING US?

WE LOST THE TIES WHEN WE JUMPED, AND THE *GHOST* CAN SCRAMBLE ITS SIGNATURE...

...SO THEY WON'T RECOGNIZE US WHEN WE RETURN.

OH. THAT'S...PRETTY COOL. SO JUST DROP ME AND MY BLASTERS OUTSIDE CAPITAL CITY AND--

THEY'RE NOT YOUR BLASTERS.

AND WE'RE NOT GOING BACK TO CAPITAL CITY. THE JOB'S NOT DONE.

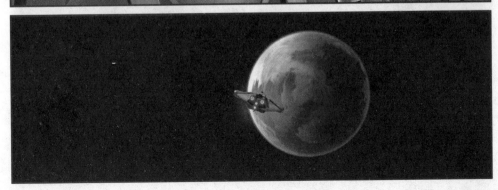

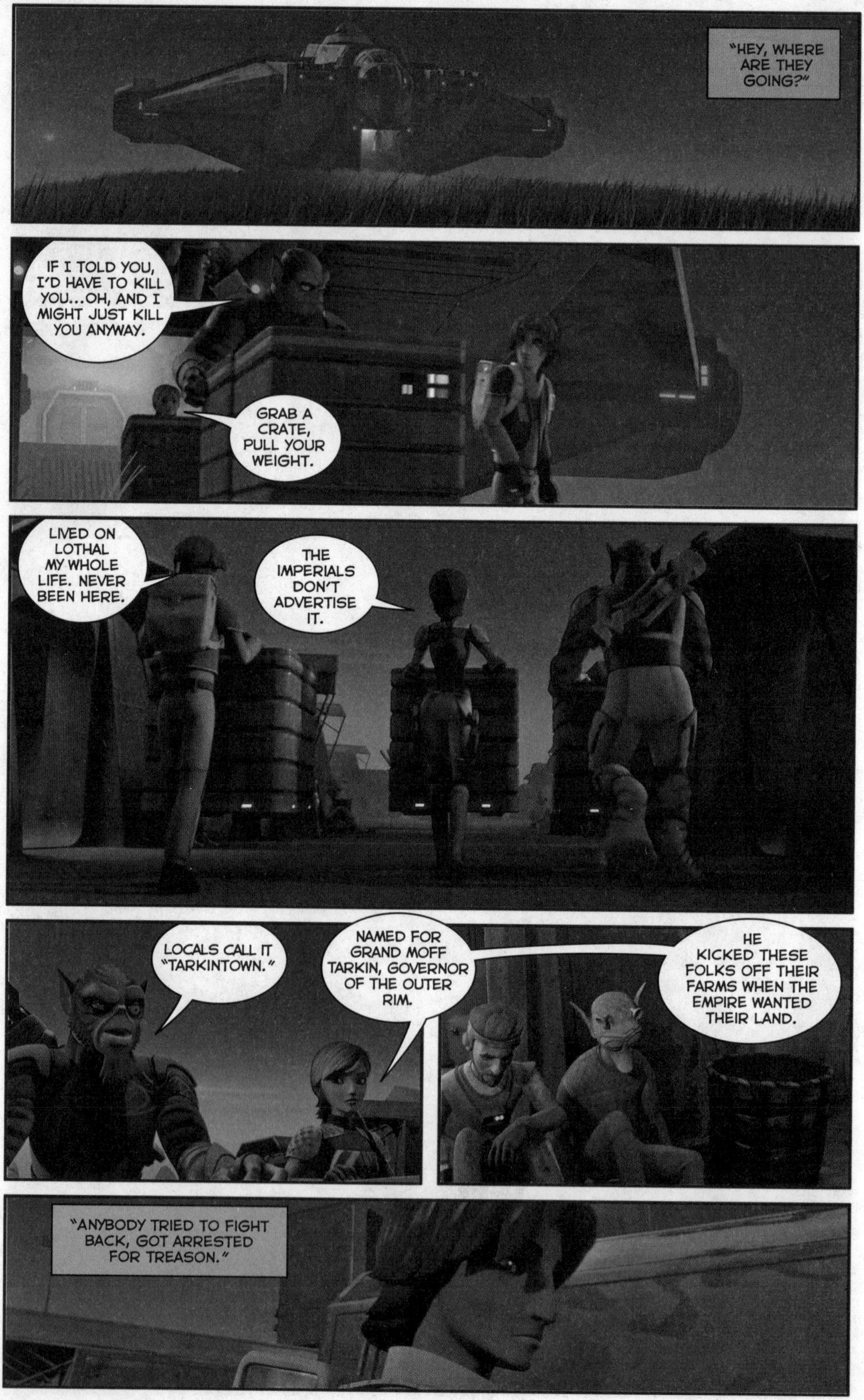
"HEY, WHERE ARE THEY GOING?"
IF I TOLD YOU, I'D HAVE TO KILL YOU...OH, AND I MIGHT JUST KILL YOU ANYWAY.
GRAB A CRATE, PULL YOUR WEIGHT.
LIVED ON LOTHAL MY WHOLE LIFE. NEVER BEEN HERE.
THE IMPERIALS DON'T ADVERTISE IT.
LOCALS CALL IT "TARKINTOWN."
NAMED FOR GRAND MOFF TARKIN, GOVERNOR OF THE OUTER RIM.
HE KICKED THESE FOLKS OFF THEIR FARMS WHEN THE EMPIRE WANTED THEIR LAND.
"ANYBODY TRIED TO FIGHT BACK, GOT ARRESTED FOR TREASON."

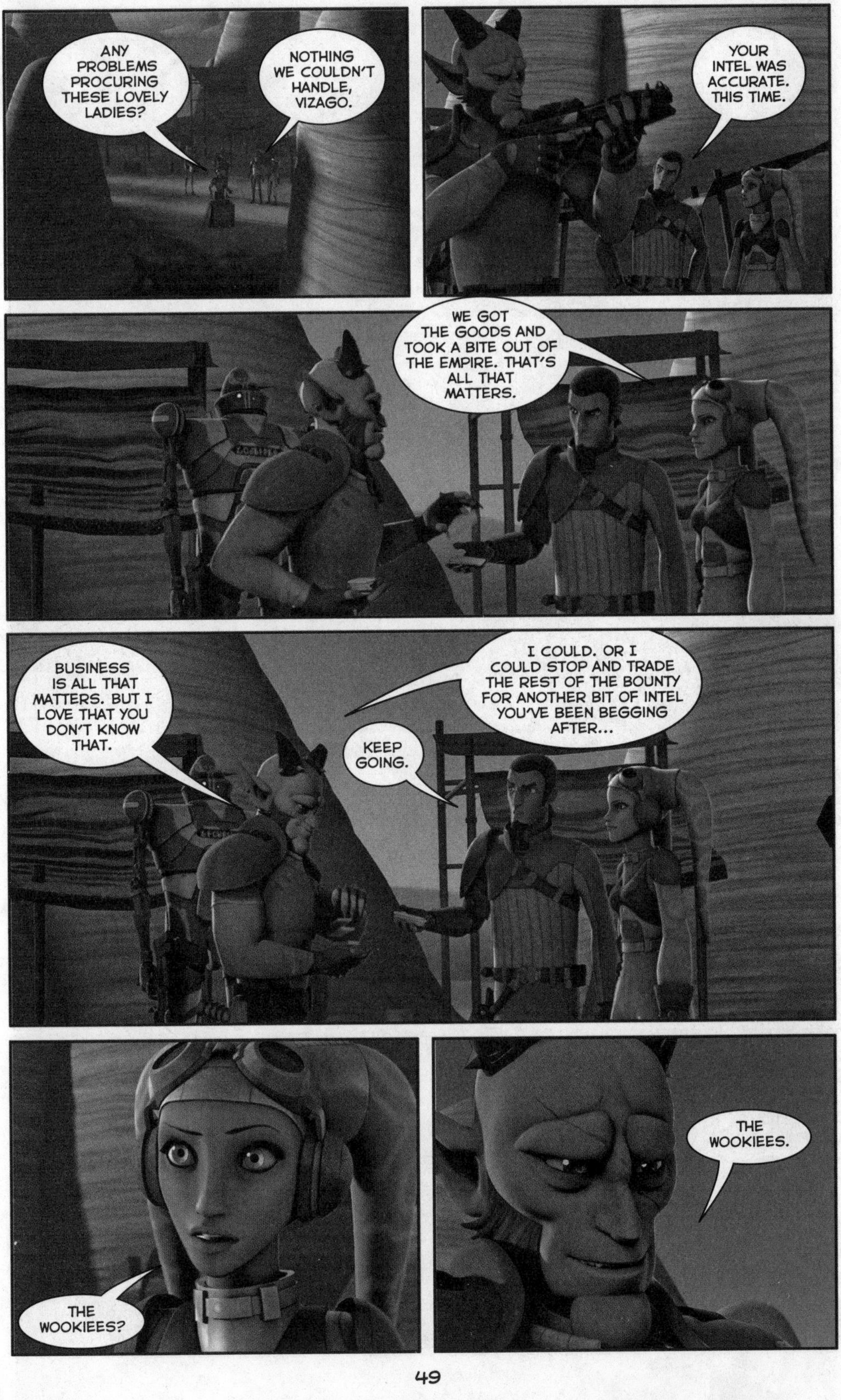
ANY PROBLEMS PROCURING THESE LOVELY LADIES?
NOTHING WE COULDN'T HANDLE, VIZAGO.
YOUR INTEL WAS ACCURATE. THIS TIME.
WE GOT THE GOODS AND TOOK A BITE OUT OF THE EMPIRE. THAT'S ALL THAT MATTERS.
BUSINESS IS ALL THAT MATTERS. BUT I LOVE THAT YOU DON'T KNOW THAT.
I COULD. OR I COULD STOP AND TRADE THE REST OF THE BOUNTY FOR ANOTHER BIT OF INTEL YOU'VE BEEN BEGGING AFTER...
KEEP GOING.
THE WOOKIEES?
THE WOOKIEES.

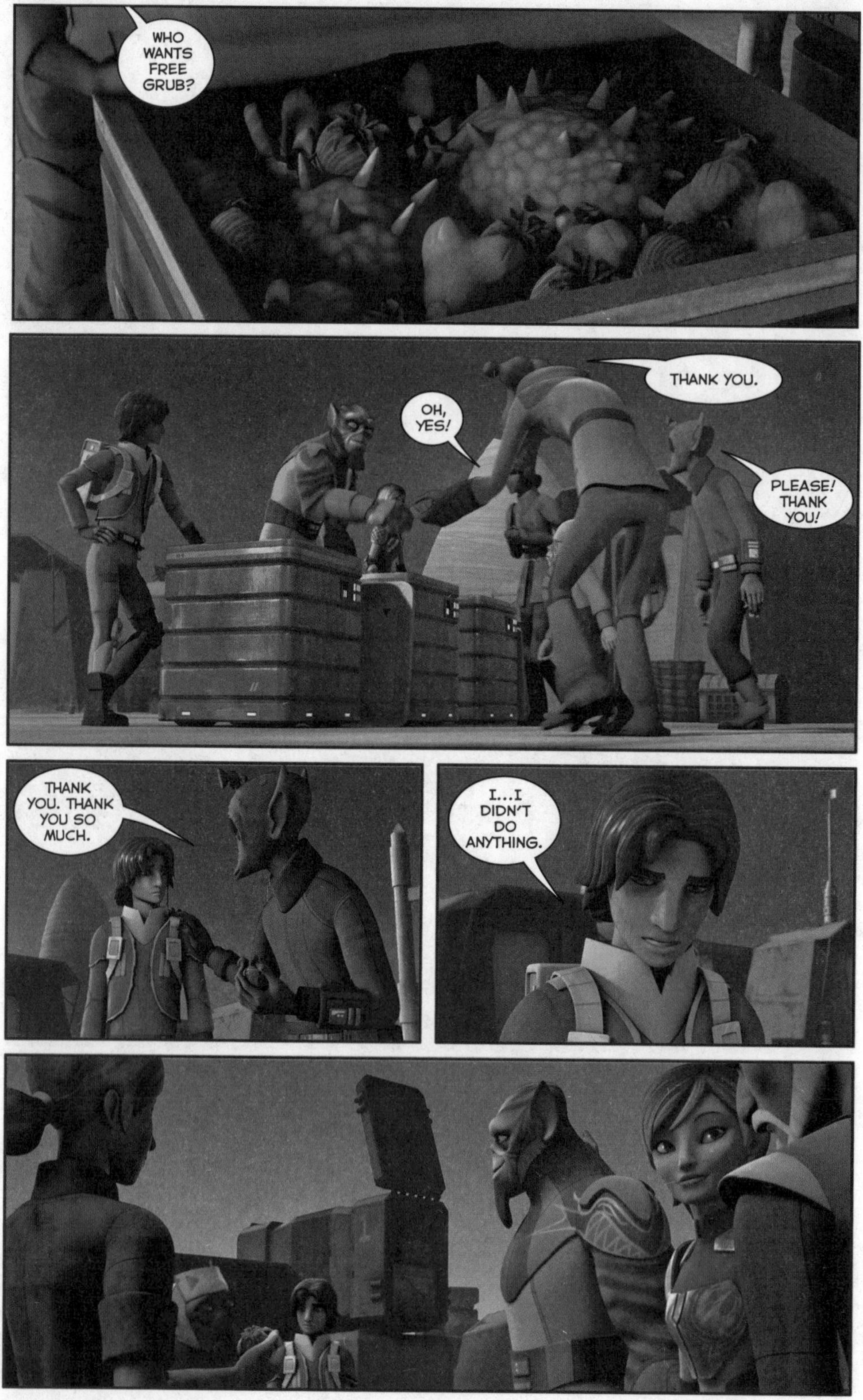
WHO WANTS FREE GRUB?
THANK YOU.
OH, YES!
PLEASE! THANK YOU!
THANK YOU. THANK YOU SO MUCH.
I...I DIDN'T DO ANYTHING.

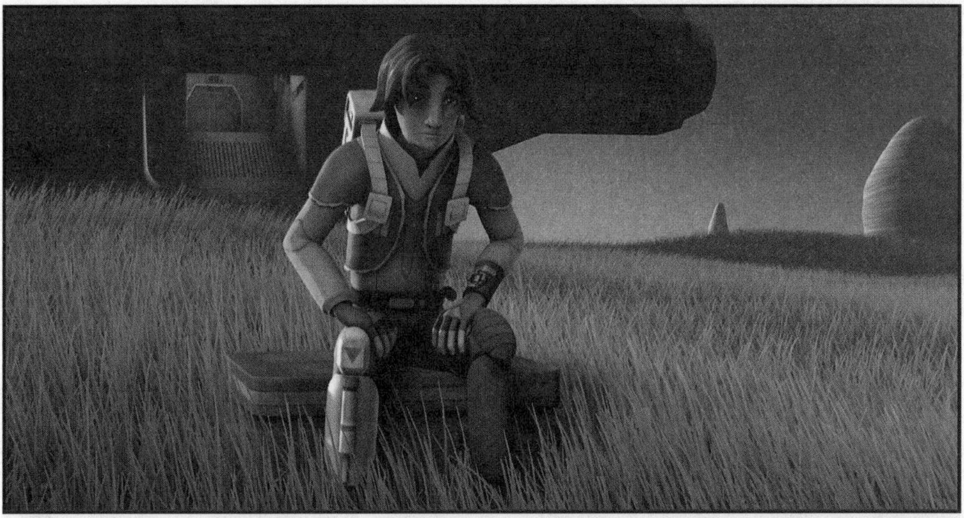

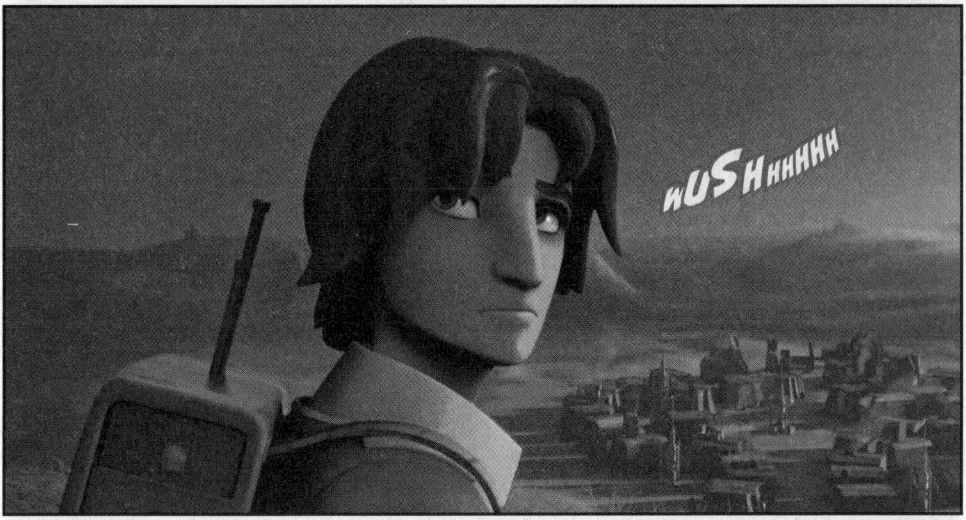
WUSHHHHHHH

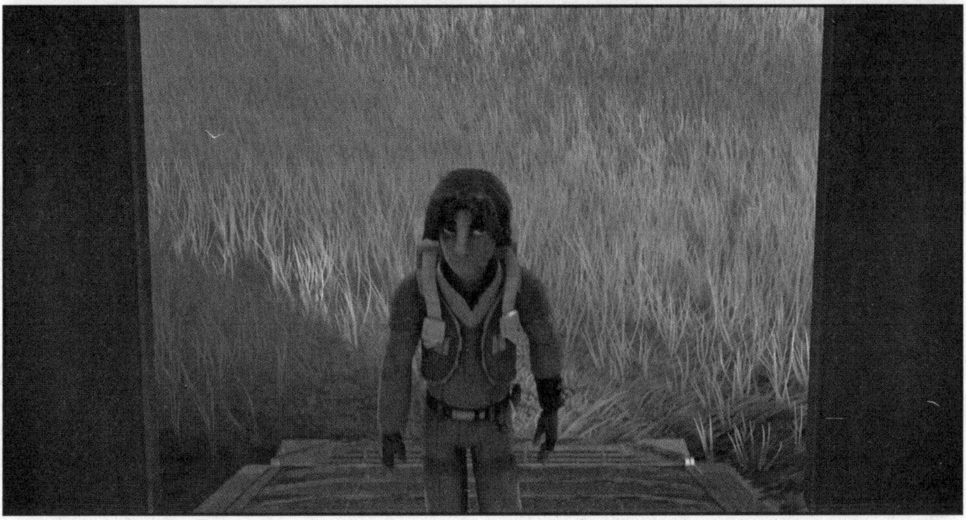

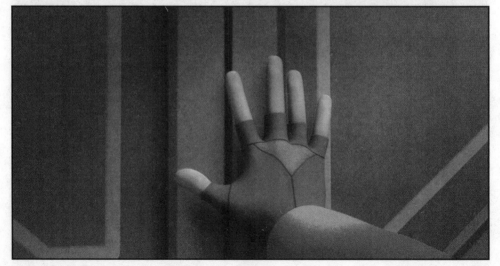

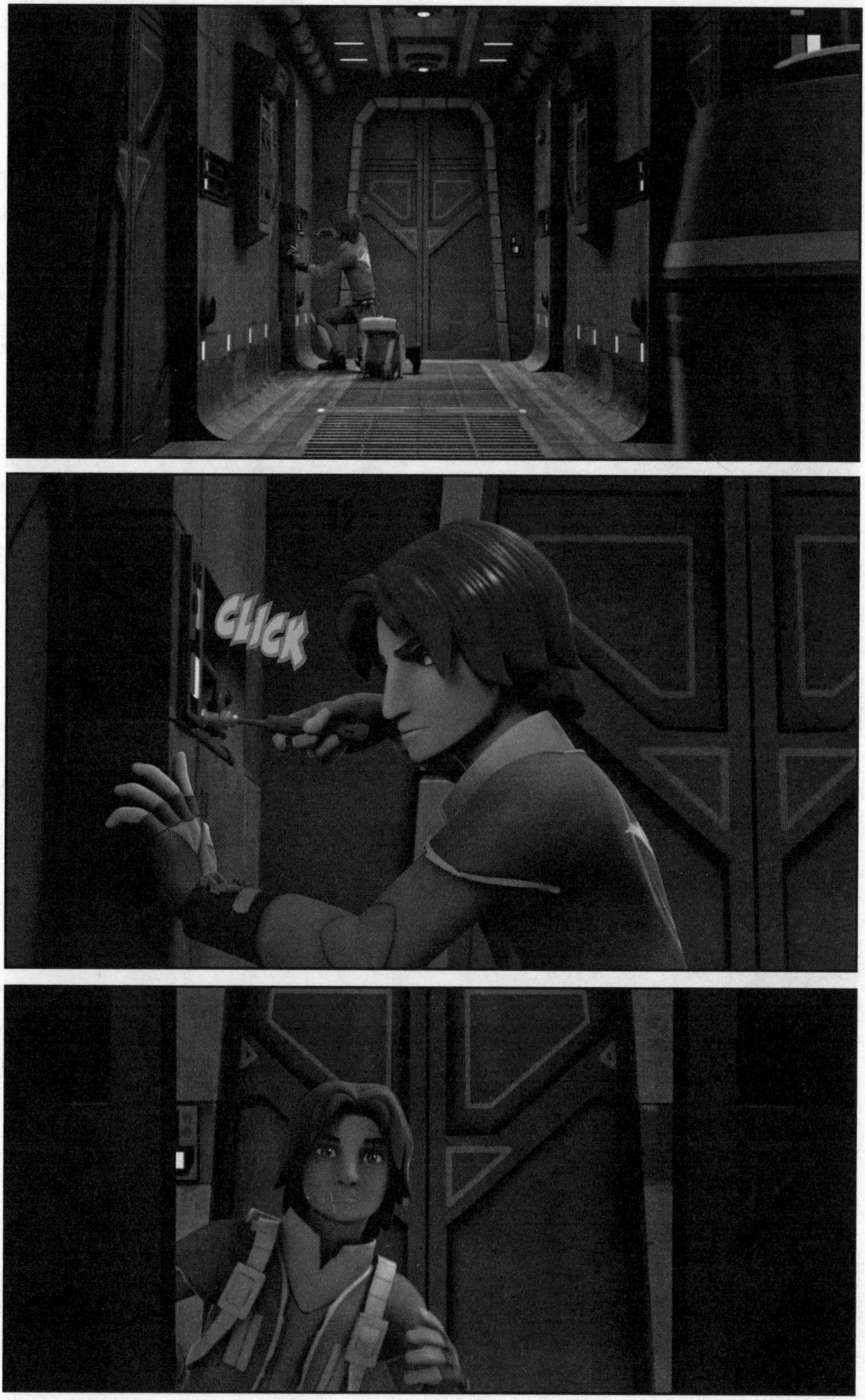
CLICK

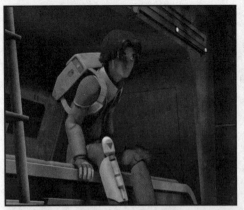

OKAY...

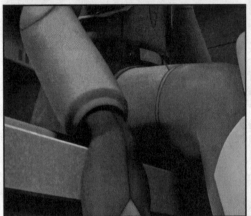

...WEIRD.

MIGHT BE WORTH SOMETHING...

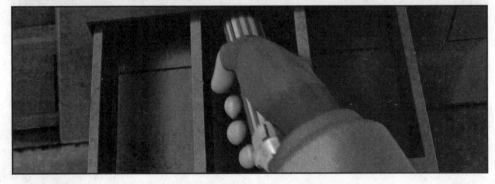

WHOA.

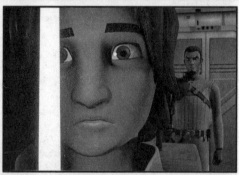

CAREFUL. YOU'LL CUT YOUR ARM OFF.

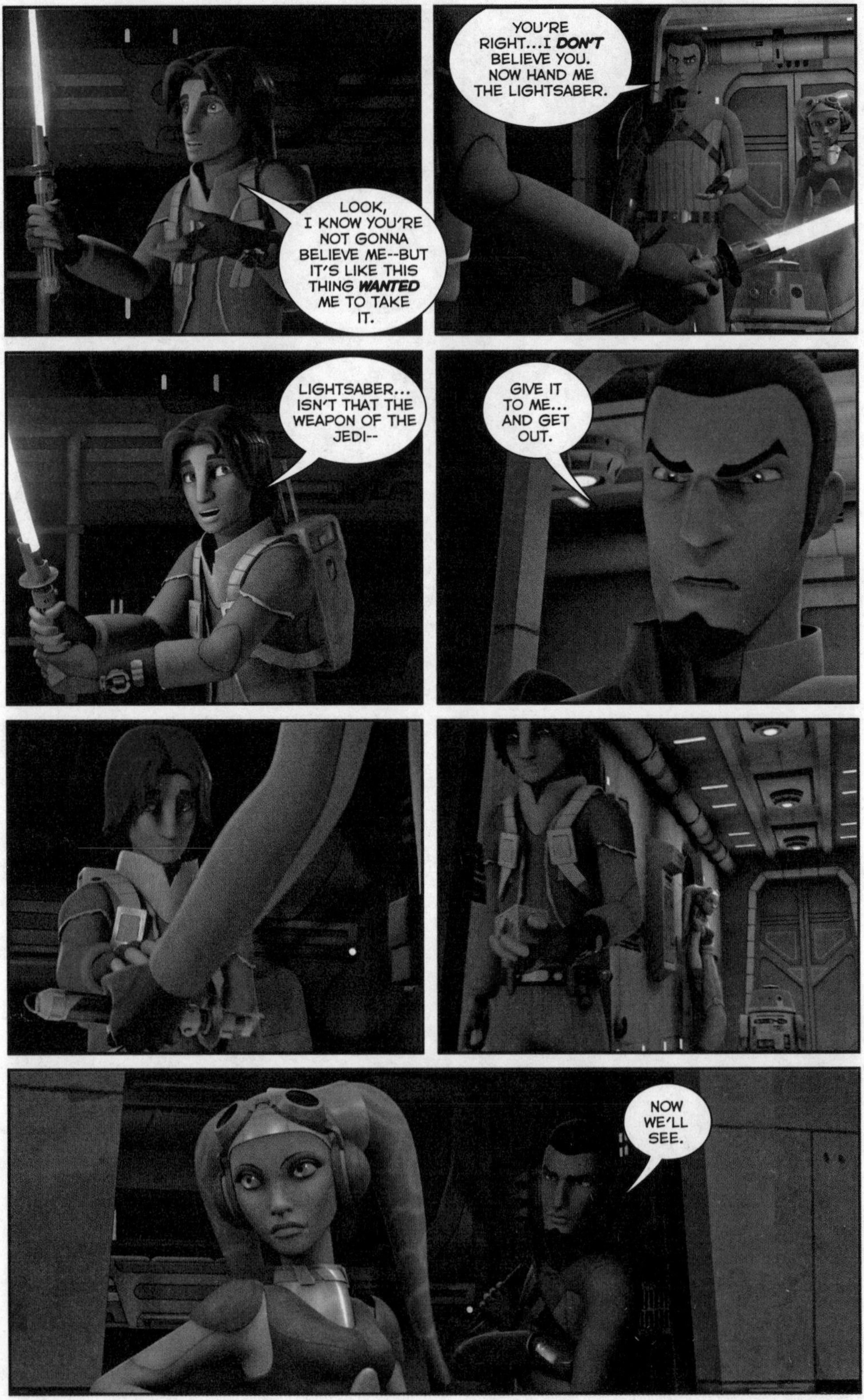
LOOK, I KNOW YOU'RE NOT GONNA BELIEVE ME--BUT IT'S LIKE THIS THING WANTED ME TO TAKE IT.
YOU'RE RIGHT...I DON'T BELIEVE YOU. NOW HAND ME THE LIGHTSABER.
LIGHTSABER... ISN'T THAT THE WEAPON OF THE JEDI--
GIVE IT TO ME... AND GET OUT.
NOW WE'LL SEE.

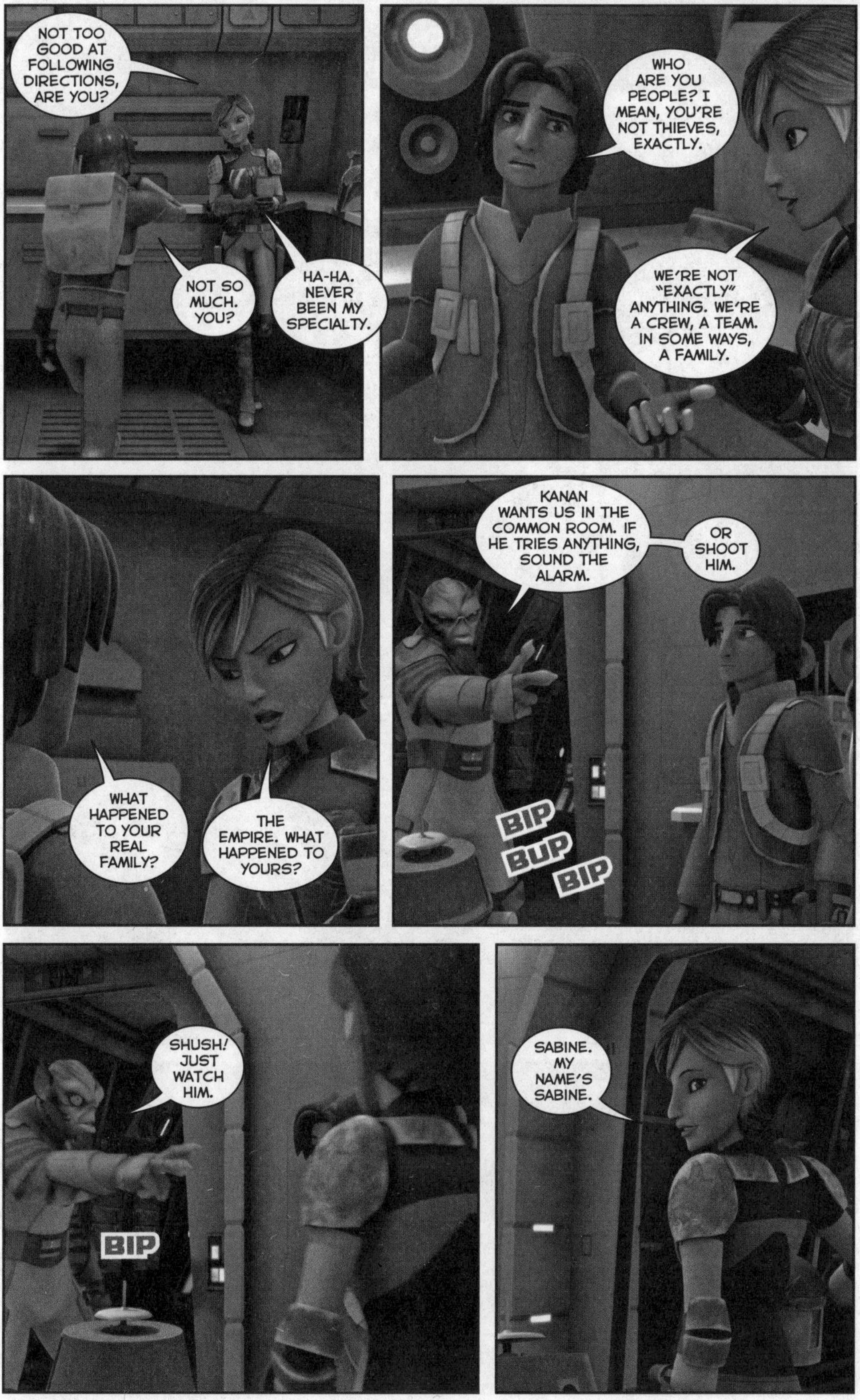
NOT TOO GOOD AT FOLLOWING DIRECTIONS, ARE YOU?
NOT SO MUCH. YOU?
HA-HA. NEVER BEEN MY SPECIALTY.
WHO ARE YOU PEOPLE? I MEAN, YOU'RE NOT THIEVES, EXACTLY.
WE'RE NOT "EXACTLY" ANYTHING. WE'RE A CREW, A TEAM. IN SOME WAYS, A FAMILY.
WHAT HAPPENED TO YOUR REAL FAMILY?
THE EMPIRE. WHAT HAPPENED TO YOURS?
KANAN WANTS US IN THE COMMON ROOM. IF HE TRIES ANYTHING, SOUND THE ALARM.
OR SHOOT HIM.
BIP
BUP
BIP
SHUSH! JUST WATCH HIM.
BIP
SABINE. MY NAME'S SABINE.

WE HAVE A NEW MISSION. VIZAGO ACQUIRED THE FLIGHT PLAN FOR AN IMPERIAL TRANSPORT SHIP FULL OF WOOKIEE PRISONERS.

MOST OF THESE WOOKIEES WERE SOLDIERS FOR THE OLD REPUBLIC.

I OWE THOSE HAIRY BEASTS-- THEY SAVED SOME OF MY PEOPLE.

MINE, TOO.

IF WE'RE GOING TO SAVE THEM, WE'VE GOT A TIGHT WINDOW. THEY'VE BEEN TAKEN TO AN UNKNOWN SLAVE-LABOR CAMP.

IF WE DON'T INTERCEPT THIS SHIP, WE'LL NEVER FIND THEM.

NOW, I HAVE A PLAN.

BUT...

CLANK

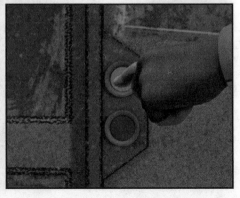

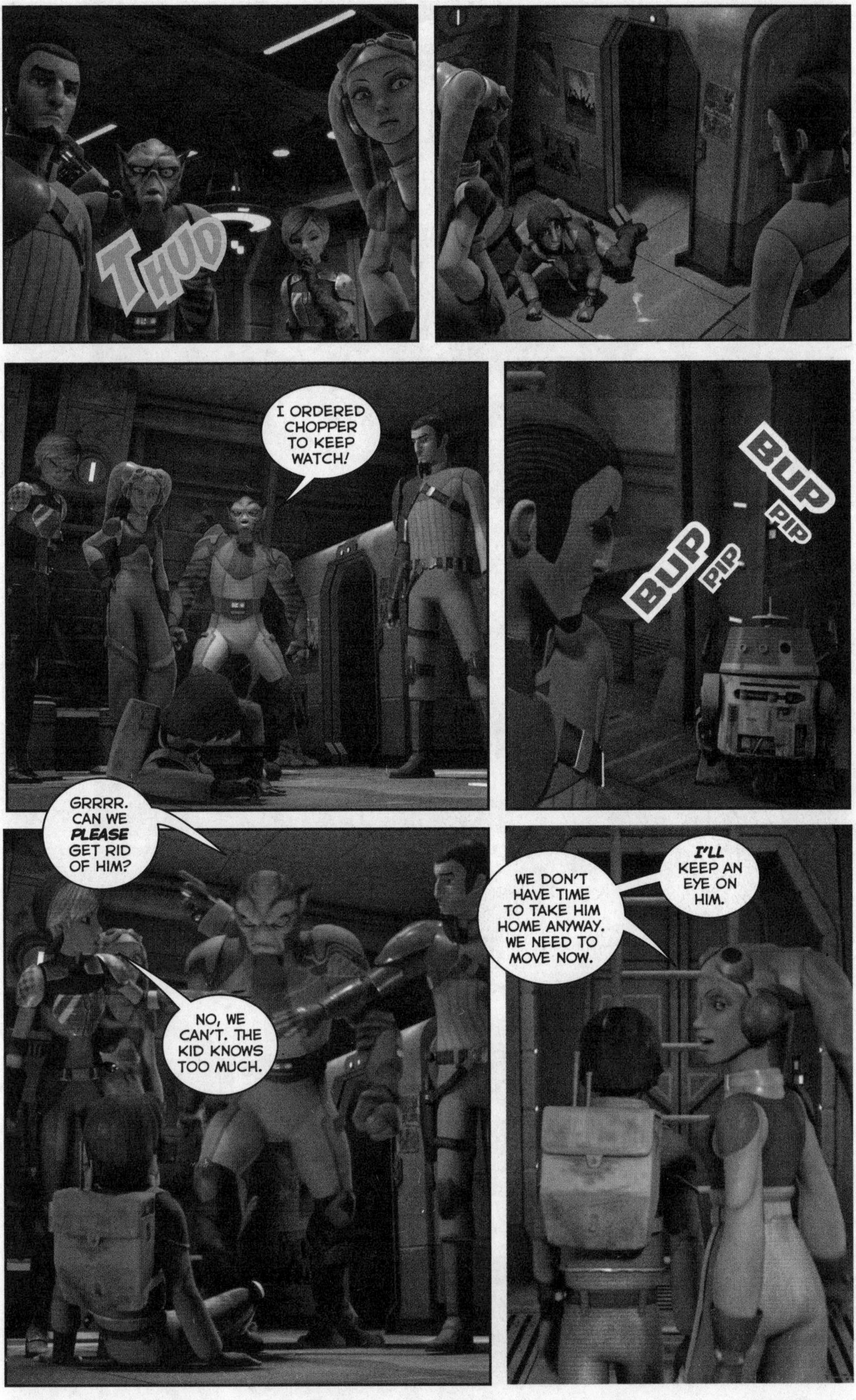
THUD
I ORDERED CHOPPER TO KEEP WATCH!
BUP PIP
BUP PIP
GRRRR. CAN WE *PLEASE* GET RID OF HIM?
NO, WE CAN'T. THE KID KNOWS TOO MUCH.
WE DON'T HAVE TIME TO TAKE HIM HOME ANYWAY. WE NEED TO MOVE NOW.
I'LL KEEP AN EYE ON HIM.

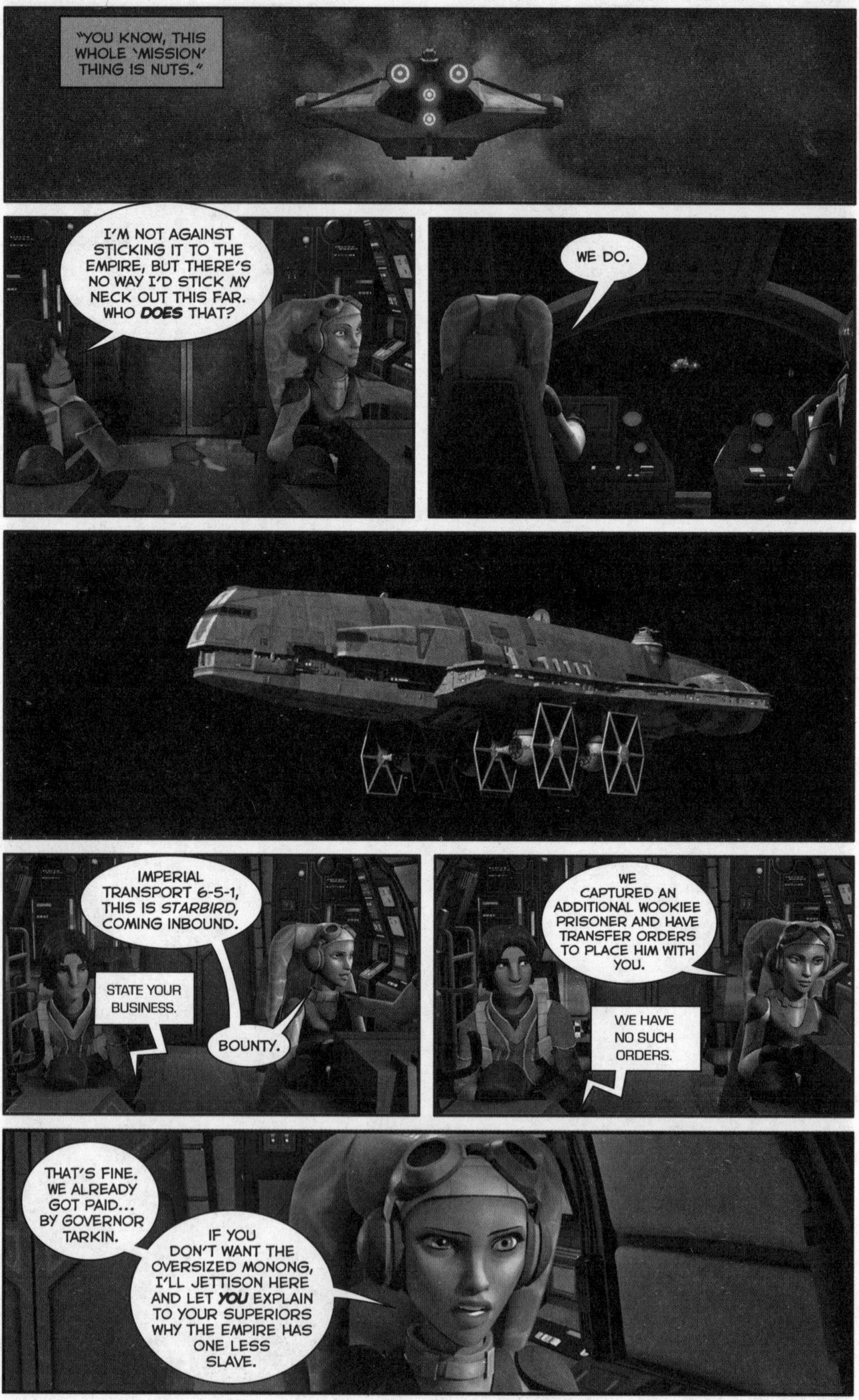
"YOU KNOW, THIS WHOLE 'MISSION' THING IS NUTS."
I'M NOT AGAINST STICKING IT TO THE EMPIRE, BUT THERE'S NO WAY I'D STICK MY NECK OUT THIS FAR. WHO *DOES* THAT?
WE DO.
IMPERIAL TRANSPORT 6-5-1, THIS IS *STARBIRD*, COMING INBOUND.
STATE YOUR BUSINESS.
BOUNTY.
WE CAPTURED AN ADDITIONAL WOOKIEE PRISONER AND HAVE TRANSFER ORDERS TO PLACE HIM WITH YOU.
WE HAVE NO SUCH ORDERS.
THAT'S FINE. WE ALREADY GOT PAID... BY GOVERNOR TARKIN.
IF YOU DON'T WANT THE OVERSIZED MONONG, I'LL JETTISON HERE AND LET *YOU* EXPLAIN TO YOUR SUPERIORS WHY THE EMPIRE HAS ONE LESS SLAVE.

PERMISSION TO DOCK. BAY ONE.

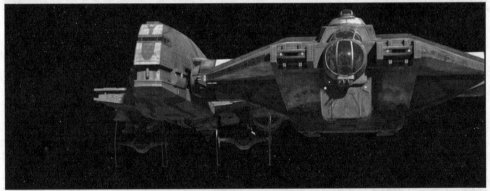

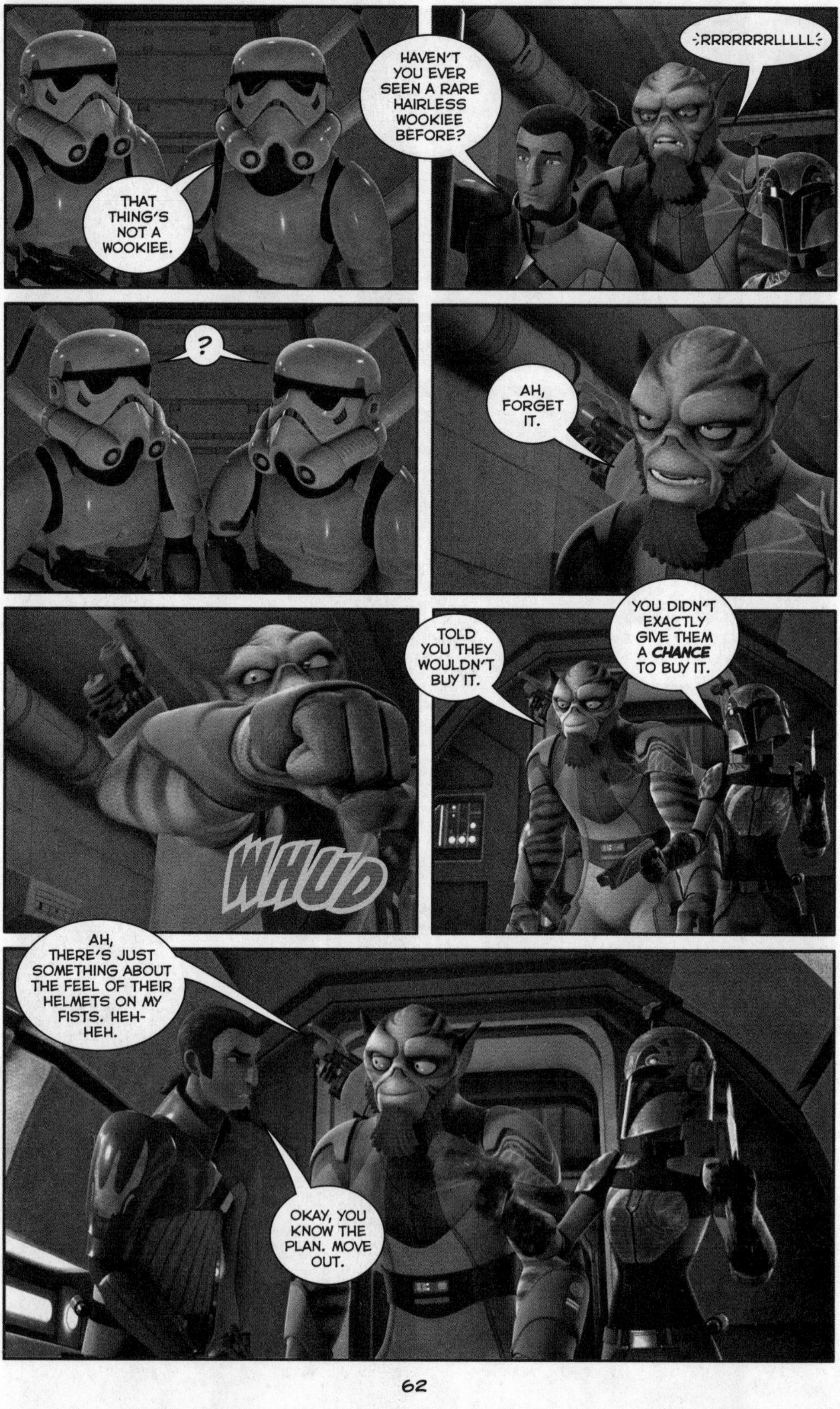
THAT THING'S NOT A WOOKIEE.
HAVEN'T YOU EVER SEEN A RARE HAIRLESS WOOKIEE BEFORE?
RRRRRRRLLLLL
?
AH, FORGET IT.
WHUD
TOLD YOU THEY WOULDN'T BUY IT.
YOU DIDN'T EXACTLY GIVE THEM A CHANCE TO BUY IT.
AH, THERE'S JUST SOMETHING ABOUT THE FEEL OF THEIR HELMETS ON MY FISTS. HEH-HEH.
OKAY, YOU KNOW THE PLAN. MOVE OUT.

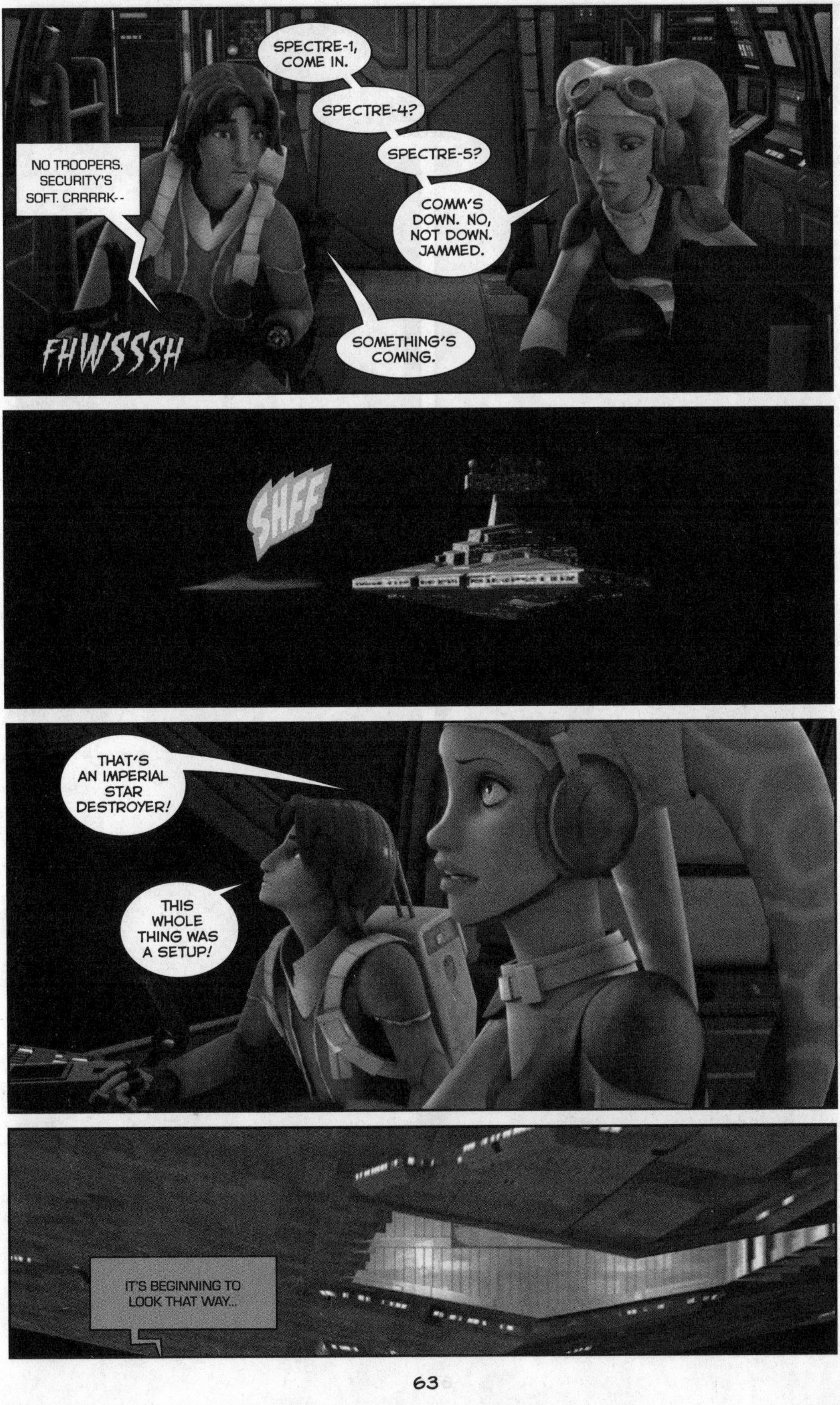
SPECTRE-1, COME IN.
SPECTRE-4?
SPECTRE-5?
NO TROOPERS. SECURITY'S SOFT. CRRRRK--
COMM'S DOWN. NO, NOT DOWN. JAMMED.
FHWSSSH
SOMETHING'S COMING.
SHFF
THAT'S AN IMPERIAL STAR DESTROYER!
THIS WHOLE THING WAS A SETUP!
IT'S BEGINNING TO LOOK THAT WAY...

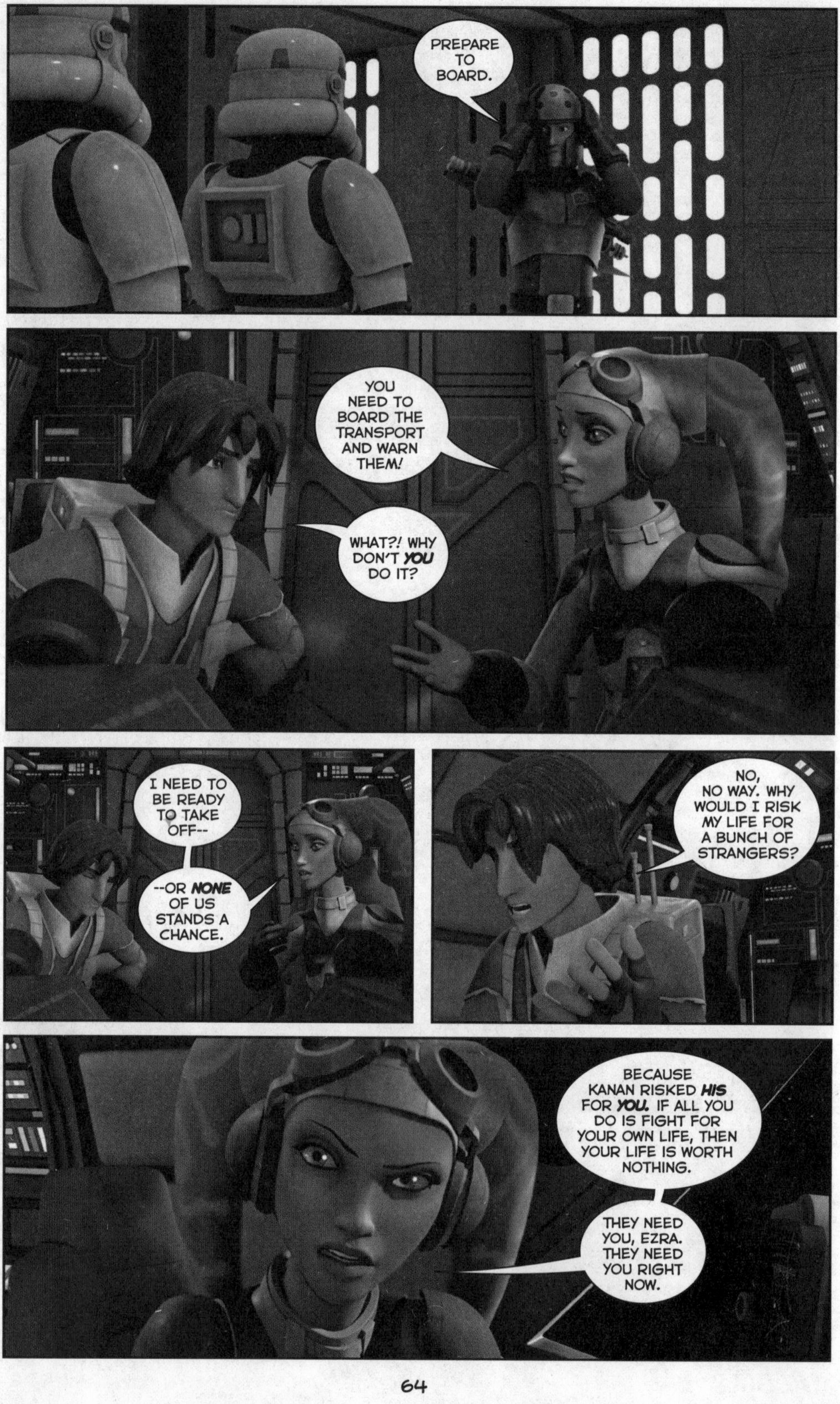
PREPARE TO BOARD.
YOU NEED TO BOARD THE TRANSPORT AND WARN THEM!
WHAT?! WHY DON'T *YOU* DO IT?
I NEED TO BE READY TO TAKE OFF--
--OR *NONE* OF US STANDS A CHANCE.
NO, NO WAY. WHY WOULD I RISK MY LIFE FOR A BUNCH OF STRANGERS?
BECAUSE KANAN RISKED *HIS* FOR *YOU.* IF ALL YOU DO IS FIGHT FOR YOUR OWN LIFE, THEN YOUR LIFE IS WORTH NOTHING.
THEY NEED YOU, EZRA. THEY NEED YOU RIGHT NOW.

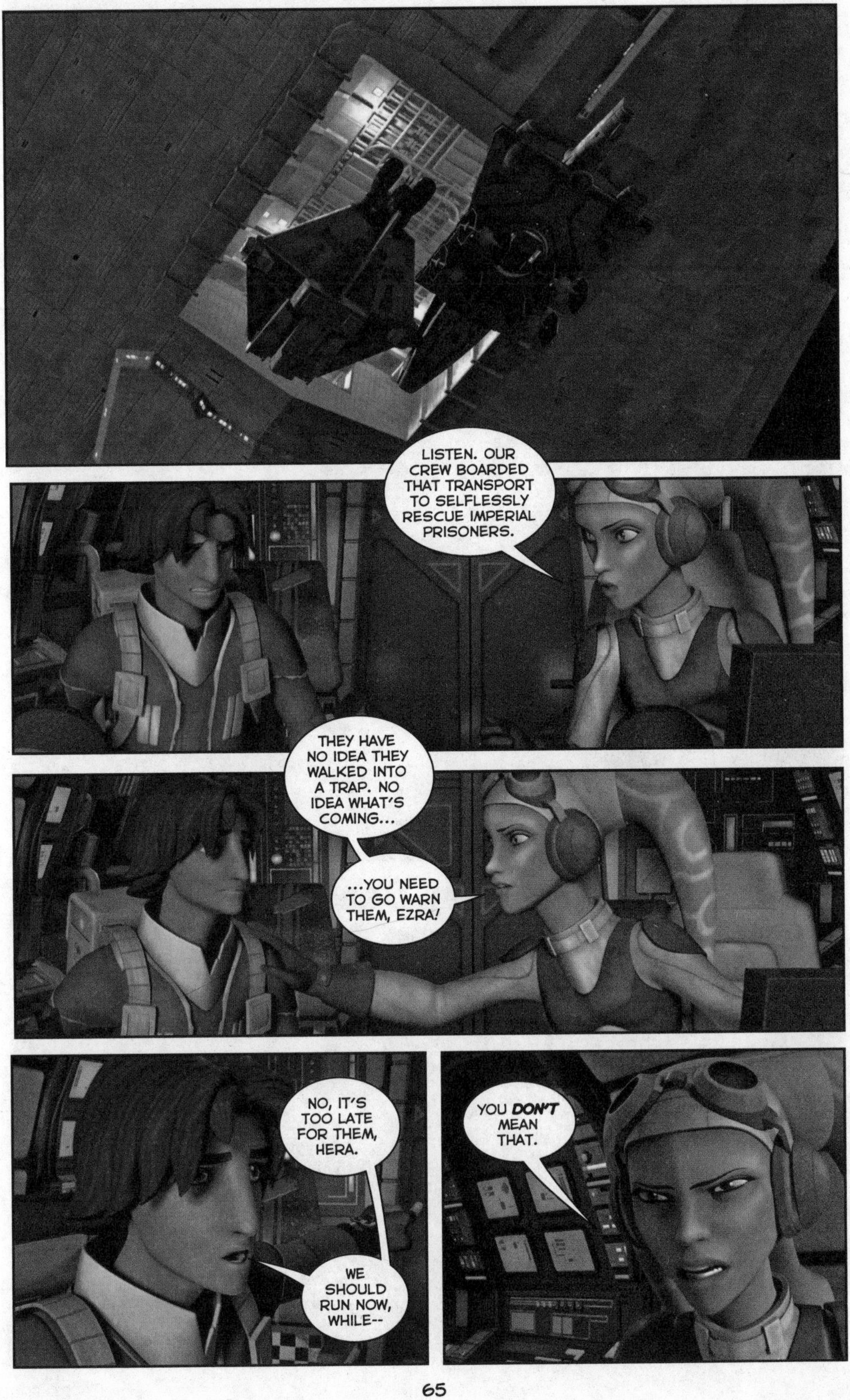
LISTEN. OUR CREW BOARDED THAT TRANSPORT TO SELFLESSLY RESCUE IMPERIAL PRISONERS.
THEY HAVE NO IDEA THEY WALKED INTO A TRAP. NO IDEA WHAT'S COMING...
...YOU NEED TO GO WARN THEM, EZRA!
NO, IT'S TOO LATE FOR THEM, HERA.
WE SHOULD RUN NOW, WHILE--
YOU **DON'T** MEAN THAT.

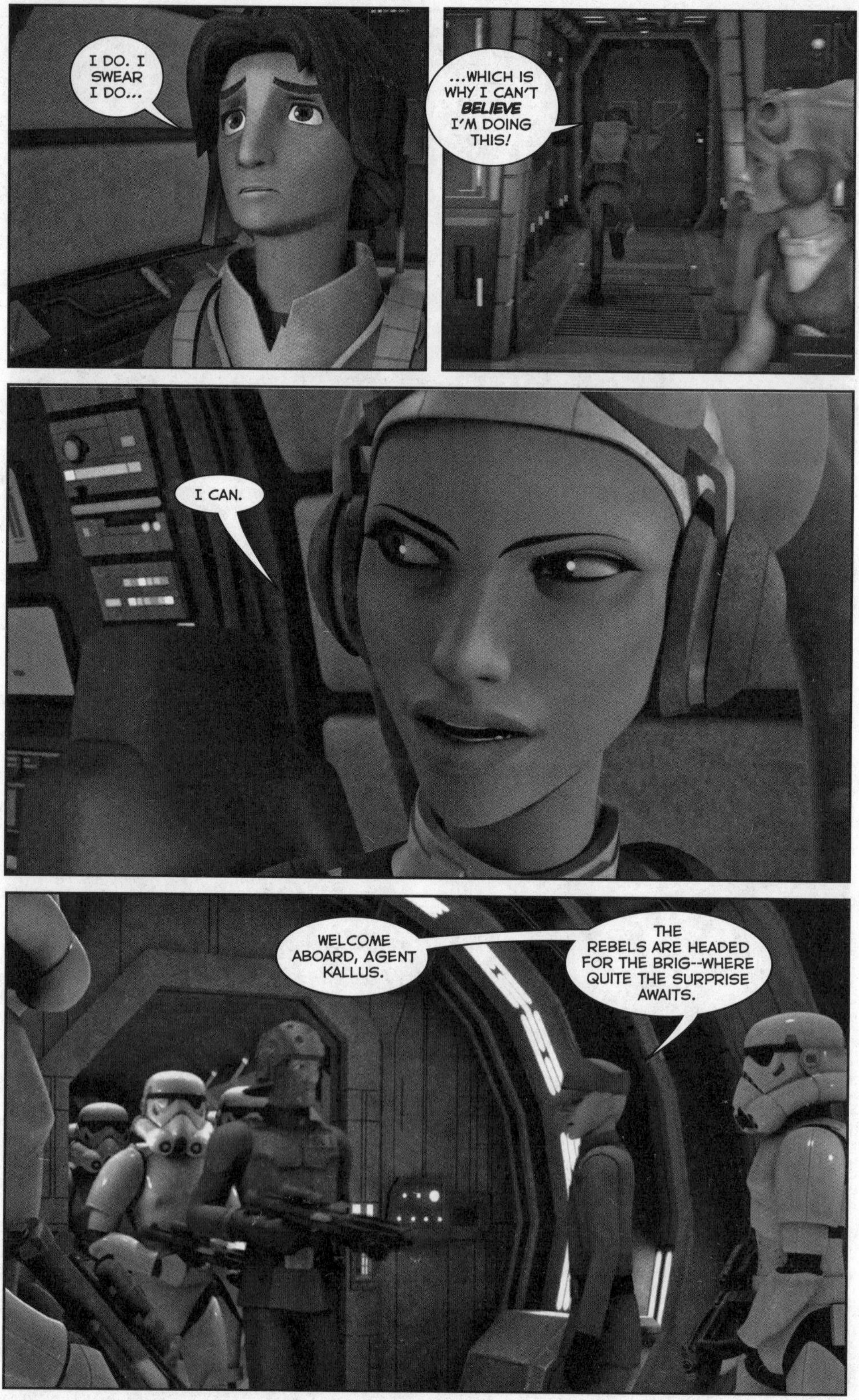
I DO. I SWEAR I DO...
...WHICH IS WHY I CAN'T BELIEVE I'M DOING THIS!
I CAN.
WELCOME ABOARD, AGENT KALLUS.
THE REBELS ARE HEADED FOR THE BRIG--WHERE QUITE THE SURPRISE AWAITS.

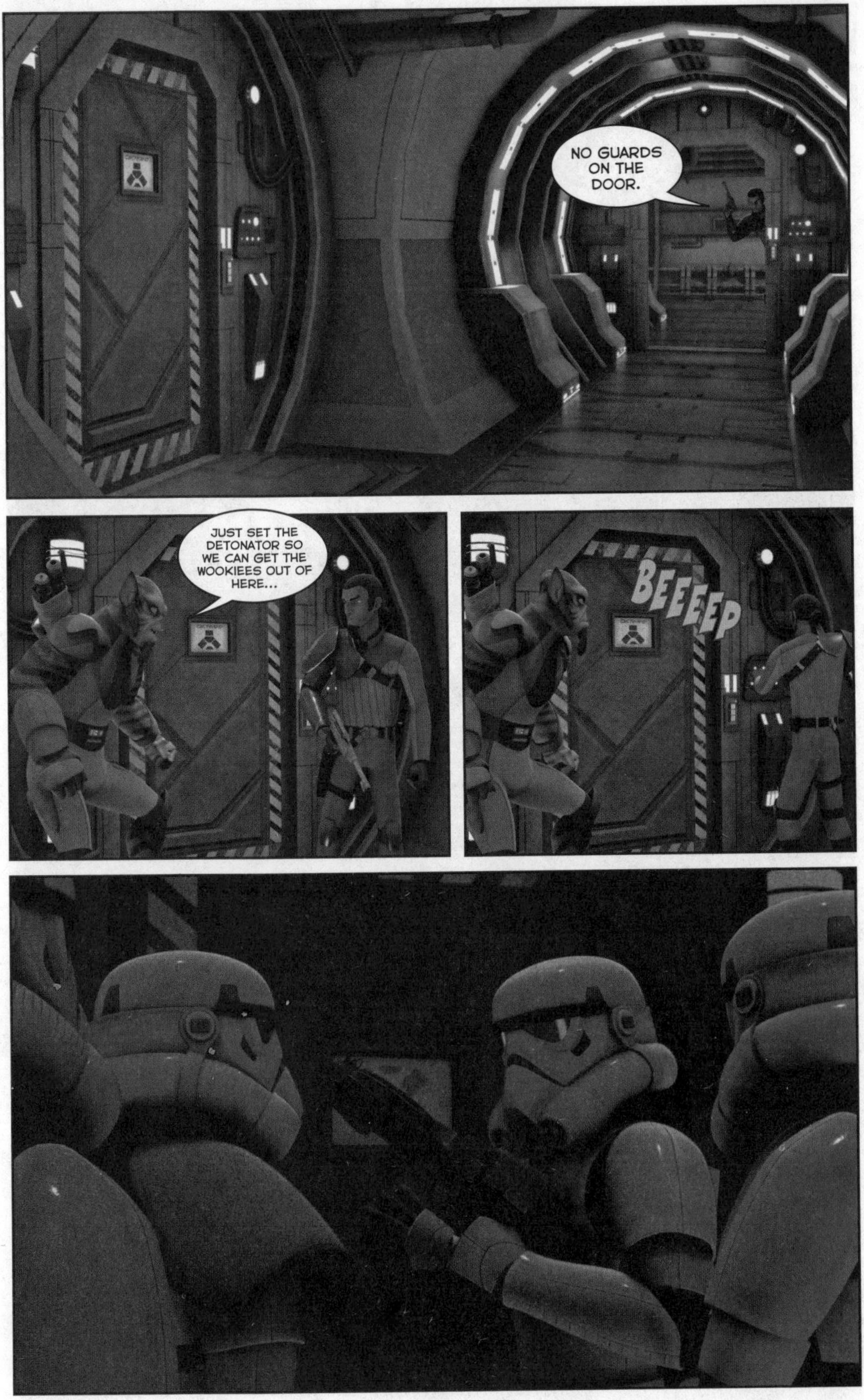
NO GUARDS ON THE DOOR.
JUST SET THE DETONATOR SO WE CAN GET THE WOOKIEES OUT OF HERE...
BEEEEP

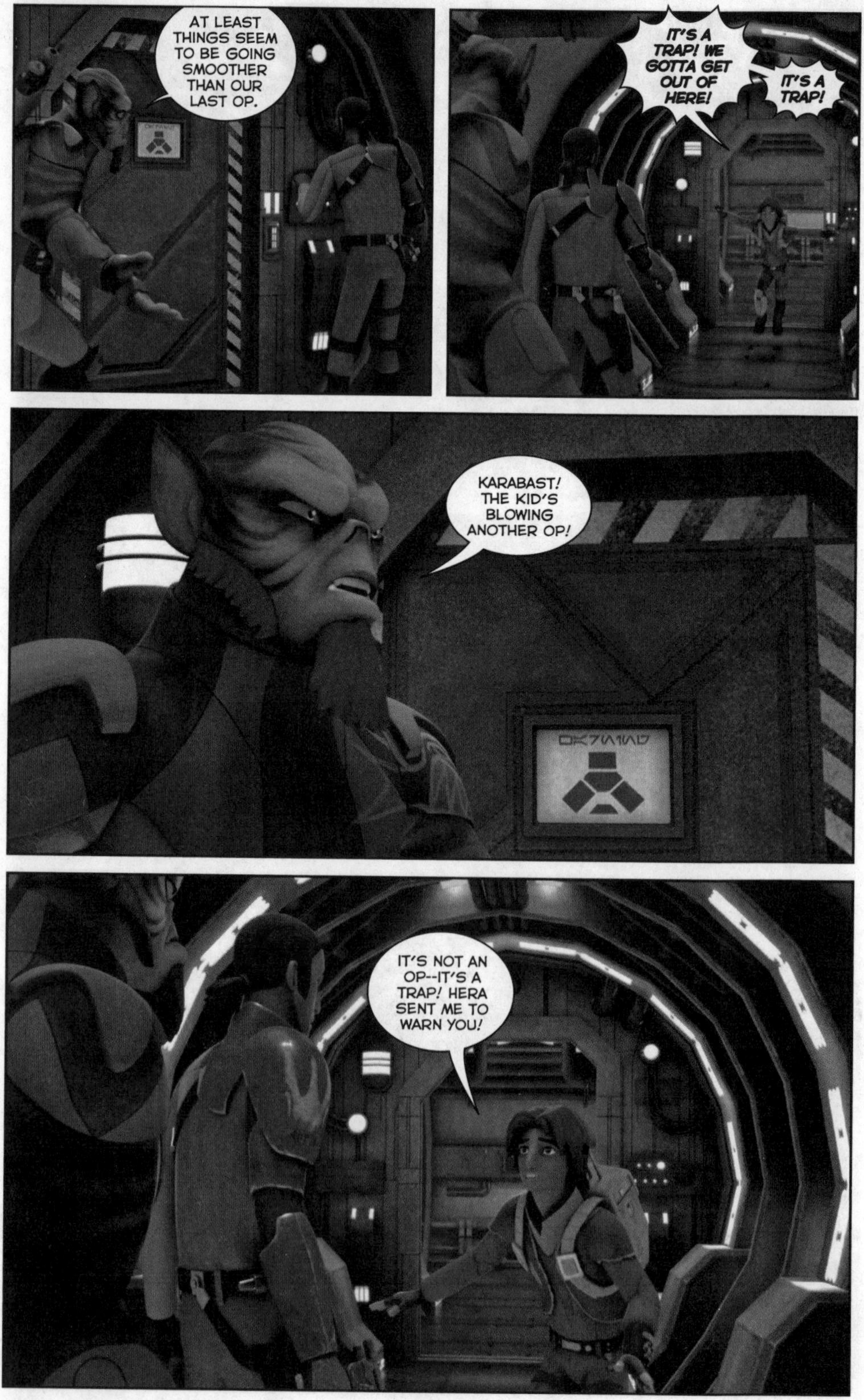
AT LEAST THINGS SEEM TO BE GOING SMOOTHER THAN OUR LAST OP.
IT'S A TRAP! WE GOTTA GET OUT OF HERE!
IT'S A TRAP!
KARABAST! THE KID'S BLOWING ANOTHER OP!
IT'S NOT AN OP--IT'S A TRAP! HERA SENT ME TO WARN YOU!

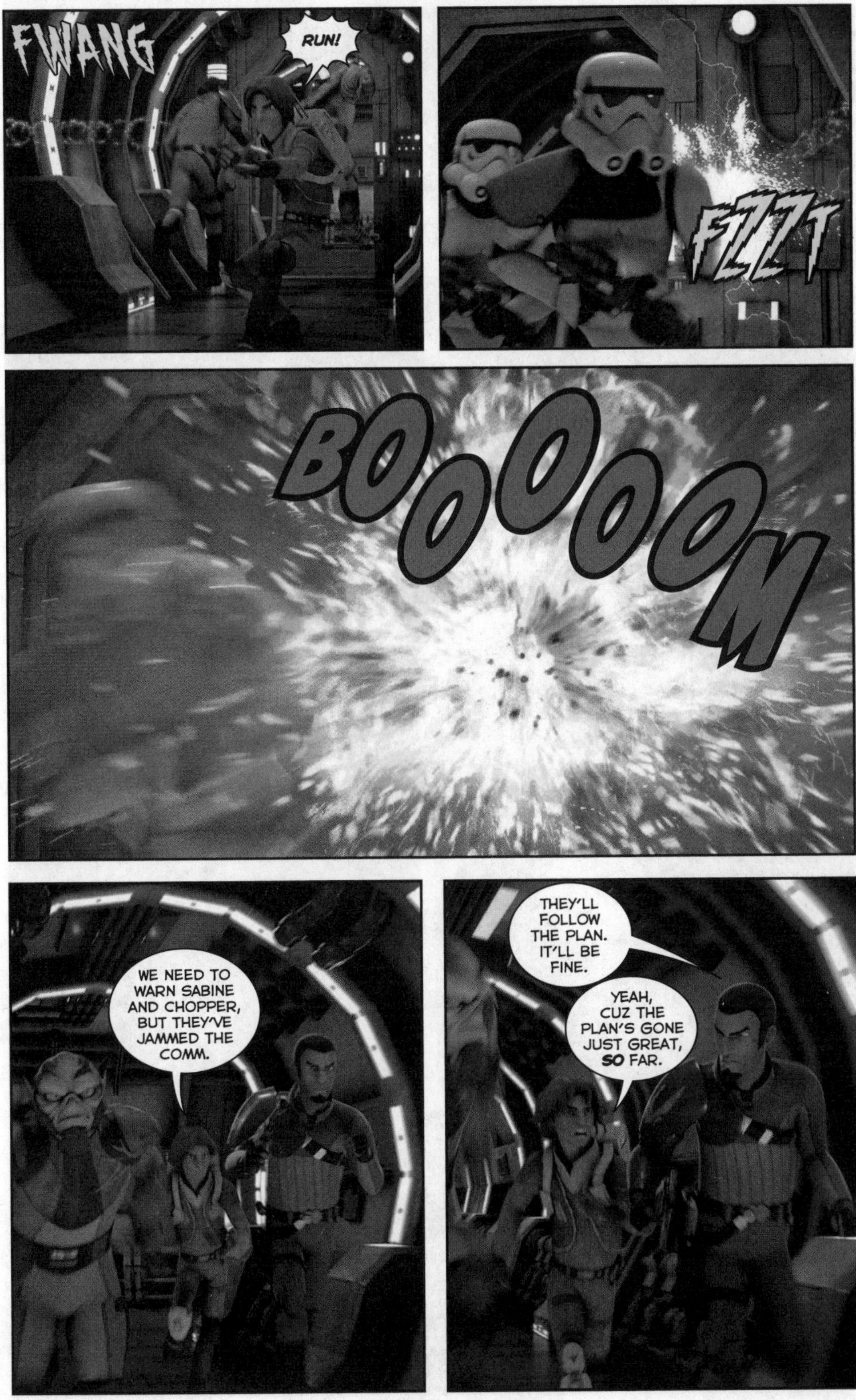
FWANG
RUN!
FZZT
BOOOOOM
WE NEED TO WARN SABINE AND CHOPPER, BUT THEY'VE JAMMED THE COMM.
THEY'LL FOLLOW THE PLAN. IT'LL BE FINE.
YEAH, CUZ THE PLAN'S GONE JUST GREAT, **SO** FAR.

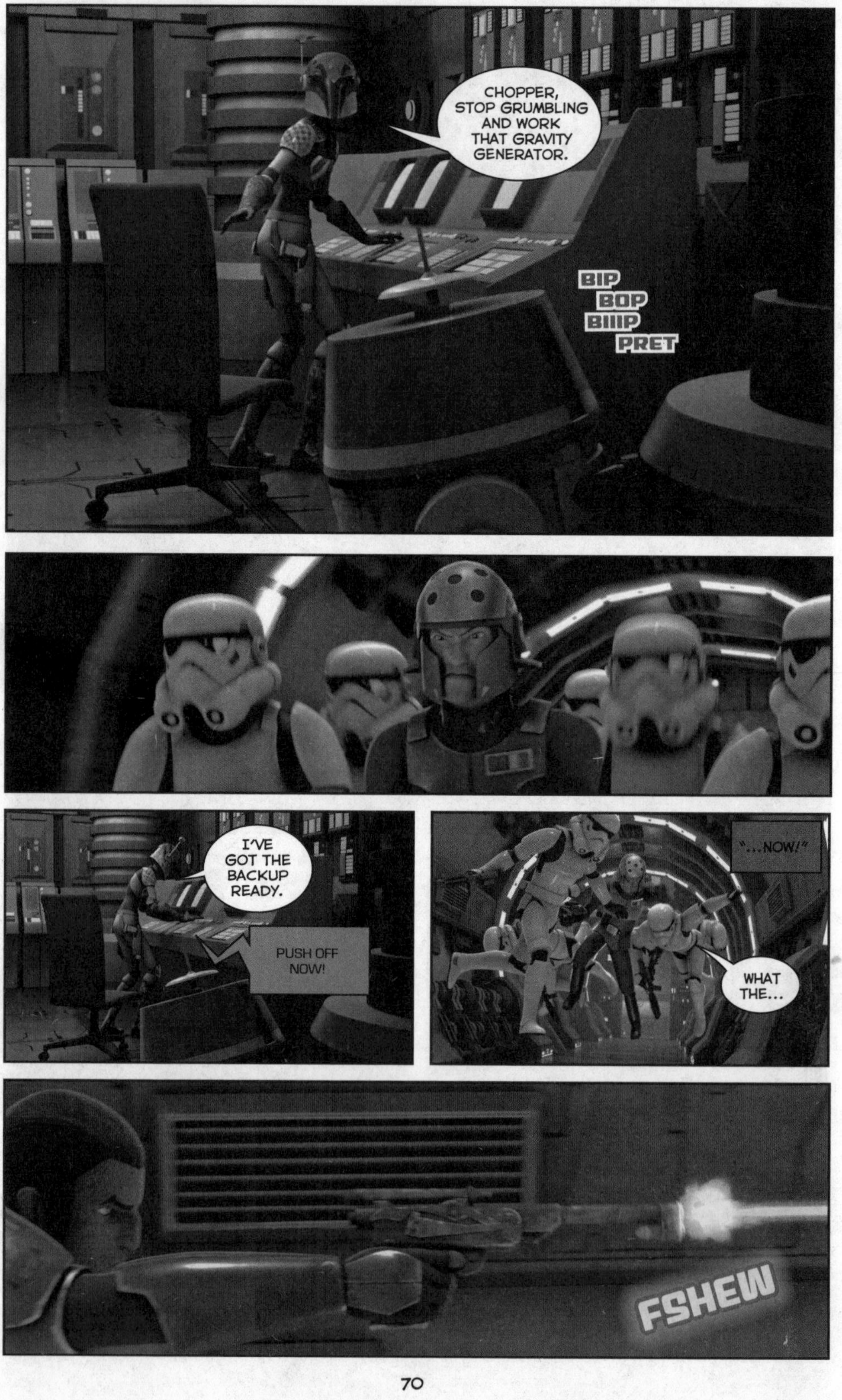
CHOPPER, STOP GRUMBLING AND WORK THAT GRAVITY GENERATOR.
BIP BOP BIIIP PRET
I'VE GOT THE BACKUP READY.
PUSH OFF NOW!
"...NOW!"
WHAT THE...
FSHEW

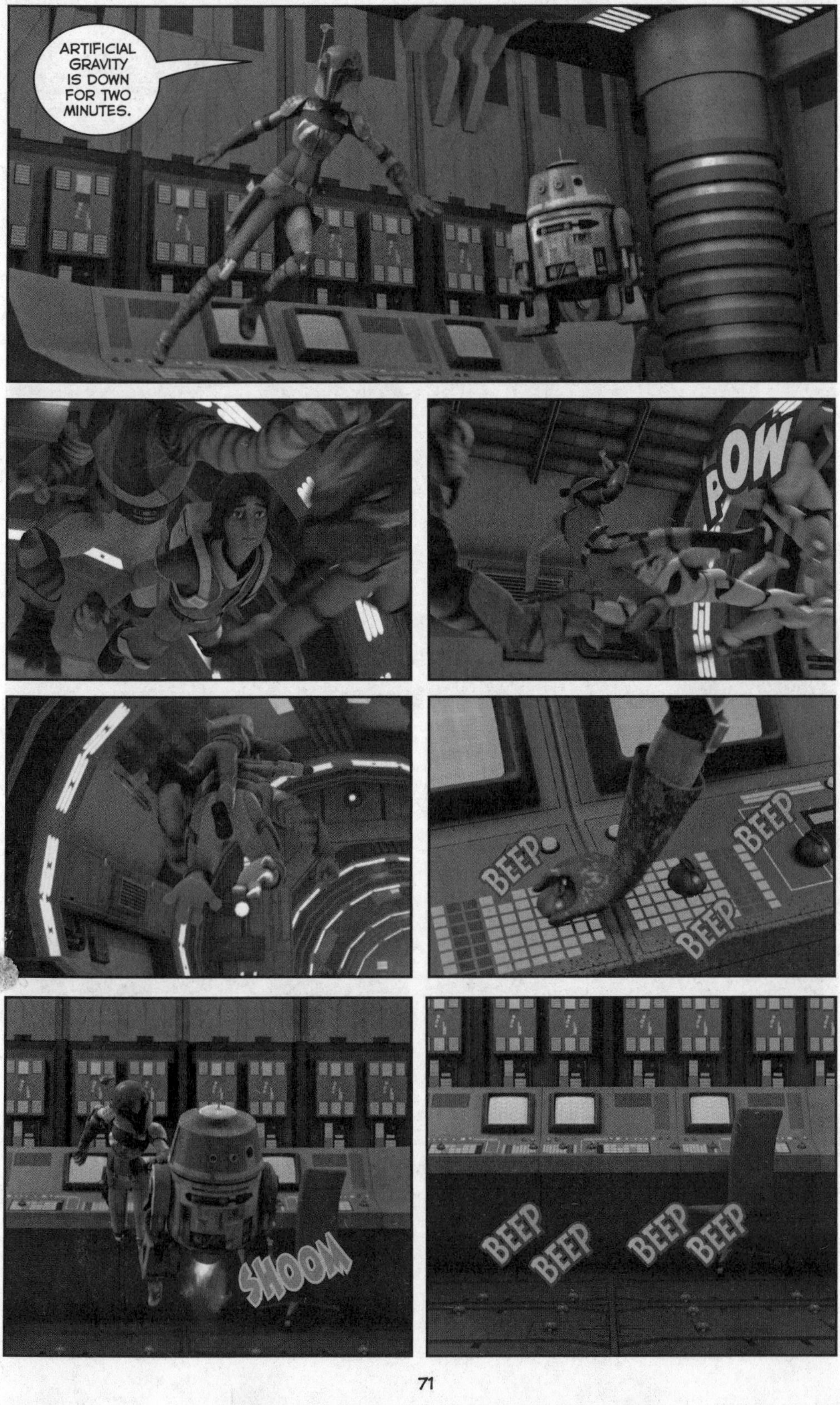
ARTIFICIAL GRAVITY IS DOWN FOR TWO MINUTES.
POW
BEEP
BEEP
BEEP
SHOOM
BEEP
BEEP
BEEP
BEEP

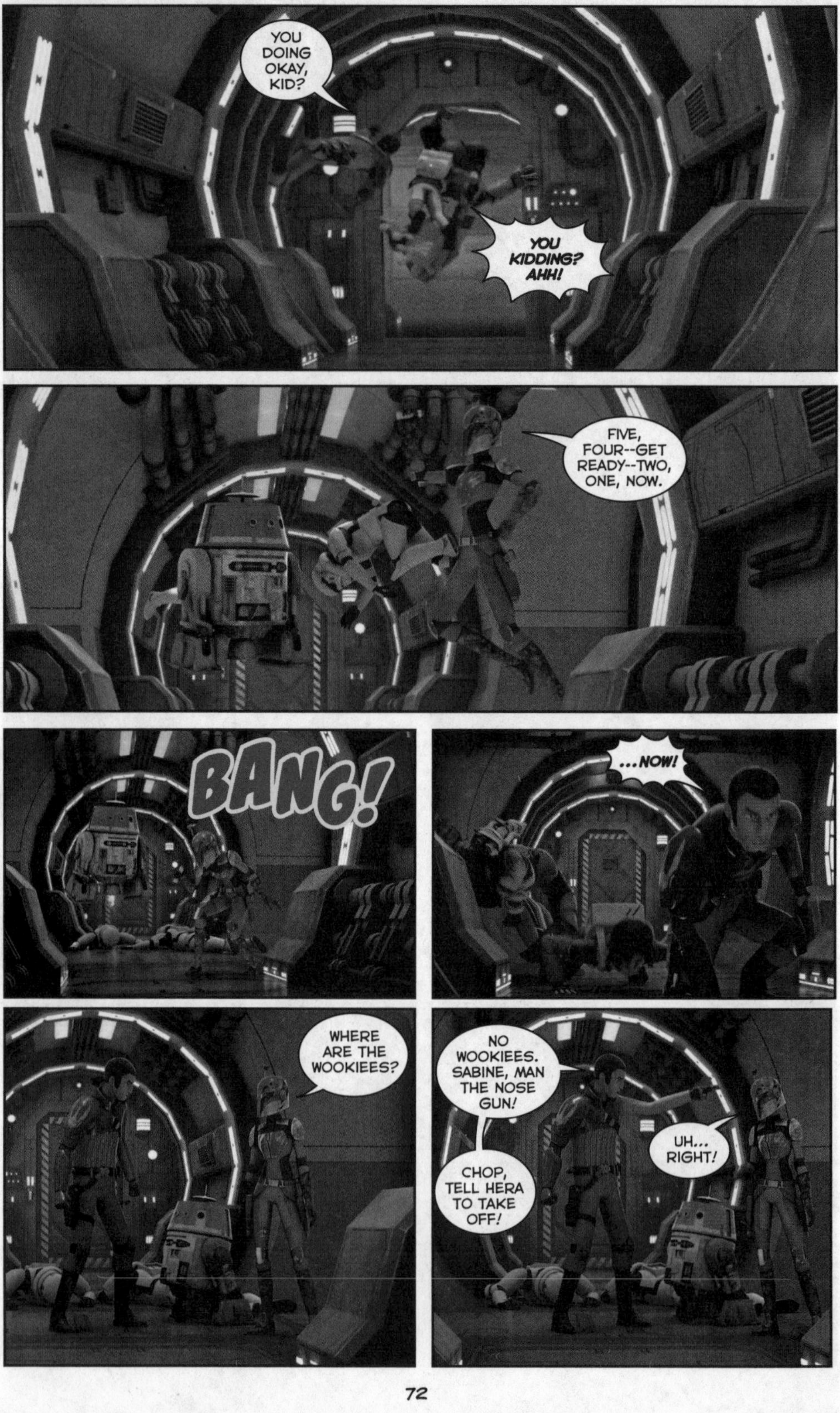
YOU DOING OKAY, KID?
YOU KIDDING? AHH!
FIVE, FOUR--GET READY--TWO, ONE, NOW.
BANG!
...NOW!
WHERE ARE THE WOOKIEES?
NO WOOKIEES. SABINE, MAN THE NOSE GUN!
CHOP, TELL HERA TO TAKE OFF!
UH... RIGHT!

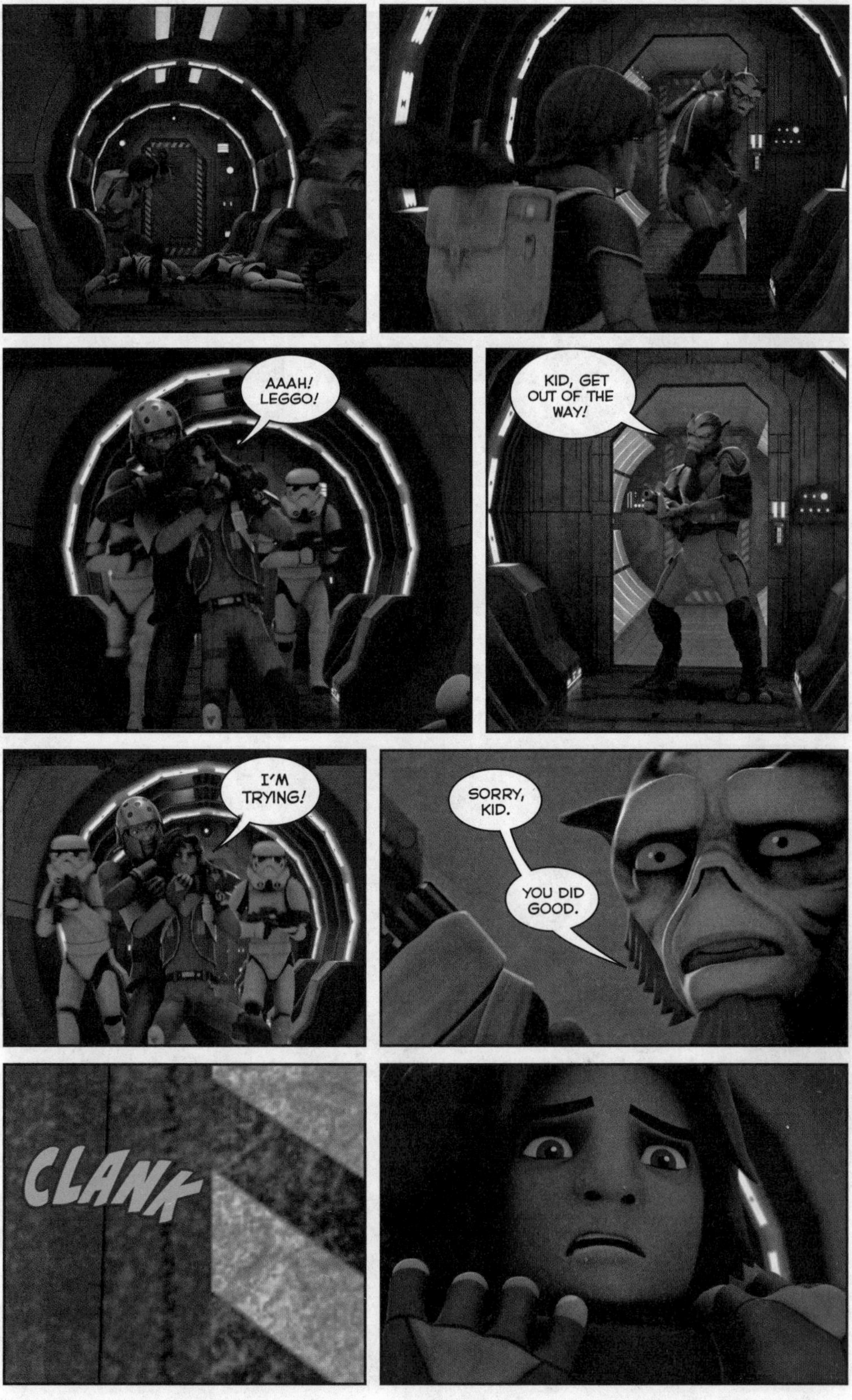
AAAH! LEGGO!
KID, GET OUT OF THE WAY!
I'M TRYING!
SORRY, KID.
YOU DID GOOD.
CLANK

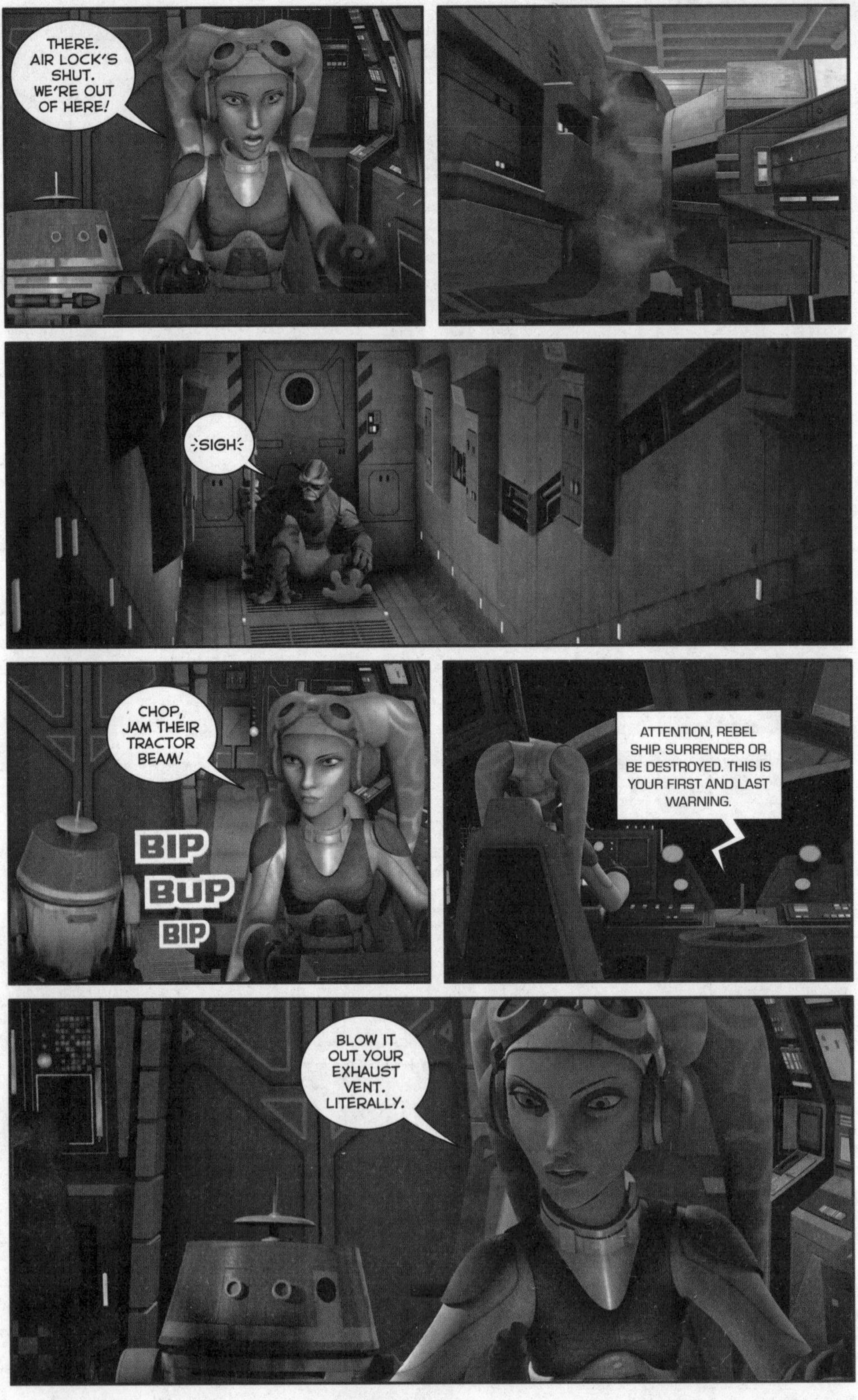
THERE. AIR LOCK'S SHUT. WE'RE OUT OF HERE!
SIGH
CHOP, JAM THEIR TRACTOR BEAM!
BIP
BUP
BIP
ATTENTION, REBEL SHIP. SURRENDER OR BE DESTROYED. THIS IS YOUR FIRST AND LAST WARNING.
BLOW IT OUT YOUR EXHAUST VENT. LITERALLY.

SABINE!

CLICK

BEEP BEEP BEEP

BOOOOOOOOOOOOOM

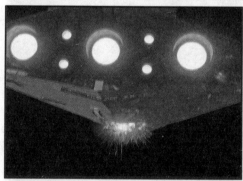

AW, I CAN'T SEE IT FROM HERE. HOW'D IT LOOK?

GORGEOUS, SABINE. AS ALWAYS.

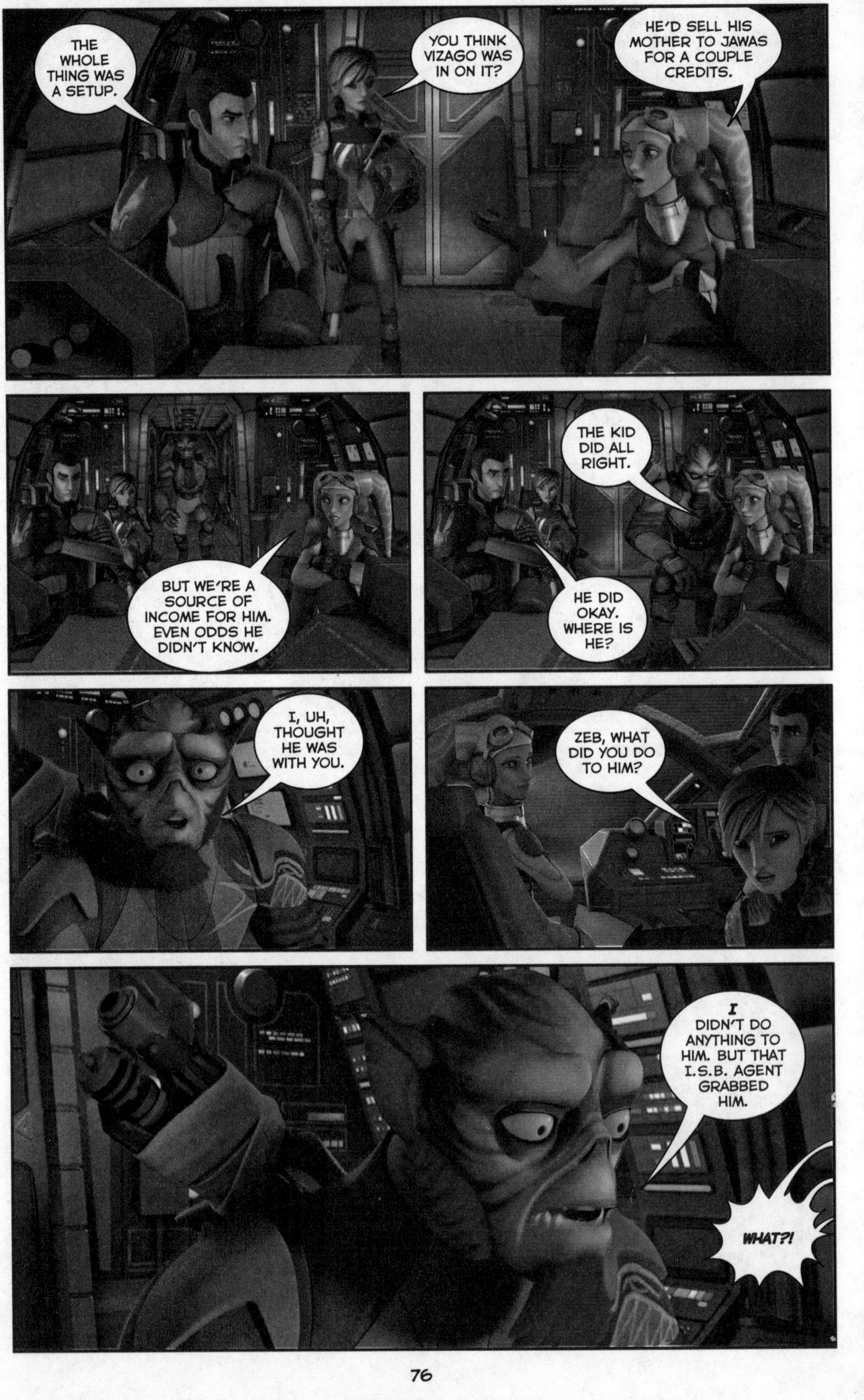

THE WHOLE THING WAS A SETUP.
YOU THINK VIZAGO WAS IN ON IT?
HE'D SELL HIS MOTHER TO JAWAS FOR A COUPLE CREDITS.
BUT WE'RE A SOURCE OF INCOME FOR HIM. EVEN ODDS HE DIDN'T KNOW.
THE KID DID ALL RIGHT.
HE DID OKAY. WHERE IS HE?
I, UH, THOUGHT HE WAS WITH YOU.
ZEB, WHAT DID YOU DO TO HIM?
I DIDN'T DO ANYTHING TO HIM. BUT THAT I.S.B. AGENT GRABBED HIM.
WHAT?!

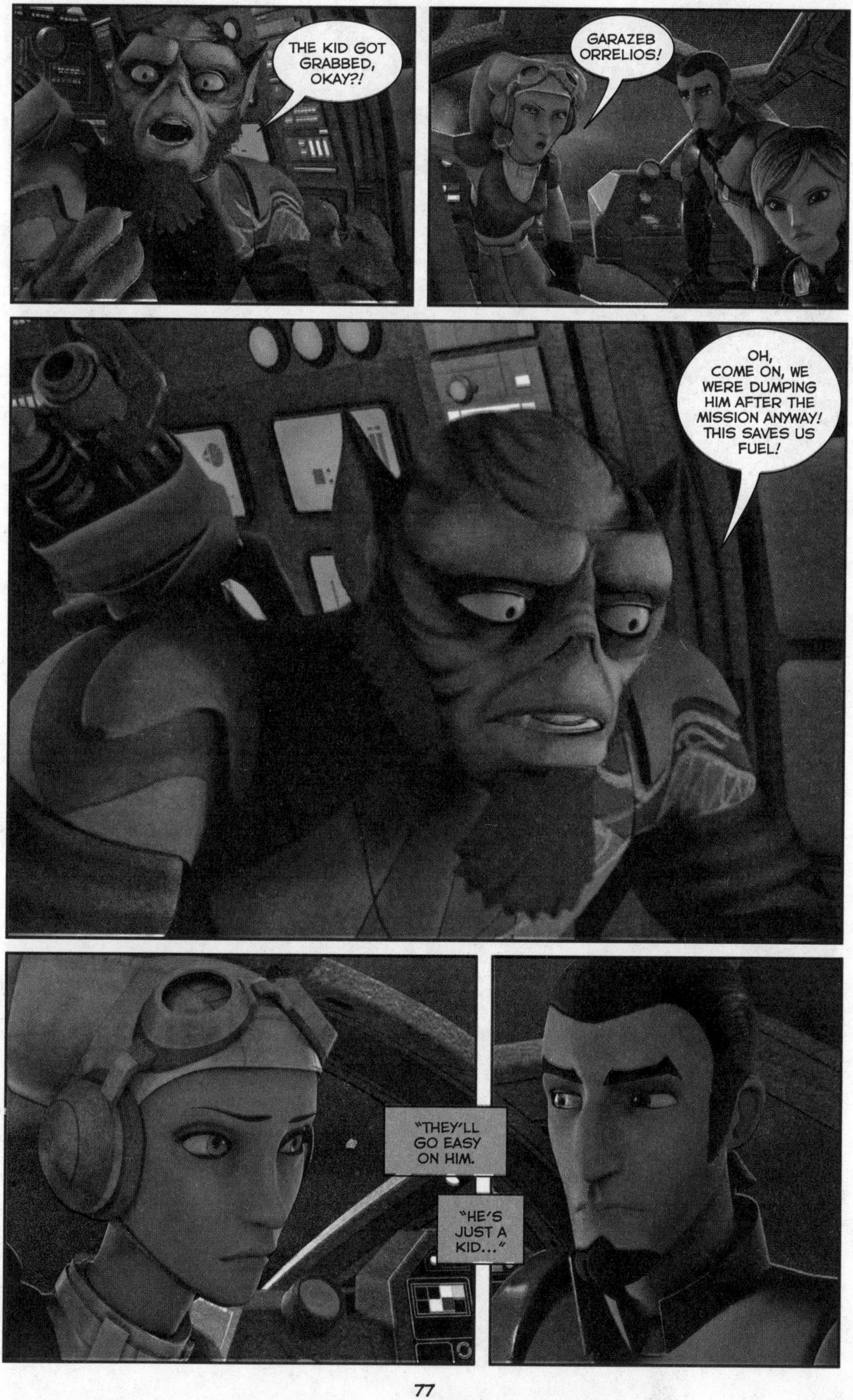
THE KID GOT GRABBED, OKAY?!
GARAZEB ORRELIOS!
OH, COME ON, WE WERE DUMPING HIM AFTER THE MISSION ANYWAY! THIS SAVES US FUEL!
"THEY'LL GO EASY ON HIM.
"HE'S JUST A KID..."

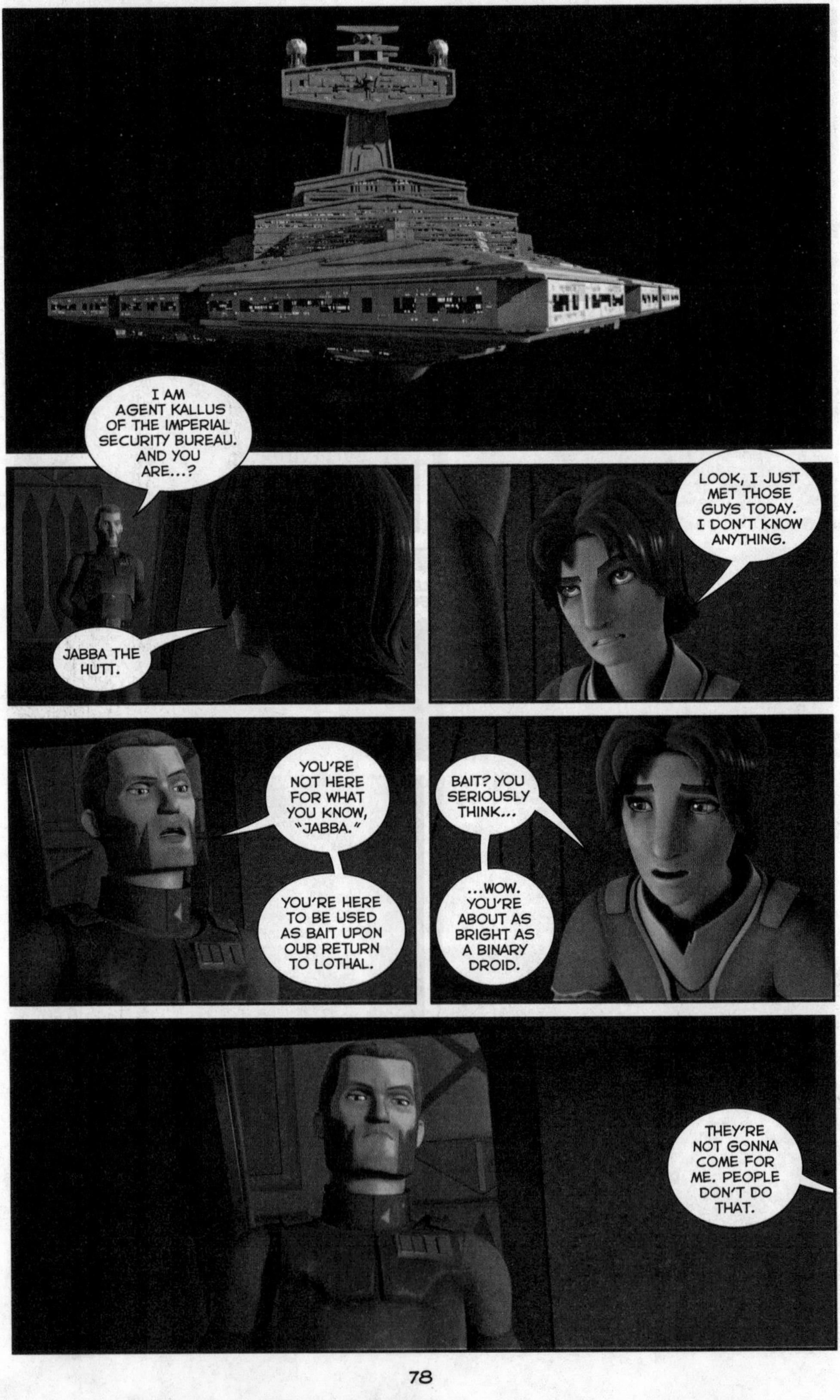
I AM AGENT KALLUS OF THE IMPERIAL SECURITY BUREAU. AND YOU ARE...?
JABBA THE HUTT.
LOOK, I JUST MET THOSE GUYS TODAY. I DON'T KNOW ANYTHING.
YOU'RE NOT HERE FOR WHAT YOU KNOW, "JABBA."
YOU'RE HERE TO BE USED AS BAIT UPON OUR RETURN TO LOTHAL.
BAIT? YOU SERIOUSLY THINK...
...WOW. YOU'RE ABOUT AS BRIGHT AS A BINARY DROID.
THEY'RE NOT GONNA COME FOR ME. PEOPLE DON'T DO THAT.

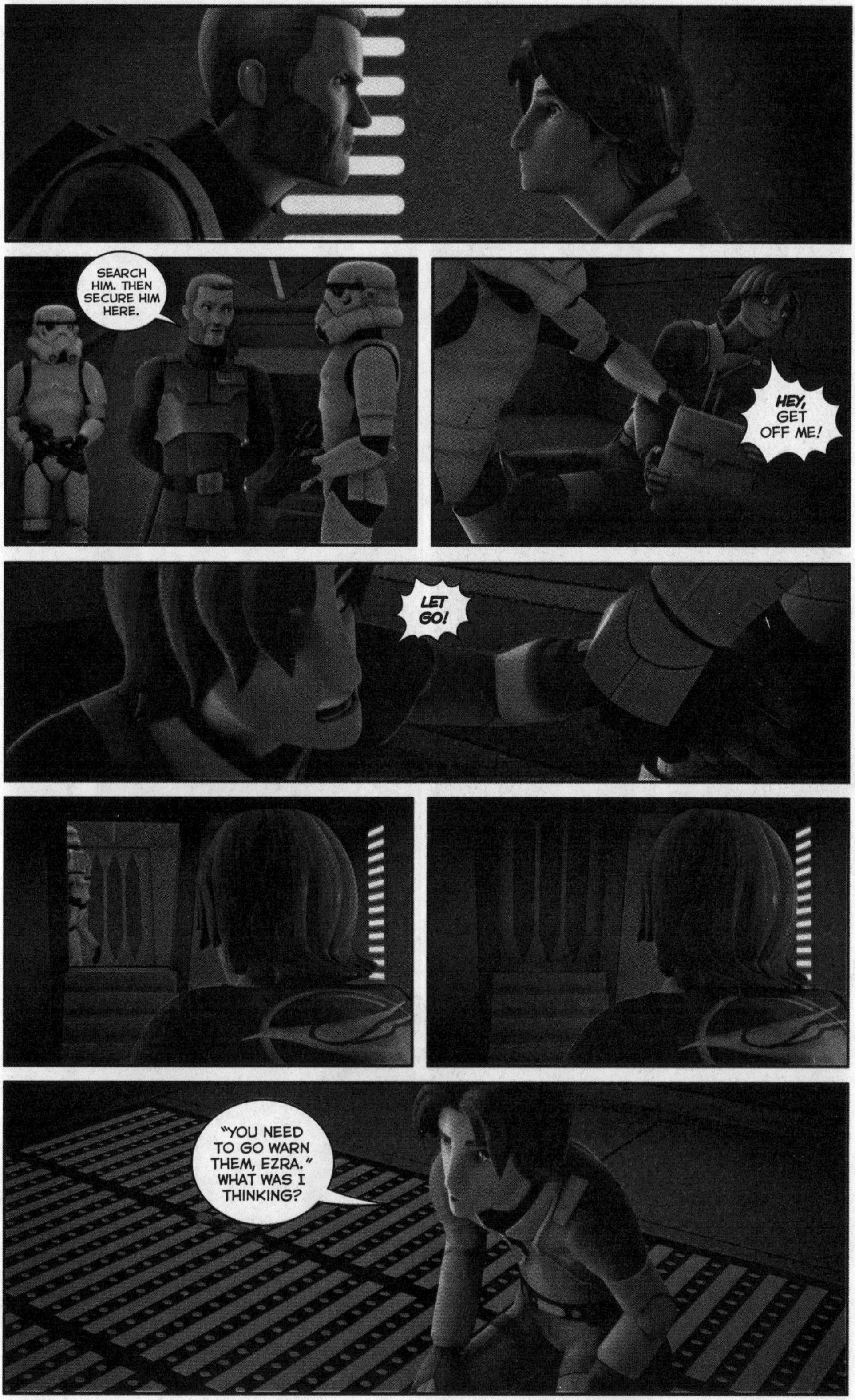
SEARCH HIM. THEN SECURE HIM HERE.
HEY, GET OFF ME!
LET GO!
"YOU NEED TO GO WARN THEM, EZRA." WHAT WAS I THINKING?

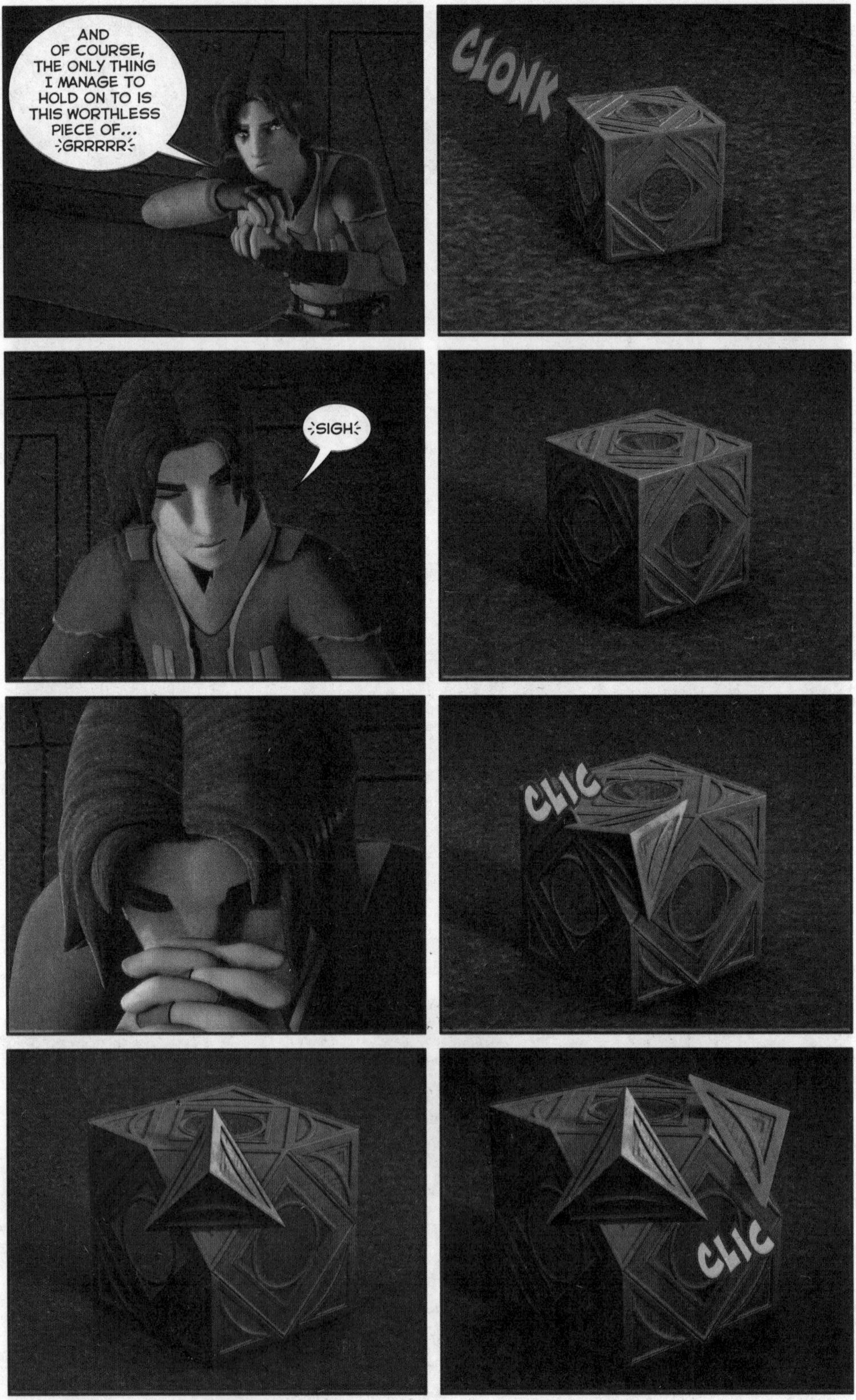
AND OF COURSE, THE ONLY THING I MANAGE TO HOLD ON TO IS THIS WORTHLESS PIECE OF... GRRRRR
CLONK
SIGH
CLIC
CLIC

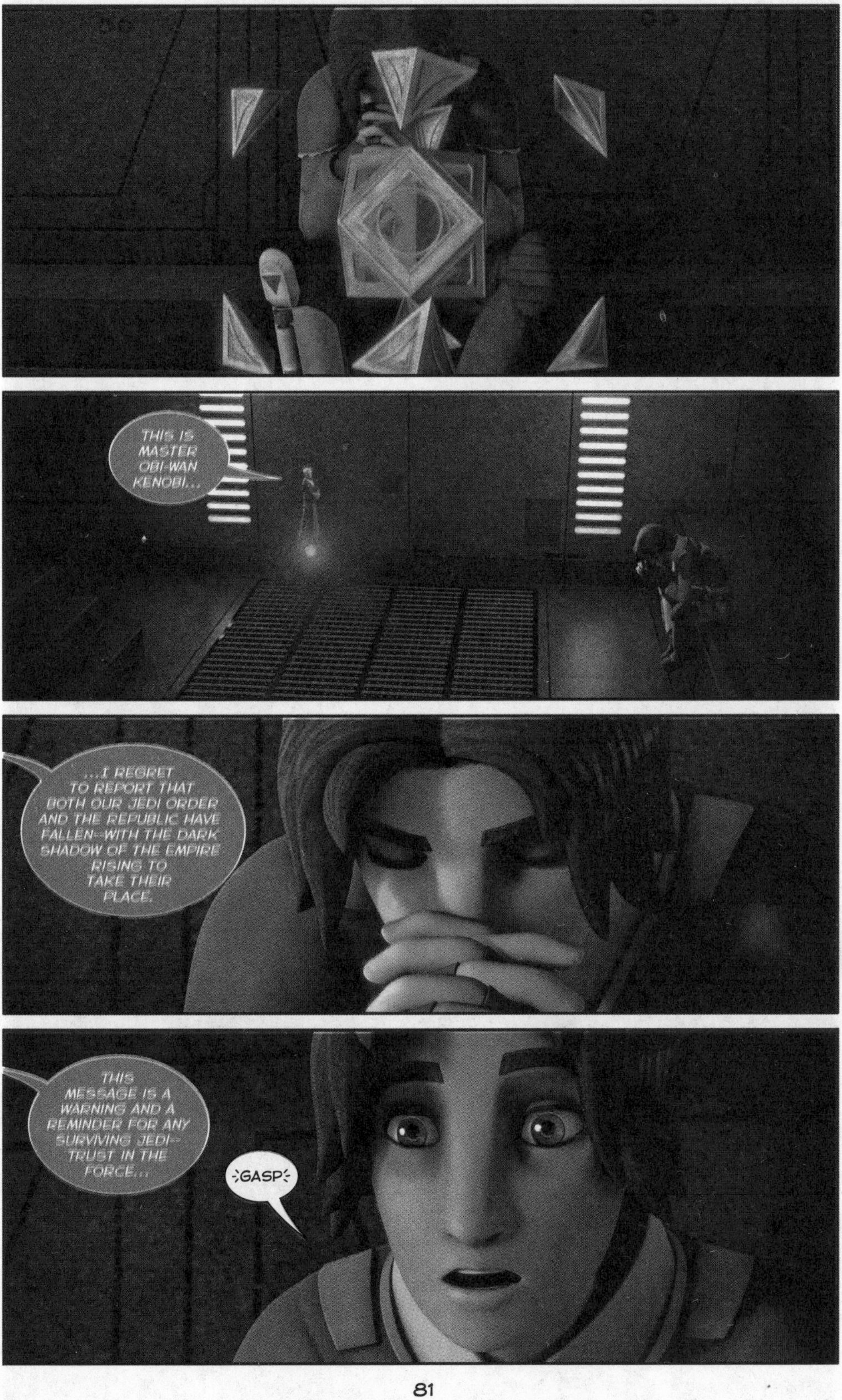
THIS IS MASTER OBI-WAN KENOBI...
...I REGRET TO REPORT THAT BOTH OUR JEDI ORDER AND THE REPUBLIC HAVE FALLEN--WITH THE DARK SHADOW OF THE EMPIRE RISING TO TAKE THEIR PLACE.
THIS MESSAGE IS A WARNING AND A REMINDER FOR ANY SURVIVING JEDI-- TRUST IN THE FORCE...
GASP

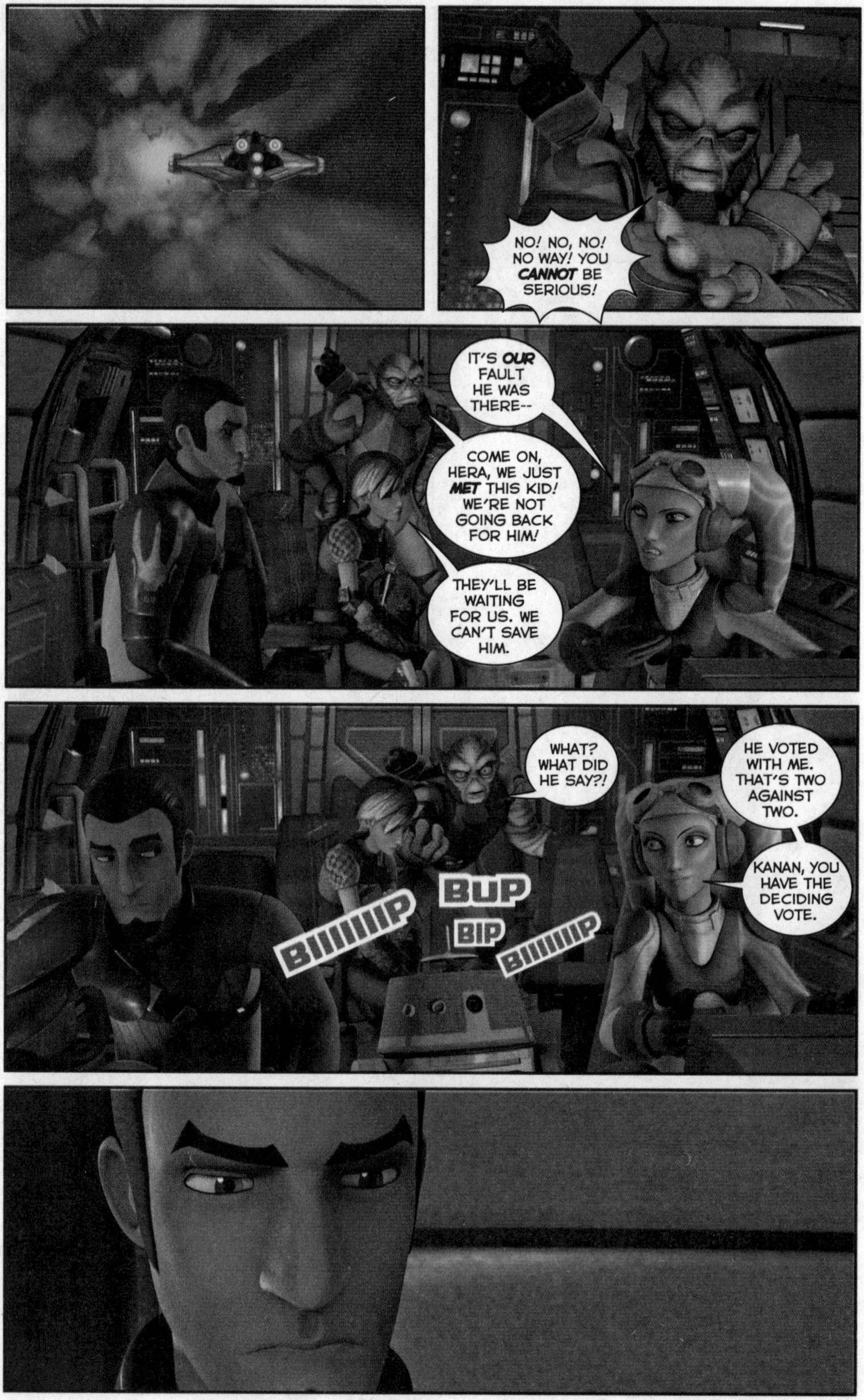
NO! NO, NO! NO WAY! YOU CANNOT BE SERIOUS!
IT'S OUR FAULT HE WAS THERE--
COME ON, HERA, WE JUST MET THIS KID! WE'RE NOT GOING BACK FOR HIM!
THEY'LL BE WAITING FOR US. WE CAN'T SAVE HIM.
WHAT? WHAT DID HE SAY?!
BIIIIIIP
BUP
BIP
BIIIIIIP
HE VOTED WITH ME. THAT'S TWO AGAINST TWO.
KANAN, YOU HAVE THE DECIDING VOTE.

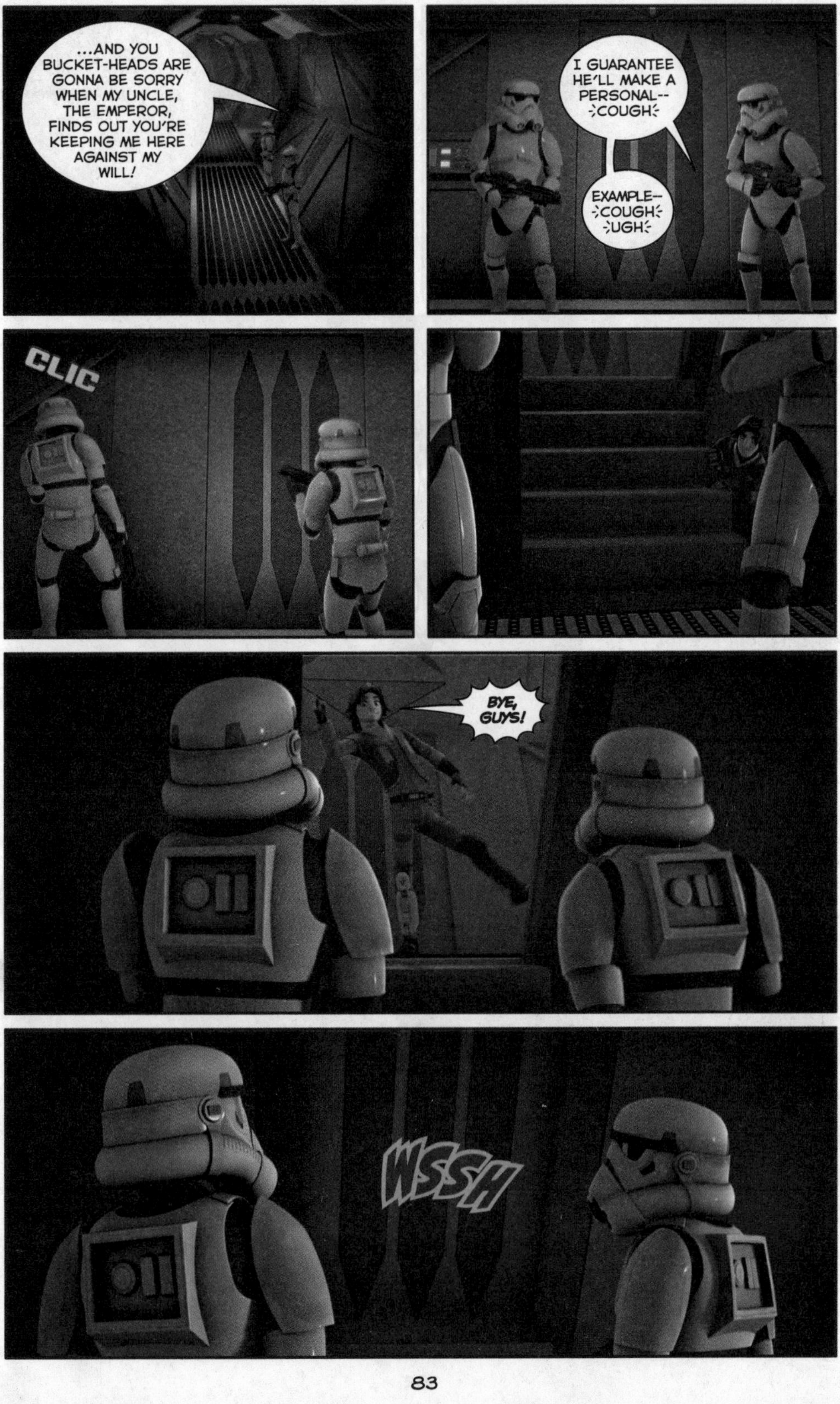
...AND YOU BUCKET-HEADS ARE GONNA BE SORRY WHEN MY UNCLE, THE EMPEROR, FINDS OUT YOU'RE KEEPING ME HERE AGAINST MY WILL!
I GUARANTEE HE'LL MAKE A PERSONAL-- COUGH
EXAMPLE-- COUGH UGH
CLIC
BYE, GUYS!
WSSH

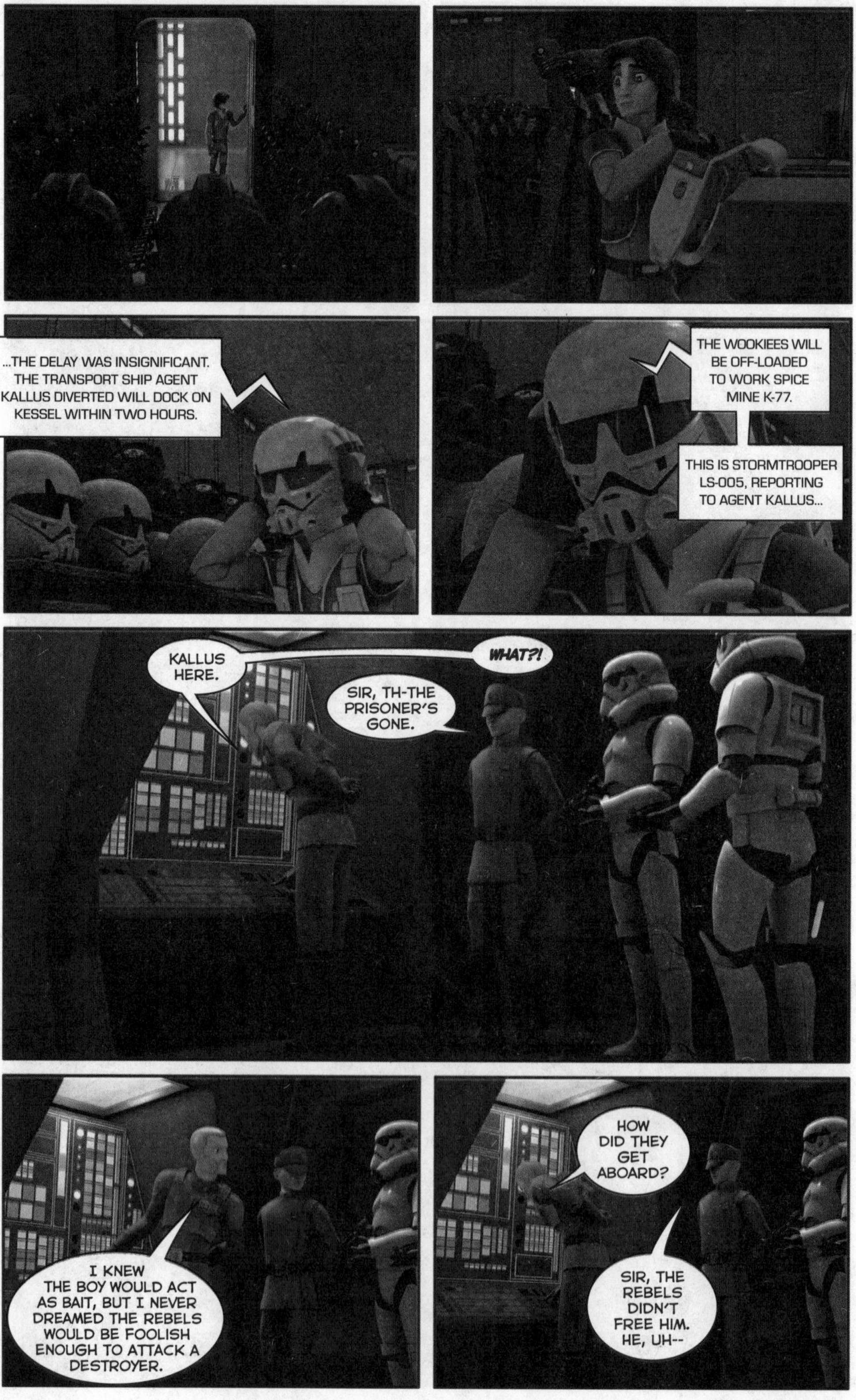
...THE DELAY WAS INSIGNIFICANT. THE TRANSPORT SHIP AGENT KALLUS DIVERTED WILL DOCK ON KESSEL WITHIN TWO HOURS.
THE WOOKIEES WILL BE OFF-LOADED TO WORK SPICE MINE K-77.
THIS IS STORMTROOPER LS-005, REPORTING TO AGENT KALLUS...
KALLUS HERE.
SIR, TH-THE PRISONER'S GONE.
WHAT?!
I KNEW THE BOY WOULD ACT AS BAIT, BUT I NEVER DREAMED THE REBELS WOULD BE FOOLISH ENOUGH TO ATTACK A DESTROYER.
HOW DID THEY GET ABOARD?
SIR, THE REBELS DIDN'T FREE HIM. HE, UH--

AGENT KALLUS! THERE'S A SECURITY BREACH IN THE LOWER HANGAR!

I DON'T KNOW HOW, BUT THE REBEL SHIP APPROACHED WITHOUT ALERTING OUR SENSORS.

THEY CAME *BACK!* I DON'T BELIEVE IT!

ORDER ALL STORMTROOPERS TO CONVERGE ON THE LOWER HANGAR. I'LL MEET THEM THERE.

⸎AHEM⸎ THIS IS TROOPER LS-123, REPORTING INTRUDERS IN THE UPPER HANGAR.

SIR, I BELIEVE THE LOWER HANGAR IS A DIVERSION.

MAYBE, MAYBE NOT. SQUADS FIVE THROUGH EIGHT DIVERT TO UPPER HANGAR. THE REST CONVERGE AS ORDERED.

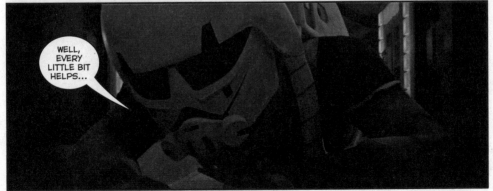
WELL, EVERY LITTLE BIT HELPS...

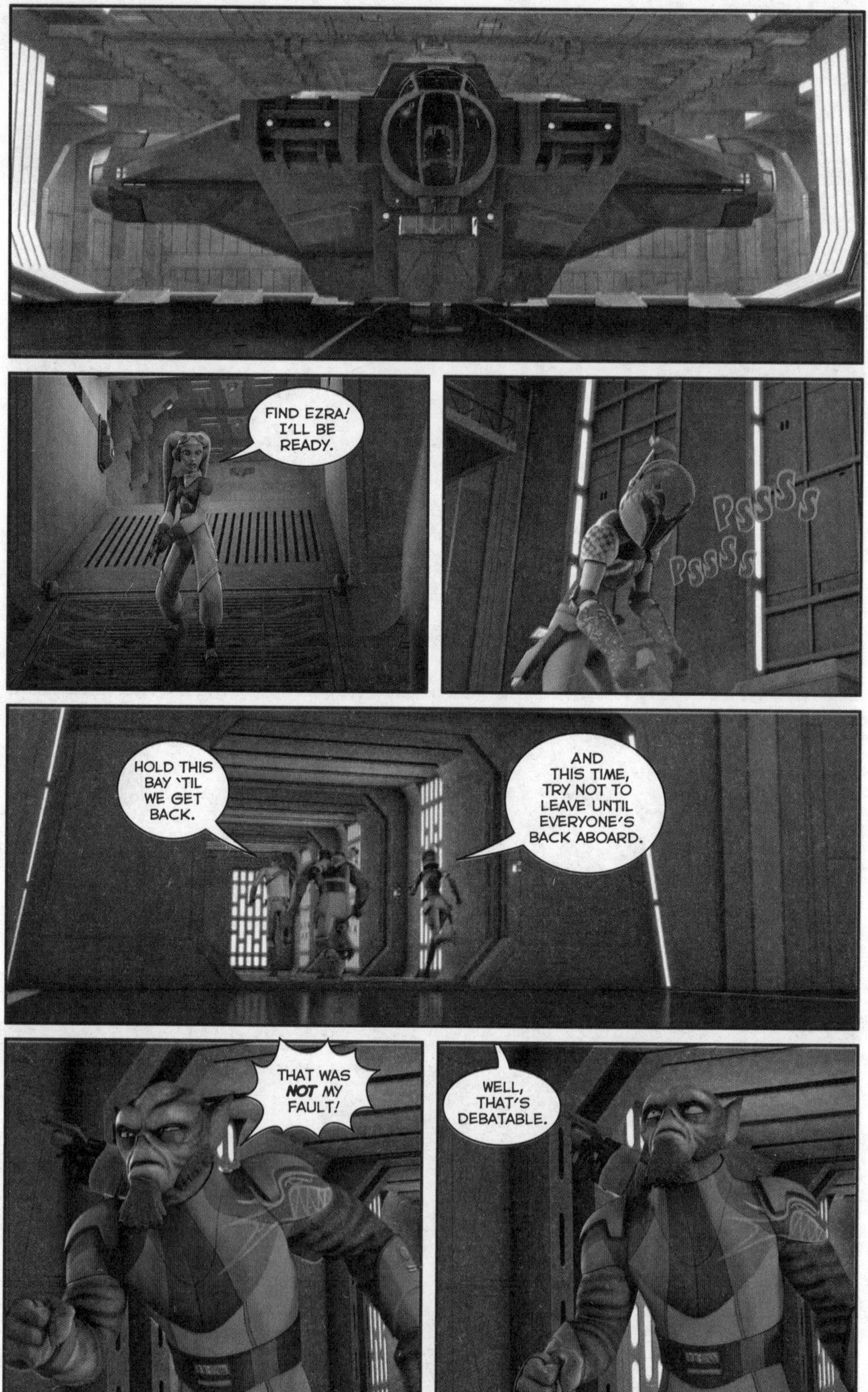
FIND EZRA! I'LL BE READY.
PSSSS
PSSSS
HOLD THIS BAY 'TIL WE GET BACK.
AND THIS TIME, TRY NOT TO LEAVE UNTIL EVERYONE'S BACK ABOARD.
THAT WAS **NOT** MY FAULT!
WELL, THAT'S DEBATABLE.

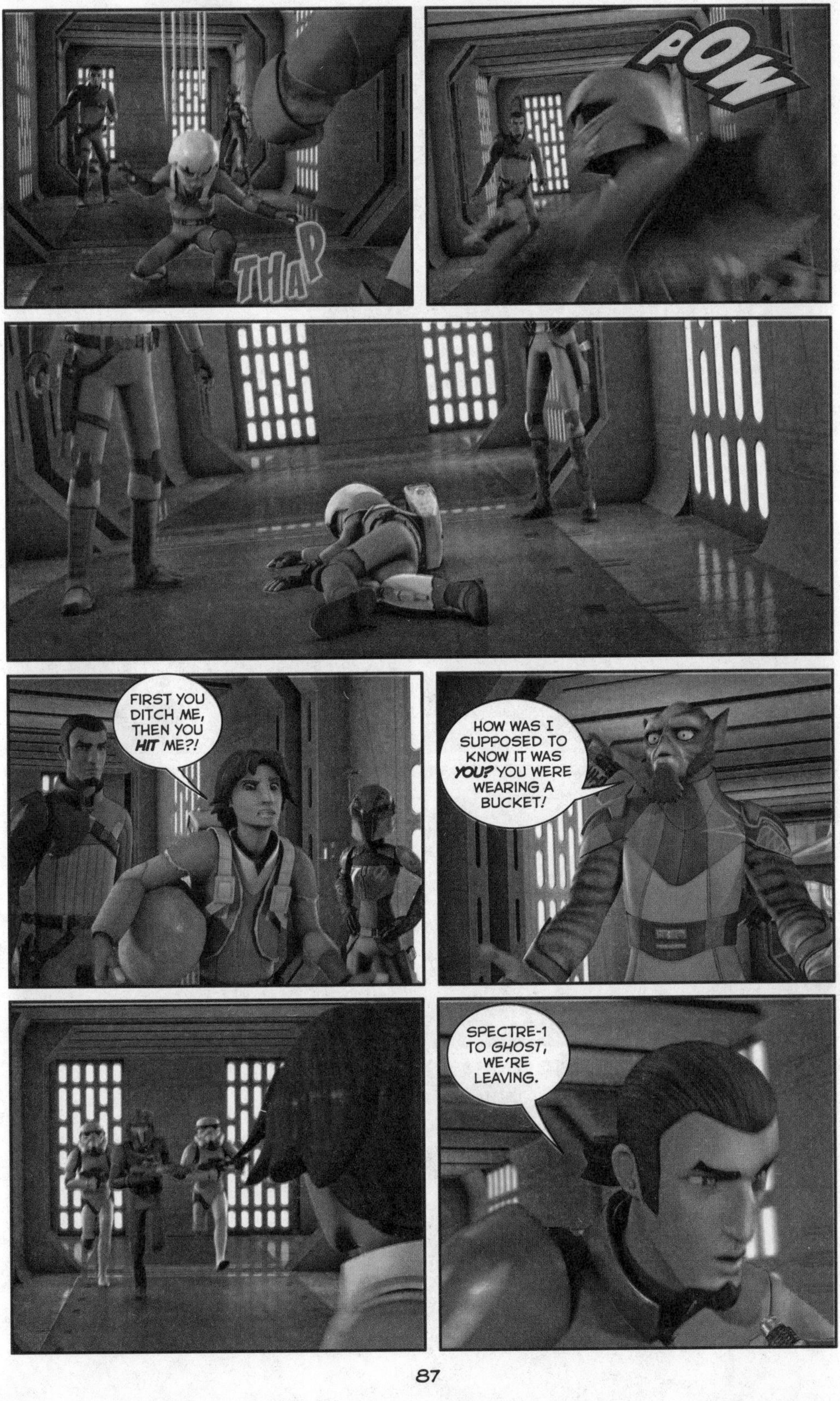
THAP
POW
FIRST YOU DITCH ME, THEN YOU *HIT* ME?!
HOW WAS I SUPPOSED TO KNOW IT WAS *YOU?* YOU WERE WEARING A BUCKET!
SPECTRE-1 TO *GHOST*, WE'RE LEAVING.

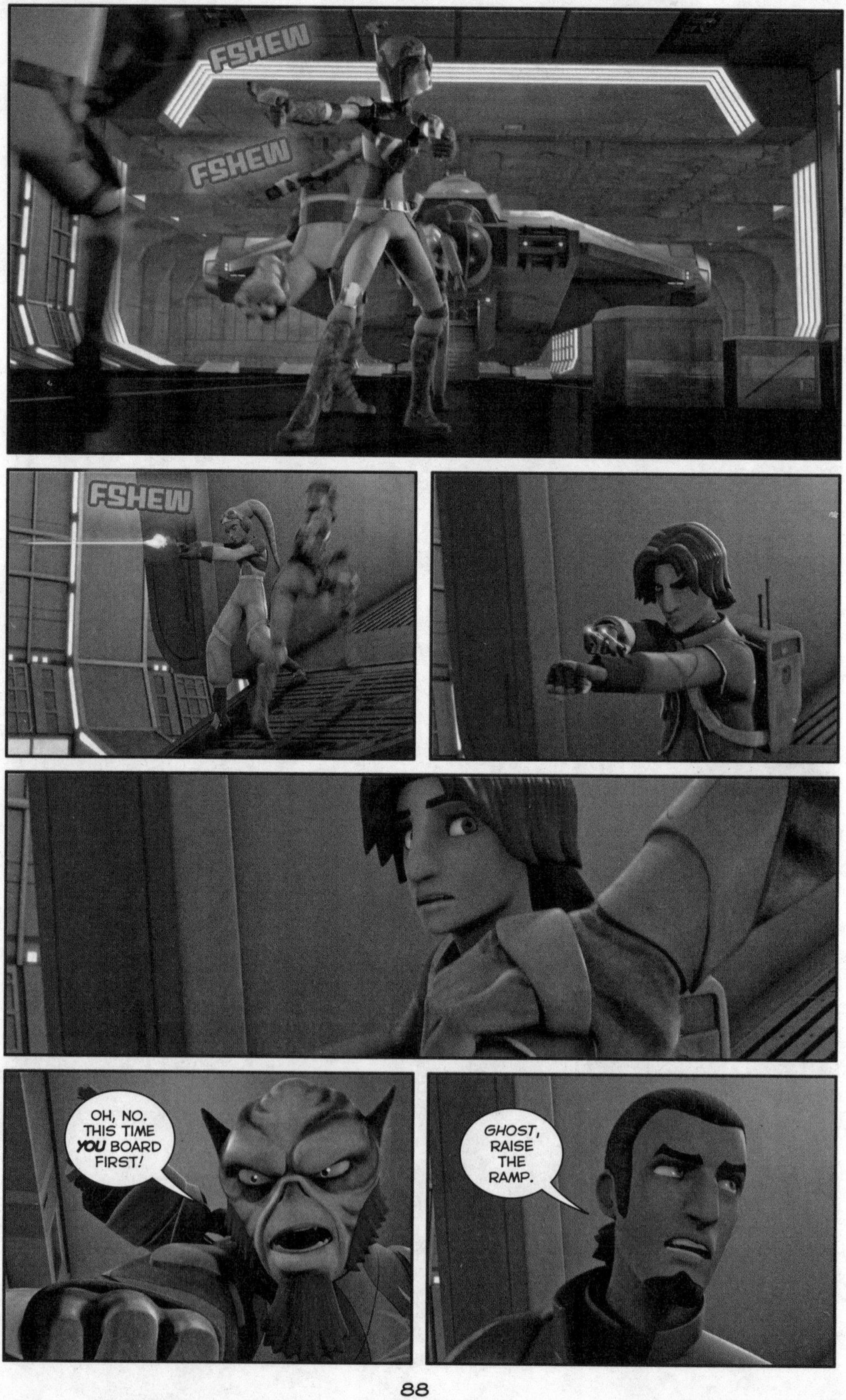
FSHEW
FSHEW
FSHEW
OH, NO. THIS TIME *YOU* BOARD FIRST!
GHOST, RAISE THE RAMP.

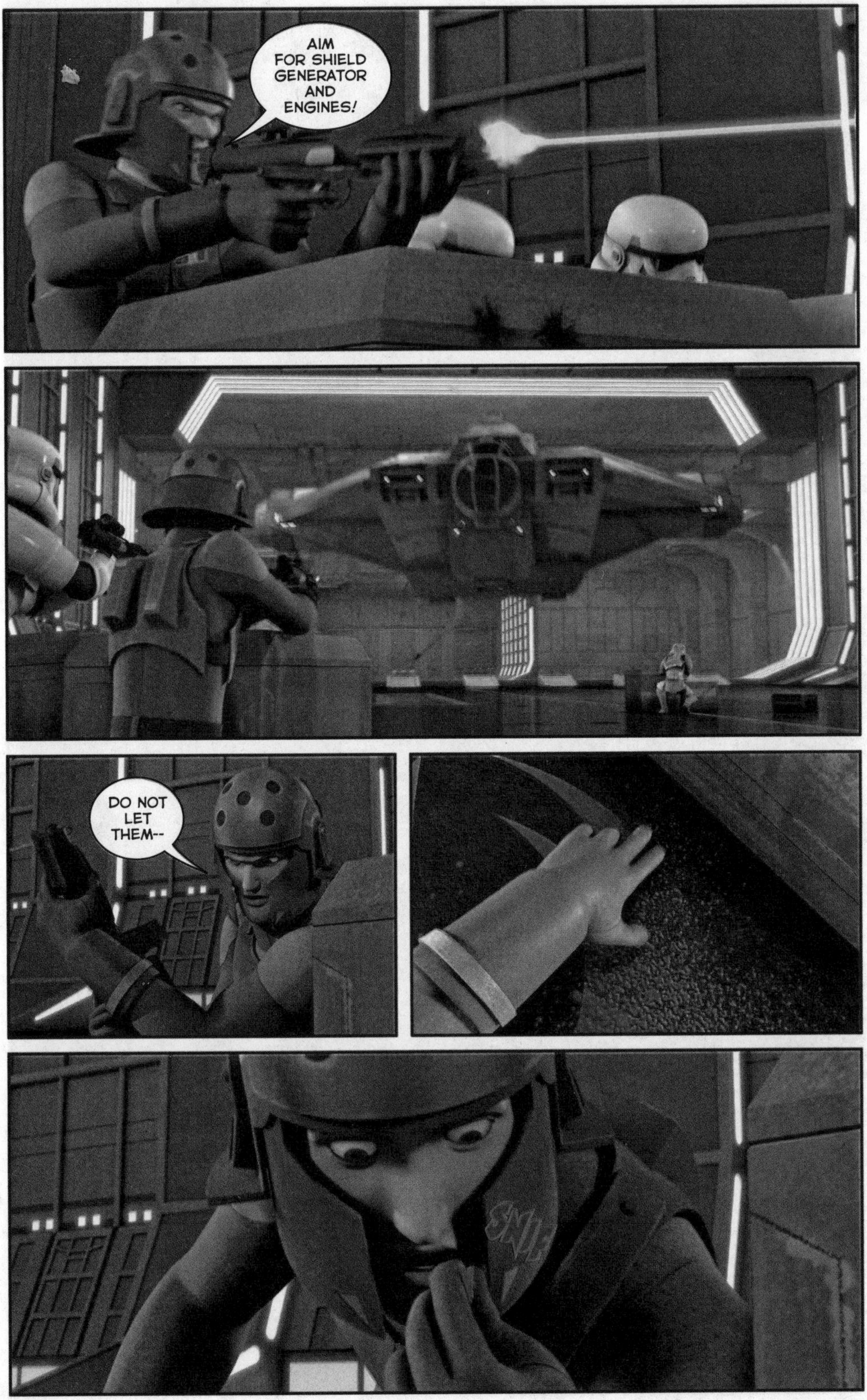
AIM FOR SHIELD GENERATOR AND ENGINES!
DO NOT LET THEM--
SNIF

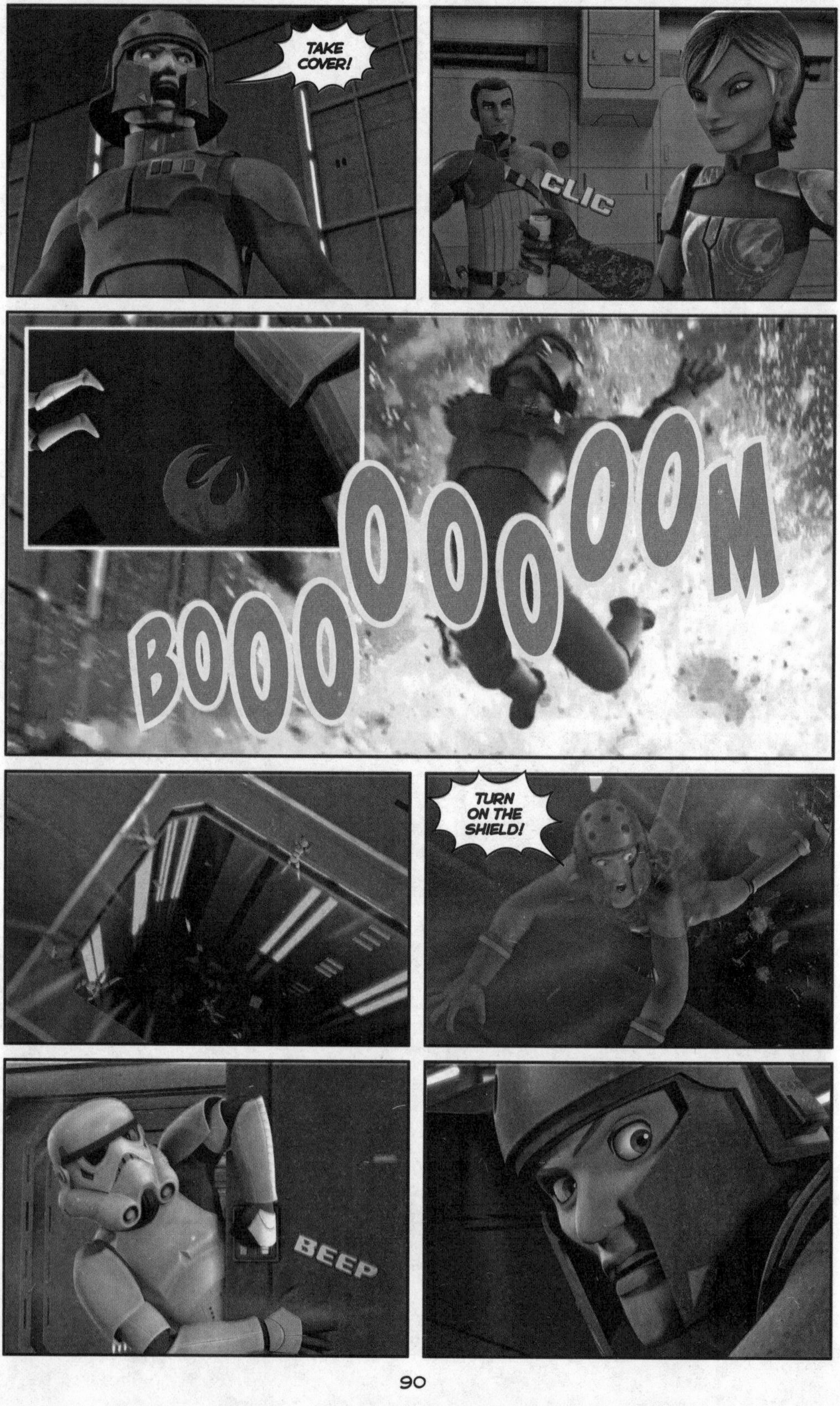
TAKE COVER!
CLIC
BOOOOOOOOM
TURN ON THE SHIELD!
BEEP

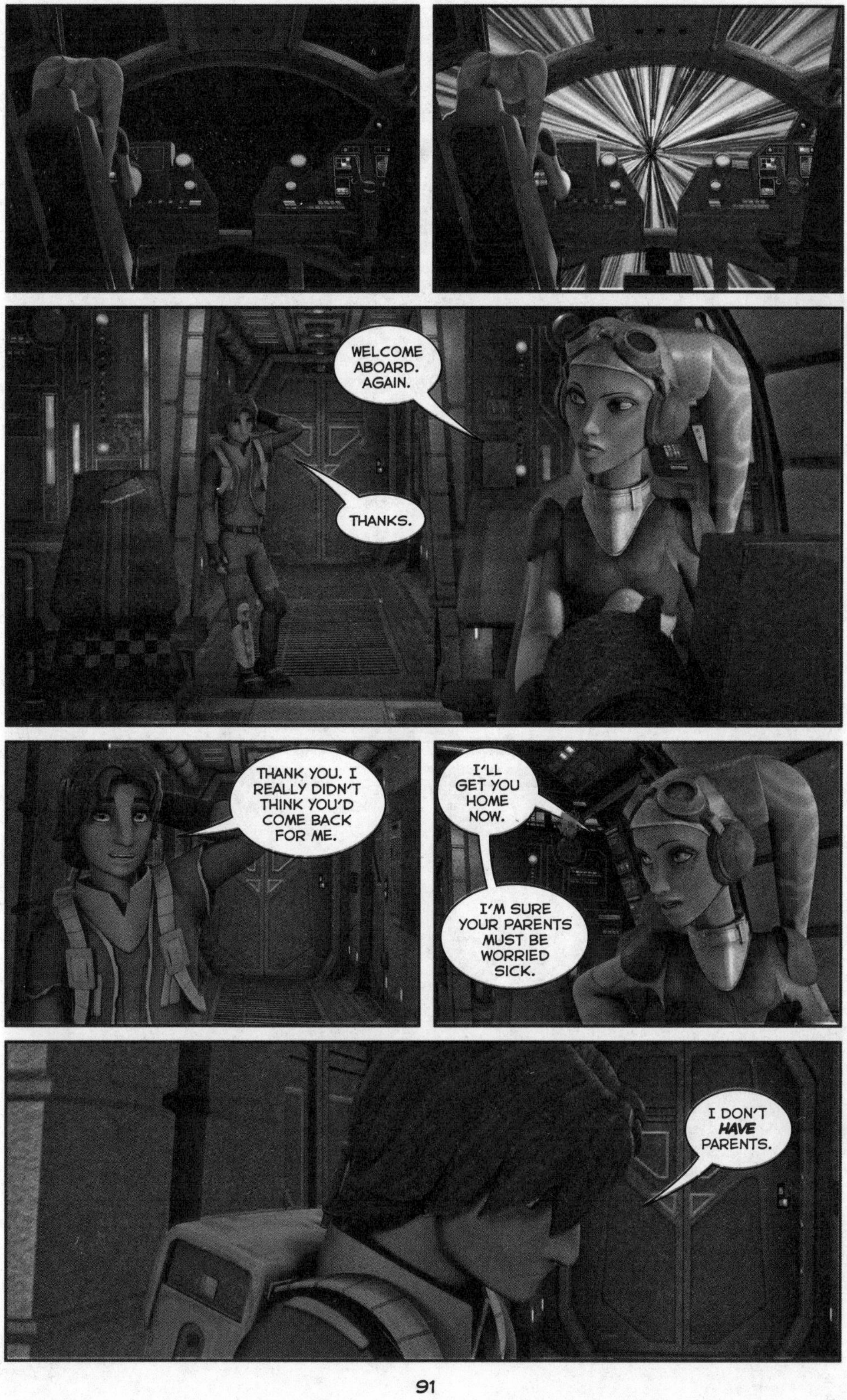
WELCOME ABOARD. AGAIN.
THANKS.
THANK YOU. I REALLY DIDN'T THINK YOU'D COME BACK FOR ME.
I'LL GET YOU HOME NOW.
I'M SURE YOUR PARENTS MUST BE WORRIED SICK.
I DON'T *HAVE* PARENTS.

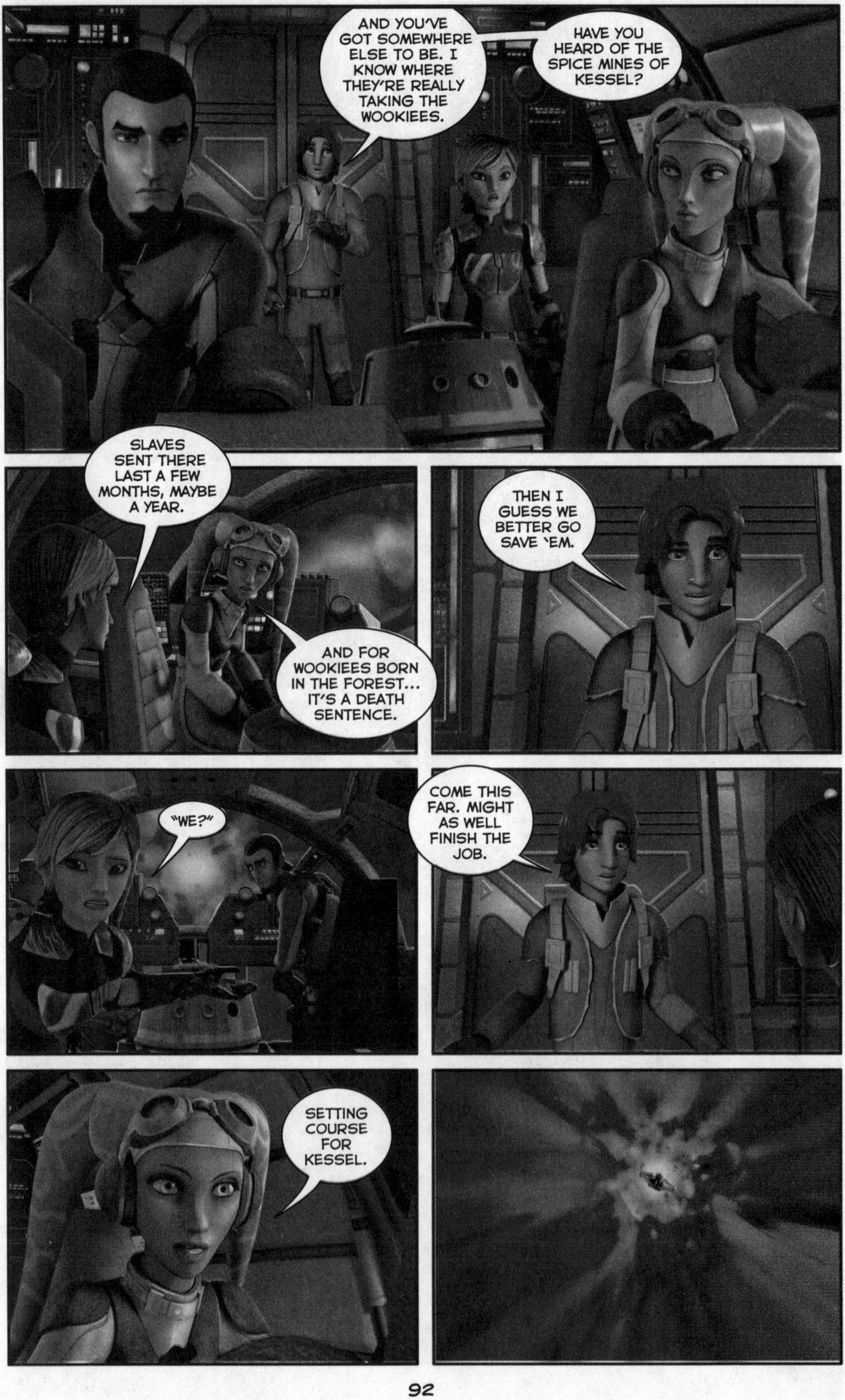
AND YOU'VE GOT SOMEWHERE ELSE TO BE. I KNOW WHERE THEY'RE REALLY TAKING THE WOOKIEES.
HAVE YOU HEARD OF THE SPICE MINES OF KESSEL?
SLAVES SENT THERE LAST A FEW MONTHS, MAYBE A YEAR.
AND FOR WOOKIEES BORN IN THE FOREST... IT'S A DEATH SENTENCE.
THEN I GUESS WE BETTER GO SAVE 'EM.
"WE?"
COME THIS FAR. MIGHT AS WELL FINISH THE JOB.
SETTING COURSE FOR KESSEL.

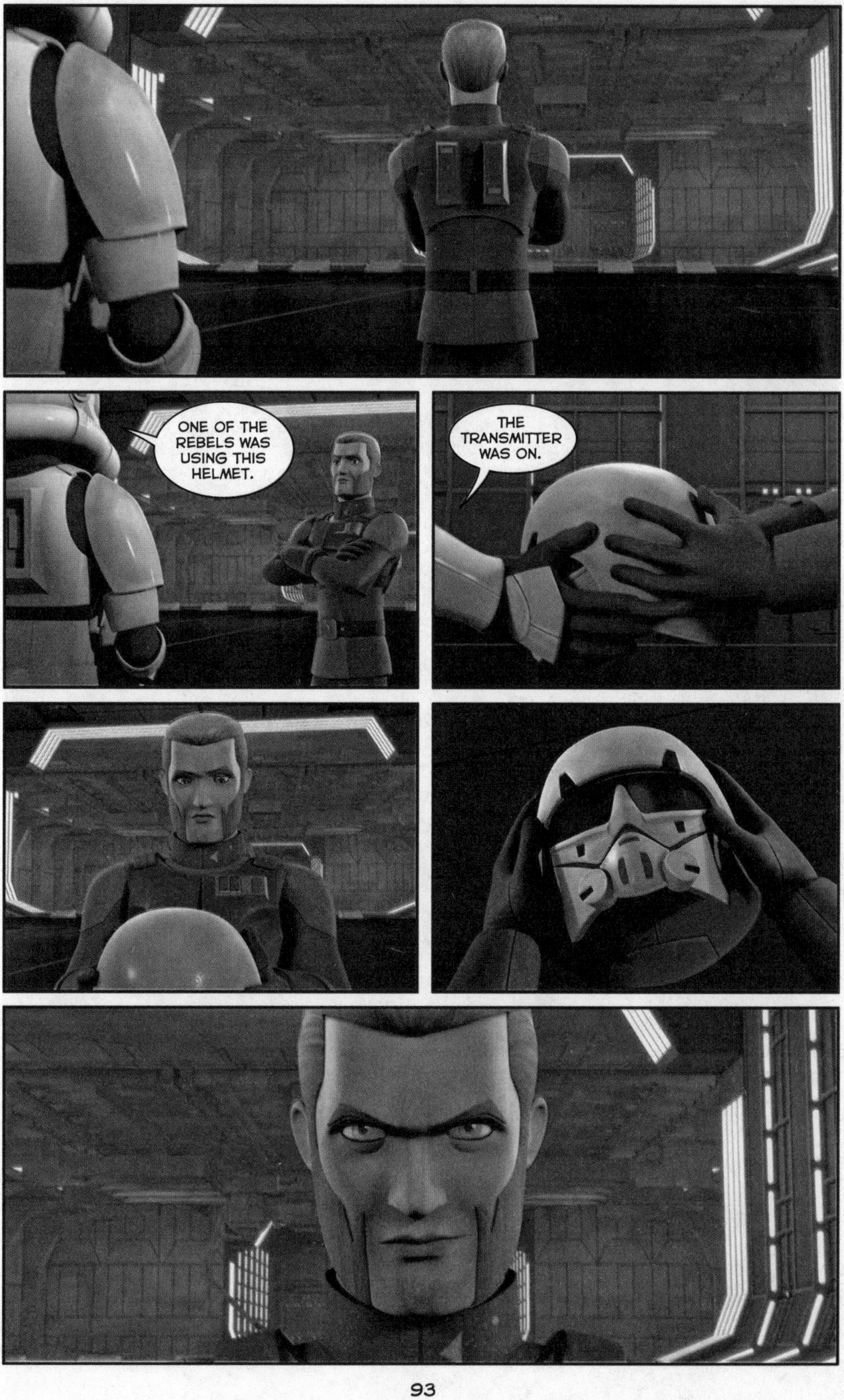
ONE OF THE REBELS WAS USING THIS HELMET.
THE TRANSMITTER WAS ON.

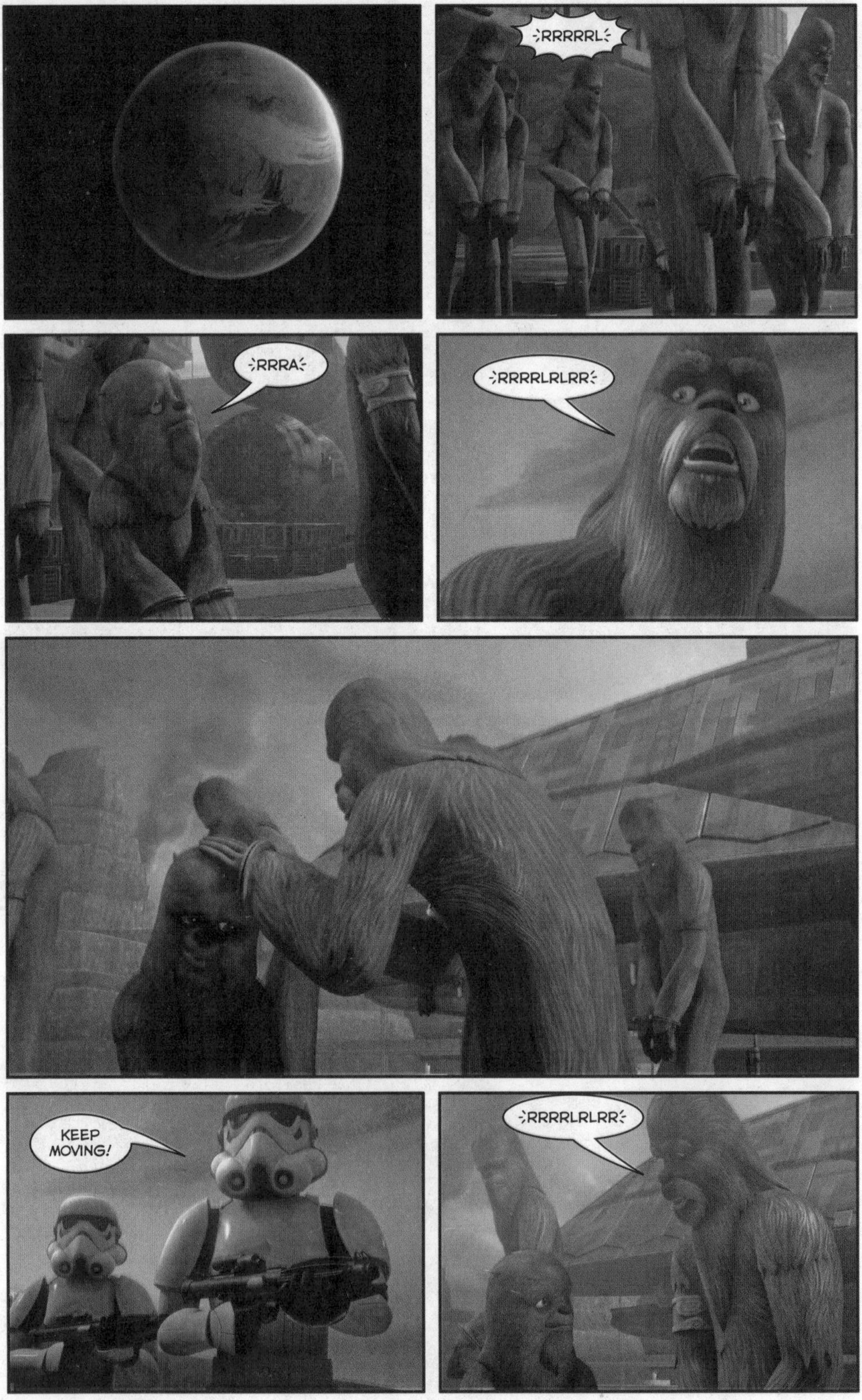
RRRRRL
RRRA
RRRRLRLRR
KEEP MOVING!
RRRRLRLRR

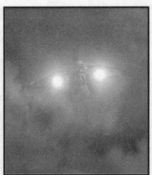

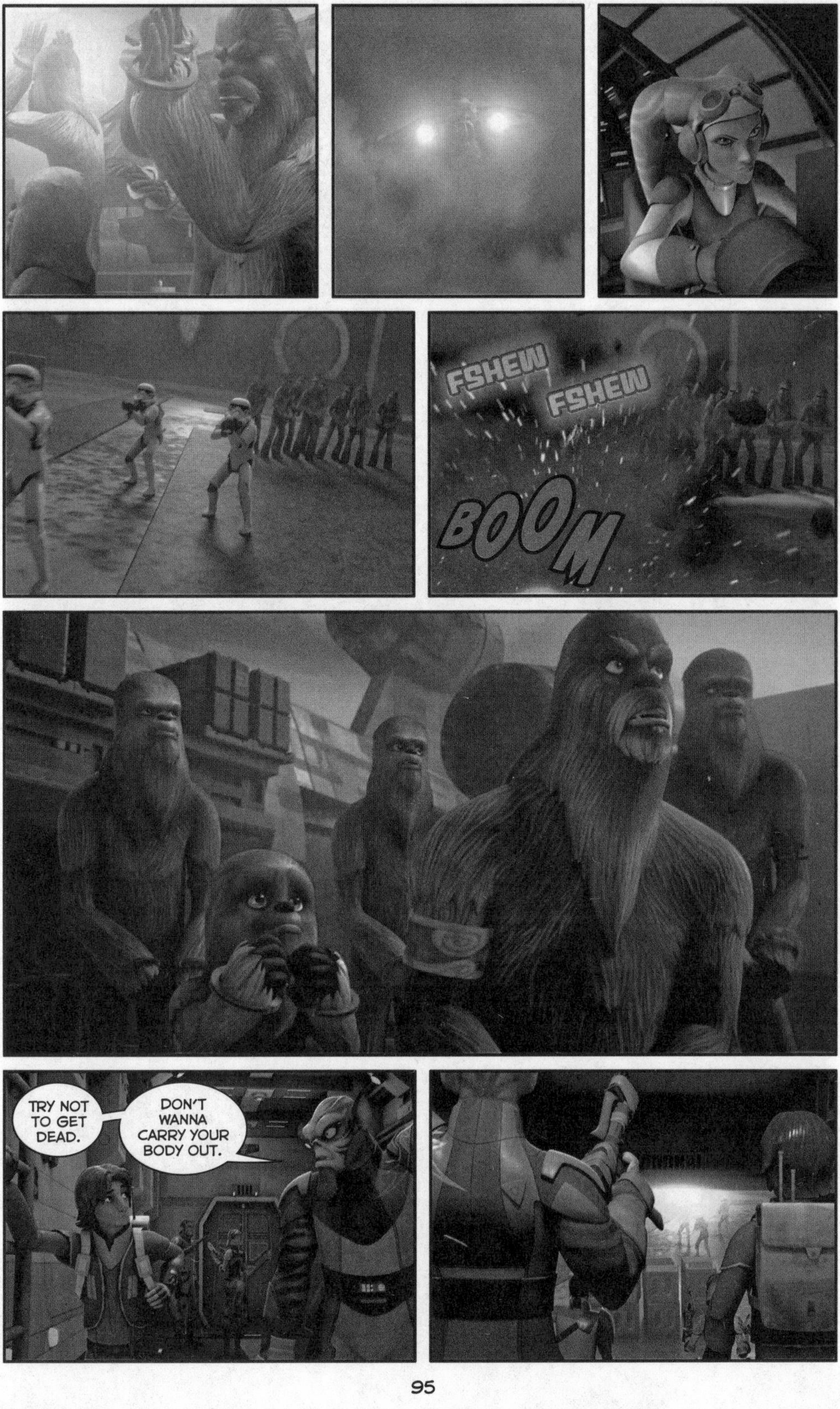
FSHEW
FSHEW
BOOM
TRY NOT TO GET DEAD.
DON'T WANNA CARRY YOUR BODY OUT.

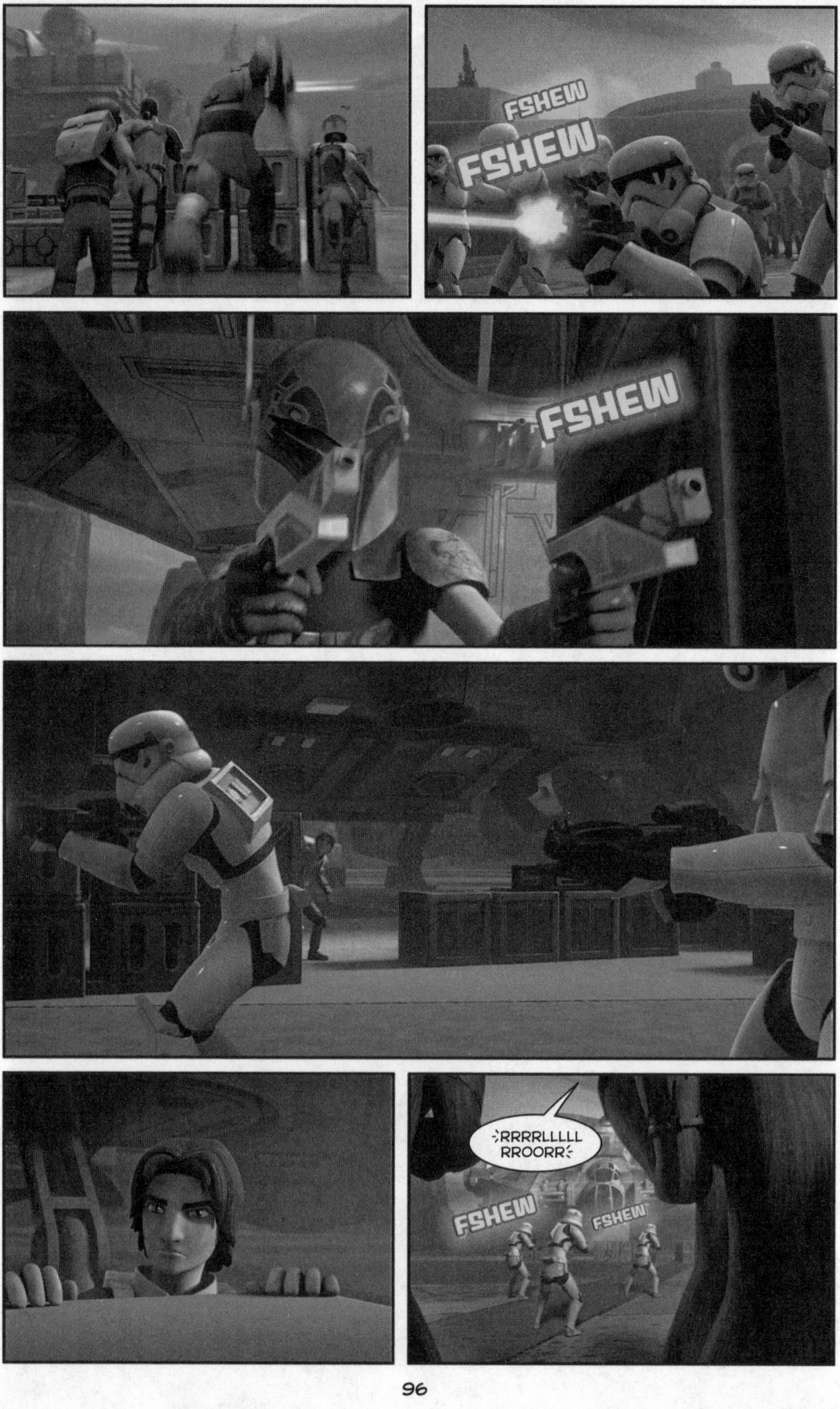
FSHEW
FSHEW
FSHEW
RRRRLLLLL RROORR
FSHEW
FSHEW

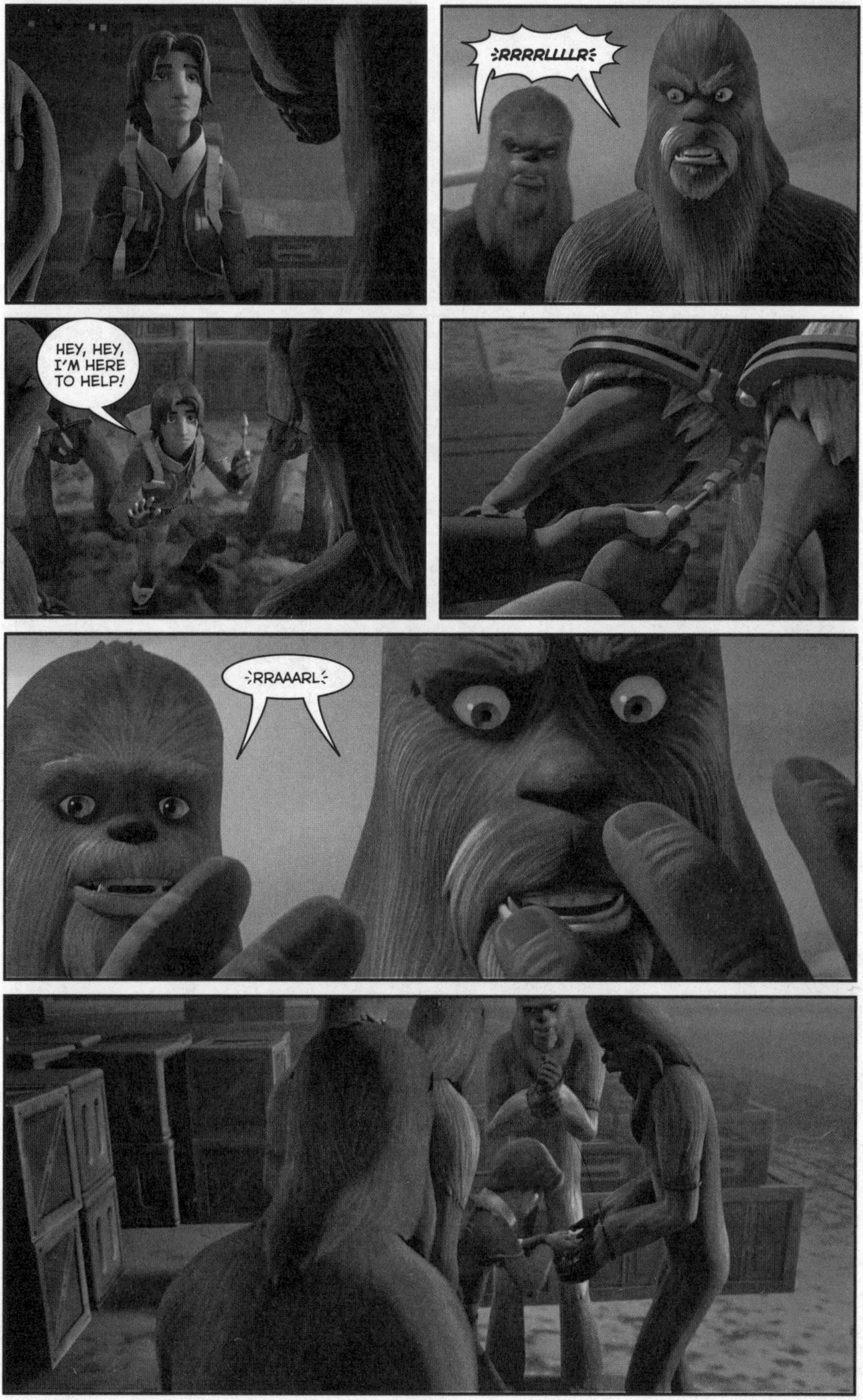
RRRRLLLLR
HEY, HEY, I'M HERE TO HELP!
RRAAARL

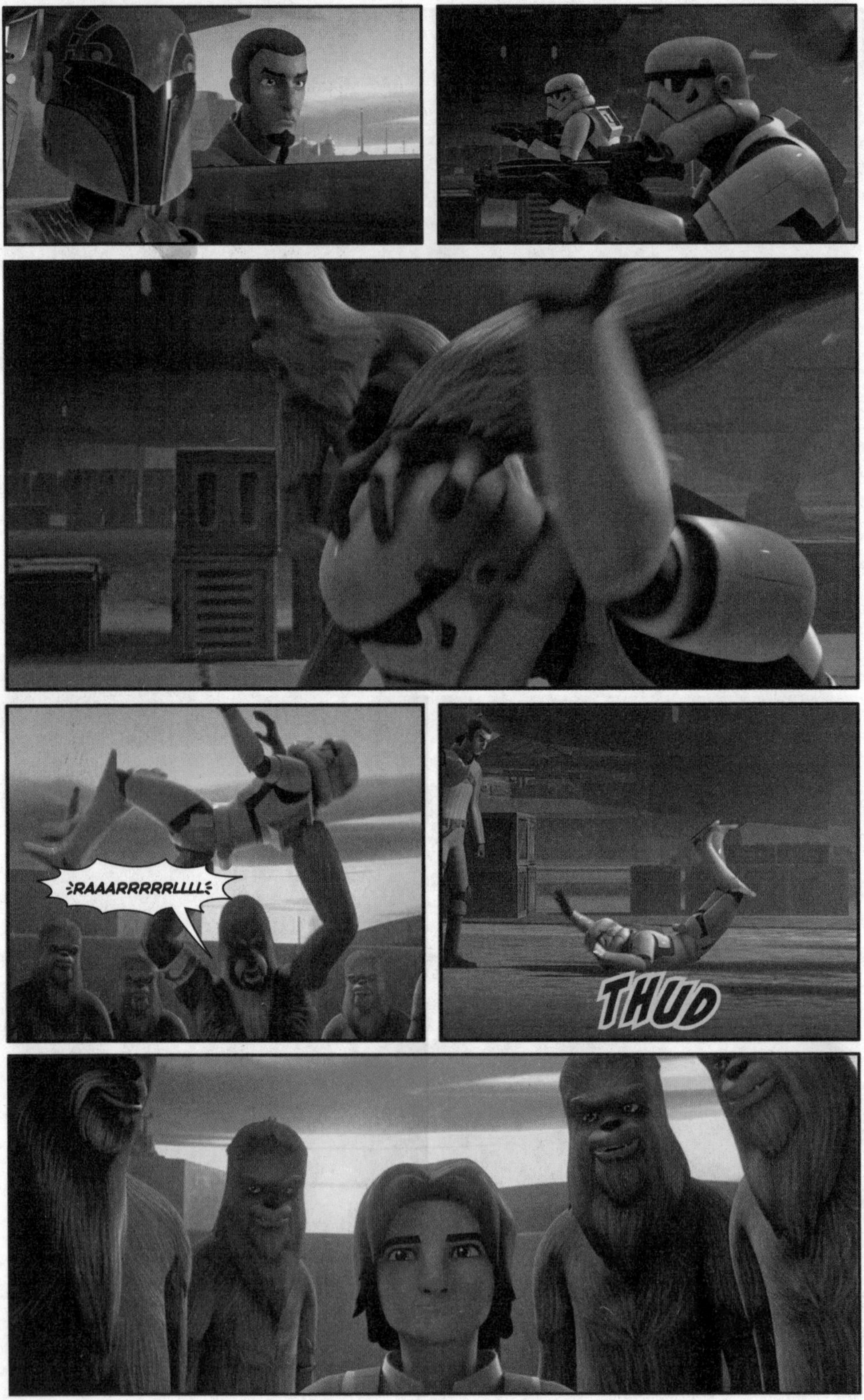
RAAARRRRRLLLL
THUD

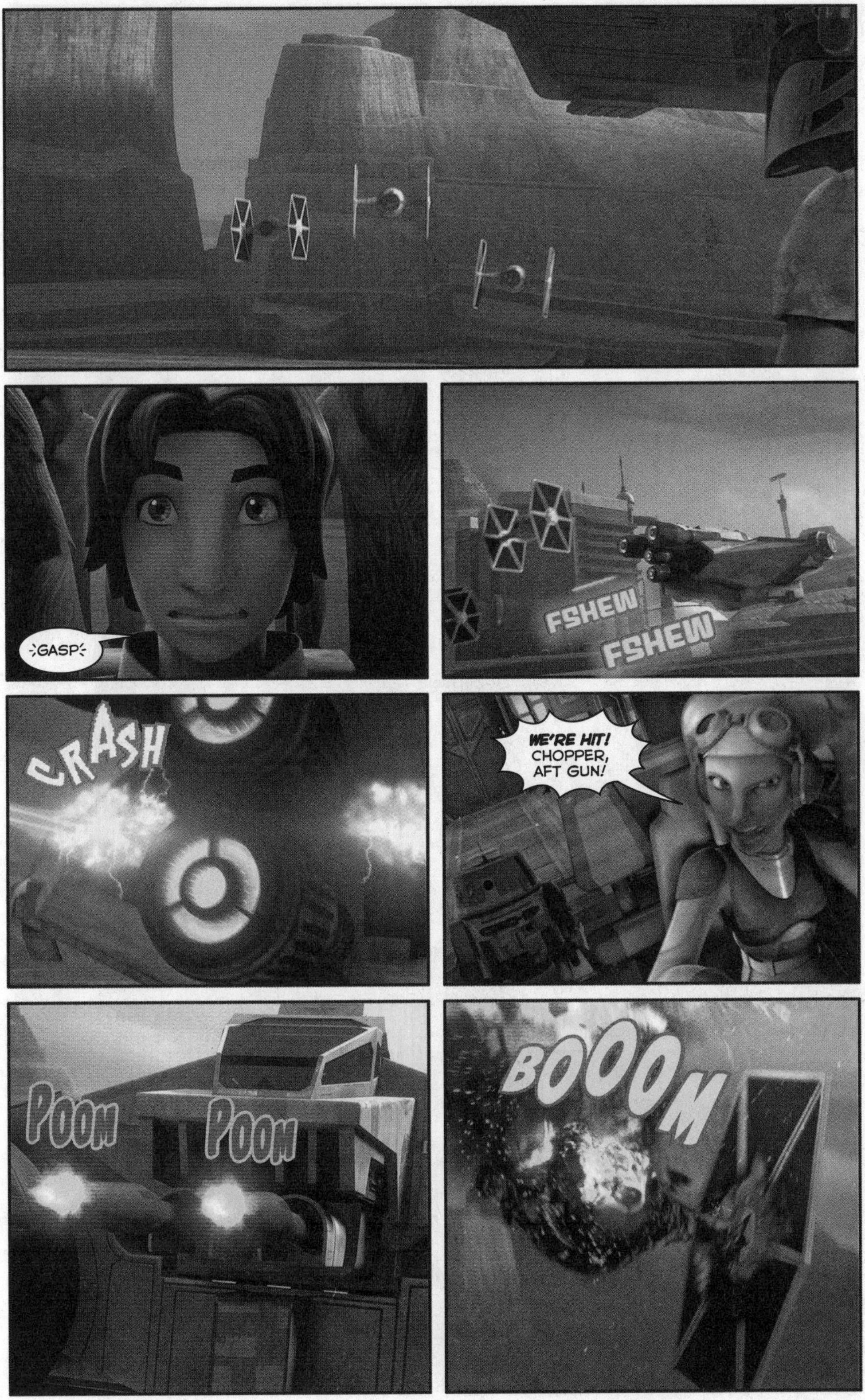
GASP
FSHEW
FSHEW
CRASH
WE'RE HIT! CHOPPER, AFT GUN!
POOM
POOM
BOOOM

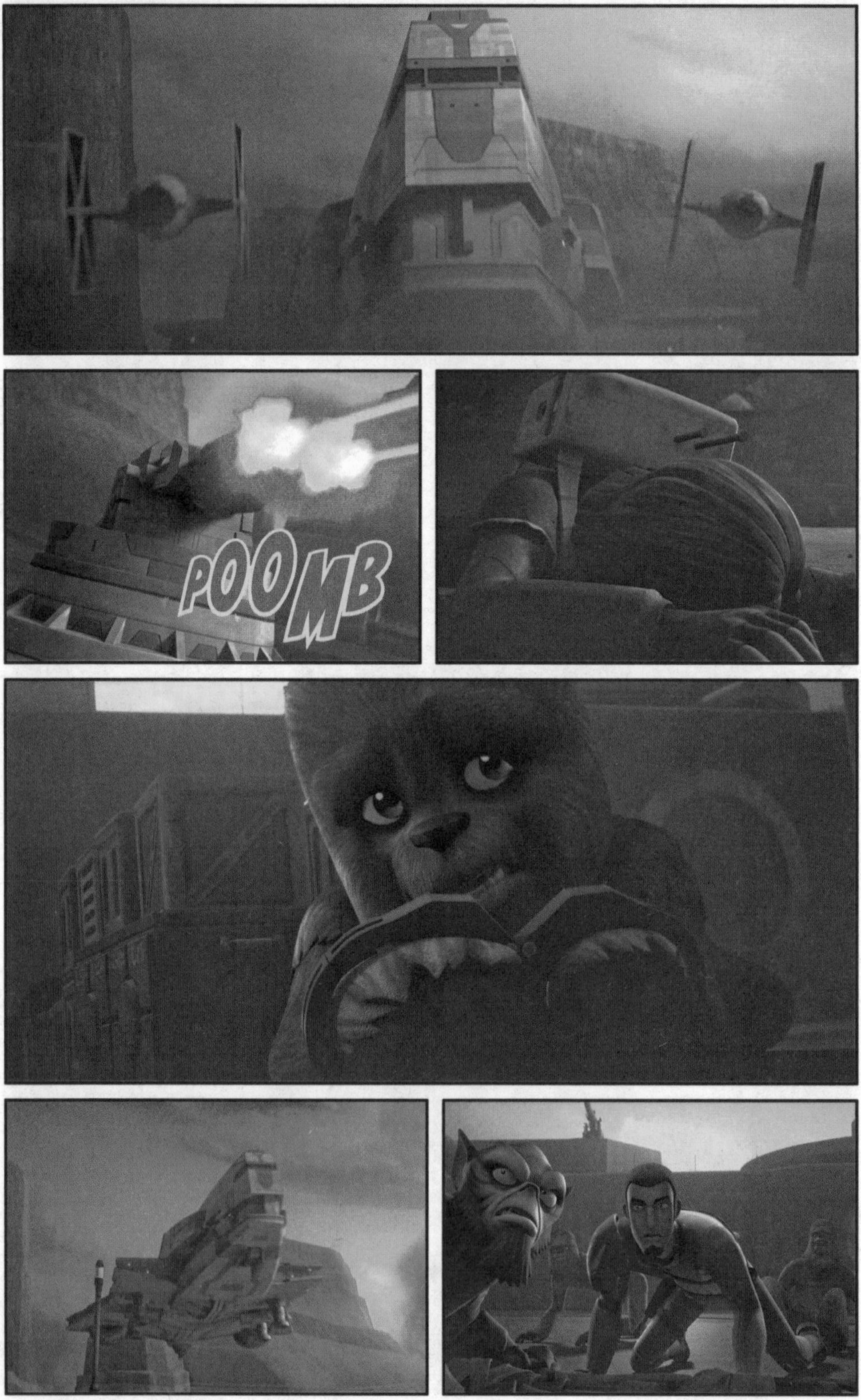
POOMB

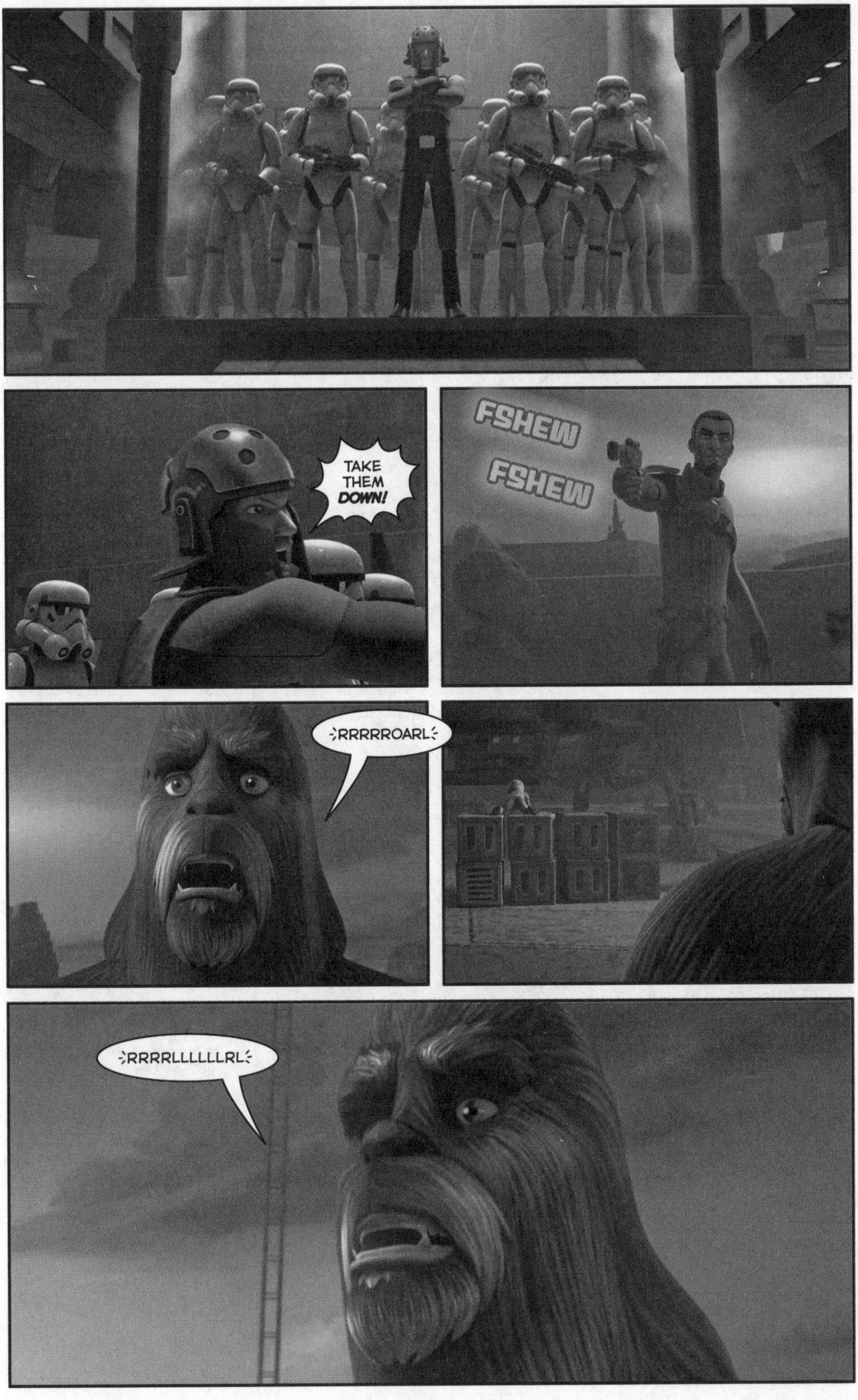
TAKE THEM DOWN!
FSHEW
FSHEW
RRRRROARL
RRRRLLLLLLRL

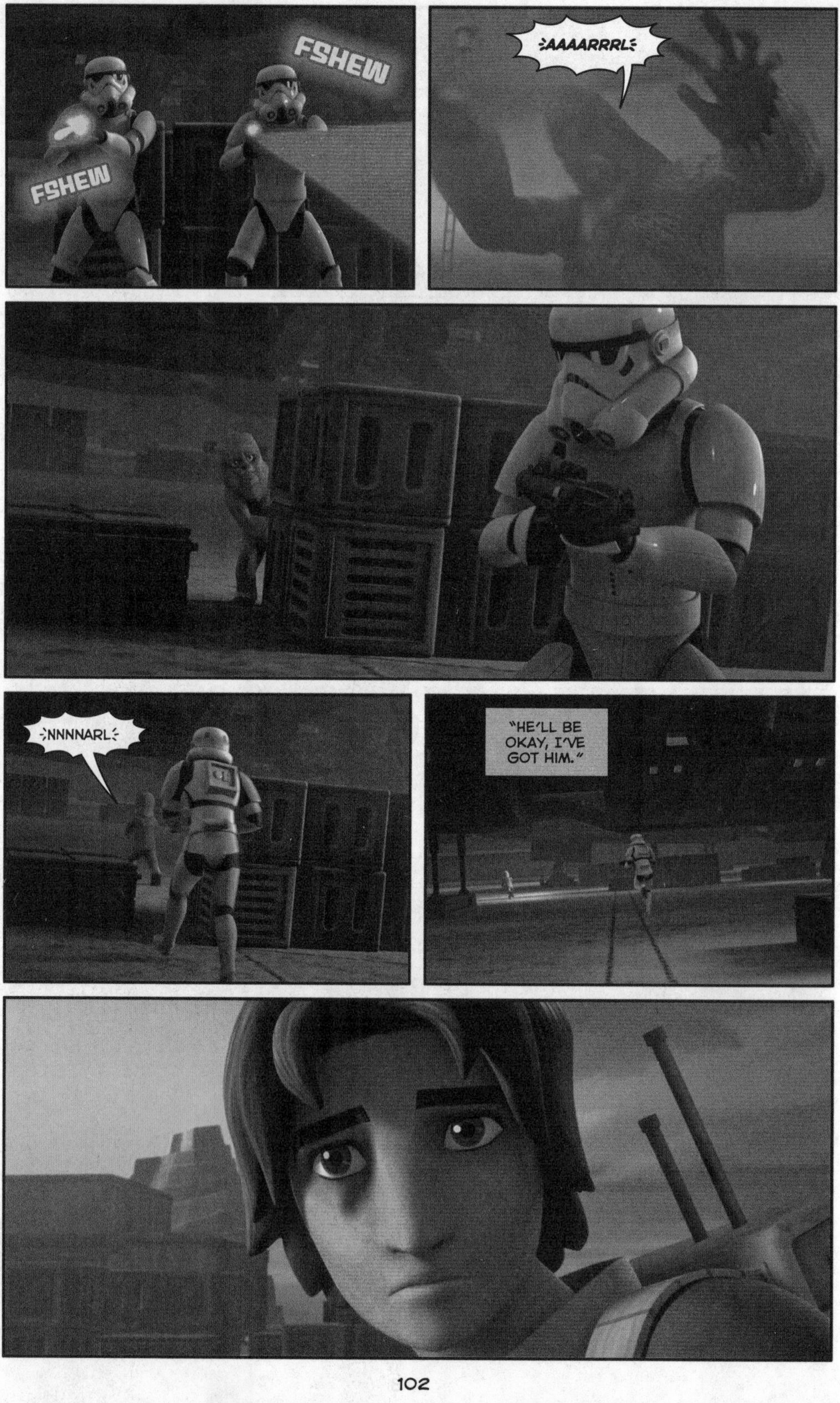
FSHEW
FSHEW
AAAARRRL
NNNNARL
"HE'LL BE OKAY, I'VE GOT HIM."

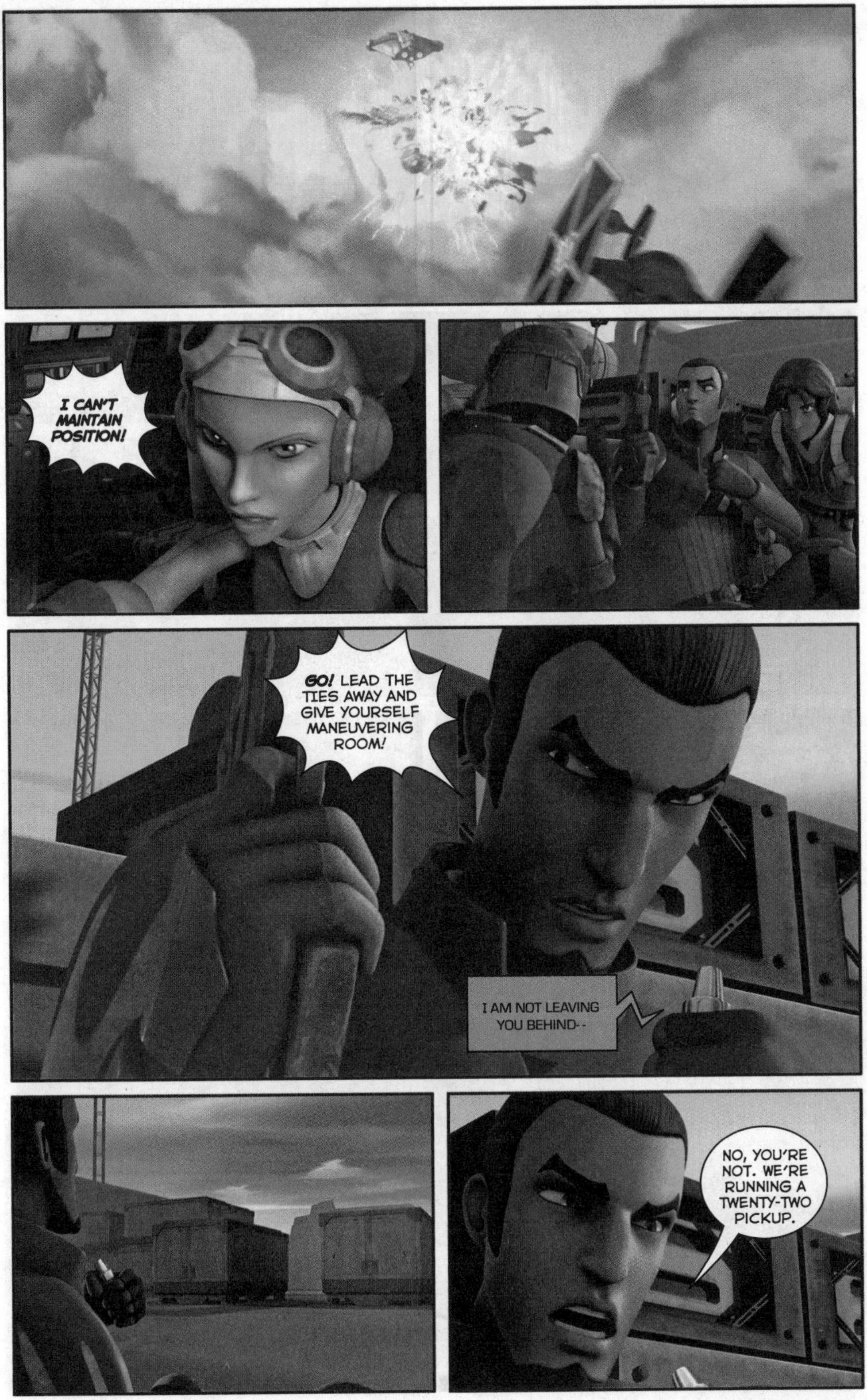
I CAN'T MAINTAIN POSITION!
GO! LEAD THE TIES AWAY AND GIVE YOURSELF MANEUVERING ROOM!
I AM NOT LEAVING YOU BEHIND--
NO, YOU'RE NOT. WE'RE RUNNING A TWENTY-TWO PICKUP.

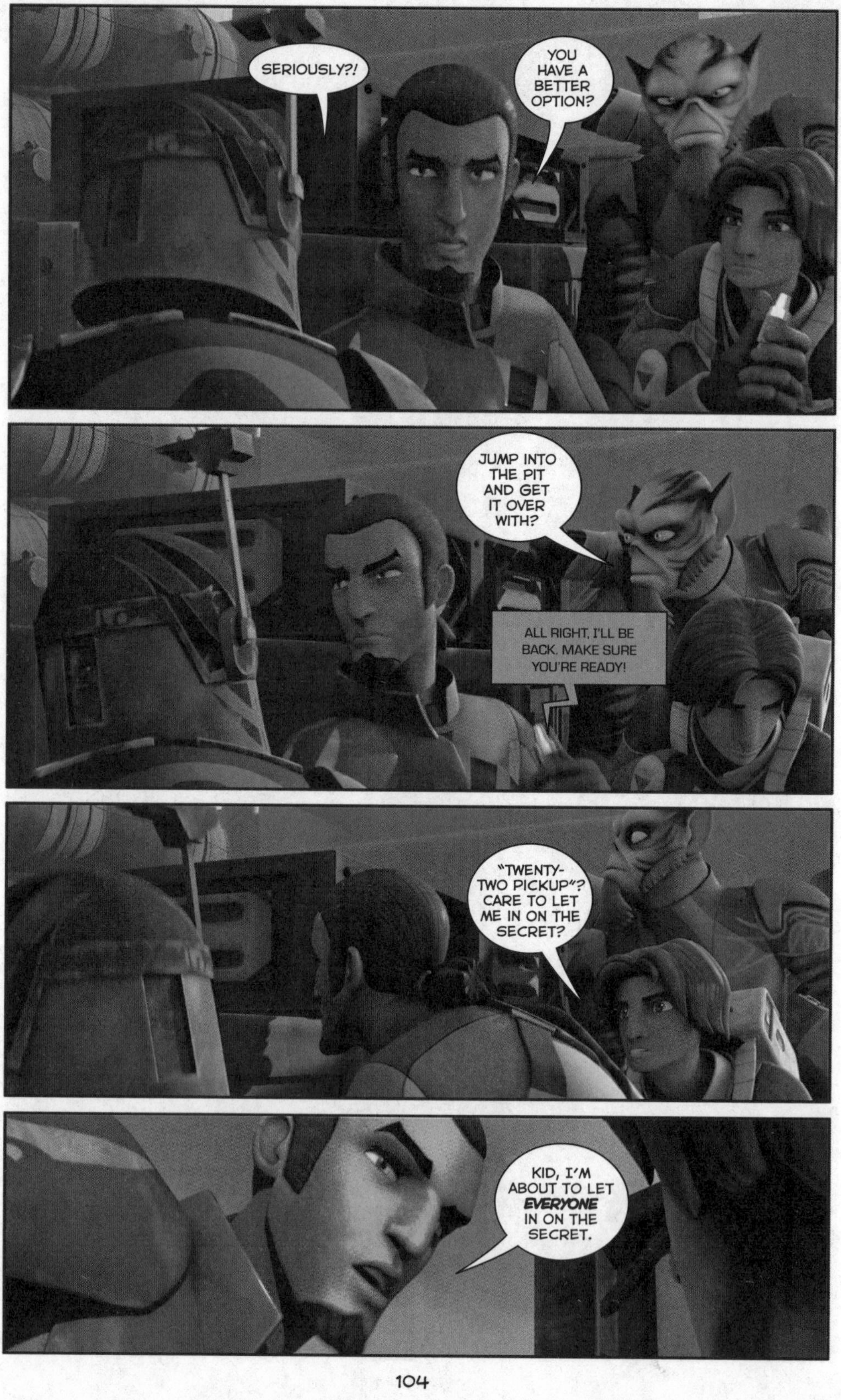
SERIOUSLY?!
YOU HAVE A BETTER OPTION?
JUMP INTO THE PIT AND GET IT OVER WITH?
ALL RIGHT, I'LL BE BACK. MAKE SURE YOU'RE READY!
"TWENTY-TWO PICKUP"? CARE TO LET ME IN ON THE SECRET?
KID, I'M ABOUT TO LET *EVERYONE* IN ON THE SECRET.

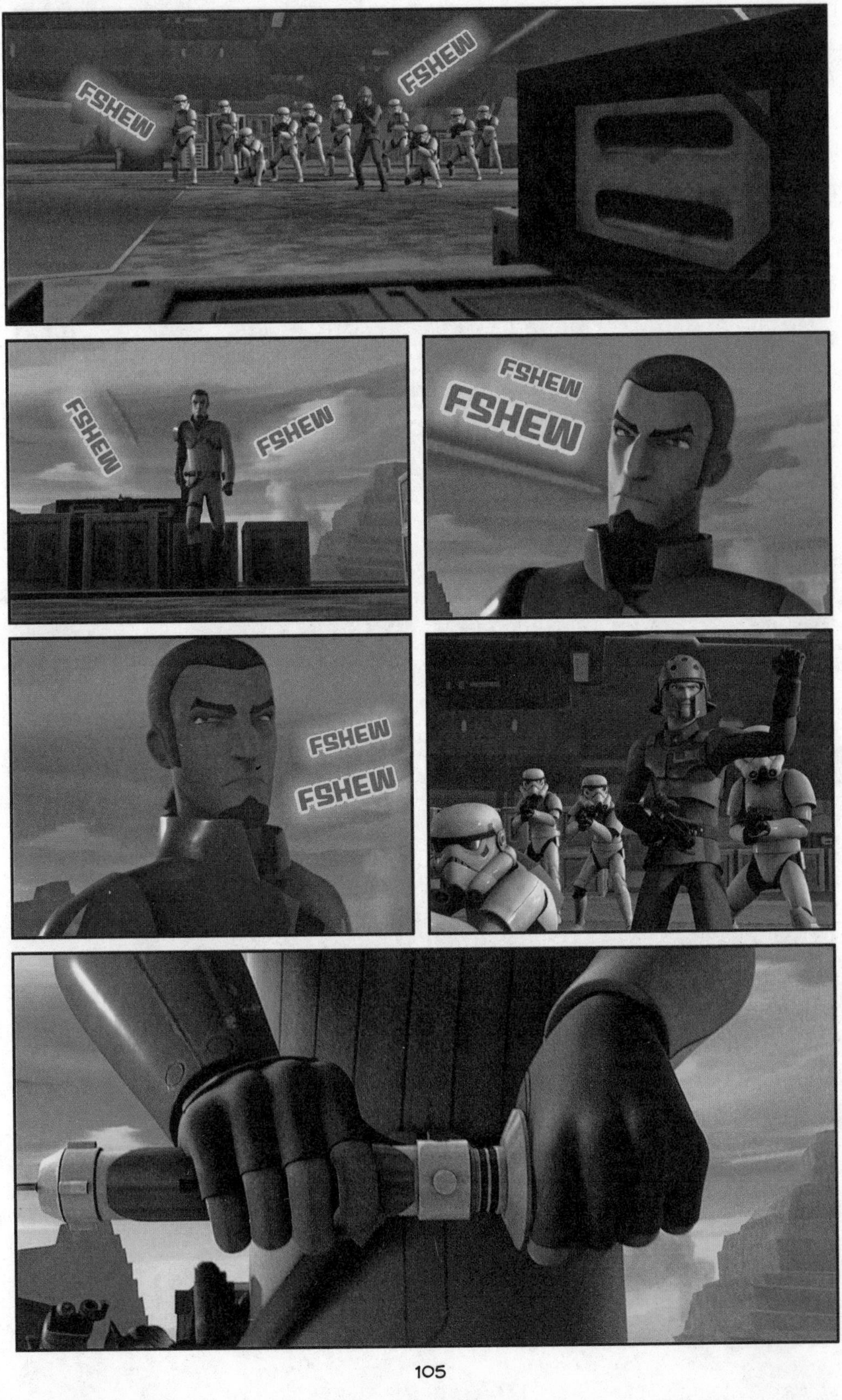
FSHEW
FSHEW
FSHEW
FSHEW
FSHEW
FSHEW
FSHEW
FSHEW

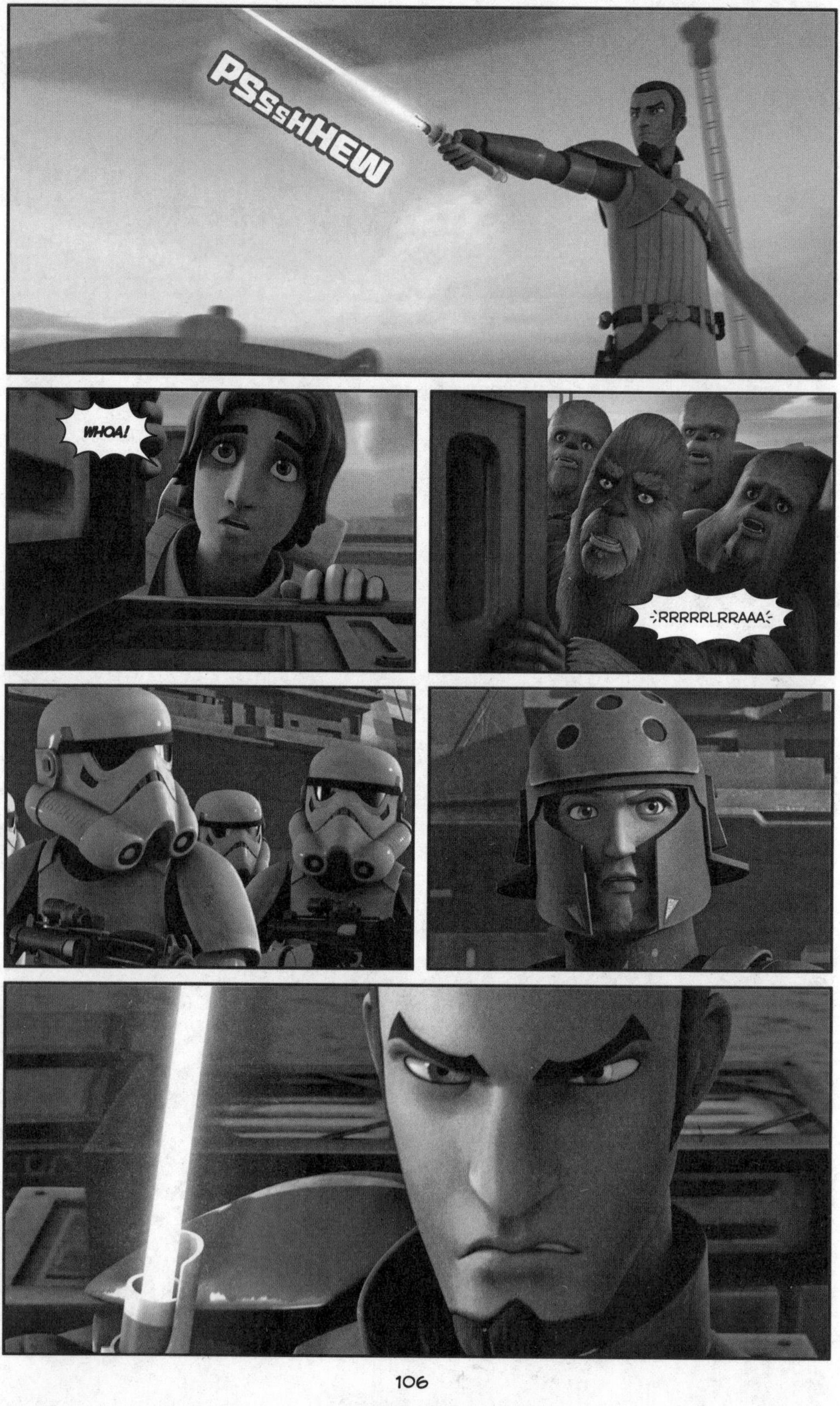
PSSSHHEW
WHOA!
RRRRRLRRAAA

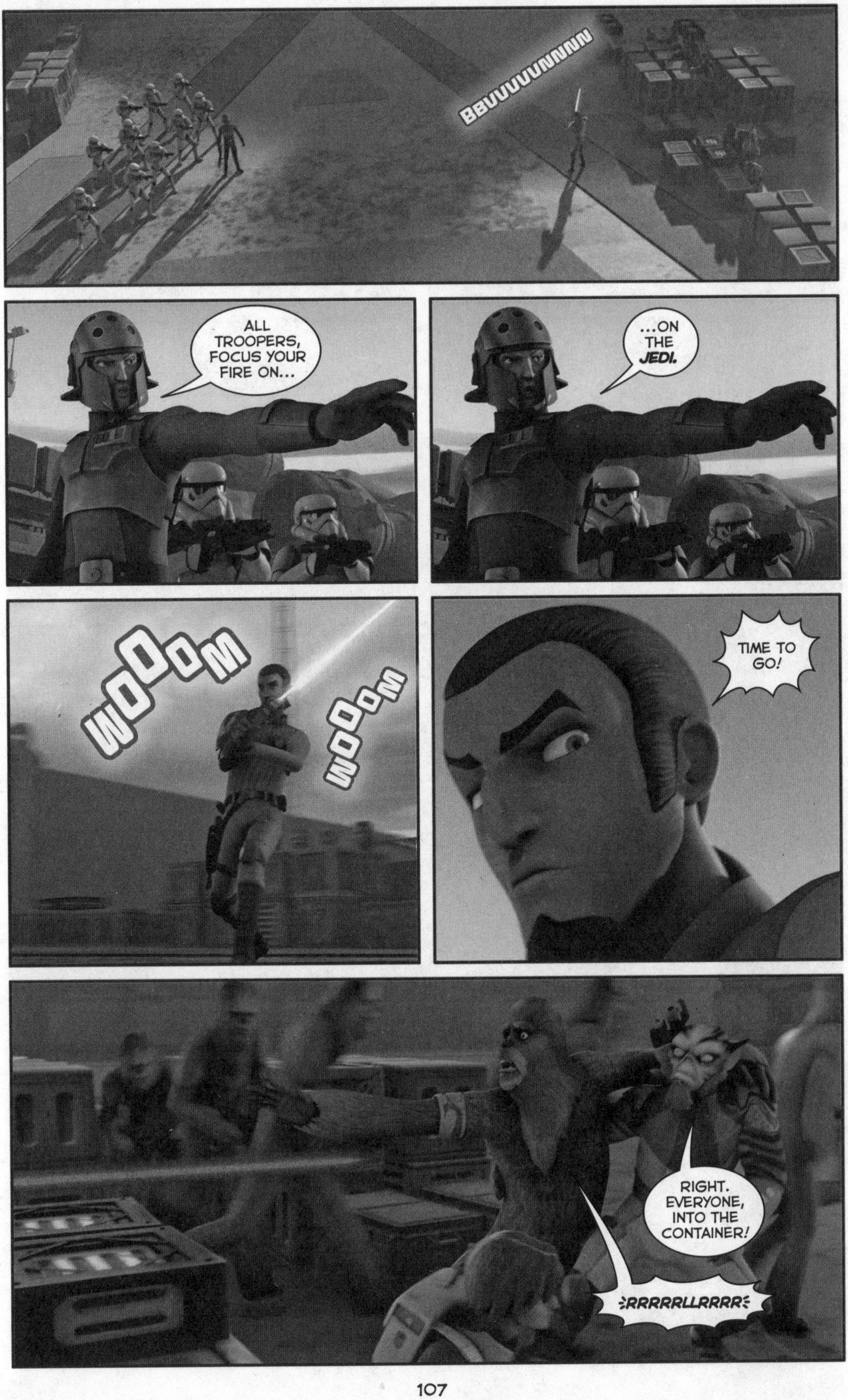
BBUUUUNNNN
ALL TROOPERS, FOCUS YOUR FIRE ON...
...ON THE JEDI.
WOOOM
WOOOM
TIME TO GO!
RIGHT. EVERYONE, INTO THE CONTAINER!
RRRRRLLRRRR

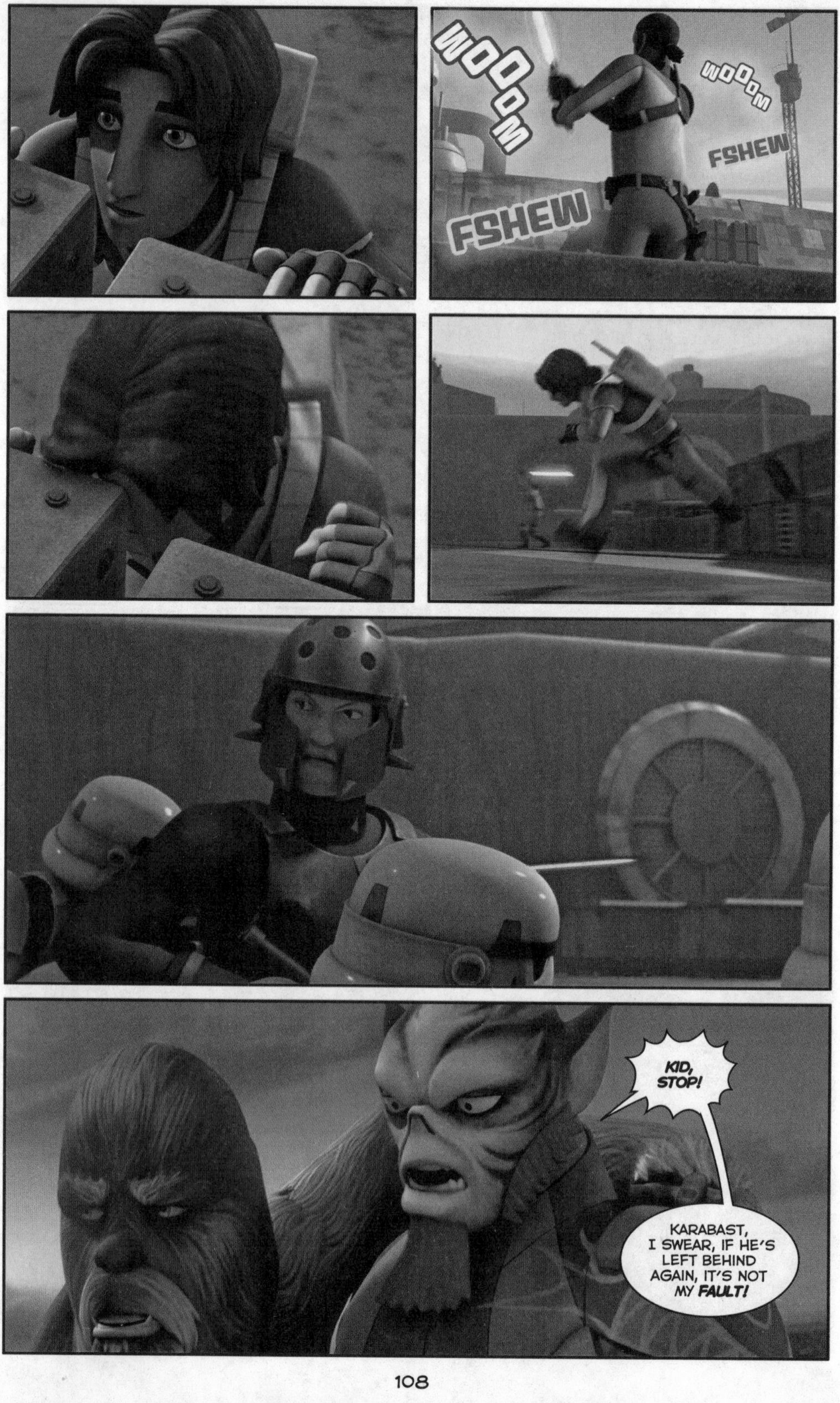
WOOOM
WOOOM
FSHEW
FSHEW
KID, STOP!
KARABAST, I SWEAR, IF HE'S LEFT BEHIND AGAIN, IT'S NOT MY **FAULT!**

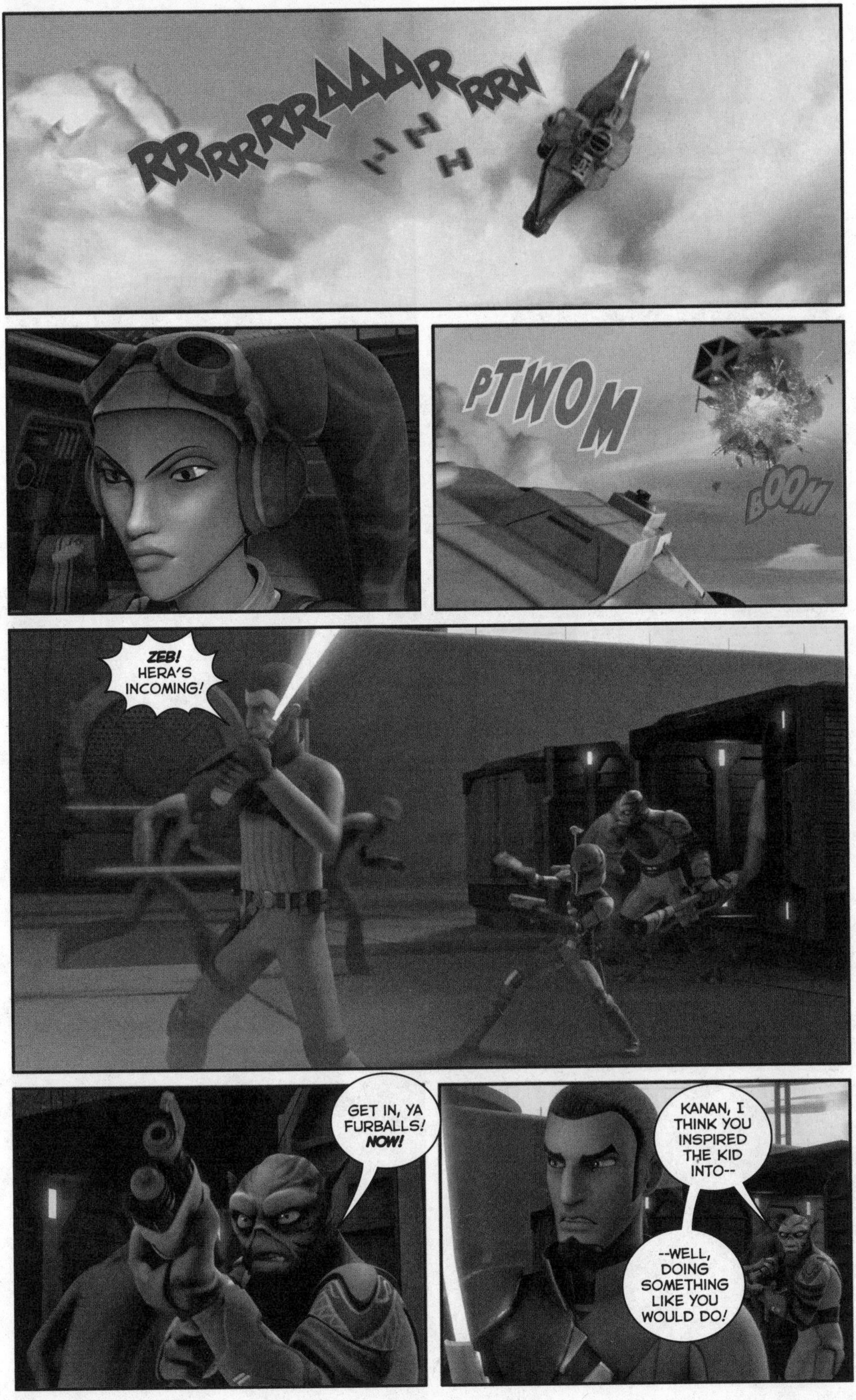
RRRRRRAAAARRRN
PTWOM
BOOM
ZEB! HERA'S INCOMING!
GET IN, YA FURBALLS! NOW!
KANAN, I THINK YOU INSPIRED THE KID INTO--
--WELL, DOING SOMETHING LIKE YOU WOULD DO!

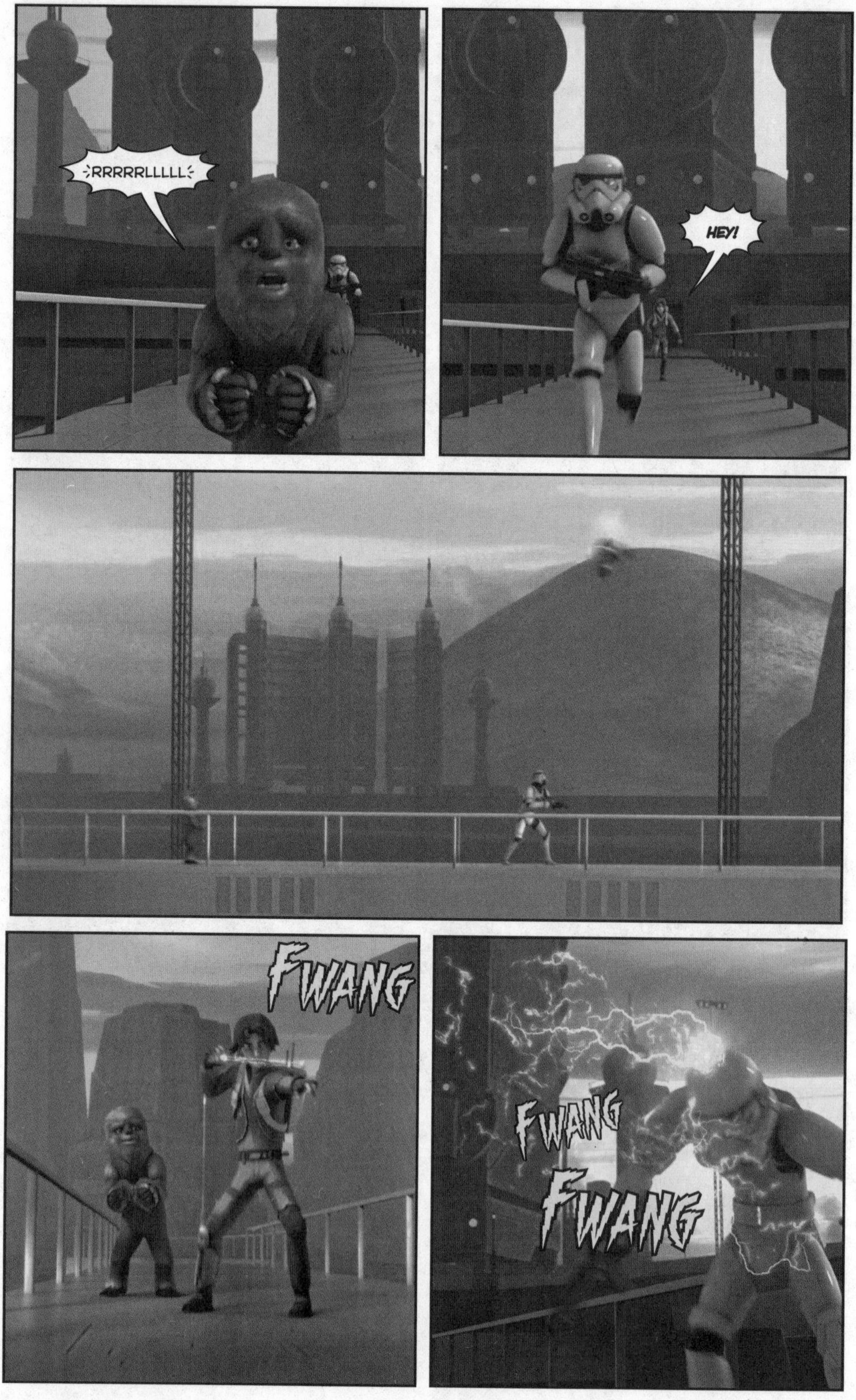
RRRRRLLLLL
HEY!
FWANG
FWANG
FWANG

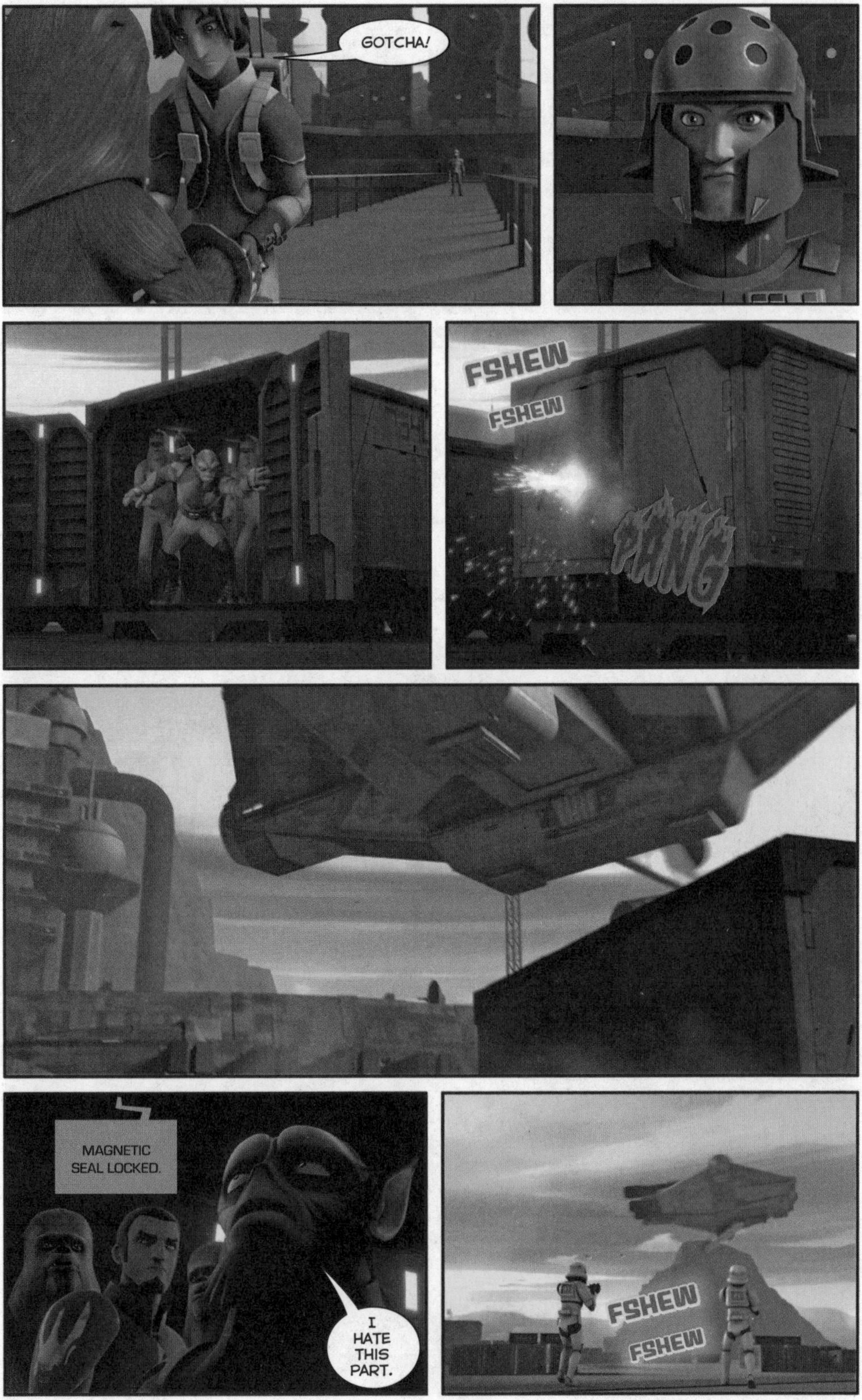
GOTCHA!
FSHEW
FSHEW
PANG
MAGNETIC SEAL LOCKED.
I HATE THIS PART.
FSHEW
FSHEW

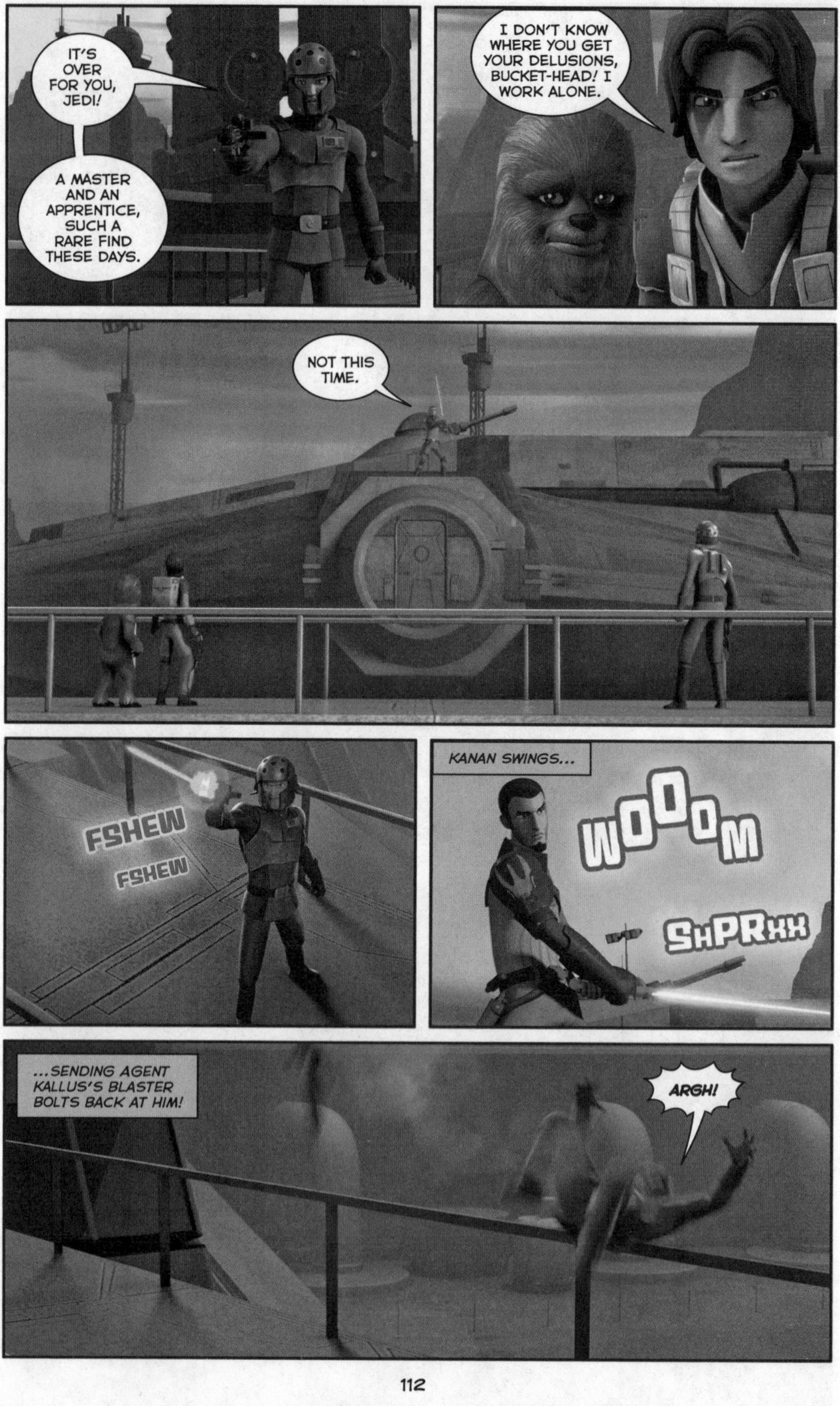
IT'S OVER FOR YOU, JEDI!
A MASTER AND AN APPRENTICE, SUCH A RARE FIND THESE DAYS.
I DON'T KNOW WHERE YOU GET YOUR DELUSIONS, BUCKET-HEAD! I WORK ALONE.
NOT THIS TIME.
FSHEW
FSHEW
KANAN SWINGS...
WOOOOM
SHPRXX
...SENDING AGENT KALLUS'S BLASTER BOLTS BACK AT HIM!
ARGH!

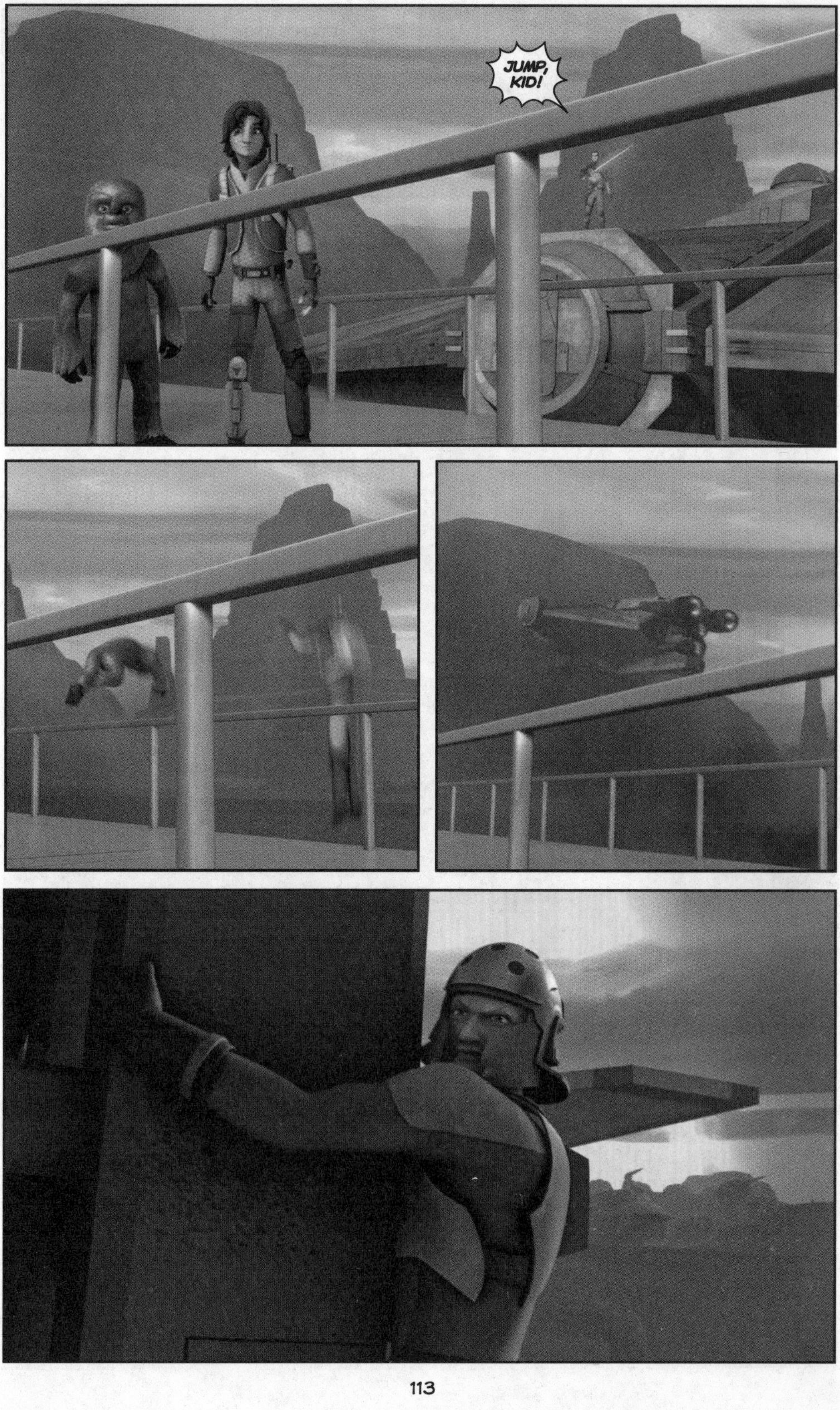
JUMP, KID!

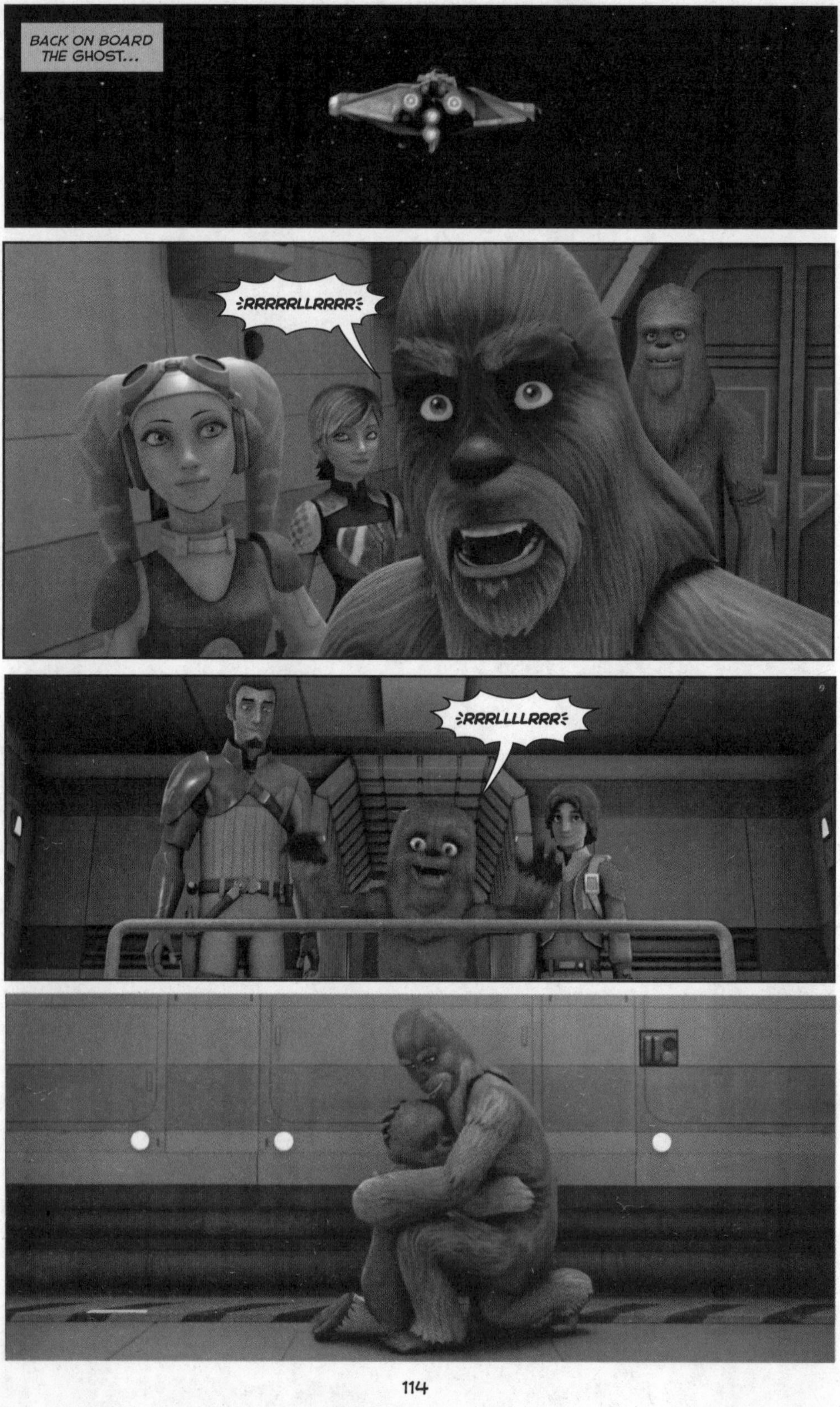
BACK ON BOARD THE GHOST...
RRRRRLLRRRR
RRRLLLLRRR

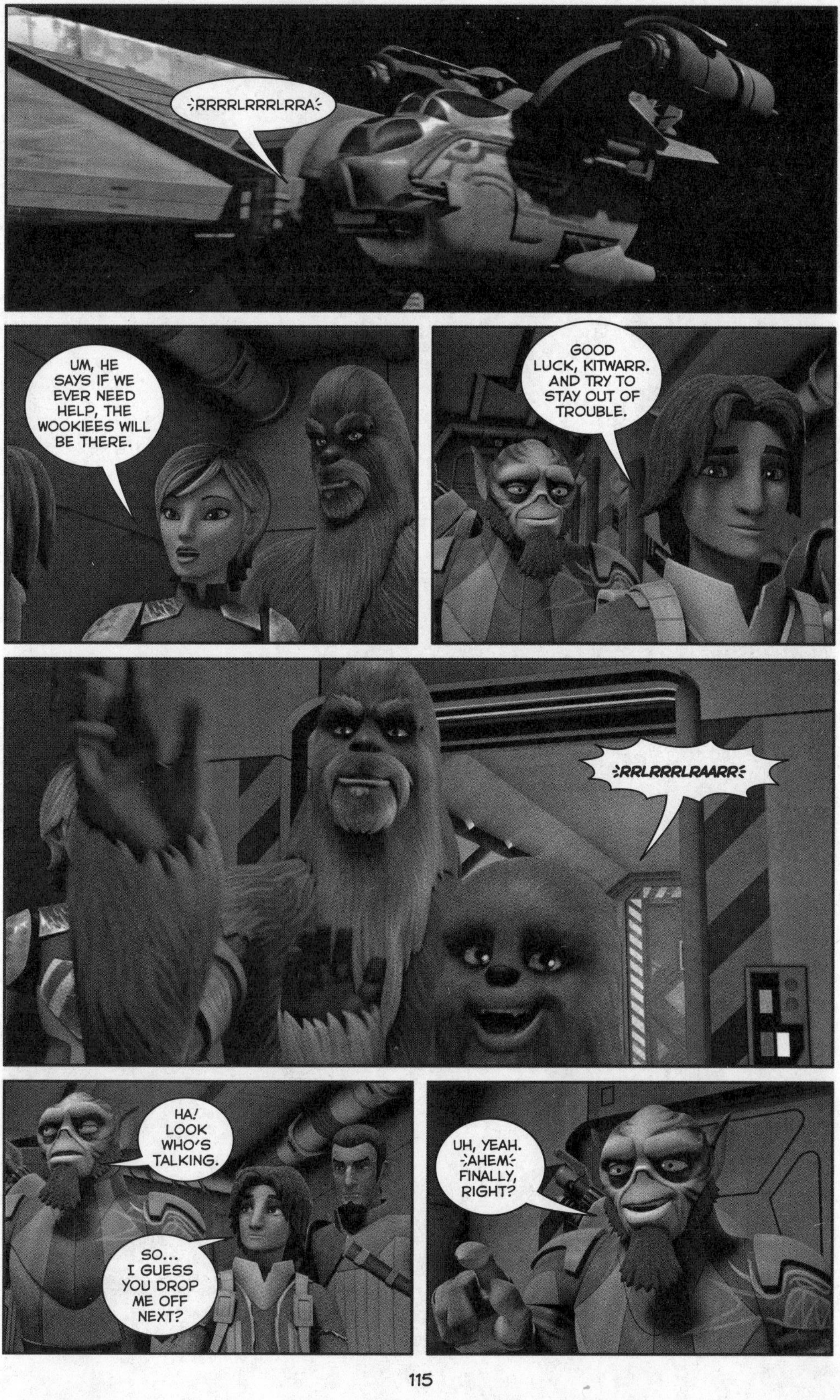

RRRRLRRRLRRA
UM, HE SAYS IF WE EVER NEED HELP, THE WOOKIEES WILL BE THERE.
GOOD LUCK, KITWARR. AND TRY TO STAY OUT OF TROUBLE.
RRLRRRLRAARR
HA! LOOK WHO'S TALKING.
SO... I GUESS YOU DROP ME OFF NEXT?
UH, YEAH. AHEM FINALLY, RIGHT?

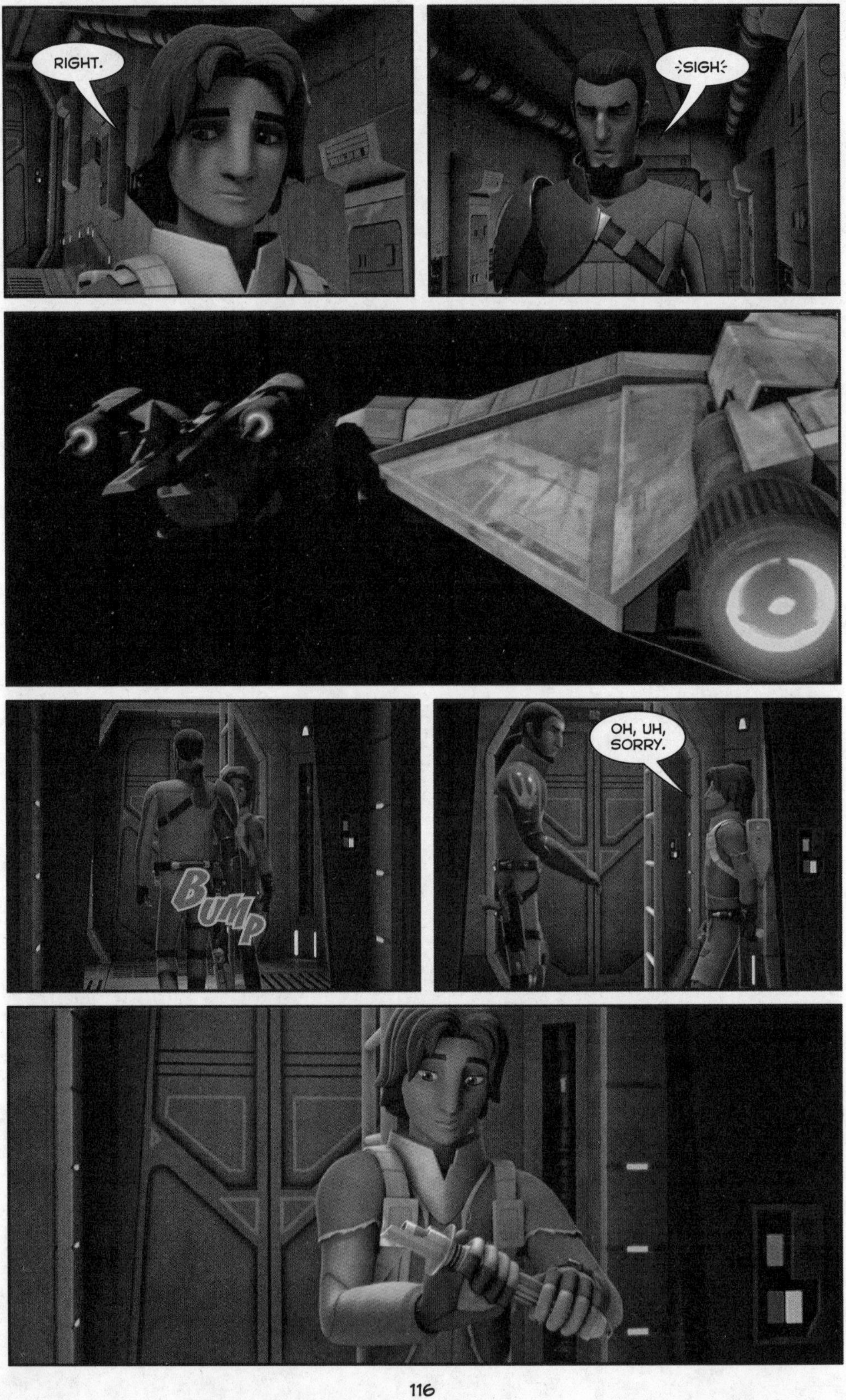
RIGHT.
-SIGH-
BUMP
OH, UH, SORRY.

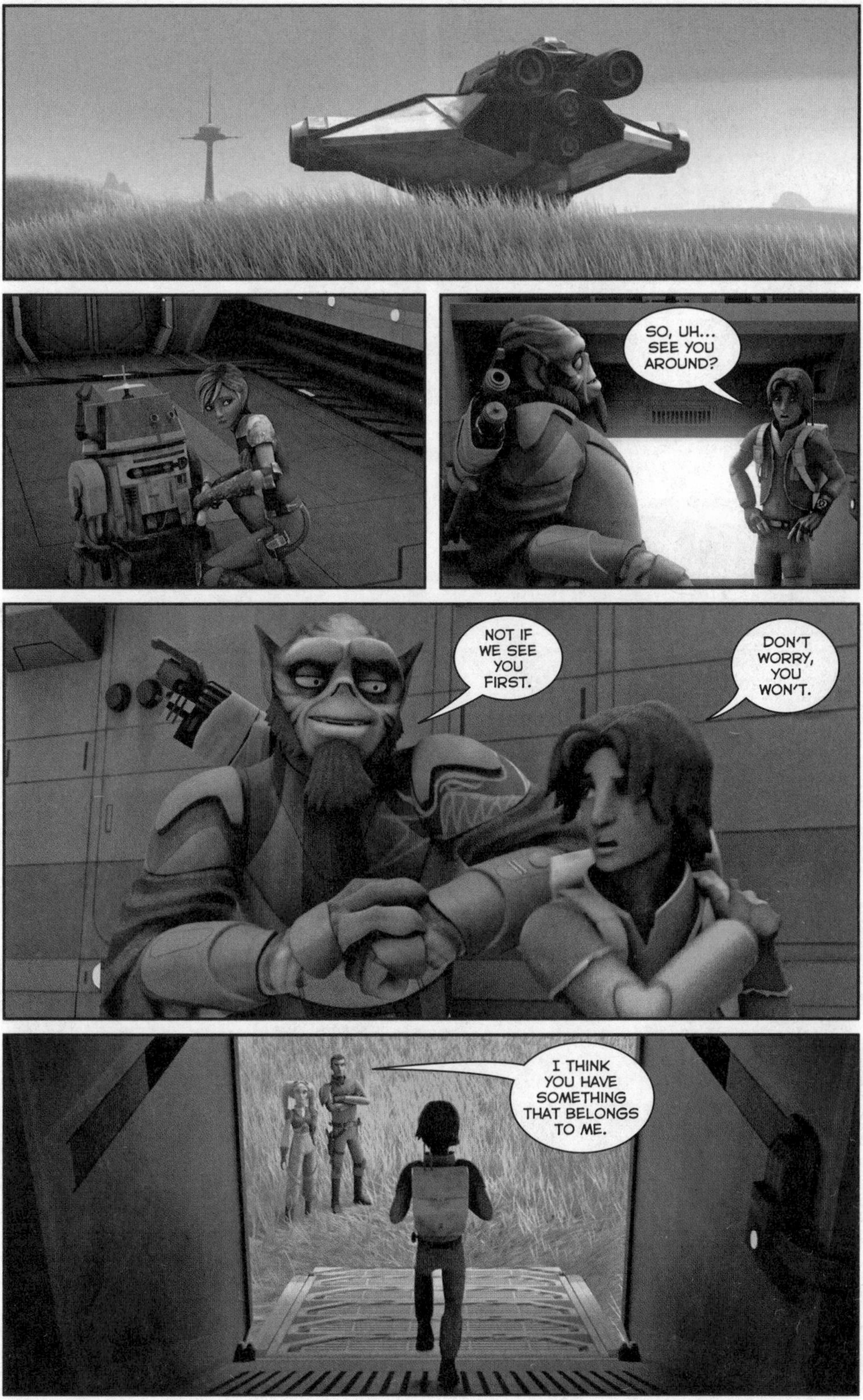
SO, UH... SEE YOU AROUND?
NOT IF WE SEE YOU FIRST.
DON'T WORRY, YOU WON'T.
I THINK YOU HAVE SOMETHING THAT BELONGS TO ME.

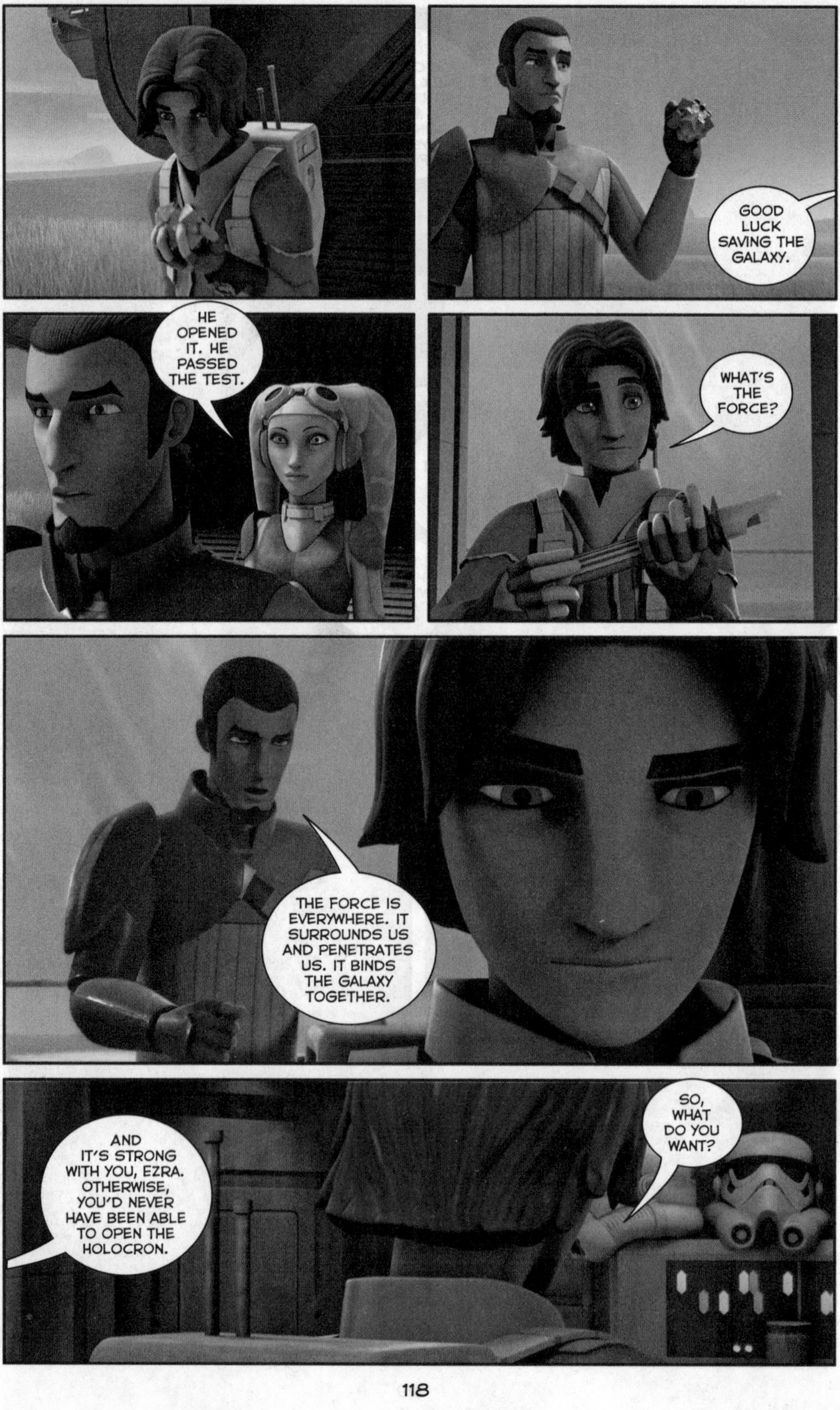
GOOD LUCK SAVING THE GALAXY.
HE OPENED IT. HE PASSED THE TEST.
WHAT'S THE FORCE?
THE FORCE IS EVERYWHERE. IT SURROUNDS US AND PENETRATES US. IT BINDS THE GALAXY TOGETHER.
AND IT'S STRONG WITH YOU, EZRA. OTHERWISE, YOU'D NEVER HAVE BEEN ABLE TO OPEN THE HOLOCRON.
SO, WHAT DO YOU WANT?

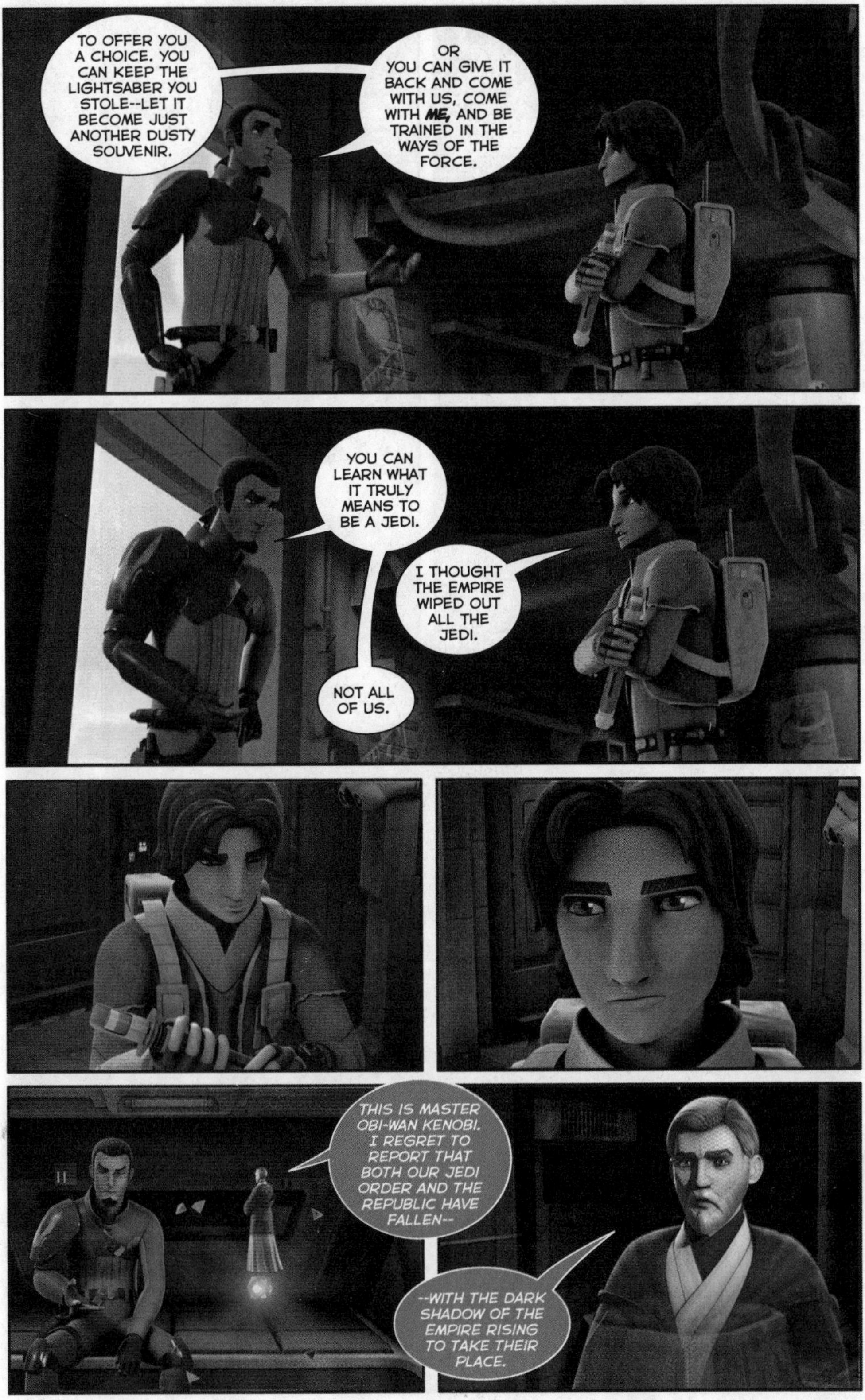
TO OFFER YOU A CHOICE. YOU CAN KEEP THE LIGHTSABER YOU STOLE--LET IT BECOME JUST ANOTHER DUSTY SOUVENIR.
OR YOU CAN GIVE IT BACK AND COME WITH US, COME WITH *ME,* AND BE TRAINED IN THE WAYS OF THE FORCE.
YOU CAN LEARN WHAT IT TRULY MEANS TO BE A JEDI.
I THOUGHT THE EMPIRE WIPED OUT ALL THE JEDI.
NOT ALL OF US.
THIS IS MASTER OBI-WAN KENOBI. I REGRET TO REPORT THAT BOTH OUR JEDI ORDER AND THE REPUBLIC HAVE FALLEN--
--WITH THE DARK SHADOW OF THE EMPIRE RISING TO TAKE THEIR PLACE.

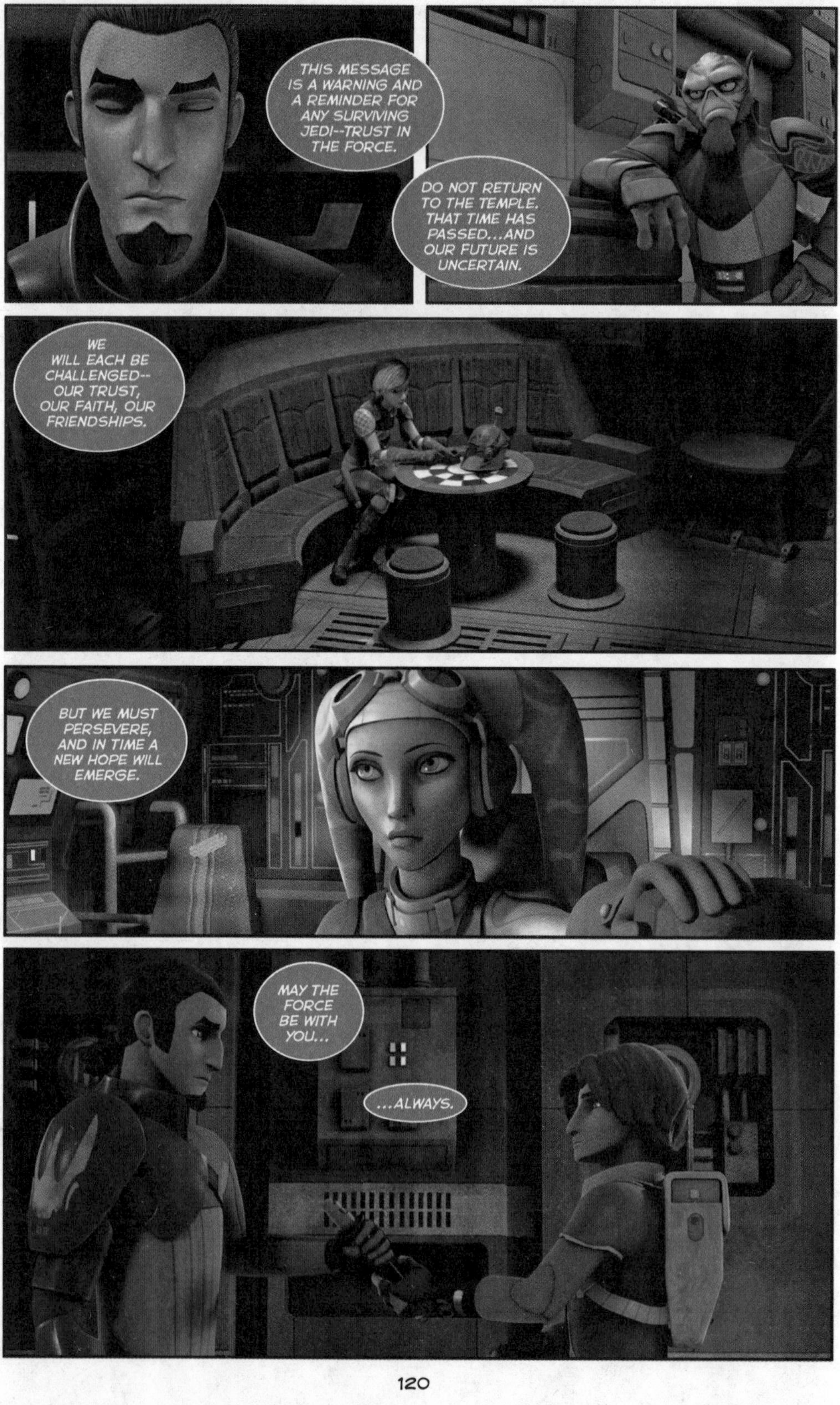
THIS MESSAGE IS A WARNING AND A REMINDER FOR ANY SURVIVING JEDI--TRUST IN THE FORCE.
DO NOT RETURN TO THE TEMPLE. THAT TIME HAS PASSED...AND OUR FUTURE IS UNCERTAIN.
WE WILL EACH BE CHALLENGED--OUR TRUST, OUR FAITH, OUR FRIENDSHIPS.
BUT WE MUST PERSEVERE, AND IN TIME A NEW HOPE WILL EMERGE.
MAY THE FORCE BE WITH YOU...
...ALWAYS.

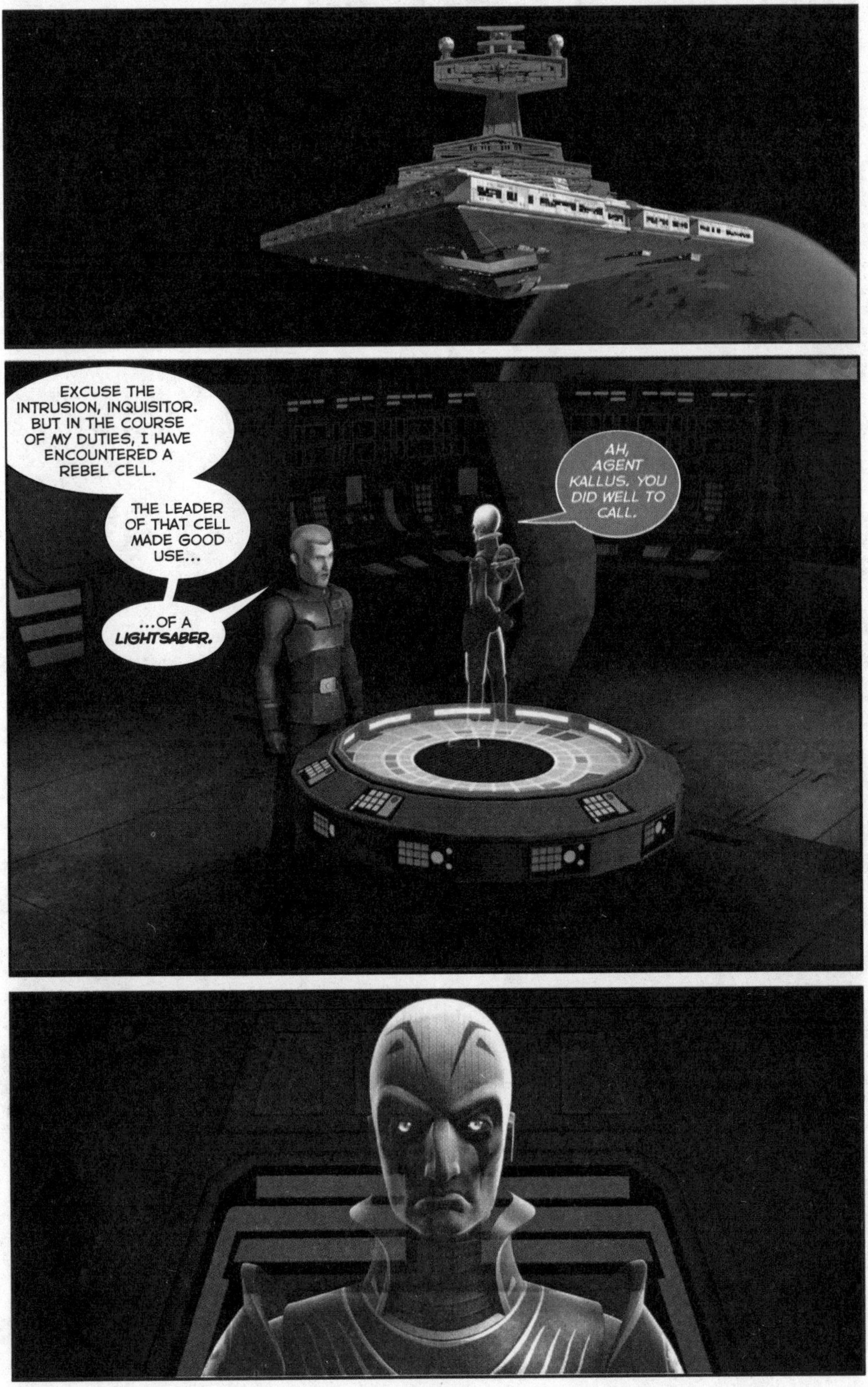
EXCUSE THE INTRUSION, INQUISITOR. BUT IN THE COURSE OF MY DUTIES, I HAVE ENCOUNTERED A REBEL CELL.
AH, AGENT KALLUS. YOU DID WELL TO CALL.
THE LEADER OF THAT CELL MADE GOOD USE...
...OF A LIGHTSABER.

STAR WARS REBELS™

DROIDS IN DISTRESS

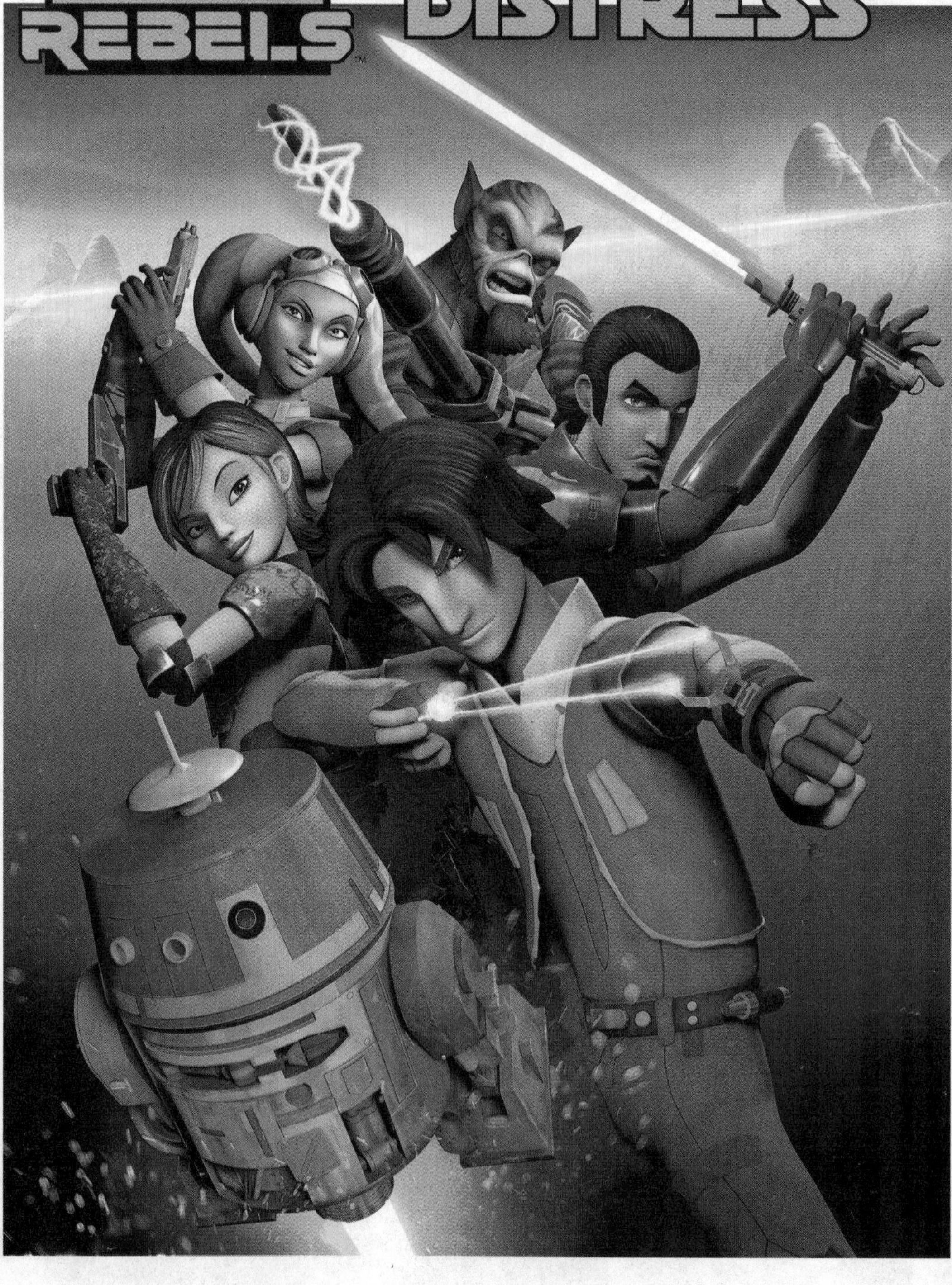

"I DON'T HAVE A SHOT!"

CHOPPER, DO YOU HAVE THE COORDINATES?

BZZZ PIP PUP

WHAT DID HE SAY?

HE SAID, "HELLO, HYPERSPACE!"

THAT'S NOT WHAT HE SAID.

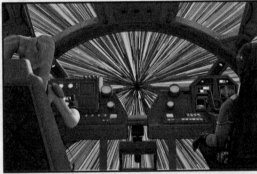

TOLD YA WE'D GET AWAY...

WITH THE SHIPMENT.

YOU SAID WE'D GET AWAY WITH THE SHIPMENT.

KANAN, WE'RE LOW ON EVERYTHING.

FOOD...

EXPLOSIVES...

FUEL! WE NEED TO MAKE SOME MONEY, OR WE MIGHT AS WELL PUT THE *GHOST* IN STORAGE.

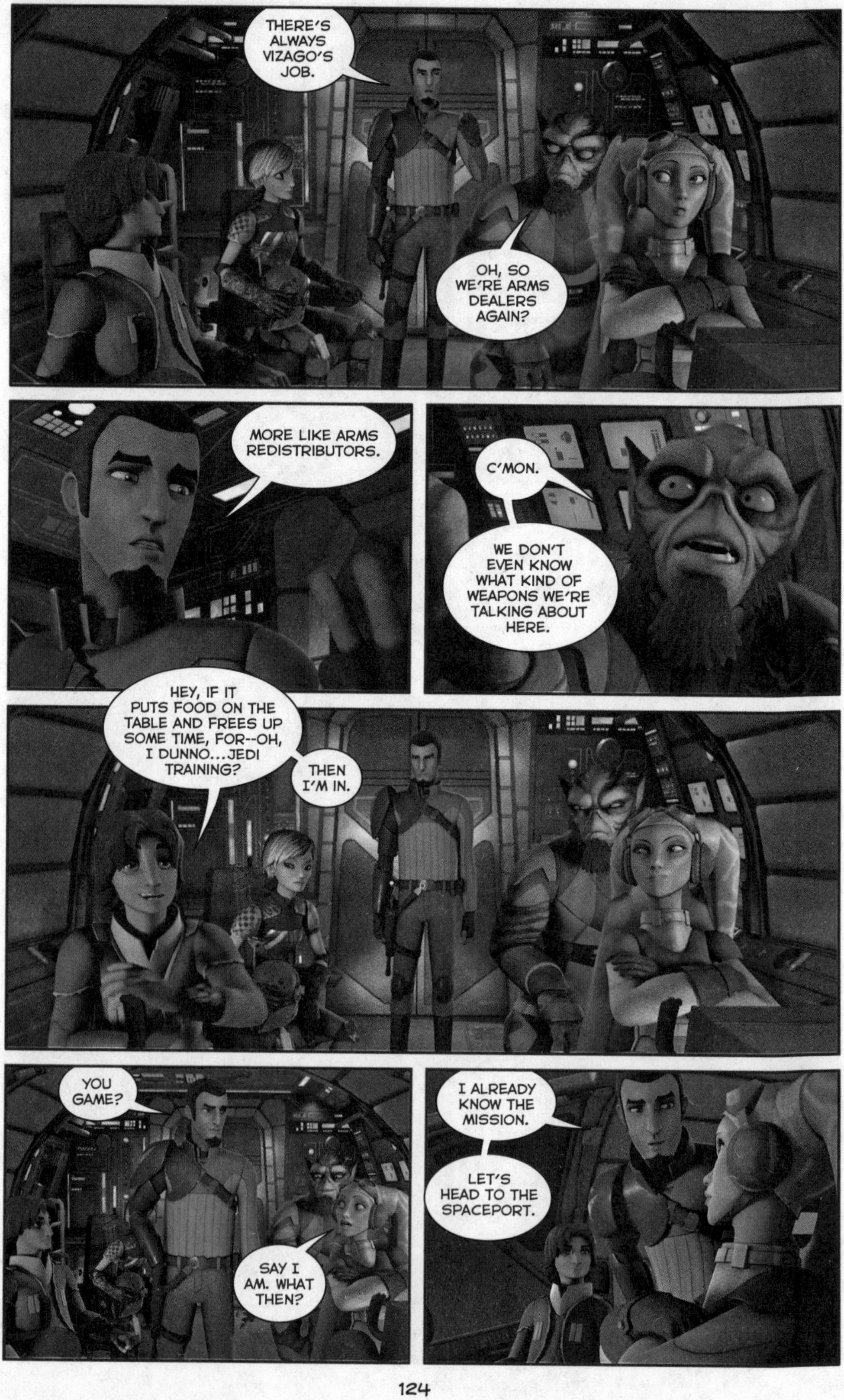
THERE'S ALWAYS VIZAGO'S JOB.
OH, SO WE'RE ARMS DEALERS AGAIN?
MORE LIKE ARMS REDISTRIBUTORS.
C'MON.
WE DON'T EVEN KNOW WHAT KIND OF WEAPONS WE'RE TALKING ABOUT HERE.
HEY, IF IT PUTS FOOD ON THE TABLE AND FREES UP SOME TIME, FOR--OH, I DUNNO...JEDI TRAINING?
THEN I'M IN.
YOU GAME?
SAY I AM. WHAT THEN?
I ALREADY KNOW THE MISSION.
LET'S HEAD TO THE SPACEPORT.

"NOW BOARDING STAR-COMMUTER SHUTTLE ST-45, BOUND FOR GAREL."

HOW RUDE!

BONK

THIS WAY, MR. WABO.

WE HAVE SEATS IN THE FRONT.

GRUA THUN, TUA, MOG BABB VILL WORN.

ARGH, WHERE IS THAT TRANSLATOR?

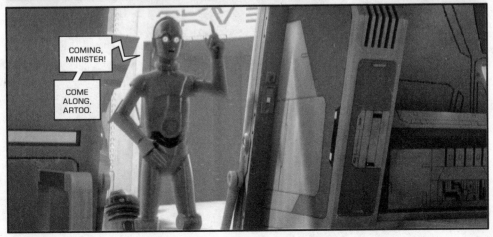

COMING, MINISTER!

COME ALONG, ARTOO.

"FINAL CALL FOR STAR-COMMUTER SHUTTLE ST-45 BOUND FOR GAREL."

UGH!

BRRRZZZ BEEP

SENTIENTS, PLEASE PREPARE FOR TAKEOFF.

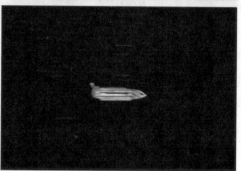

MEK MEK MEKEKEKEKKK

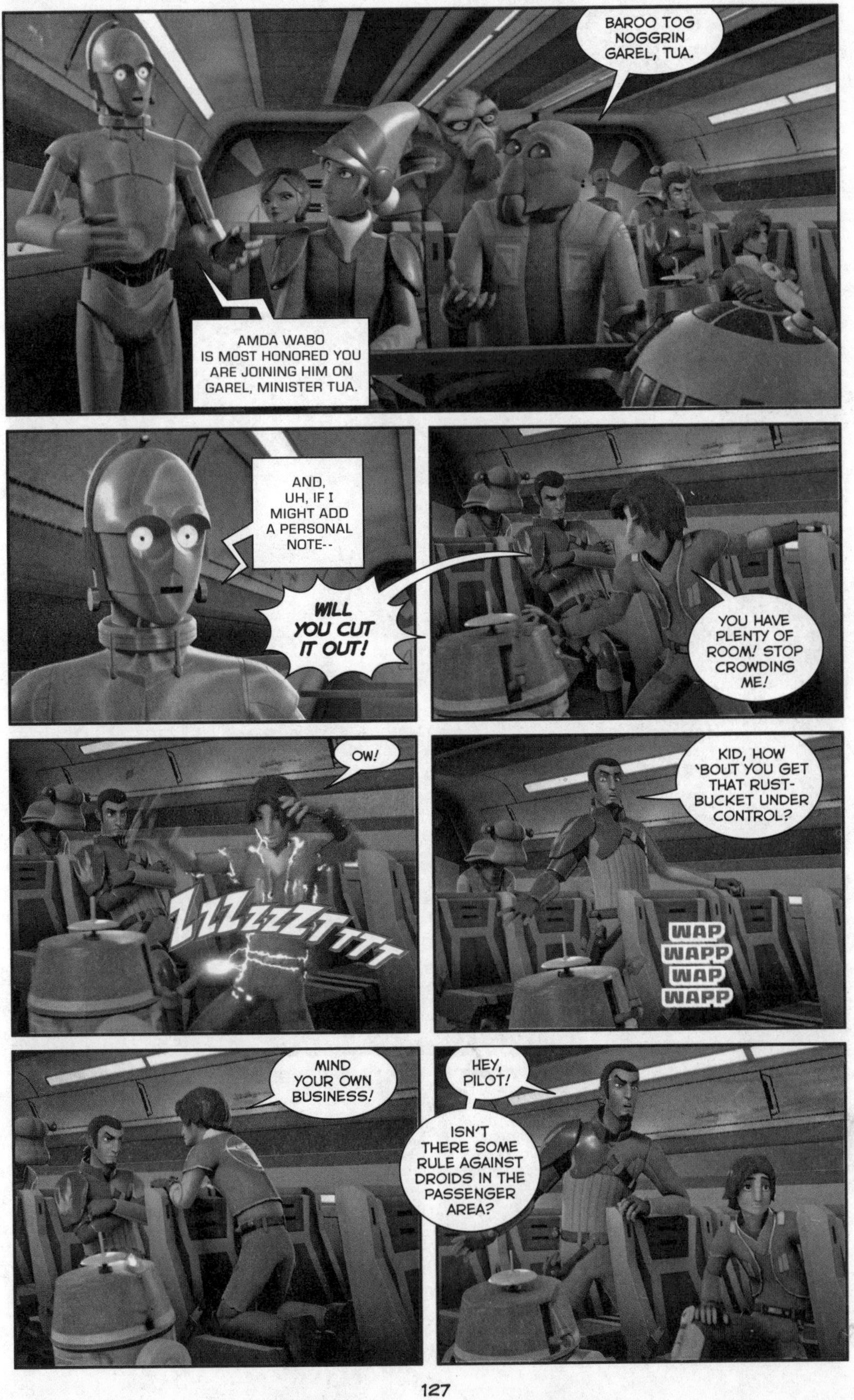
BAROO TOG NOGGRIN GAREL, TUA.
AMDA WABO IS MOST HONORED YOU ARE JOINING HIM ON GAREL, MINISTER TUA.
AND, UH, IF I MIGHT ADD A PERSONAL NOTE--
WILL YOU CUT IT OUT!
YOU HAVE PLENTY OF ROOM! STOP CROWDING ME!
OW!
ZZZzzzZTTTT
KID, HOW 'BOUT YOU GET THAT RUST-BUCKET UNDER CONTROL?
WAP
WAPP
WAP
WAPP
MIND YOUR OWN BUSINESS!
HEY, PILOT!
ISN'T THERE SOME RULE AGAINST DROIDS IN THE PASSENGER AREA?

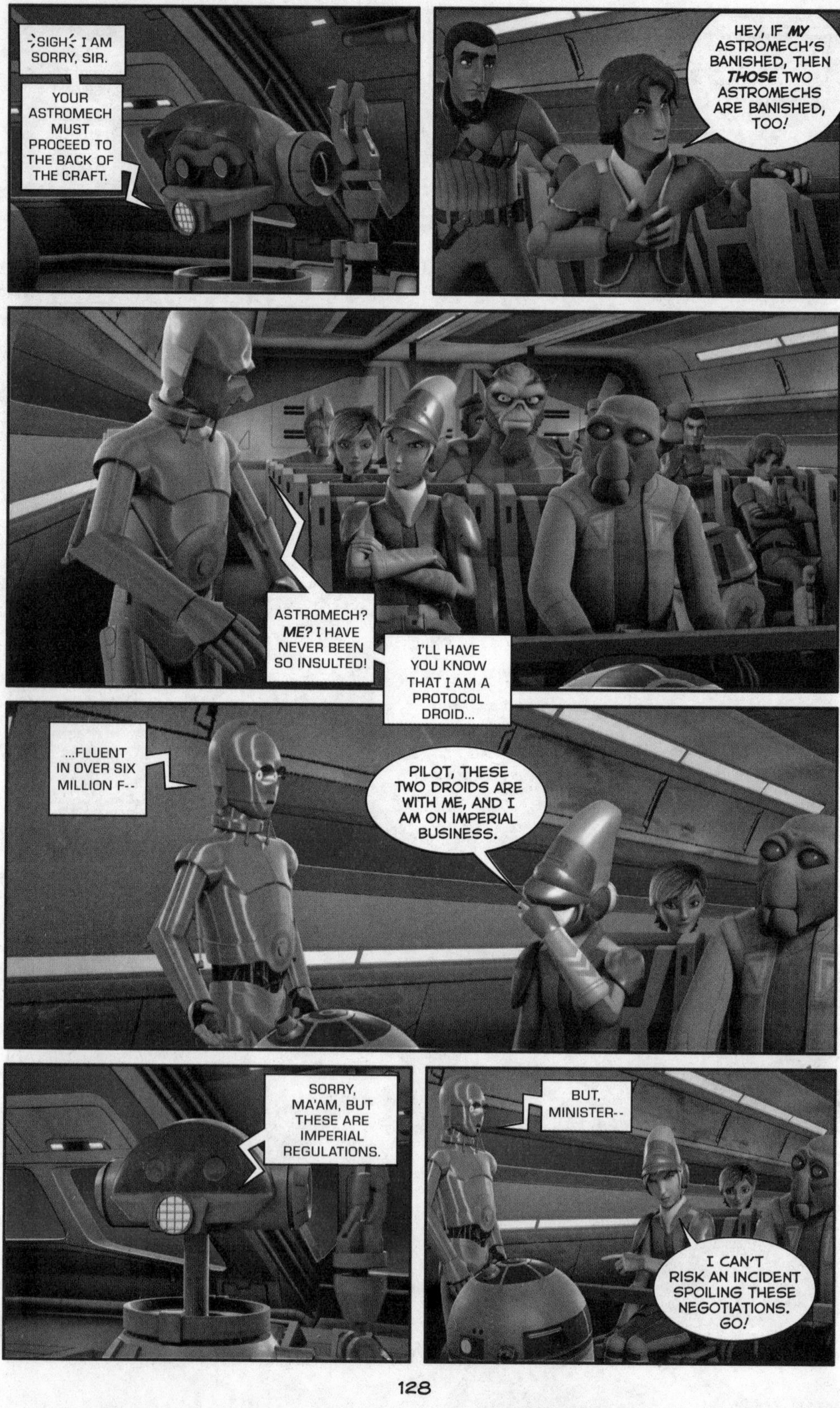

SIGH I AM SORRY, SIR.
YOUR ASTROMECH MUST PROCEED TO THE BACK OF THE CRAFT.
HEY, IF *MY* ASTROMECH'S BANISHED, THEN *THOSE* TWO ASTROMECHS ARE BANISHED, TOO!
ASTROMECH? *ME?* I HAVE NEVER BEEN SO INSULTED!
I'LL HAVE YOU KNOW THAT I AM A PROTOCOL DROID...
...FLUENT IN OVER SIX MILLION F--
PILOT, THESE TWO DROIDS ARE WITH ME, AND I AM ON IMPERIAL BUSINESS.
SORRY, MA'AM, BUT THESE ARE IMPERIAL REGULATIONS.
BUT, MINISTER--
I CAN'T RISK AN INCIDENT SPOILING THESE NEGOTIATIONS. GO!

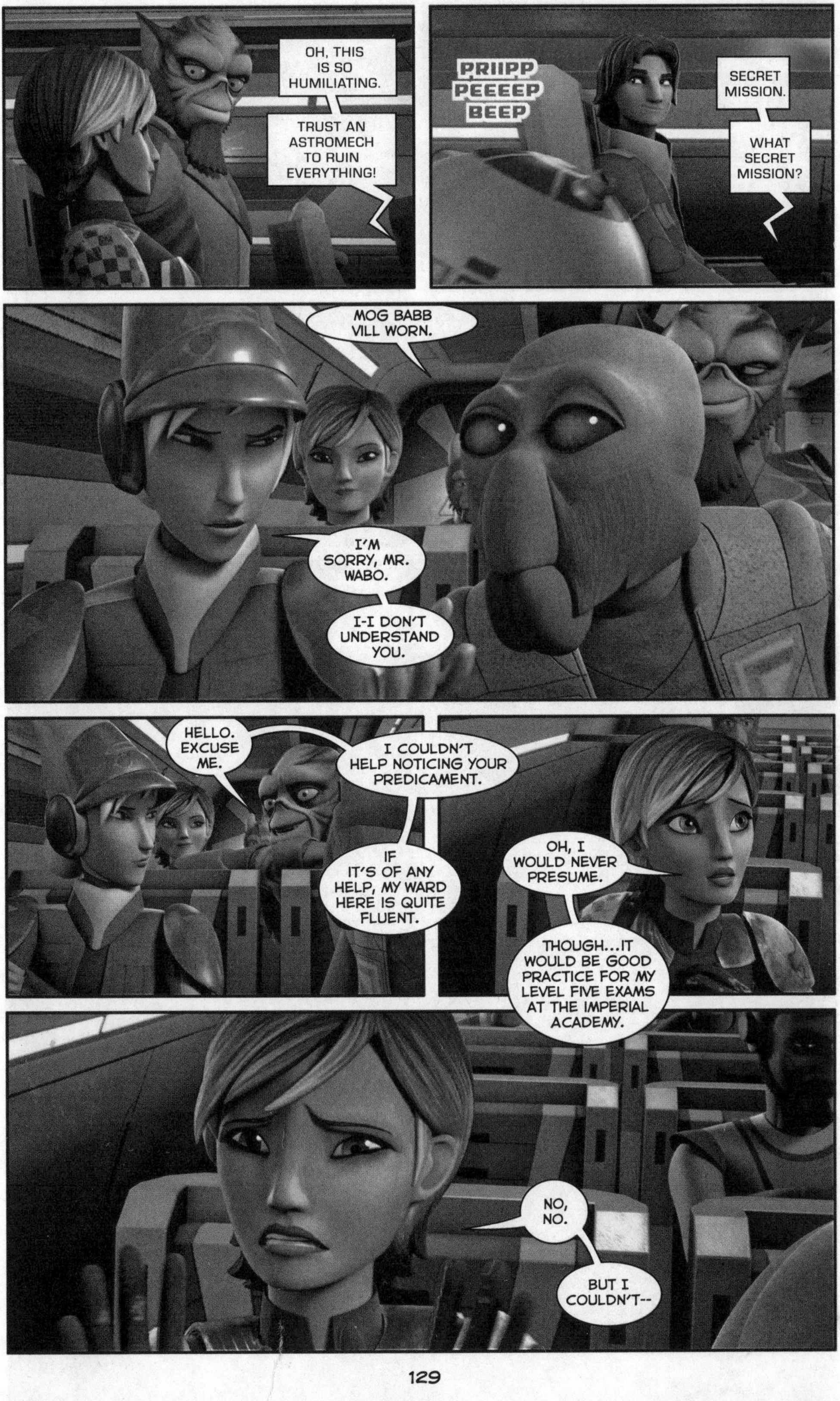
OH, THIS IS SO HUMILIATING.
TRUST AN ASTROMECH TO RUIN EVERYTHING!
PRIIPP PEEEEP BEEP
SECRET MISSION.
WHAT SECRET MISSION?
MOG BABB VILL WORN.
I'M SORRY, MR. WABO.
I-I DON'T UNDERSTAND YOU.
HELLO. EXCUSE ME.
I COULDN'T HELP NOTICING YOUR PREDICAMENT.
IF IT'S OF ANY HELP, MY WARD HERE IS QUITE FLUENT.
OH, I WOULD NEVER PRESUME.
THOUGH...IT WOULD BE GOOD PRACTICE FOR MY LEVEL FIVE EXAMS AT THE IMPERIAL ACADEMY.
NO, NO.
BUT I COULDN'T--

YOU'RE A LEVEL FIVE ACADEMY STUDENT?

I WAS TOO, ONCE UPON A TIME.

THAT YOUNG CREATURE CAN'T POSSIBLY TAKE THE PLACE OF A FULLY PROGRAMMED PROTOCOL DROID SUCH AS I.

THE ODDS OF OUR MISSION BECOMING A COMPLETE DEBACLE ARE--

CLANK

BEEP

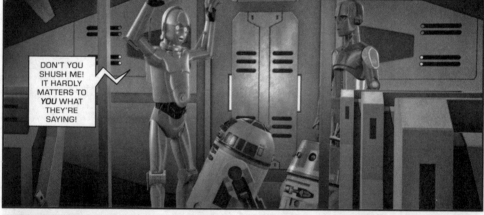

DON'T YOU SHUSH ME! IT HARDLY MATTERS TO *YOU* WHAT THEY'RE SAYING!

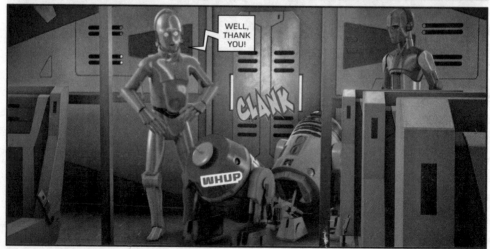

WELL, THANK YOU!

CLANK

WHUP

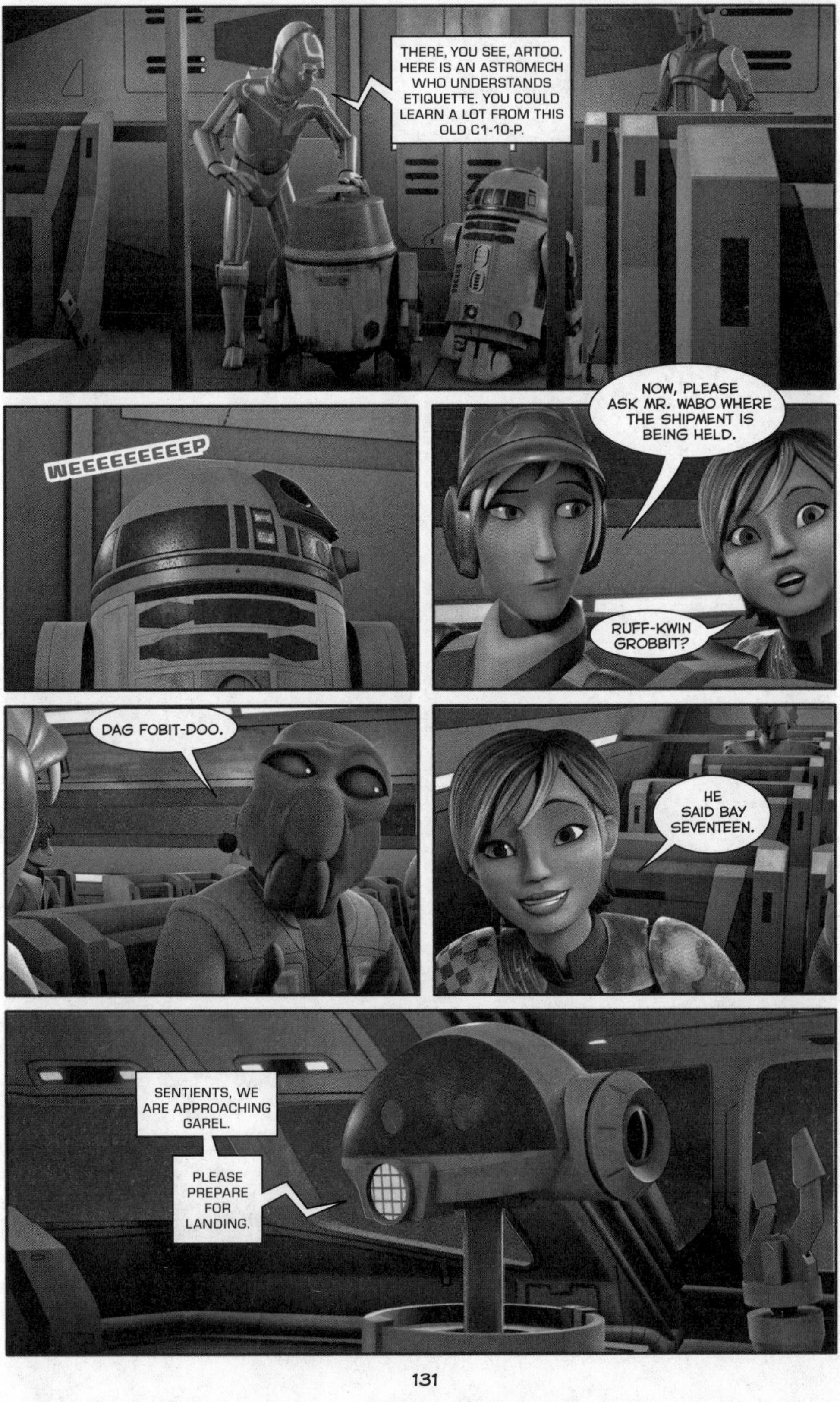
THERE, YOU SEE, ARTOO. HERE IS AN ASTROMECH WHO UNDERSTANDS ETIQUETTE. YOU COULD LEARN A LOT FROM THIS OLD C1-10-P.
WEEEEEEEEEP
NOW, PLEASE ASK MR. WABO WHERE THE SHIPMENT IS BEING HELD.
RUFF-KWIN GROBBIT?
DAG FOBIT-DOO.
HE SAID BAY SEVENTEEN.
SENTIENTS, WE ARE APPROACHING GAREL.
PLEASE PREPARE FOR LANDING.

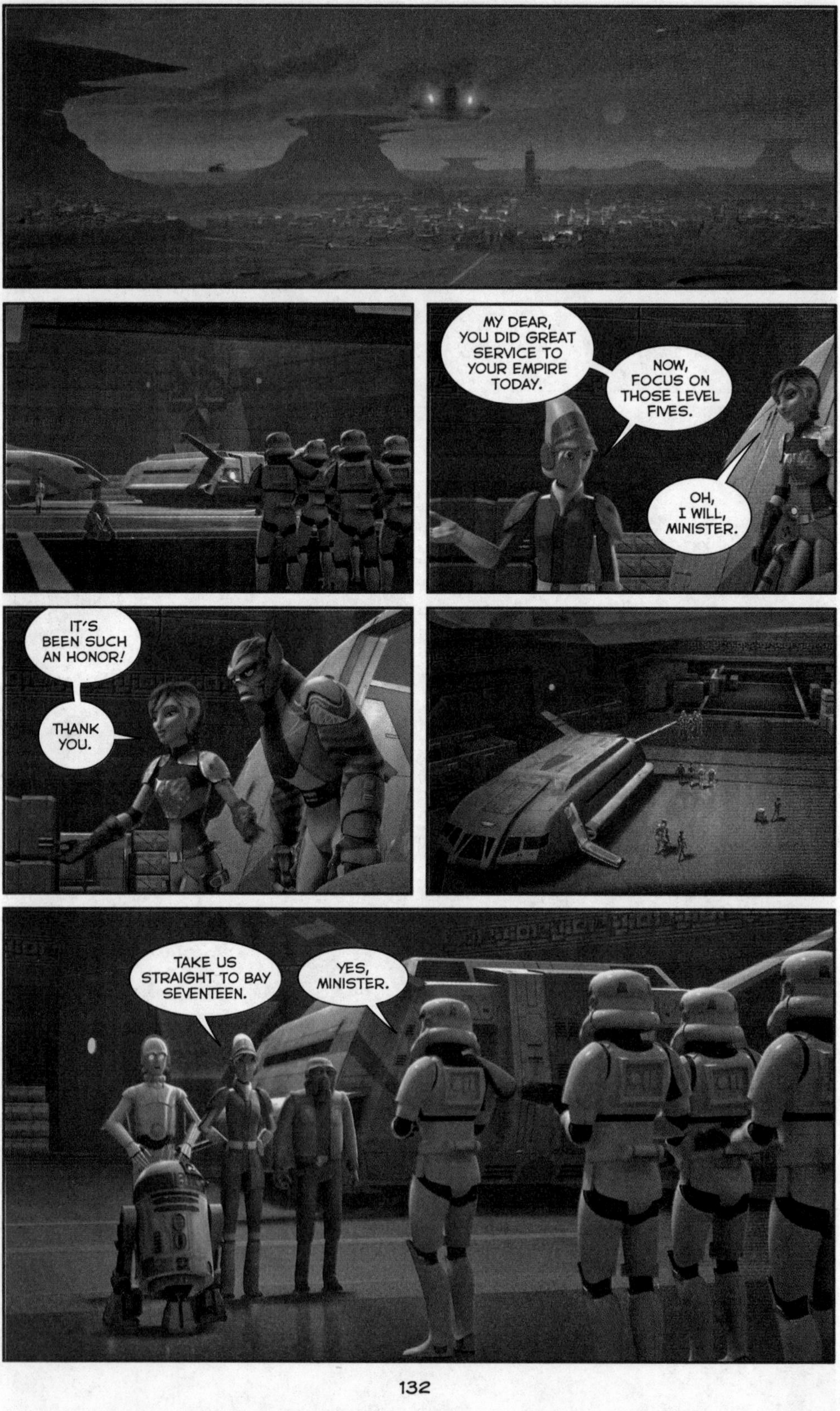
MY DEAR, YOU DID GREAT SERVICE TO YOUR EMPIRE TODAY.
NOW, FOCUS ON THOSE LEVEL FIVES.
OH, I WILL, MINISTER.
IT'S BEEN SUCH AN HONOR!
THANK YOU.
TAKE US STRAIGHT TO BAY SEVENTEEN.
YES, MINISTER.

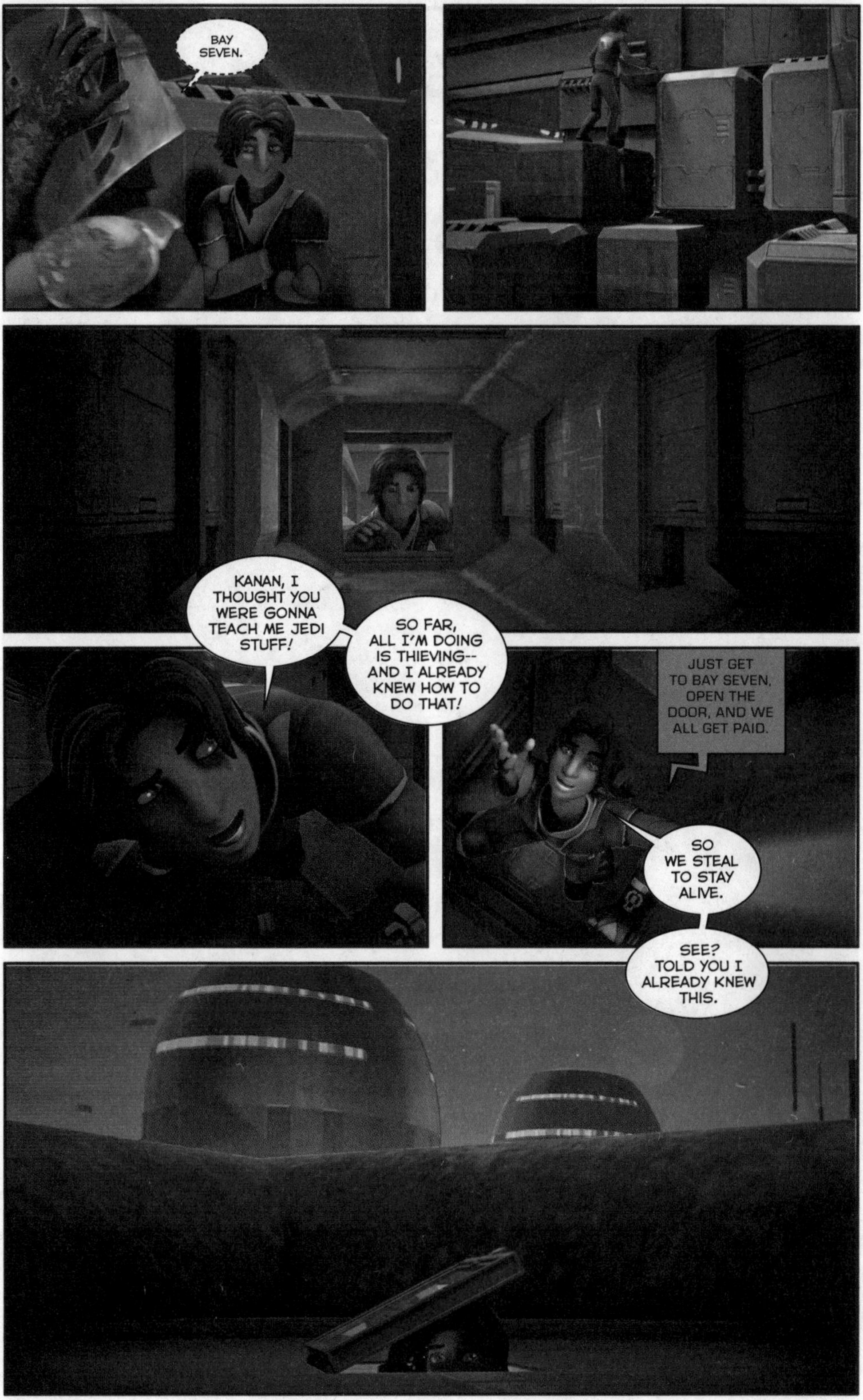
BAY SEVEN.
KANAN, I THOUGHT YOU WERE GONNA TEACH ME JEDI STUFF!
SO FAR, ALL I'M DOING IS THIEVING-- AND I ALREADY KNEW HOW TO DO THAT!
JUST GET TO BAY SEVEN, OPEN THE DOOR, AND WE ALL GET PAID.
SO WE STEAL TO STAY ALIVE.
SEE? TOLD YOU I ALREADY KNEW THIS.

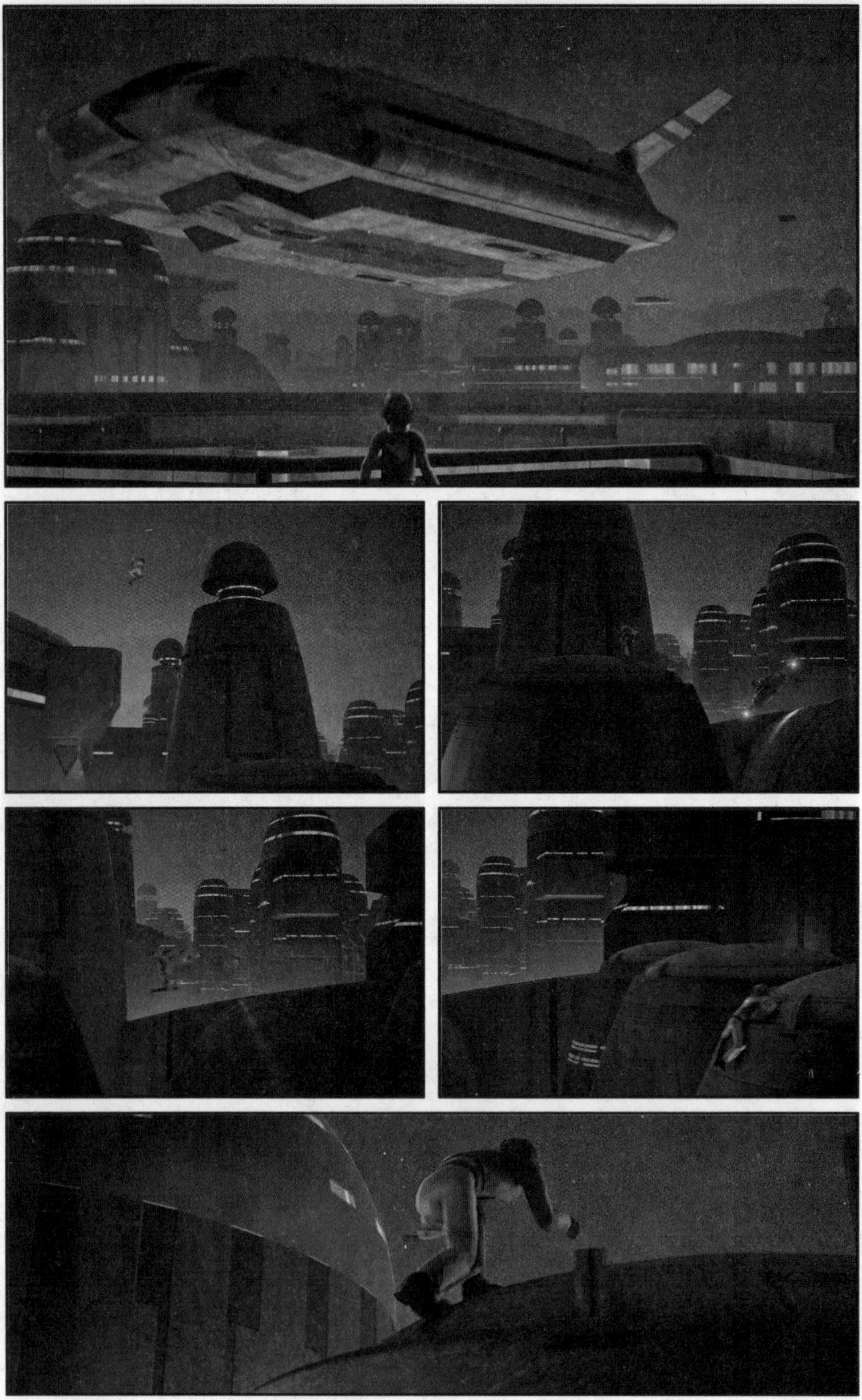

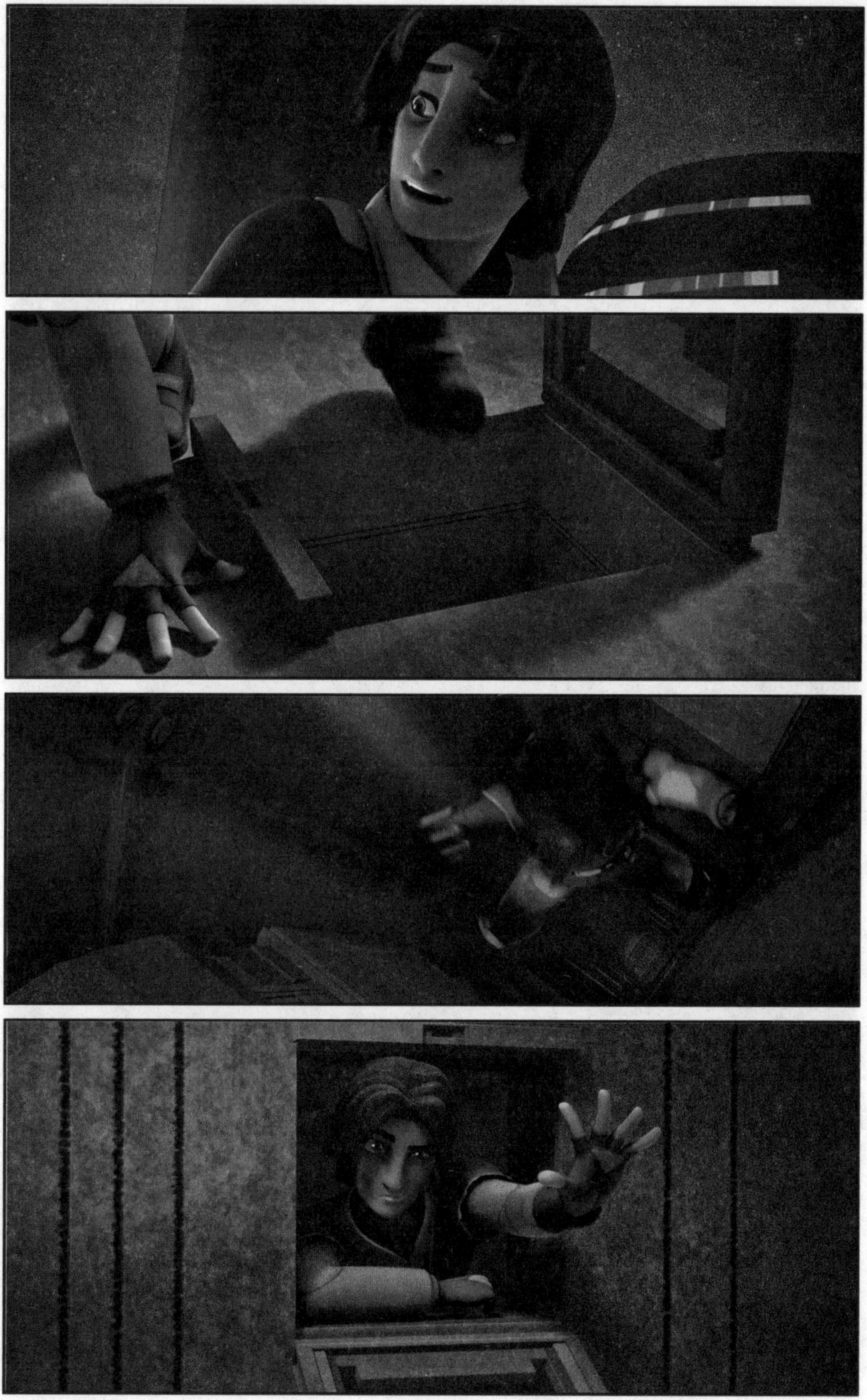

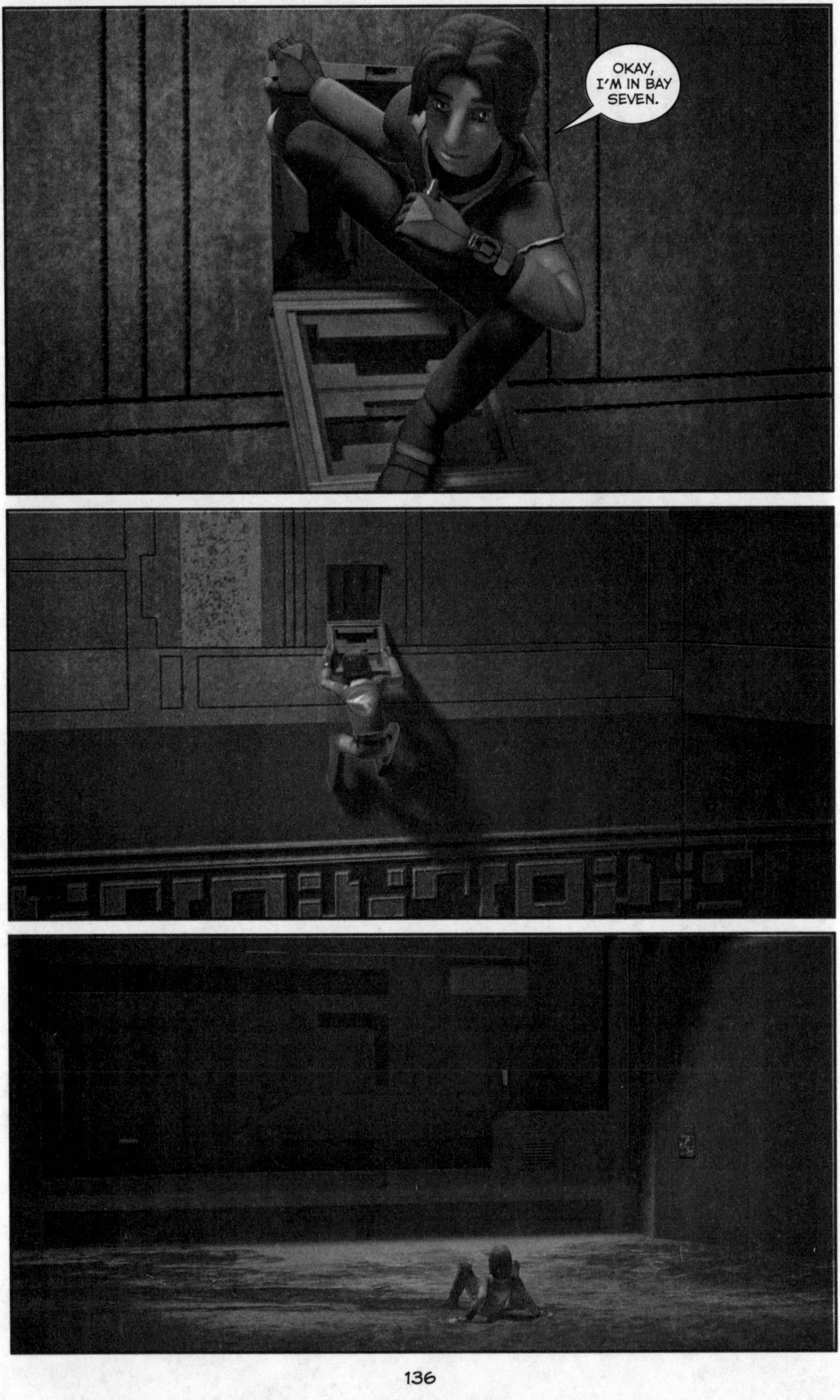
OKAY, I'M IN BAY SEVEN.

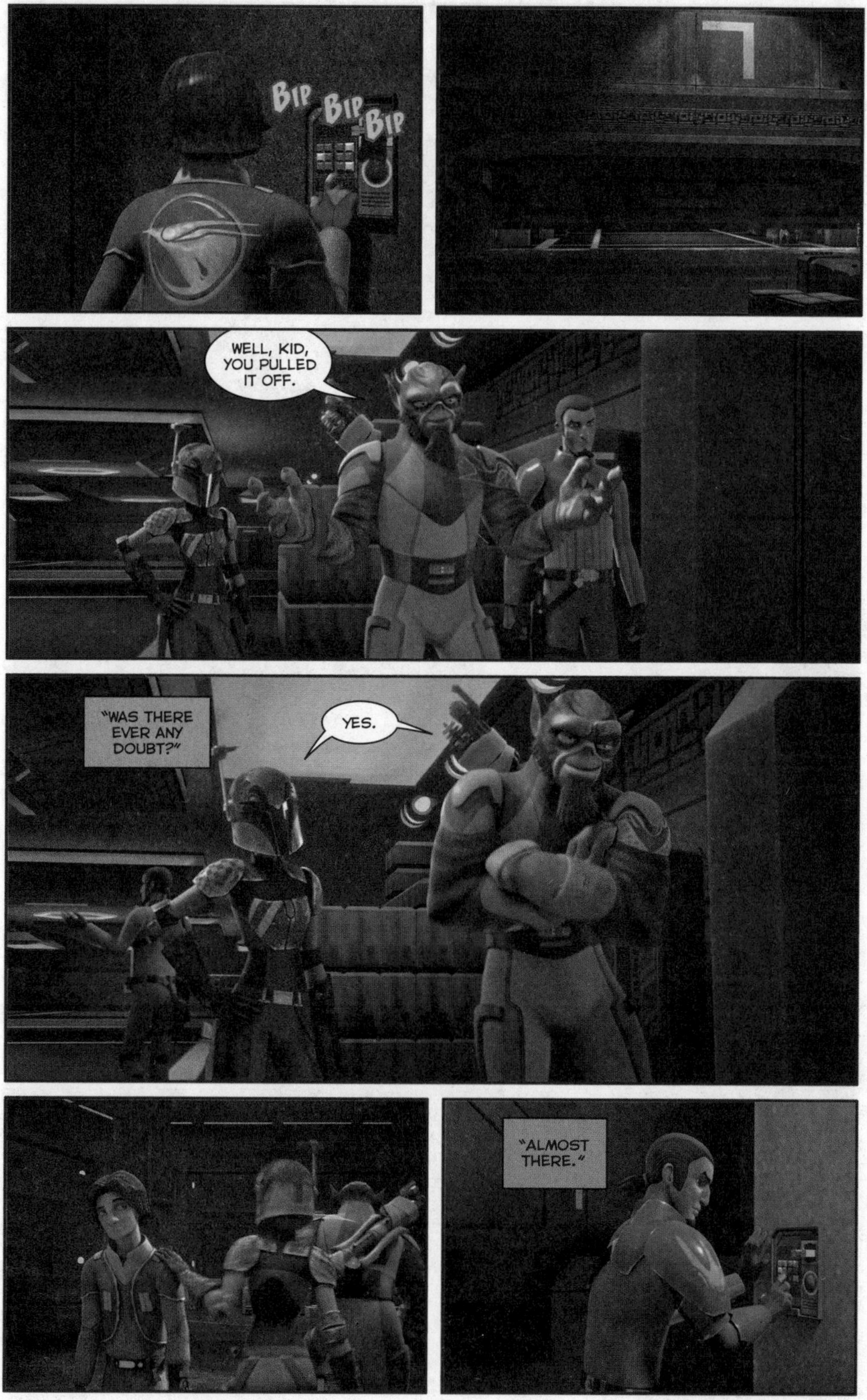
BIP BIP BIP
WELL, KID, YOU PULLED IT OFF.
"WAS THERE EVER ANY DOUBT?"
YES.
"ALMOST THERE."

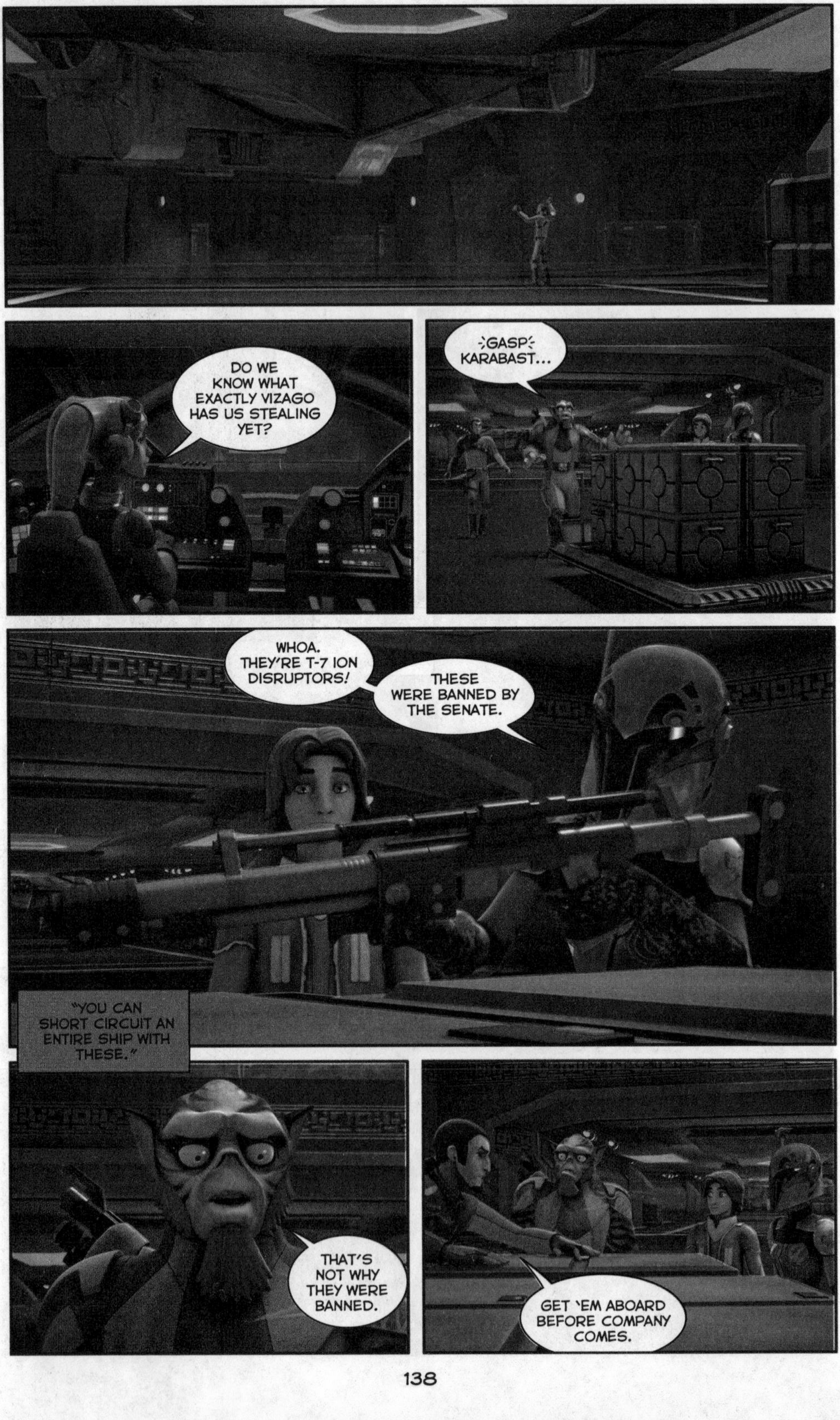
DO WE KNOW WHAT EXACTLY VIZAGO HAS US STEALING YET?
GASP KARABAST...
WHOA. THEY'RE T-7 ION DISRUPTORS!
THESE WERE BANNED BY THE SENATE.
"YOU CAN SHORT CIRCUIT AN ENTIRE SHIP WITH THESE."
THAT'S NOT WHY THEY WERE BANNED.
GET 'EM ABOARD BEFORE COMPANY COMES.

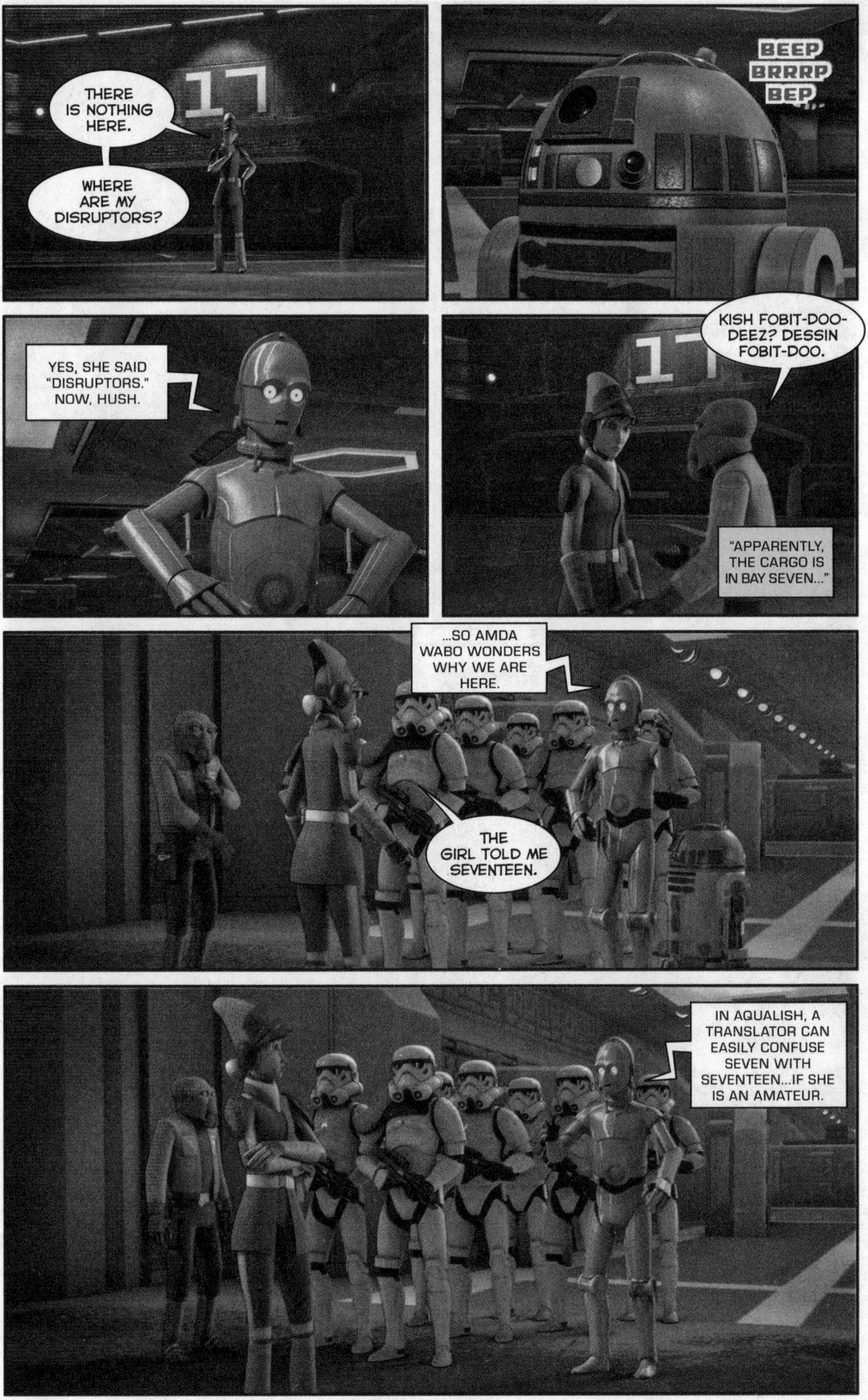
THERE IS NOTHING HERE.
WHERE ARE MY DISRUPTORS?
BEEP BRRRP BEP...
YES, SHE SAID "DISRUPTORS." NOW, HUSH.
KISH FOBIT-DOO-DEEZ? DESSIN FOBIT-DOO.
"APPARENTLY, THE CARGO IS IN BAY SEVEN..."
...SO AMDA WABO WONDERS WHY WE ARE HERE.
THE GIRL TOLD ME SEVENTEEN.
IN AQUALISH, A TRANSLATOR CAN EASILY CONFUSE SEVEN WITH SEVENTEEN...IF SHE IS AN AMATEUR.

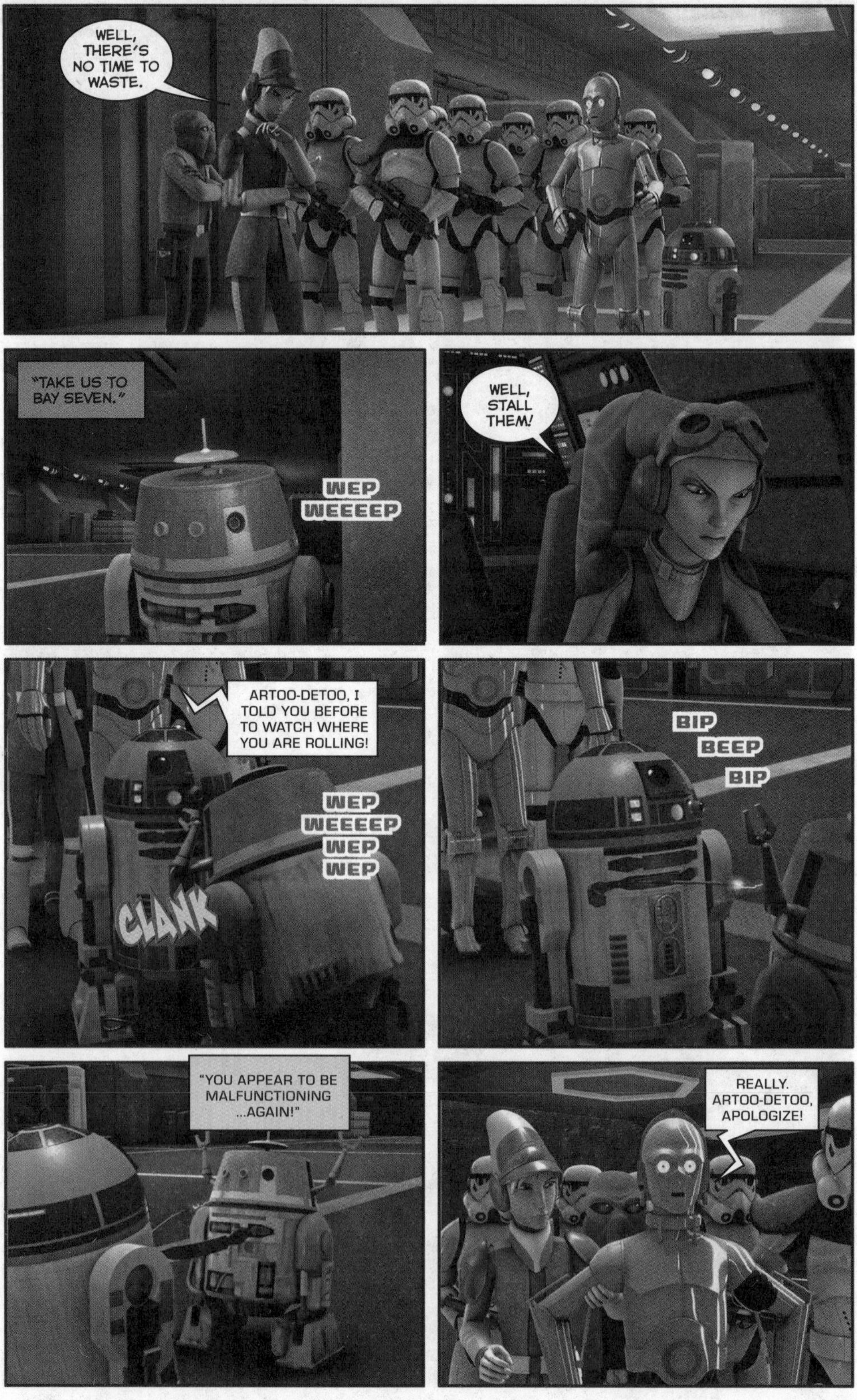

WELL, THERE'S NO TIME TO WASTE.
"TAKE US TO BAY SEVEN."
WEP WEEEEP
WELL, STALL THEM!
ARTOO-DETOO, I TOLD YOU BEFORE TO WATCH WHERE YOU ARE ROLLING!
WEP WEEEEP WEP WEP
CLANK
BIP BEEP BIP
"YOU APPEAR TO BE MALFUNCTIONING ...AGAIN!"
REALLY. ARTOO-DETOO, APOLOGIZE!

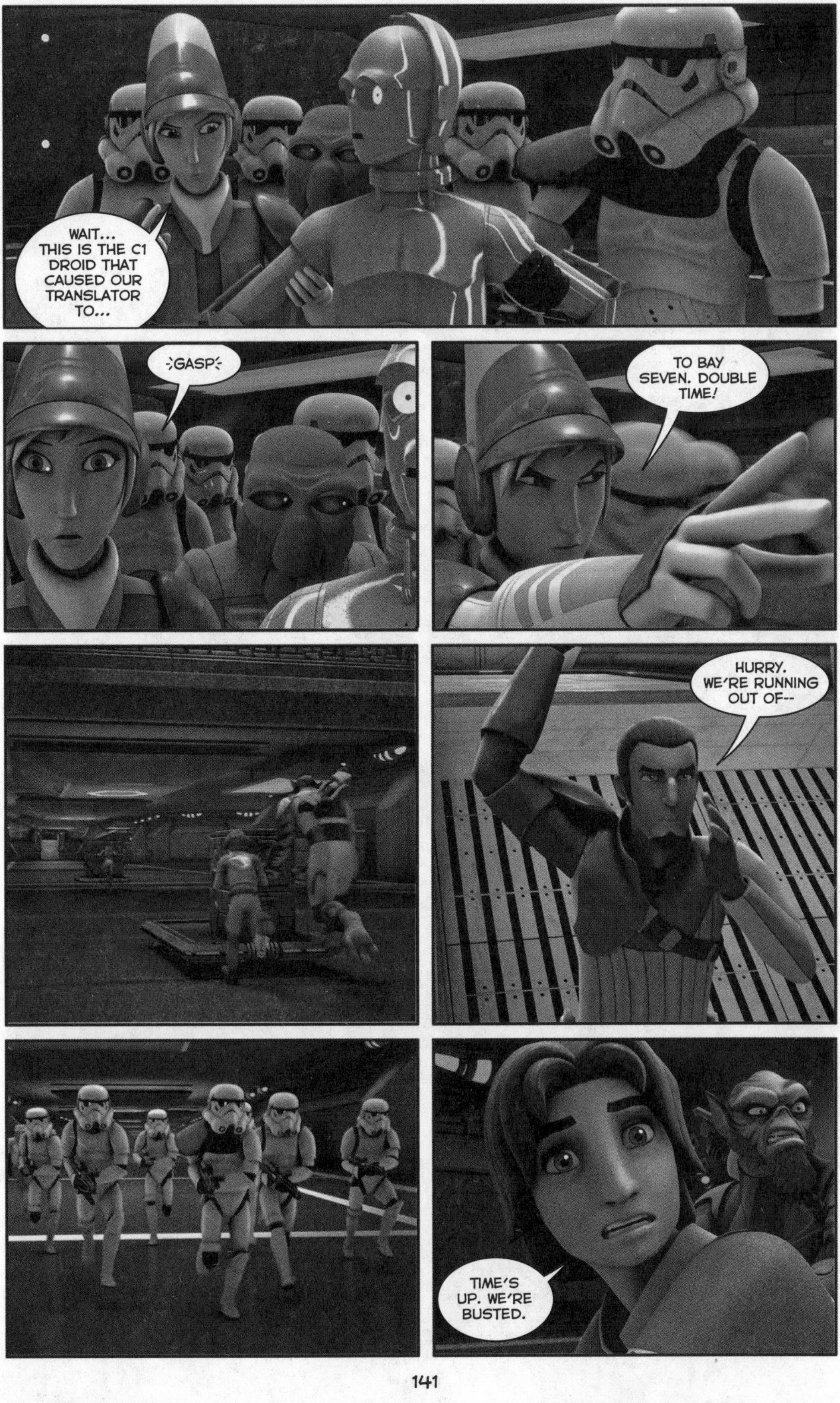
WAIT... THIS IS THE C1 DROID THAT CAUSED OUR TRANSLATOR TO...
GASP
TO BAY SEVEN. DOUBLE TIME!
HURRY. WE'RE RUNNING OUT OF--
TIME'S UP. WE'RE BUSTED.

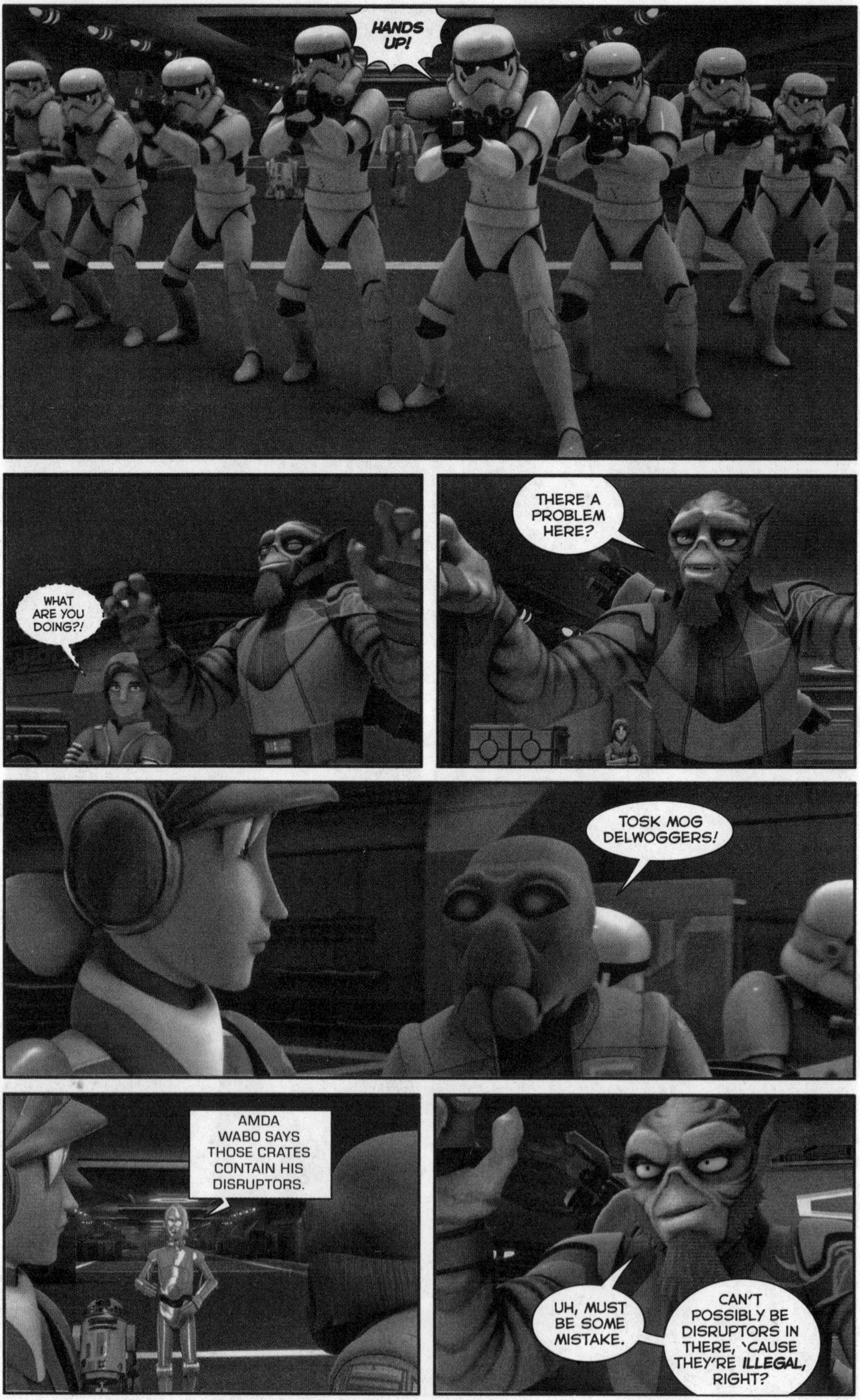
HANDS UP!
WHAT ARE YOU DOING?!
THERE A PROBLEM HERE?
TOSK MOG DELWOGGERS!
AMDA WABO SAYS THOSE CRATES CONTAIN HIS DISRUPTORS.
UH, MUST BE SOME MISTAKE.
CAN'T POSSIBLY BE DISRUPTORS IN THERE, 'CAUSE THEY'RE ILLEGAL, RIGHT?

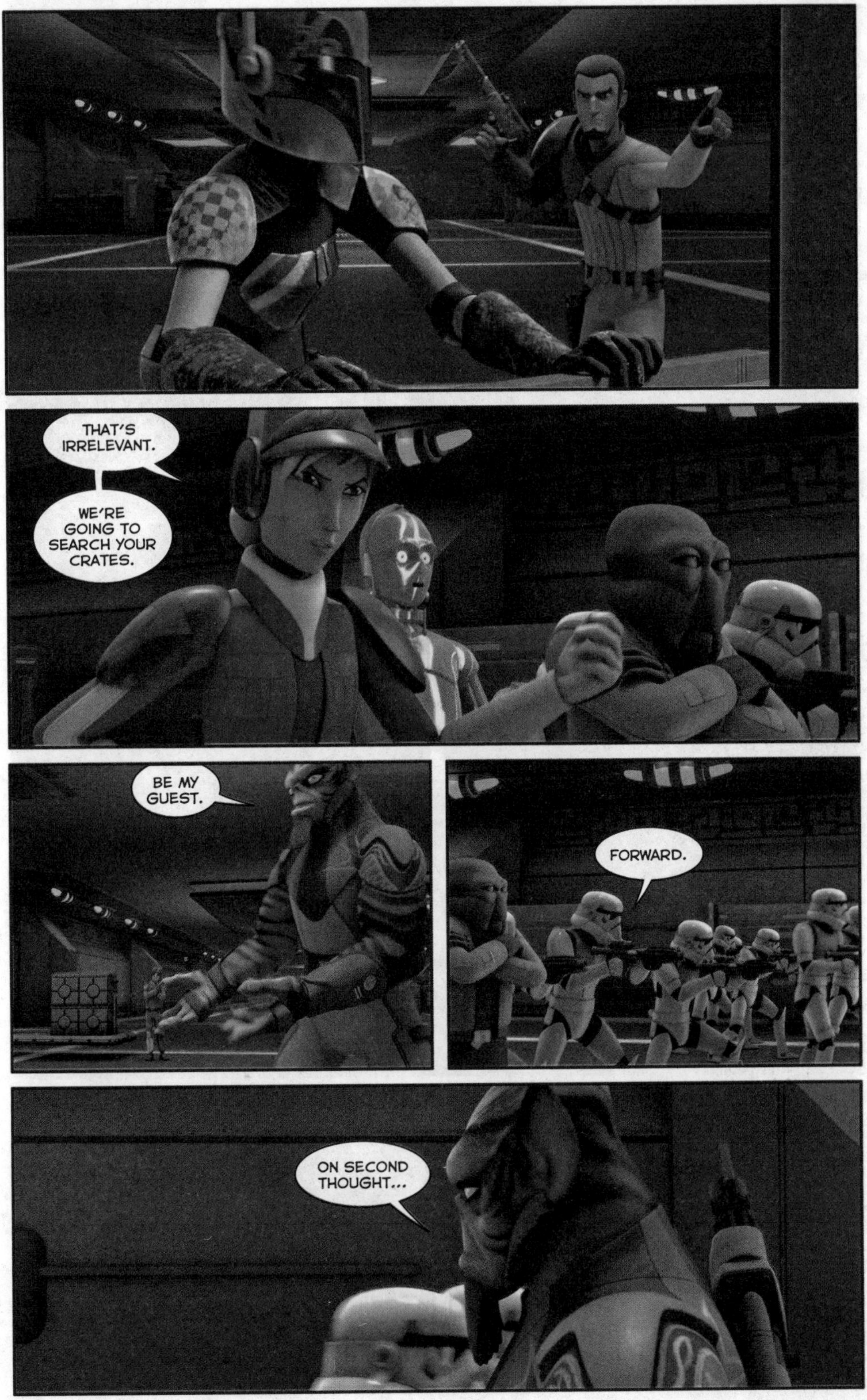
THAT'S IRRELEVANT.
WE'RE GOING TO SEARCH YOUR CRATES.
BE MY GUEST.
FORWARD.
ON SECOND THOUGHT...

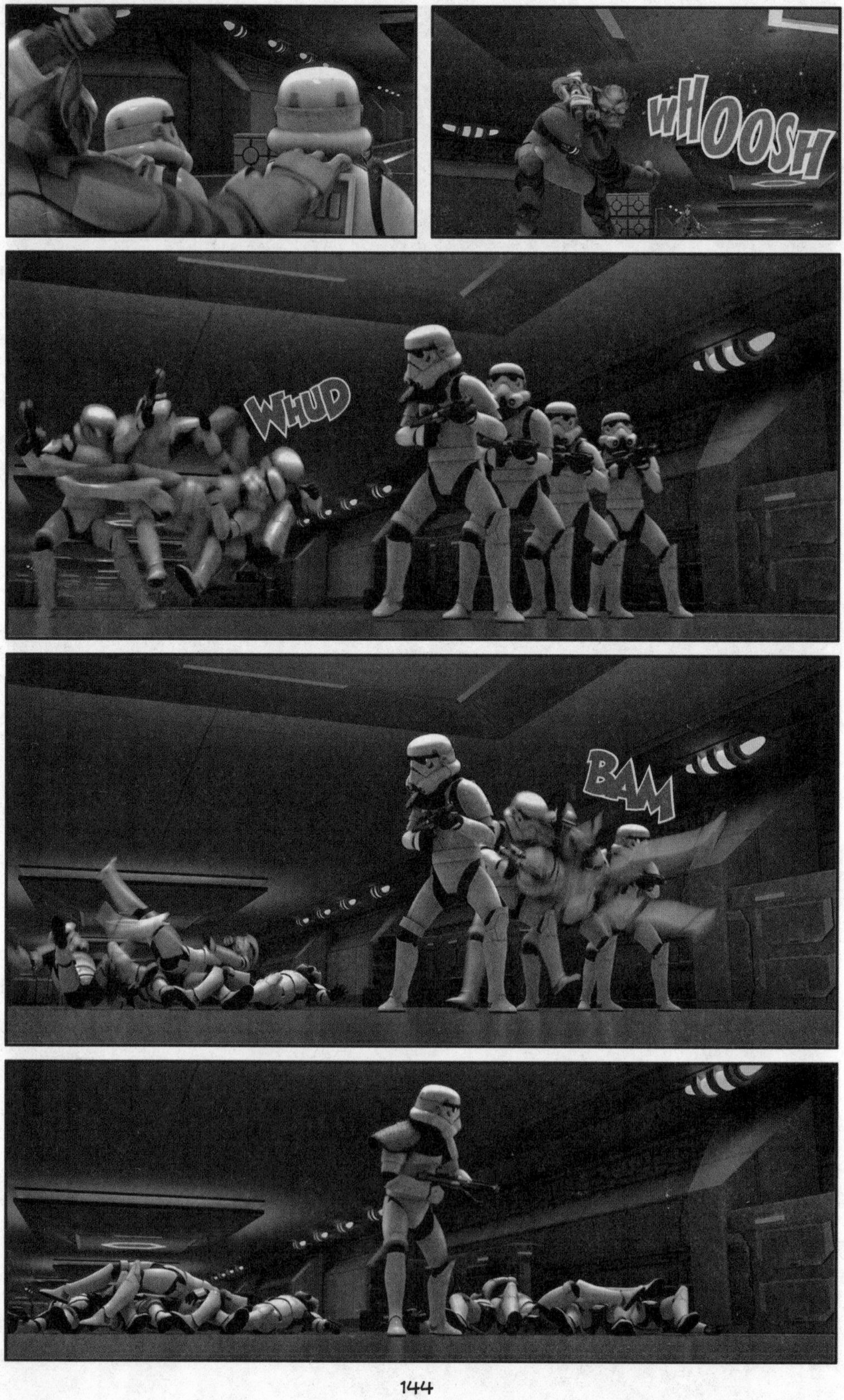
WHOOSH
WHUD
BAM

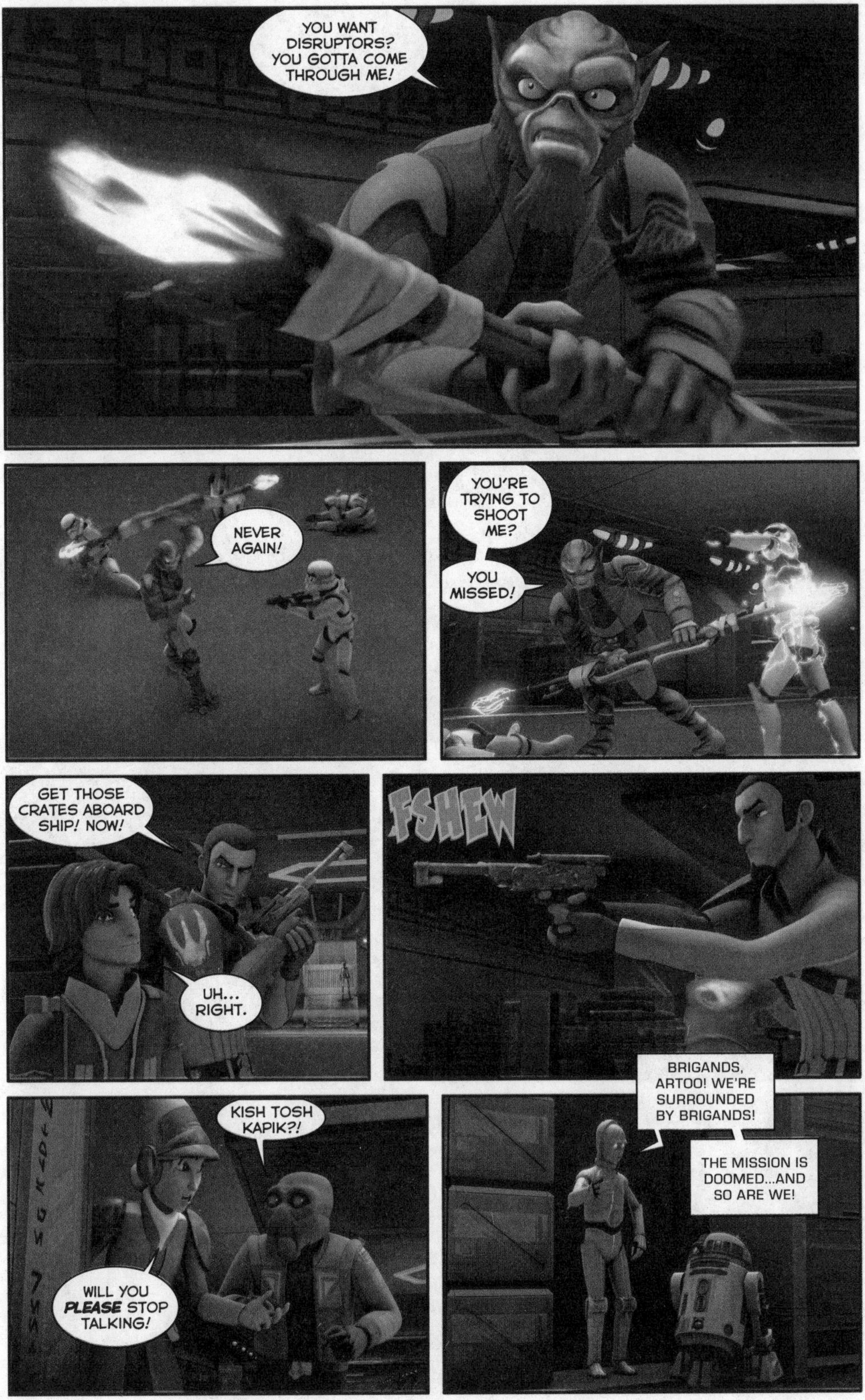
YOU WANT DISRUPTORS? YOU GOTTA COME THROUGH ME!
NEVER AGAIN!
YOU'RE TRYING TO SHOOT ME?
YOU MISSED!
GET THOSE CRATES ABOARD SHIP! NOW!
UH... RIGHT.
FSHEW
KISH TOSH KAPIK?!
WILL YOU **PLEASE** STOP TALKING!
BRIGANDS, ARTOO! WE'RE SURROUNDED BY BRIGANDS!
THE MISSION IS DOOMED...AND SO ARE WE!

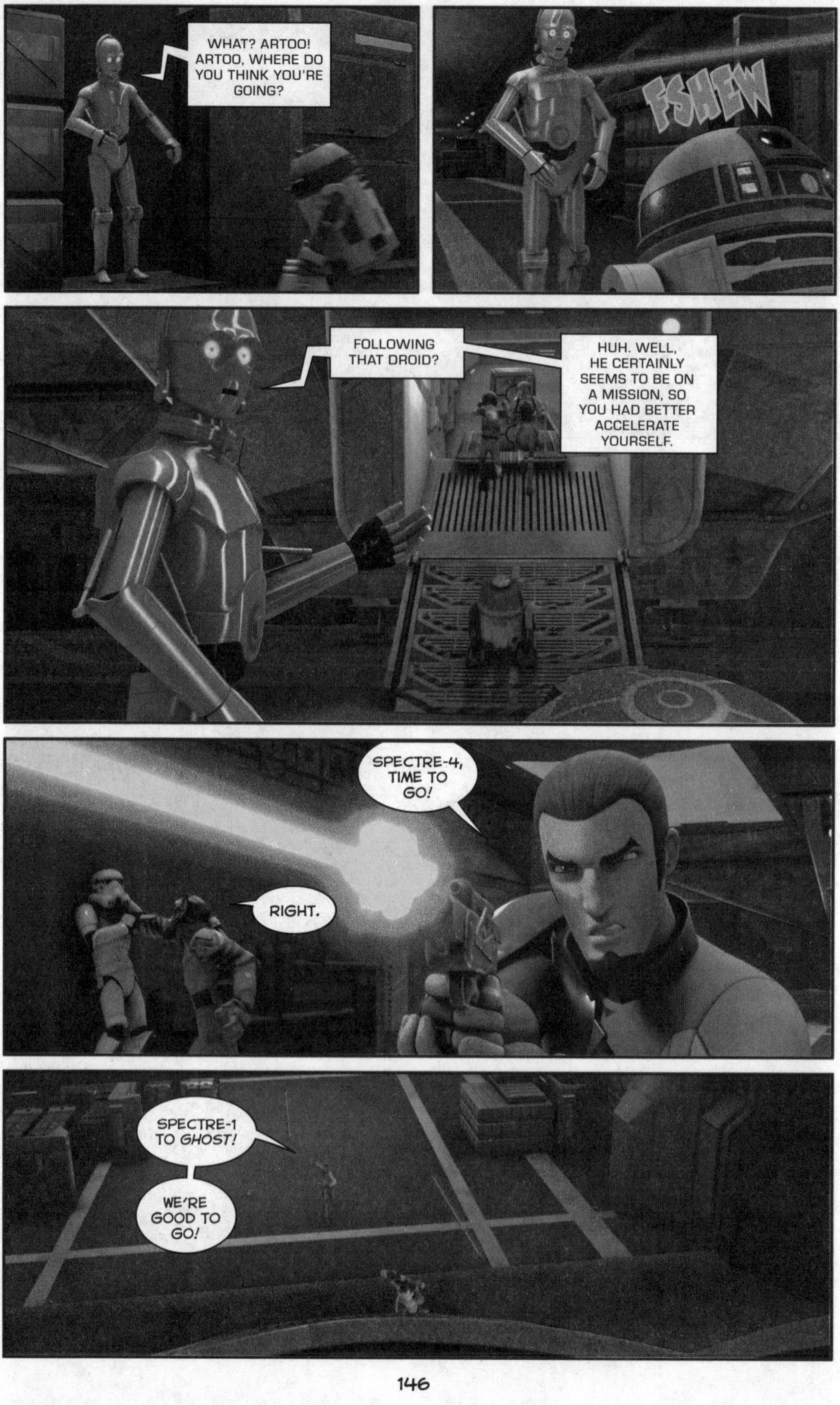
WHAT? ARTOO! ARTOO, WHERE DO YOU THINK YOU'RE GOING?
FSHEW
FOLLOWING THAT DROID?
HUH. WELL, HE CERTAINLY SEEMS TO BE ON A MISSION, SO YOU HAD BETTER ACCELERATE YOURSELF.
SPECTRE-4, TIME TO GO!
RIGHT.
SPECTRE-1 TO GHOST!
WE'RE GOOD TO GO!

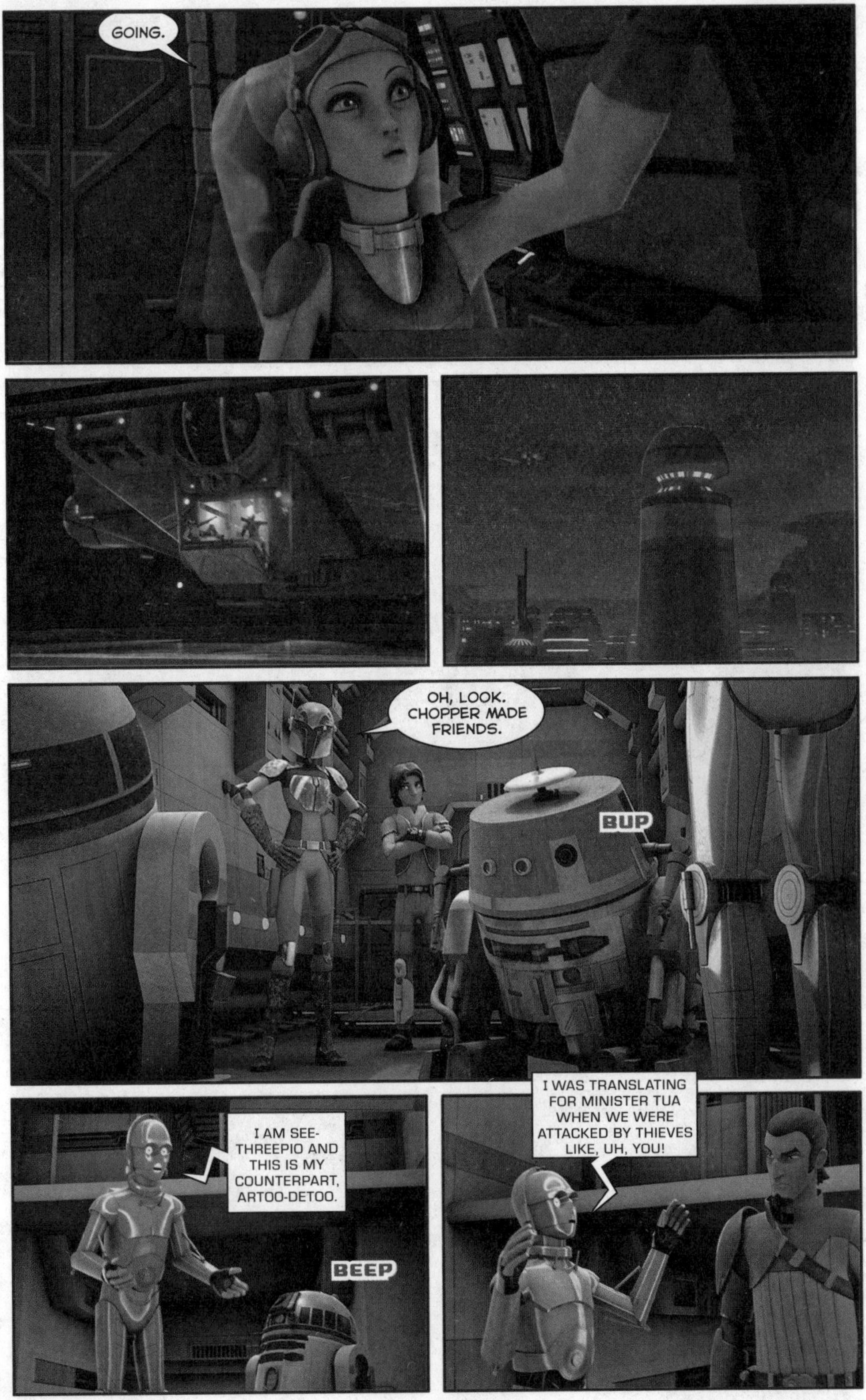
GOING.
OH, LOOK. CHOPPER MADE FRIENDS.
BUP
I AM SEE-THREEPIO AND THIS IS MY COUNTERPART, ARTOO-DETOO.
BEEP
I WAS TRANSLATING FOR MINISTER TUA WHEN WE WERE ATTACKED BY THIEVES LIKE, UH, YOU!

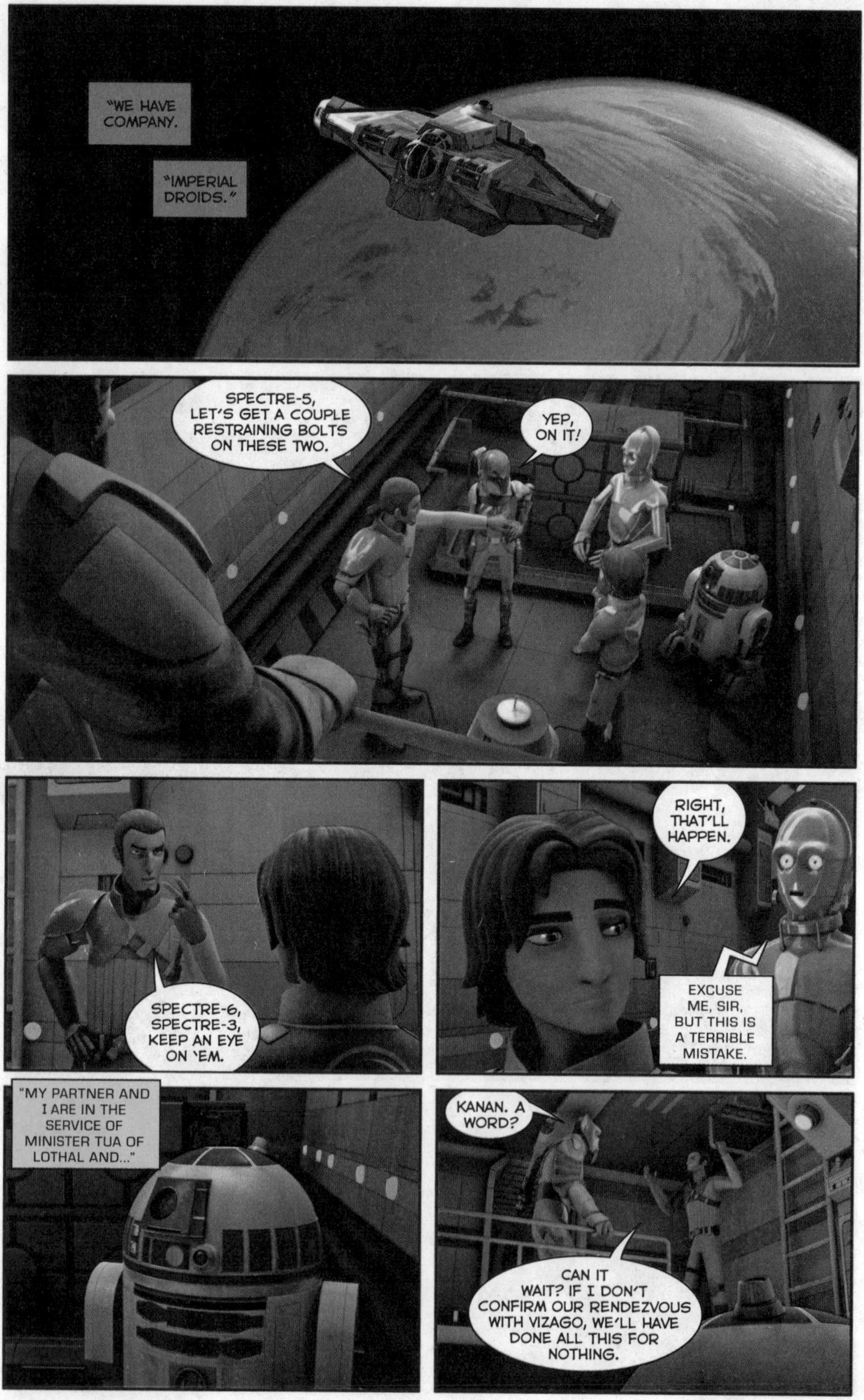
"WE HAVE COMPANY.
"IMPERIAL DROIDS."
SPECTRE-5, LET'S GET A COUPLE RESTRAINING BOLTS ON THESE TWO.
YEP, ON IT!
SPECTRE-6, SPECTRE-3, KEEP AN EYE ON 'EM.
RIGHT, THAT'LL HAPPEN.
EXCUSE ME, SIR, BUT THIS IS A TERRIBLE MISTAKE.
"MY PARTNER AND I ARE IN THE SERVICE OF MINISTER TUA OF LOTHAL AND..."
KANAN. A WORD?
CAN IT WAIT? IF I DON'T CONFIRM OUR RENDEZVOUS WITH VIZAGO, WE'LL HAVE DONE ALL THIS FOR NOTHING.

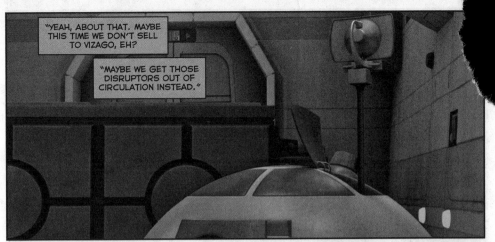

"YEAH, ABOUT THAT. MAYBE THIS TIME WE DON'T SELL TO VIZAGO, EH?

"MAYBE WE GET THOSE DISRUPTORS OUT OF CIRCULATION INSTEAD."

LEAST WE GOT 'EM OUT OF *IMPERIAL* CIRCULATION.

WHEN I WAS TRANSLATING, I FOUND OUT THEY WERE SHIPPING THOSE T-7S AS PROTOTYPES--SO THE EMPIRE COULD MASS PRODUCE THEM ON LOTHAL.

SEE, ZEB? PERFECT CRIME.

WE STEAL WEAPONS MEANT FOR THE EMPIRE--

--AND SELL THEM FOR CREDITS WE DESPERATELY NEED TO KEEP THIS BIRD FLYING.

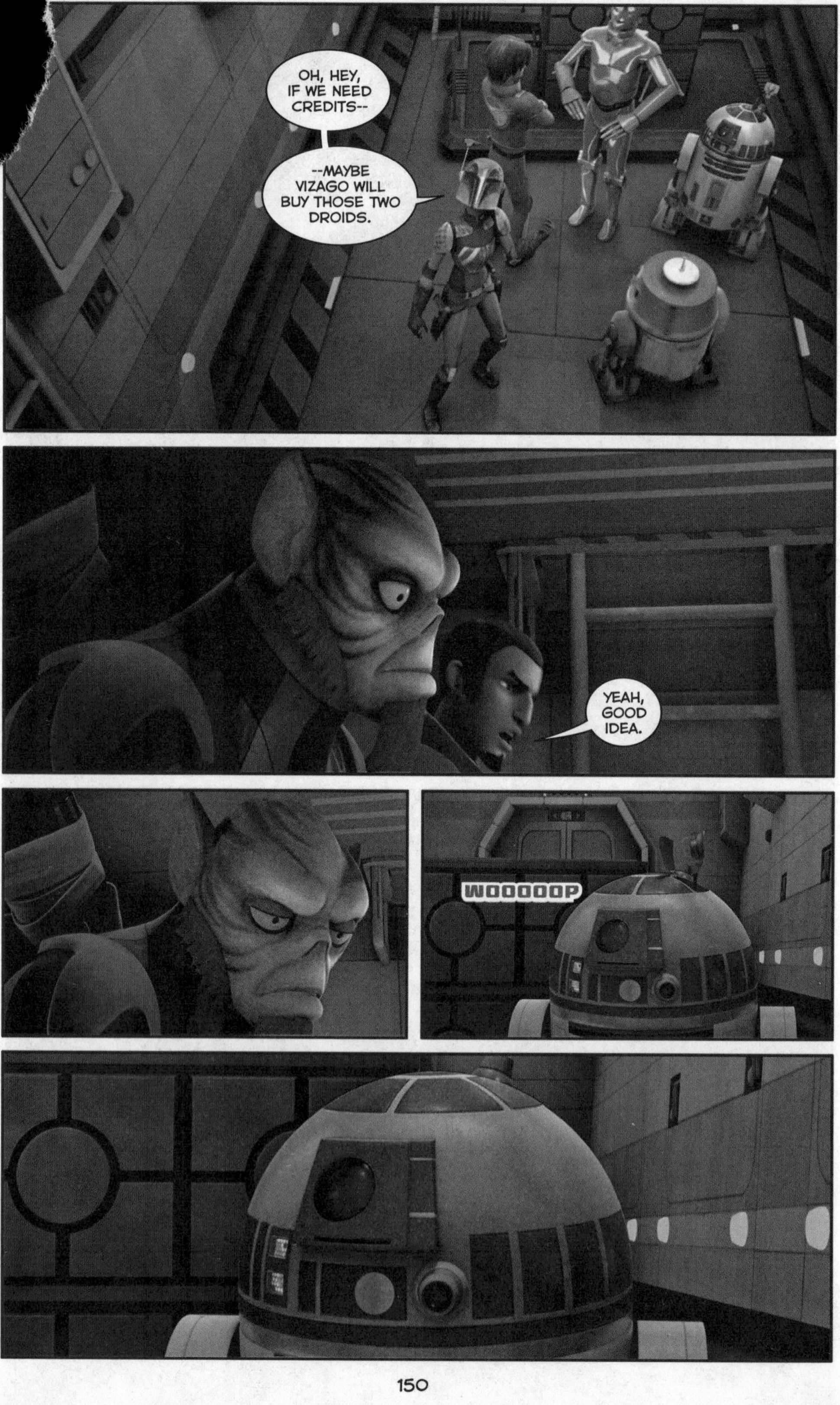
OH, HEY, IF WE NEED CREDITS--
--MAYBE VIZAGO WILL BUY THOSE TWO DROIDS.
YEAH, GOOD IDEA.
WOOOOOP

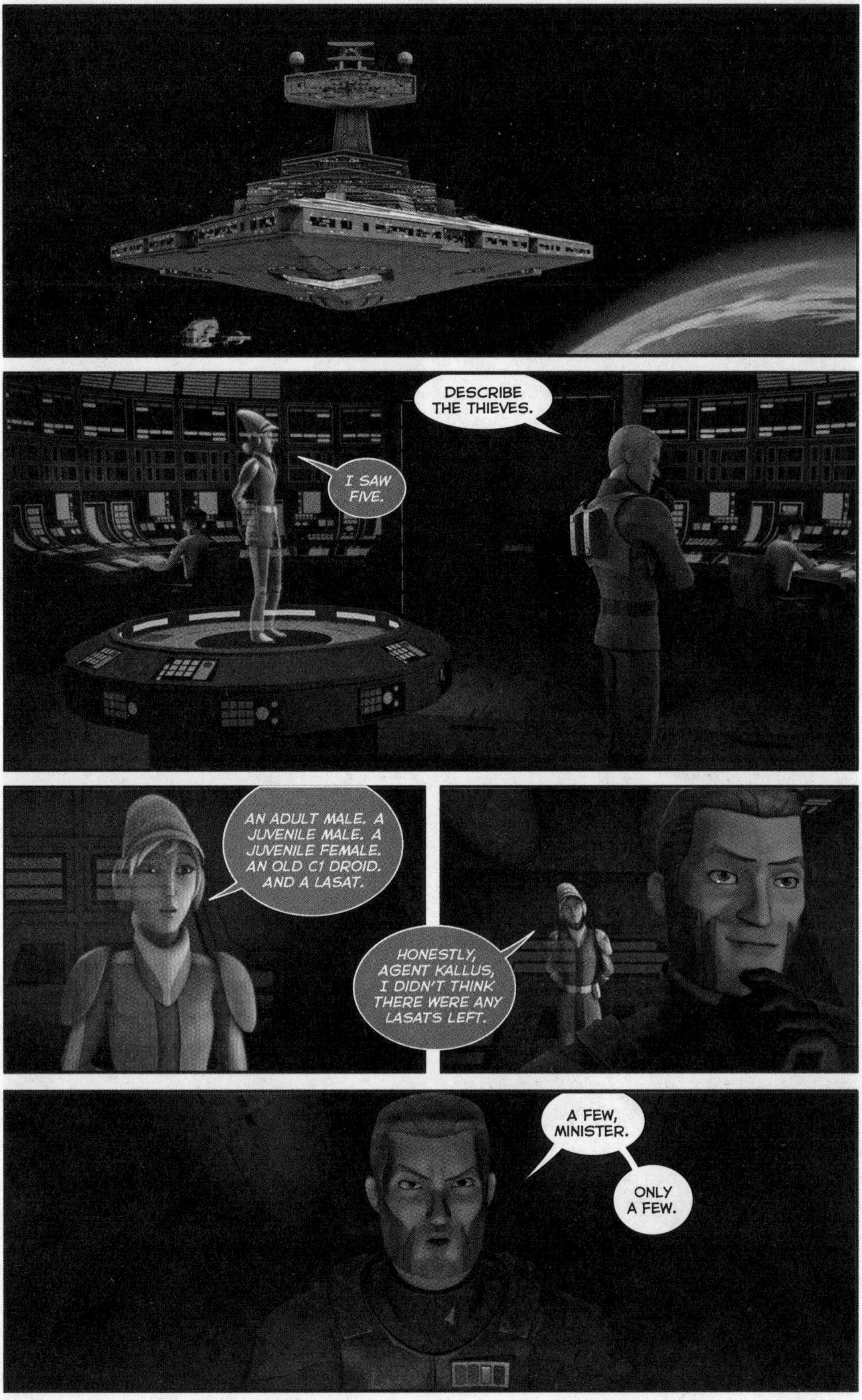
DESCRIBE THE THIEVES.
I SAW FIVE.
AN ADULT MALE. A JUVENILE MALE. A JUVENILE FEMALE. AN OLD C1 DROID. AND A LASAT.
HONESTLY, AGENT KALLUS, I DIDN'T THINK THERE WERE ANY LASATS LEFT.
A FEW, MINISTER.
ONLY A FEW.

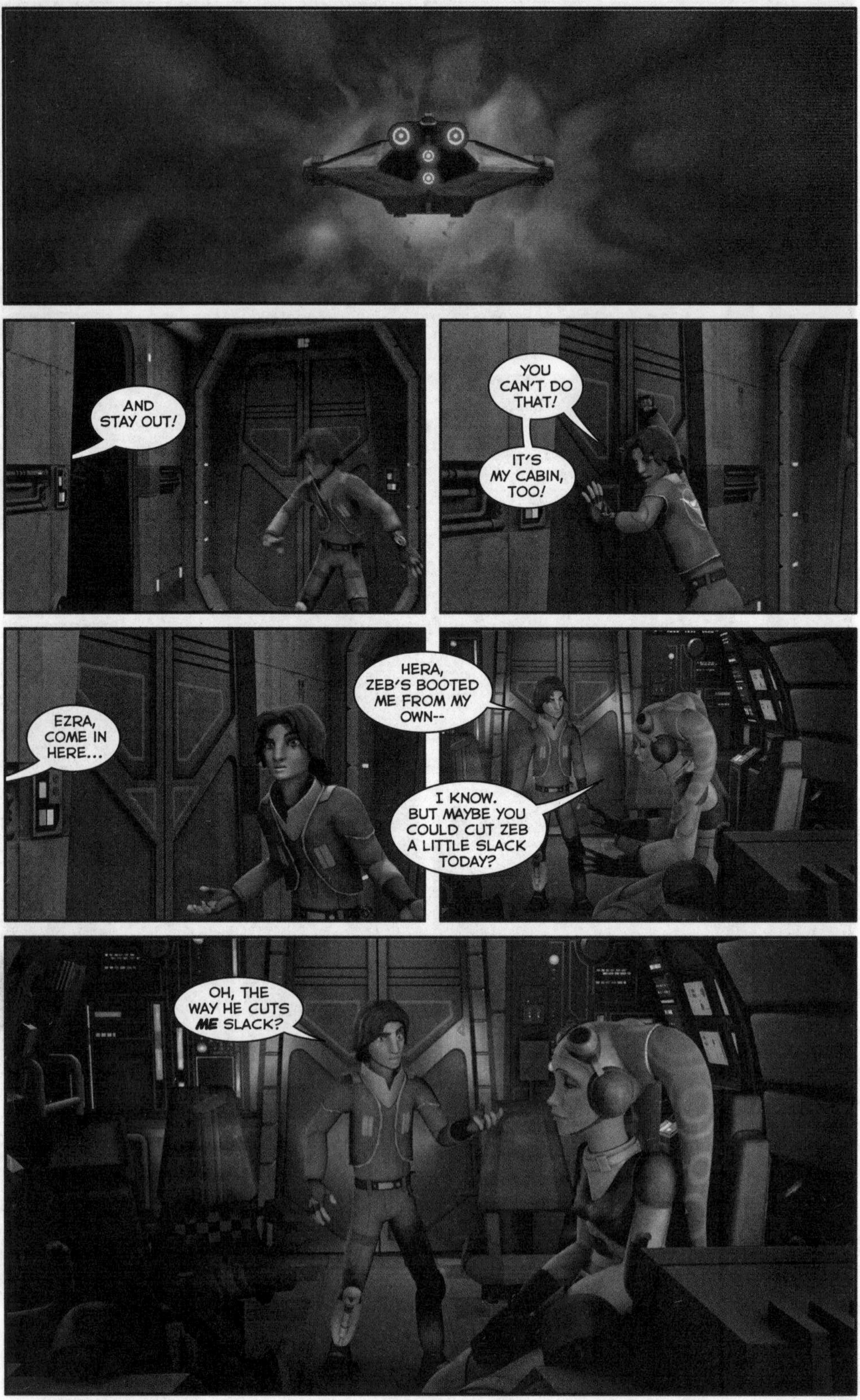
AND STAY OUT!
YOU CAN'T DO THAT!
IT'S MY CABIN, TOO!
EZRA, COME IN HERE...
HERA, ZEB'S BOOTED ME FROM MY OWN--
I KNOW. BUT MAYBE YOU COULD CUT ZEB A LITTLE SLACK TODAY?
OH, THE WAY HE CUTS ME SLACK?

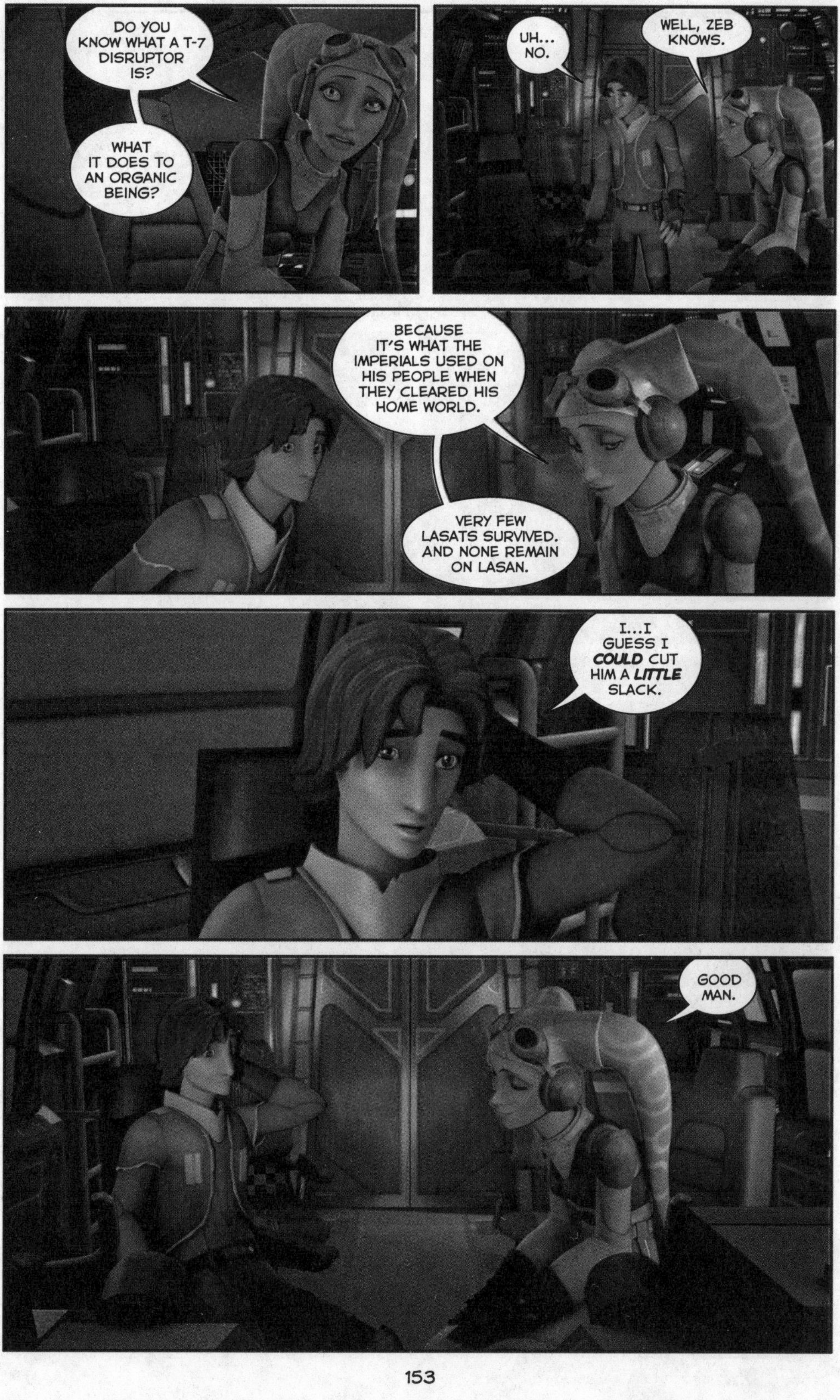
DO YOU KNOW WHAT A T-7 DISRUPTOR IS?
WHAT IT DOES TO AN ORGANIC BEING?
UH... NO.
WELL, ZEB KNOWS.
BECAUSE IT'S WHAT THE IMPERIALS USED ON HIS PEOPLE WHEN THEY CLEARED HIS HOME WORLD.
VERY FEW LASATS SURVIVED. AND NONE REMAIN ON LASAN.
I...I GUESS I **COULD** CUT HIM A **LITTLE** SLACK.
GOOD MAN.

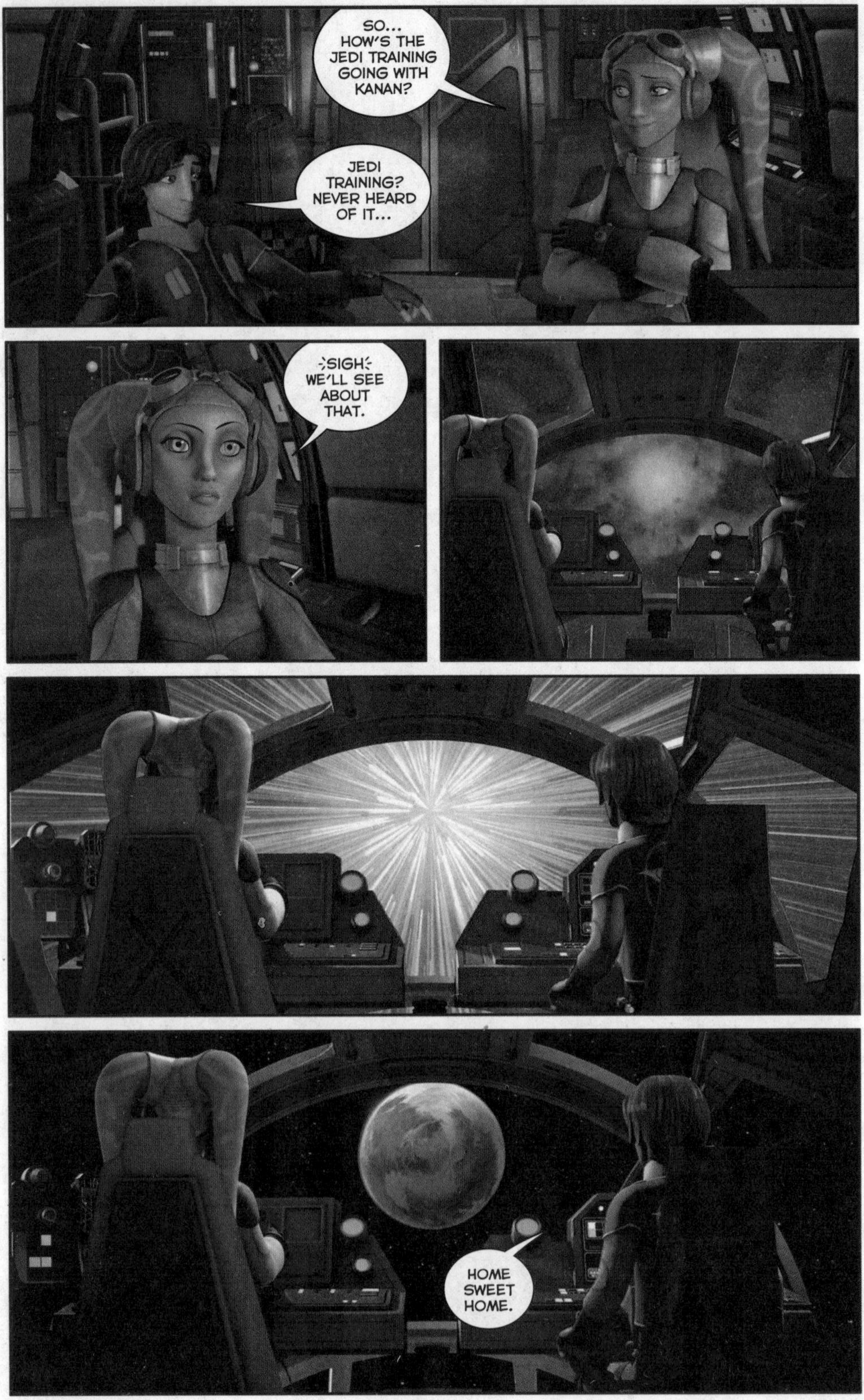
SO... HOW'S THE JEDI TRAINING GOING WITH KANAN?
JEDI TRAINING? NEVER HEARD OF IT...
-SIGH- WE'LL SEE ABOUT THAT.
HOME SWEET HOME.

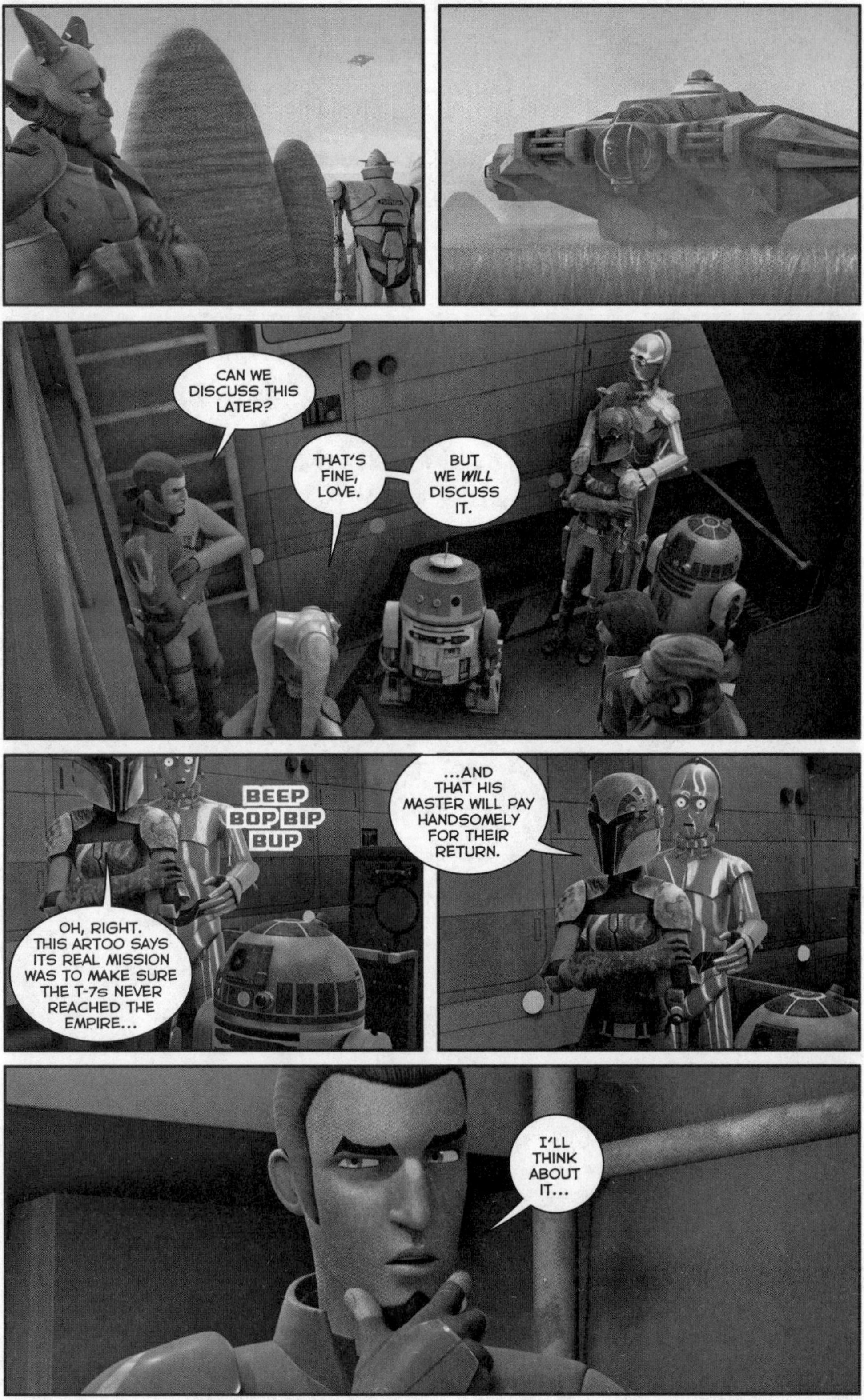
CAN WE DISCUSS THIS LATER?
THAT'S FINE, LOVE.
BUT WE *WILL* DISCUSS IT.
BEEP BOP BIP BUP
OH, RIGHT. THIS ARTOO SAYS ITS REAL MISSION WAS TO MAKE SURE THE T-7s NEVER REACHED THE EMPIRE...
...AND THAT HIS MASTER WILL PAY HANDSOMELY FOR THEIR RETURN.
I'LL THINK ABOUT IT...

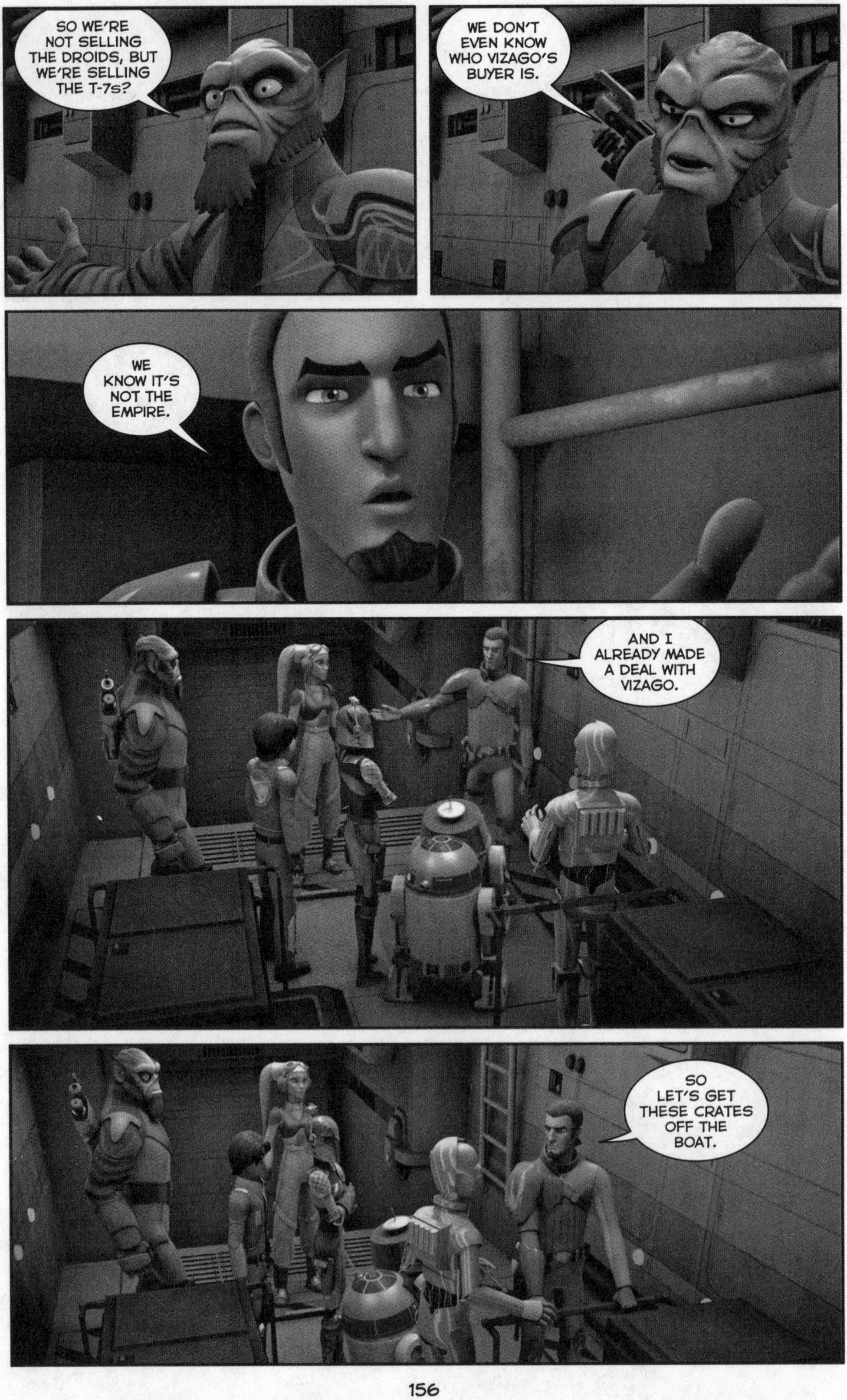
SO WE'RE NOT SELLING THE DROIDS, BUT WE'RE SELLING THE T-7s?
WE DON'T EVEN KNOW WHO VIZAGO'S BUYER IS.
WE KNOW IT'S NOT THE EMPIRE.
AND I ALREADY MADE A DEAL WITH VIZAGO.
SO LET'S GET THESE CRATES OFF THE BOAT.

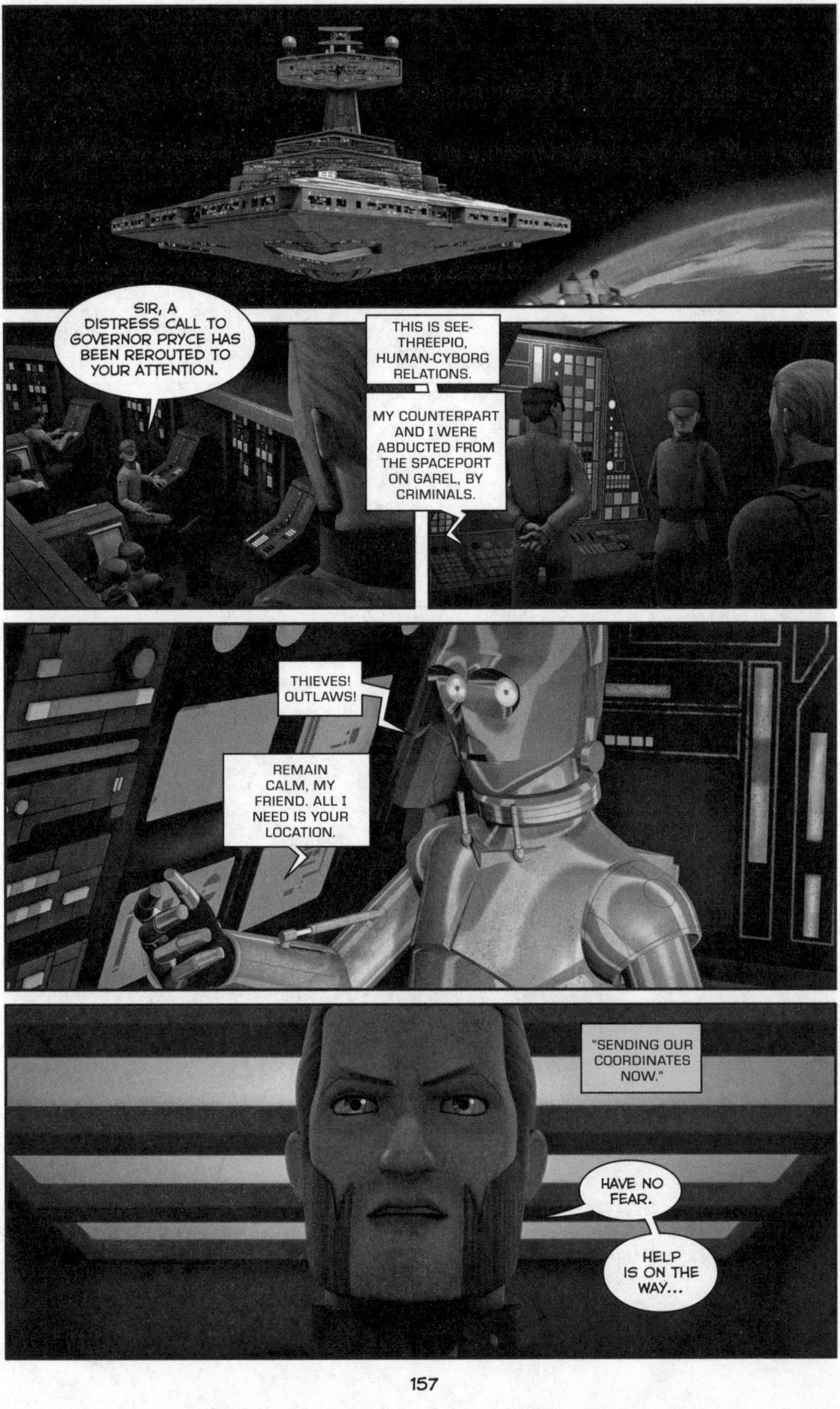
SIR, A DISTRESS CALL TO GOVERNOR PRYCE HAS BEEN REROUTED TO YOUR ATTENTION.
THIS IS SEE-THREEPIO, HUMAN-CYBORG RELATIONS.
MY COUNTERPART AND I WERE ABDUCTED FROM THE SPACEPORT ON GAREL, BY CRIMINALS.
THIEVES! OUTLAWS!
REMAIN CALM, MY FRIEND. ALL I NEED IS YOUR LOCATION.
"SENDING OUR COORDINATES NOW."
HAVE NO FEAR.
HELP IS ON THE WAY...

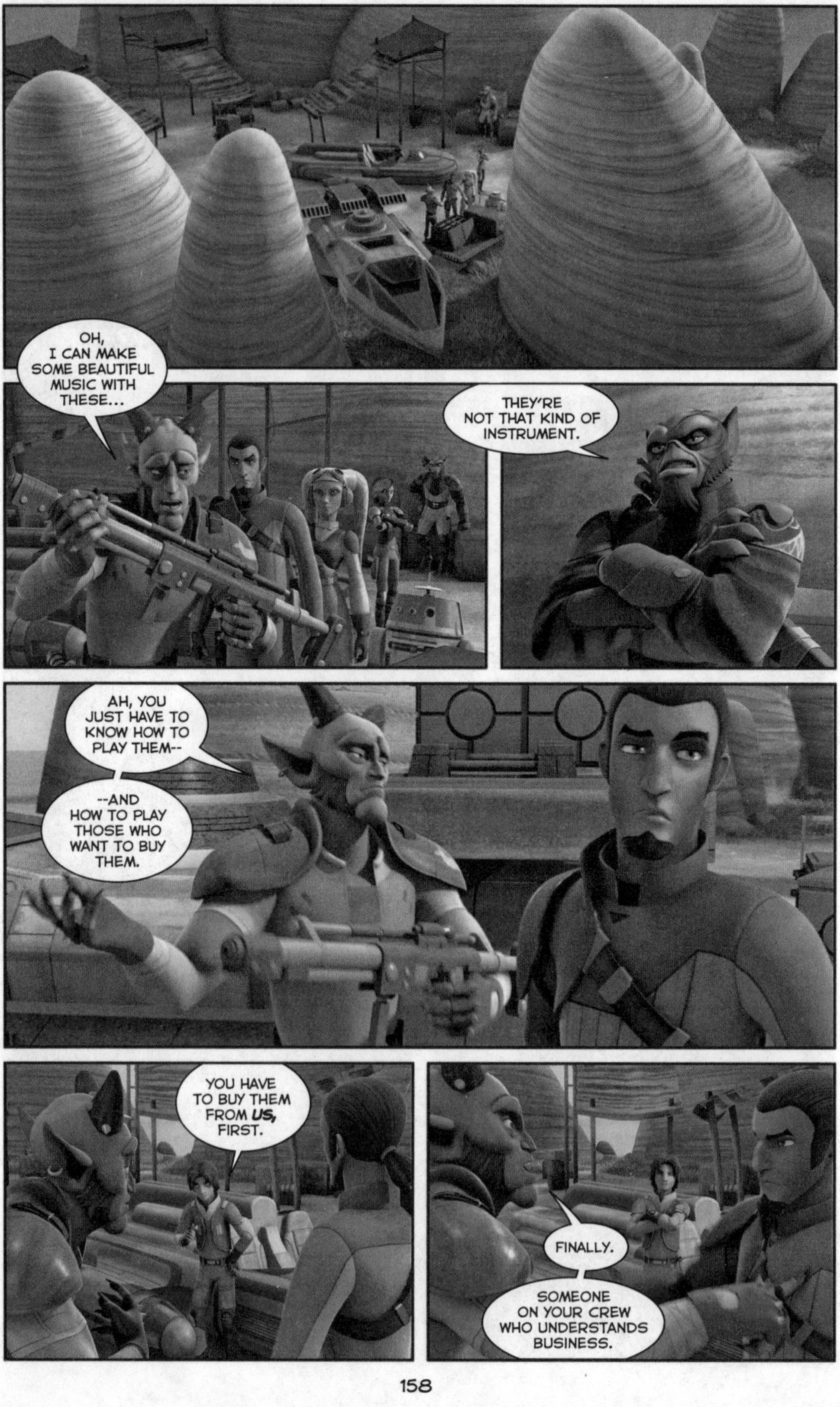
OH, I CAN MAKE SOME BEAUTIFUL MUSIC WITH THESE...
THEY'RE NOT THAT KIND OF INSTRUMENT.
AH, YOU JUST HAVE TO KNOW HOW TO PLAY THEM--
--AND HOW TO PLAY THOSE WHO WANT TO BUY THEM.
YOU HAVE TO BUY THEM FROM *US,* FIRST.
FINALLY.
SOMEONE ON YOUR CREW WHO UNDERSTANDS BUSINESS.

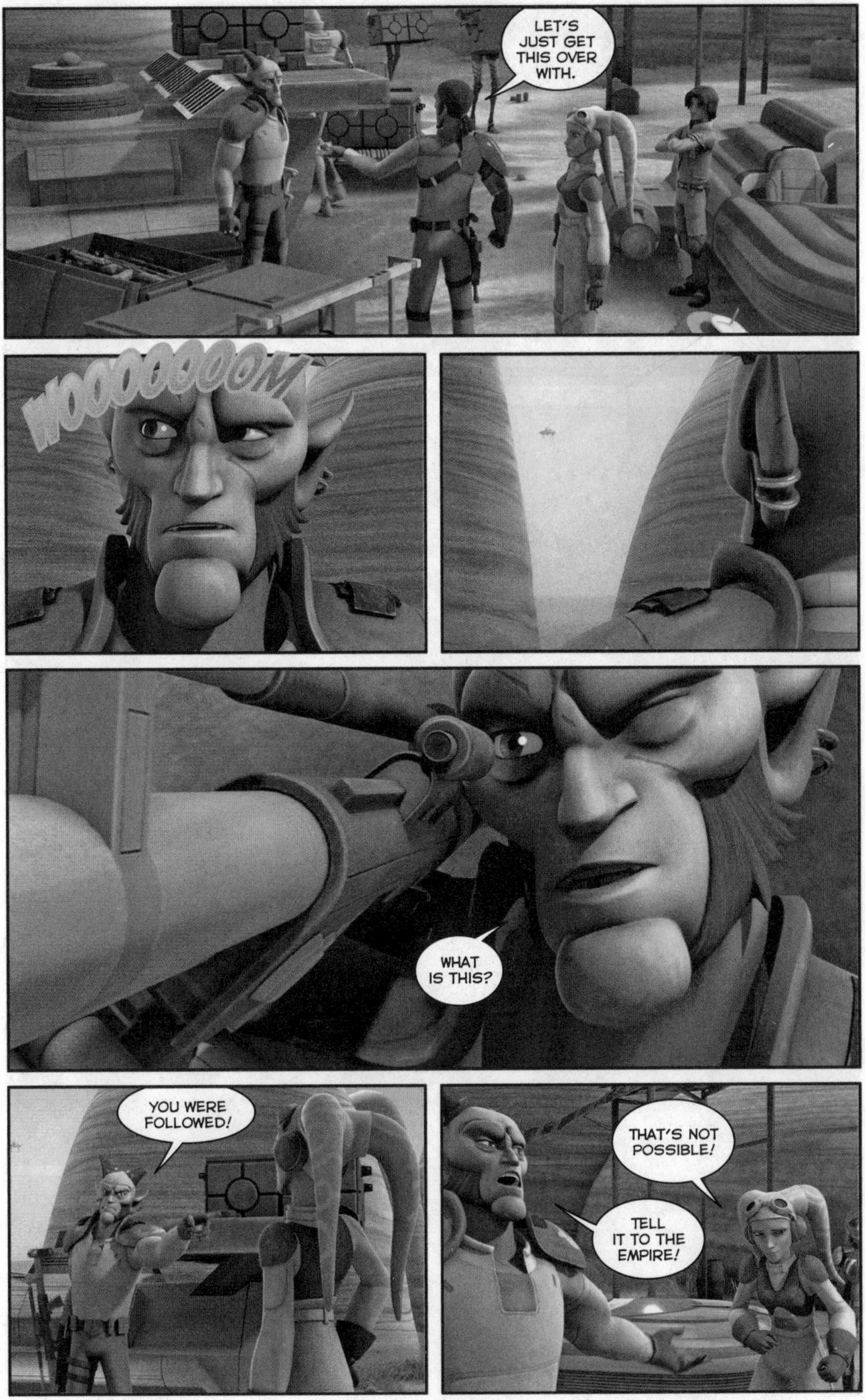
LET'S JUST GET THIS OVER WITH.
WOOOOOOOM
WHAT IS THIS?
YOU WERE FOLLOWED!
THAT'S NOT POSSIBLE!
TELL IT TO THE EMPIRE!

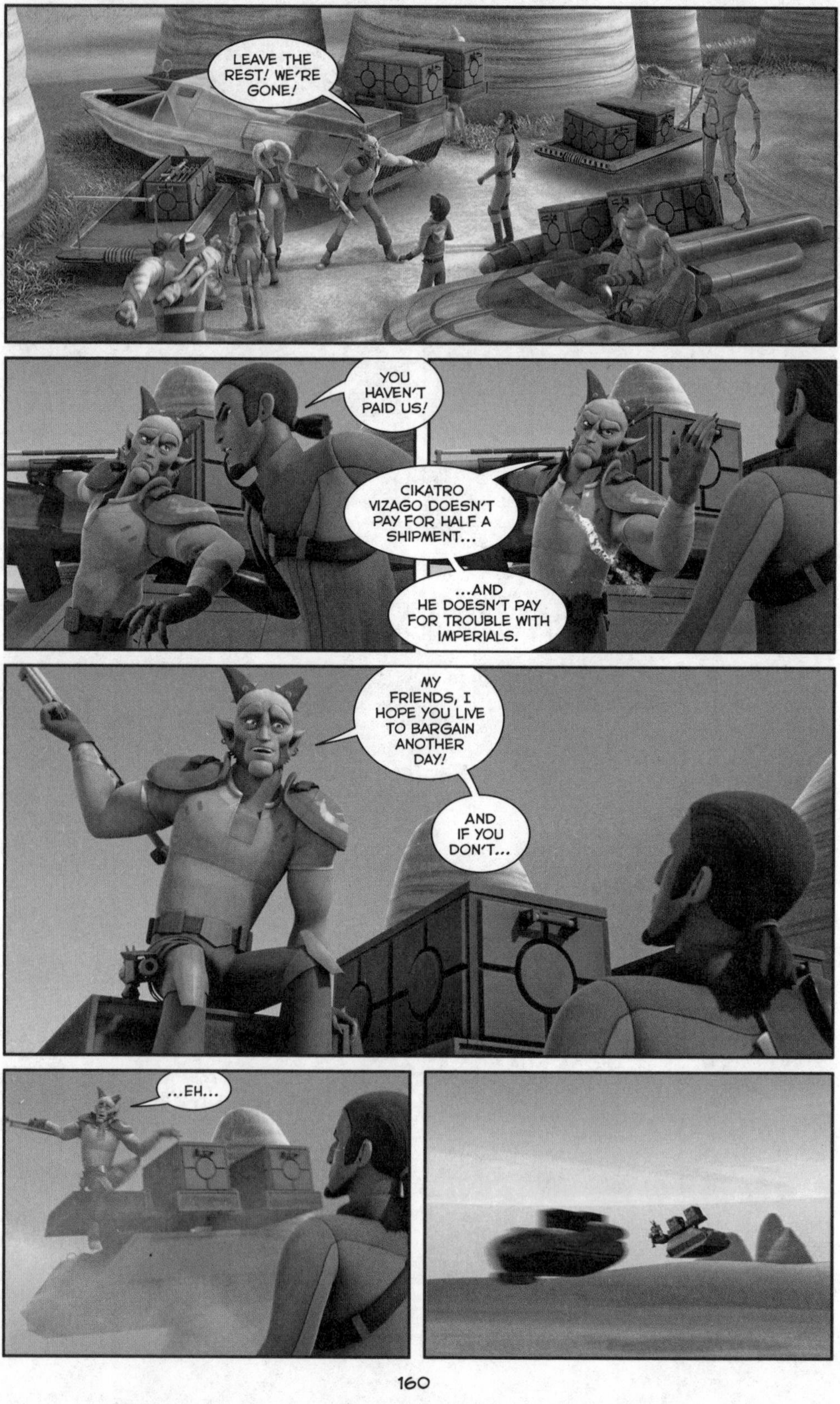
LEAVE THE REST! WE'RE GONE!
YOU HAVEN'T PAID US!
CIKATRO VIZAGO DOESN'T PAY FOR HALF A SHIPMENT...
...AND HE DOESN'T PAY FOR TROUBLE WITH IMPERIALS.
MY FRIENDS, I HOPE YOU LIVE TO BARGAIN ANOTHER DAY!
AND IF YOU DON'T...
...EH...

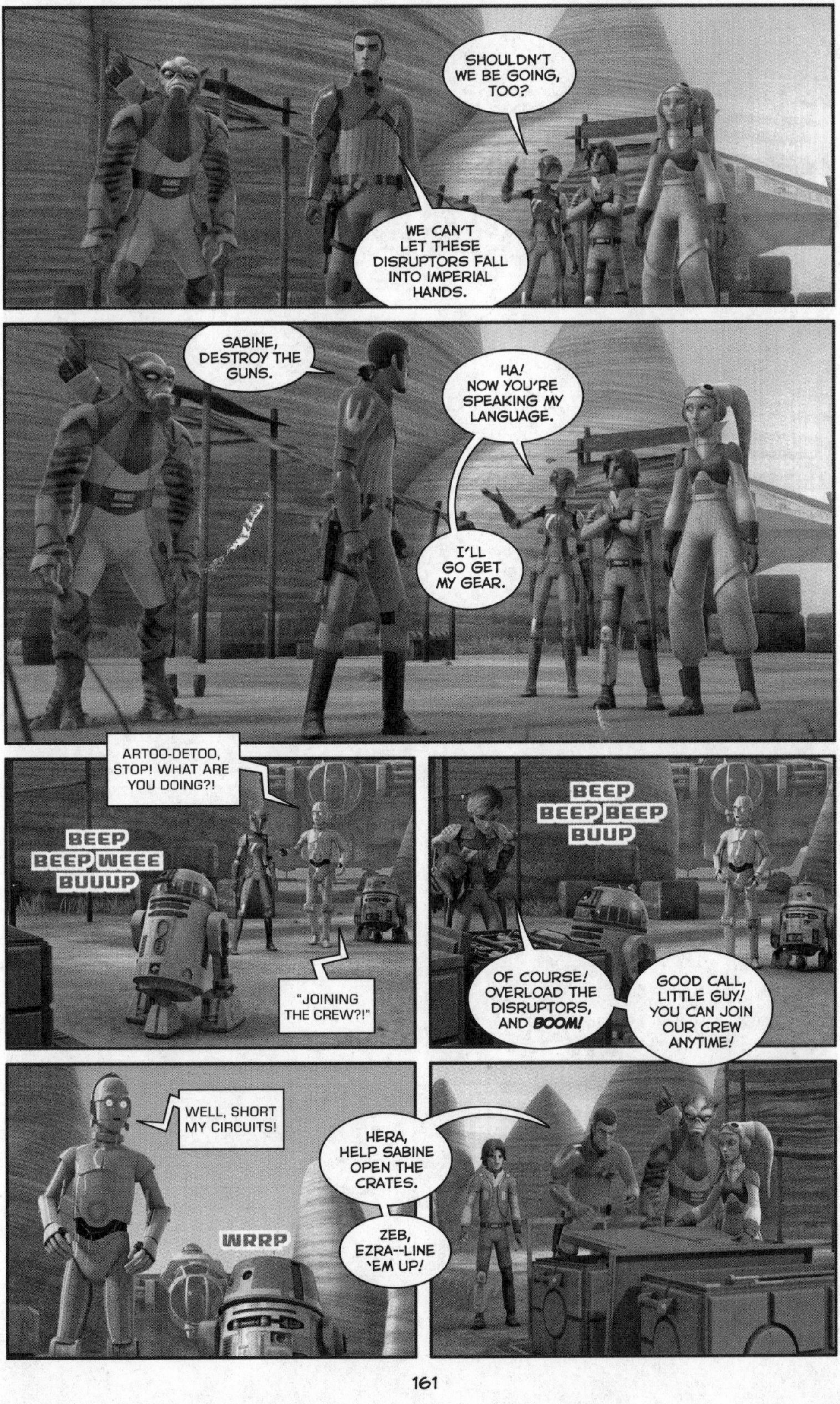
SHOULDN'T WE BE GOING, TOO?
WE CAN'T LET THESE DISRUPTORS FALL INTO IMPERIAL HANDS.
SABINE, DESTROY THE GUNS.
HA! NOW YOU'RE SPEAKING MY LANGUAGE.
I'LL GO GET MY GEAR.
ARTOO-DETOO, STOP! WHAT ARE YOU DOING?!
BEEP BEEP WEEE BUUUP
"JOINING THE CREW?!"
BEEP BEEP BEEP BUUP
OF COURSE! OVERLOAD THE DISRUPTORS, AND BOOM!
GOOD CALL, LITTLE GUY! YOU CAN JOIN OUR CREW ANYTIME!
WELL, SHORT MY CIRCUITS!
WRRP
HERA, HELP SABINE OPEN THE CRATES.
ZEB, EZRA--LINE 'EM UP!

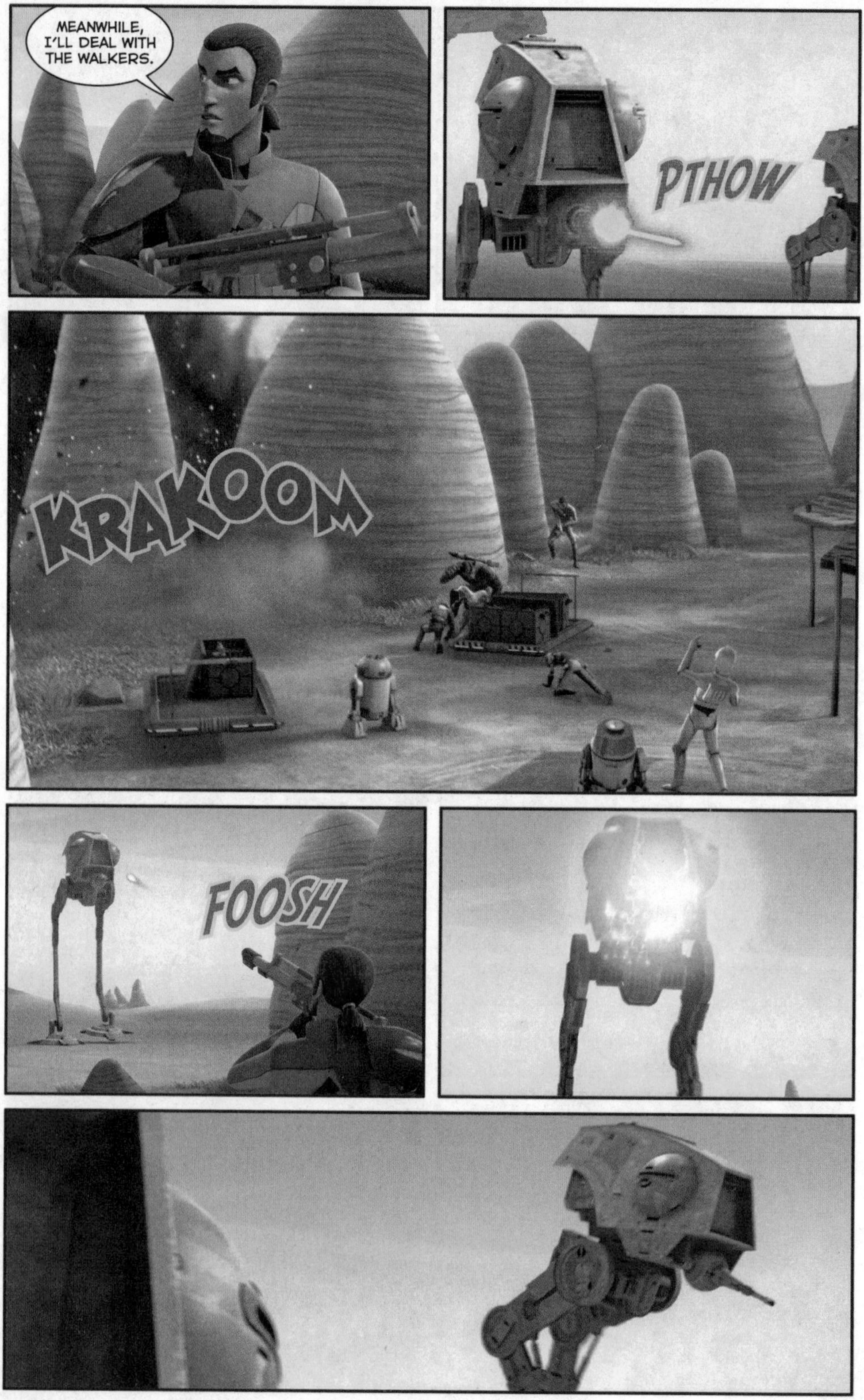
MEANWHILE, I'LL DEAL WITH THE WALKERS.
PTHOW
KRAKOOM
FOOSH

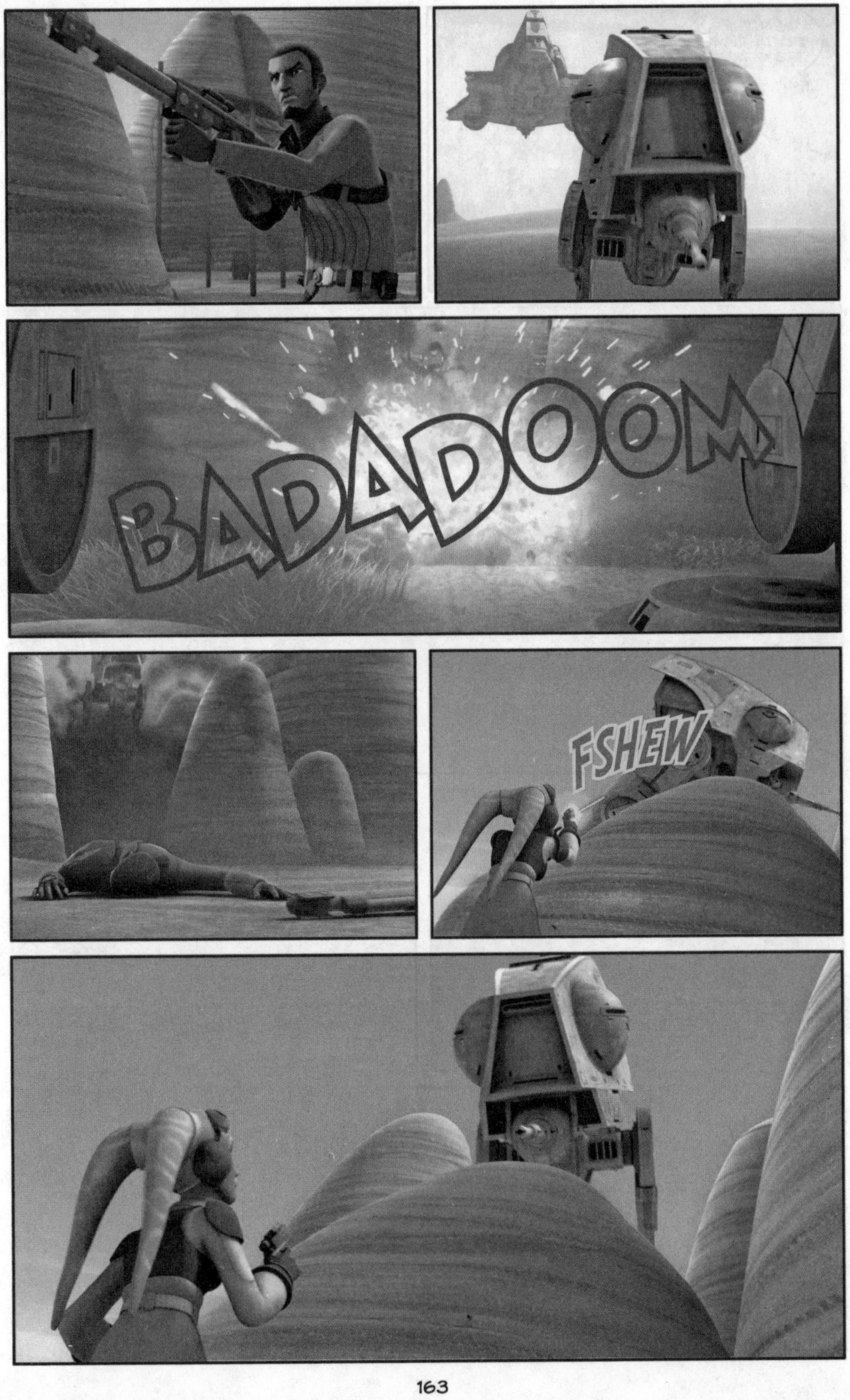
BADADOOM
FSHEW

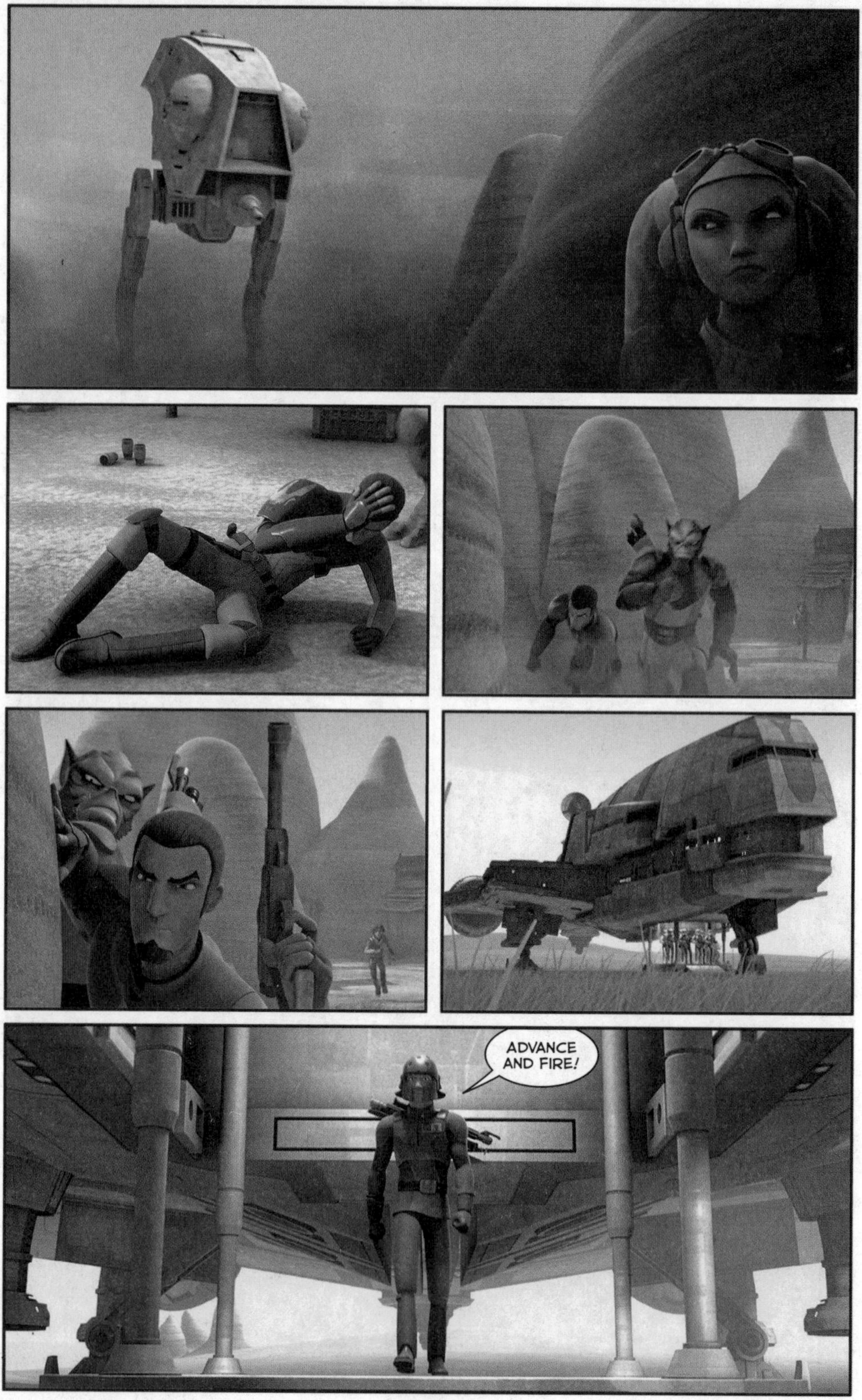
ADVANCE AND FIRE!

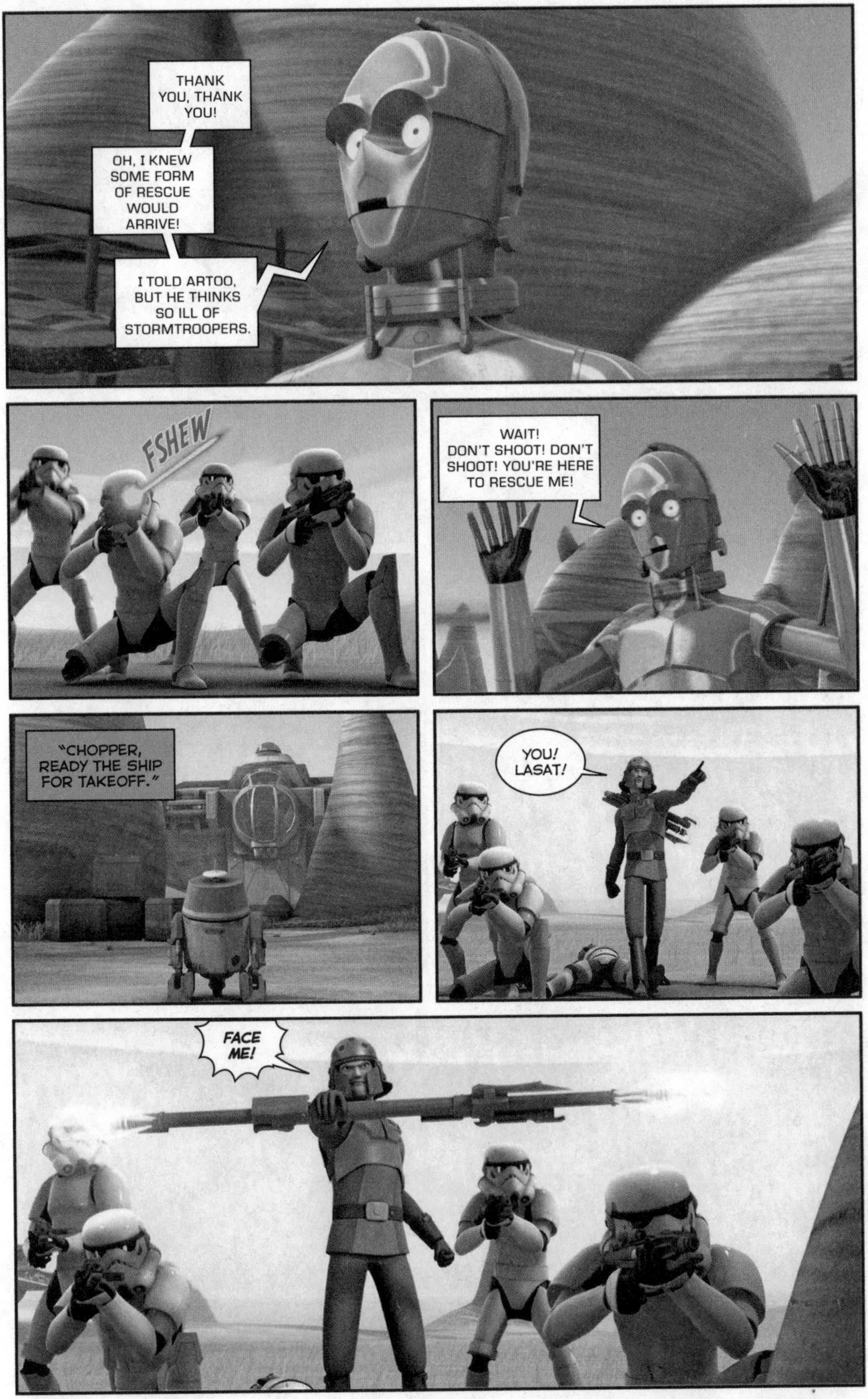
THANK YOU, THANK YOU!
OH, I KNEW SOME FORM OF RESCUE WOULD ARRIVE!
I TOLD ARTOO, BUT HE THINKS SO ILL OF STORMTROOPERS.
FSHEW
WAIT! DON'T SHOOT! DON'T SHOOT! YOU'RE HERE TO RESCUE ME!
"CHOPPER, READY THE SHIP FOR TAKEOFF."
YOU! LASAT!
FACE ME!

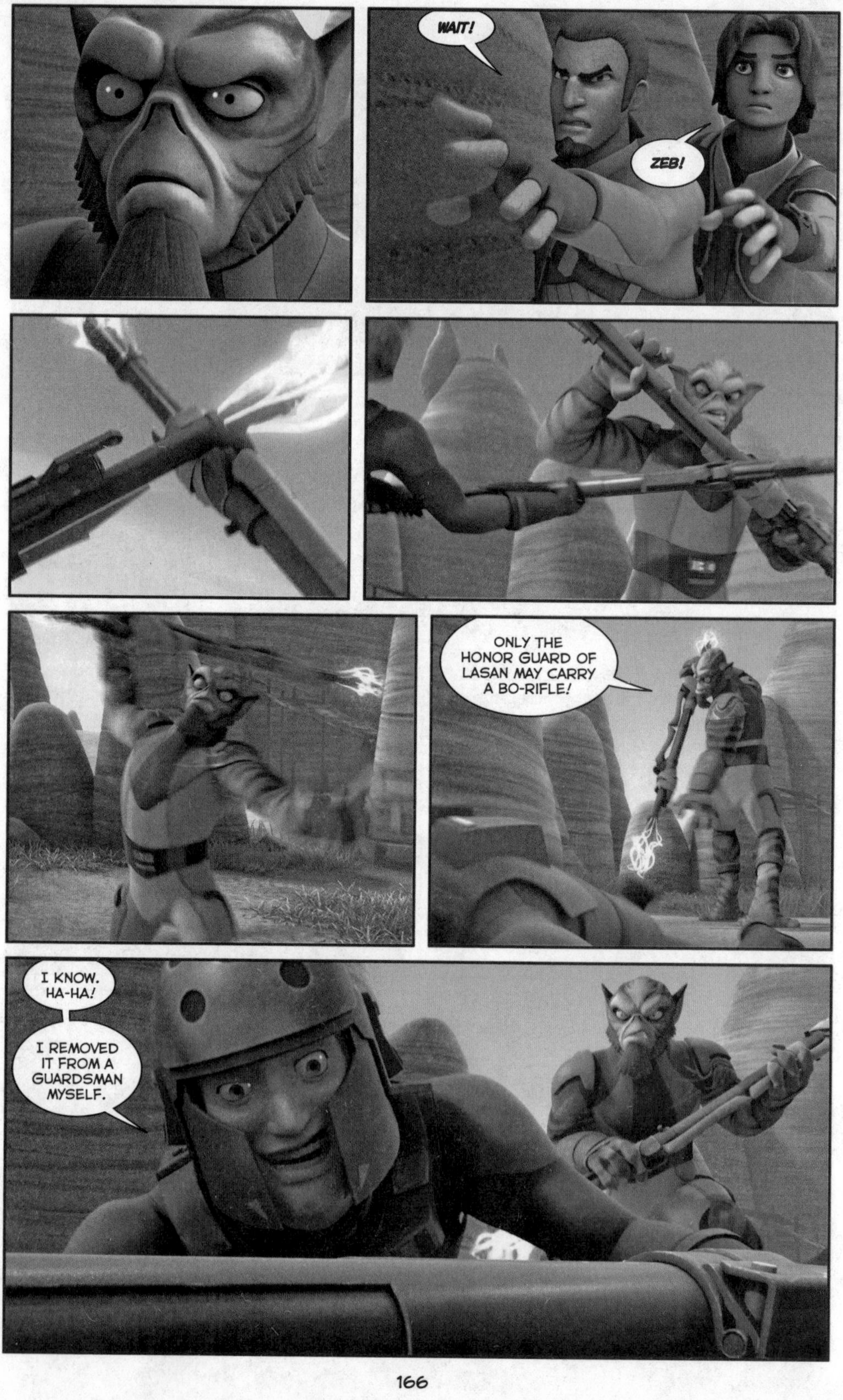
WAIT!
ZEB!
ONLY THE HONOR GUARD OF LASAN MAY CARRY A BO-RIFLE!
I KNOW. HA-HA!
I REMOVED IT FROM A GUARDSMAN MYSELF.

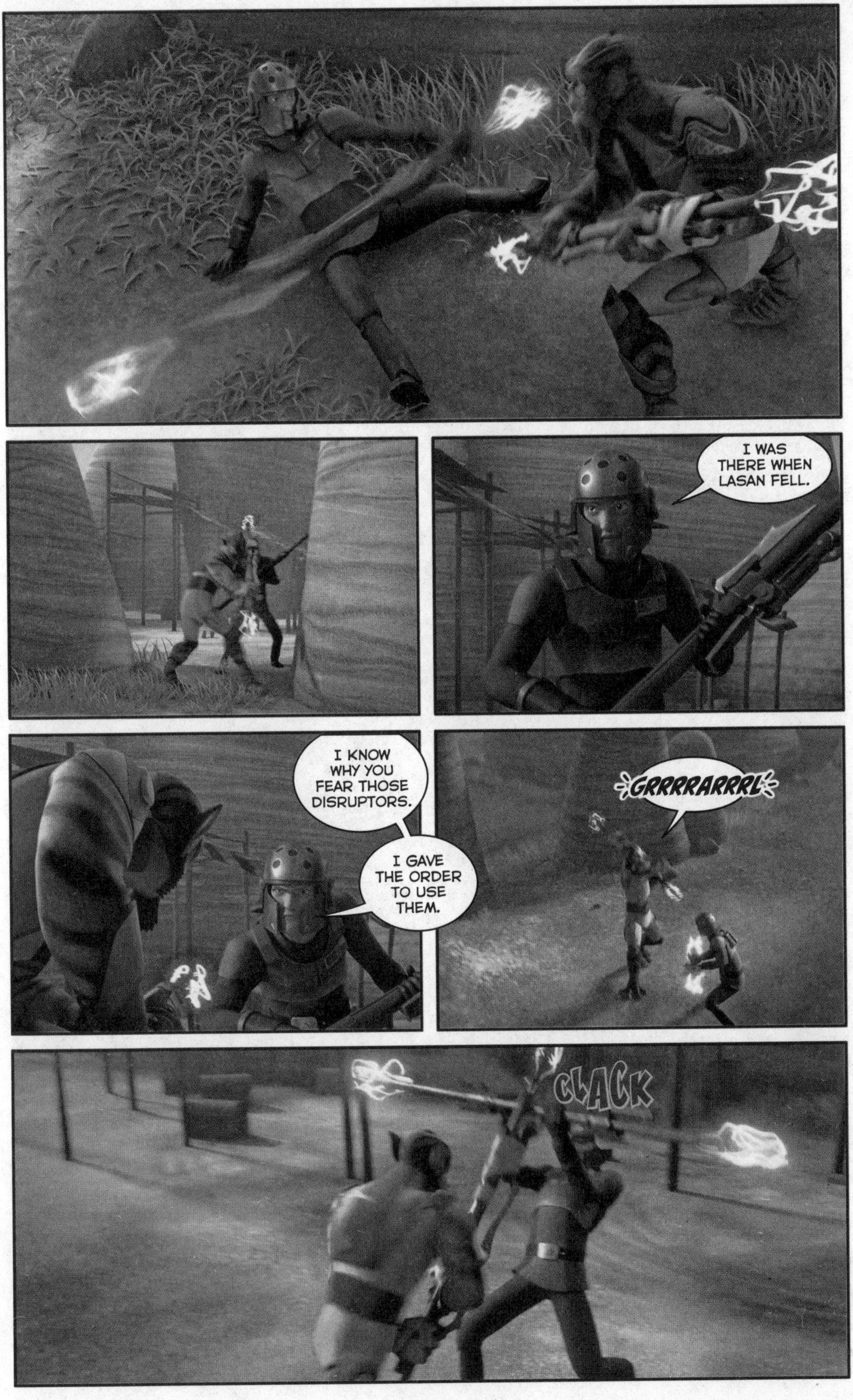
I WAS THERE WHEN LASAN FELL.
I KNOW WHY YOU FEAR THOSE DISRUPTORS.
I GAVE THE ORDER TO USE THEM.
GRRRRARRRL
CLACK

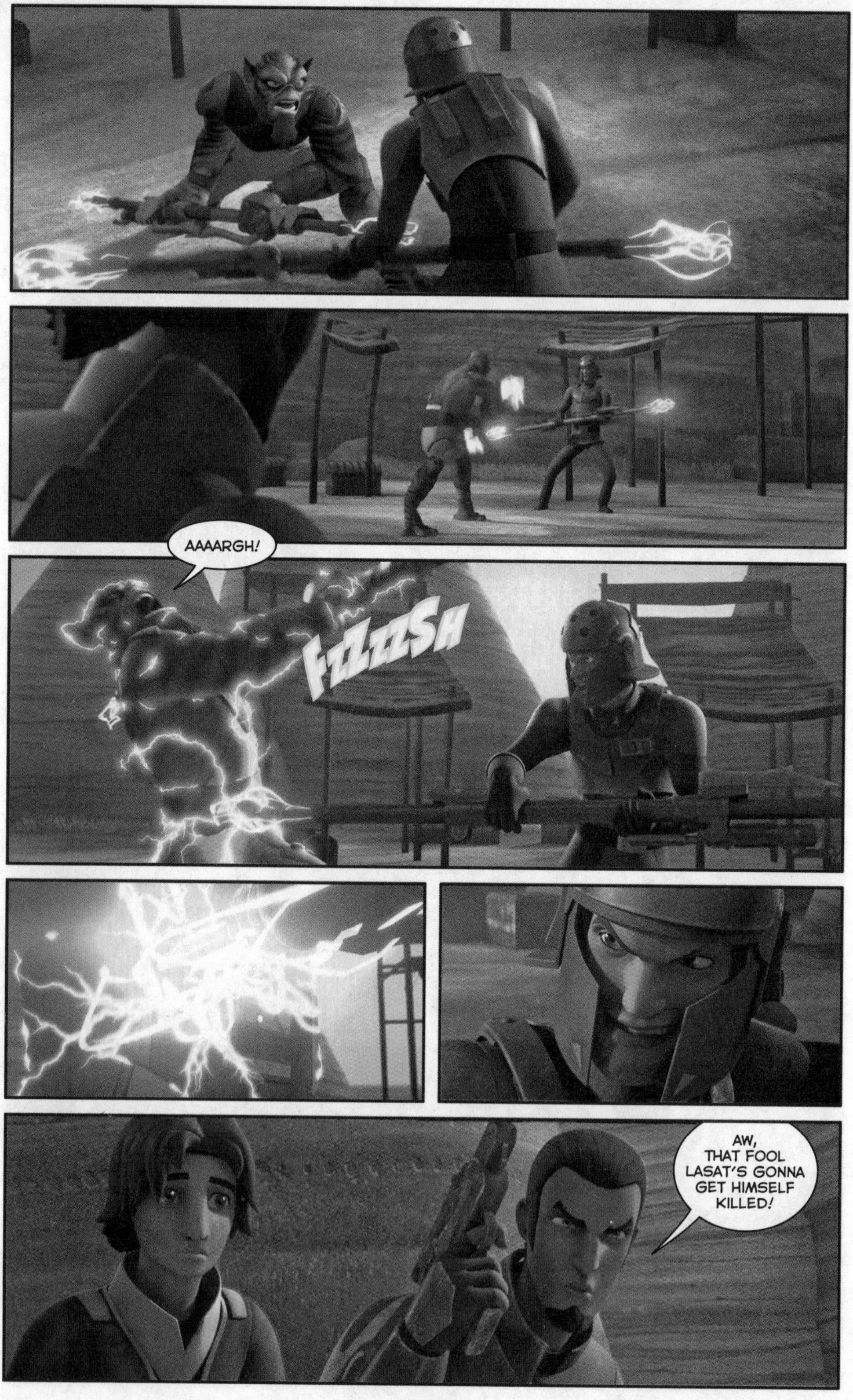
AAAARGH!
FZZZZSH
AW, THAT FOOL LASAT'S GONNA GET HIMSELF KILLED!

OKAY, WE'RE READY.

EVERYONE, PUSH!

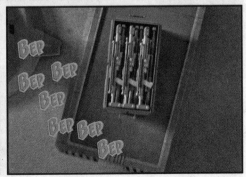

BER
BER BER
BER
BER BER
BER

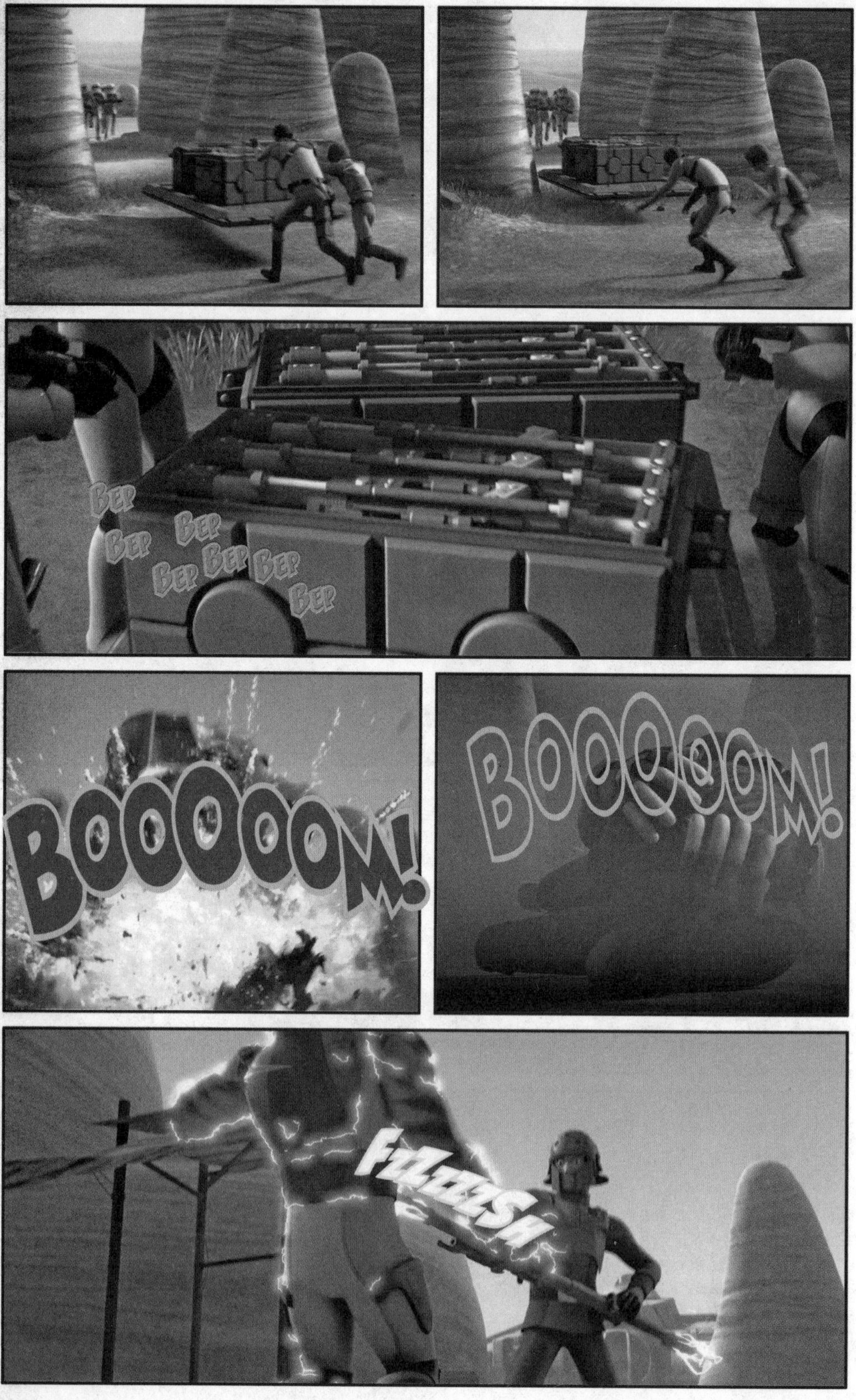
BEP
BEP BEP
BEP BEP BEP
BEP
BOOOOOM!
BOOOOOM!
FZZZZSH

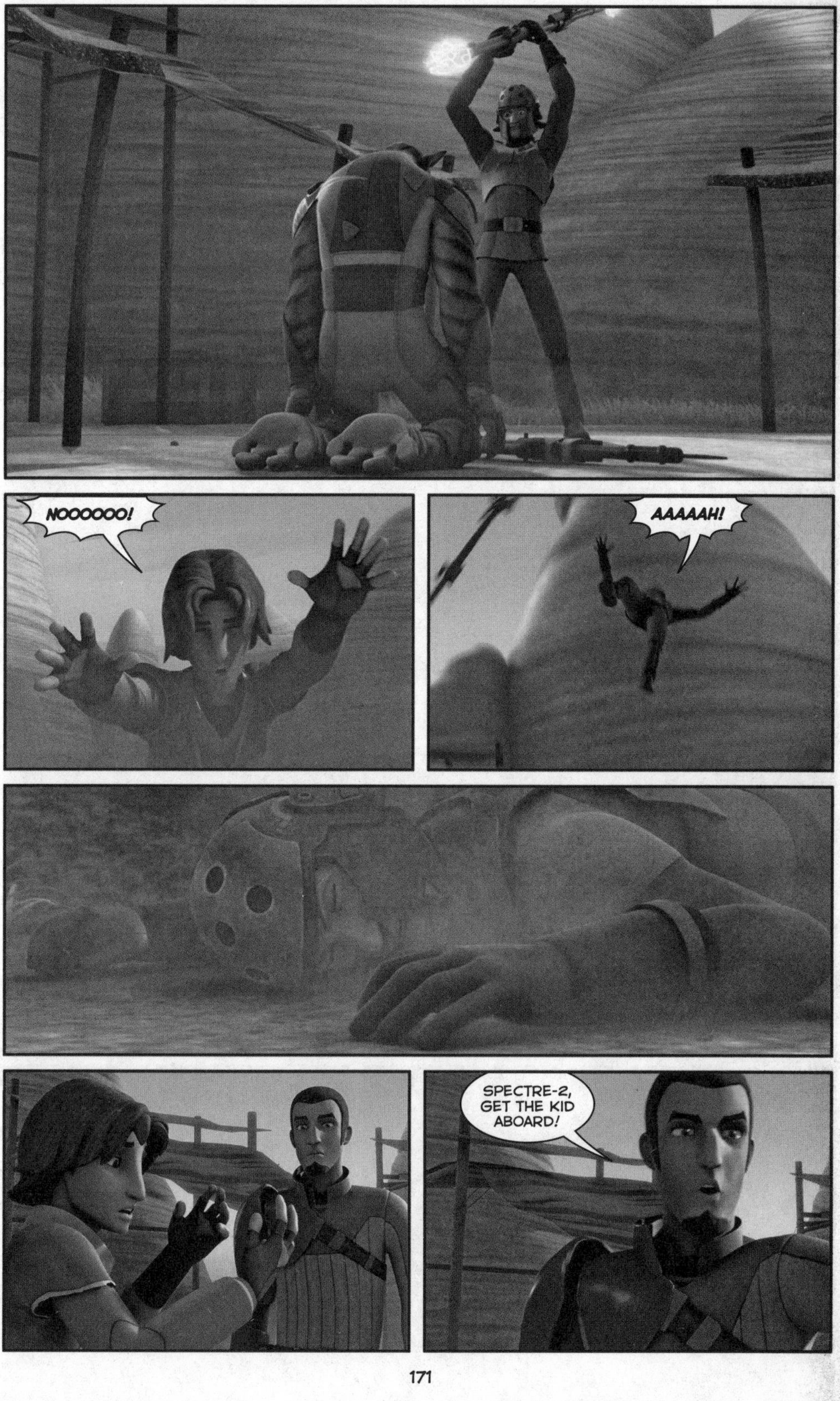
NOOOOOO!
AAAAAH!
SPECTRE-2, GET THE KID ABOARD!

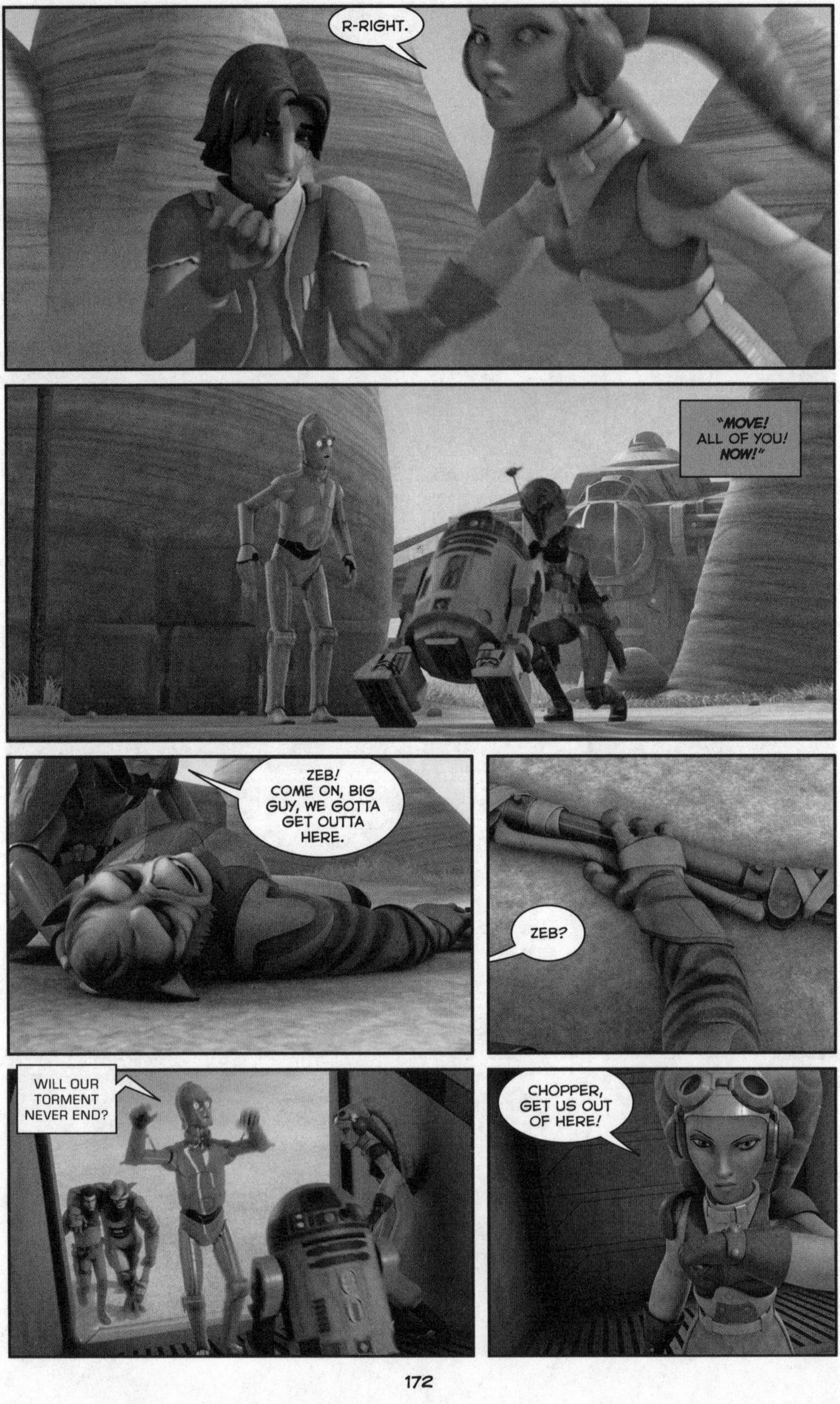
R-RIGHT.
"MOVE! ALL OF YOU! NOW!"
ZEB! COME ON, BIG GUY, WE GOTTA GET OUTTA HERE.
ZEB?
WILL OUR TORMENT NEVER END?
CHOPPER, GET US OUT OF HERE!

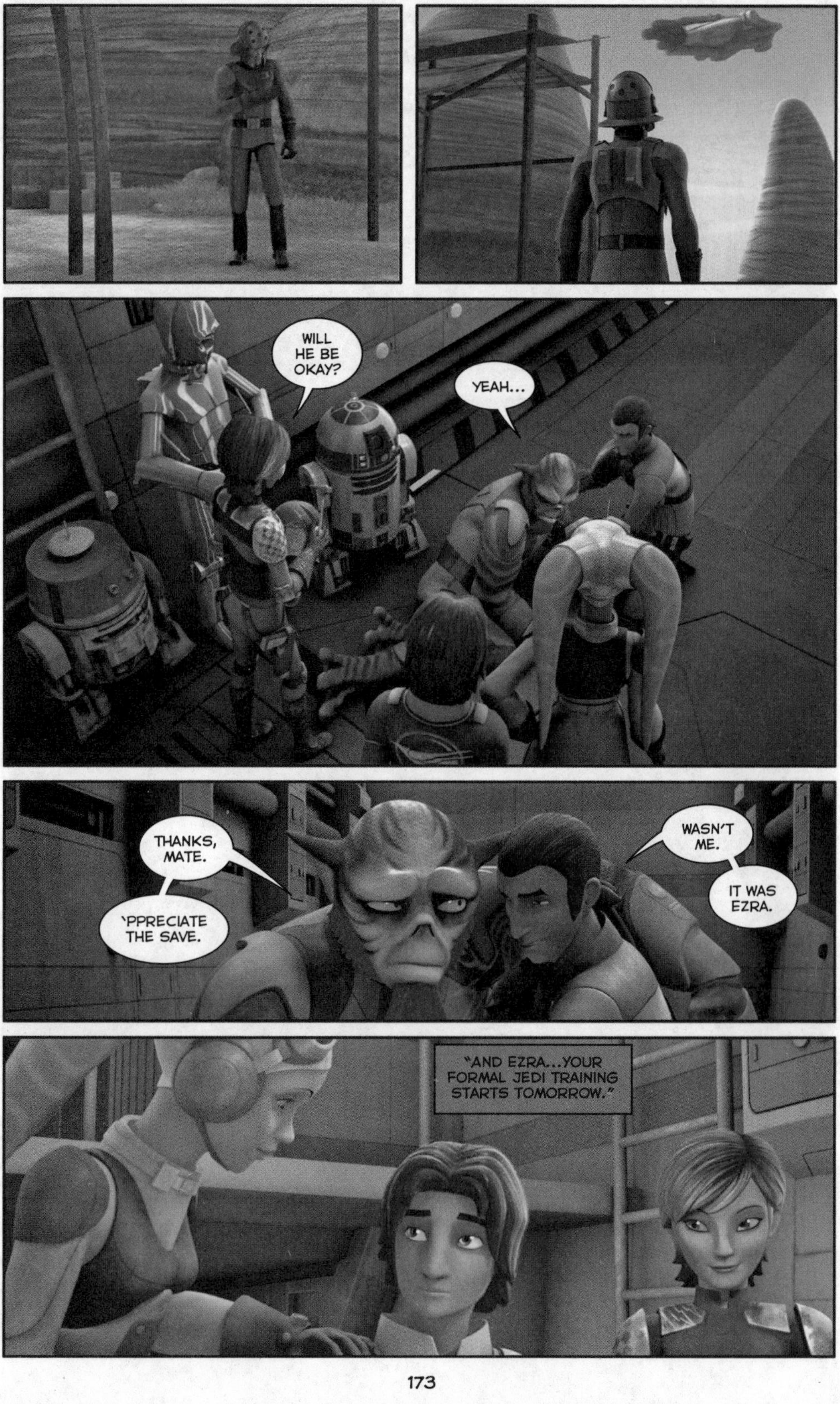
WILL HE BE OKAY?
YEAH...
THANKS, MATE.
'PPRECIATE THE SAVE.
WASN'T ME.
IT WAS EZRA.
"AND EZRA...YOUR FORMAL JEDI TRAINING STARTS TOMORROW."

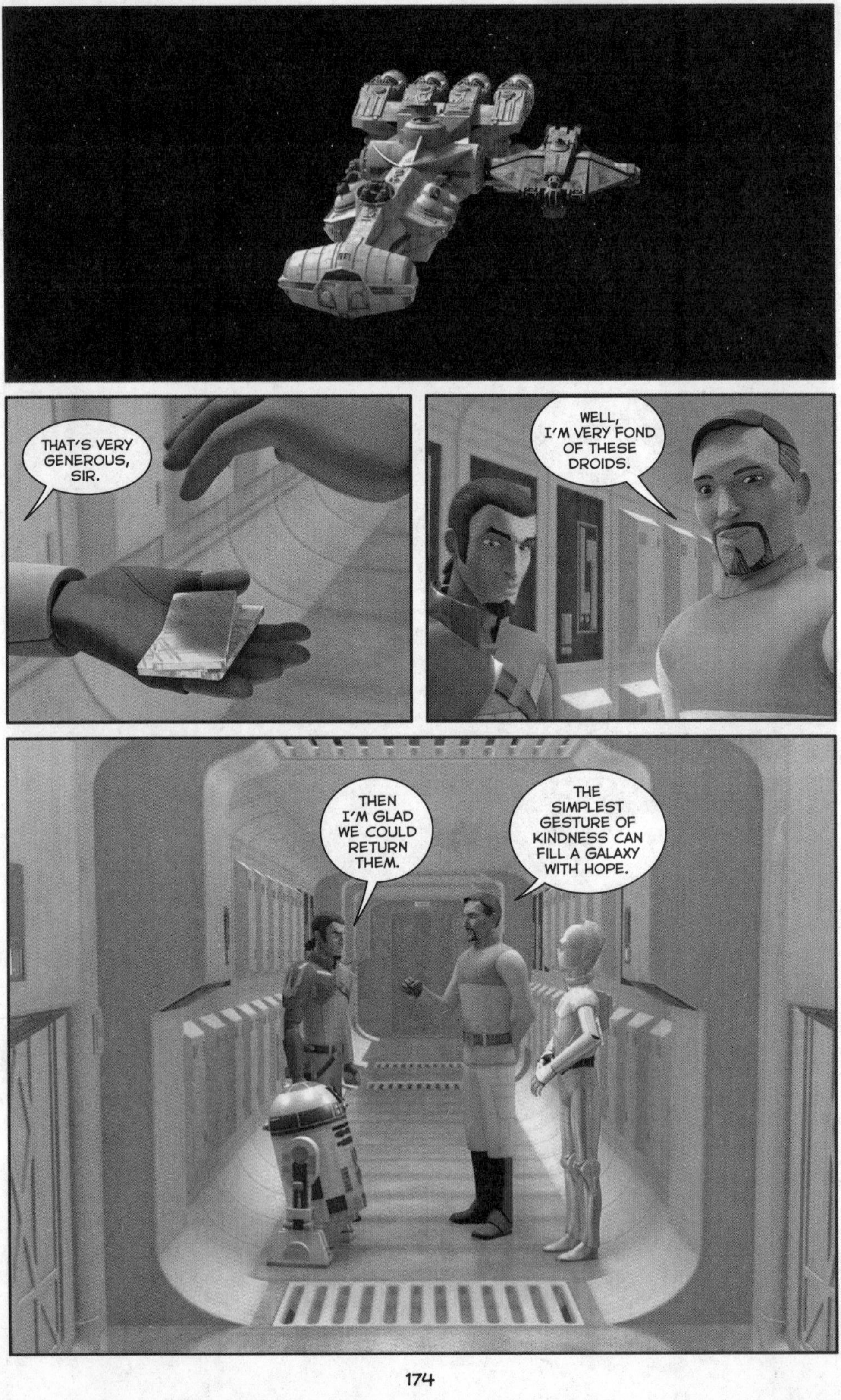
THAT'S VERY GENEROUS, SIR.
WELL, I'M VERY FOND OF THESE DROIDS.
THEN I'M GLAD WE COULD RETURN THEM.
THE SIMPLEST GESTURE OF KINDNESS CAN FILL A GALAXY WITH HOPE.

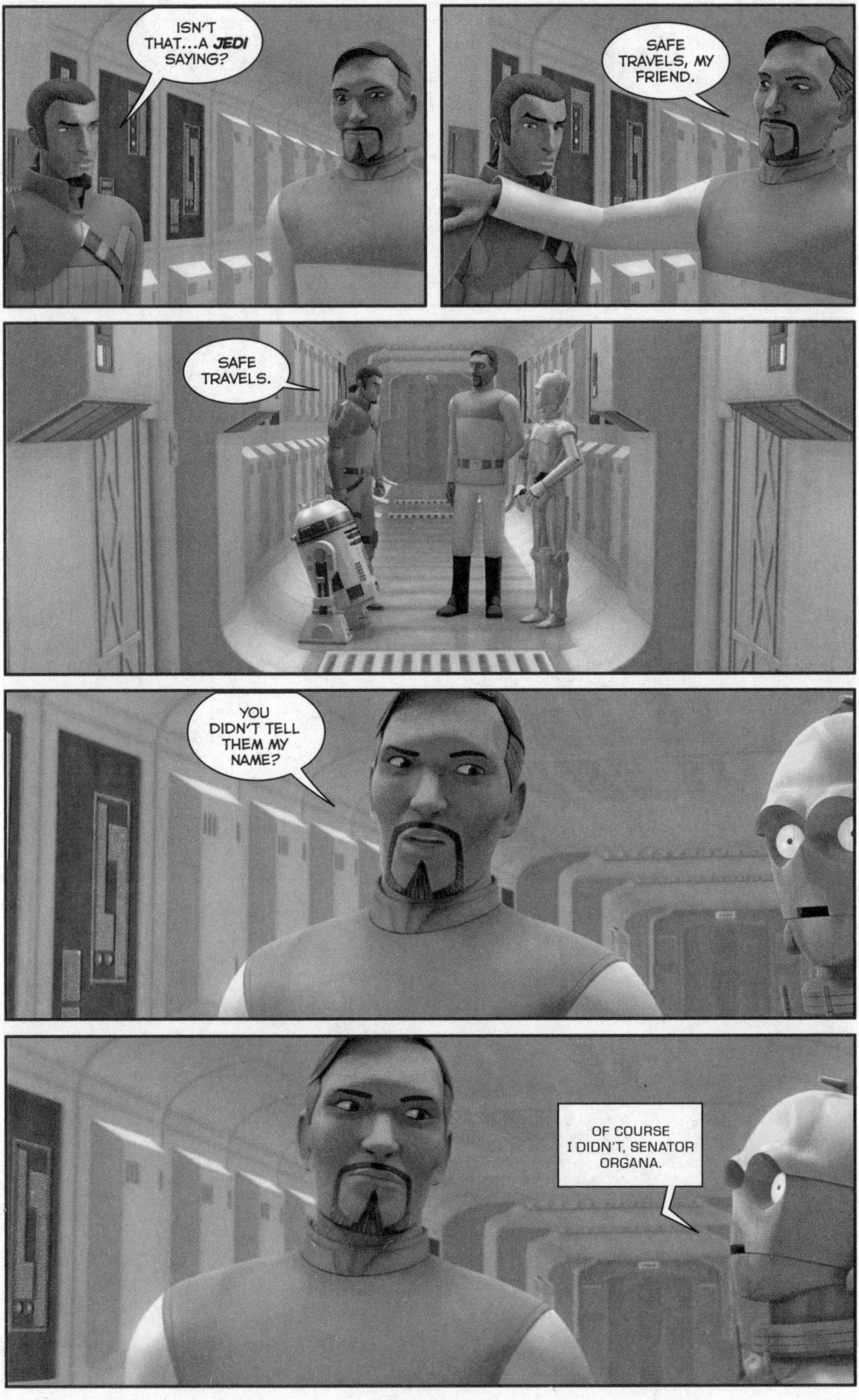
ISN'T THAT...A **JEDI** SAYING?
SAFE TRAVELS, MY FRIEND.
SAFE TRAVELS.
YOU DIDN'T TELL THEM MY NAME?
OF COURSE I DIDN'T, SENATOR ORGANA.

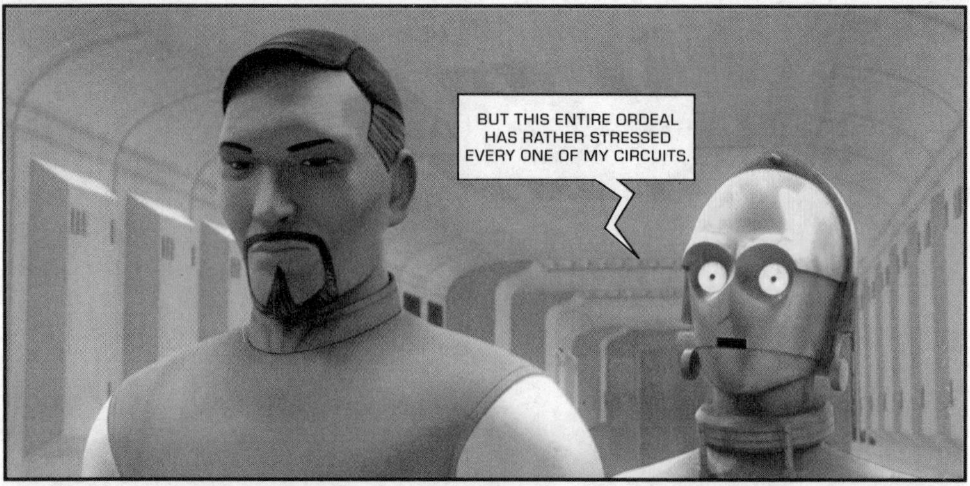
BUT THIS ENTIRE ORDEAL HAS RATHER STRESSED EVERY ONE OF MY CIRCUITS.

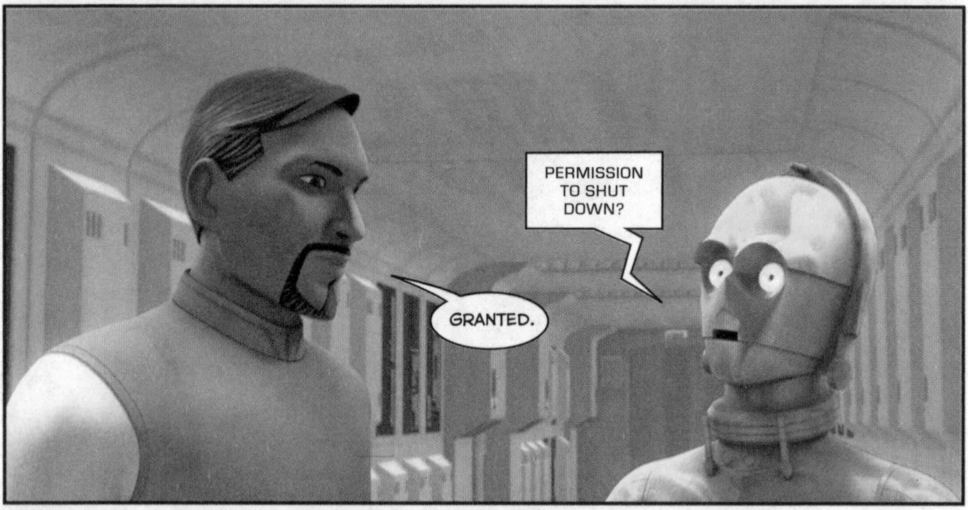
PERMISSION TO SHUT DOWN?
GRANTED.

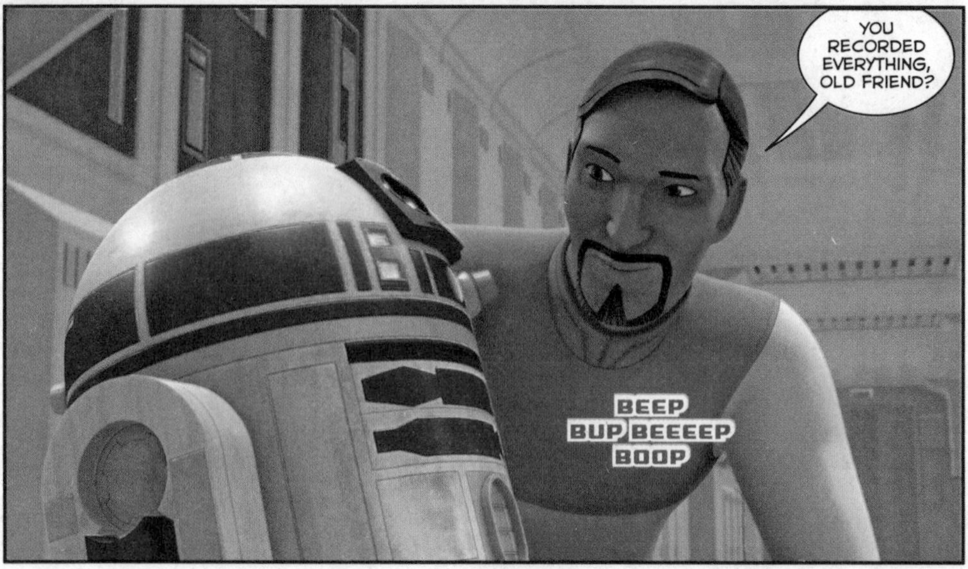
YOU RECORDED EVERYTHING, OLD FRIEND?
BEEP BUP BEEEEP BOOP

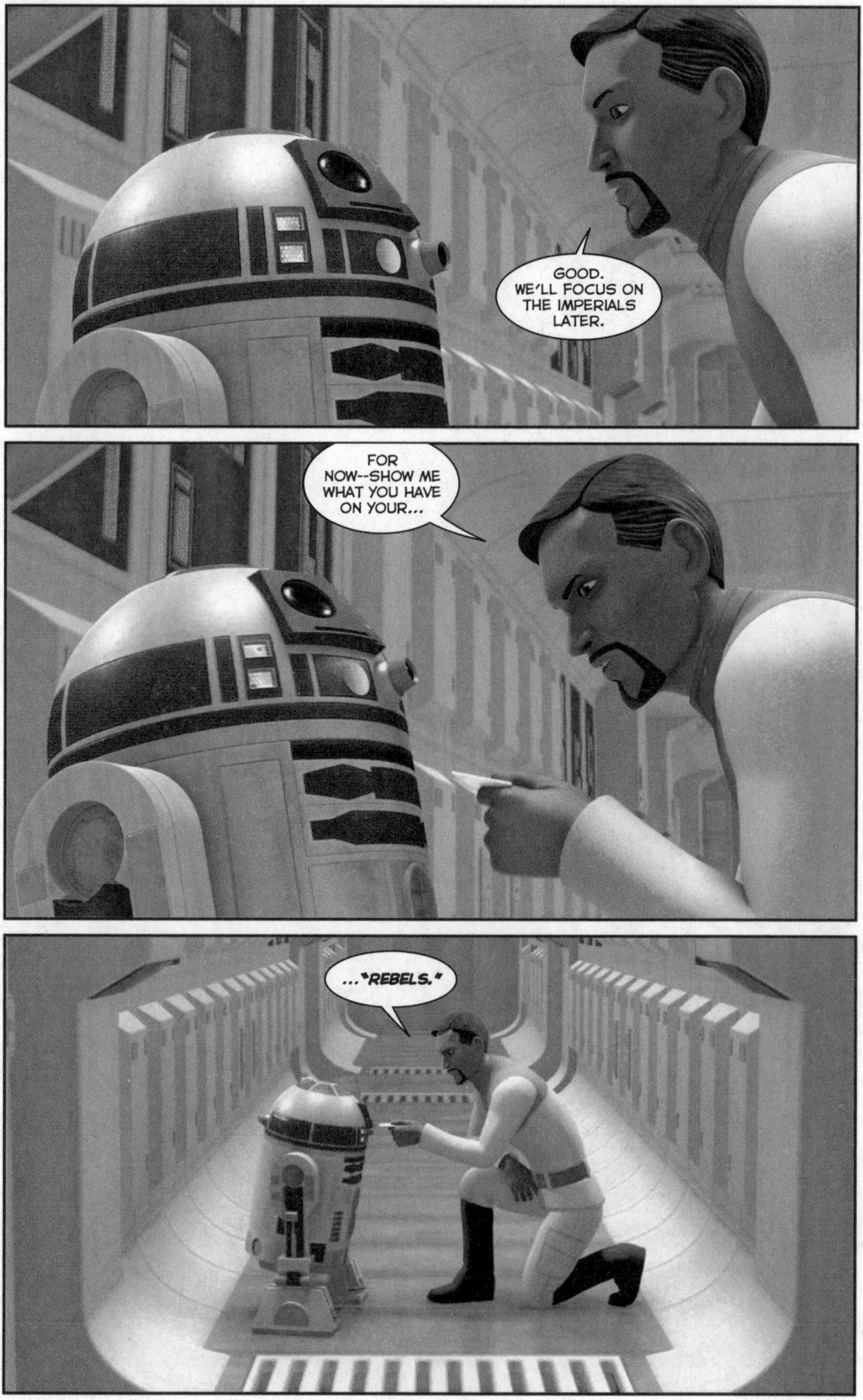
GOOD. WE'LL FOCUS ON THE IMPERIALS LATER.
FOR NOW--SHOW ME WHAT YOU HAVE ON YOUR...
..."REBELS."

STAR WARS REBELS™

FIGHTER FLIGHT

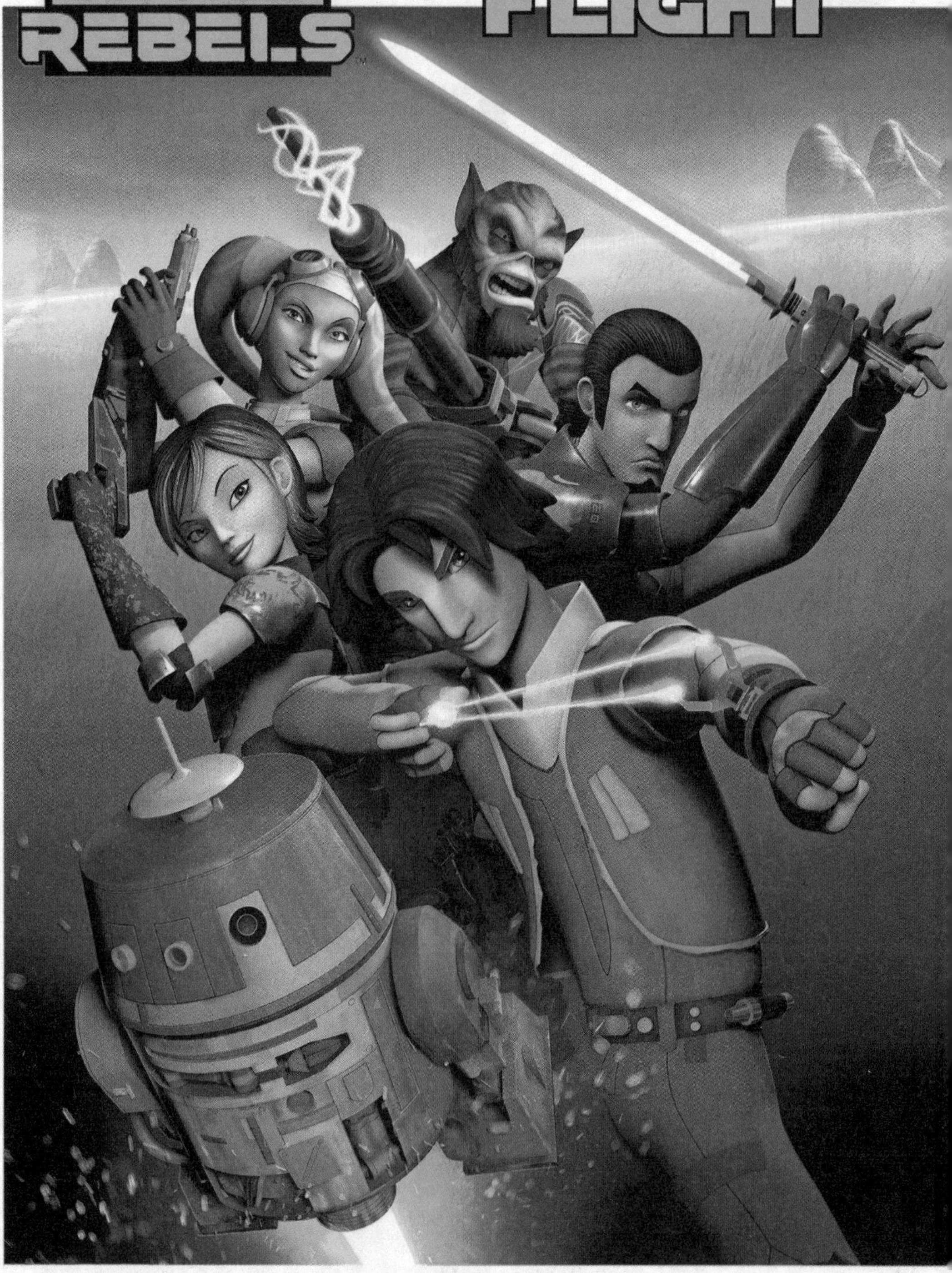

OKAY, YOU CAN DO THIS...

CLONK

BIP BUP BIP

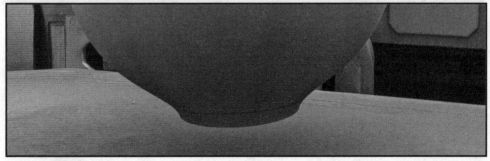

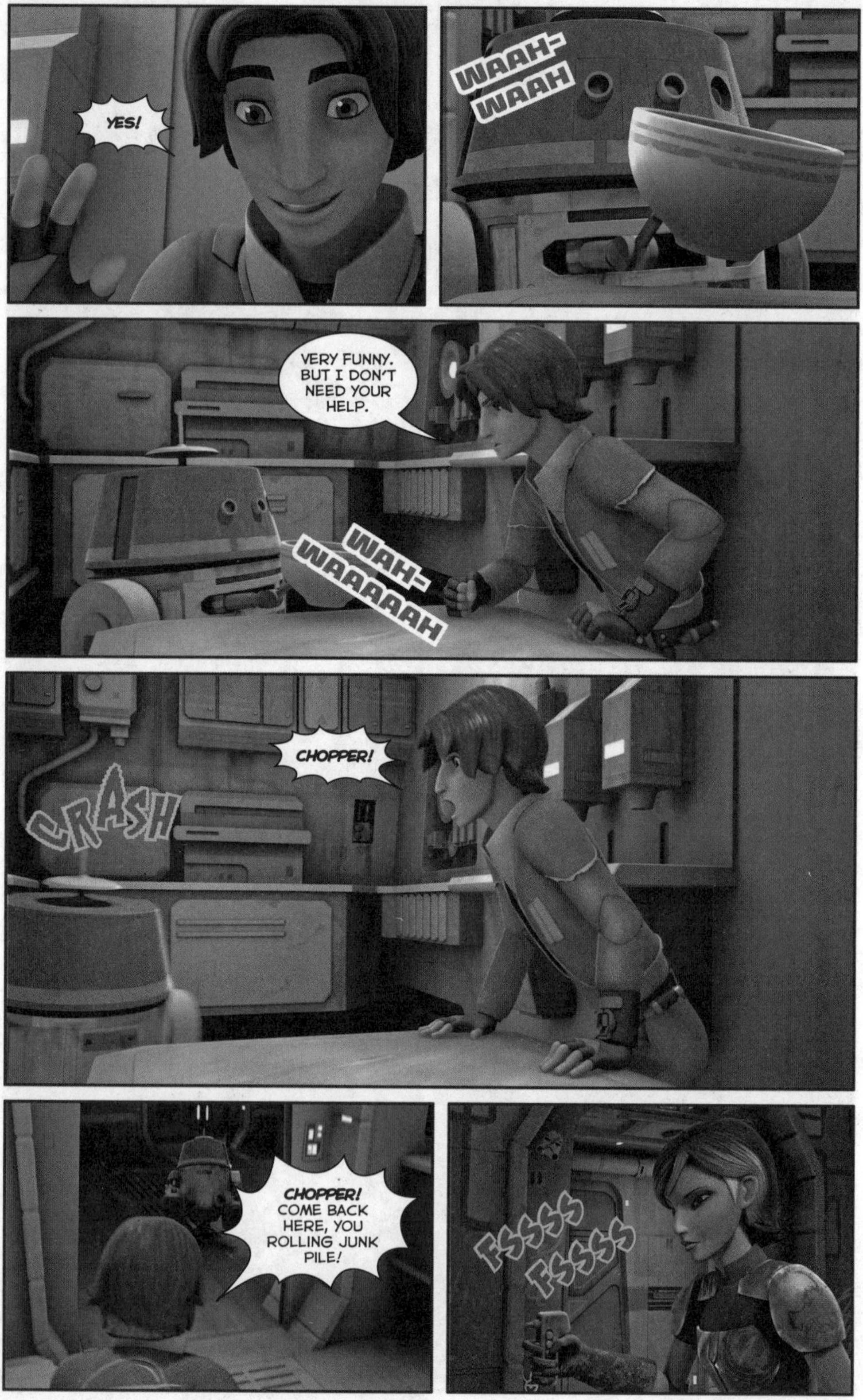
YES!
WAAH-WAAH
VERY FUNNY. BUT I DON'T NEED YOUR HELP.
WAH-WAAAAAAH
CHOPPER!
CRASH
CHOPPER! COME BACK HERE, YOU ROLLING JUNK PILE!
FSSSS FSSSS

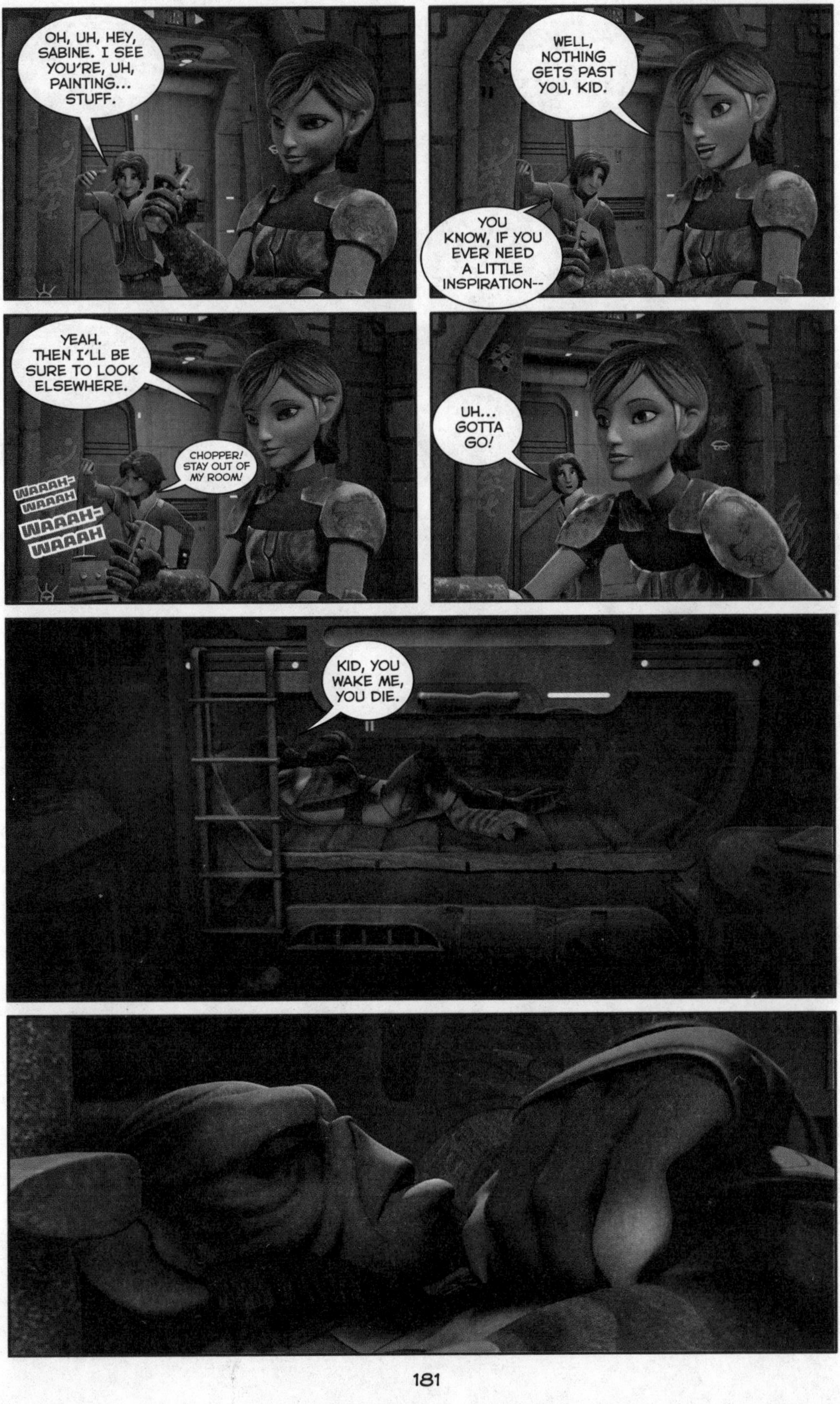
OH, UH, HEY, SABINE. I SEE YOU'RE, UH, PAINTING... STUFF.
WELL, NOTHING GETS PAST YOU, KID.
YOU KNOW, IF YOU EVER NEED A LITTLE INSPIRATION--
YEAH. THEN I'LL BE SURE TO LOOK ELSEWHERE.
CHOPPER! STAY OUT OF MY ROOM!
WAAAH-WAAAH
WAAAH-WAAAH
UH... GOTTA GO!
KID, YOU WAKE ME, YOU DIE.

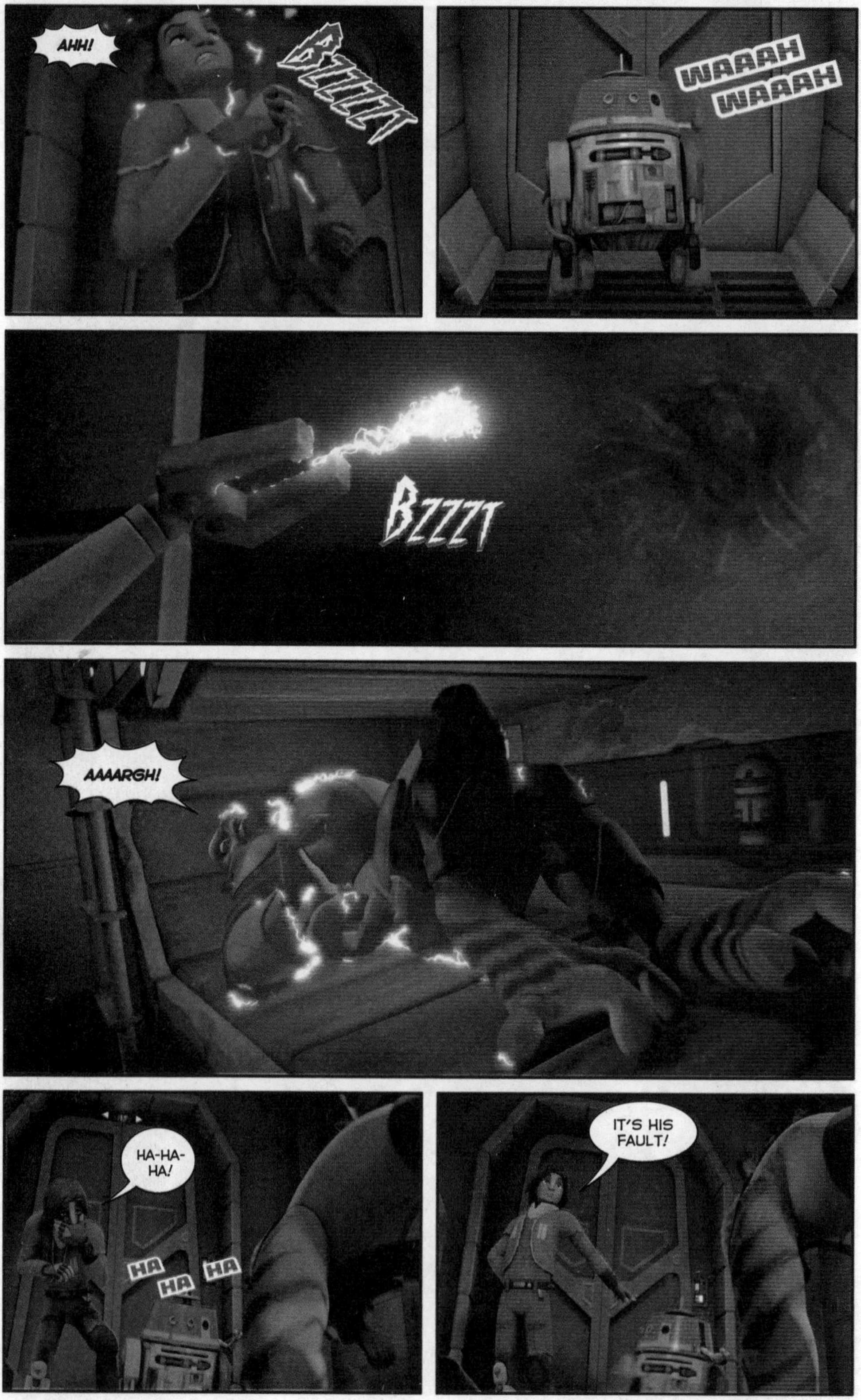
AHH!
BZZZT
WAAAH
WAAAH
BZZZT
AAAARGH!
HA-HA-HA!
HA
HA
HA
IT'S HIS FAULT!

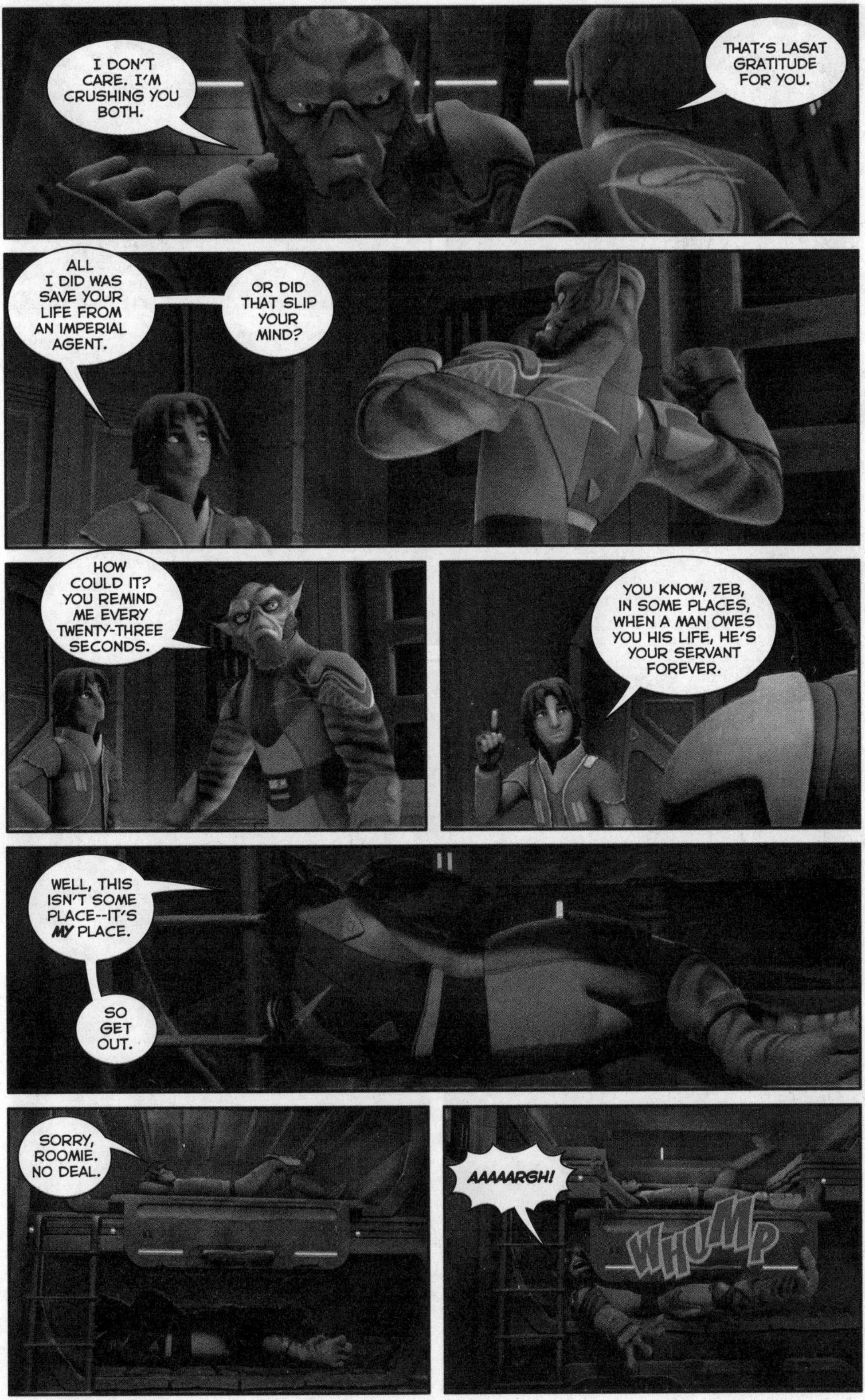
I DON'T CARE. I'M CRUSHING YOU BOTH.
THAT'S LASAT GRATITUDE FOR YOU.
ALL I DID WAS SAVE YOUR LIFE FROM AN IMPERIAL AGENT.
OR DID THAT SLIP YOUR MIND?
HOW COULD IT? YOU REMIND ME EVERY TWENTY-THREE SECONDS.
YOU KNOW, ZEB, IN SOME PLACES, WHEN A MAN OWES YOU HIS LIFE, HE'S YOUR SERVANT FOREVER.
WELL, THIS ISN'T SOME PLACE--IT'S *MY* PLACE.
SO GET OUT.
SORRY, ROOMIE. NO DEAL.
AAAAARGH!
WHUMP

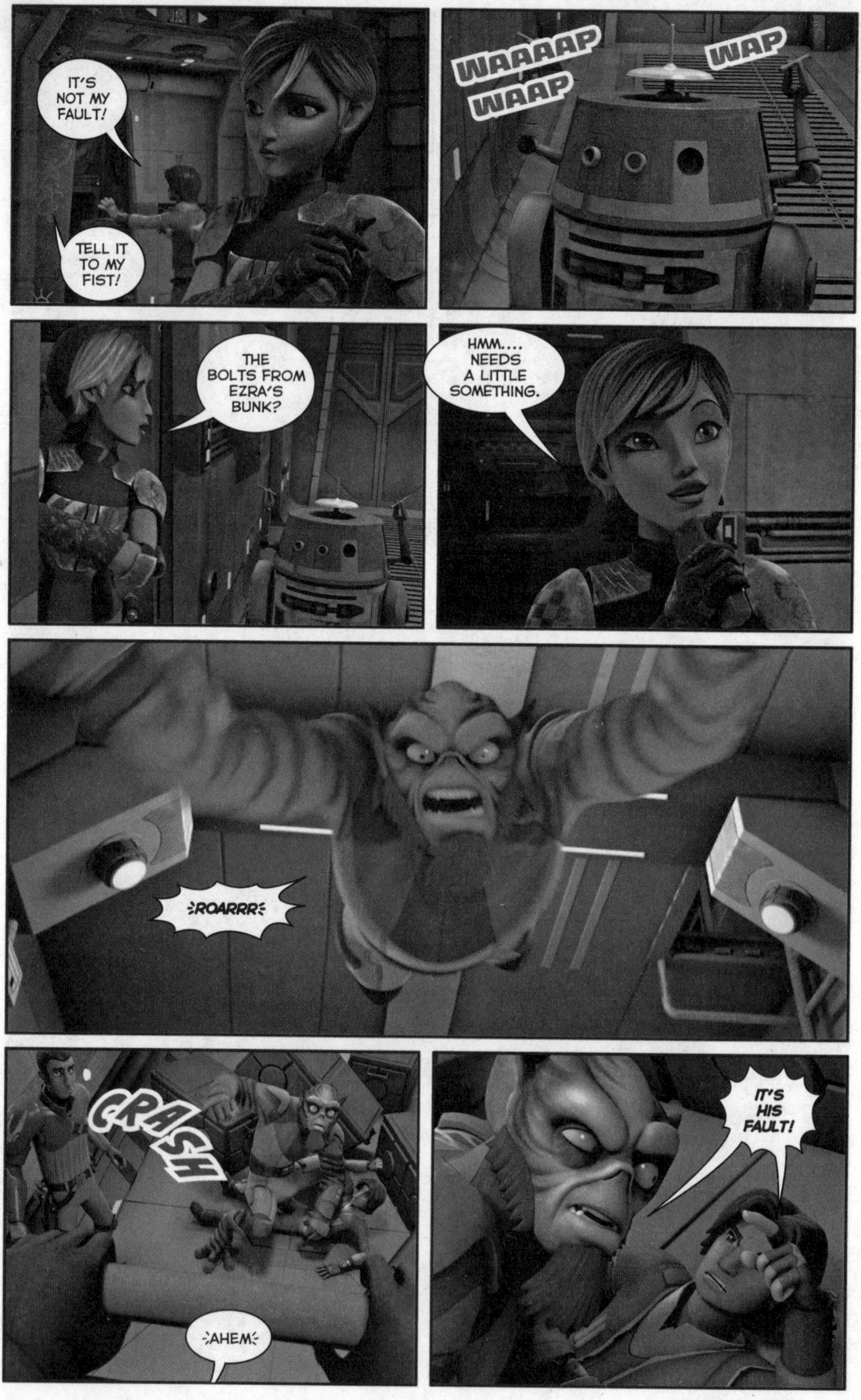
IT'S NOT MY FAULT!
TELL IT TO MY FIST!
WAAAAP
WAAP
WAP
THE BOLTS FROM EZRA'S BUNK?
HMM.... NEEDS A LITTLE SOMETHING.
ROARRR
CRASH
AHEM
IT'S HIS FAULT!

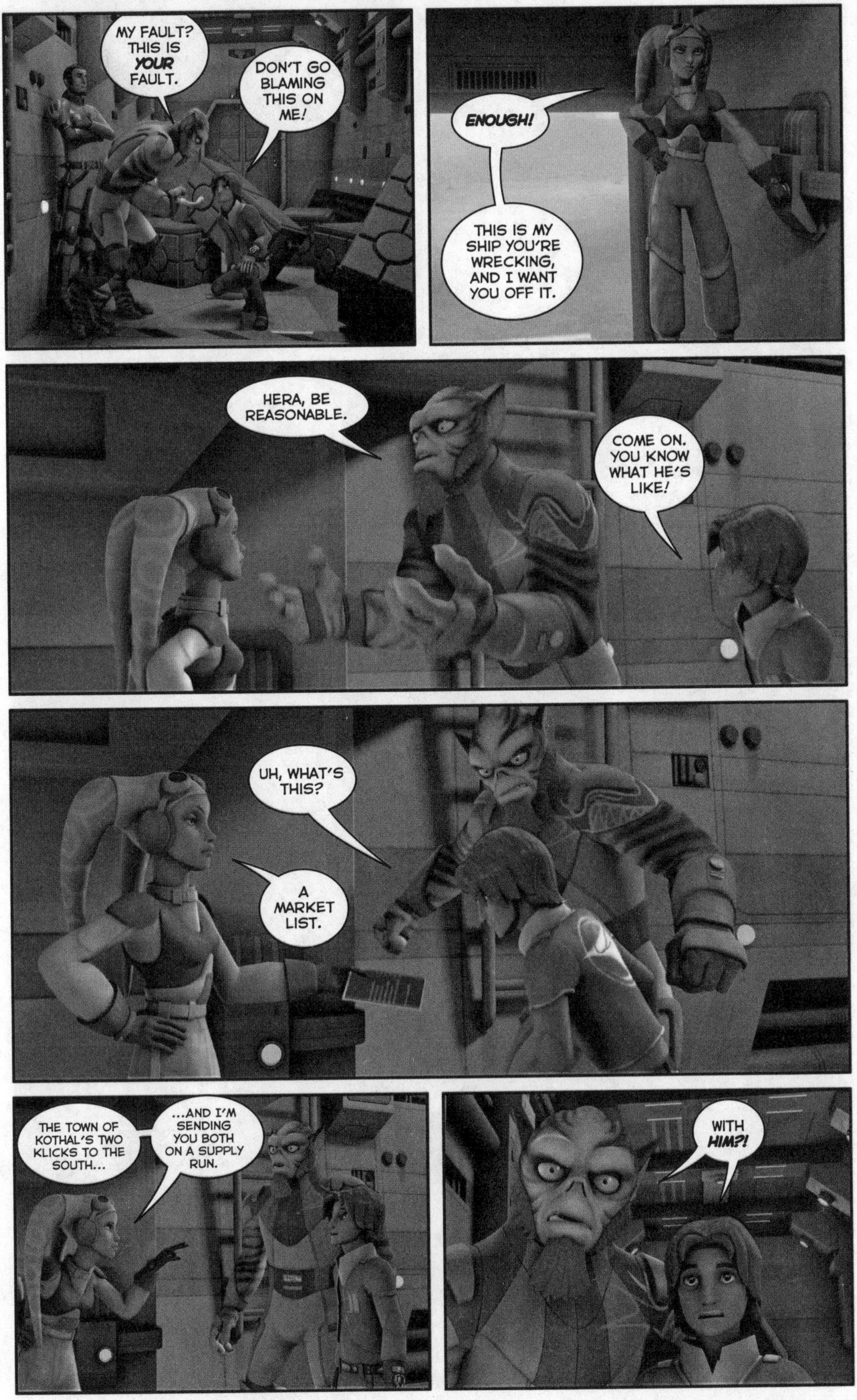
MY FAULT? THIS IS **YOUR** FAULT.
DON'T GO BLAMING THIS ON ME!
ENOUGH!
THIS IS MY SHIP YOU'RE WRECKING, AND I WANT YOU OFF IT.
HERA, BE REASONABLE.
COME ON. YOU KNOW WHAT HE'S LIKE!
UH, WHAT'S THIS?
A MARKET LIST.
THE TOWN OF KOTHAL'S TWO KLICKS TO THE SOUTH...
...AND I'M SENDING YOU BOTH ON A SUPPLY RUN.
WITH **HIM?!**

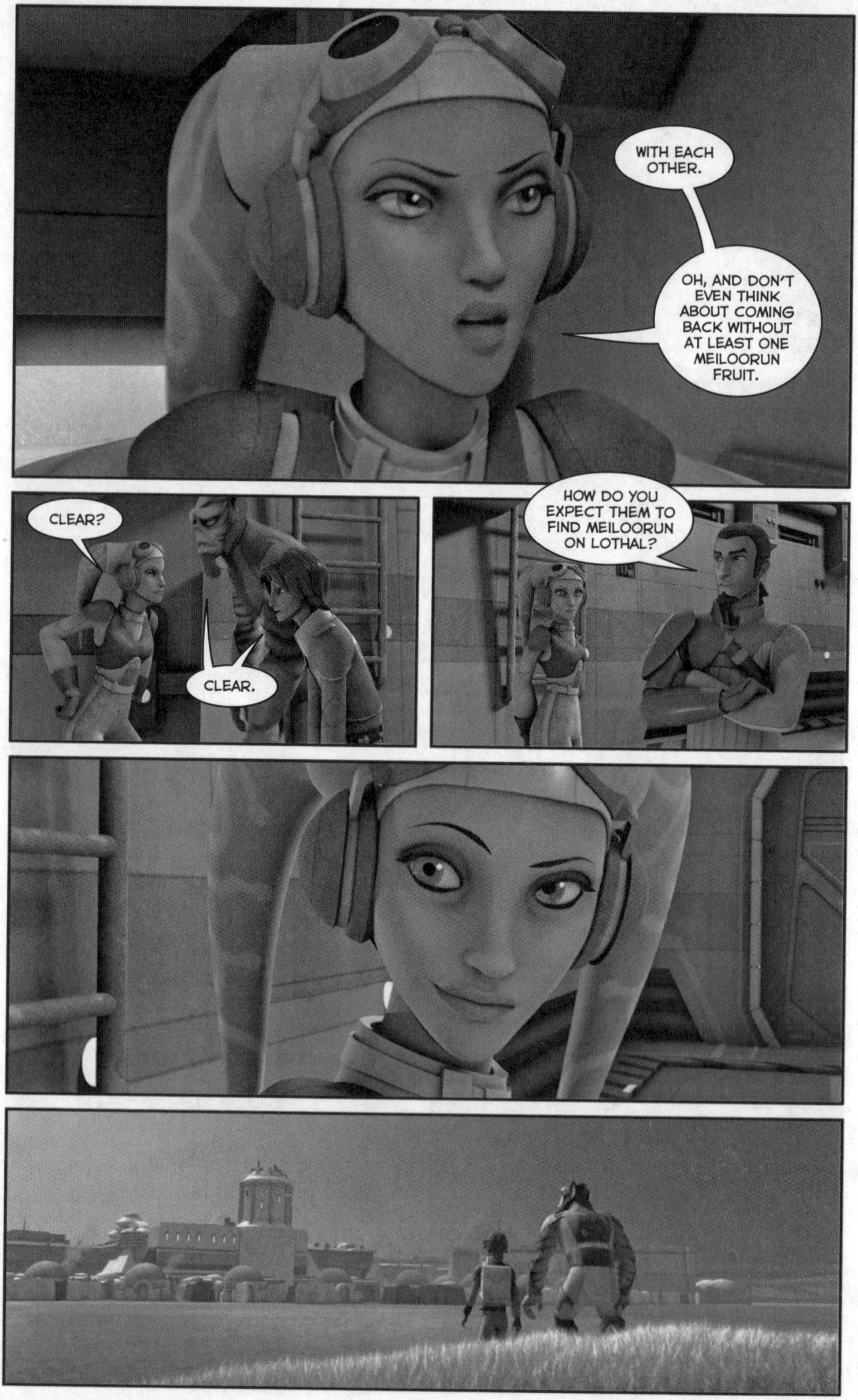
WITH EACH OTHER.
OH, AND DON'T EVEN THINK ABOUT COMING BACK WITHOUT AT LEAST ONE MEILOORUN FRUIT.
CLEAR?
CLEAR.
HOW DO YOU EXPECT THEM TO FIND MEILOORUN ON LOTHAL?

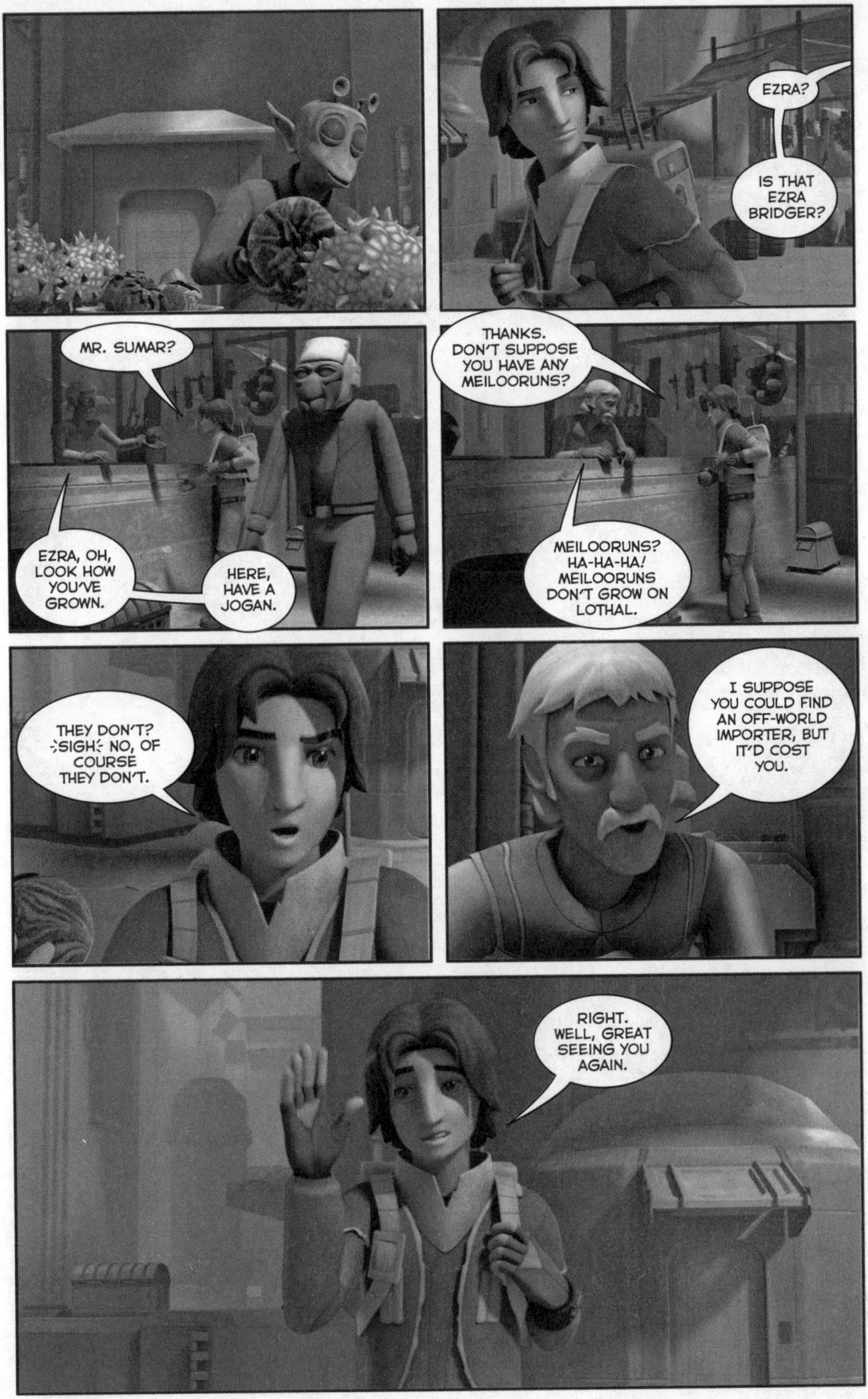
EZRA?
IS THAT EZRA BRIDGER?
MR. SUMAR?
EZRA, OH, LOOK HOW YOU'VE GROWN.
HERE, HAVE A JOGAN.
THANKS. DON'T SUPPOSE YOU HAVE ANY MEILOORUNS?
MEILOORUNS? HA-HA-HA! MEILOORUNS DON'T GROW ON LOTHAL.
THEY DON'T? *SIGH* NO, OF COURSE THEY DON'T.
I SUPPOSE YOU COULD FIND AN OFF-WORLD IMPORTER, BUT IT'D COST YOU.
RIGHT. WELL, GREAT SEEING YOU AGAIN.

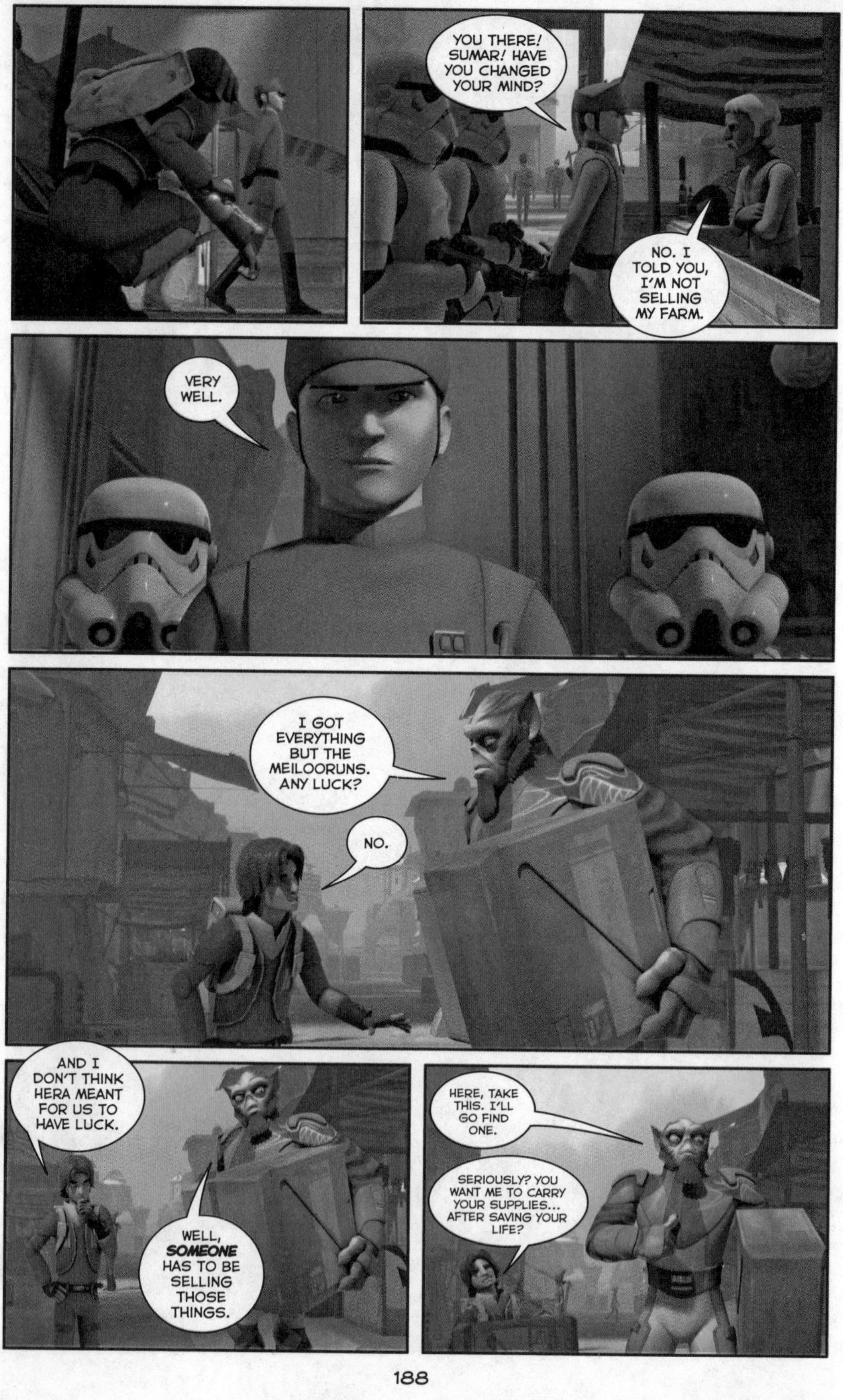
YOU THERE! SUMAR! HAVE YOU CHANGED YOUR MIND?
NO. I TOLD YOU, I'M NOT SELLING MY FARM.
VERY WELL.
I GOT EVERYTHING BUT THE MEILOORUNS. ANY LUCK?
NO.
AND I DON'T THINK HERA MEANT FOR US TO HAVE LUCK.
WELL, ***SOMEONE*** HAS TO BE SELLING THOSE THINGS.
HERE, TAKE THIS. I'LL GO FIND ONE.
SERIOUSLY? YOU WANT ME TO CARRY YOUR SUPPLIES... AFTER SAVING YOUR LIFE?

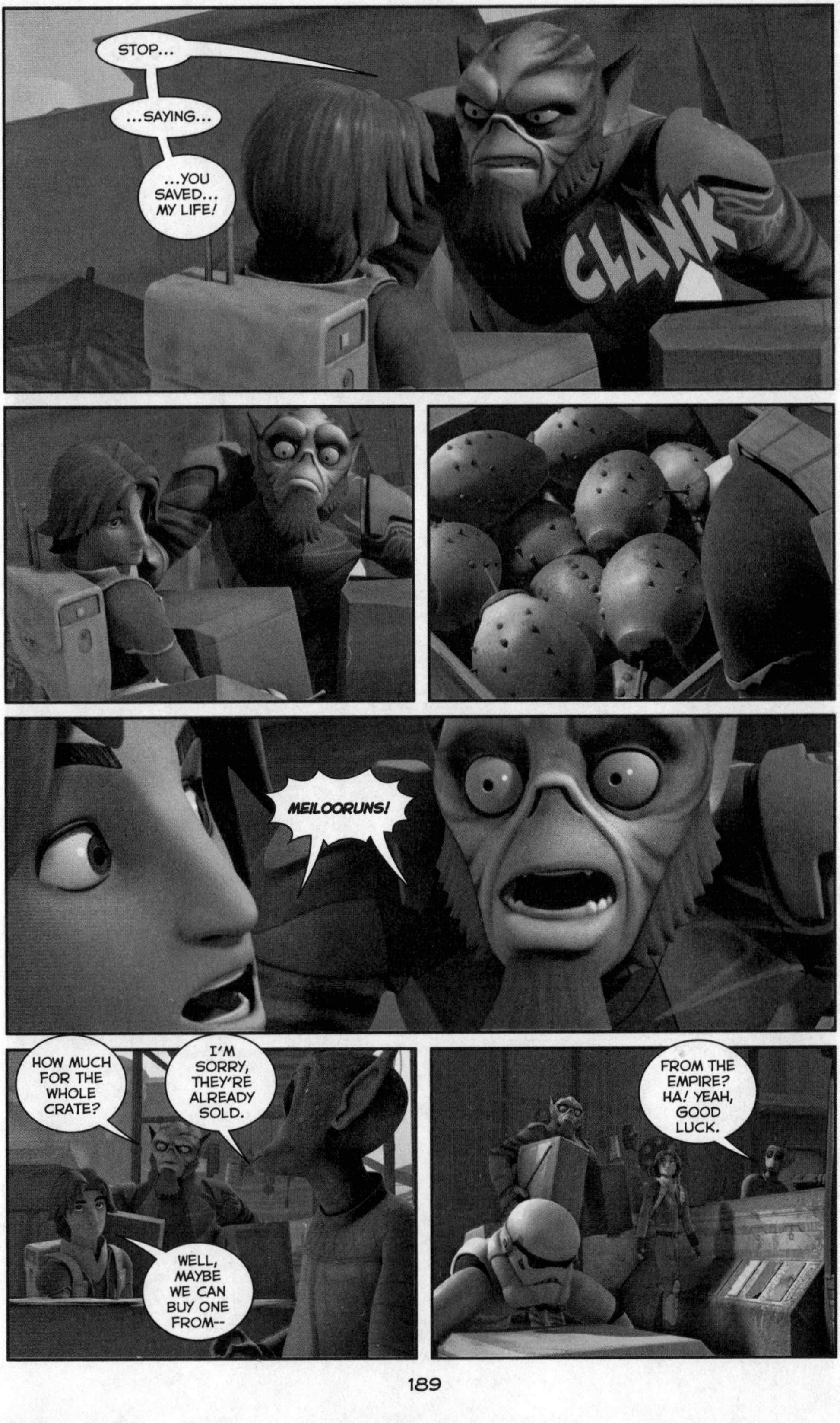
STOP...
...SAYING...
...YOU SAVED... MY LIFE!
CLANK
MEILOORUNS!
HOW MUCH FOR THE WHOLE CRATE?
I'M SORRY, THEY'RE ALREADY SOLD.
WELL, MAYBE WE CAN BUY ONE FROM--
FROM THE EMPIRE? HA! YEAH, GOOD LUCK.

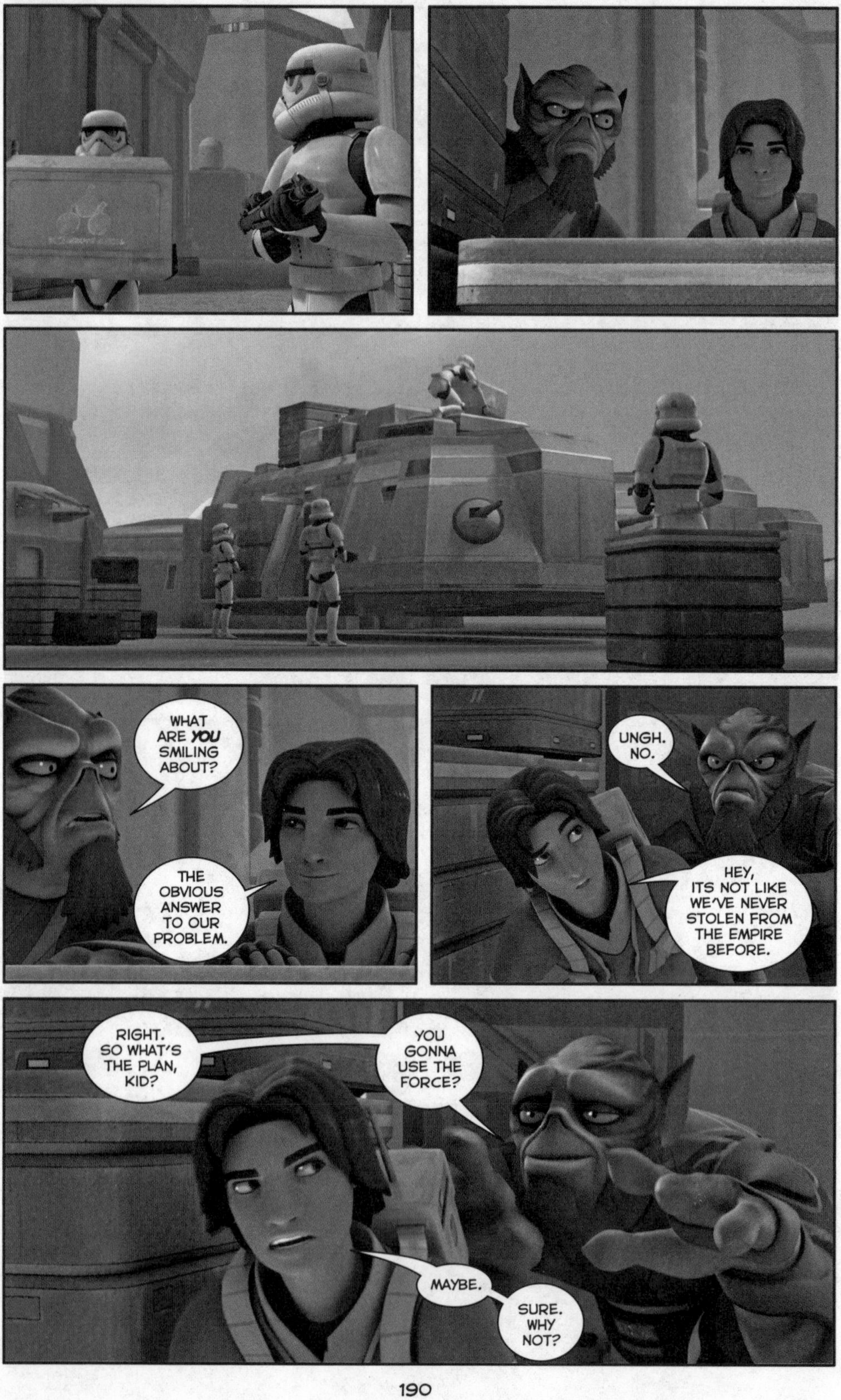
WHAT ARE *YOU* SMILING ABOUT?
THE OBVIOUS ANSWER TO OUR PROBLEM.
UNGH. NO.
HEY, ITS NOT LIKE WE'VE NEVER STOLEN FROM THE EMPIRE BEFORE.
RIGHT. SO WHAT'S THE PLAN, KID?
YOU GONNA USE THE FORCE?
MAYBE.
SURE. WHY NOT?

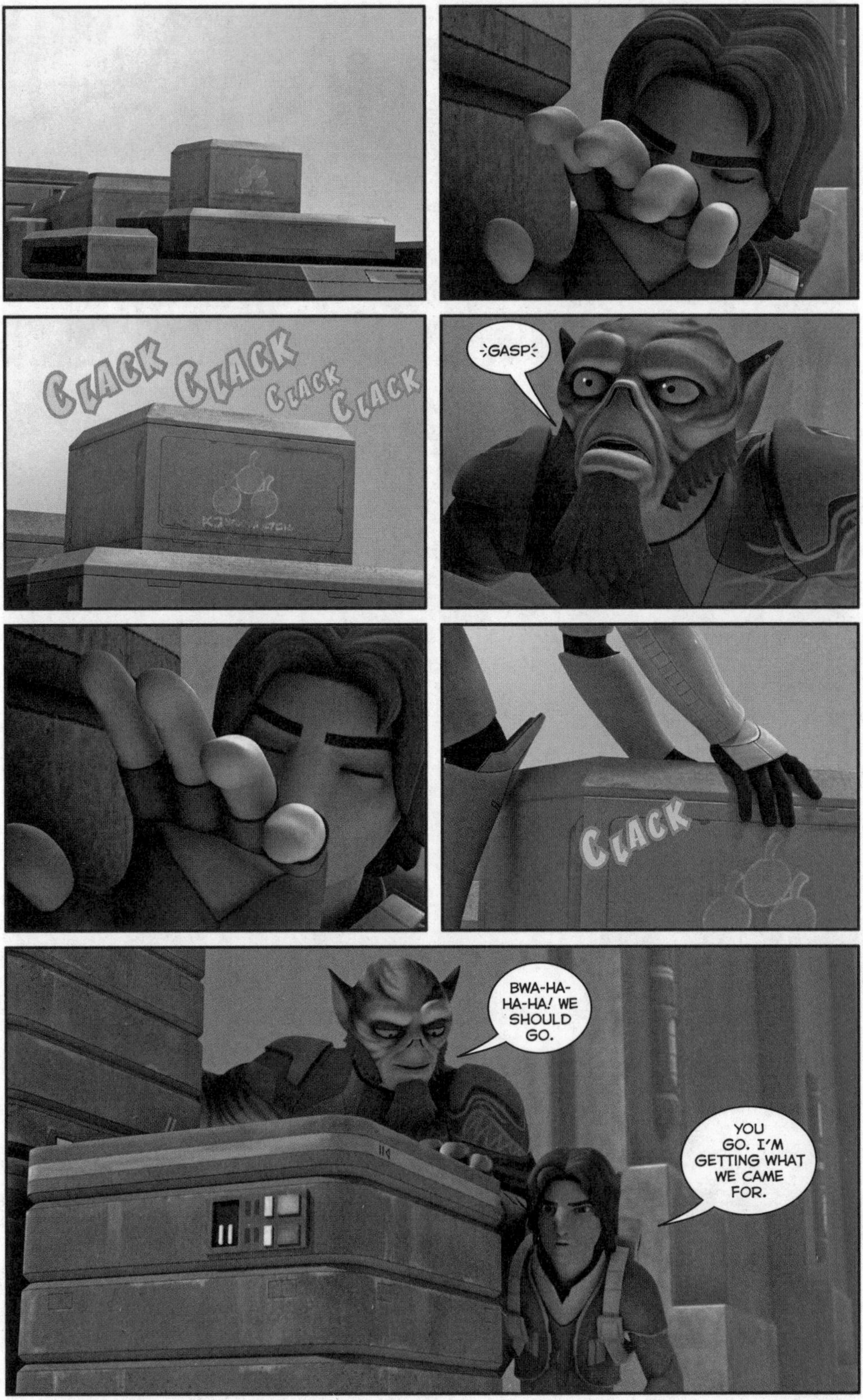
CLACK CLACK CLACK CLACK
GASP
CLACK
BWA-HA-HA-HA! WE SHOULD GO.
YOU GO. I'M GETTING WHAT WE CAME FOR.

WAIT,
KID...
ARGH.

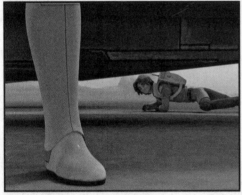

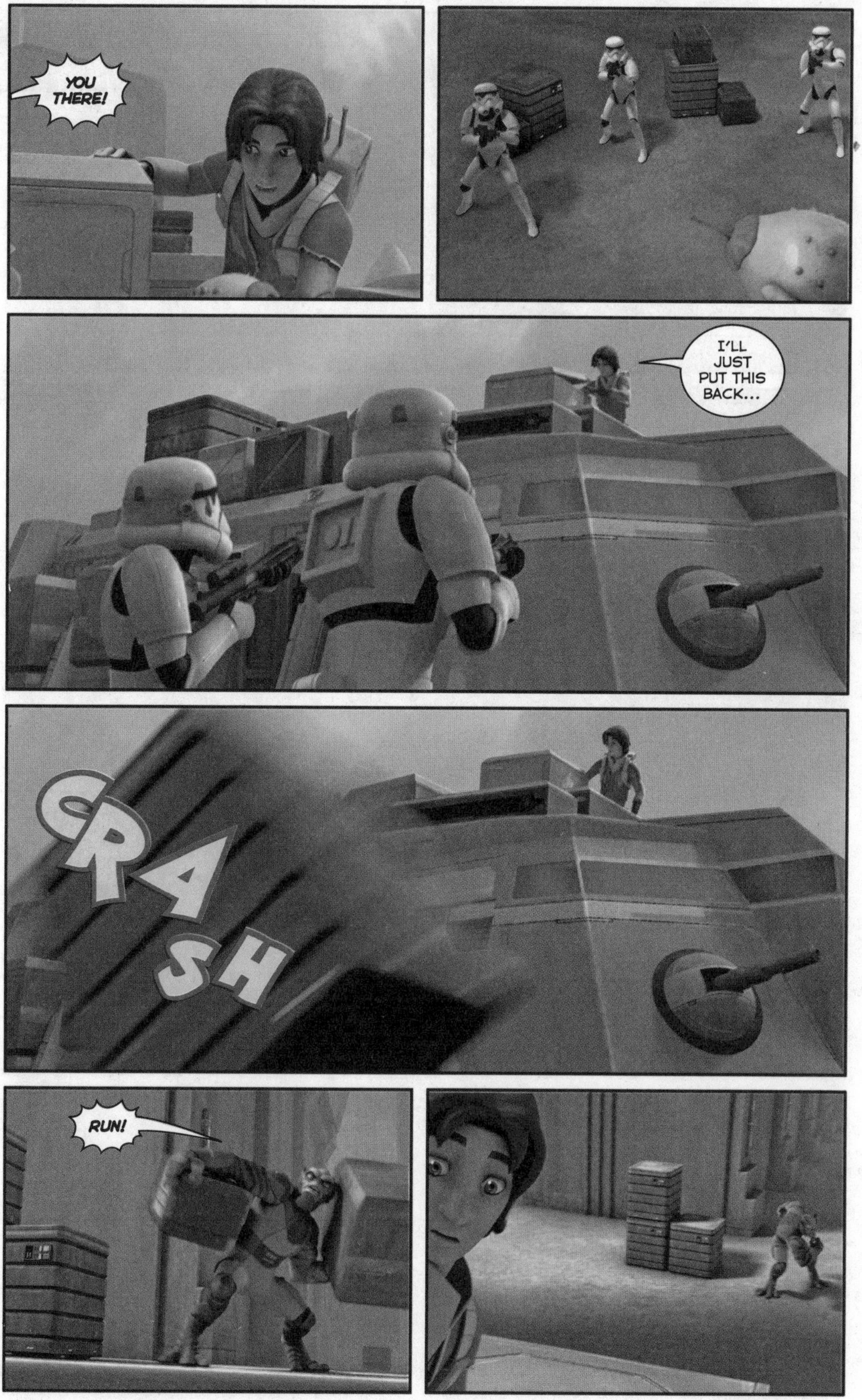
YOU THERE!
I'LL JUST PUT THIS BACK...
CRASH
RUN!

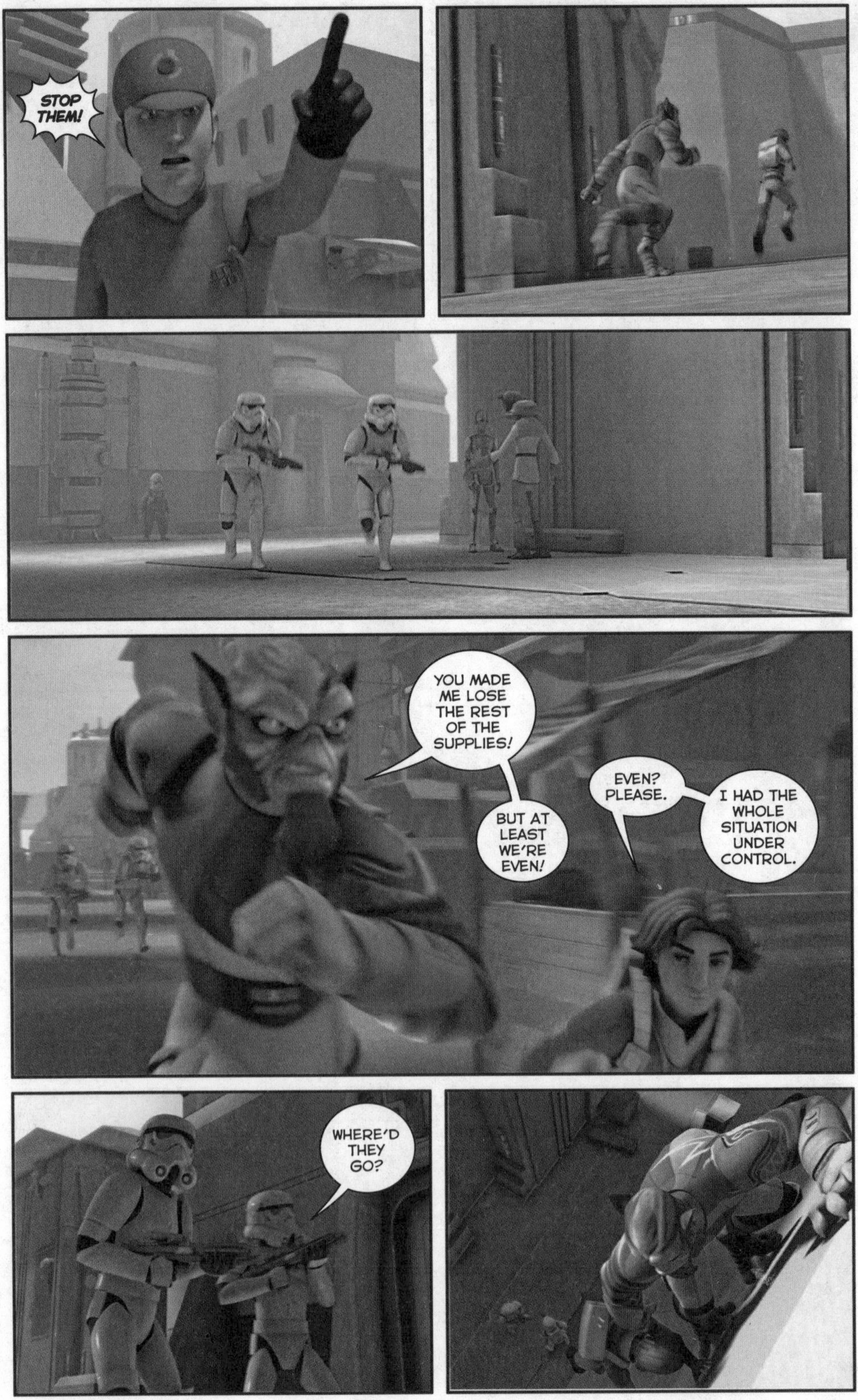
STOP THEM!
YOU MADE ME LOSE THE REST OF THE SUPPLIES!
BUT AT LEAST WE'RE EVEN!
EVEN? PLEASE.
I HAD THE WHOLE SITUATION UNDER CONTROL.
WHERE'D THEY GO?

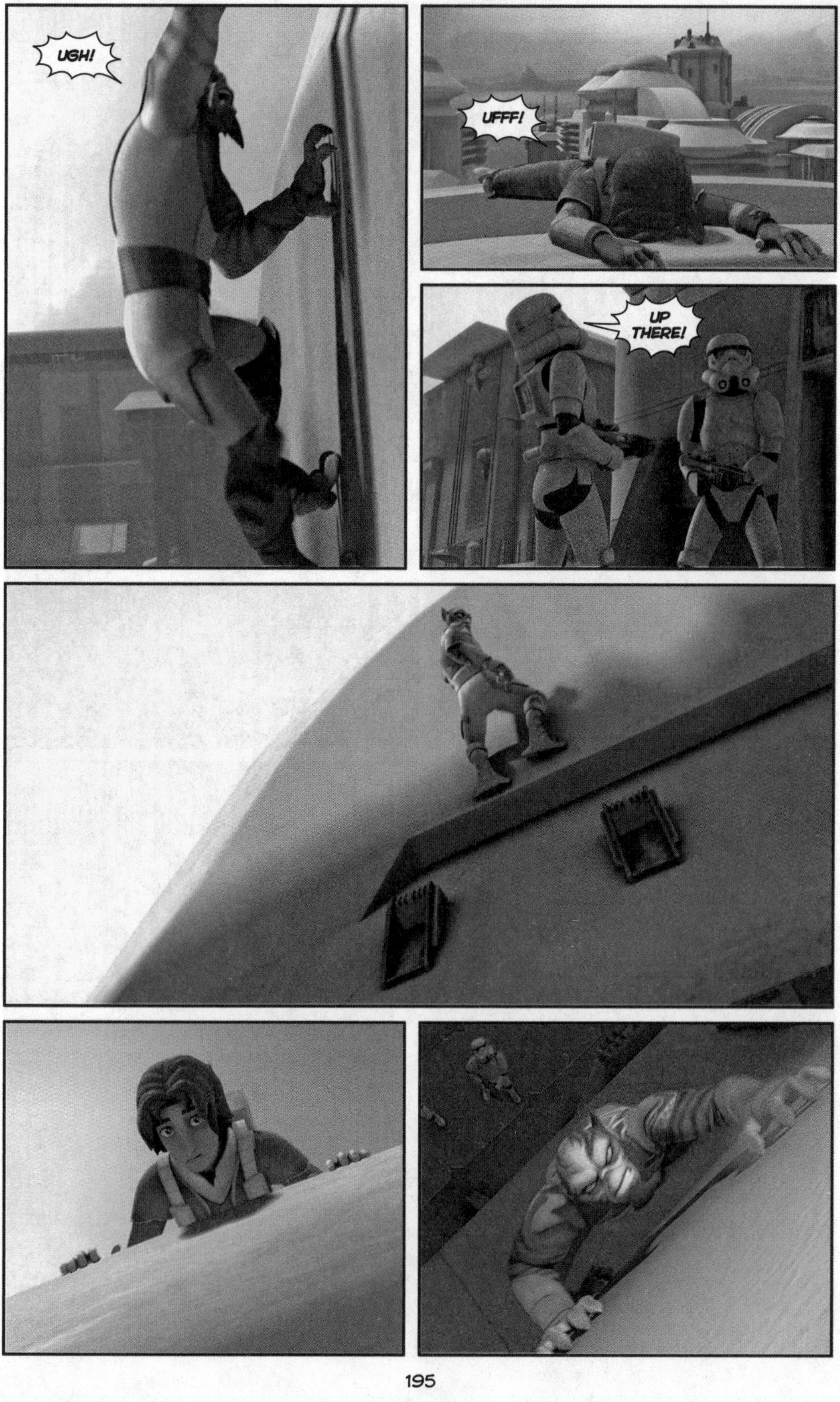
UGH!
UFFF!
UP THERE!

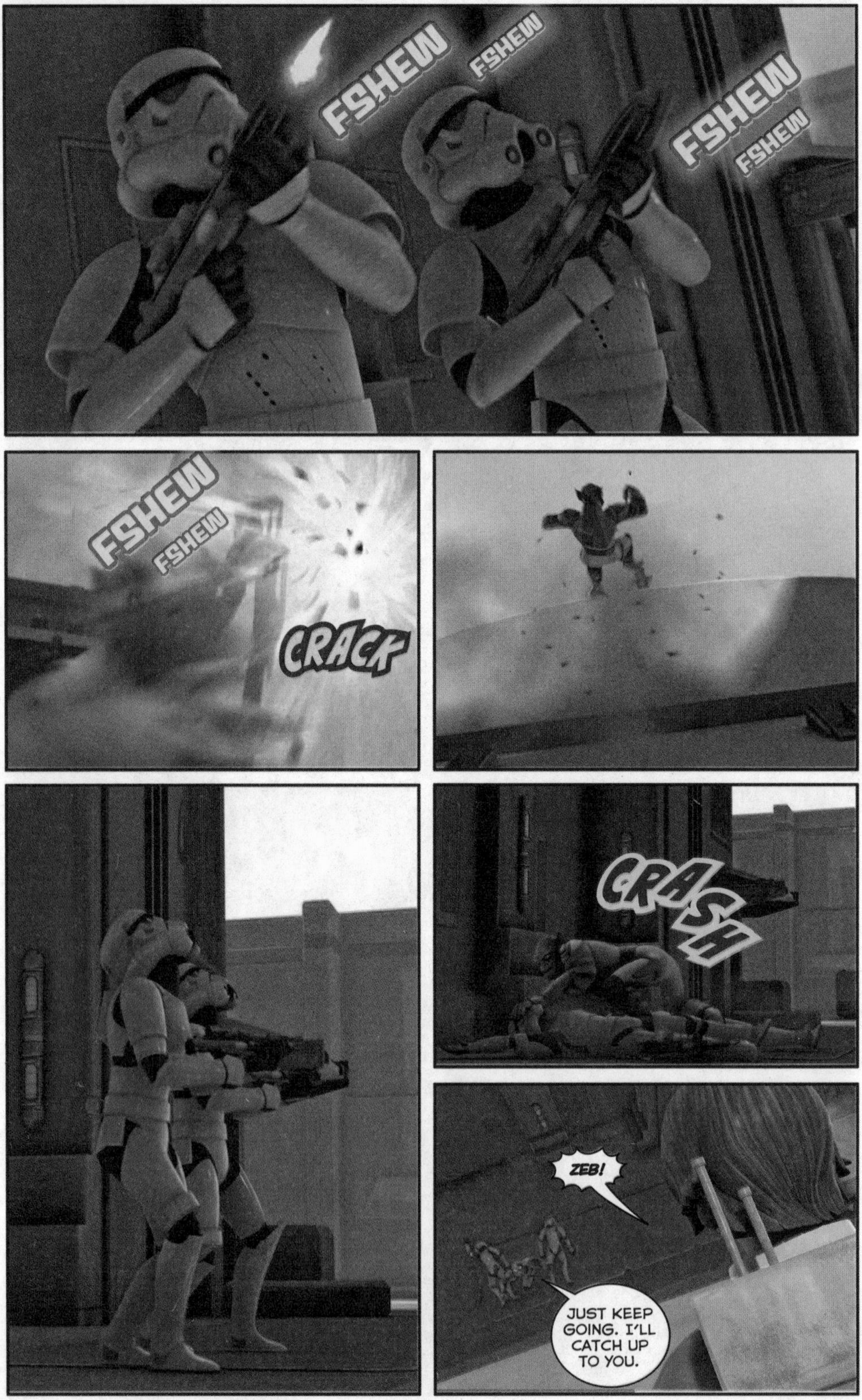
FSHEW
FSHEW
FSHEW
FSHEW
FSHEW
FSHEW
CRACK
CRASH
ZEB!
JUST KEEP GOING. I'LL CATCH UP TO YOU.

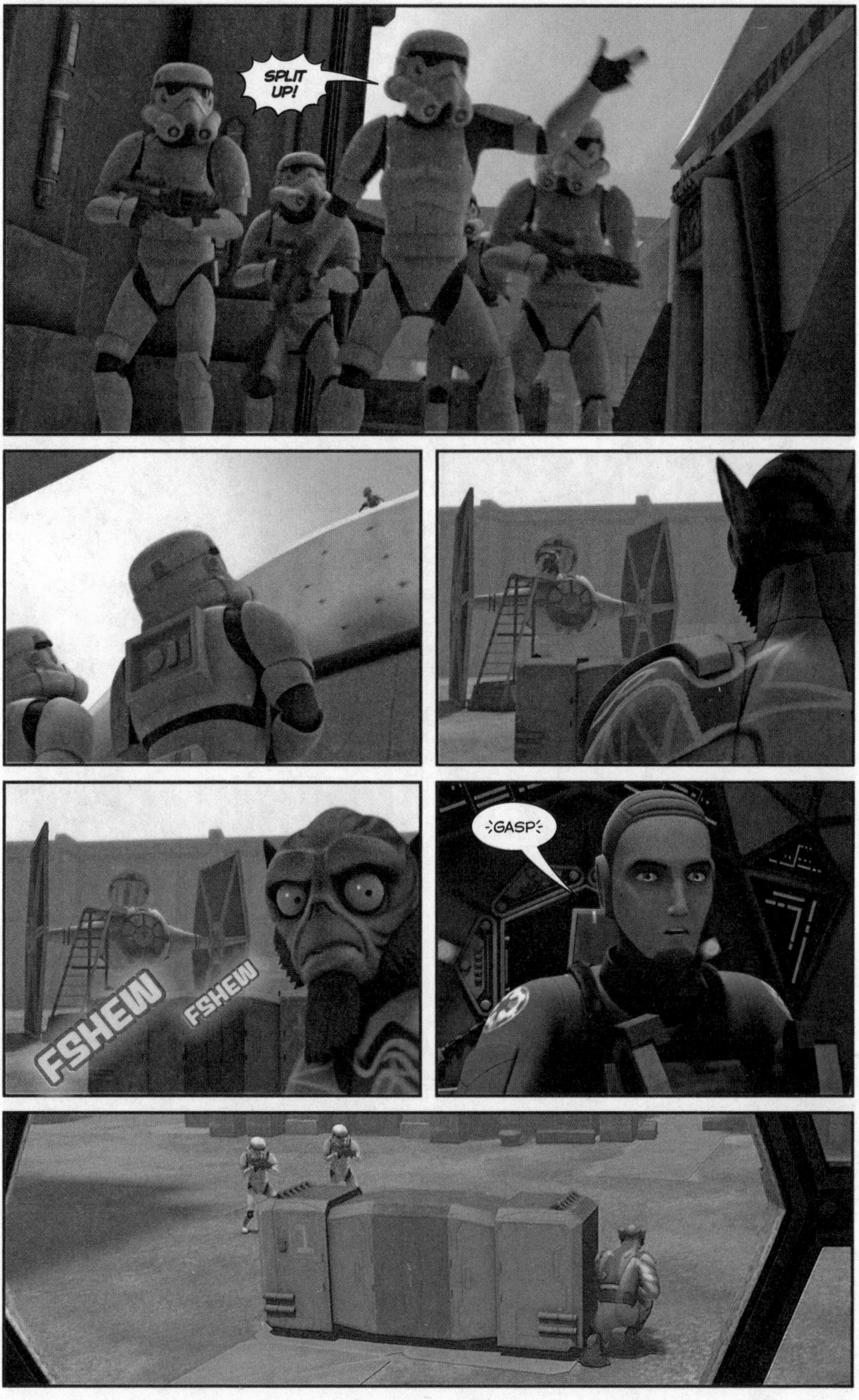
SPLIT UP!
FSHEW
FSHEW
GASP

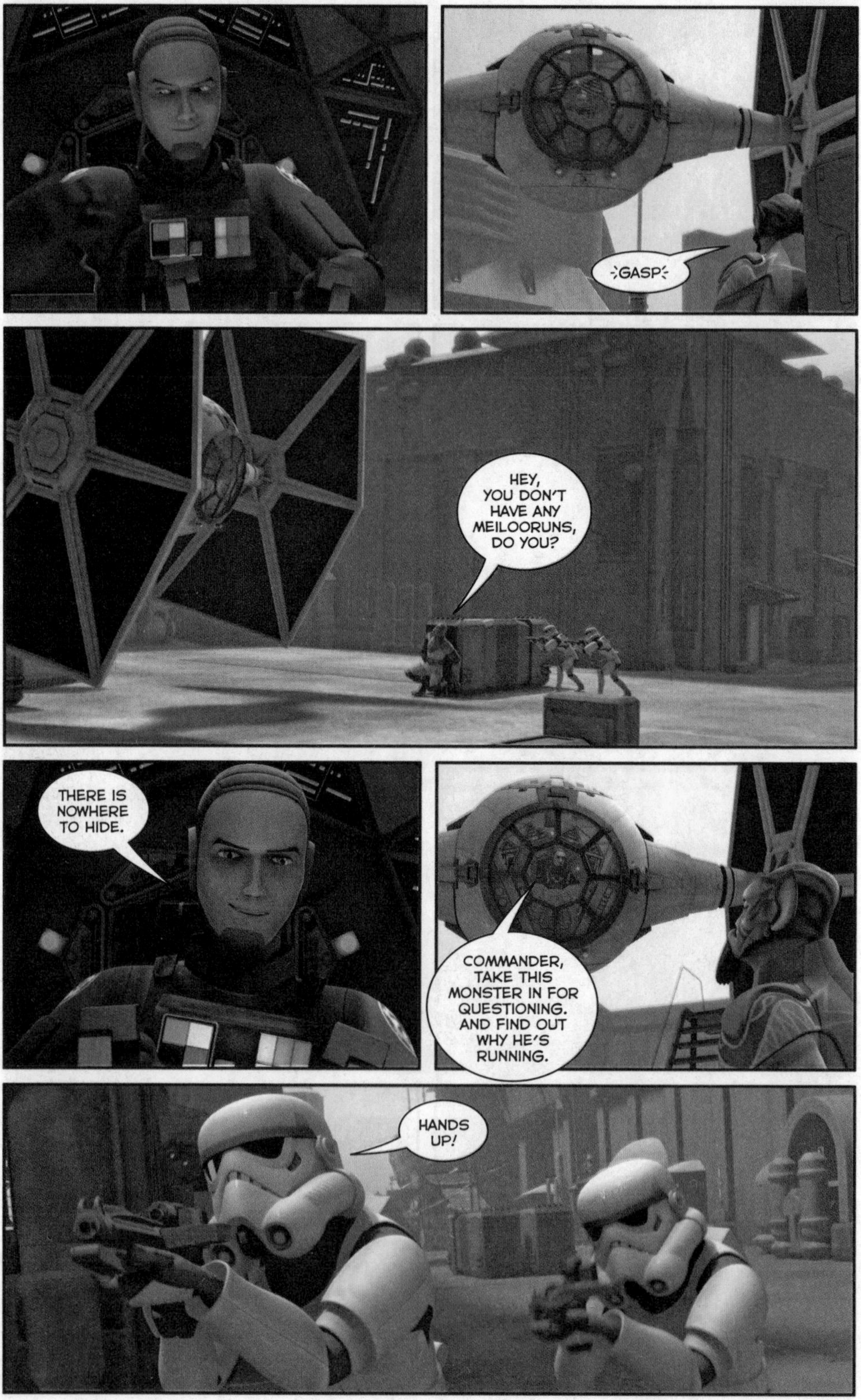
GASP
HEY, YOU DON'T HAVE ANY MEILOORUNS, DO YOU?
THERE IS NOWHERE TO HIDE.
COMMANDER, TAKE THIS MONSTER IN FOR QUESTIONING. AND FIND OUT WHY HE'S RUNNING.
HANDS UP!

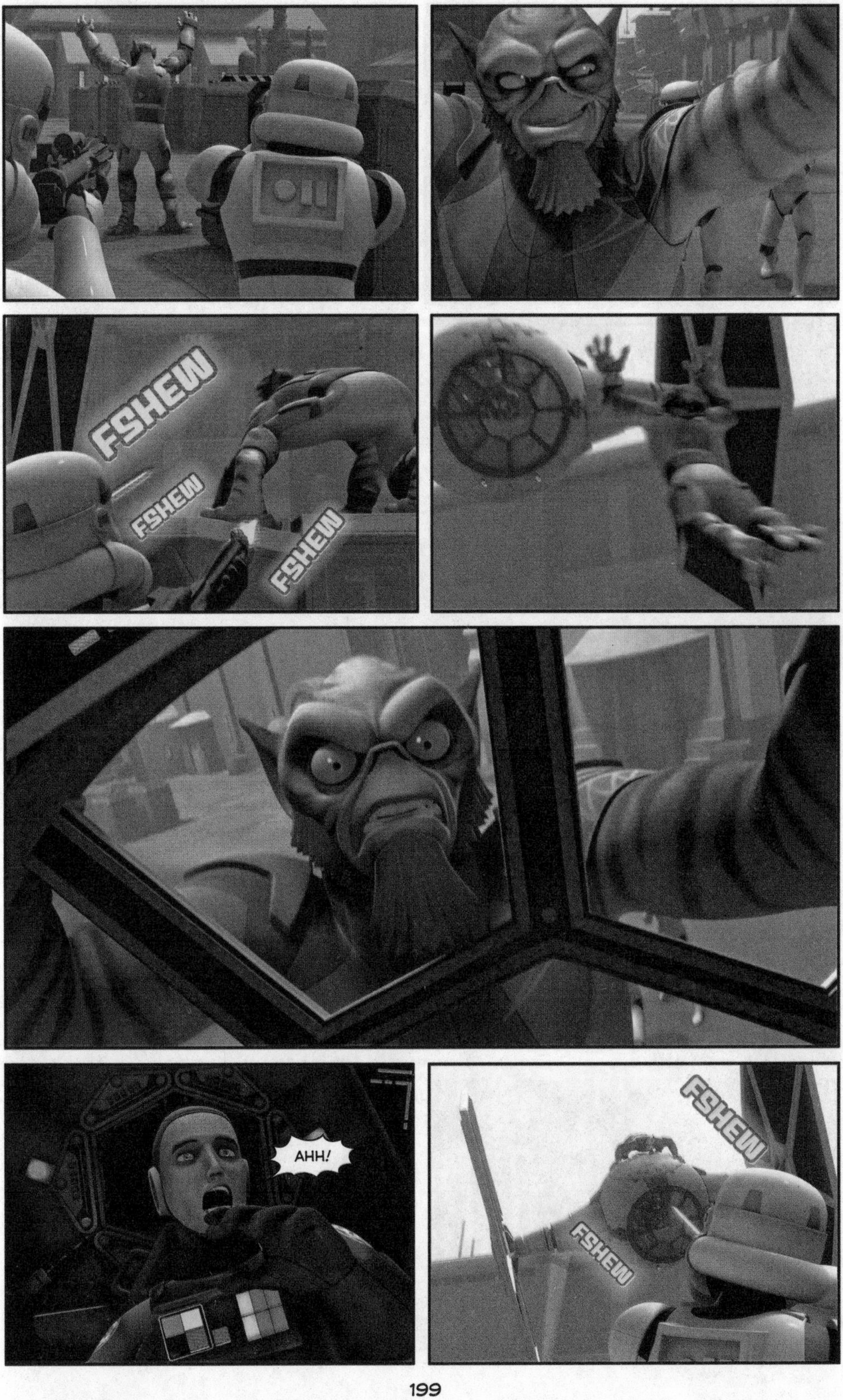
FSHEW
FSHEW
FSHEW
AHH!
FSHEW
FSHEW

NEVER ACTUALLY FLOWN ONE OF THESE BEFORE.

WHOA!

FSHEW

FSHEW

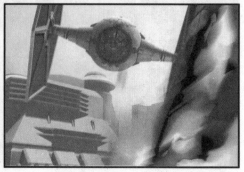

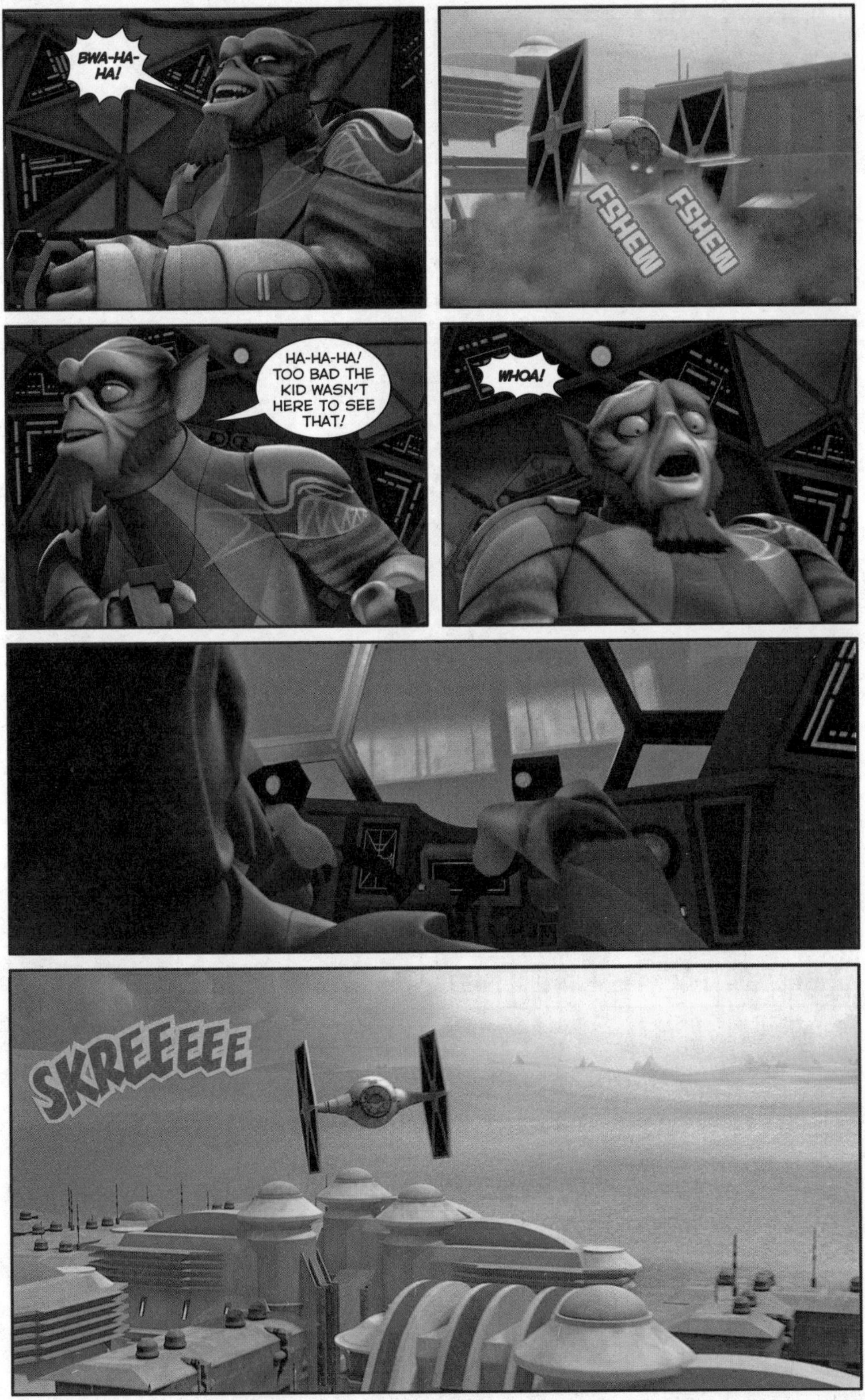
BWA-HA-HA!
FSHEW
FSHEW
HA-HA-HA! TOO BAD THE KID WASN'T HERE TO SEE THAT!
WHOA!
SKREEEEE

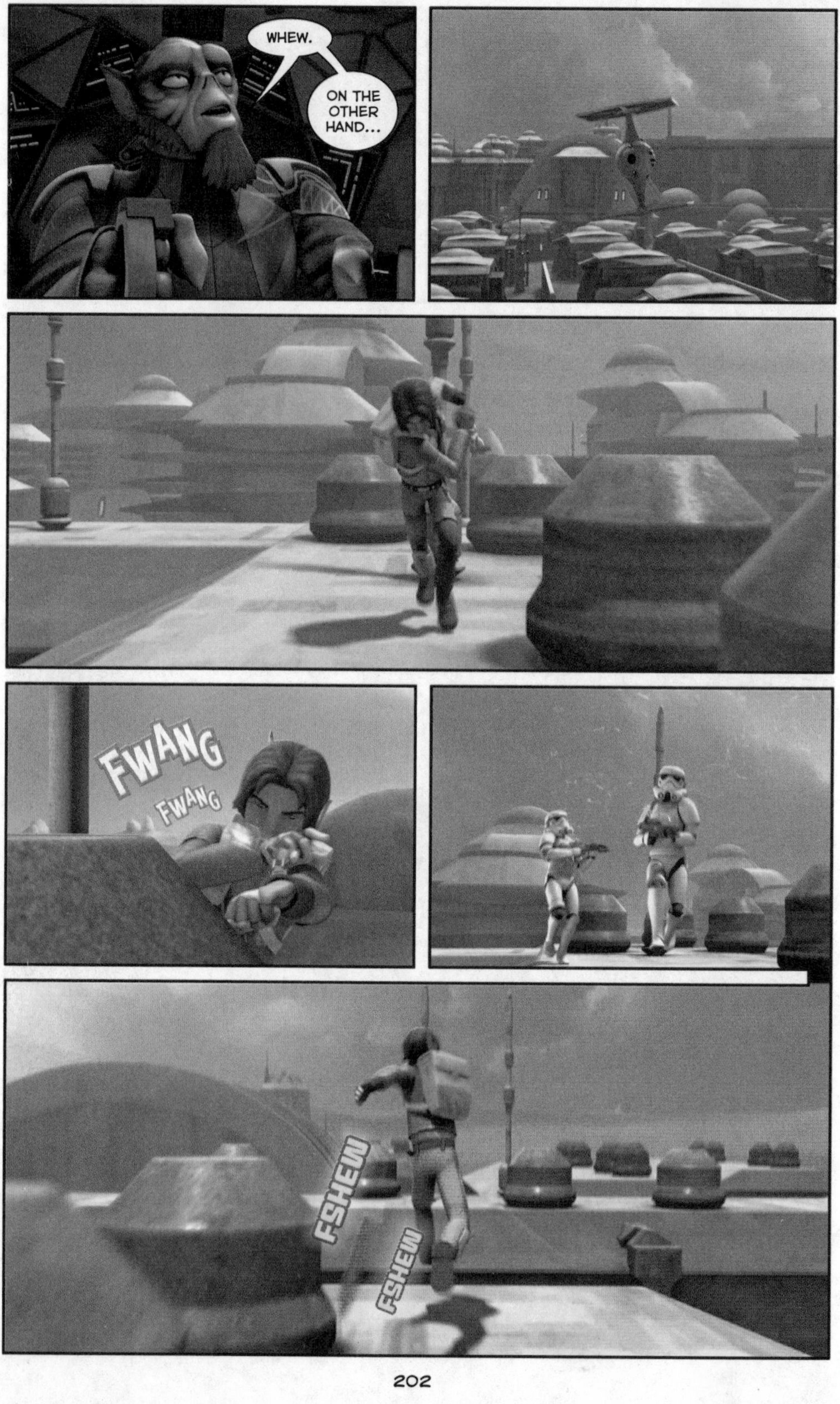
WHEW.
ON THE OTHER HAND...
FWANG
FWANG
FSHEW
FSHEW

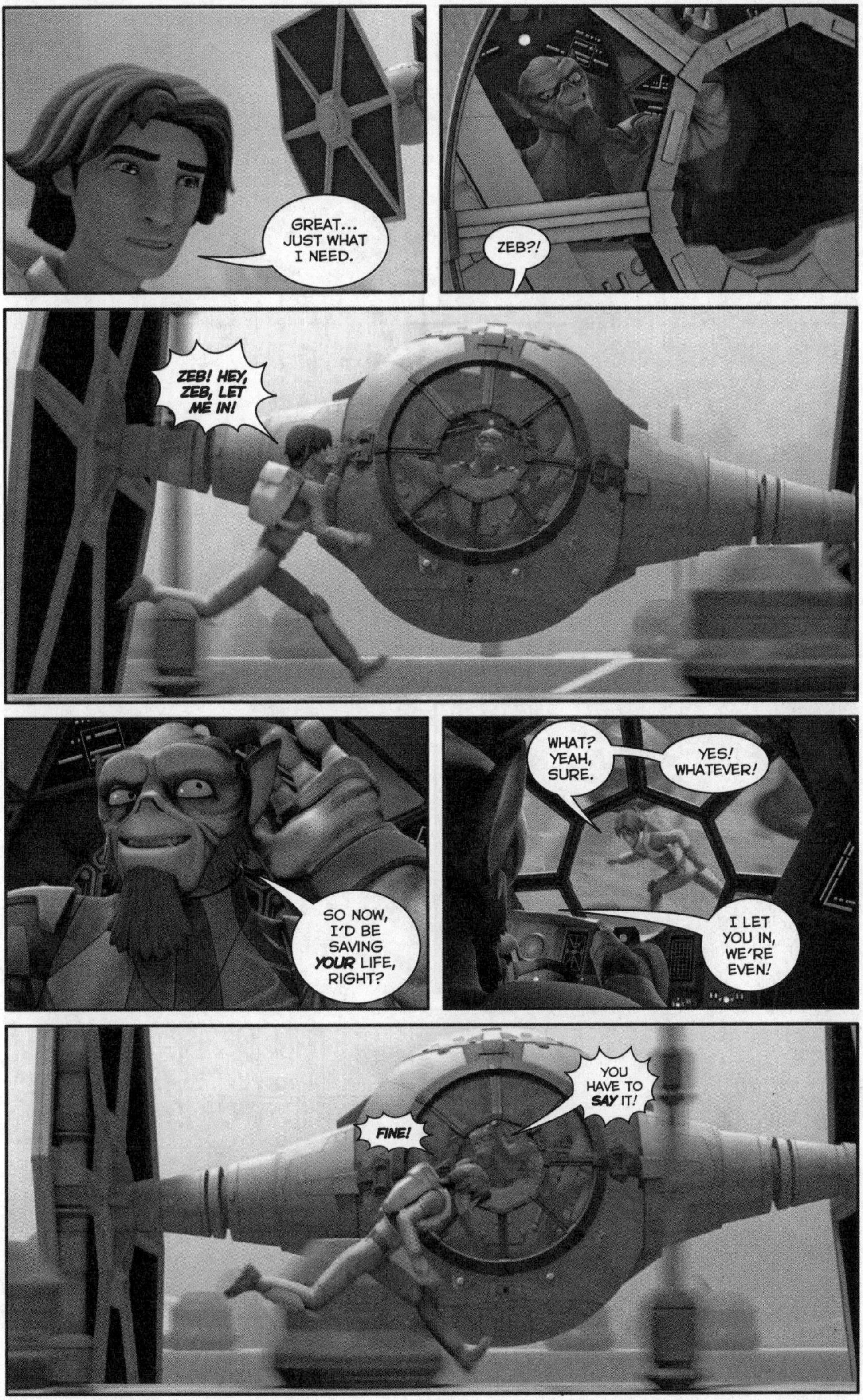
GREAT... JUST WHAT I NEED.
ZEB?!
ZEB! HEY, ZEB, LET ME IN!
SO NOW, I'D BE SAVING YOUR LIFE, RIGHT?
WHAT? YEAH, SURE.
YES! WHATEVER!
I LET YOU IN, WE'RE EVEN!
YOU HAVE TO SAY IT!
FINE!

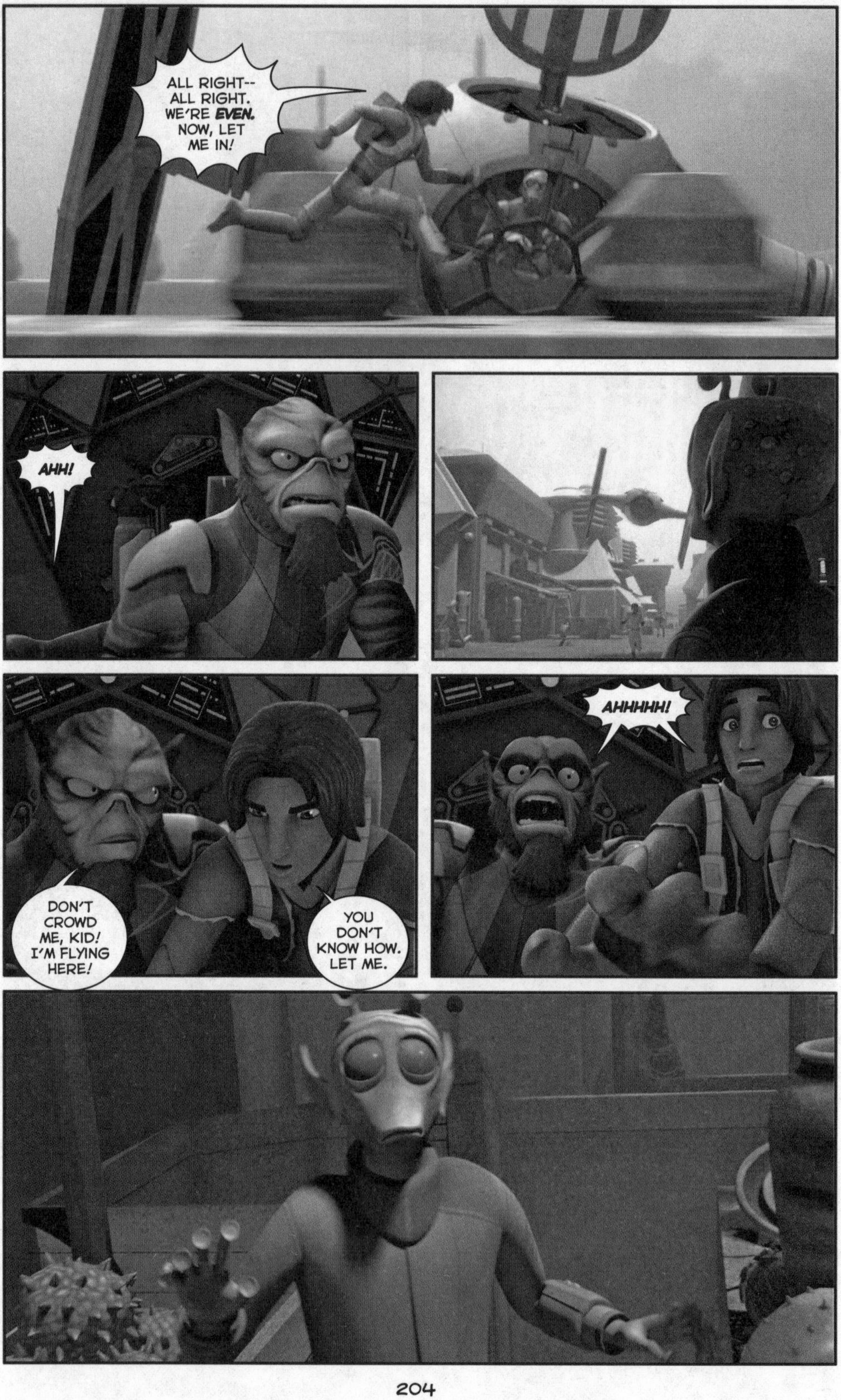
ALL RIGHT--
ALL RIGHT.
WE'RE **EVEN.**
NOW, LET
ME IN!
AHH!
DON'T CROWD ME, KID! I'M FLYING HERE!
YOU DON'T KNOW HOW. LET ME.
AHHHHH!

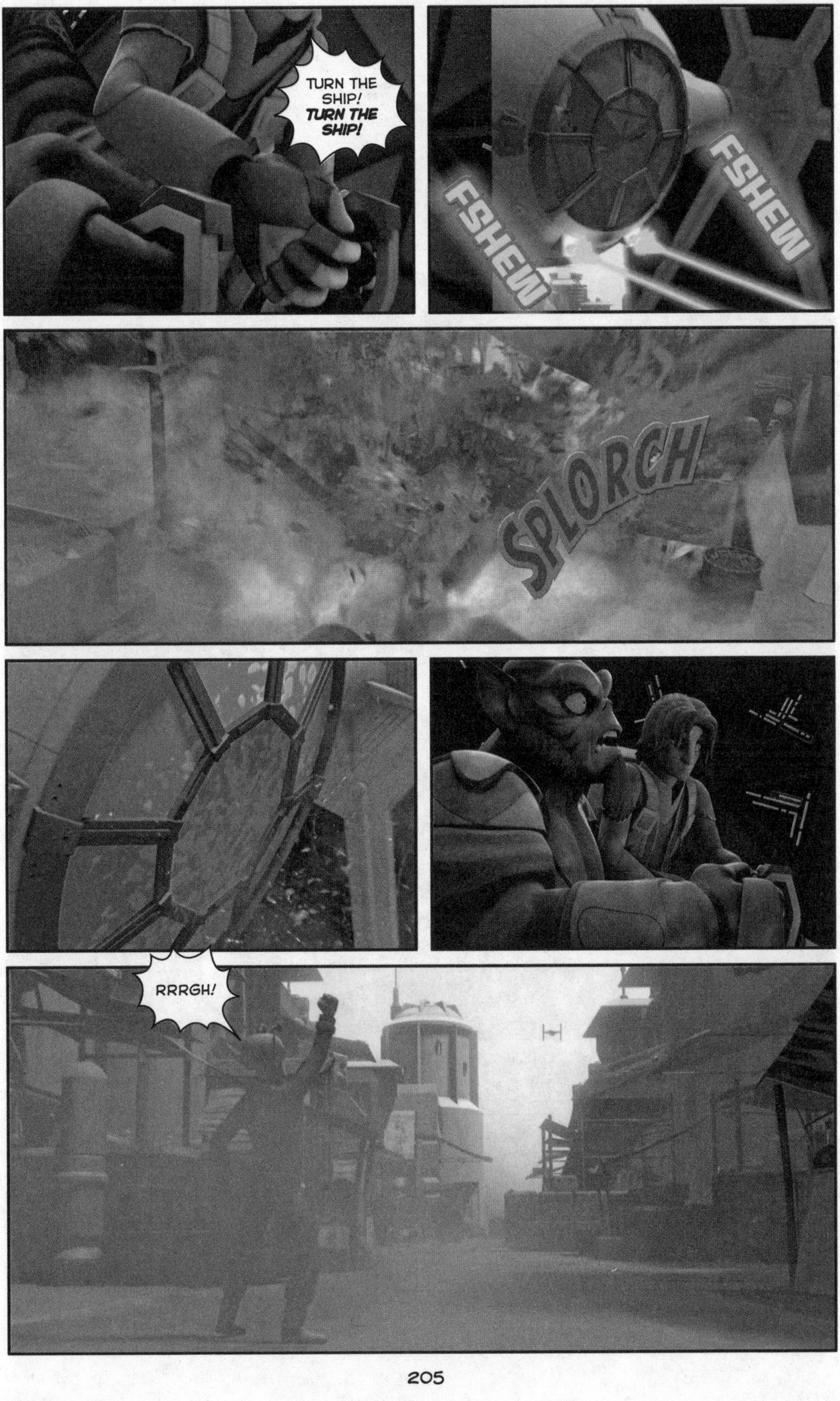
TURN THE SHIP! TURN THE SHIP!
FSHEW
FSHEW
SPLORCH
RRRGH!

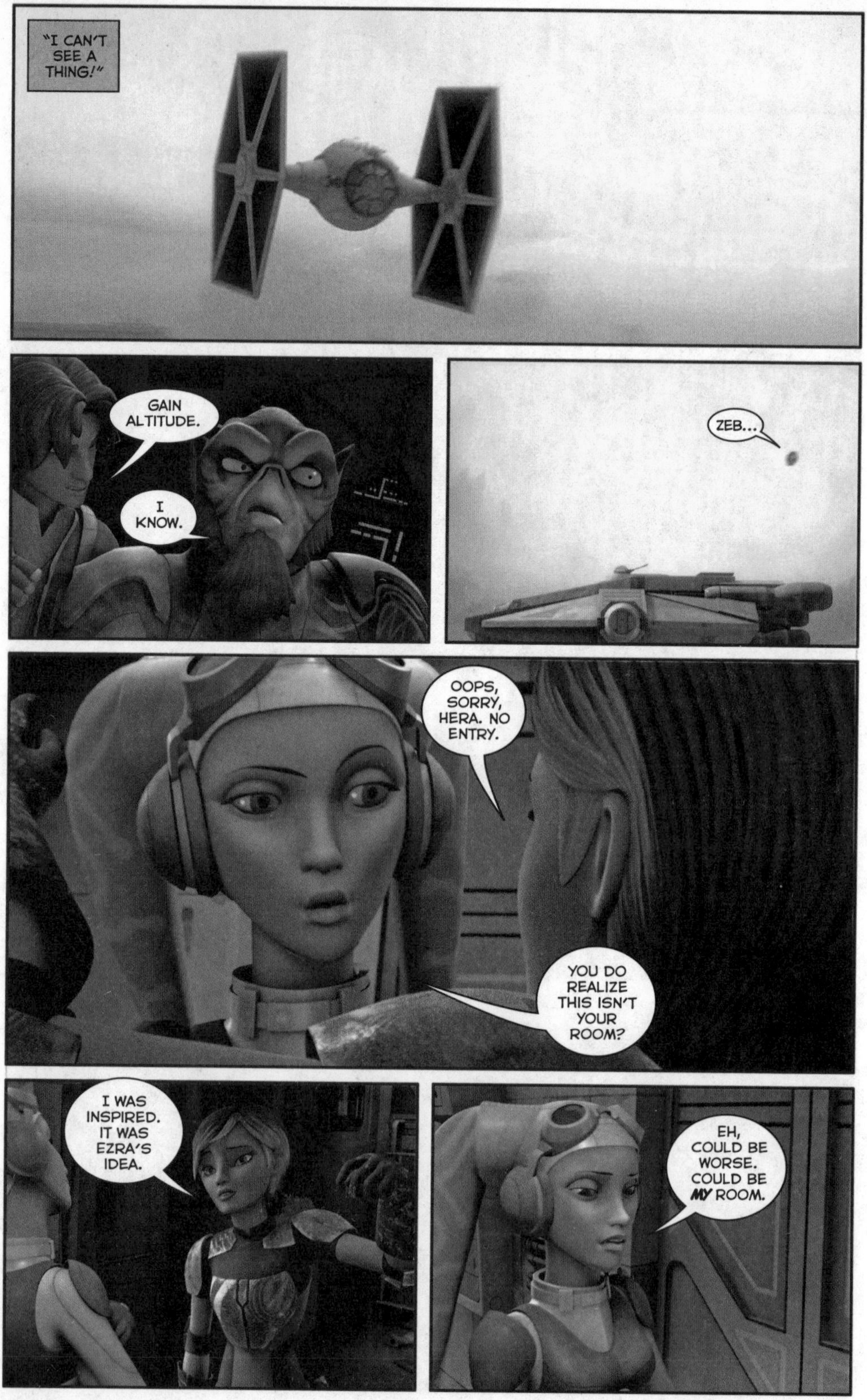
"I CAN'T SEE A THING!"
GAIN ALTITUDE.
I KNOW.
ZEB...
OOPS, SORRY, HERA. NO ENTRY.
YOU DO REALIZE THIS ISN'T YOUR ROOM?
I WAS INSPIRED. IT WAS EZRA'S IDEA.
EH, COULD BE WORSE. COULD BE *MY* ROOM.

I THINK WE'RE TOO LOW.

HOW CAN *YOU* TELL?

"WHY DON'T YOU GO CLEAN THE WINDOW?"

WE NEED TO TURN.

TURN!

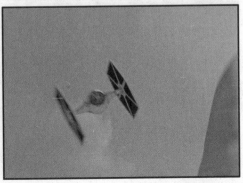

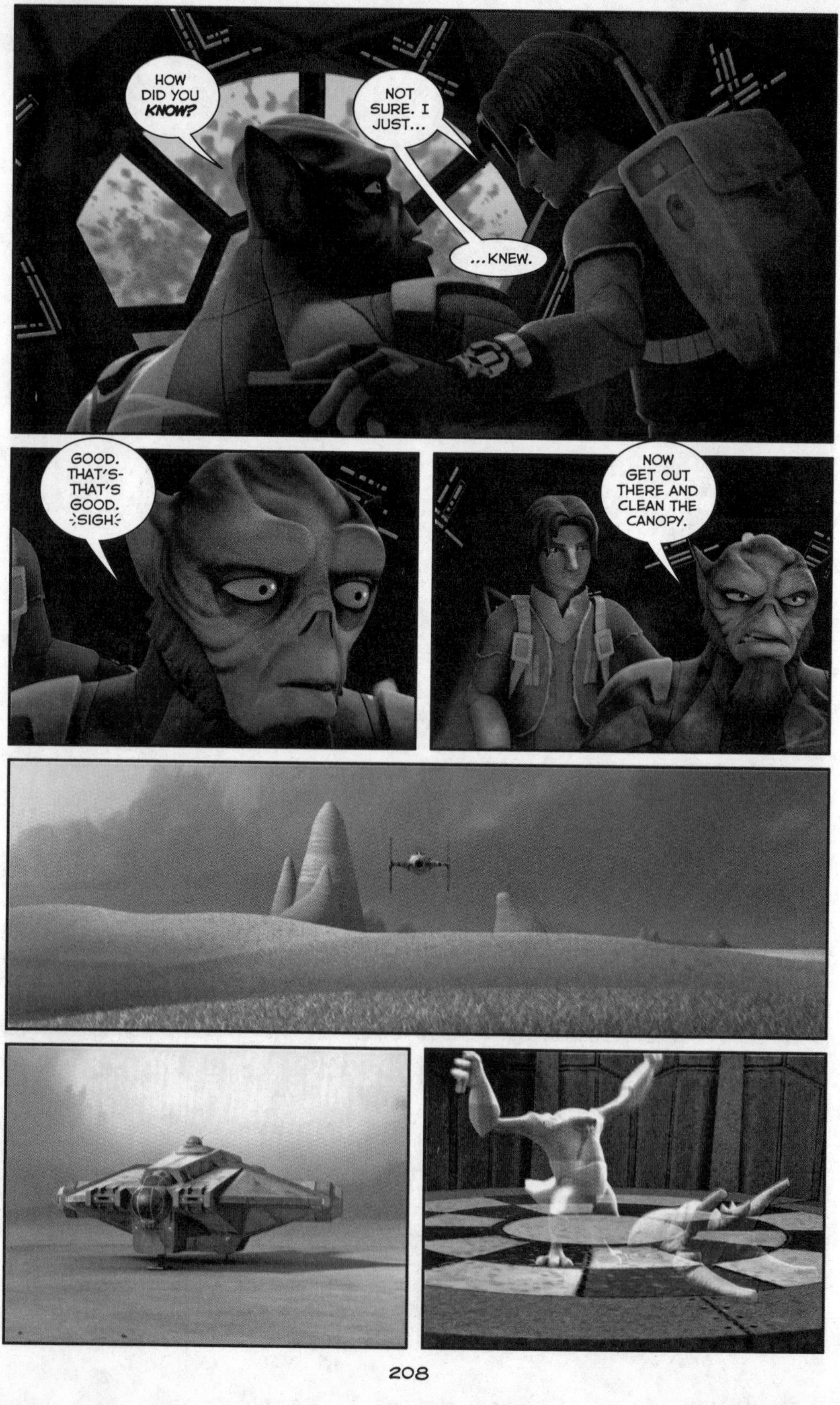
HOW DID YOU *KNOW?*
NOT SURE. I JUST...
...KNEW.
GOOD. THAT'S- THAT'S GOOD. -SIGH-
NOW GET OUT THERE AND CLEAN THE CANOPY.

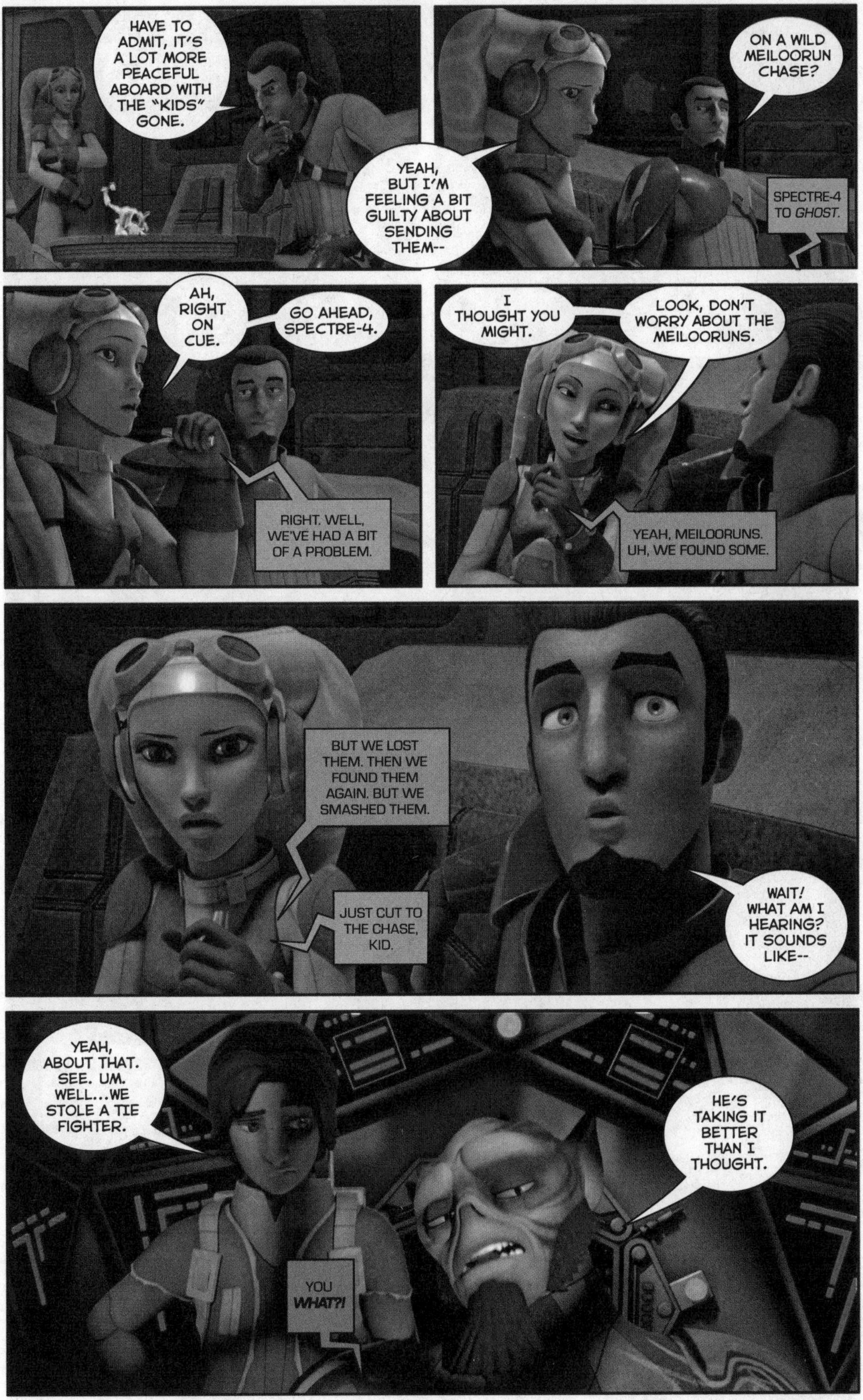
HAVE TO ADMIT, IT'S A LOT MORE PEACEFUL ABOARD WITH THE "KIDS" GONE.
YEAH, BUT I'M FEELING A BIT GUILTY ABOUT SENDING THEM--
ON A WILD MEILOORUN CHASE?
SPECTRE-4 TO *GHOST*.
AH, RIGHT ON CUE.
GO AHEAD, SPECTRE-4.
RIGHT. WELL, WE'VE HAD A BIT OF A PROBLEM.
LOOK, DON'T WORRY ABOUT THE MEILOORUNS.
I THOUGHT YOU MIGHT.
YEAH, MEILOORUNS. UH, WE FOUND SOME.
BUT WE LOST THEM. THEN WE FOUND THEM AGAIN. BUT WE SMASHED THEM.
JUST CUT TO THE CHASE, KID.
WAIT! WHAT AM I HEARING? IT SOUNDS LIKE--
YEAH, ABOUT THAT. SEE. UM. WELL...WE STOLE A TIE FIGHTER.
YOU ***WHAT?!***
HE'S TAKING IT BETTER THAN I THOUGHT.

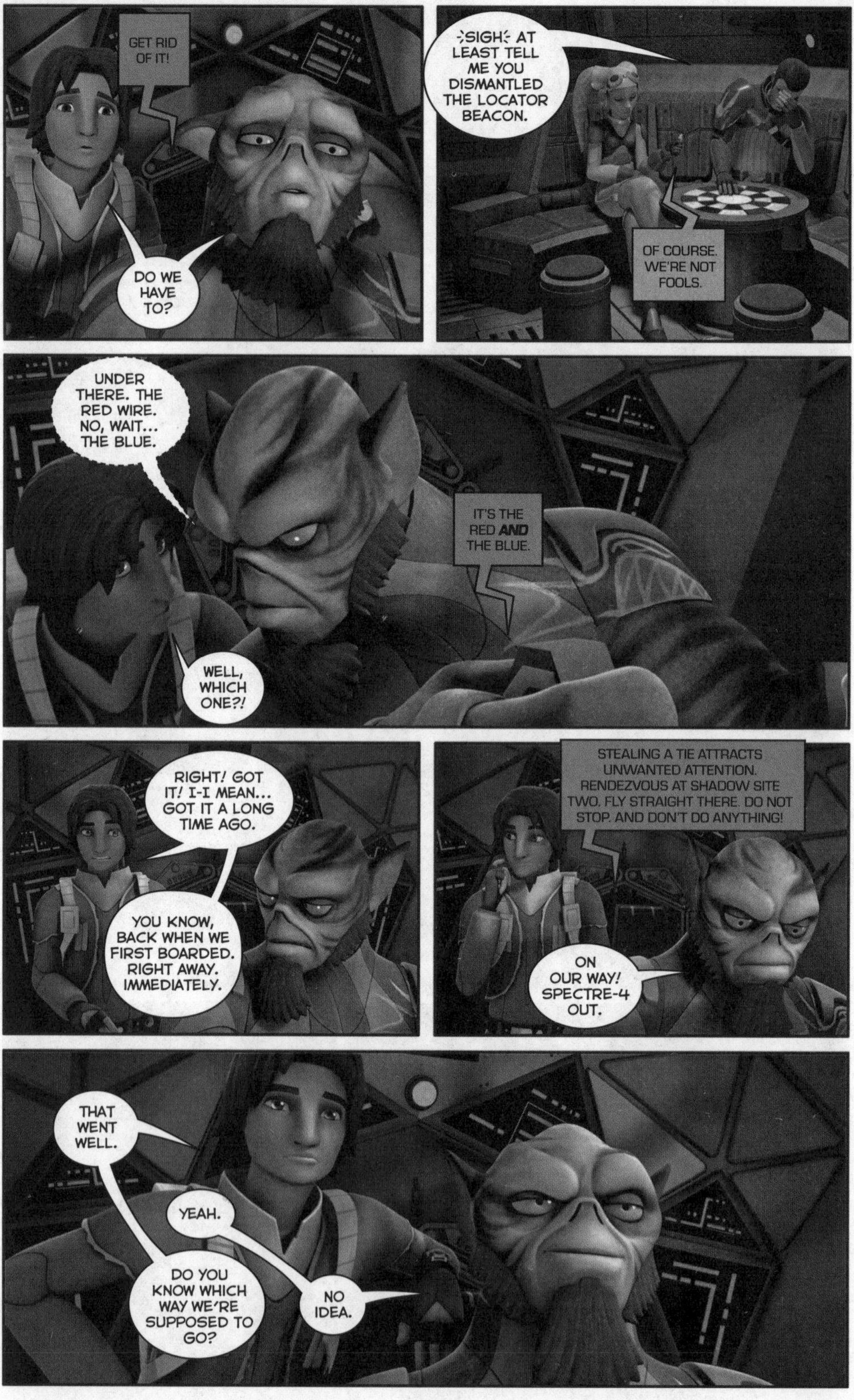
GET RID OF IT!
DO WE HAVE TO?
⊰SIGH⊱ AT LEAST TELL ME YOU DISMANTLED THE LOCATOR BEACON.
OF COURSE. WE'RE NOT FOOLS.
UNDER THERE. THE RED WIRE. NO, WAIT... THE BLUE.
WELL, WHICH ONE?!
IT'S THE RED **AND** THE BLUE.
RIGHT! GOT IT! I-I MEAN... GOT IT A LONG TIME AGO.
YOU KNOW, BACK WHEN WE FIRST BOARDED. RIGHT AWAY. IMMEDIATELY.
STEALING A TIE ATTRACTS UNWANTED ATTENTION. RENDEZVOUS AT SHADOW SITE TWO. FLY STRAIGHT THERE. DO NOT STOP. AND DON'T DO ANYTHING!
ON OUR WAY! SPECTRE-4 OUT.
THAT WENT WELL.
YEAH.
DO YOU KNOW WHICH WAY WE'RE SUPPOSED TO GO?
NO IDEA.

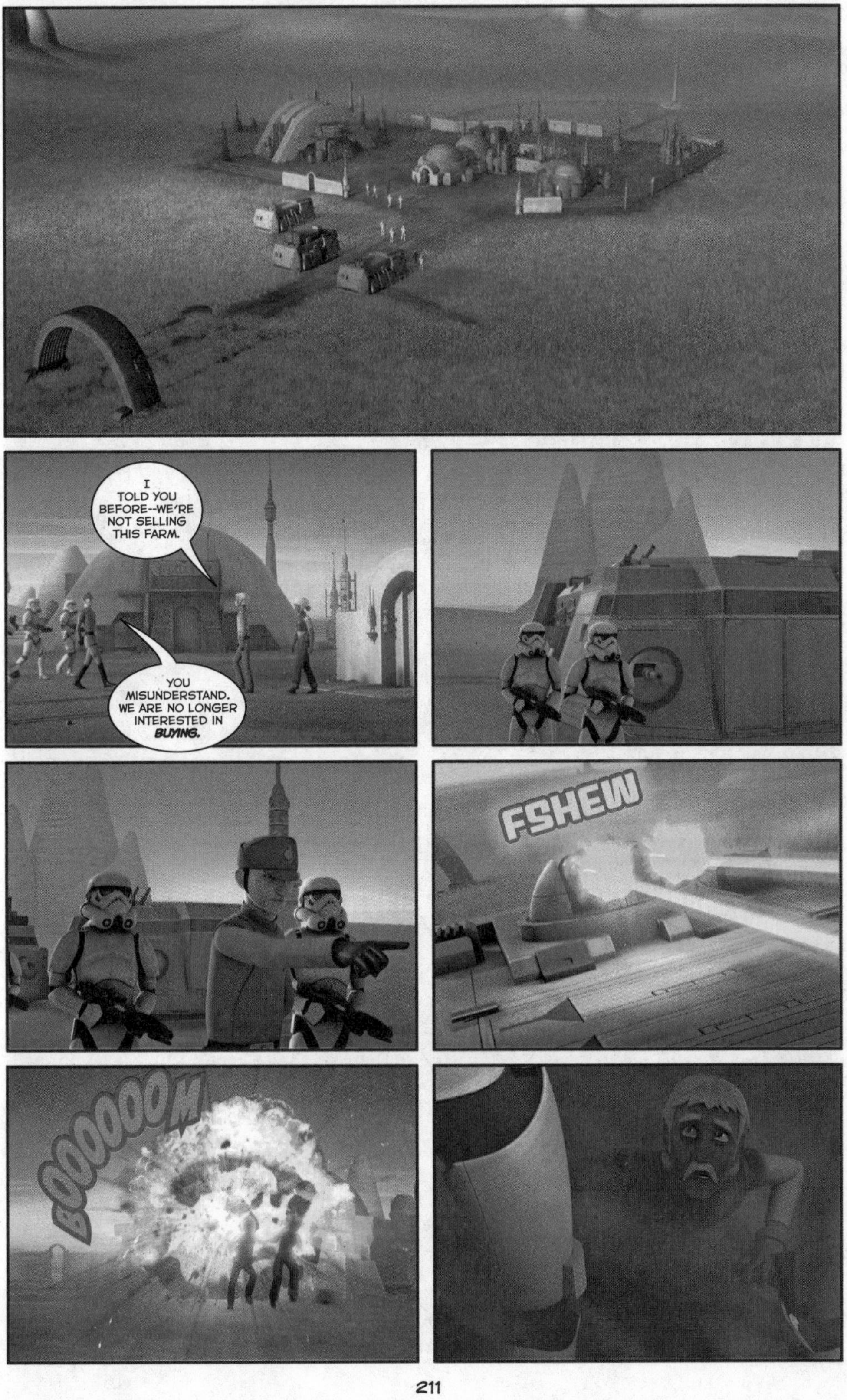
I TOLD YOU BEFORE--WE'RE NOT SELLING THIS FARM.
YOU MISUNDERSTAND. WE ARE NO LONGER INTERESTED IN *BUYING.*
FSHEW
BOOOOOOM

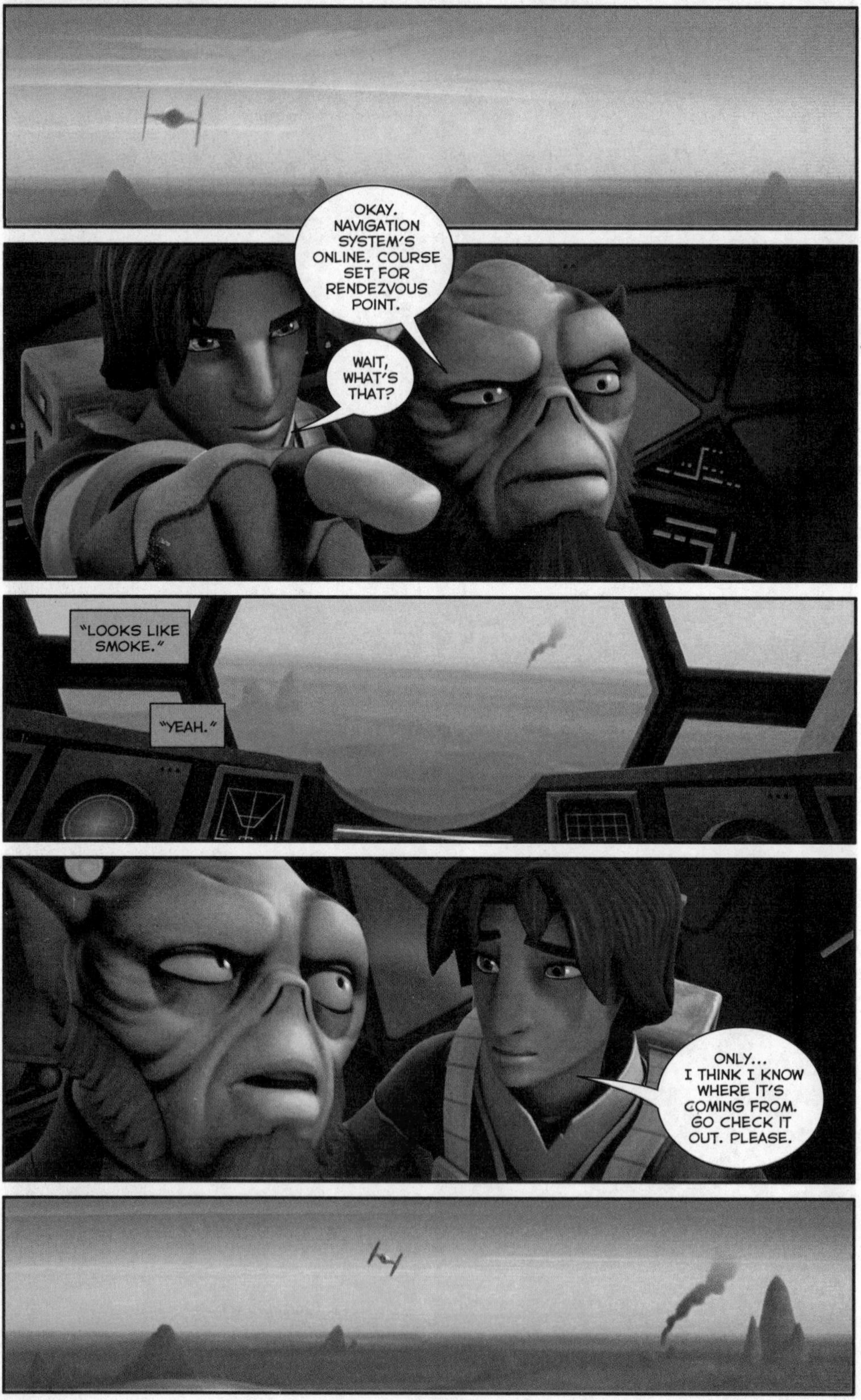

OKAY. NAVIGATION SYSTEM'S ONLINE. COURSE SET FOR RENDEZVOUS POINT.
WAIT, WHAT'S THAT?
"LOOKS LIKE SMOKE."
"YEAH."
ONLY... I THINK I KNOW WHERE IT'S COMING FROM. GO CHECK IT OUT. PLEASE.

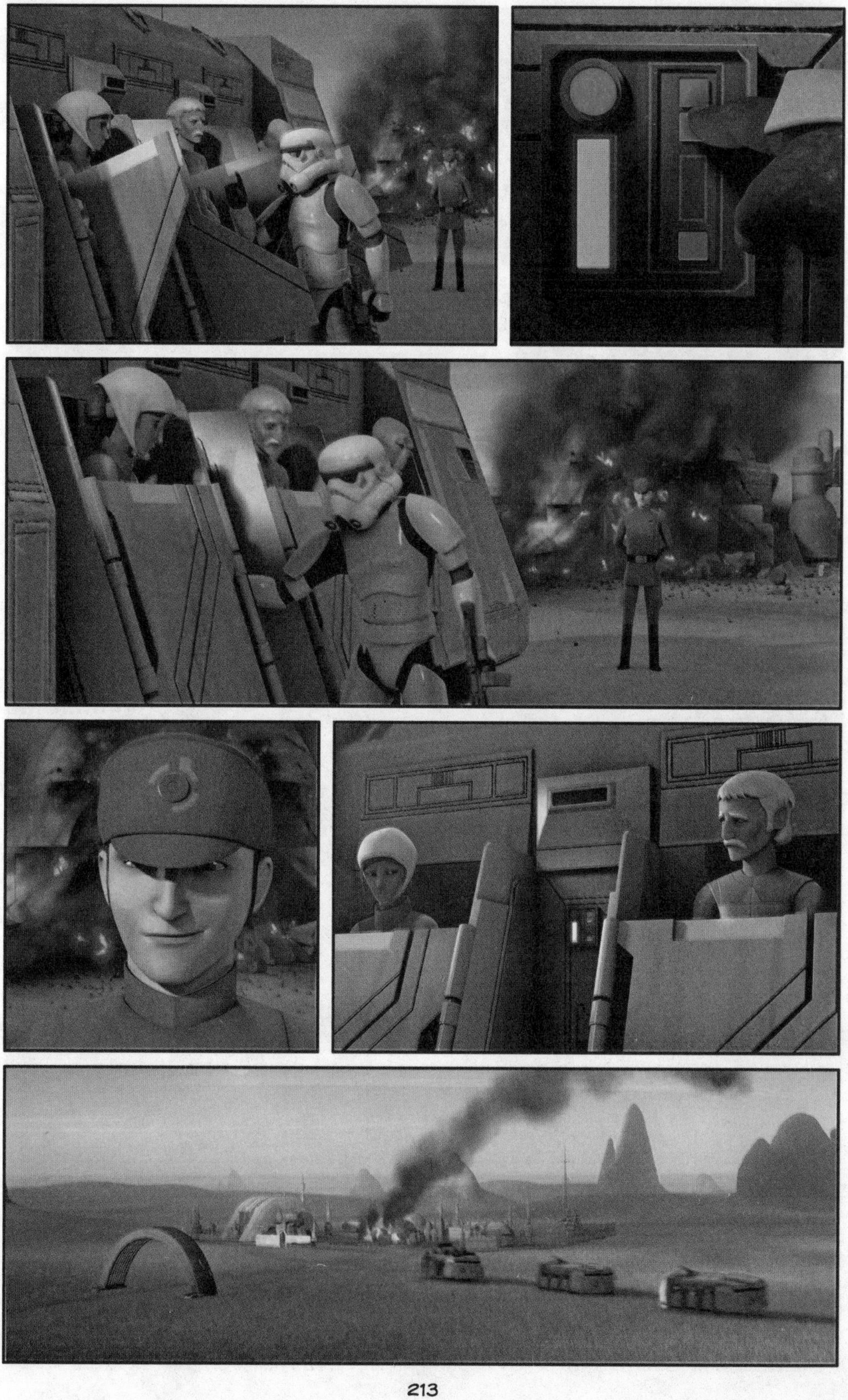

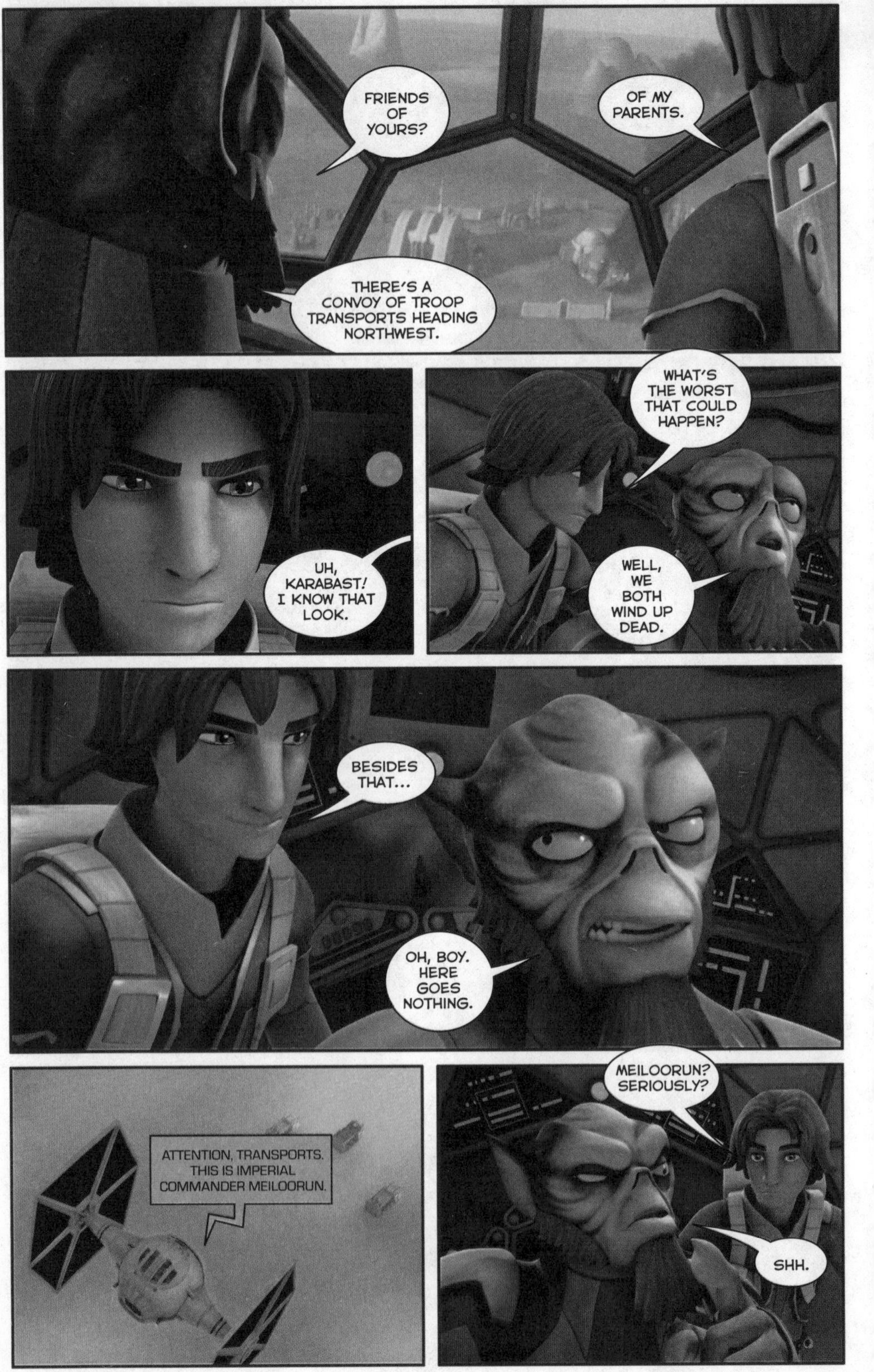
FRIENDS OF YOURS?
OF MY PARENTS.
THERE'S A CONVOY OF TROOP TRANSPORTS HEADING NORTHWEST.
UH, KARABAST! I KNOW THAT LOOK.
WHAT'S THE WORST THAT COULD HAPPEN?
WELL, WE BOTH WIND UP DEAD.
BESIDES THAT...
OH, BOY. HERE GOES NOTHING.
ATTENTION, TRANSPORTS. THIS IS IMPERIAL COMMANDER MEILOORUN.
MEILOORUN? SERIOUSLY?
SHH.

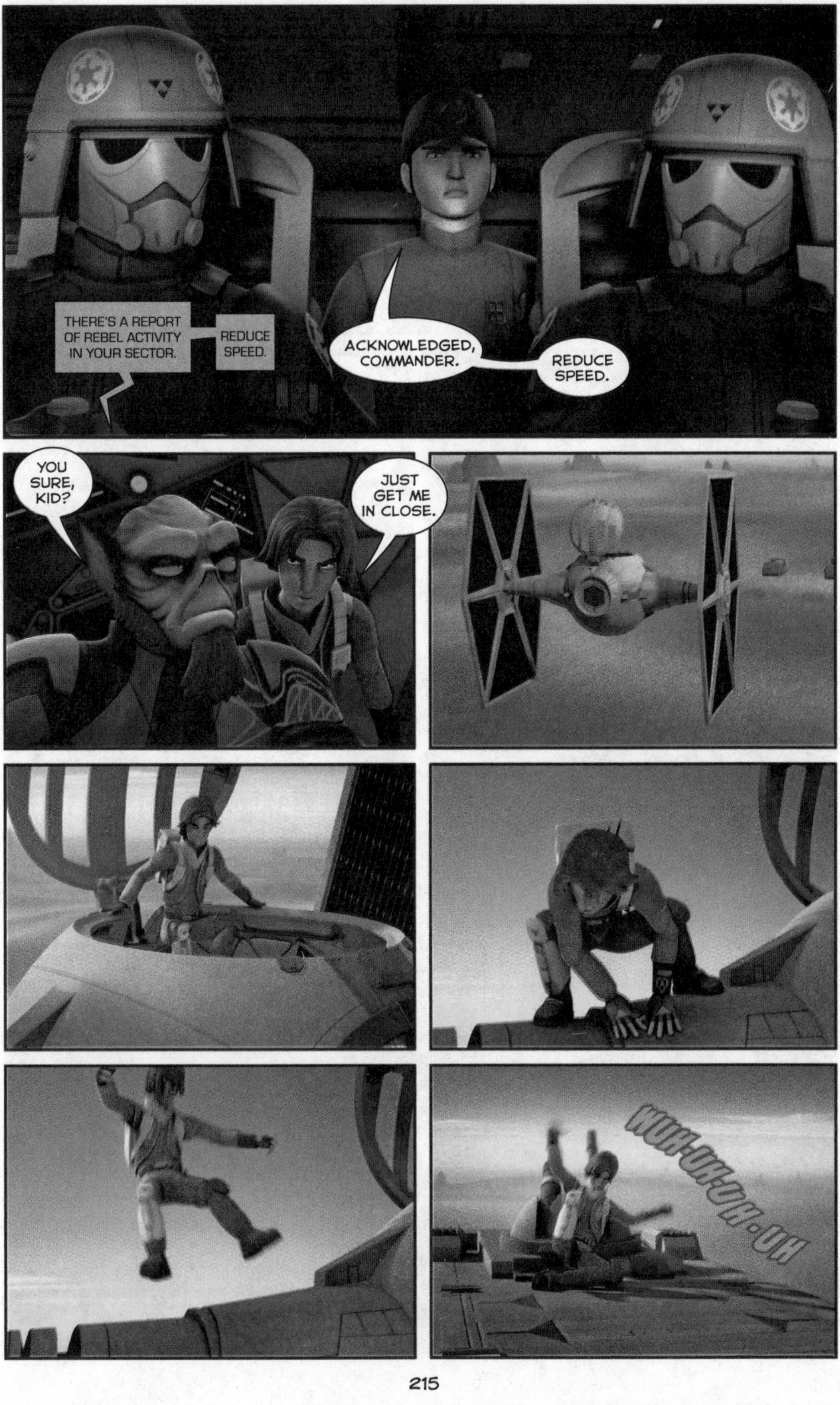
THERE'S A REPORT OF REBEL ACTIVITY IN YOUR SECTOR.
REDUCE SPEED.
ACKNOWLEDGED, COMMANDER.
REDUCE SPEED.
YOU SURE, KID?
JUST GET ME IN CLOSE.
WUH-UH-UH-UH - UH

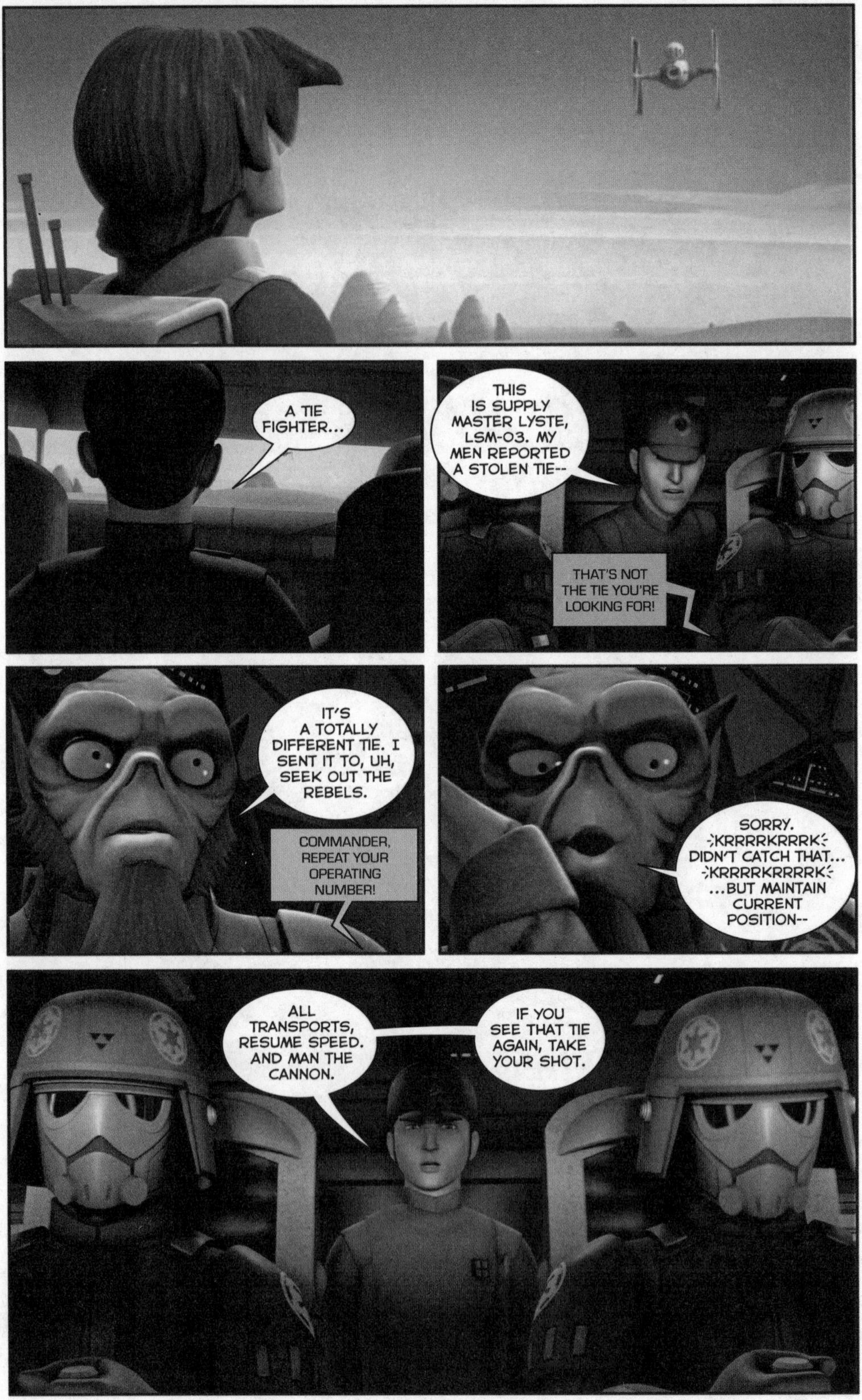
A TIE FIGHTER...
THIS IS SUPPLY MASTER LYSTE, LSM-03. MY MEN REPORTED A STOLEN TIE--
THAT'S NOT THE TIE YOU'RE LOOKING FOR!
IT'S A TOTALLY DIFFERENT TIE. I SENT IT TO, UH, SEEK OUT THE REBELS.
COMMANDER, REPEAT YOUR OPERATING NUMBER!
SORRY. KRRRRKRRRK DIDN'T CATCH THAT... KRRRRKRRRRK ...BUT MAINTAIN CURRENT POSITION--
ALL TRANSPORTS, RESUME SPEED. AND MAN THE CANNON.
IF YOU SEE THAT TIE AGAIN, TAKE YOUR SHOT.

DON'T THINK HE'S TAKING COMMANDER MEILOORUN'S ORDERS ANYMORE...

FSHEW

MR. SUMAR!

EZRA?!

HOLD ON, I'LL HAVE YOU OUT SOON!

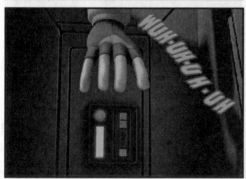

WUH-UH-UH-UH

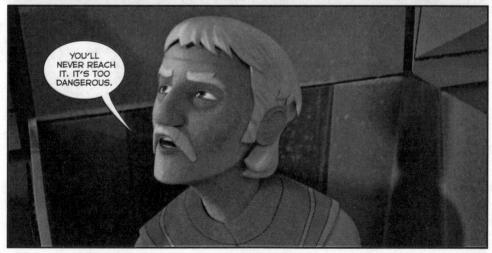

YOU'LL NEVER REACH IT. IT'S TOO DANGEROUS.

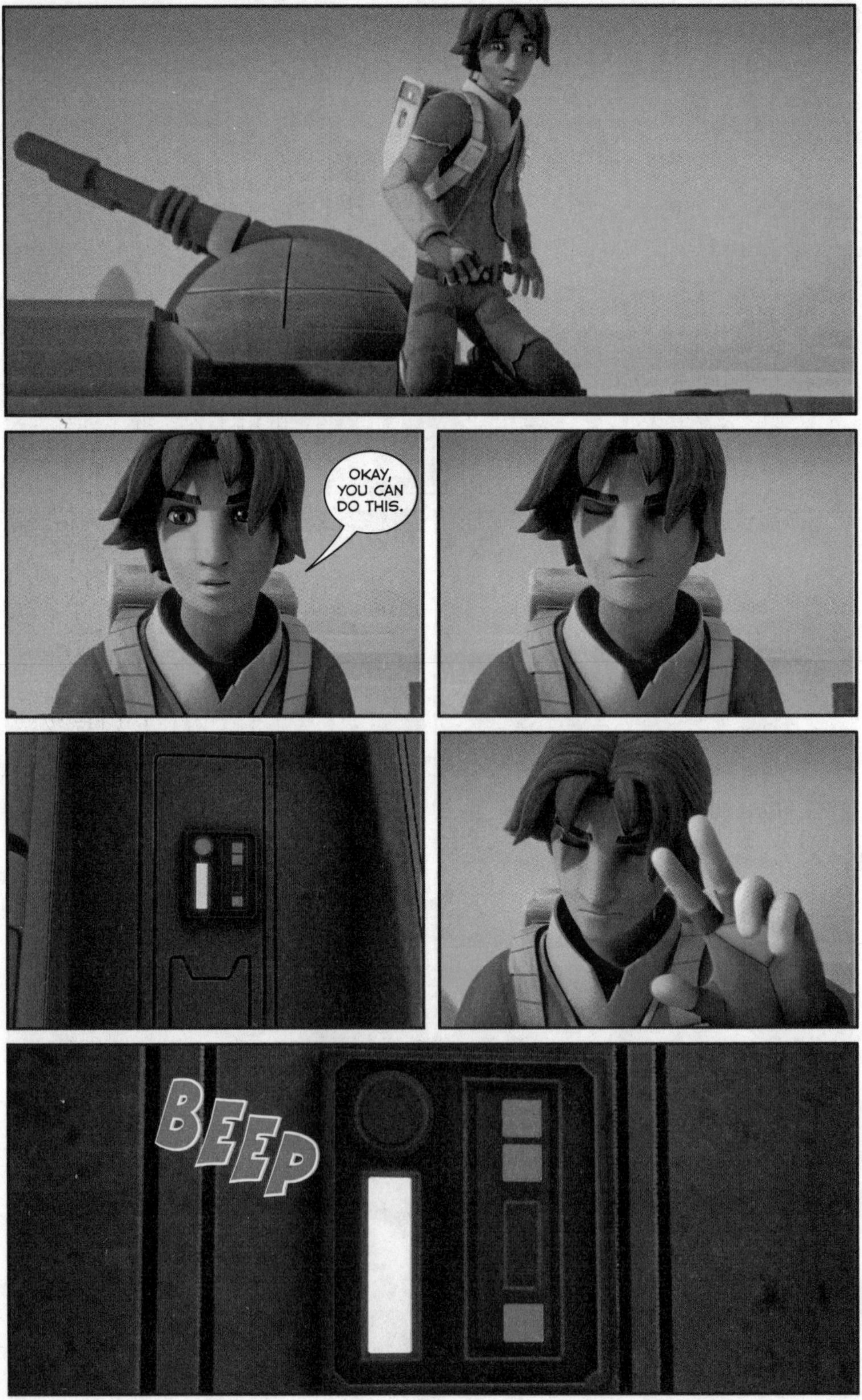
OKAY, YOU CAN DO THIS.
BEEP

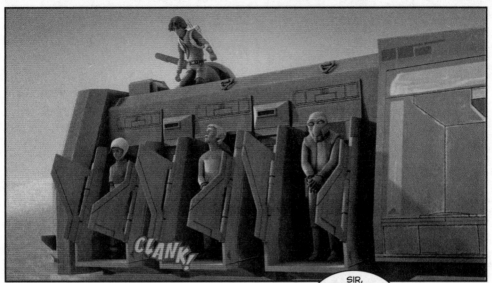

CLANK!

I KNEW I'D GET THE HANG OF THAT.

SIR, SOMEONE'S UNLOCKED THE PRISONERS ON TRANSPORT THREE.

I WANT TROOPERS UP TOP! *NOW!*

YOU HAVE TO JUMP!

JUMP AND SCATTER!

WE'RE MOVING TOO FAST!

SO YOU'D RATHER STAY PRISONERS?!

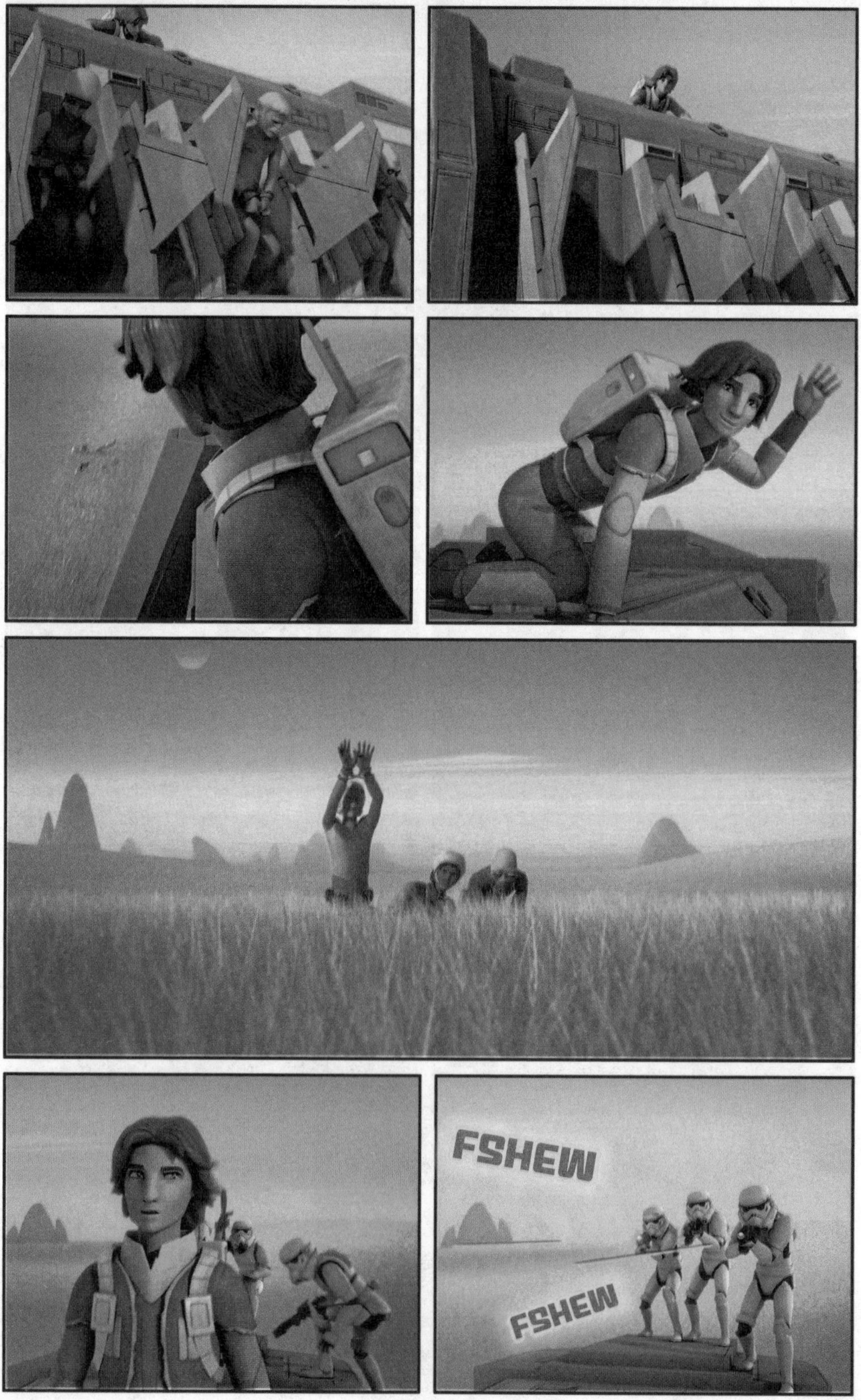
FSHEW
FSHEW

SIR, THE PRISONERS ARE ESCAPING.

OPEN FIRE.

FSHEW

FSHEW
FSHEW

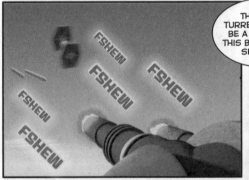

FSHEW
FSHEW
FSHEW
FSHEW
FSHEW

THAT GUN TURRET'S GONNA BE A PROBLEM. THIS BIRD HAS NO SHIELDS.

WORKING ON IT!

FSHEW
FSHEW

CLANK

WELL, HELLO, STRANGER.

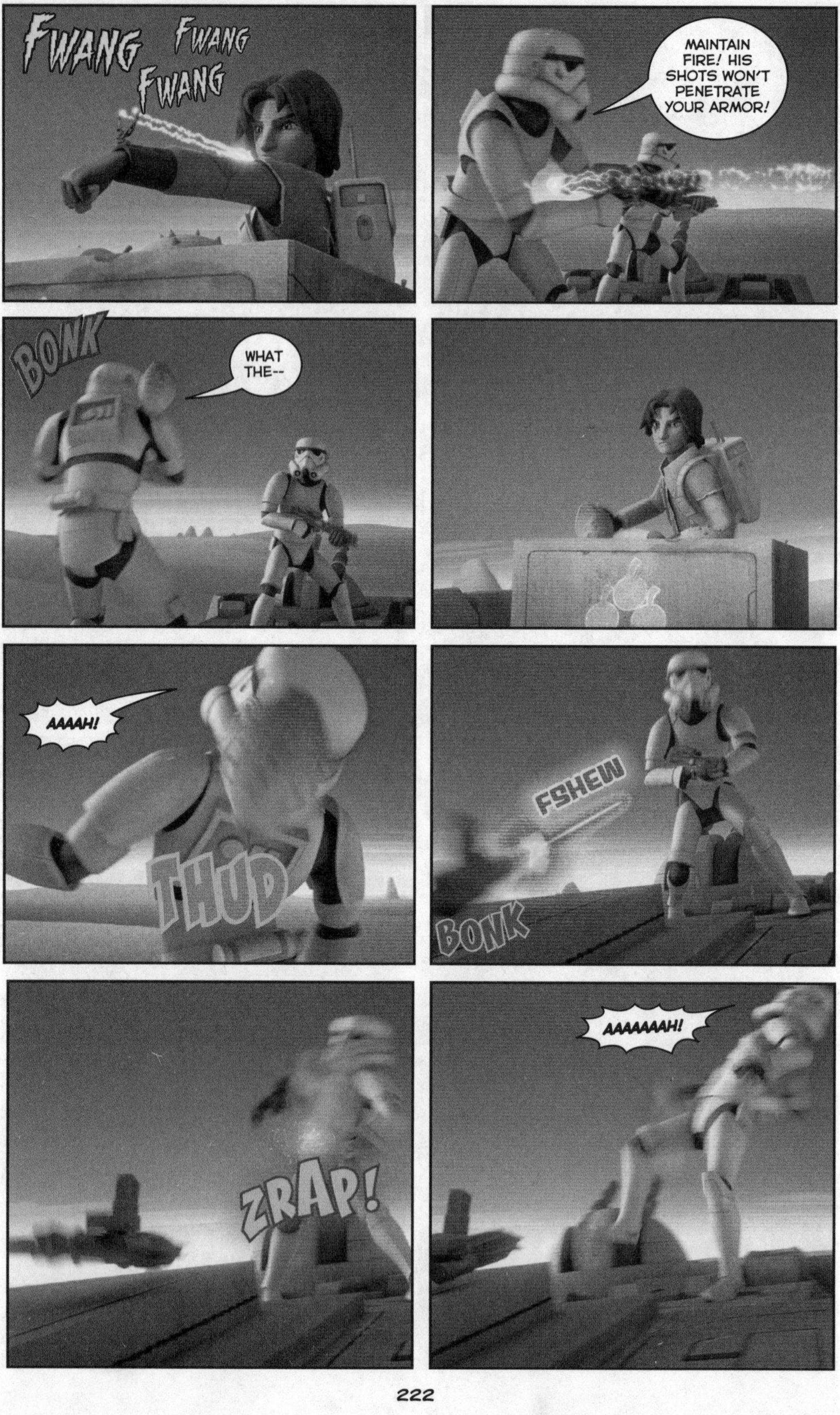
FWANG FWANG FWANG
MAINTAIN FIRE! HIS SHOTS WON'T PENETRATE YOUR ARMOR!
BONK
WHAT THE--
AAAAH!
THUD
FSHEW
BONK
ZRAP!
AAAAAAAH!

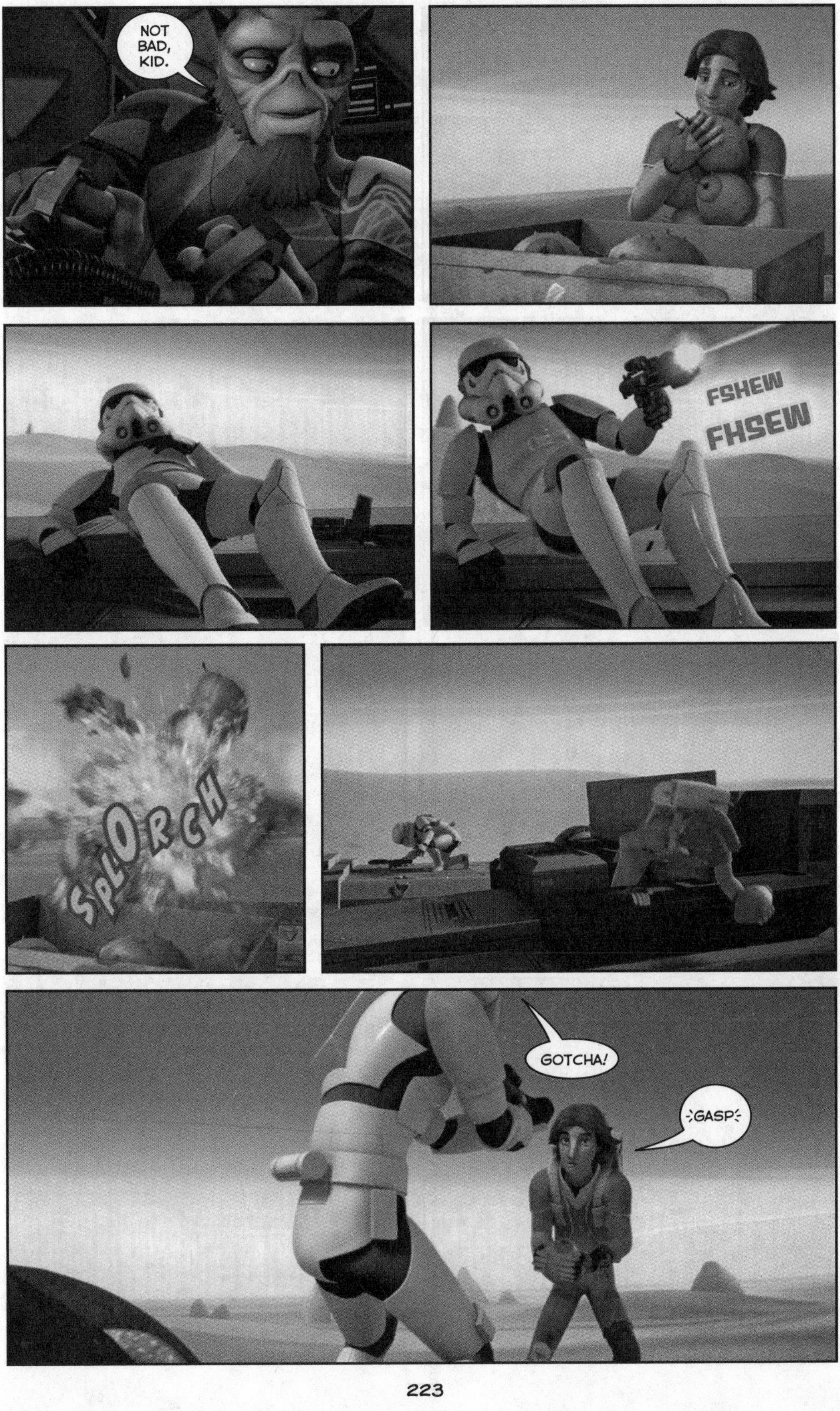
NOT BAD, KID.
FSHEW
FHSEW
SPLORCH
GOTCHA!
GASP

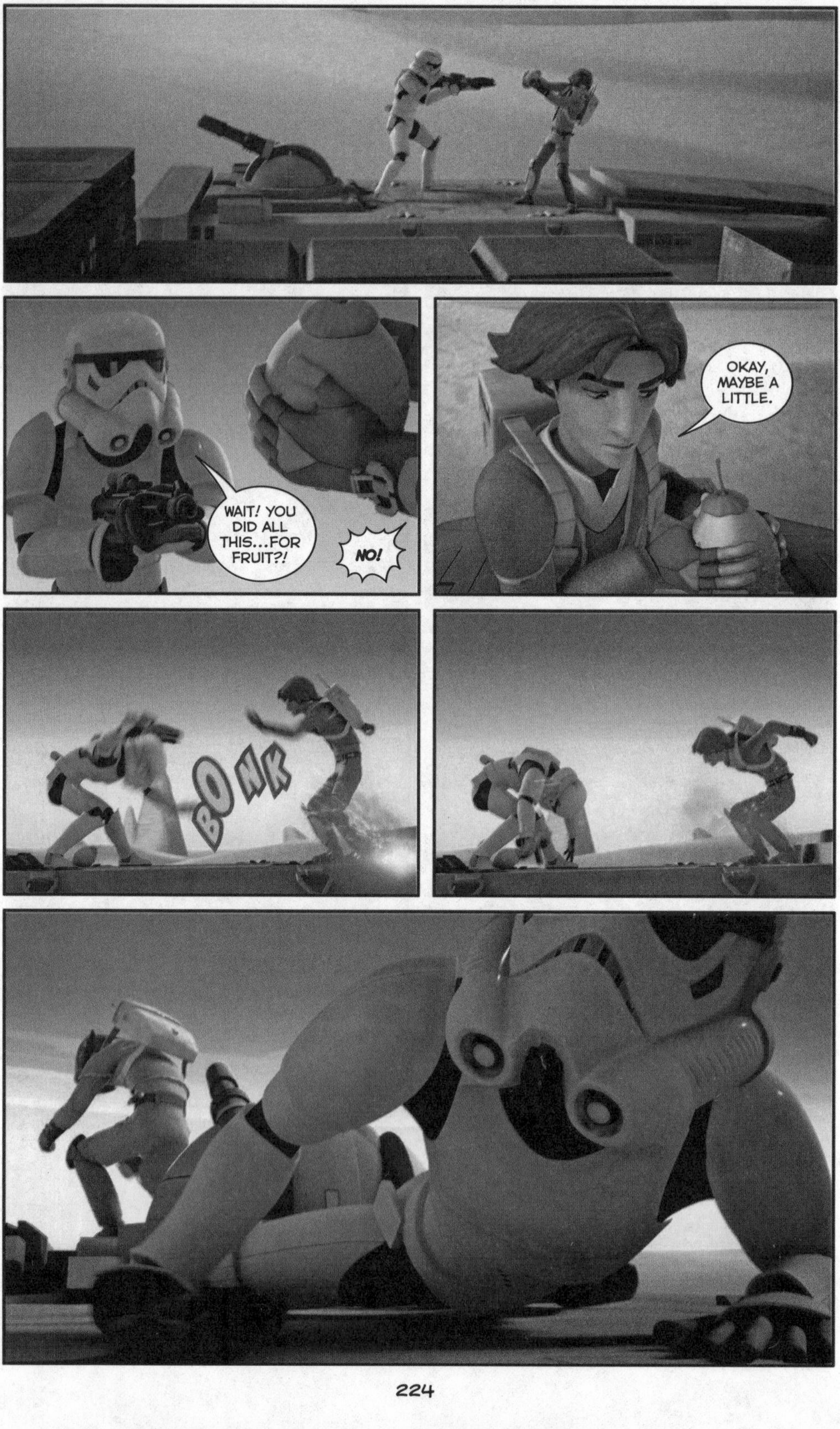

WAIT! YOU DID ALL THIS...FOR FRUIT?!
NO!
OKAY, MAYBE A LITTLE.
BONK

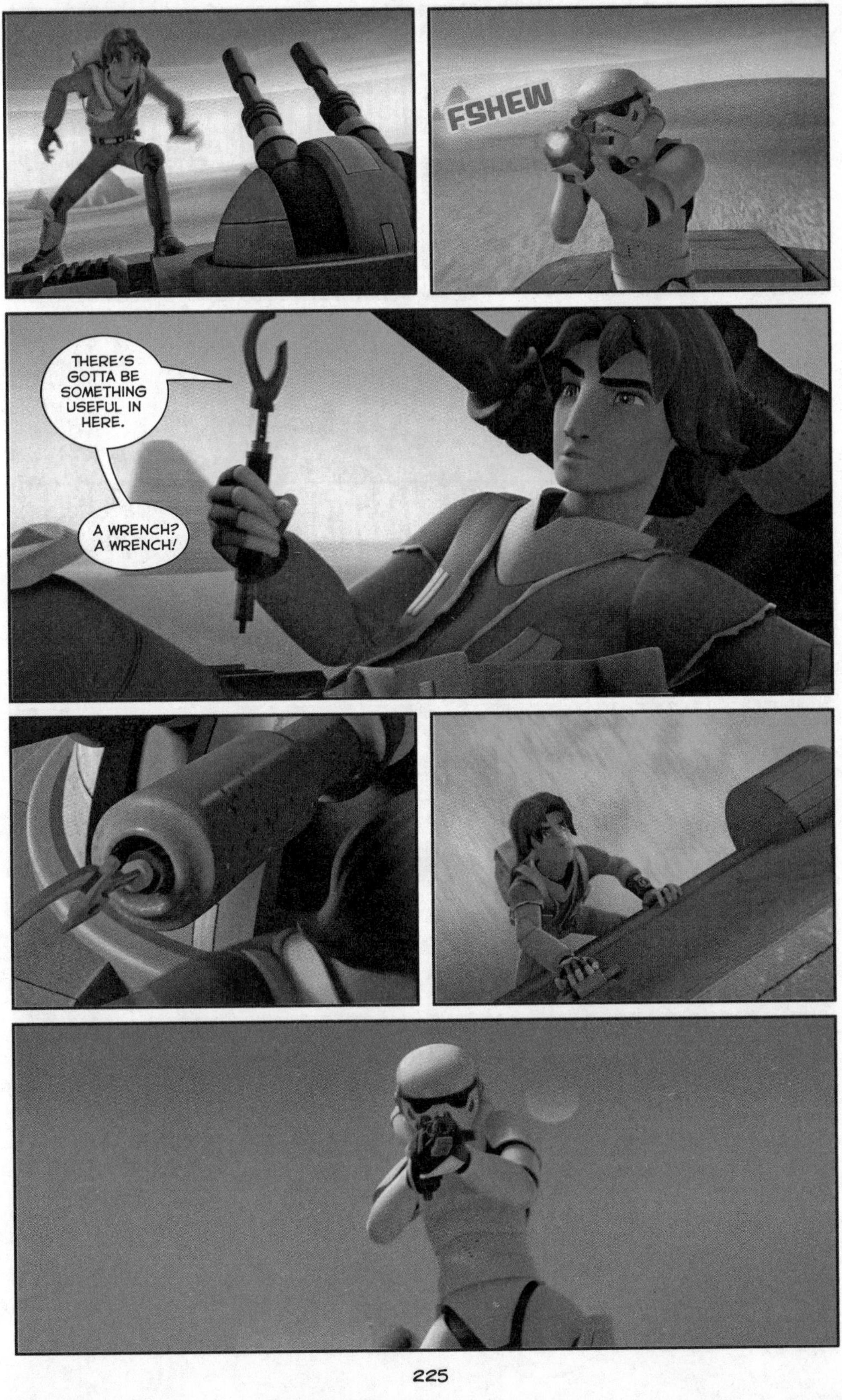
FSHEW
THERE'S GOTTA BE SOMETHING USEFUL IN HERE.
A WRENCH? A WRENCH!

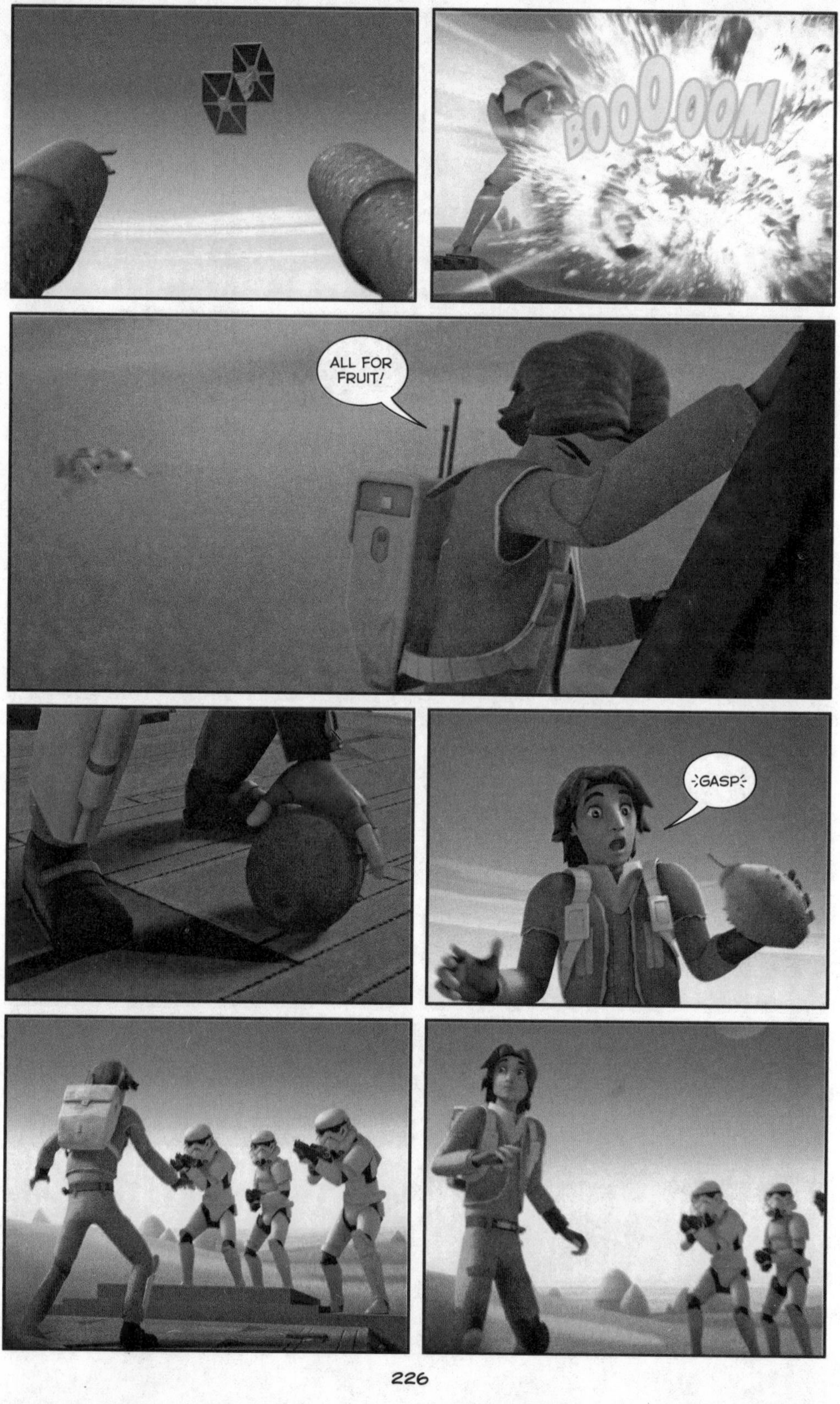
BOOOOOM
ALL FOR FRUIT!
GASP

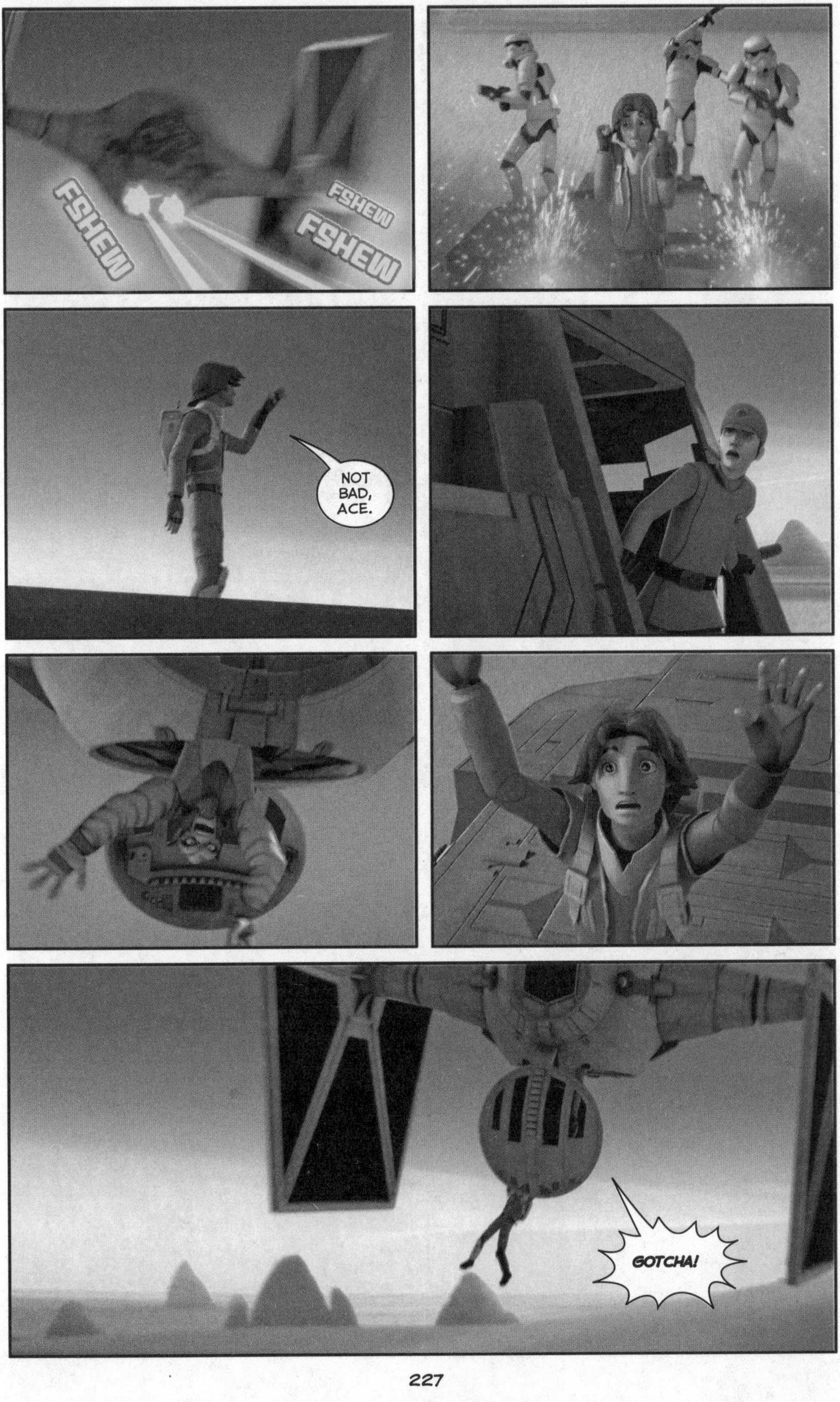
FSHEW
FSHEW
FSHEW
NOT BAD, ACE.
GOTCHA!

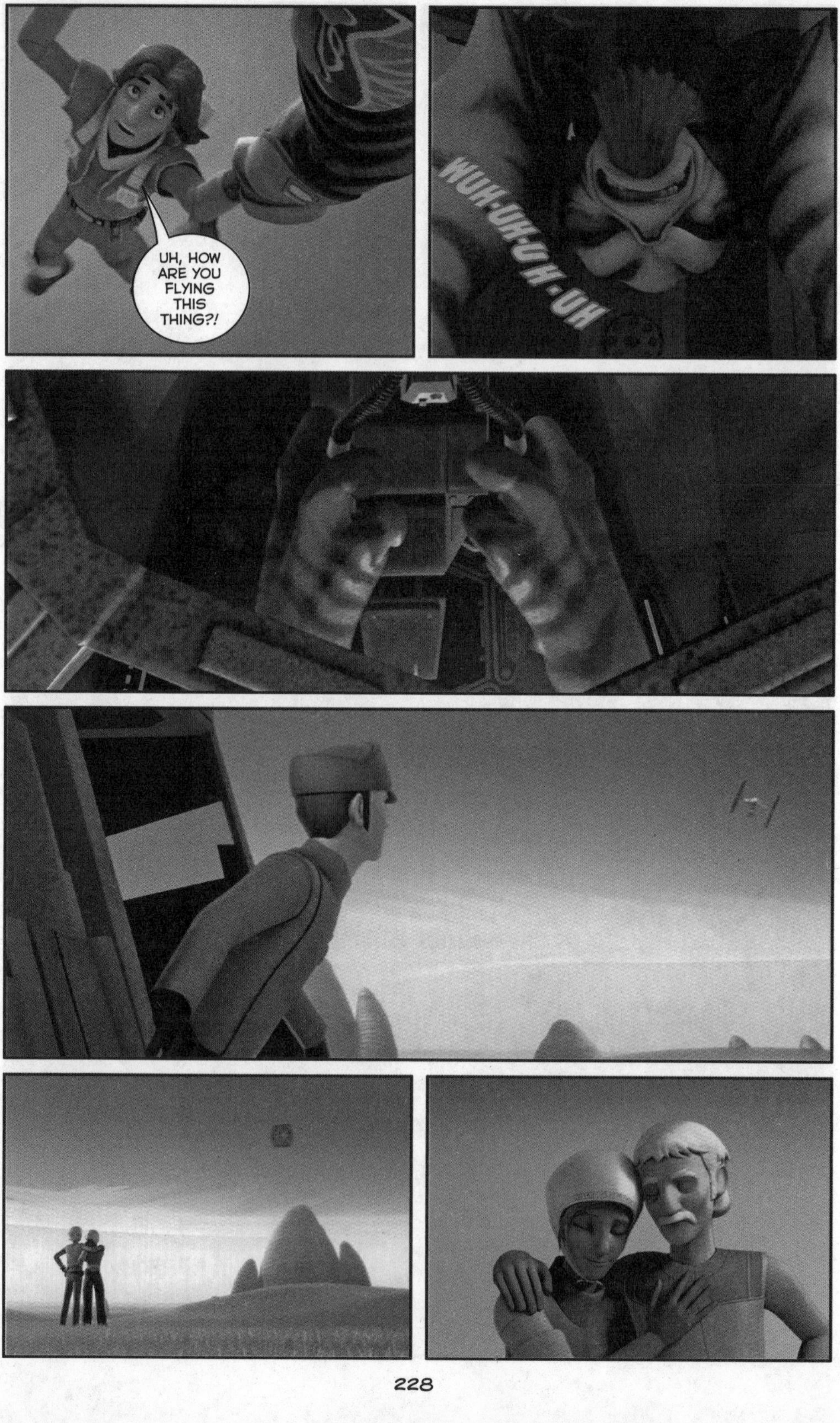
UH, HOW ARE YOU FLYING THIS THING?!

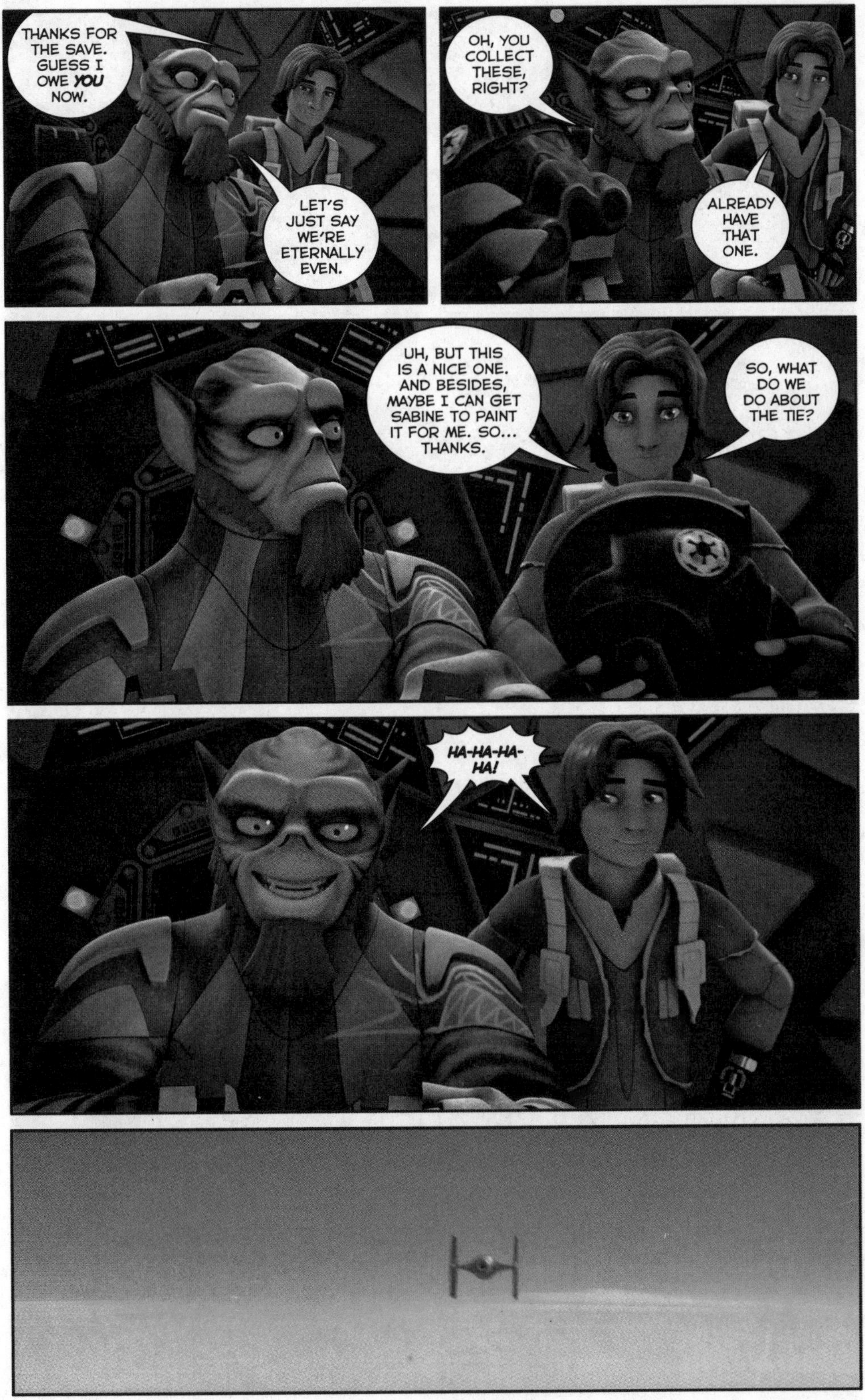
THANKS FOR THE SAVE. GUESS I OWE *YOU* NOW.
LET'S JUST SAY WE'RE ETERNALLY EVEN.
OH, YOU COLLECT THESE, RIGHT?
ALREADY HAVE THAT ONE.
UH, BUT THIS IS A NICE ONE. AND BESIDES, MAYBE I CAN GET SABINE TO PAINT IT FOR ME. SO... THANKS.
SO, WHAT DO WE DO ABOUT THE TIE?
HA-HA-HA-HA!

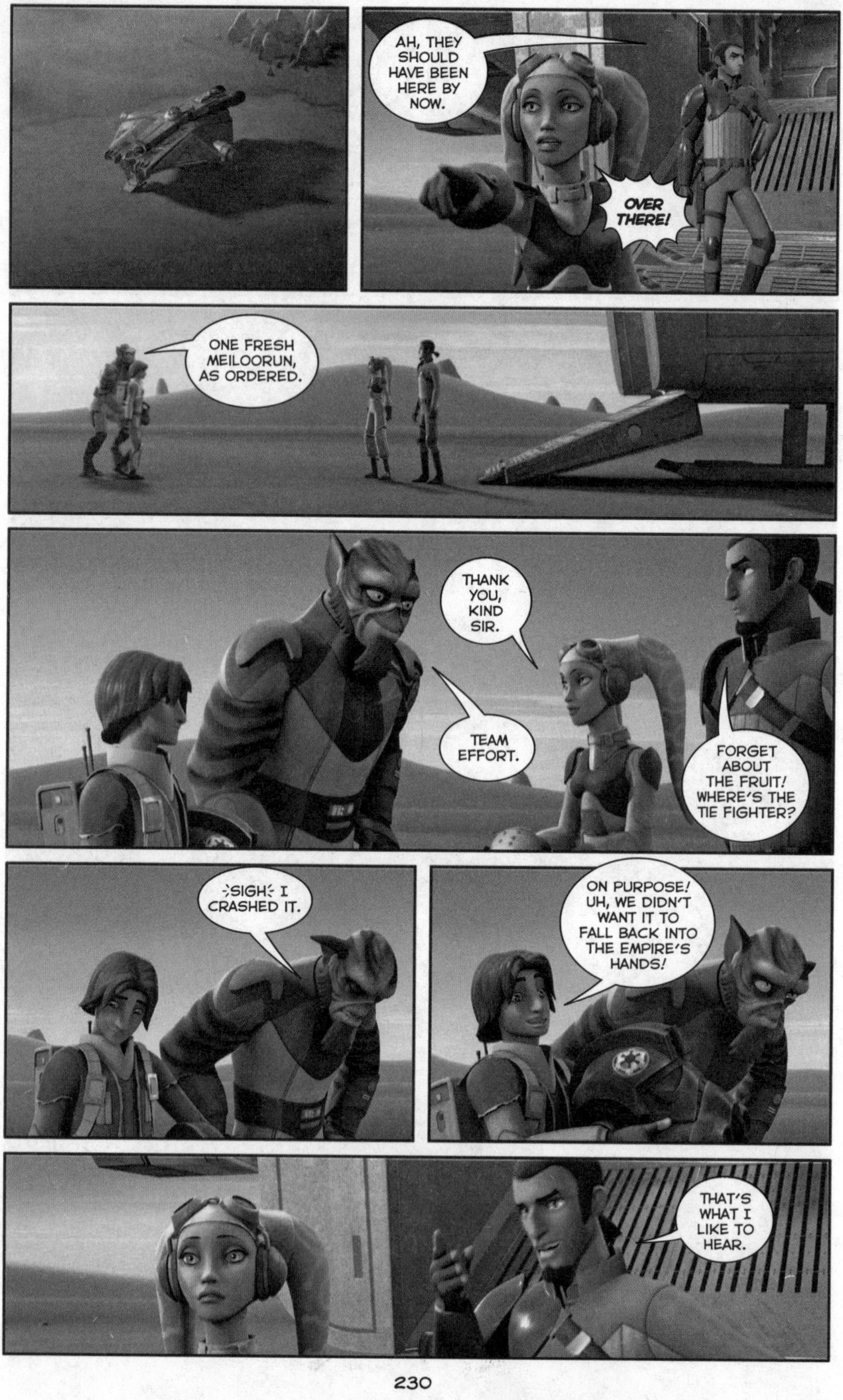

AH, THEY SHOULD HAVE BEEN HERE BY NOW.
OVER THERE!
ONE FRESH MEILOORUN, AS ORDERED.
THANK YOU, KIND SIR.
TEAM EFFORT.
FORGET ABOUT THE FRUIT! WHERE'S THE TIE FIGHTER?
-SIGH- I CRASHED IT.
ON PURPOSE! UH, WE DIDN'T WANT IT TO FALL BACK INTO THE EMPIRE'S HANDS!
THAT'S WHAT I LIKE TO HEAR.

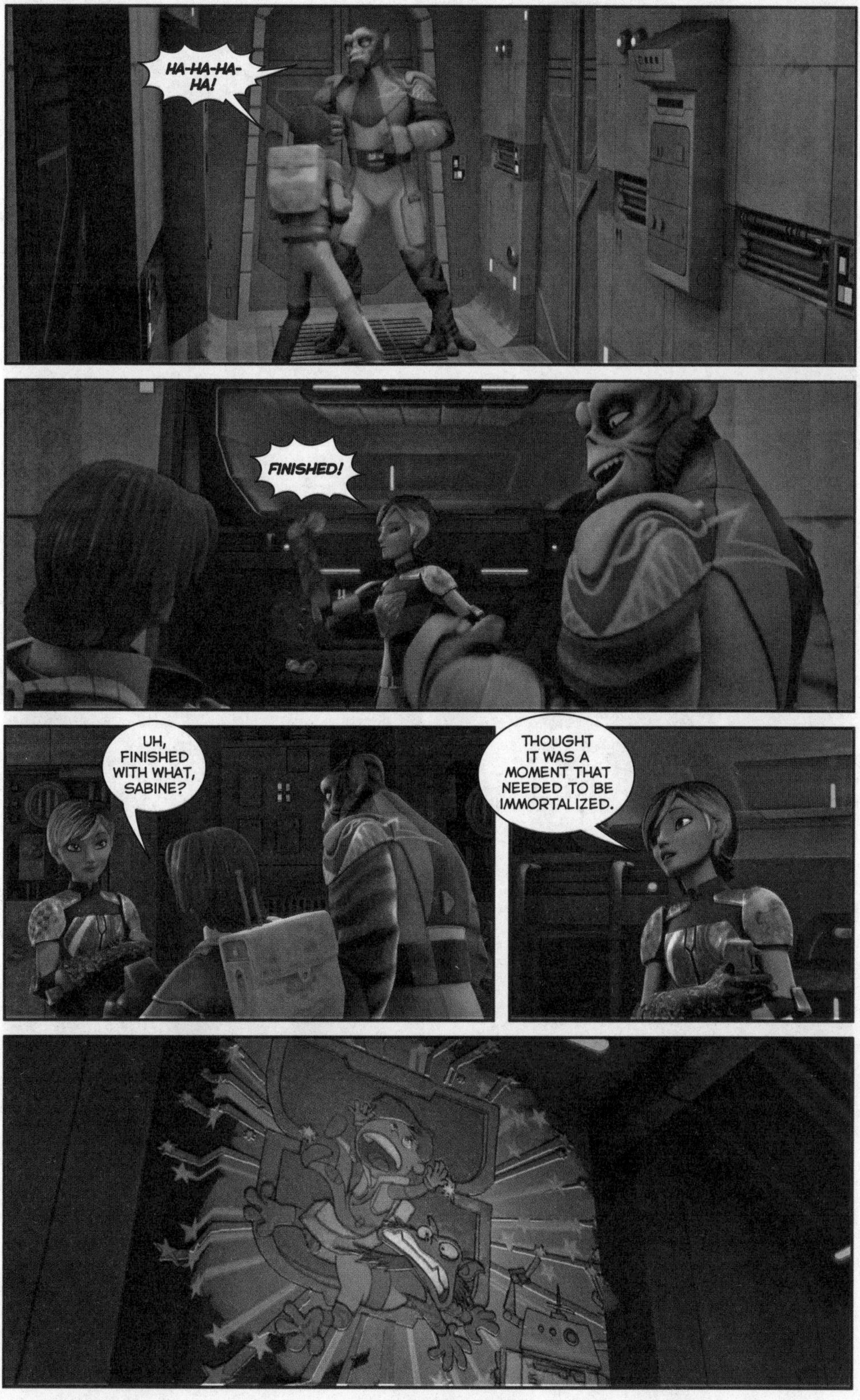
HA-HA-HA-HA!
FINISHED!
UH, FINISHED WITH WHAT, SABINE?
THOUGHT IT WAS A MOMENT THAT NEEDED TO BE IMMORTALIZED.

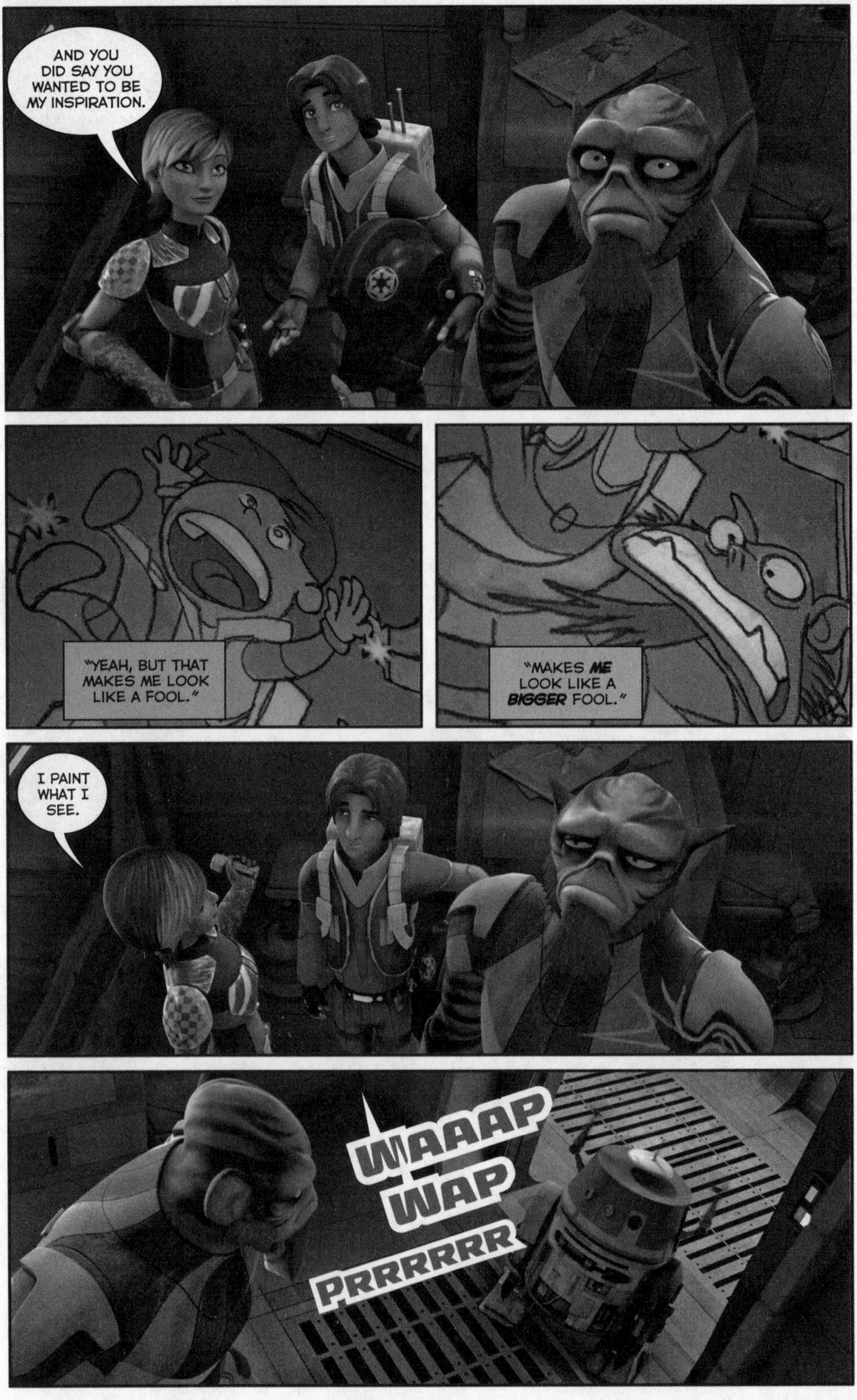
AND YOU DID SAY YOU WANTED TO BE MY INSPIRATION.
"YEAH, BUT THAT MAKES ME LOOK LIKE A FOOL."
"MAKES *ME* LOOK LIKE A *BIGGER* FOOL."
I PAINT WHAT I SEE.
WAAAP
WAP
PRRRRRR

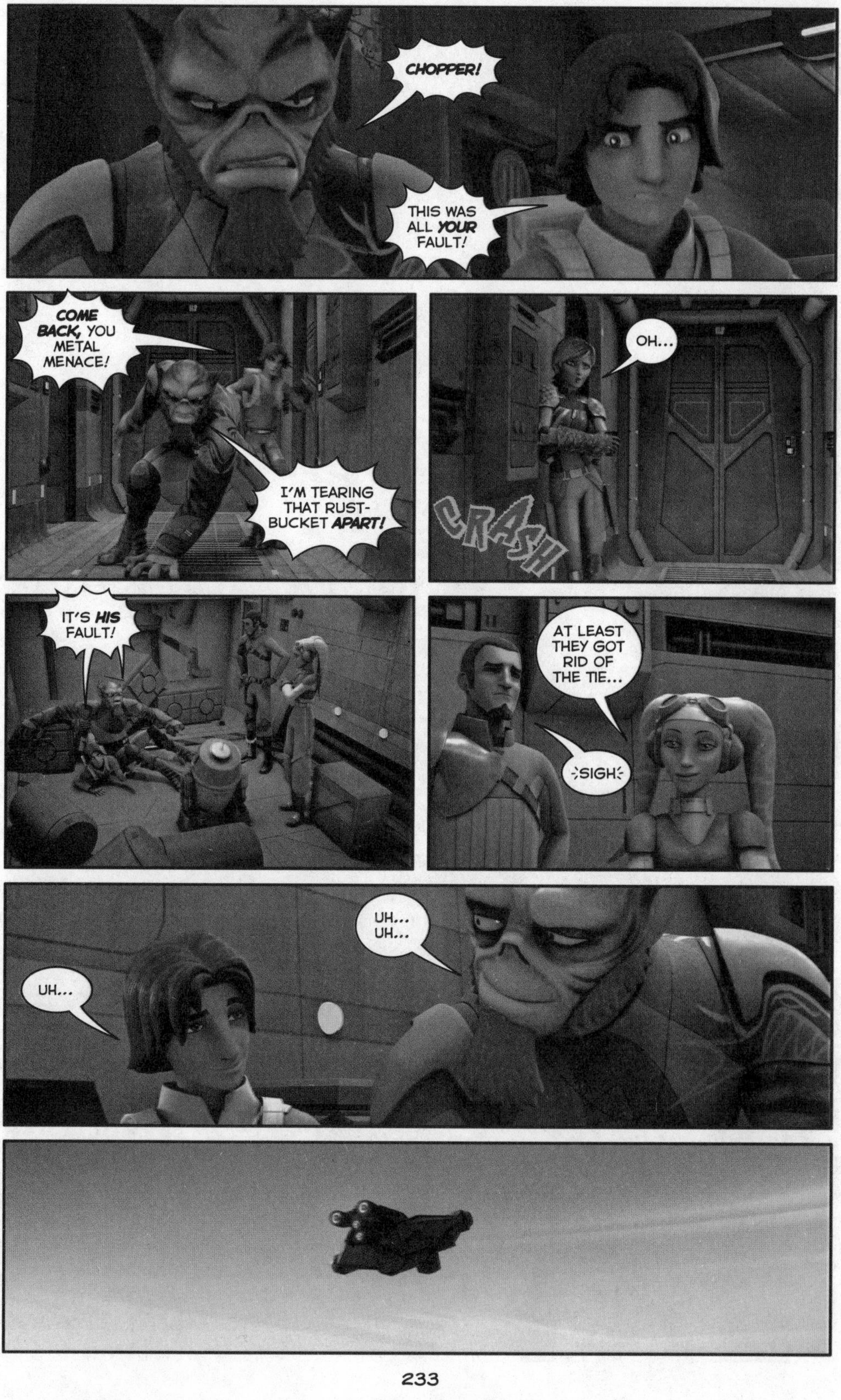
CHOPPER!
THIS WAS ALL YOUR FAULT!
COME BACK, YOU METAL MENACE!
I'M TEARING THAT RUST-BUCKET APART!
OH...
CRASH
IT'S HIS FAULT!
AT LEAST THEY GOT RID OF THE TIE...
SIGH
UH... UH...
UH...

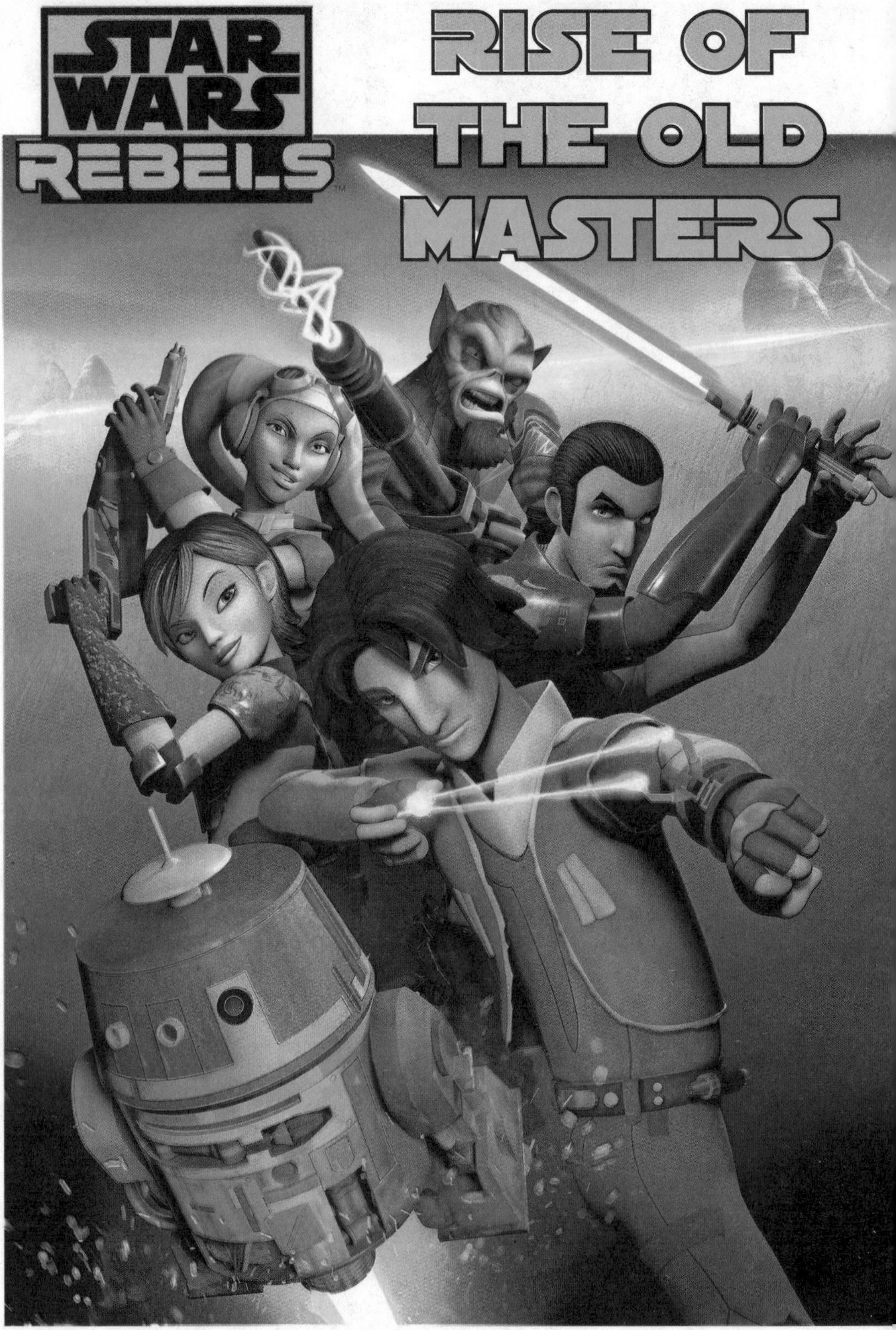
STAR WARS REBELS™
RISE OF THE OLD MASTERS

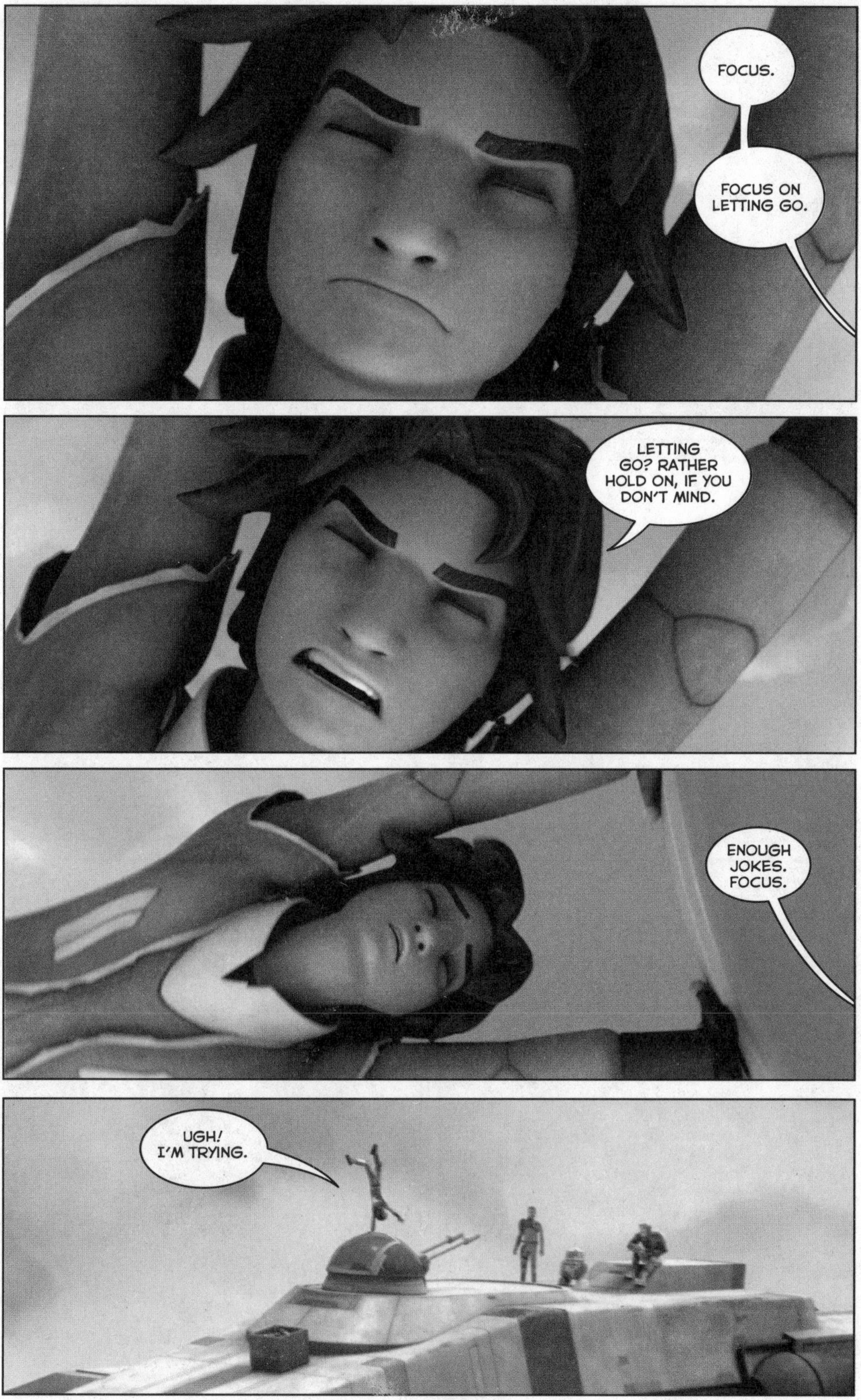
FOCUS.
FOCUS ON LETTING GO.
LETTING GO? RATHER HOLD ON, IF YOU DON'T MIND.
ENOUGH JOKES. FOCUS.
UGH! I'M TRYING.

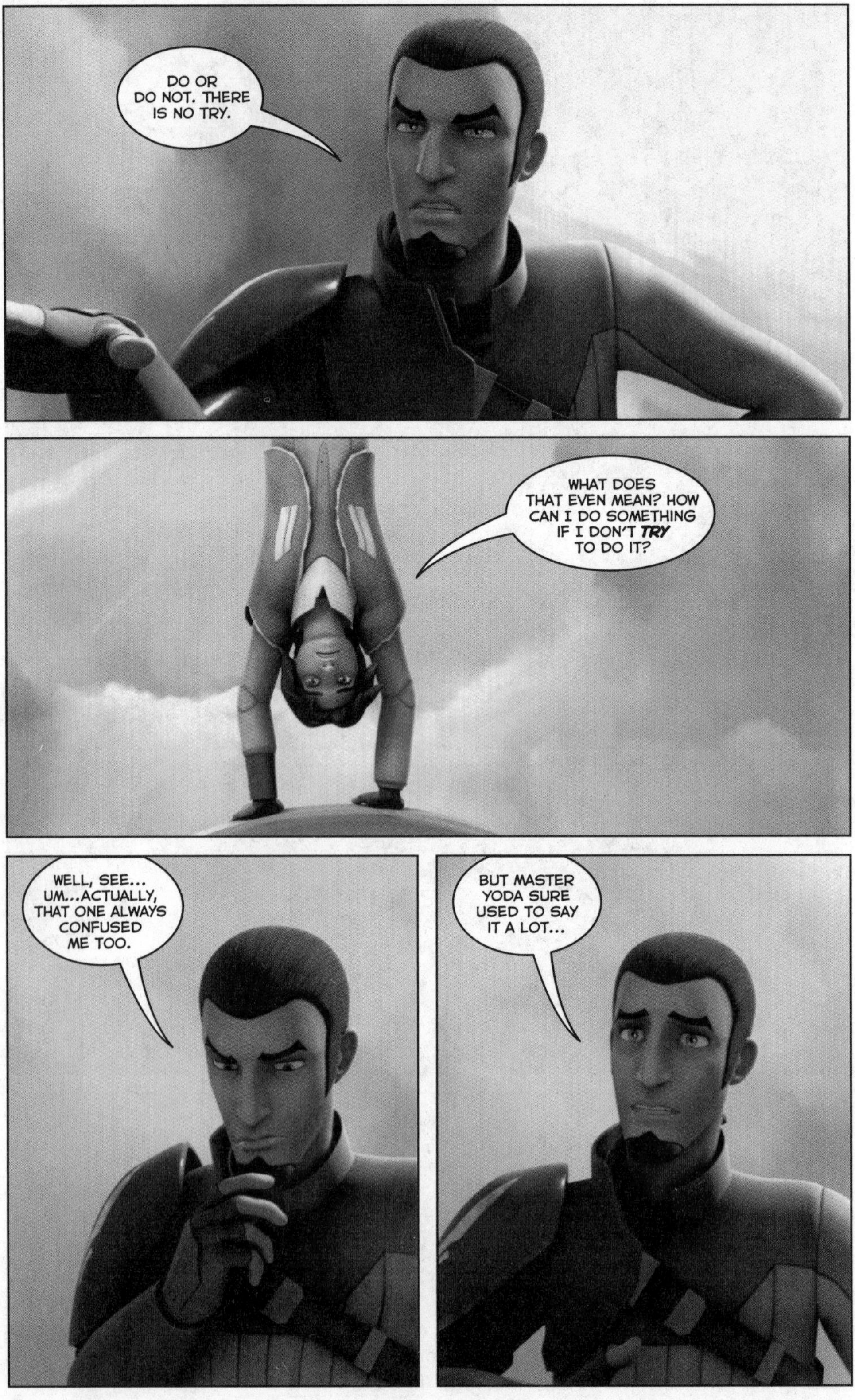
DO OR DO NOT. THERE IS NO TRY.
WHAT DOES THAT EVEN MEAN? HOW CAN I DO SOMETHING IF I DON'T *TRY* TO DO IT?
WELL, SEE... UM...ACTUALLY, THAT ONE ALWAYS CONFUSED ME TOO.
BUT MASTER YODA SURE USED TO SAY IT A LOT...

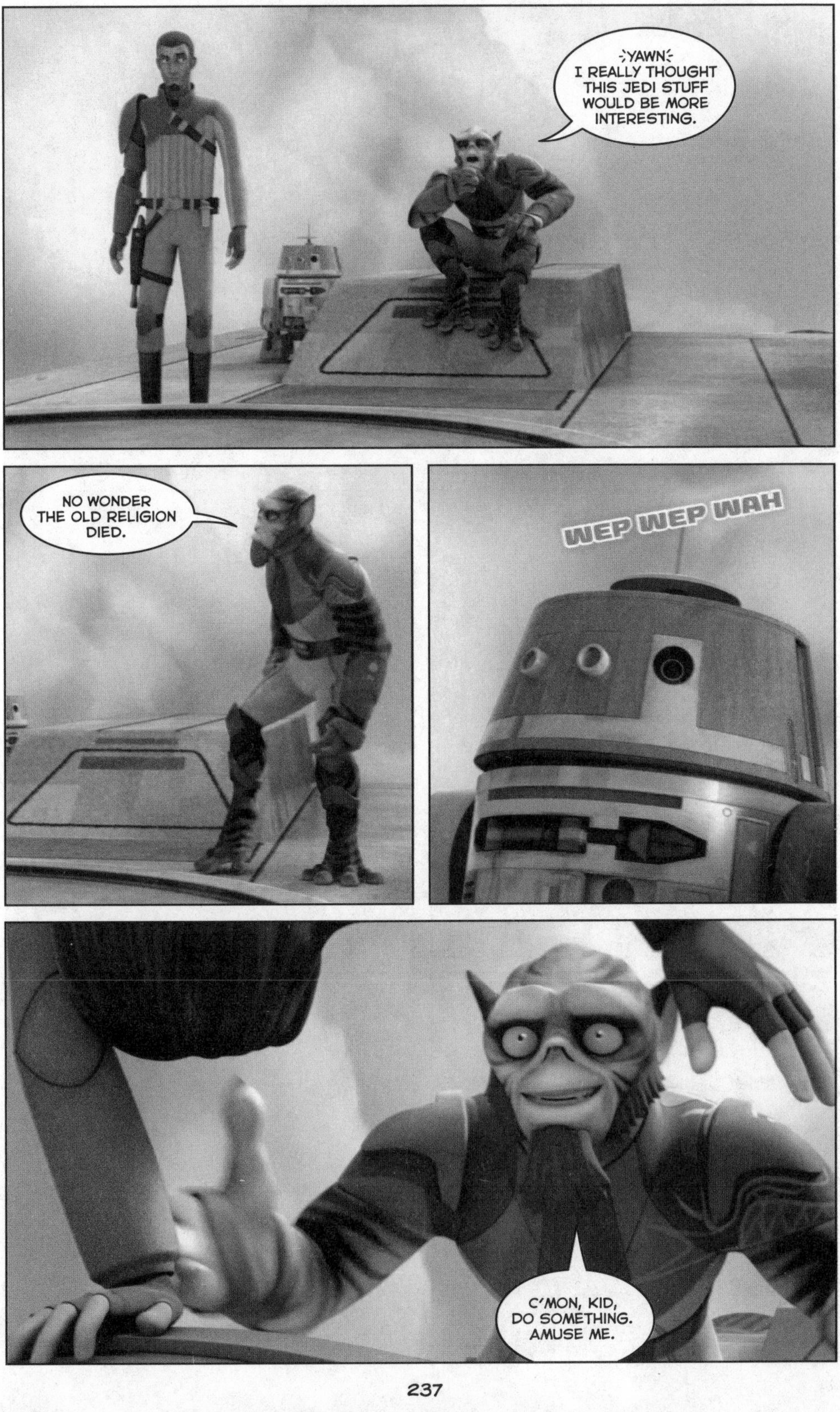
YAWN I REALLY THOUGHT THIS JEDI STUFF WOULD BE MORE INTERESTING.
NO WONDER THE OLD RELIGION DIED.
WEP WEP WAH
C'MON, KID, DO SOMETHING. AMUSE ME.

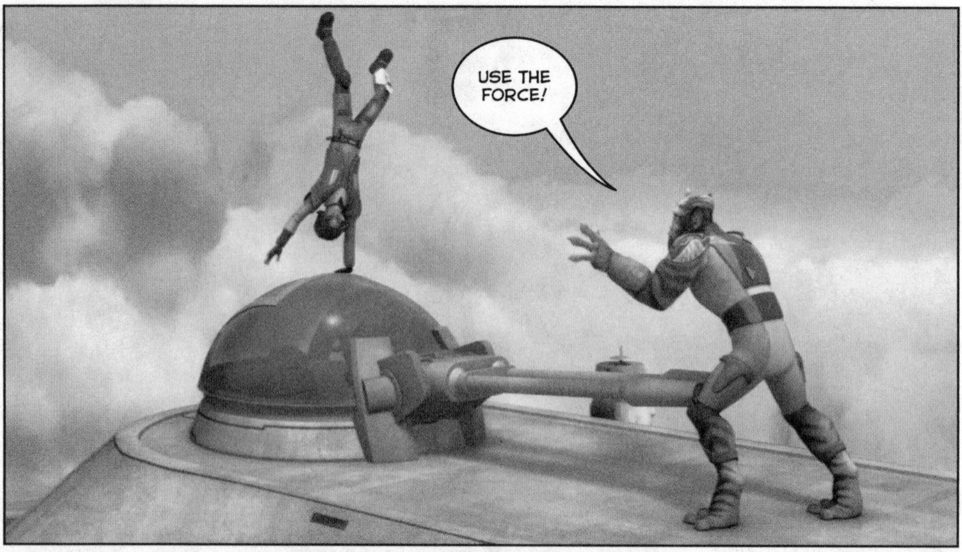
USE THE FORCE!

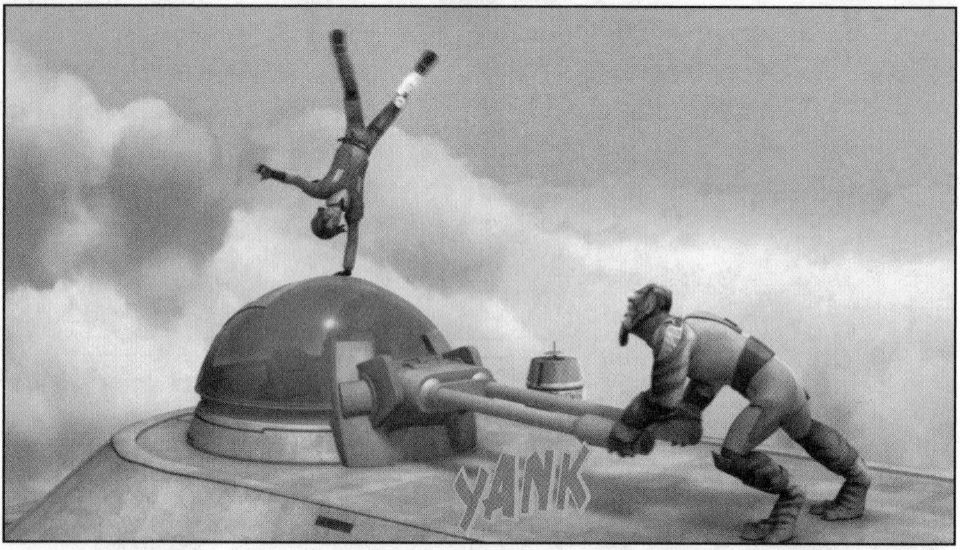
YANK

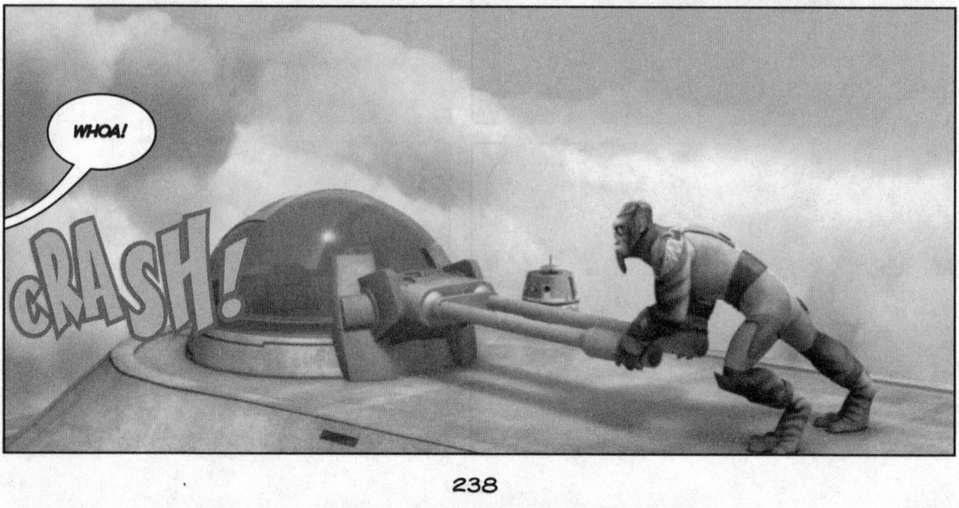
WHOA!
CRASH!

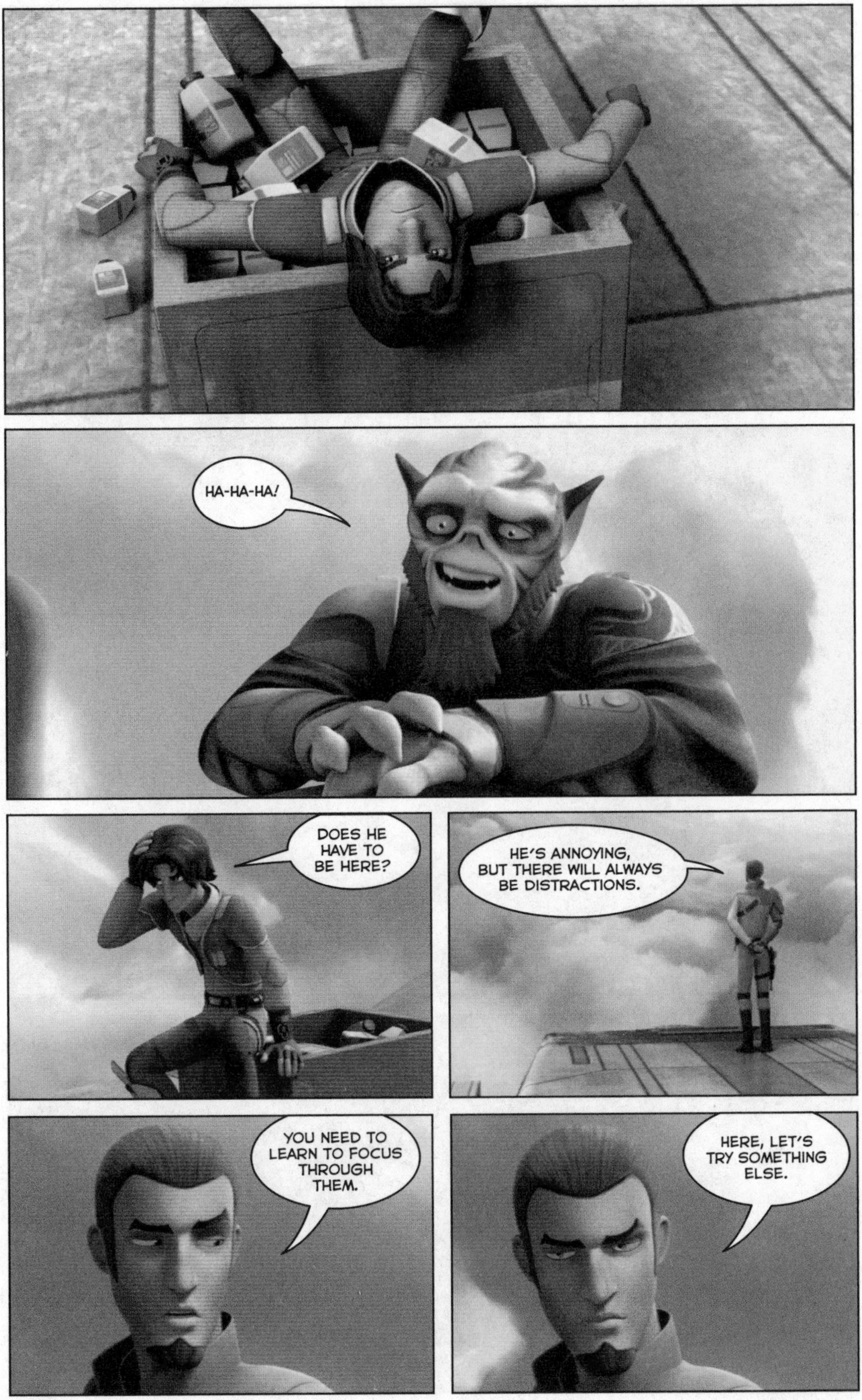
HA-HA-HA!
DOES HE HAVE TO BE HERE?
HE'S ANNOYING, BUT THERE WILL ALWAYS BE DISTRACTIONS.
YOU NEED TO LEARN TO FOCUS THROUGH THEM.
HERE, LET'S TRY SOMETHING ELSE.

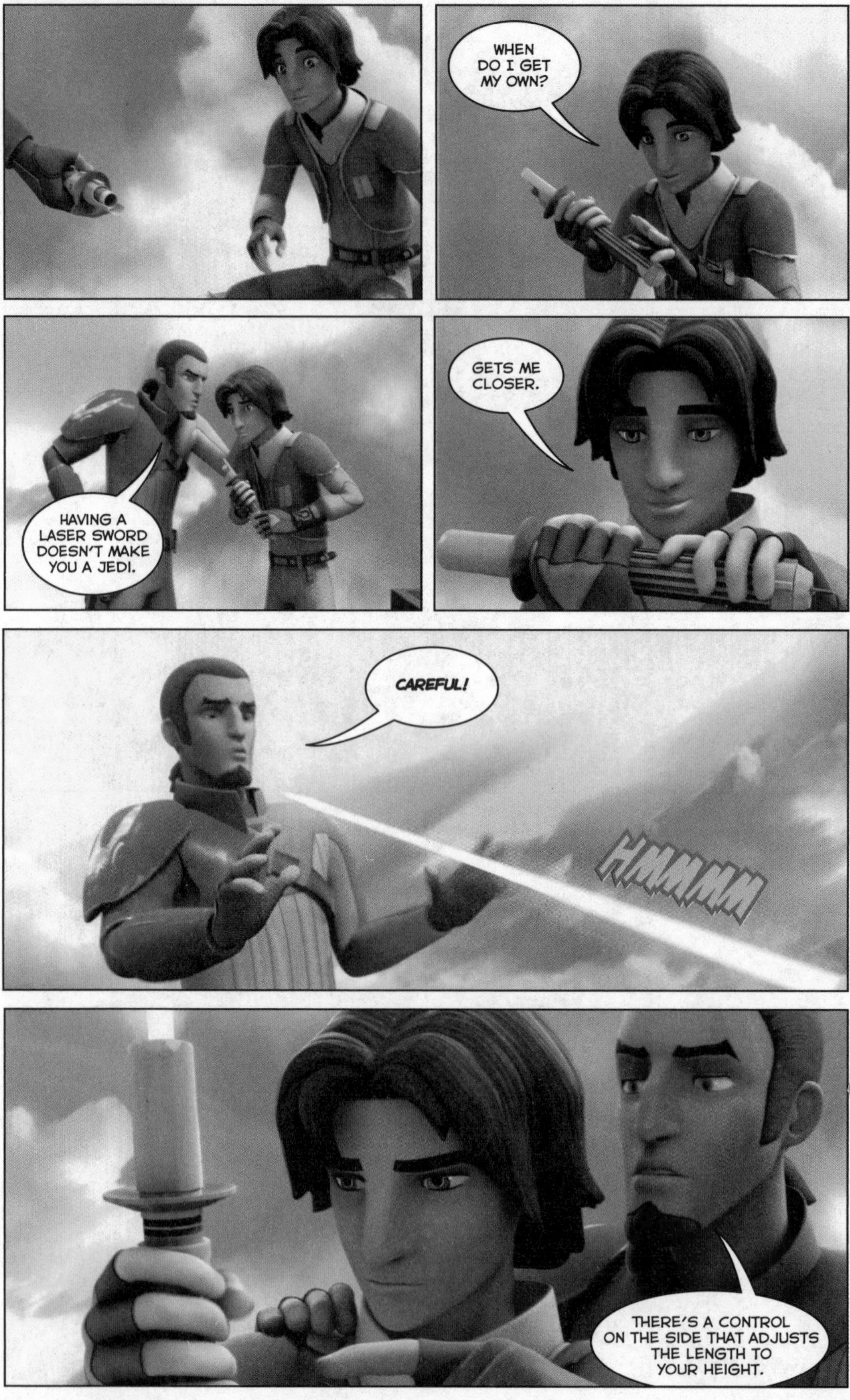
WHEN DO I GET MY OWN?
HAVING A LASER SWORD DOESN'T MAKE YOU A JEDI.
GETS ME CLOSER.
CAREFUL!
HMMMMM
THERE'S A CONTROL ON THE SIDE THAT ADJUSTS THE LENGTH TO YOUR HEIGHT.

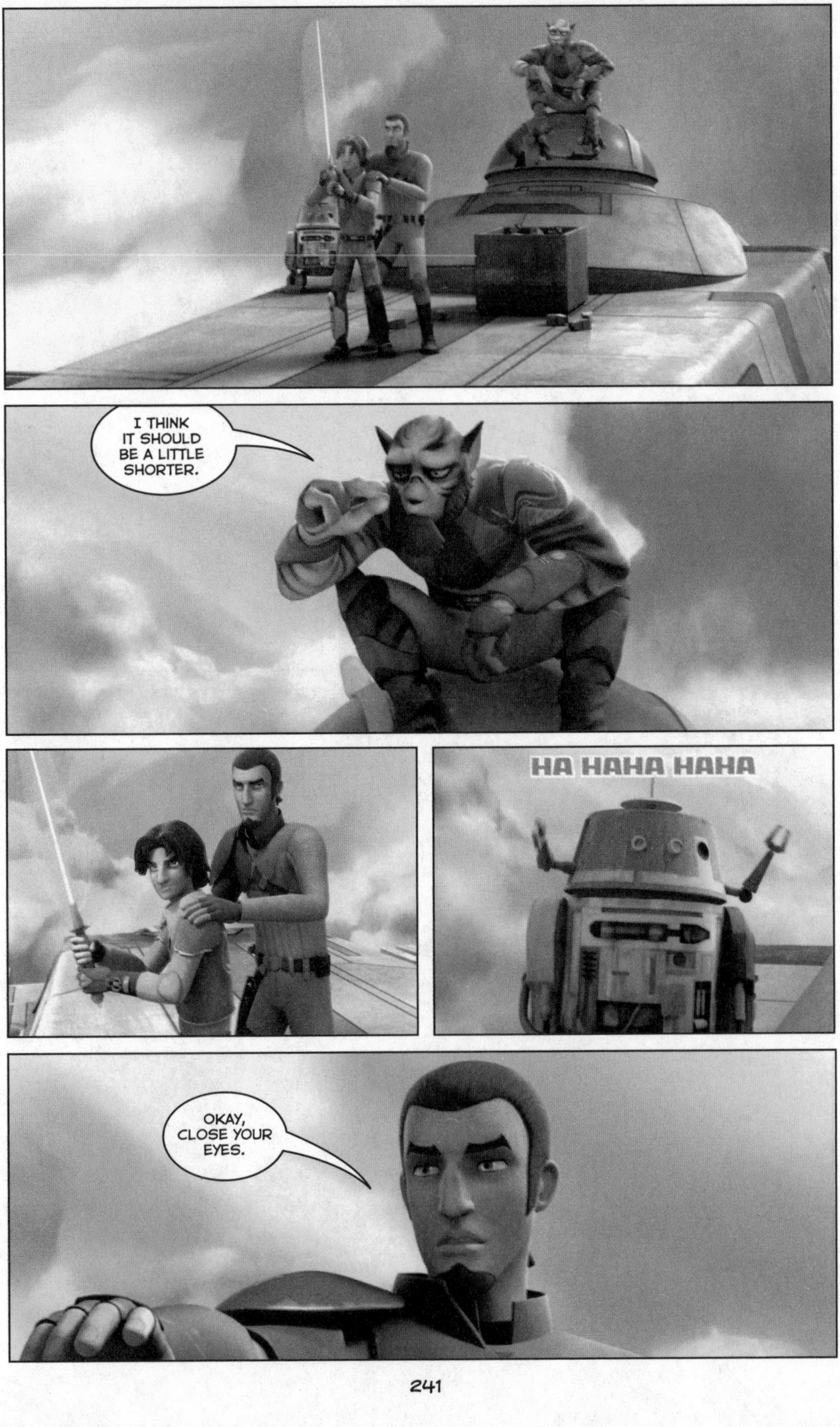
I THINK IT SHOULD BE A LITTLE SHORTER.
HA HAHA HAHA
OKAY, CLOSE YOUR EYES.

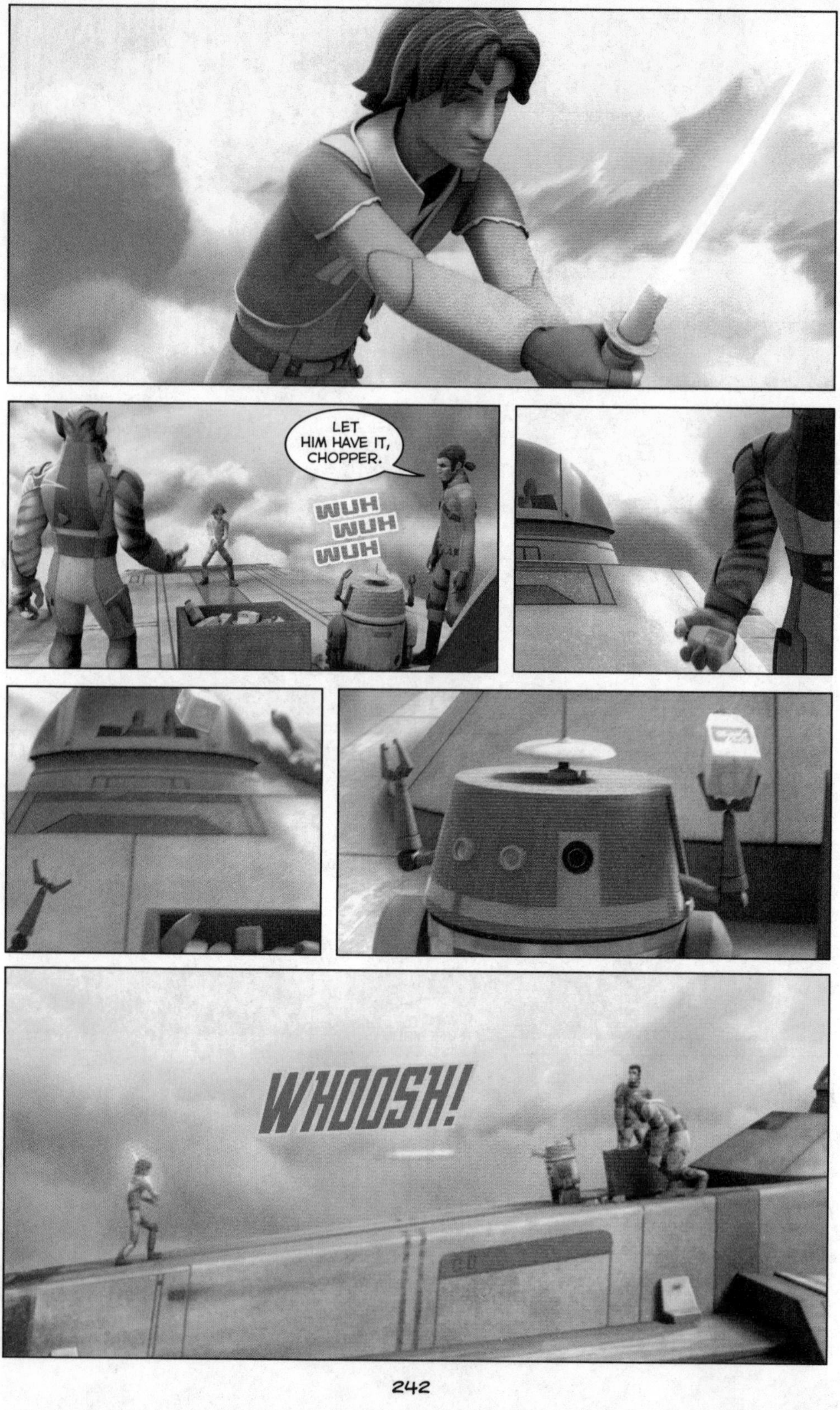
LET HIM HAVE IT, CHOPPER.
WUH WUH WUH
WHOOSH!

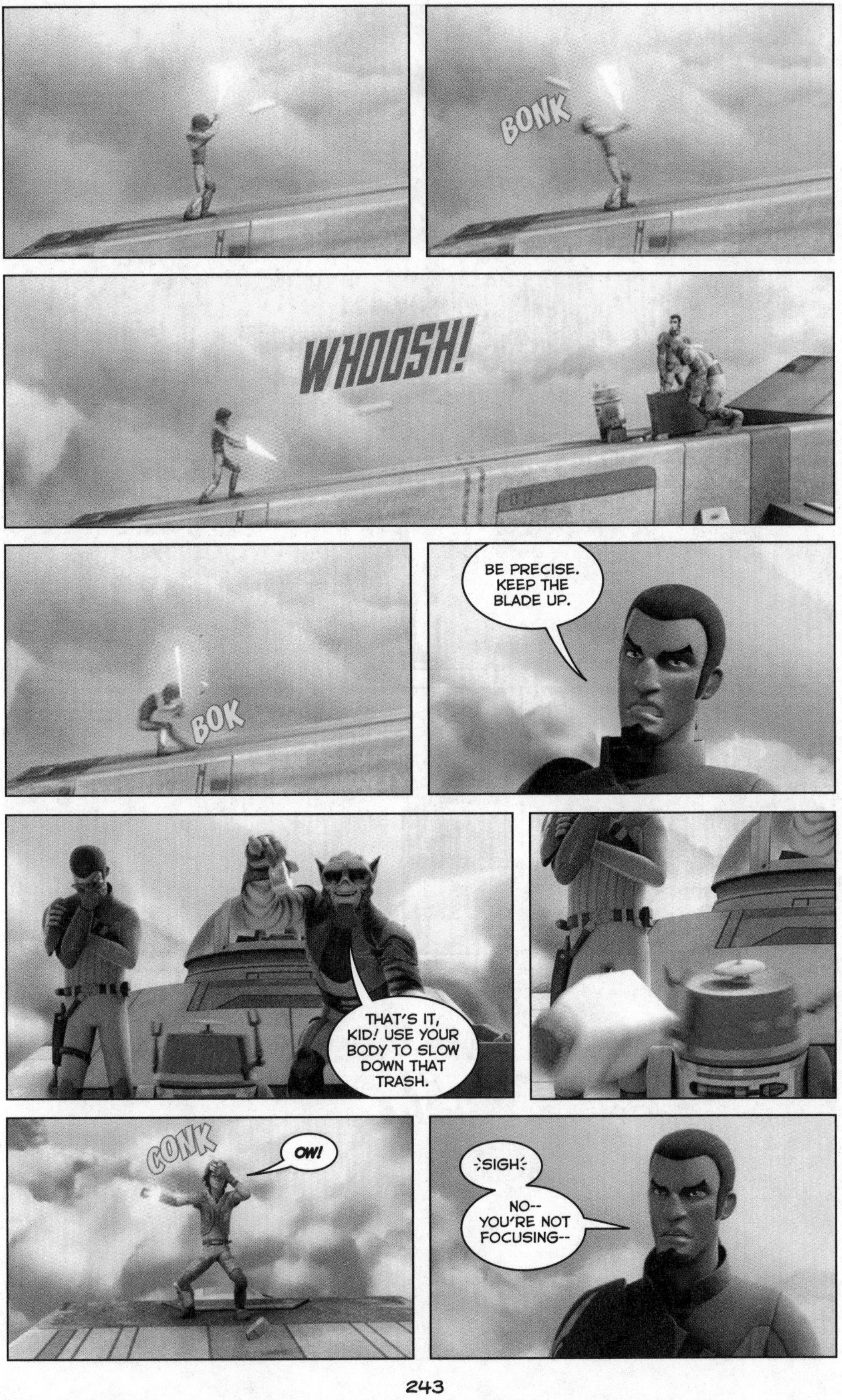
BONK
WHOOSH!
BOK
BE PRECISE. KEEP THE BLADE UP.
THAT'S IT, KID! USE YOUR BODY TO SLOW DOWN THAT TRASH.
CONK
OW!
-SIGH-
NO-- YOU'RE NOT FOCUSING--

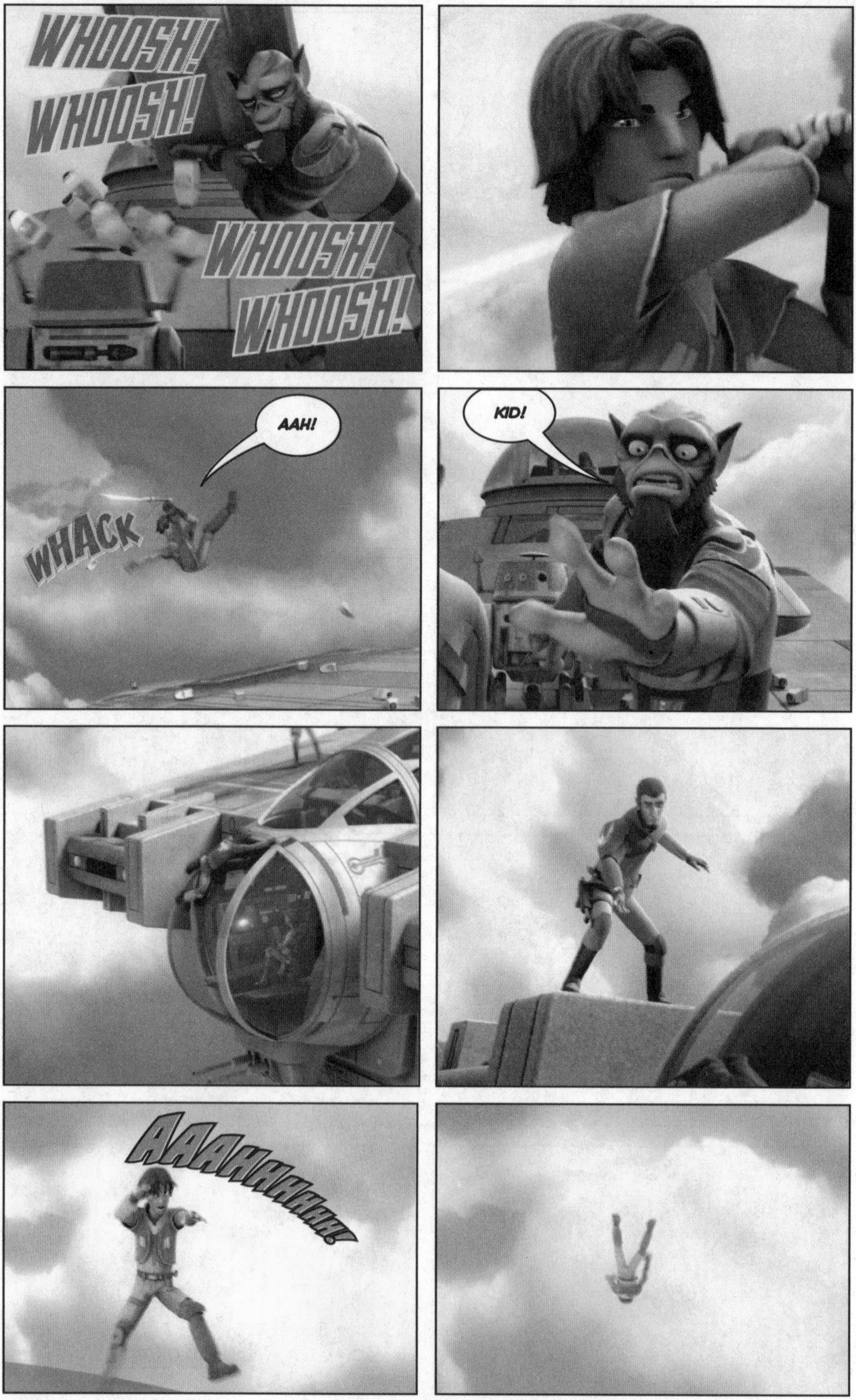
WHOOSH!
WHOOSH!
WHOOSH!
WHOOSH!
AAH!
WHACK
KID!
AAAHHHHHH!

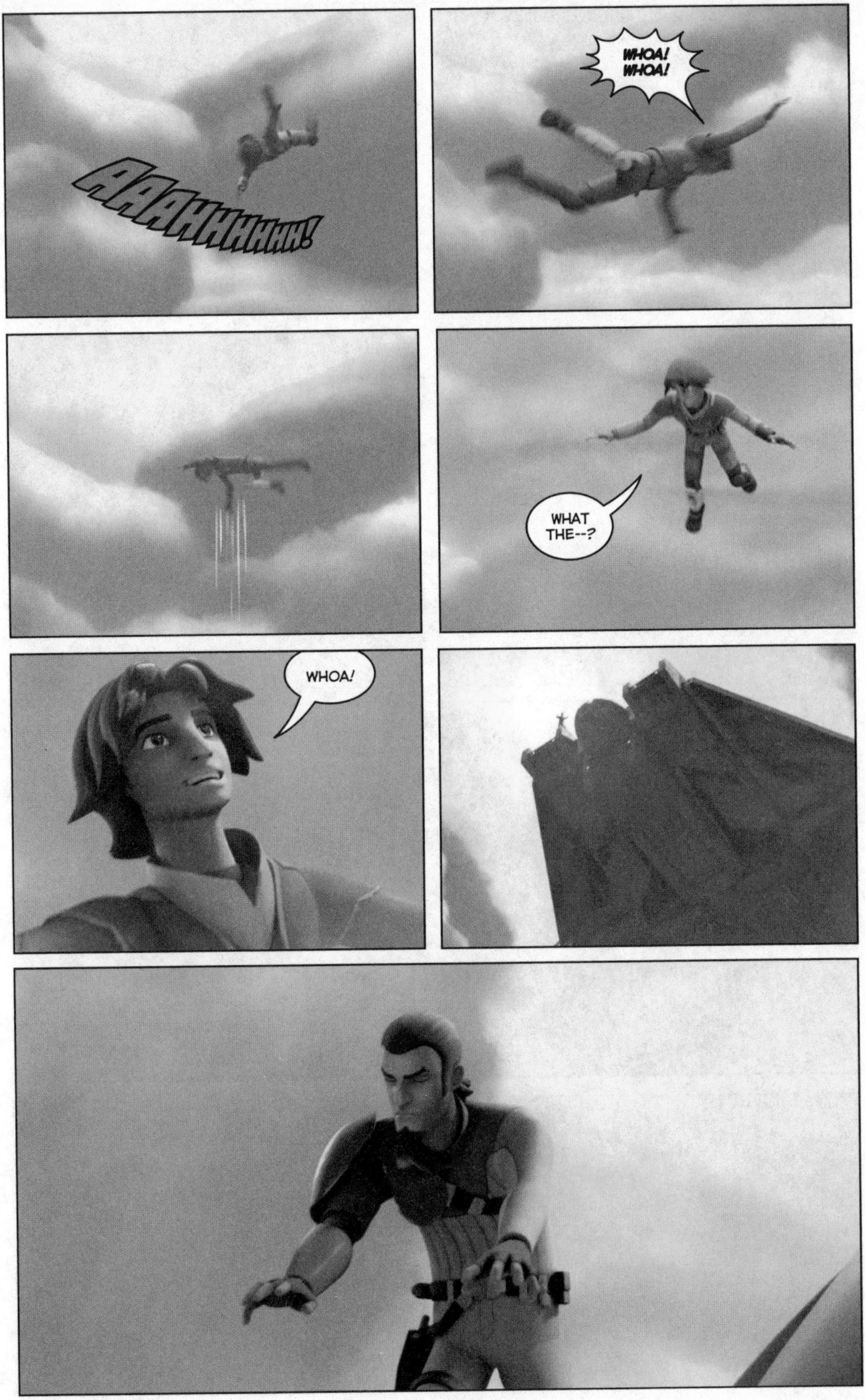
AAAAHHHHHH!
WHOA! WHOA!
WHAT THE--?
WHOA!

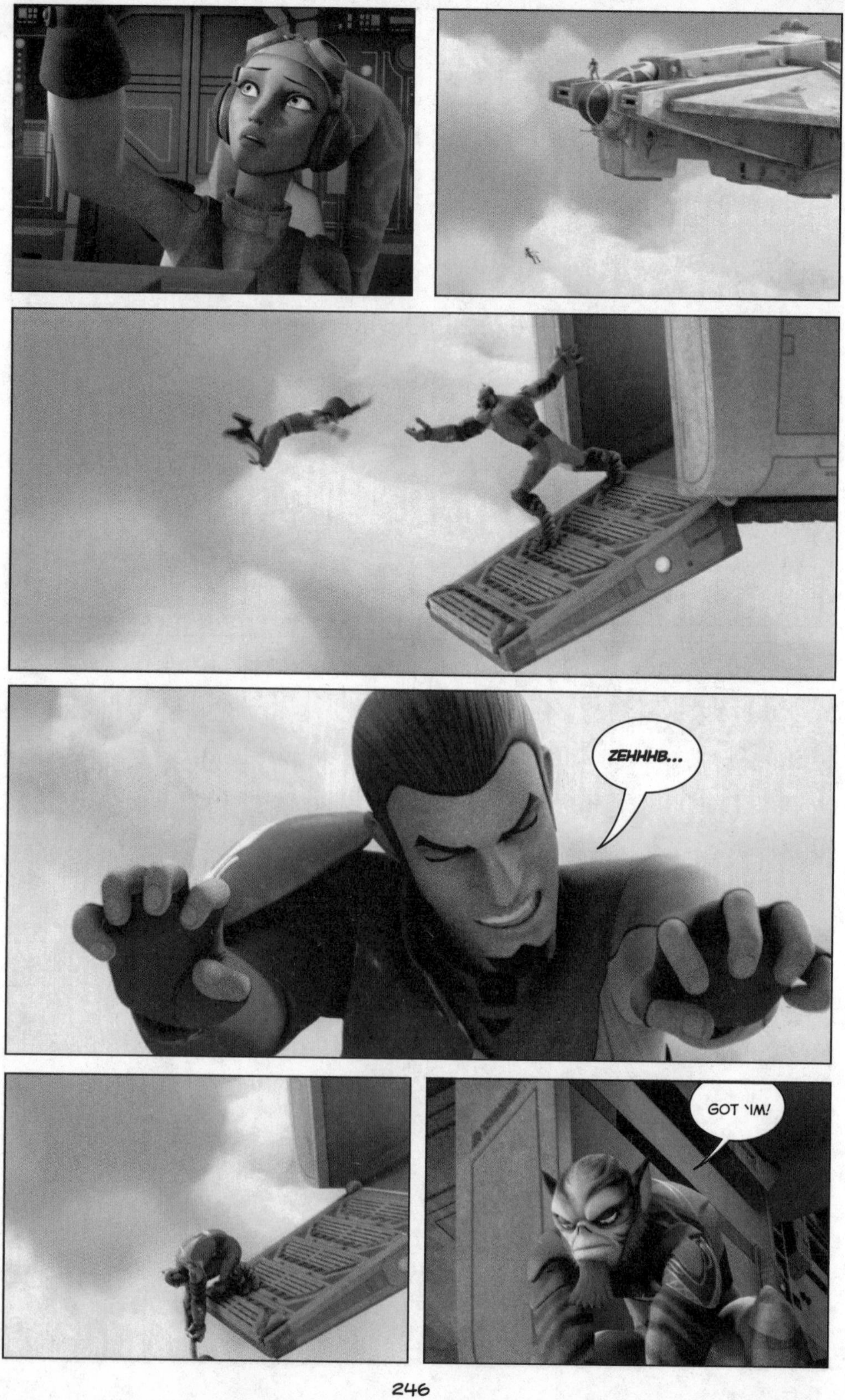
ZEHHHB...
GOT 'IM!

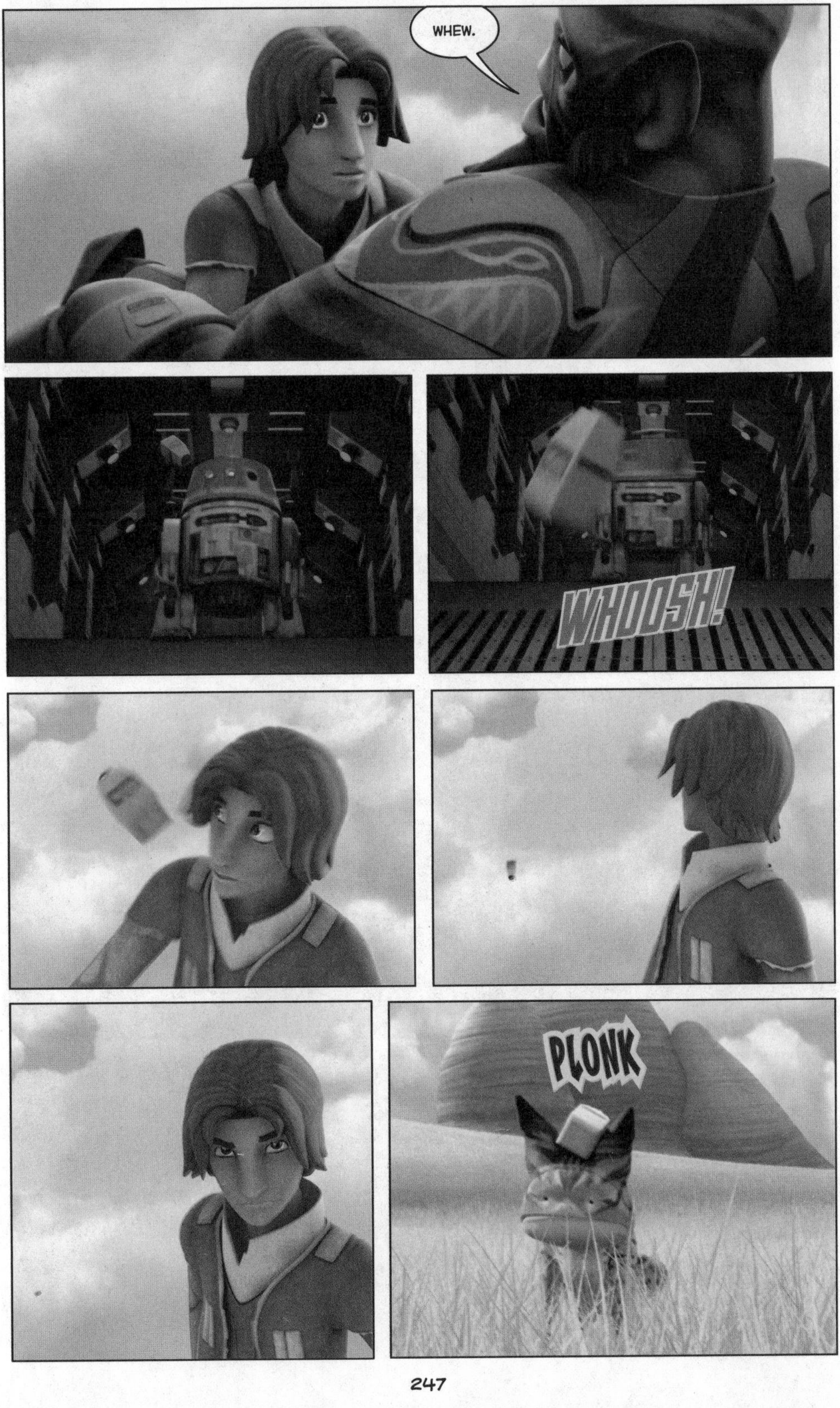
WHEW.
WHOOSH!
PLONK

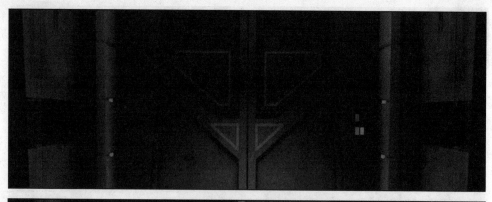

YOU WEREN'T FOCUSED.

TOUGH TO FOCUS WHEN I'M FALLING TO MY DEATH!

YOU WOULDN'T HAVE BEEN FALLING TO YOUR DEATH IF YOU WERE FOCUSED!

YOU'RE UNDISCIPLINED AND FULL OF SELF-DOUBT.

AND WHOSE FAULT IS THAT, *MASTER?*

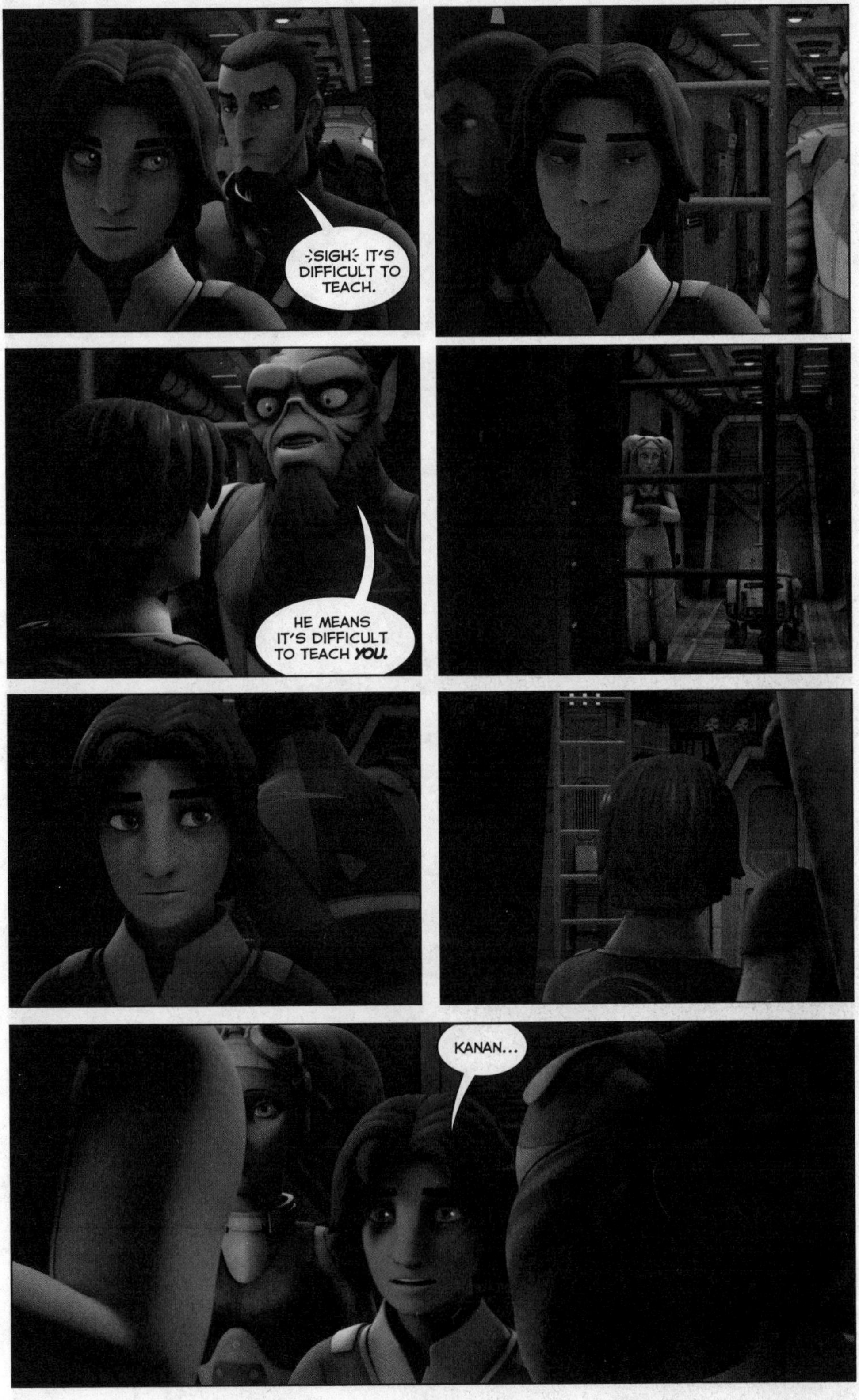
⁃SIGH⁃ IT'S DIFFICULT TO TEACH.
HE MEANS IT'S DIFFICULT TO TEACH *YOU.*
KANAN...

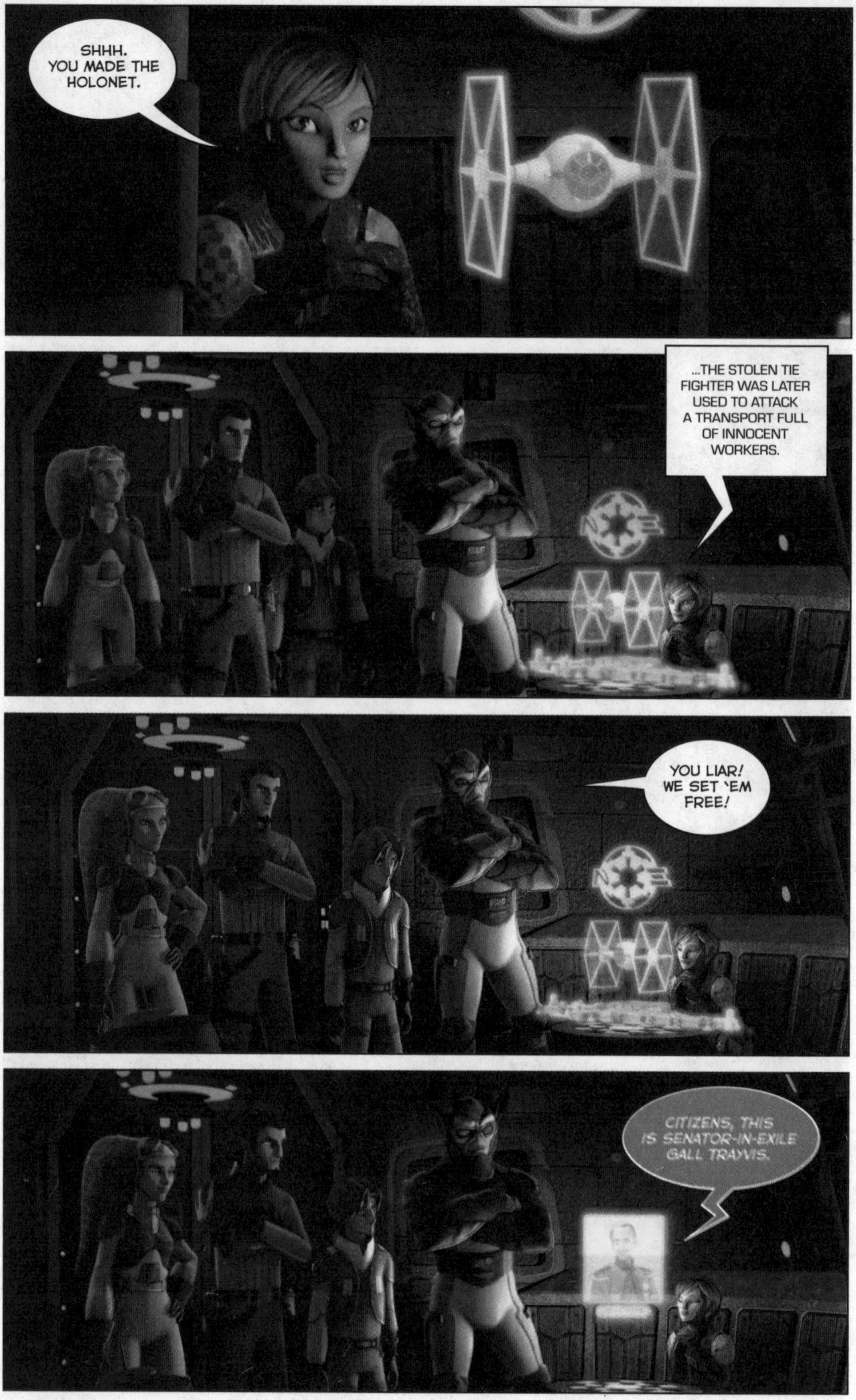
SHHH. YOU MADE THE HOLONET.
...THE STOLEN TIE FIGHTER WAS LATER USED TO ATTACK A TRANSPORT FULL OF INNOCENT WORKERS.
YOU LIAR! WE SET 'EM FREE!
CITIZENS, THIS IS SENATOR-IN-EXILE GALL TRAYVIS.

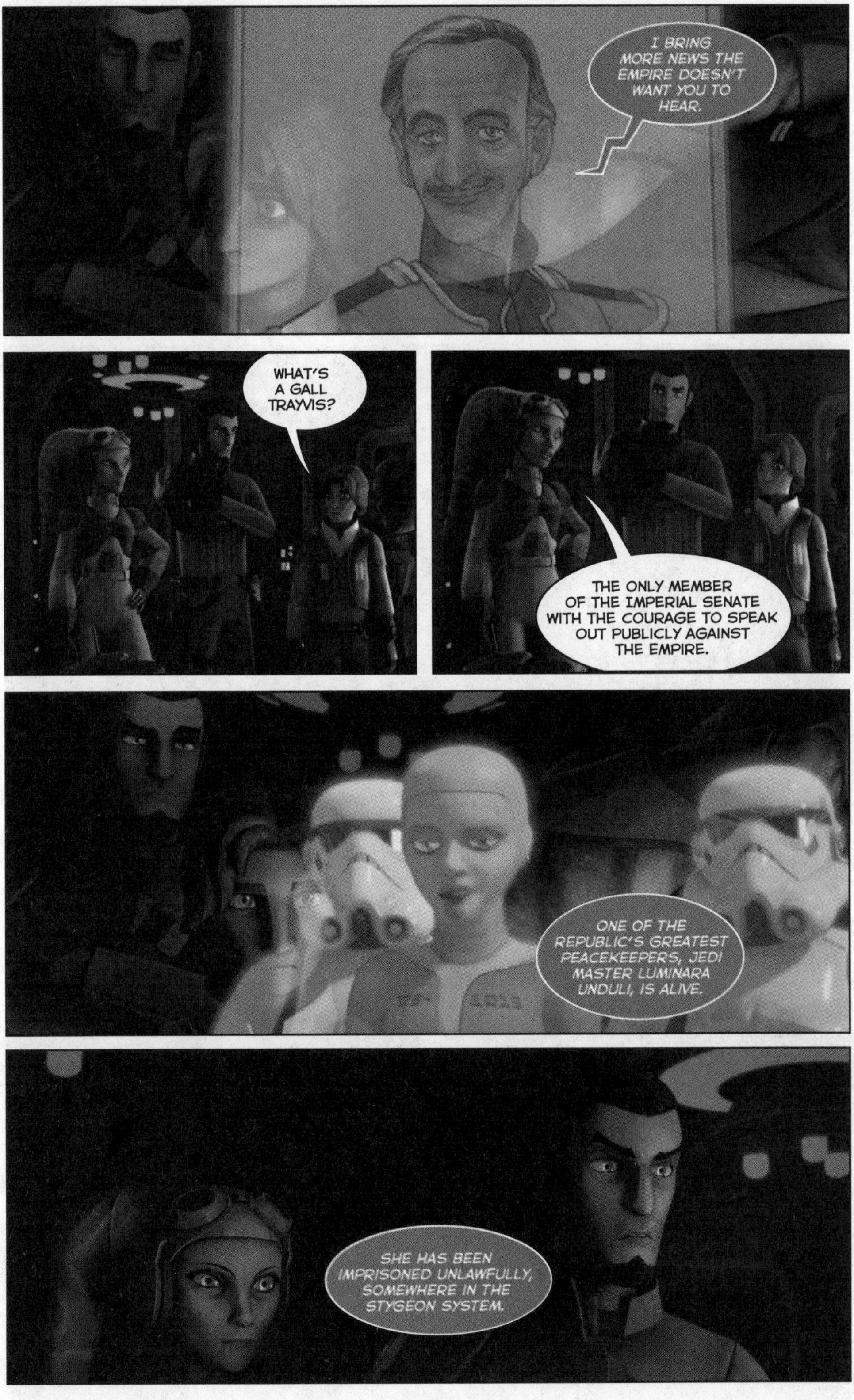
I BRING MORE NEWS THE EMPIRE DOESN'T WANT YOU TO HEAR.
WHAT'S A GALL TRAYVIS?
THE ONLY MEMBER OF THE IMPERIAL SENATE WITH THE COURAGE TO SPEAK OUT PUBLICLY AGAINST THE EMPIRE.
ONE OF THE REPUBLIC'S GREATEST PEACEKEEPERS, JEDI MASTER LUMINARA UNDULI, IS ALIVE.
SHE HAS BEEN IMPRISONED UNLAWFULLY, SOMEWHERE IN THE STYGEON SYSTEM.

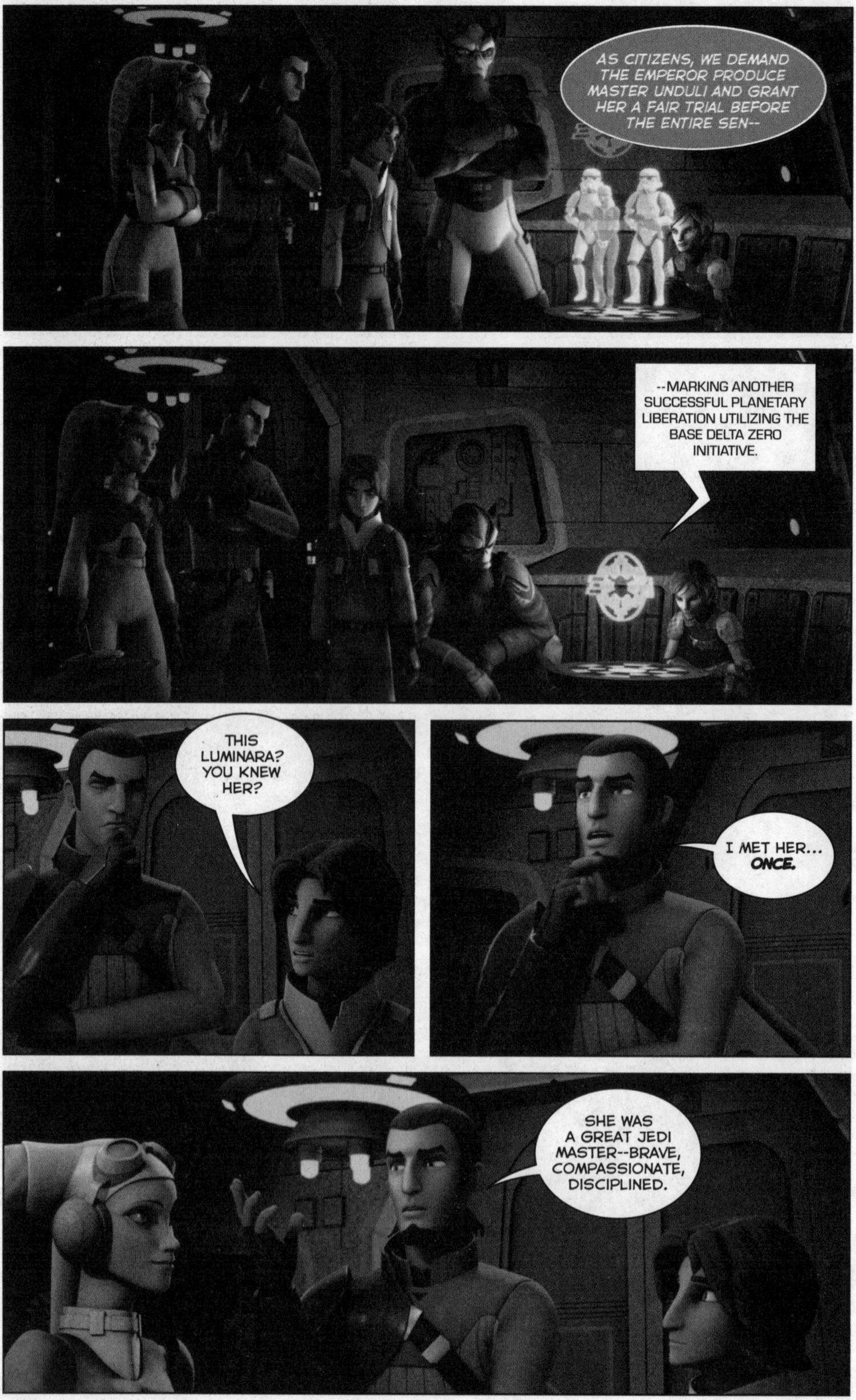
AS CITIZENS, WE DEMAND THE EMPEROR PRODUCE MASTER UNDULI AND GRANT HER A FAIR TRIAL BEFORE THE ENTIRE SEN--
--MARKING ANOTHER SUCCESSFUL PLANETARY LIBERATION UTILIZING THE BASE DELTA ZERO INITIATIVE.
THIS LUMINARA? YOU KNEW HER?
I MET HER... ONCE.
SHE WAS A GREAT JEDI MASTER--BRAVE, COMPASSIONATE, DISCIPLINED.

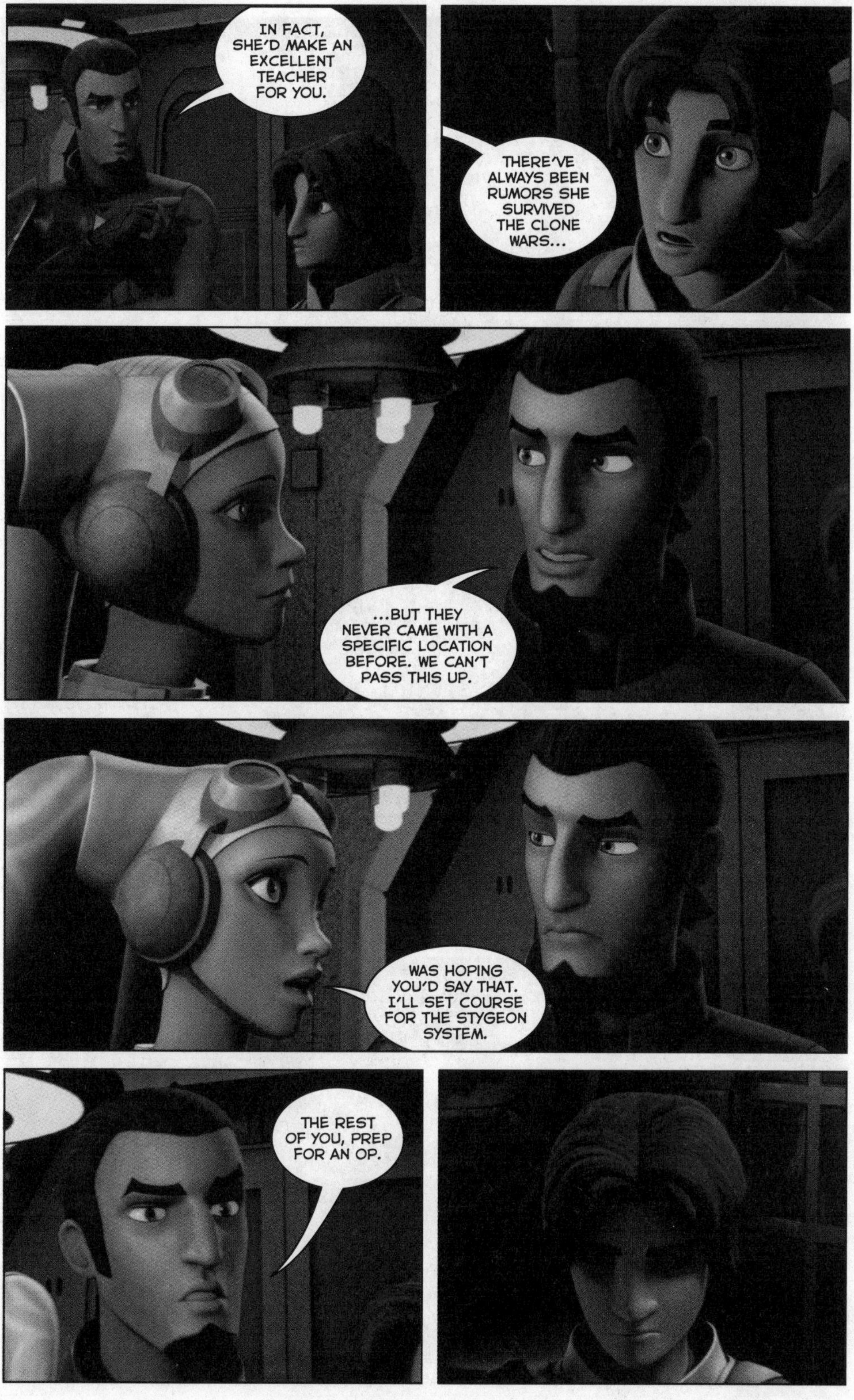
IN FACT, SHE'D MAKE AN EXCELLENT TEACHER FOR YOU.
THERE'VE ALWAYS BEEN RUMORS SHE SURVIVED THE CLONE WARS...
...BUT THEY NEVER CAME WITH A SPECIFIC LOCATION BEFORE. WE CAN'T PASS THIS UP.
WAS HOPING YOU'D SAY THAT. I'LL SET COURSE FOR THE STYGEON SYSTEM.
THE REST OF YOU, PREP FOR AN OP.

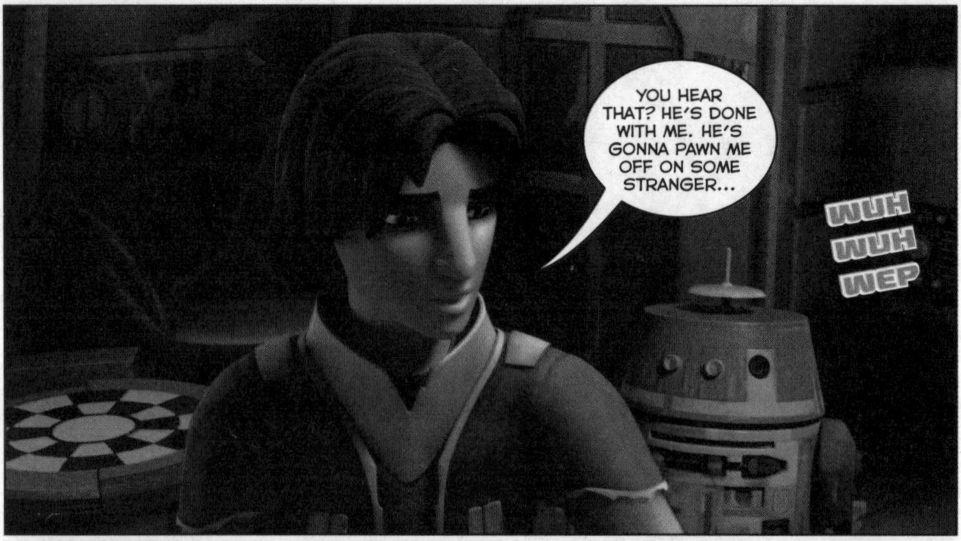
YOU HEAR THAT? HE'S DONE WITH ME. HE'S GONNA PAWN ME OFF ON SOME STRANGER...
WUH
WUH
WEP

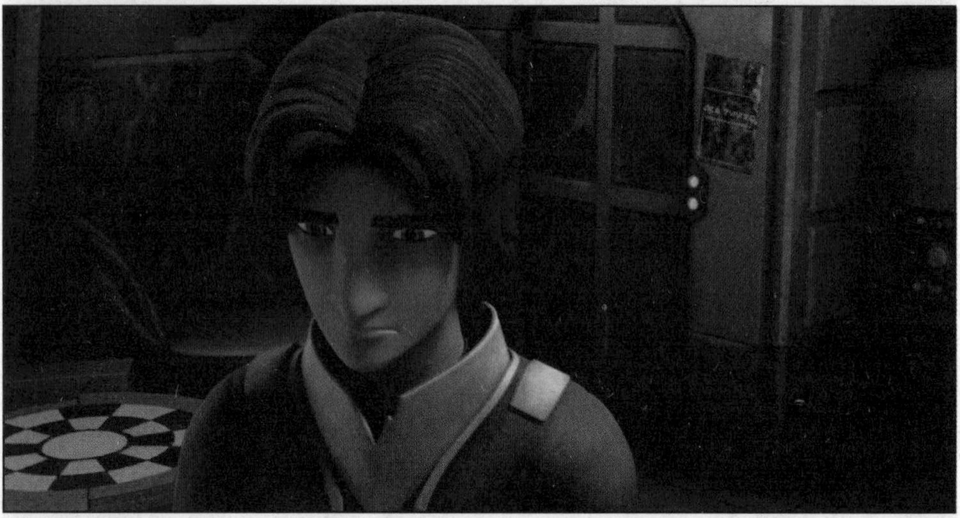

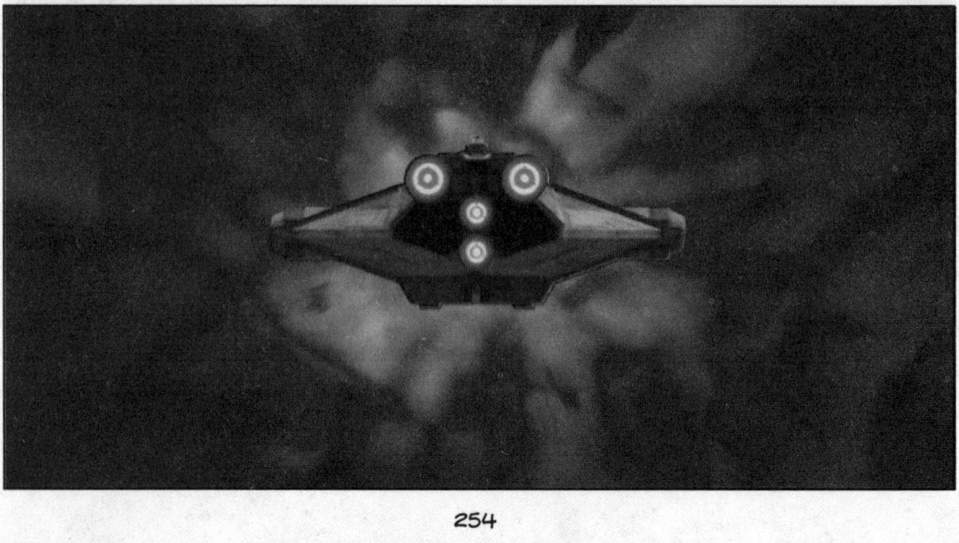

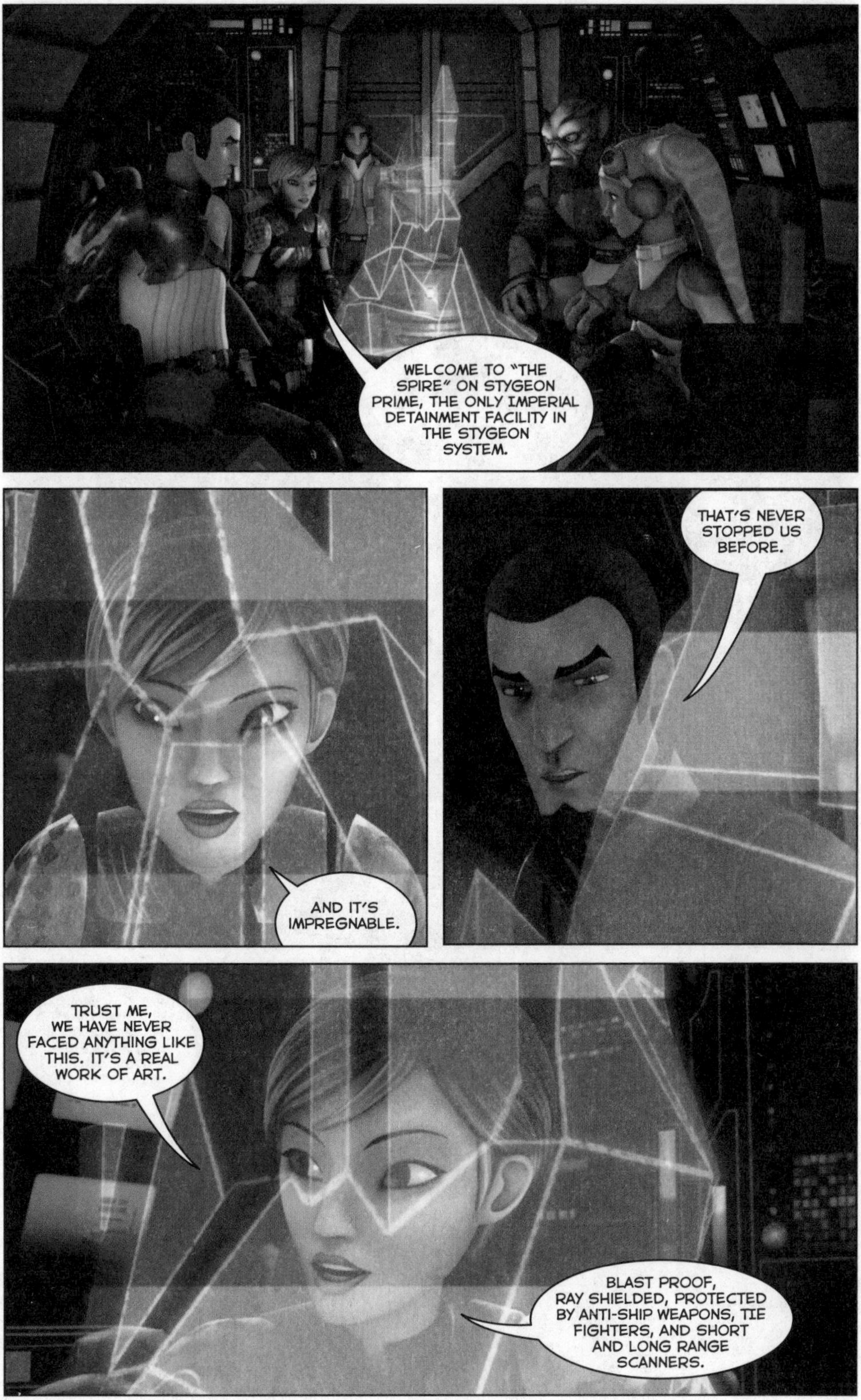
WELCOME TO "THE SPIRE" ON STYGEON PRIME, THE ONLY IMPERIAL DETAINMENT FACILITY IN THE STYGEON SYSTEM.
AND IT'S IMPREGNABLE.
THAT'S NEVER STOPPED US BEFORE.
TRUST ME, WE HAVE NEVER FACED ANYTHING LIKE THIS. IT'S A REAL WORK OF ART.
BLAST PROOF, RAY SHIELDED, PROTECTED BY ANTI-SHIP WEAPONS, TIE FIGHTERS, AND SHORT AND LONG RANGE SCANNERS.

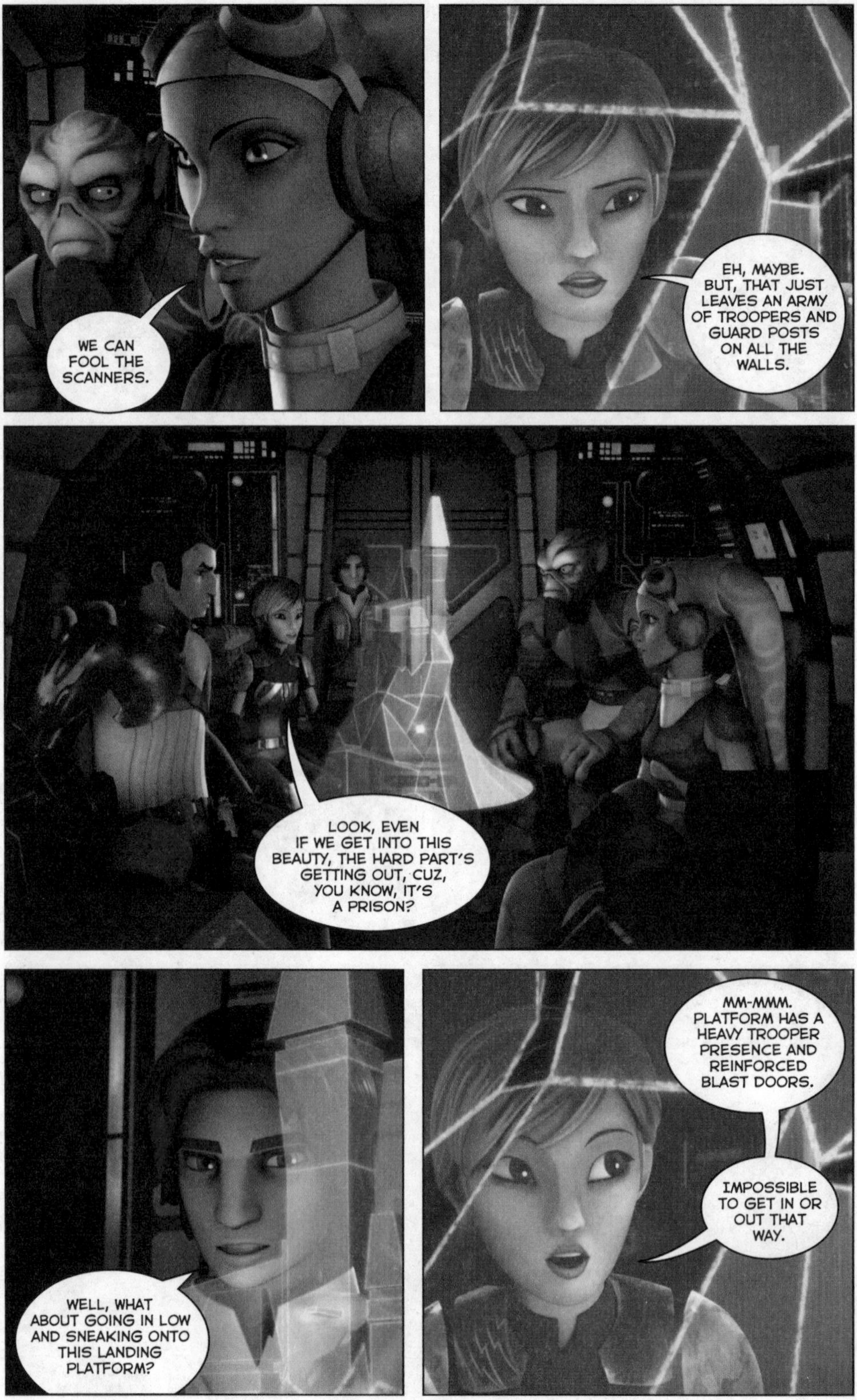
WE CAN FOOL THE SCANNERS.
EH, MAYBE. BUT, THAT JUST LEAVES AN ARMY OF TROOPERS AND GUARD POSTS ON ALL THE WALLS.
LOOK, EVEN IF WE GET INTO THIS BEAUTY, THE HARD PART'S GETTING OUT, CUZ, YOU KNOW, IT'S A PRISON?
WELL, WHAT ABOUT GOING IN LOW AND SNEAKING ONTO THIS LANDING PLATFORM?
MM-MMM. PLATFORM HAS A HEAVY TROOPER PRESENCE AND REINFORCED BLAST DOORS.
IMPOSSIBLE TO GET IN OR OUT THAT WAY.

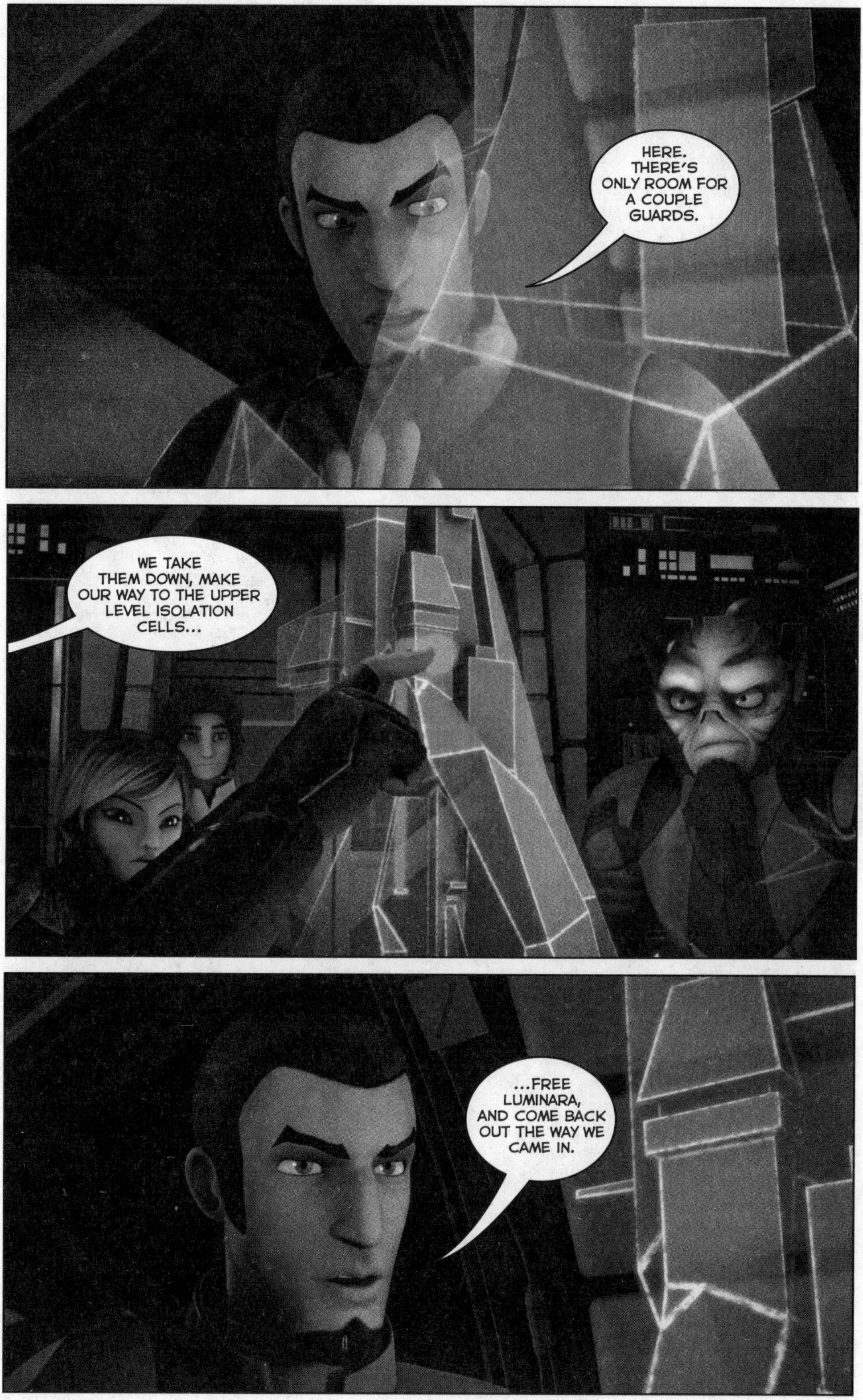
HERE. THERE'S ONLY ROOM FOR A COUPLE GUARDS.
WE TAKE THEM DOWN, MAKE OUR WAY TO THE UPPER LEVEL ISOLATION CELLS...
...FREE LUMINARA, AND COME BACK OUT THE WAY WE CAME IN.

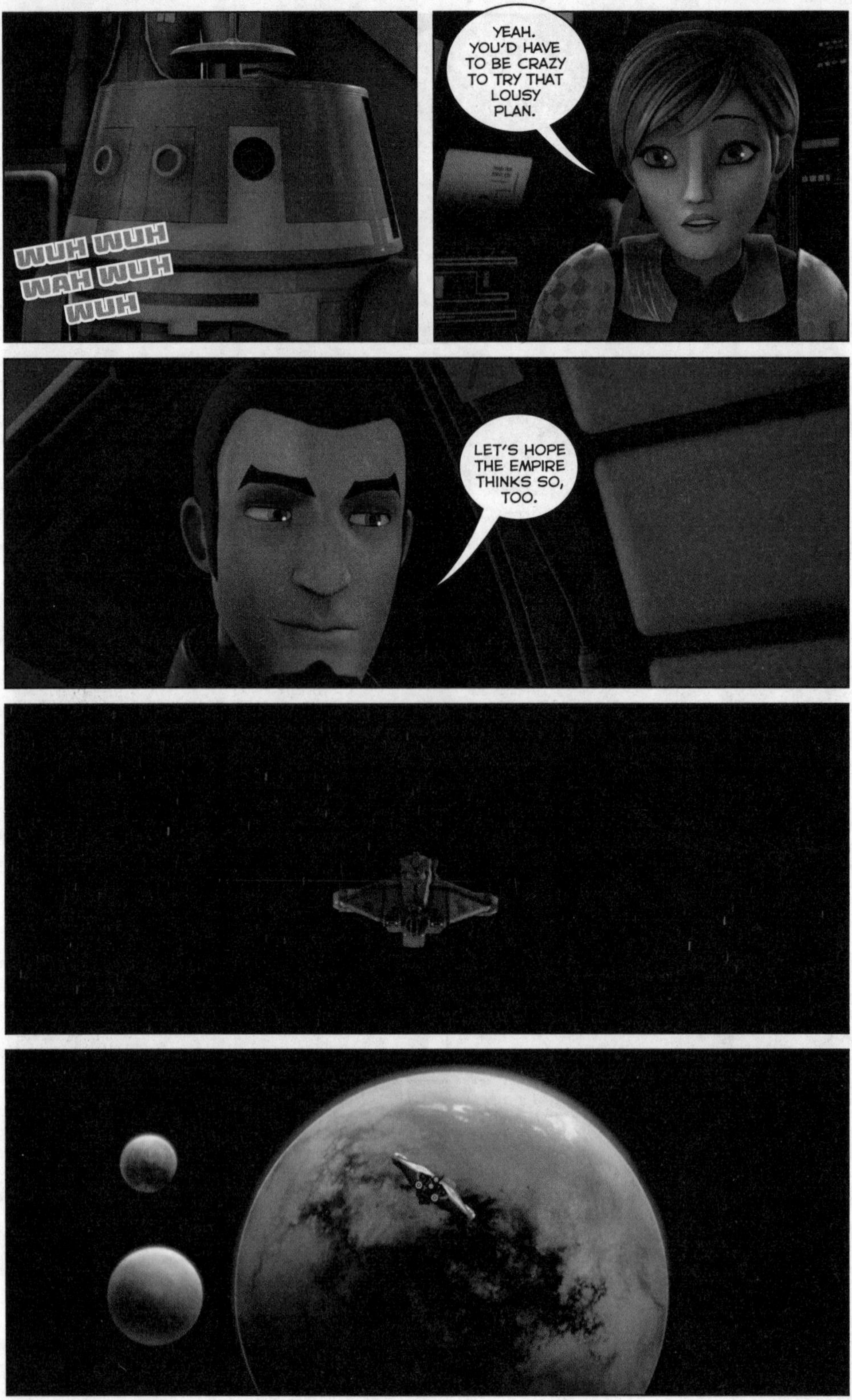
WUH WUH
WAH WUH
WUH
YEAH. YOU'D HAVE TO BE CRAZY TO TRY THAT LOUSY PLAN.
LET'S HOPE THE EMPIRE THINKS SO, TOO.

WUH WUH WAP WUH WUH WAP.

OH, I'M SORRY, CHOP. WE JUST DON'T NEED YOUR DAMAGED LOGIC CIRCUITS ON THIS ONE.

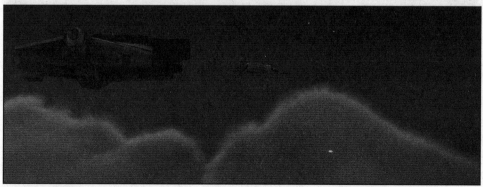

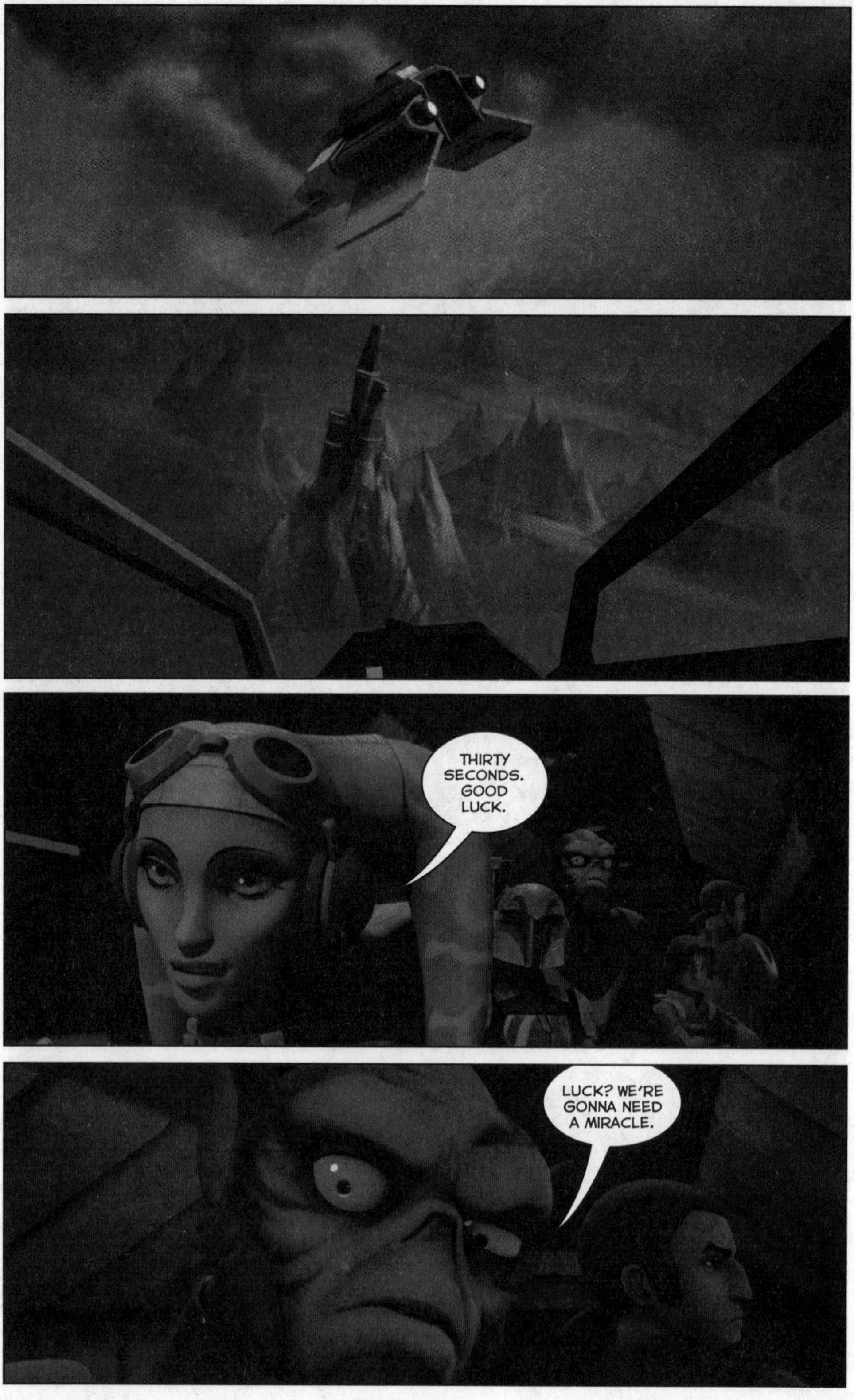
THIRTY SECONDS. GOOD LUCK.
LUCK? WE'RE GONNA NEED A MIRACLE.

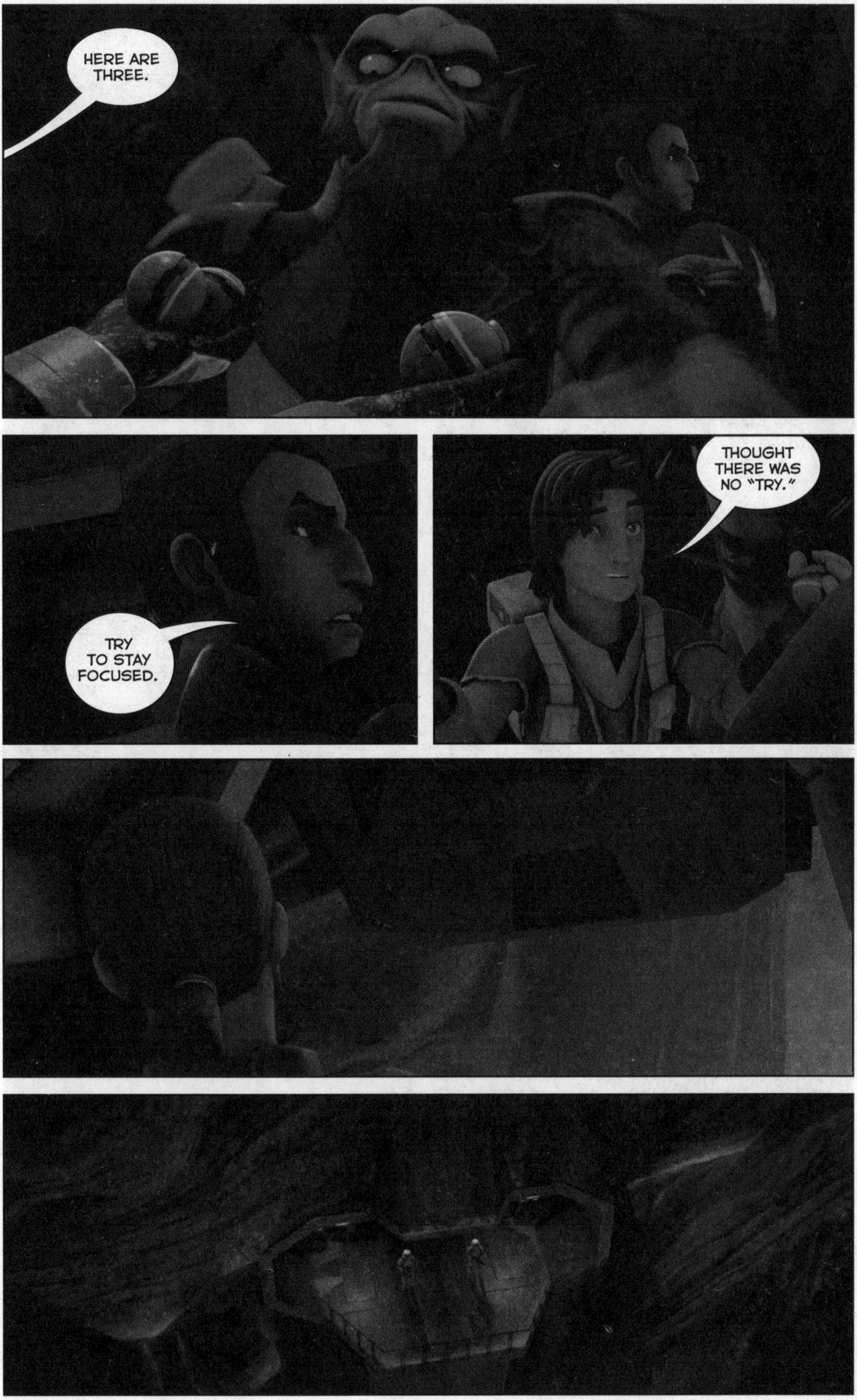
HERE ARE THREE.
TRY TO STAY FOCUSED.
THOUGHT THERE WAS NO "TRY."

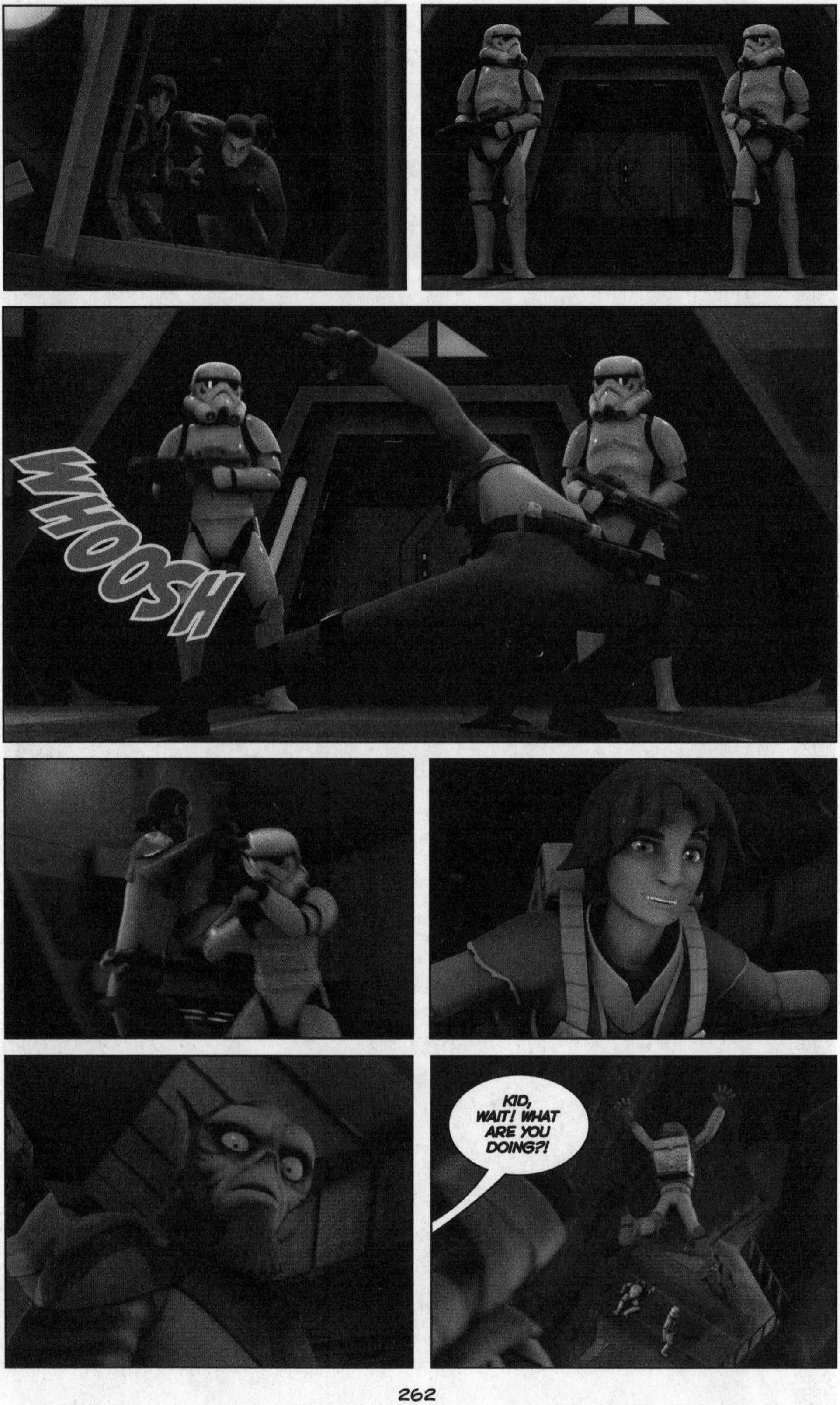
WHOOSH
KID, WAIT! WHAT ARE YOU DOING?!

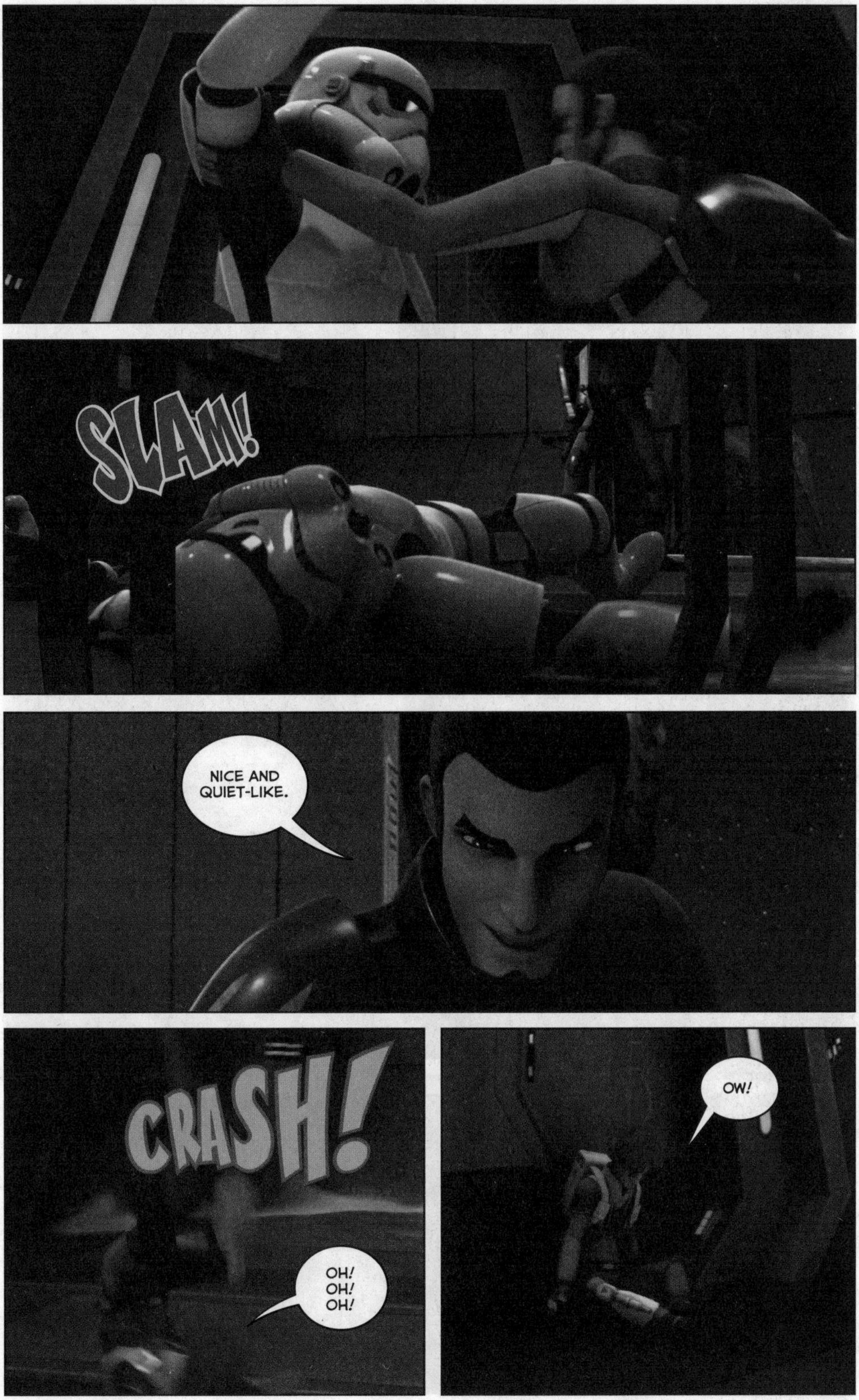
SLAM!
NICE AND QUIET-LIKE.
CRASH!
OH! OH! OH!
OW!

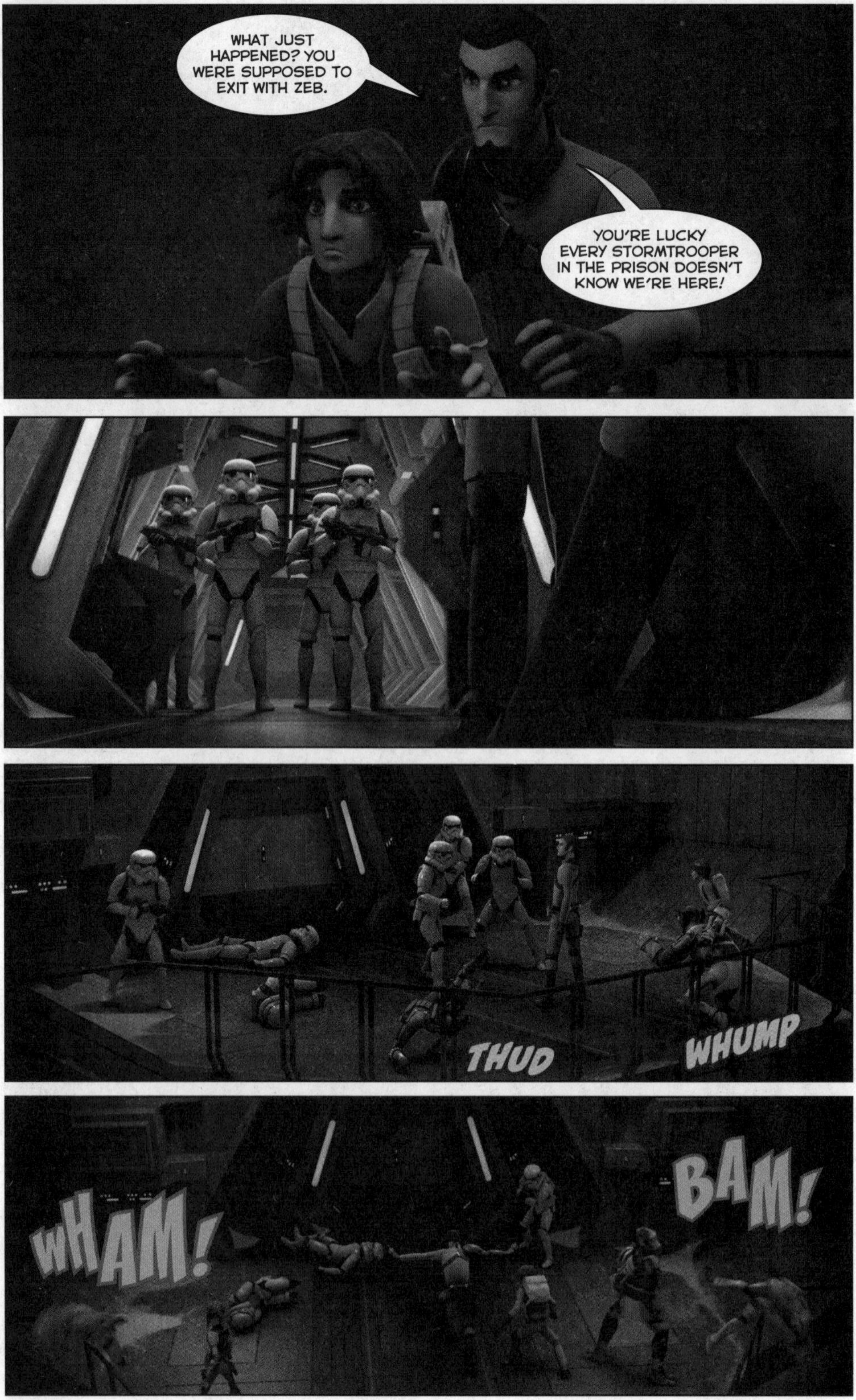
WHAT JUST HAPPENED? YOU WERE SUPPOSED TO EXIT WITH ZEB.
YOU'RE LUCKY EVERY STORMTROOPER IN THE PRISON DOESN'T KNOW WE'RE HERE!
THUD
WHUMP
WHAM!
BAM!

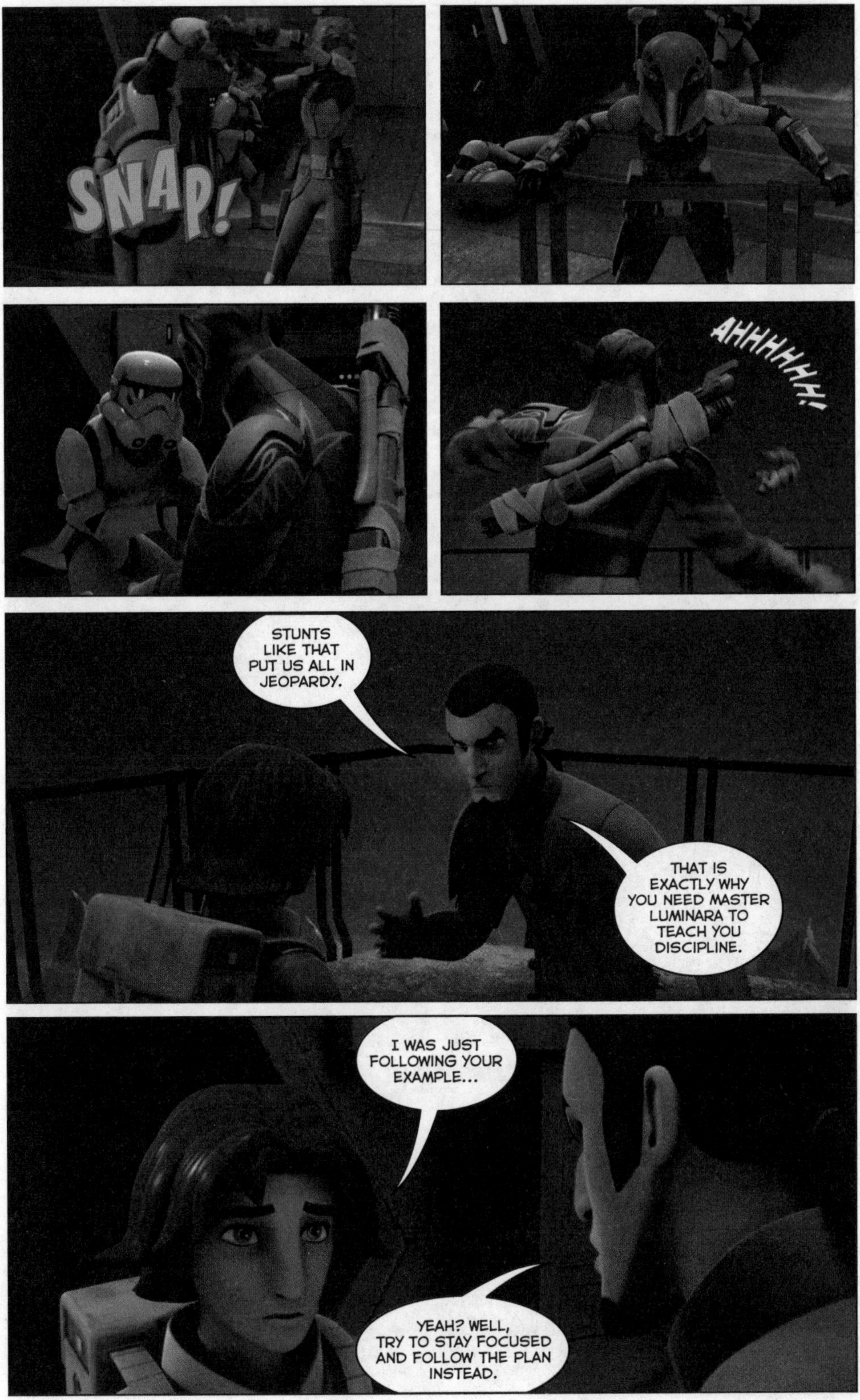
SNAP!
AHHHHHH!
STUNTS LIKE THAT PUT US ALL IN JEOPARDY.
THAT IS EXACTLY WHY YOU NEED MASTER LUMINARA TO TEACH YOU DISCIPLINE.
I WAS JUST FOLLOWING YOUR EXAMPLE...
YEAH? WELL, TRY TO STAY FOCUSED AND FOLLOW THE PLAN INSTEAD.

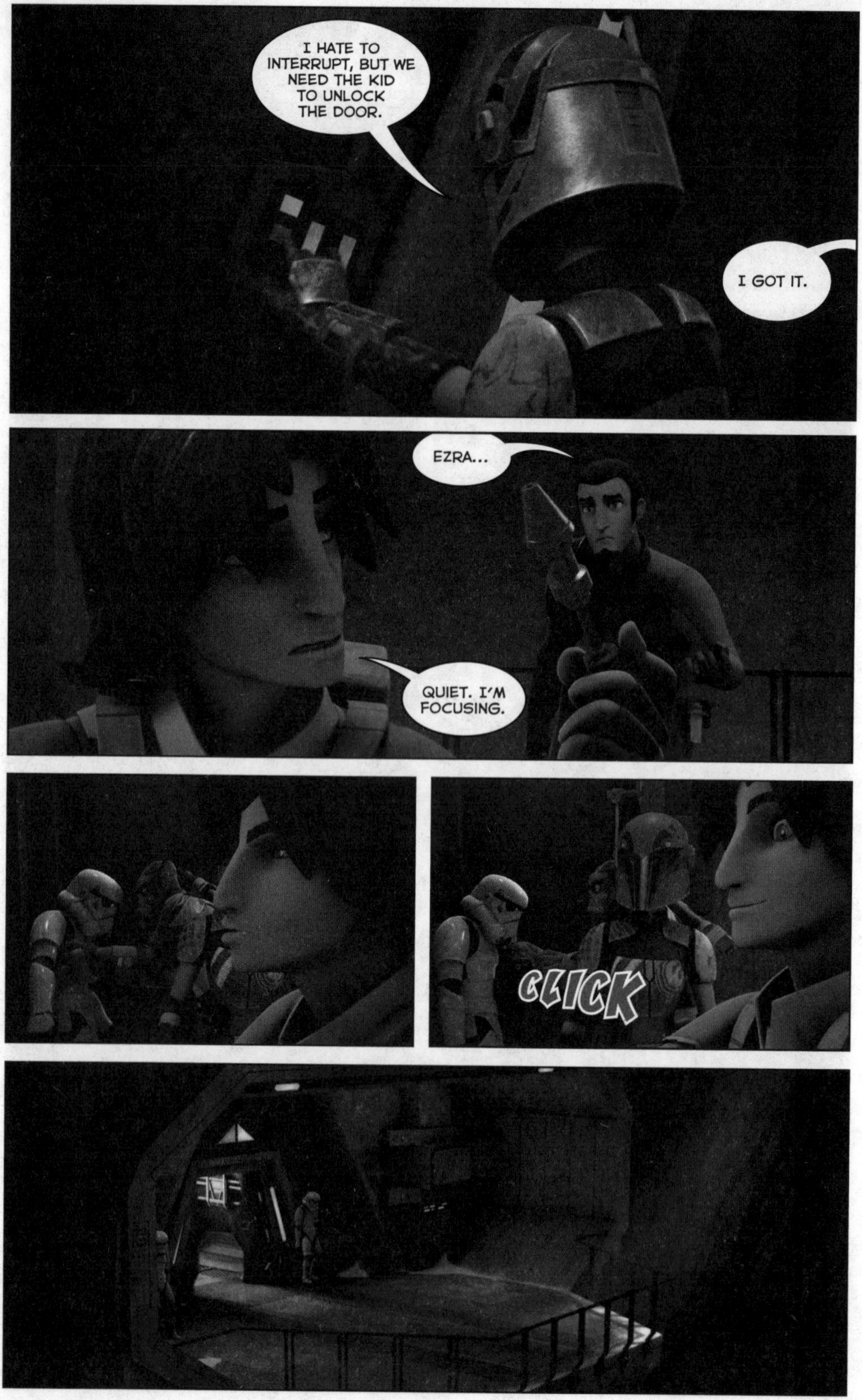
I HATE TO INTERRUPT, BUT WE NEED THE KID TO UNLOCK THE DOOR.
I GOT IT.
EZRA...
QUIET. I'M FOCUSING.
CLICK

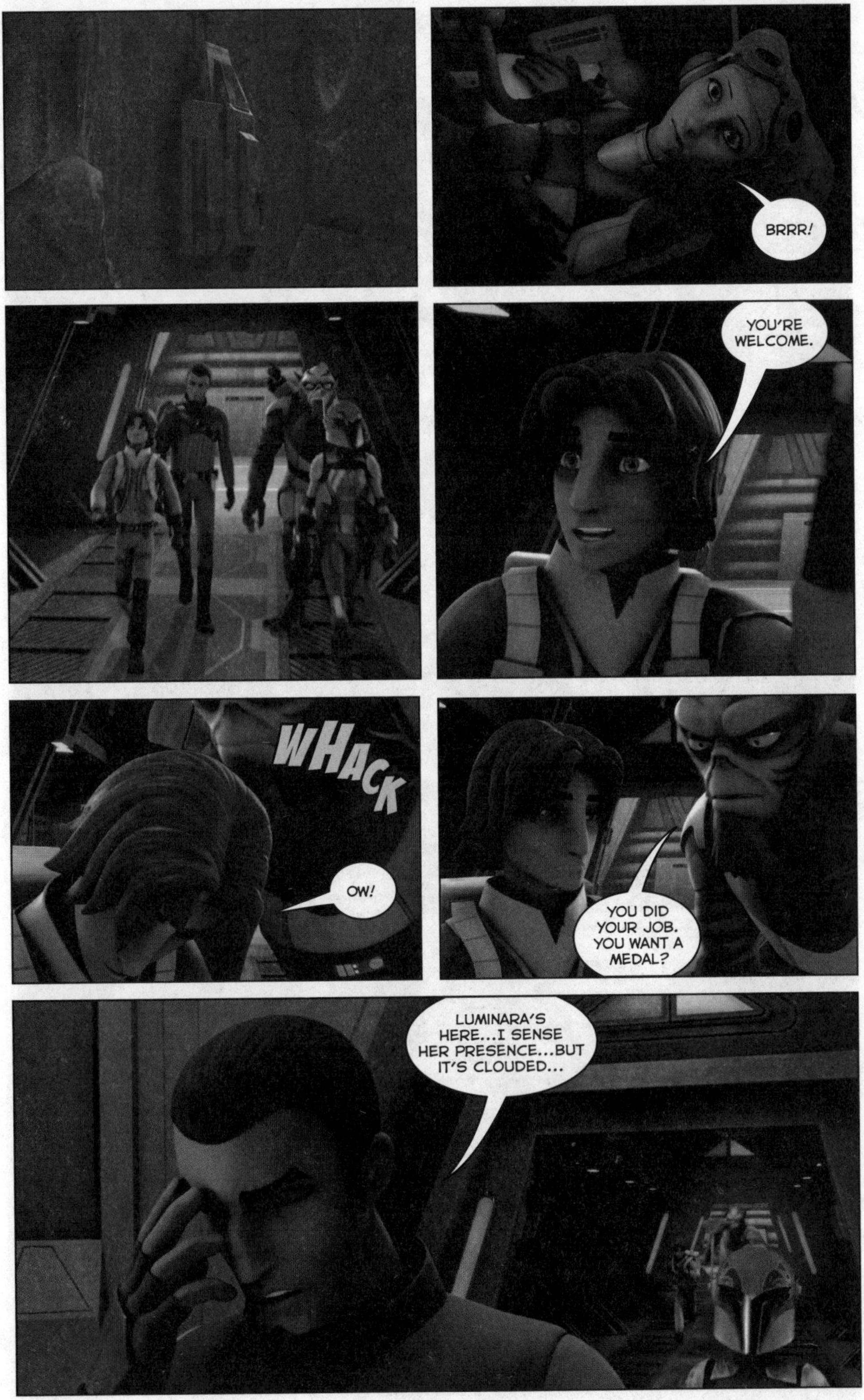
BRRR!
YOU'RE WELCOME.
WHACK
OW!
YOU DID YOUR JOB. YOU WANT A MEDAL?
LUMINARA'S HERE...I SENSE HER PRESENCE...BUT IT'S CLOUDED...

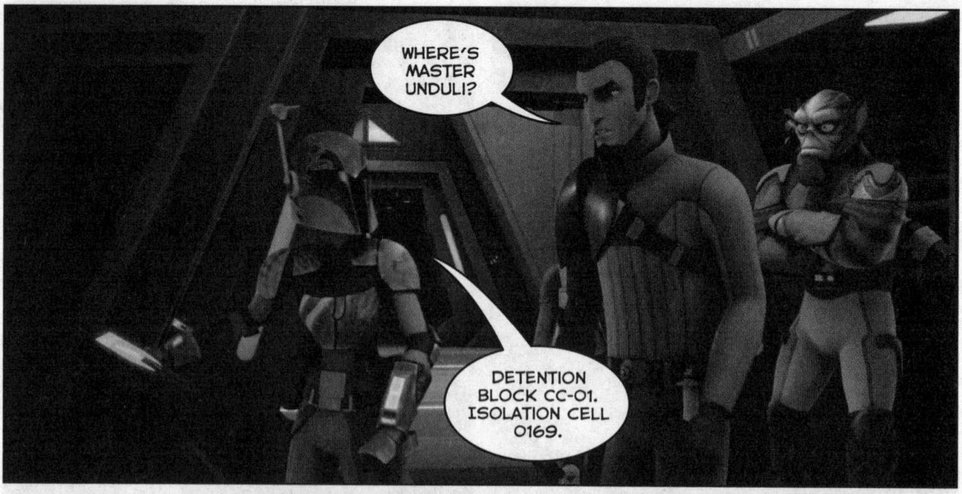
WHERE'S MASTER UNDULI?
DETENTION BLOCK CC-01. ISOLATION CELL 0169.

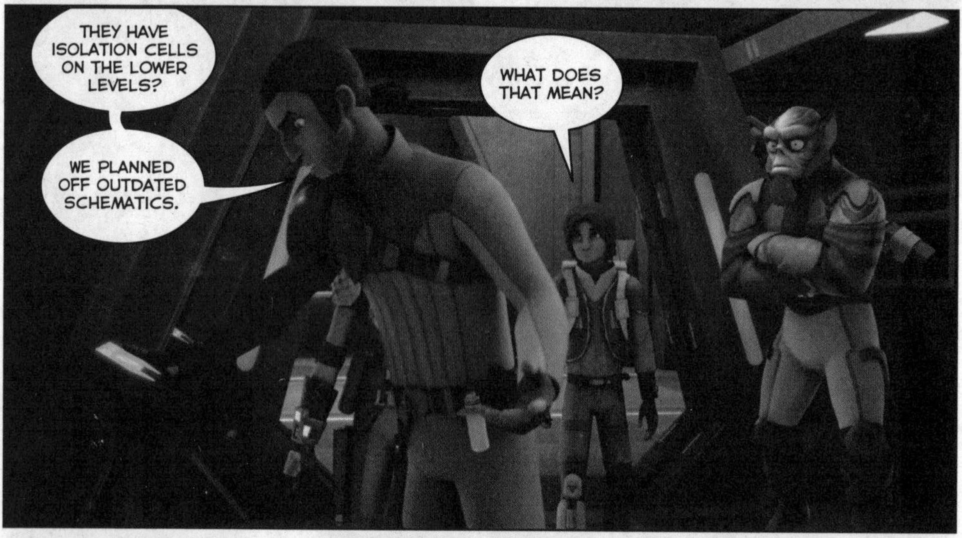
THEY HAVE ISOLATION CELLS ON THE LOWER LEVELS?
WE PLANNED OFF OUTDATED SCHEMATICS.
WHAT DOES THAT MEAN?

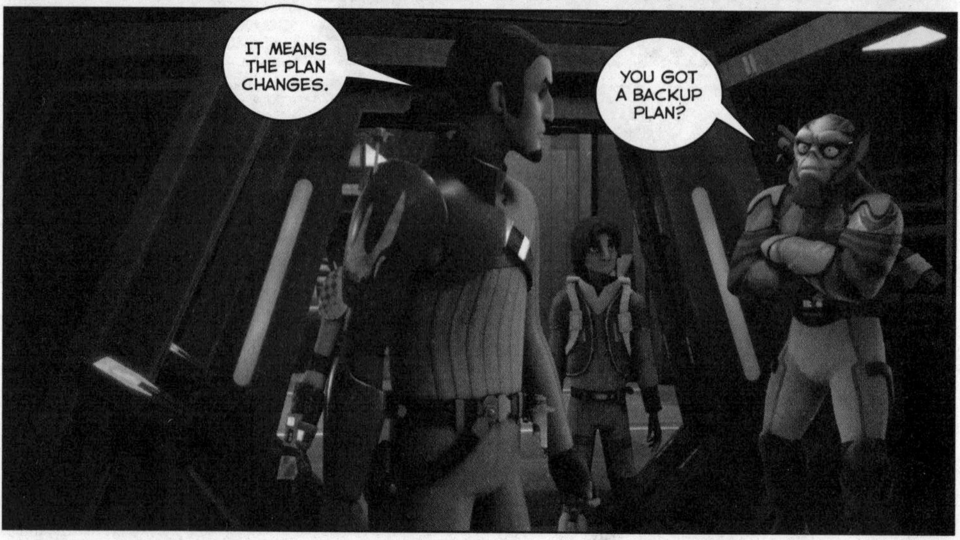
IT MEANS THE PLAN CHANGES.
YOU GOT A BACKUP PLAN?

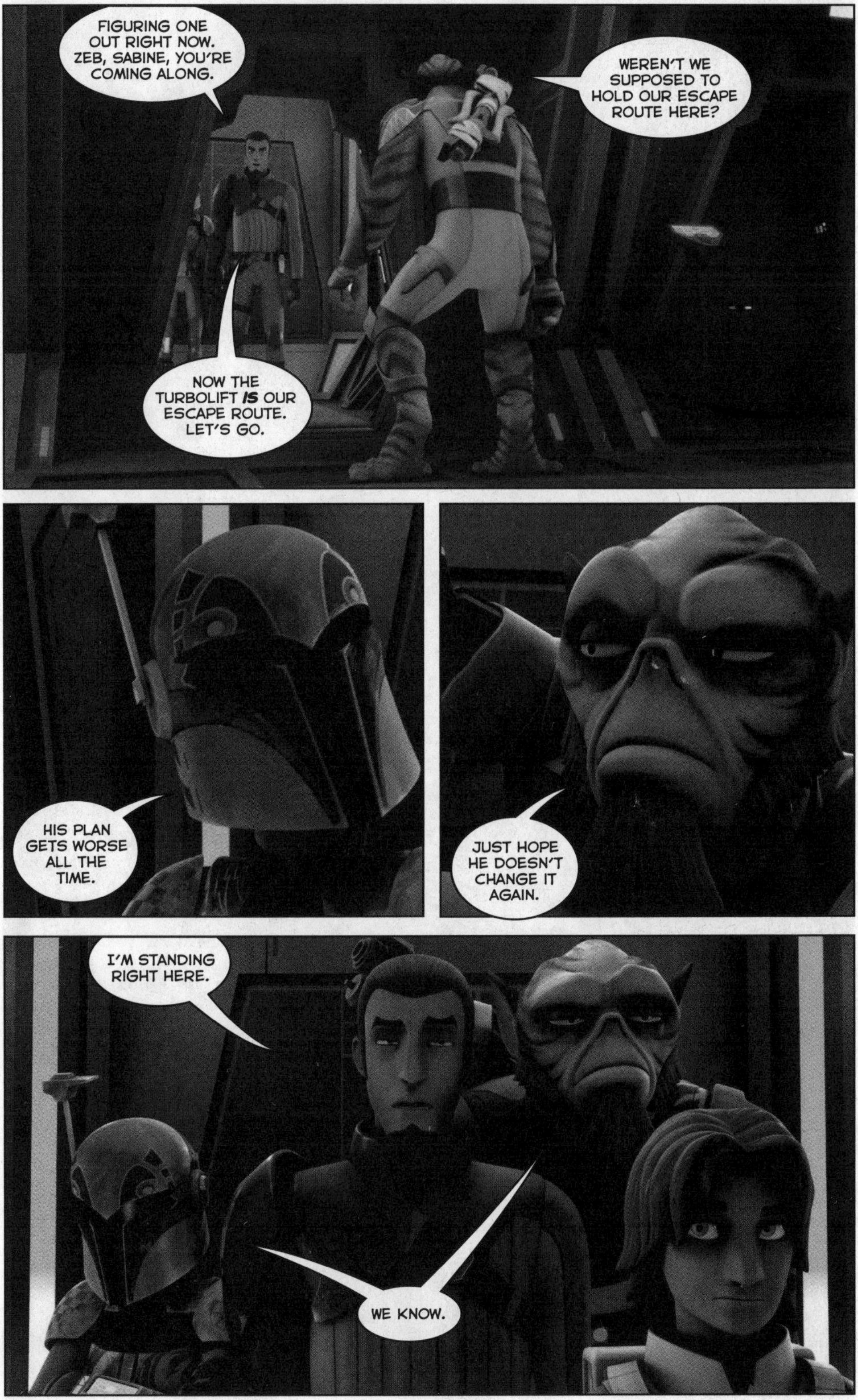
FIGURING ONE OUT RIGHT NOW. ZEB, SABINE, YOU'RE COMING ALONG.
WEREN'T WE SUPPOSED TO HOLD OUR ESCAPE ROUTE HERE?
NOW THE TURBOLIFT *IS* OUR ESCAPE ROUTE. LET'S GO.
HIS PLAN GETS WORSE ALL THE TIME.
JUST HOPE HE DOESN'T CHANGE IT AGAIN.
I'M STANDING RIGHT HERE.
WE KNOW.

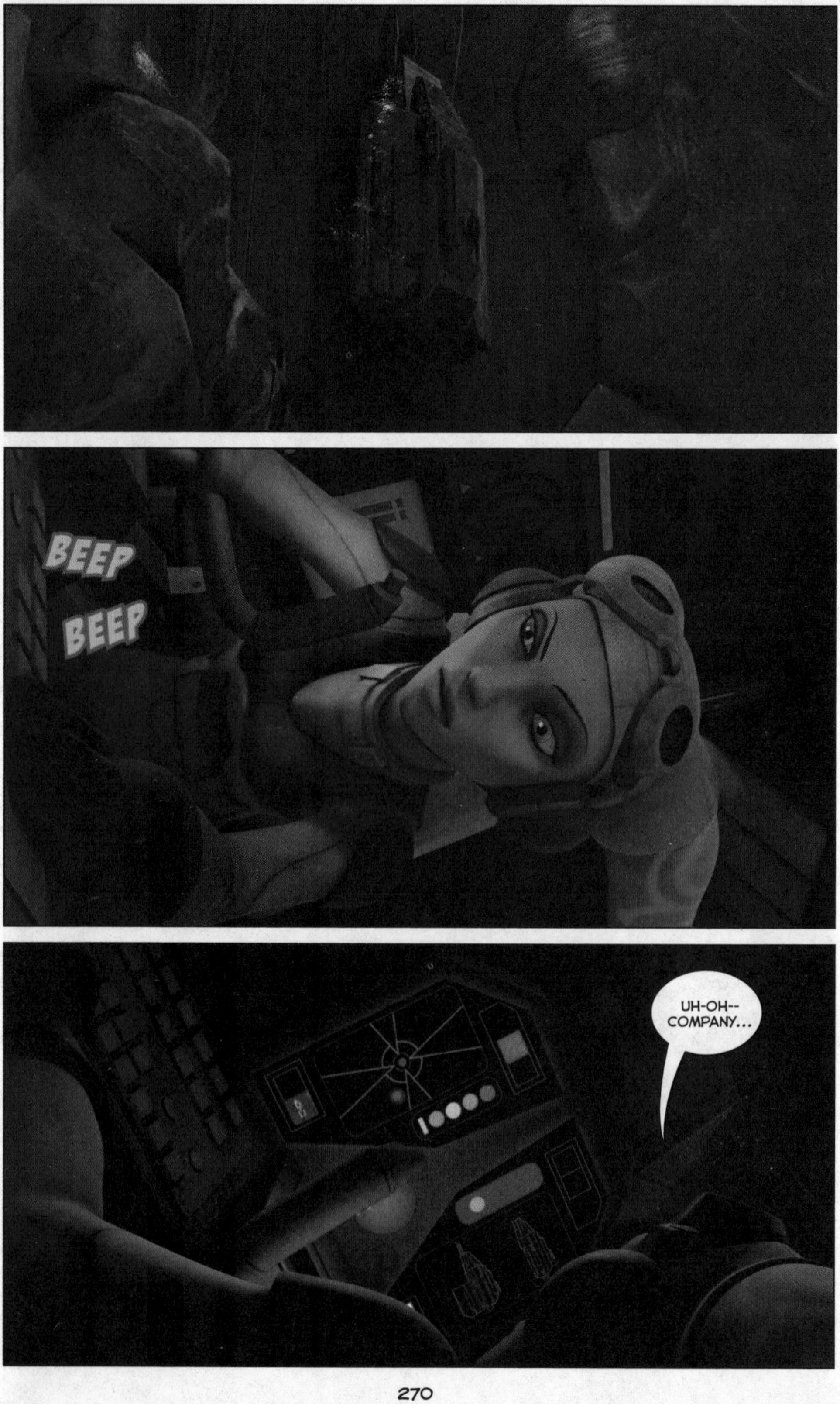
BEEP
BEEP
UH-OH--
COMPANY...

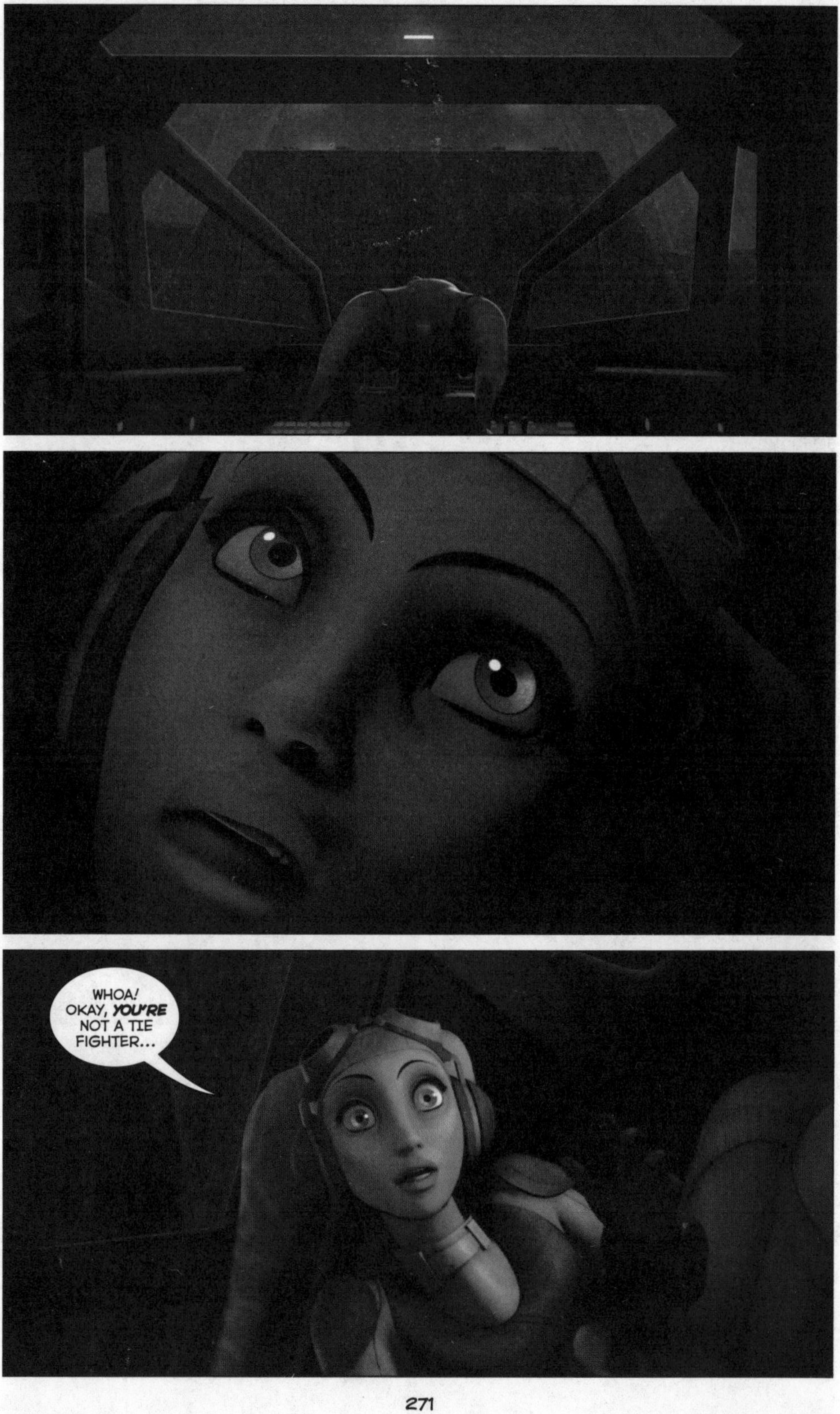
WHOA! OKAY, ***YOU'RE*** NOT A TIE FIGHTER...

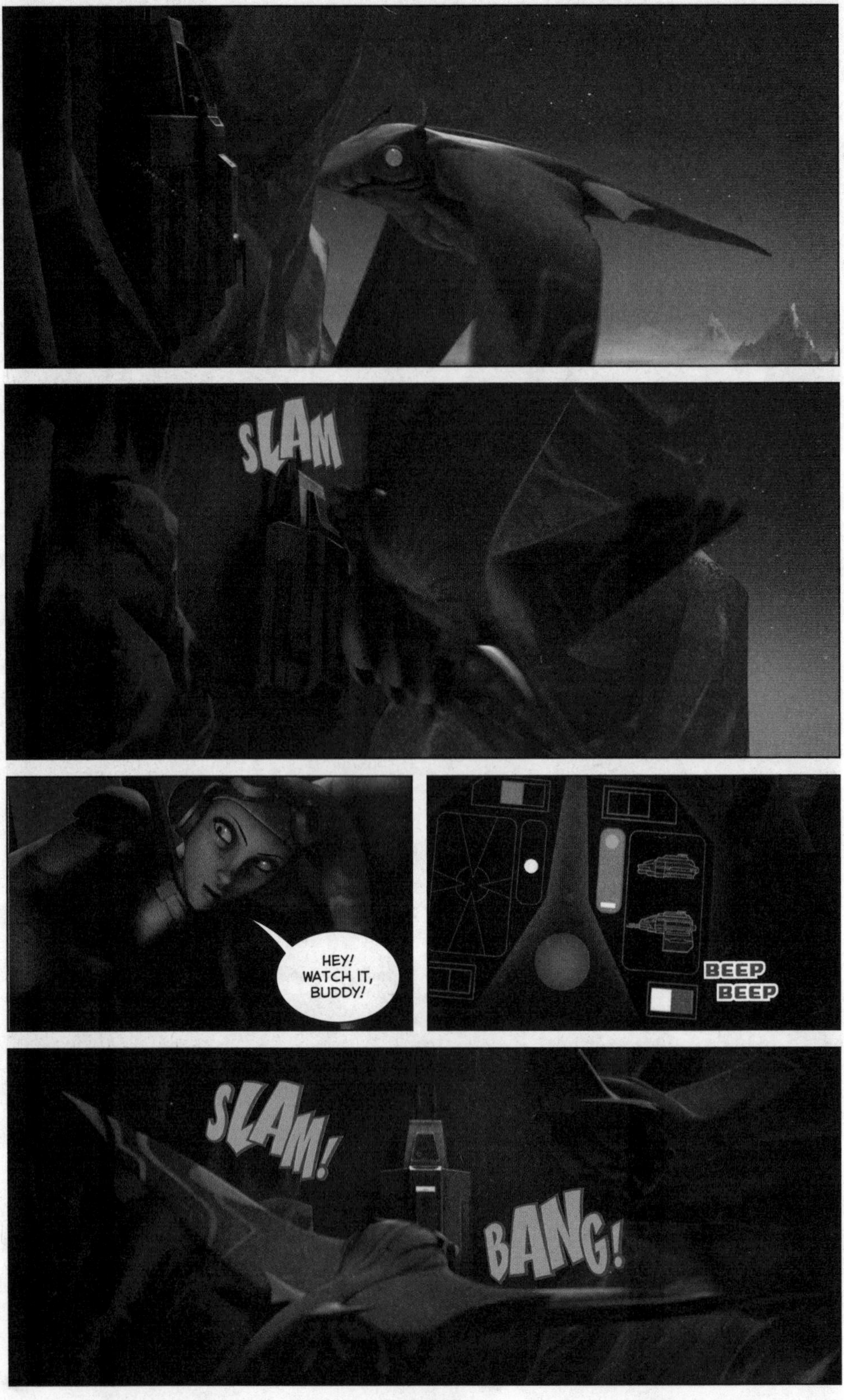
SLAM
HEY! WATCH IT, BUDDY!
BEEP BEEP
SLAM!
BANG!

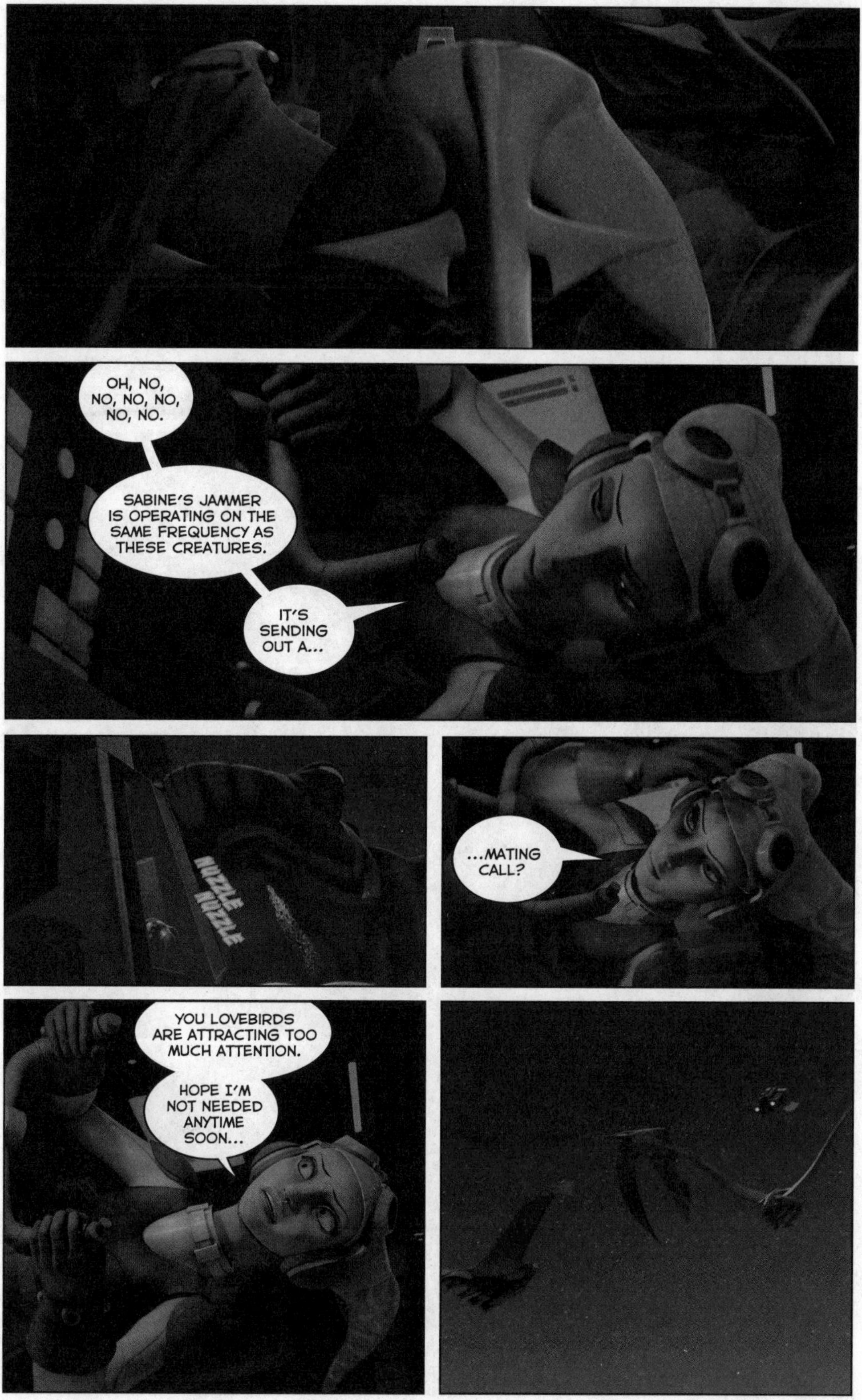
OH, NO, NO, NO, NO, NO, NO.
SABINE'S JAMMER IS OPERATING ON THE SAME FREQUENCY AS THESE CREATURES.
IT'S SENDING OUT A...
...MATING CALL?
YOU LOVEBIRDS ARE ATTRACTING TOO MUCH ATTENTION.
HOPE I'M NOT NEEDED ANYTIME SOON...

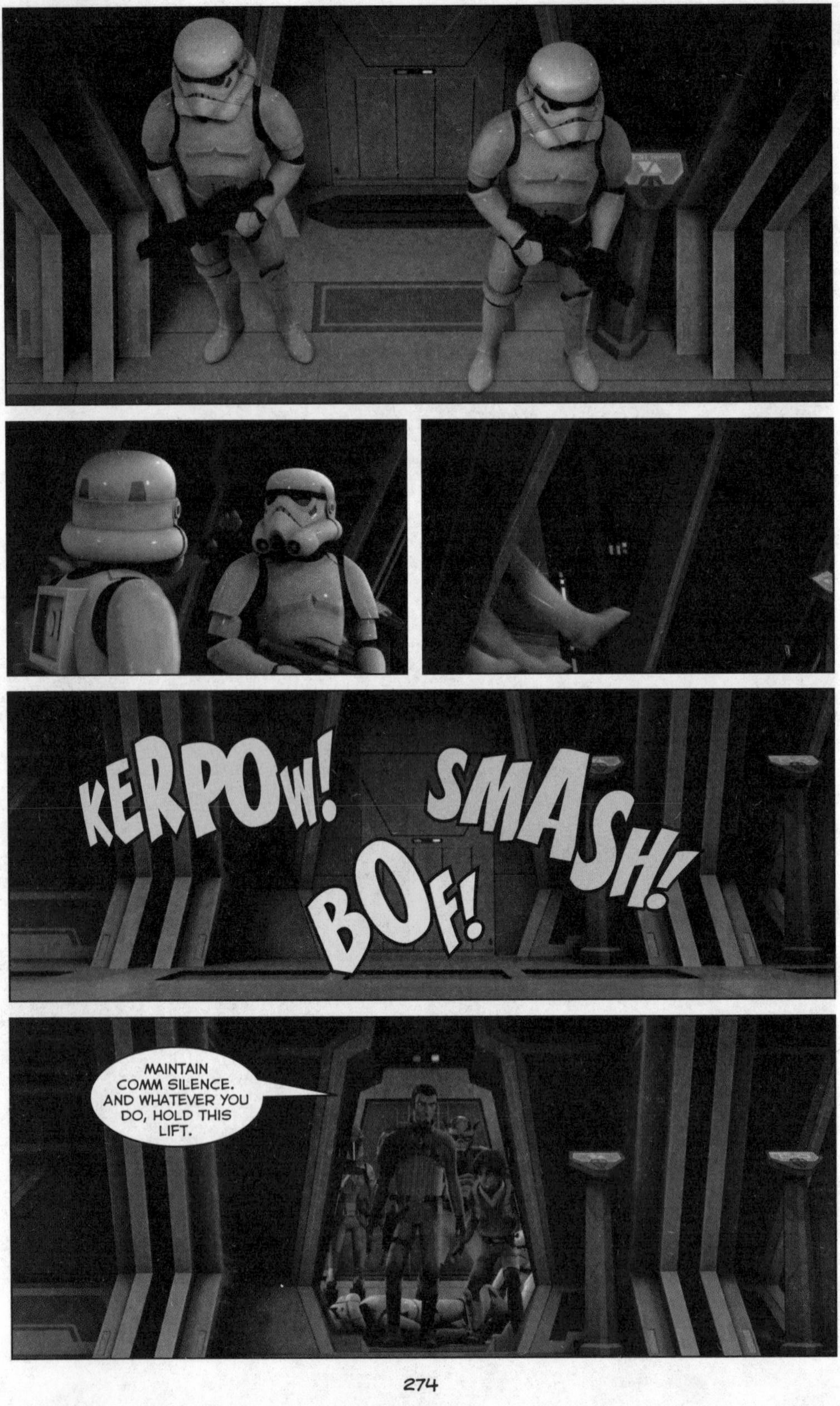
KERPOW!
SMASH!
BOF!
MAINTAIN COMM SILENCE. AND WHATEVER YOU DO, HOLD THIS LIFT.

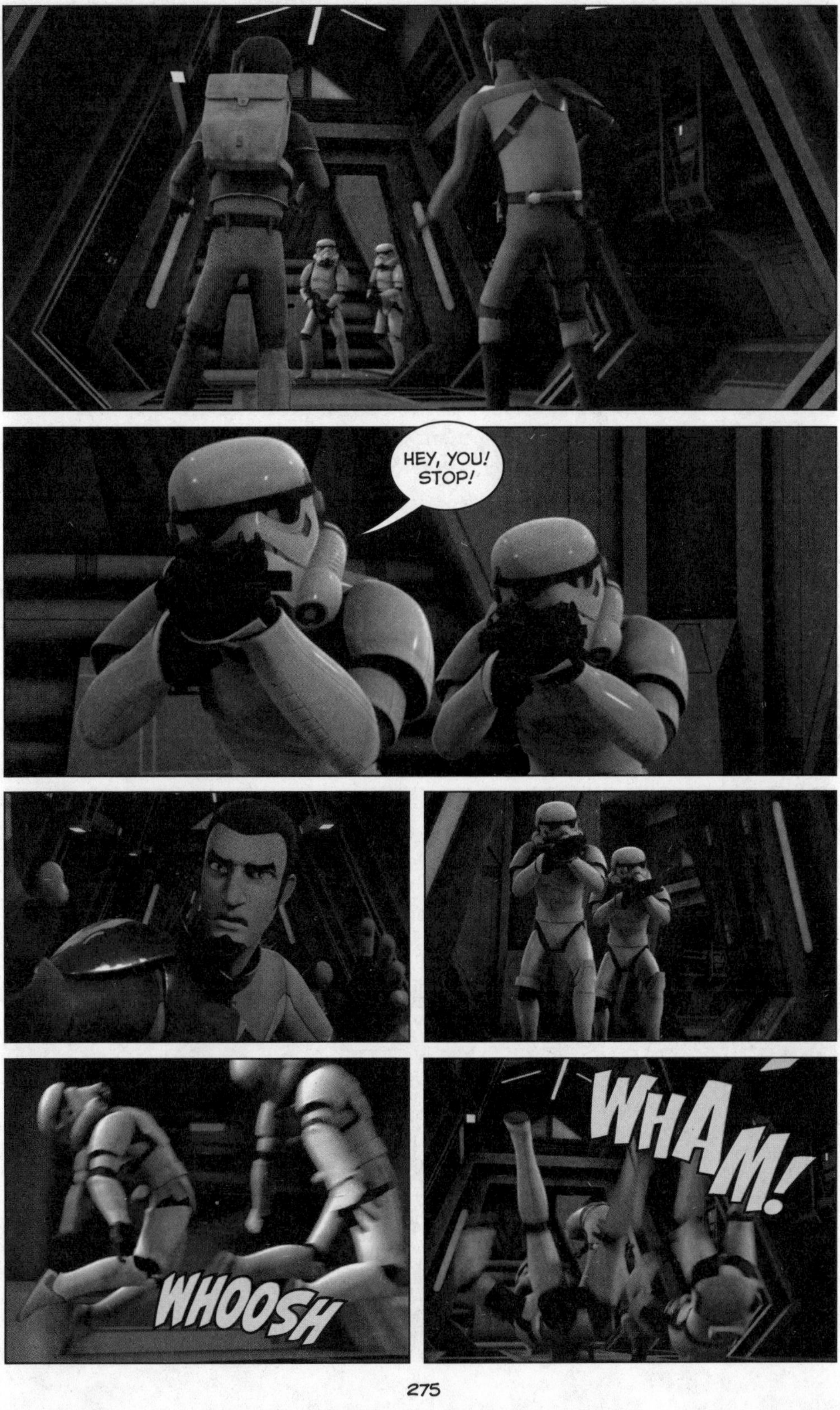
HEY, YOU! STOP!
WHOOSH
WHAM!

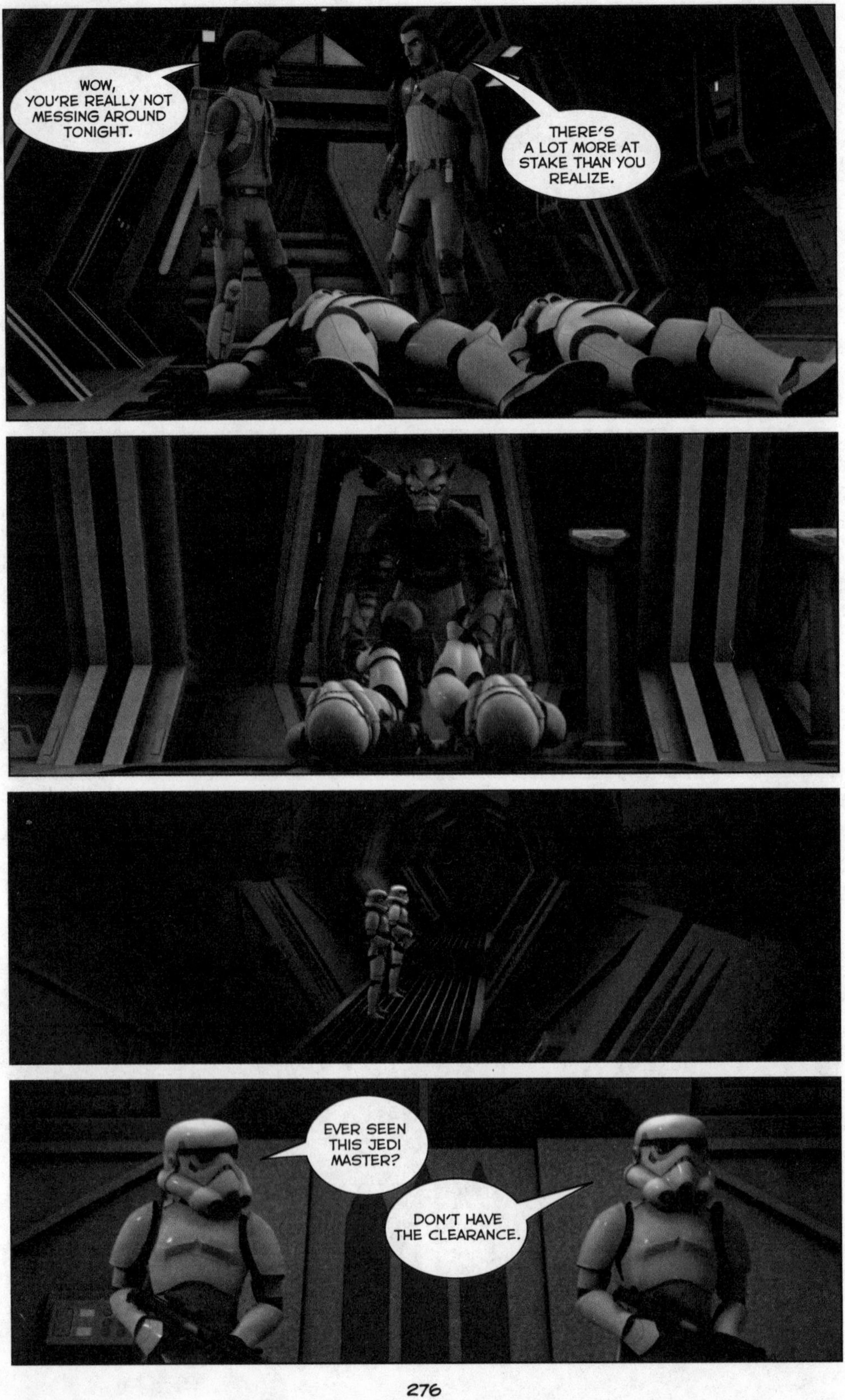
WOW, YOU'RE REALLY NOT MESSING AROUND TONIGHT.
THERE'S A LOT MORE AT STAKE THAN YOU REALIZE.
EVER SEEN THIS JEDI MASTER?
DON'T HAVE THE CLEARANCE.

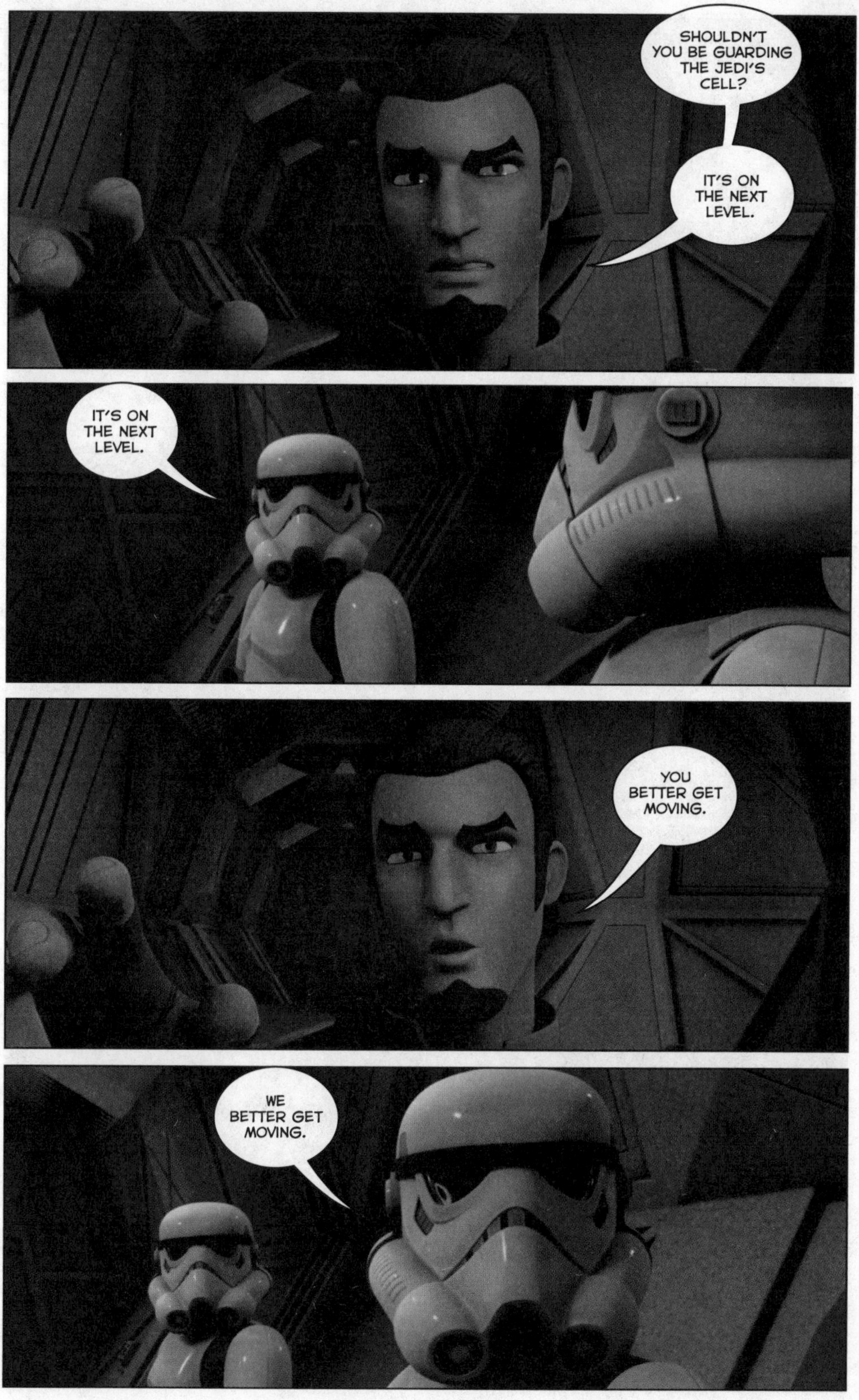
SHOULDN'T YOU BE GUARDING THE JEDI'S CELL?
IT'S ON THE NEXT LEVEL.
IT'S ON THE NEXT LEVEL.
YOU BETTER GET MOVING.
WE BETTER GET MOVING.

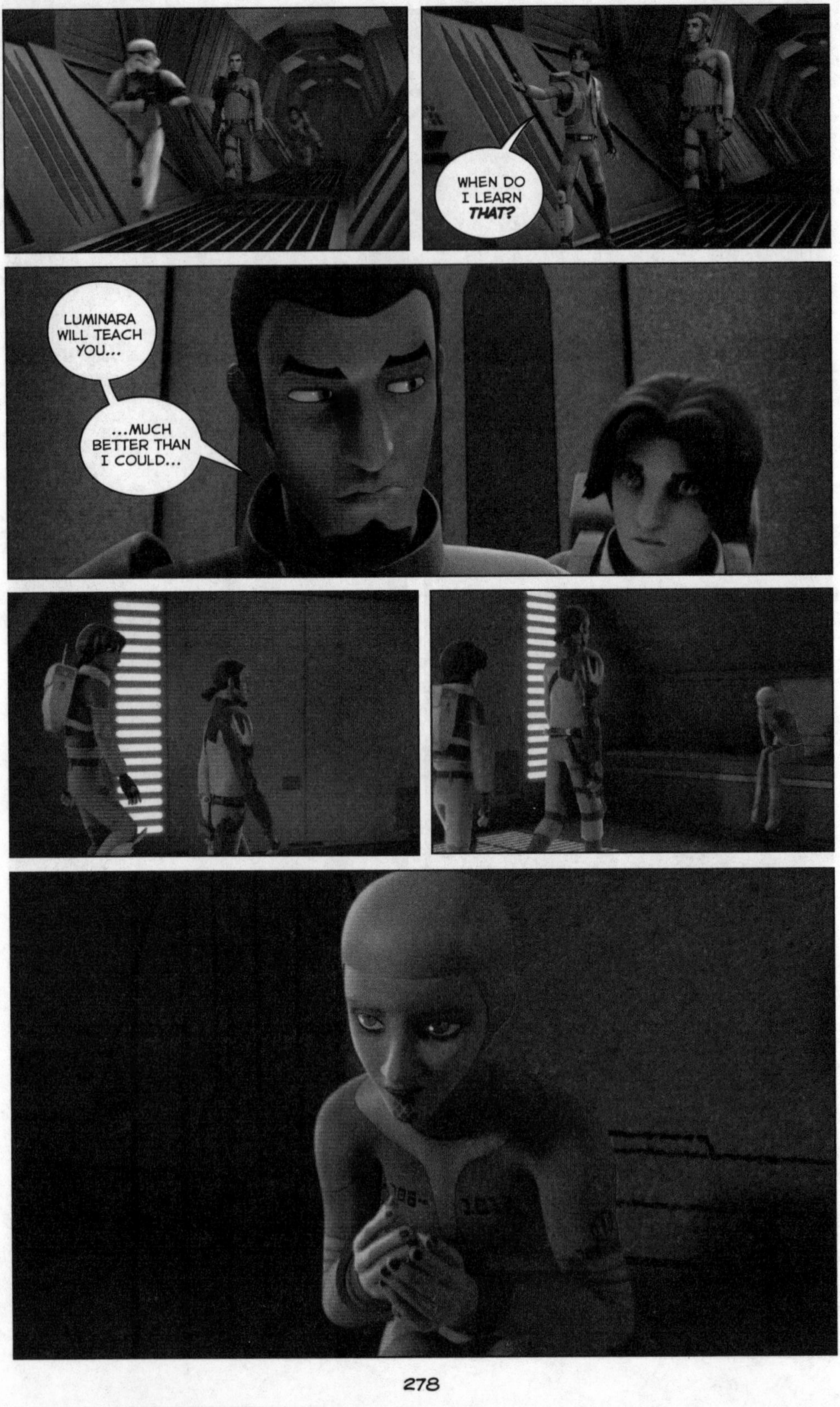
WHEN DO I LEARN *THAT?*
LUMINARA WILL TEACH YOU...
...MUCH BETTER THAN I COULD...

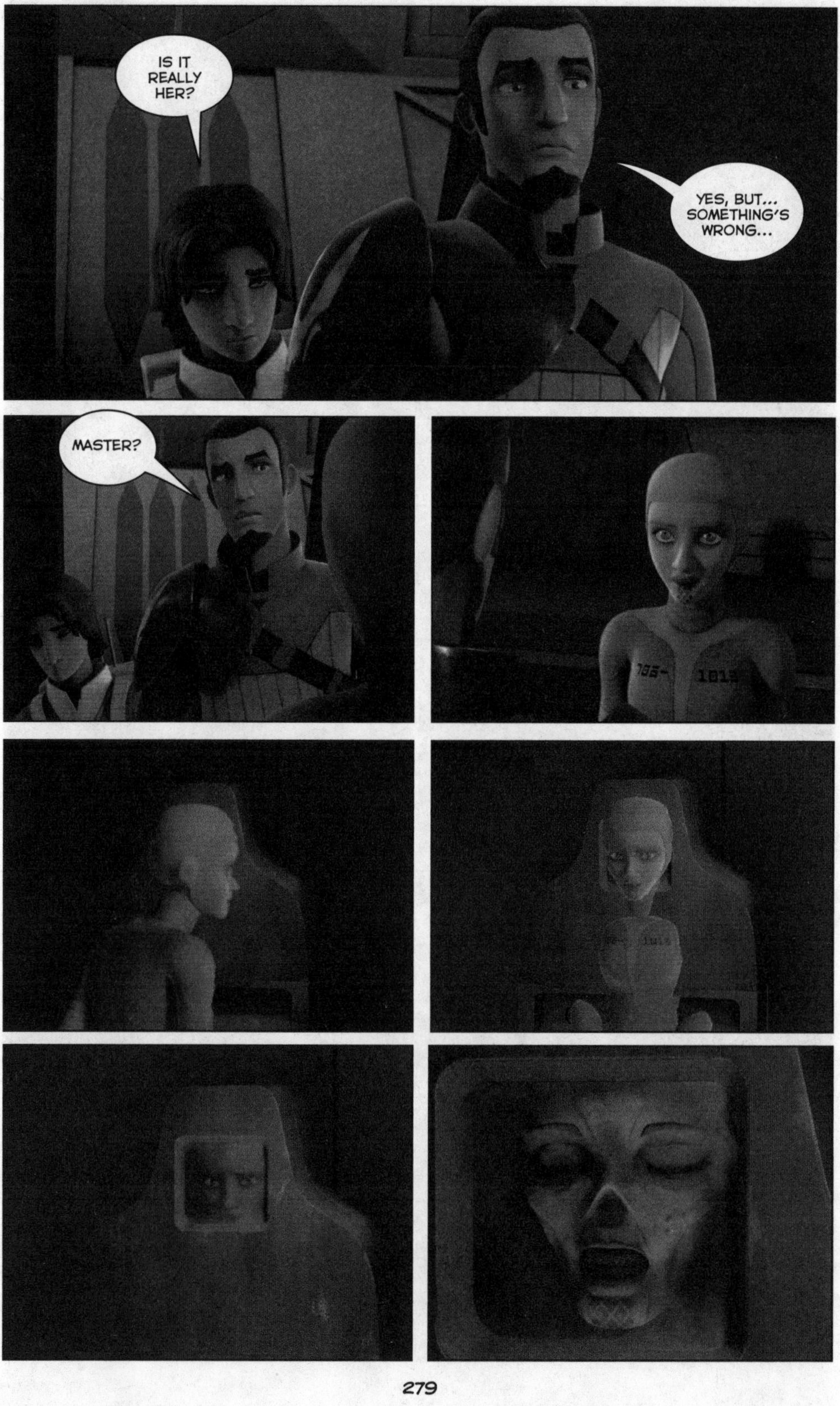
IS IT REALLY HER?
YES, BUT... SOMETHING'S WRONG...
MASTER?

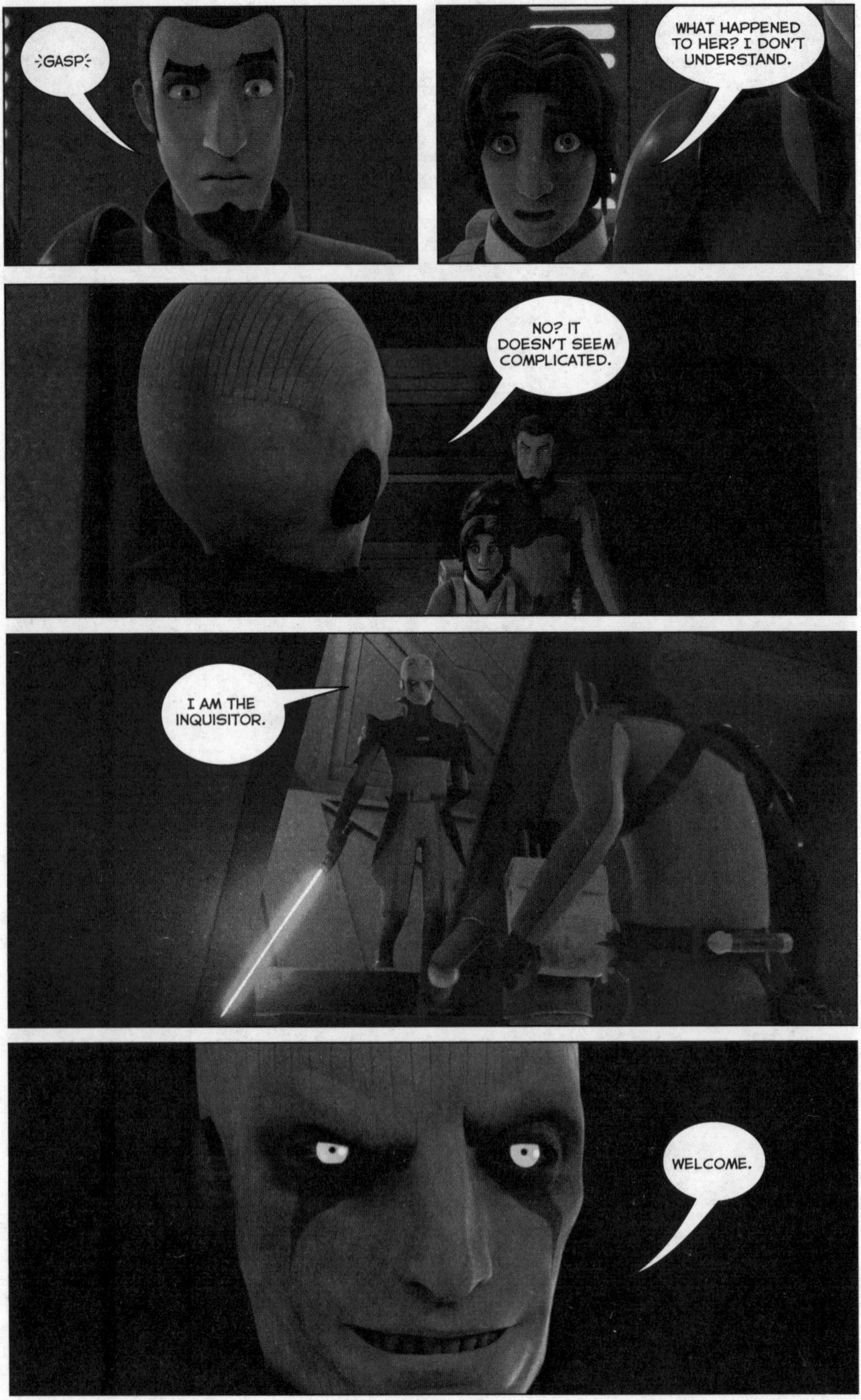
GASP
WHAT HAPPENED TO HER? I DON'T UNDERSTAND.
NO? IT DOESN'T SEEM COMPLICATED.
I AM THE INQUISITOR.
WELCOME.

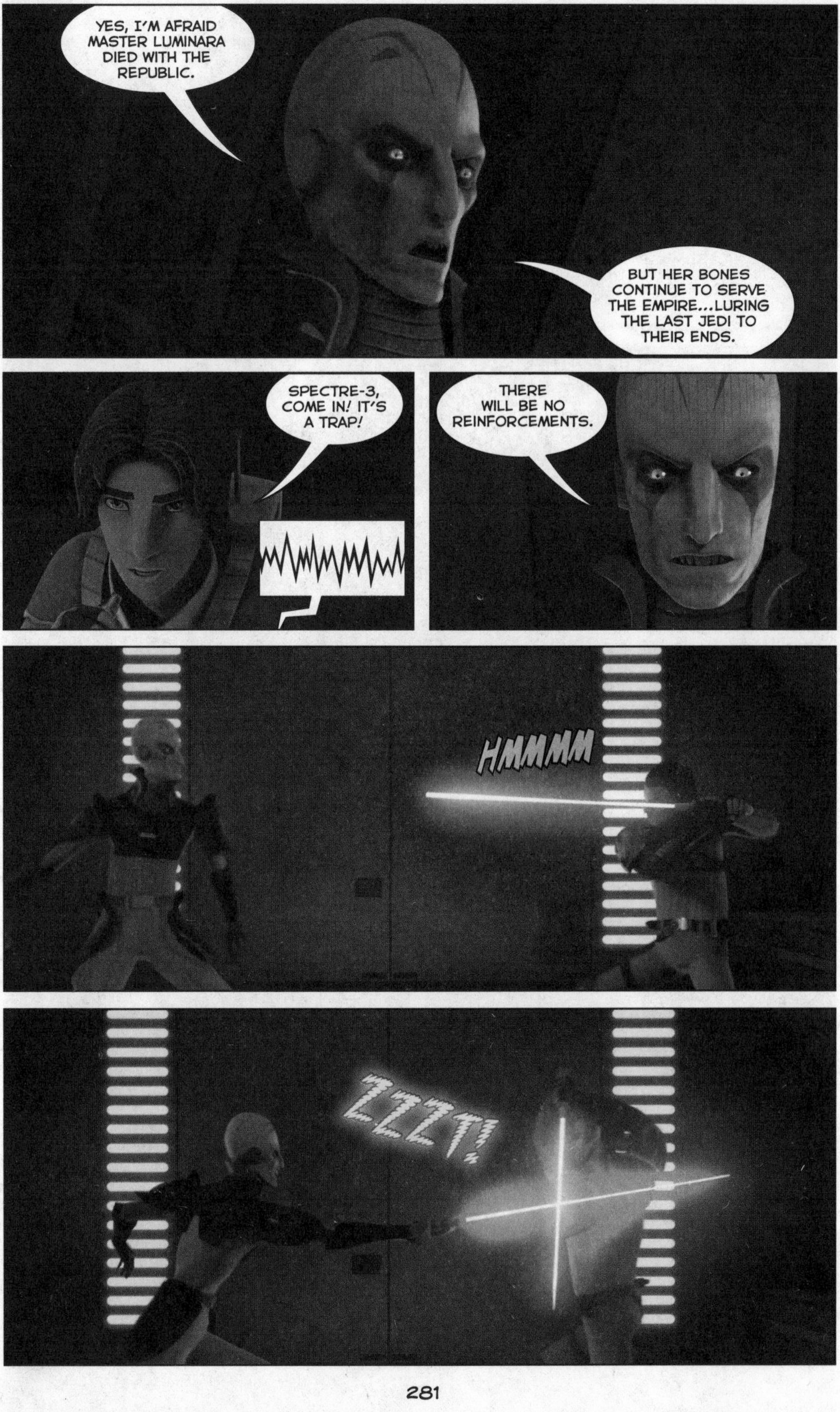
YES, I'M AFRAID MASTER LUMINARA DIED WITH THE REPUBLIC.
BUT HER BONES CONTINUE TO SERVE THE EMPIRE...LURING THE LAST JEDI TO THEIR ENDS.
SPECTRE-3, COME IN! IT'S A TRAP!
THERE WILL BE NO REINFORCEMENTS.
HMMMM
ZZZT!

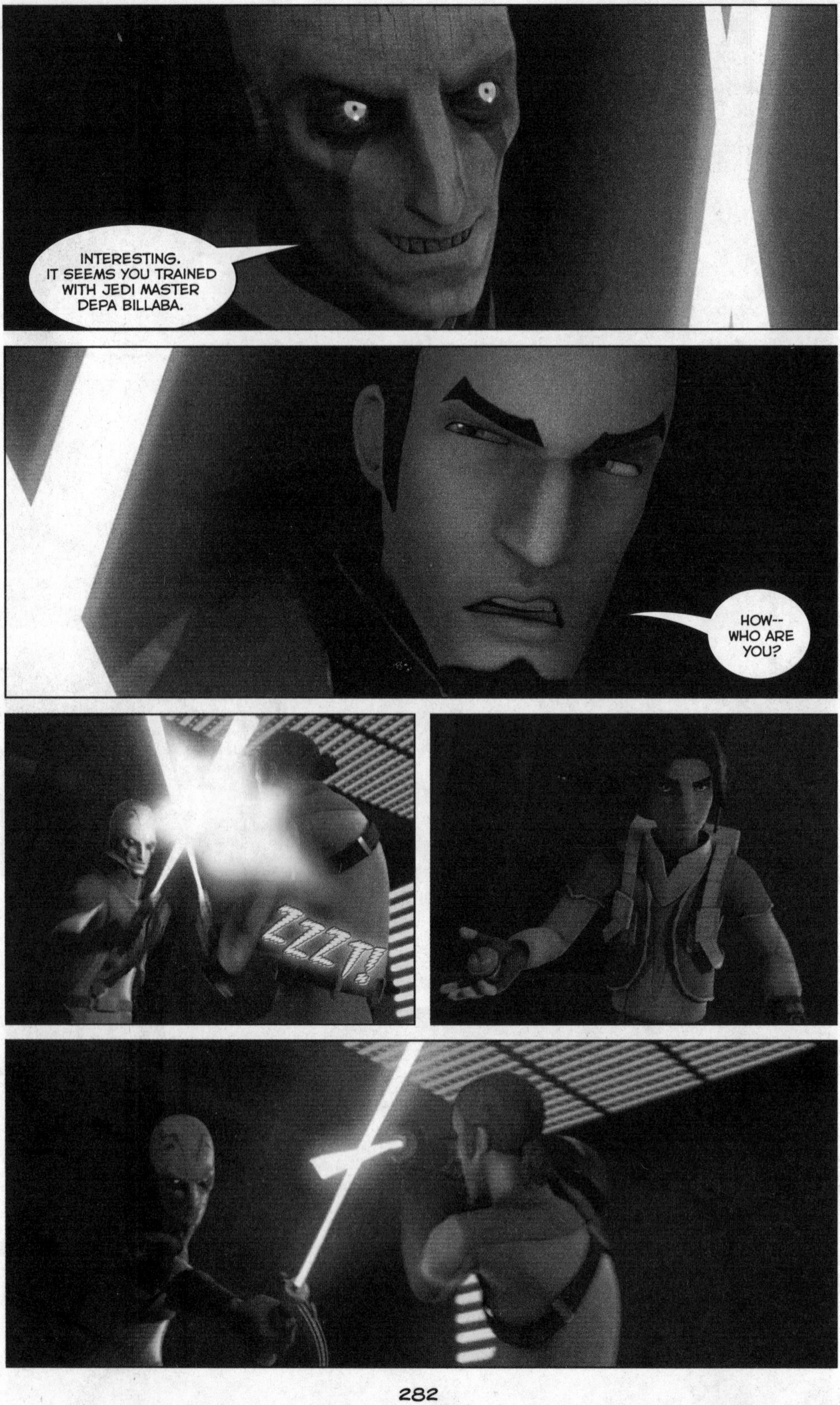
INTERESTING. IT SEEMS YOU TRAINED WITH JEDI MASTER DEPA BILLABA.
HOW-- WHO ARE YOU?
ZZZT!

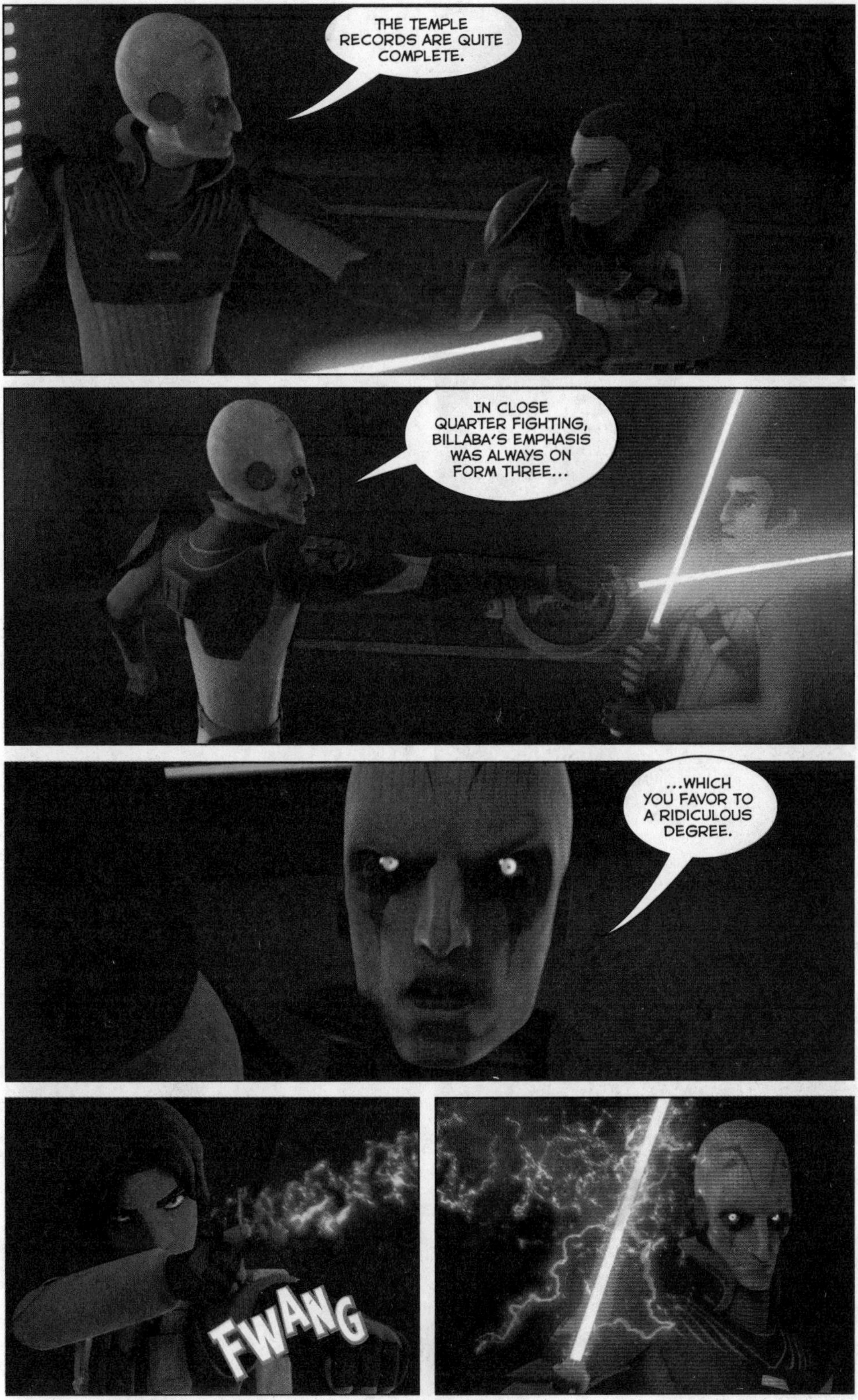
THE TEMPLE RECORDS ARE QUITE COMPLETE.
IN CLOSE QUARTER FIGHTING, BILLABA'S EMPHASIS WAS ALWAYS ON FORM THREE...
...WHICH YOU FAVOR TO A RIDICULOUS DEGREE.
FWANG

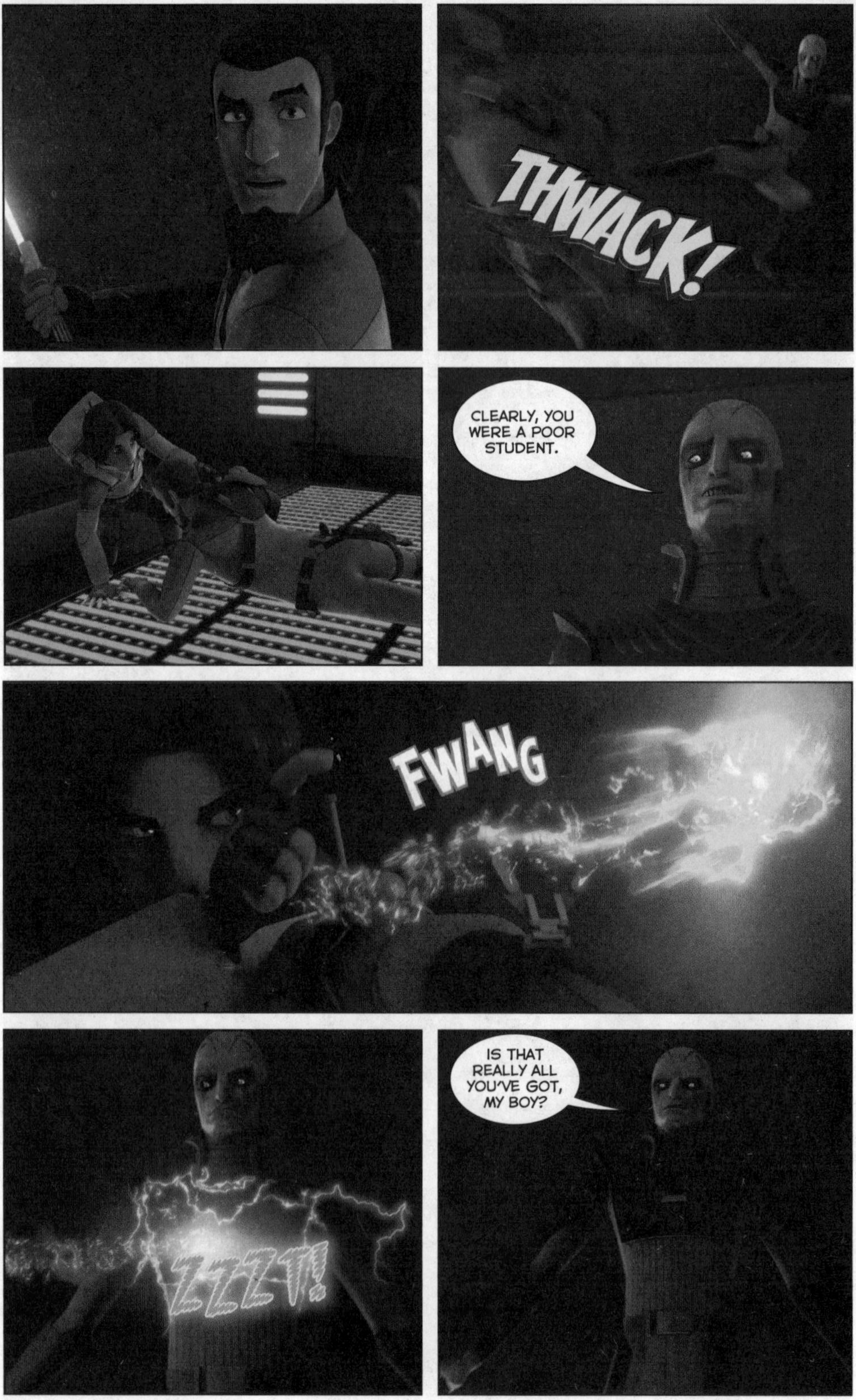
THWACK!
CLEARLY, YOU WERE A POOR STUDENT.
FWANG
ZZZT!
IS THAT REALLY ALL YOU'VE GOT, MY BOY?

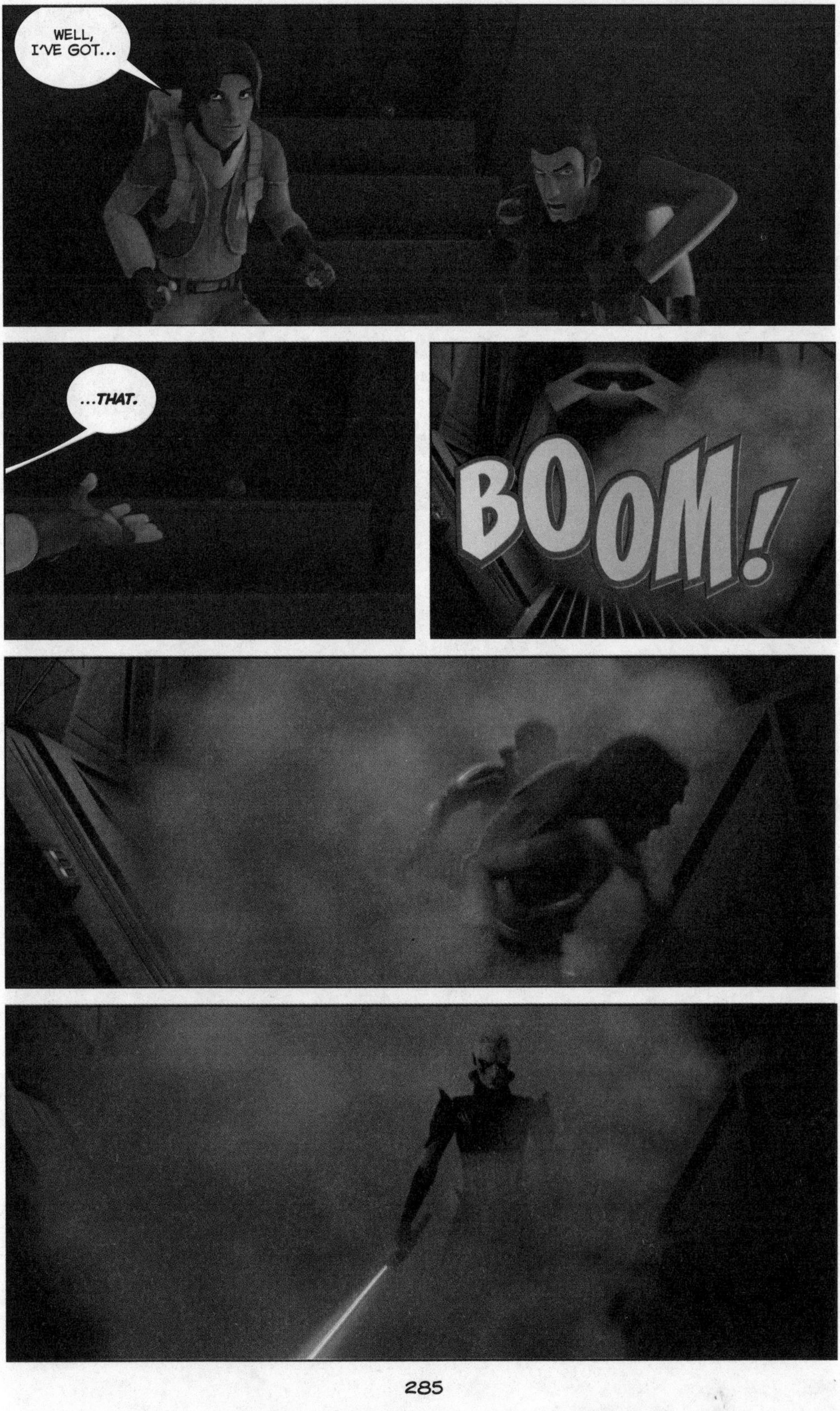
WELL, I'VE GOT...
...THAT.
BOOM!

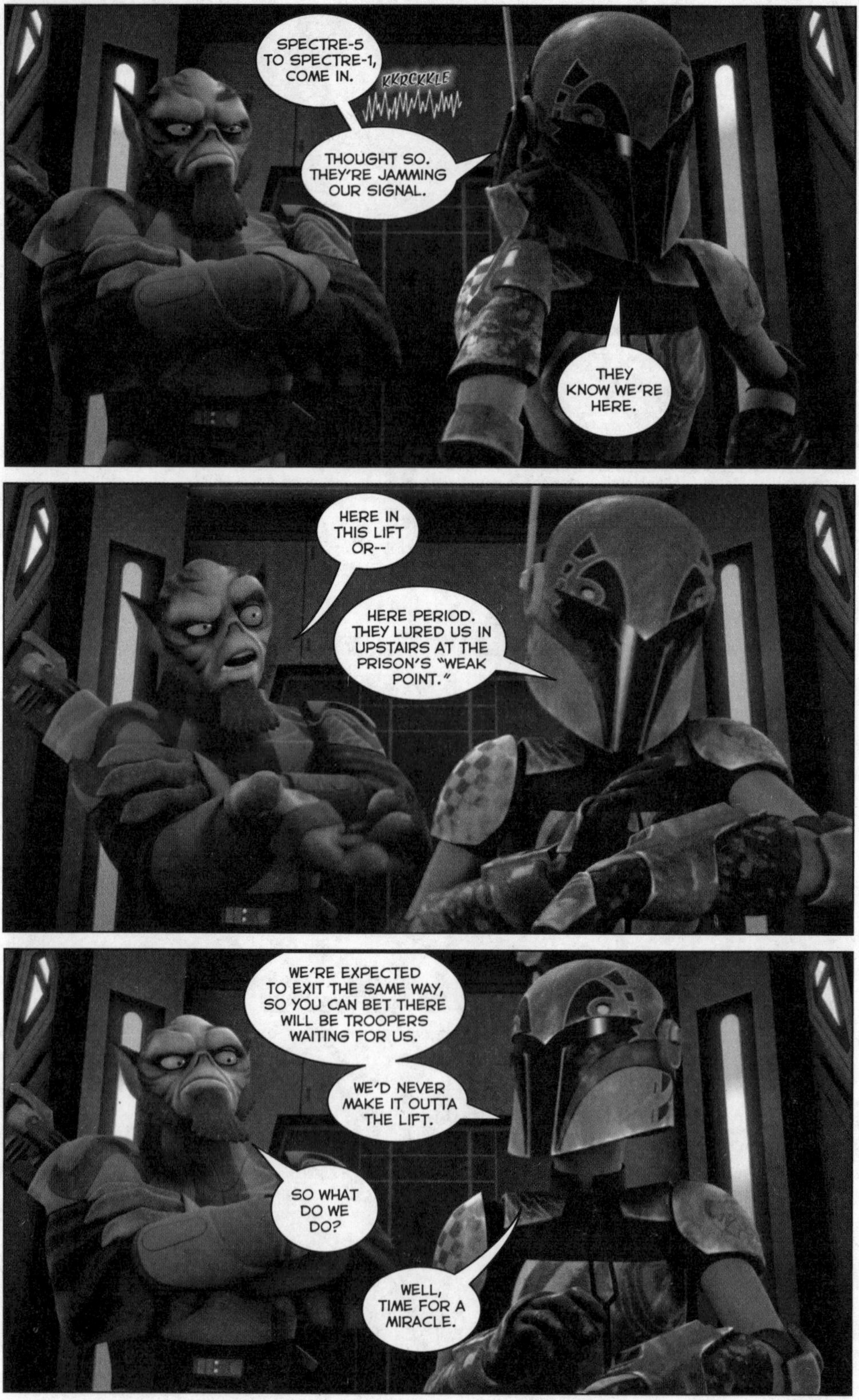
SPECTRE-5 TO SPECTRE-1, COME IN.
KKRCKKLE
THOUGHT SO. THEY'RE JAMMING OUR SIGNAL.
THEY KNOW WE'RE HERE.
HERE IN THIS LIFT OR--
HERE PERIOD. THEY LURED US IN UPSTAIRS AT THE PRISON'S "WEAK POINT."
WE'RE EXPECTED TO EXIT THE SAME WAY, SO YOU CAN BET THERE WILL BE TROOPERS WAITING FOR US.
WE'D NEVER MAKE IT OUTTA THE LIFT.
SO WHAT DO WE DO?
WELL, TIME FOR A MIRACLE.

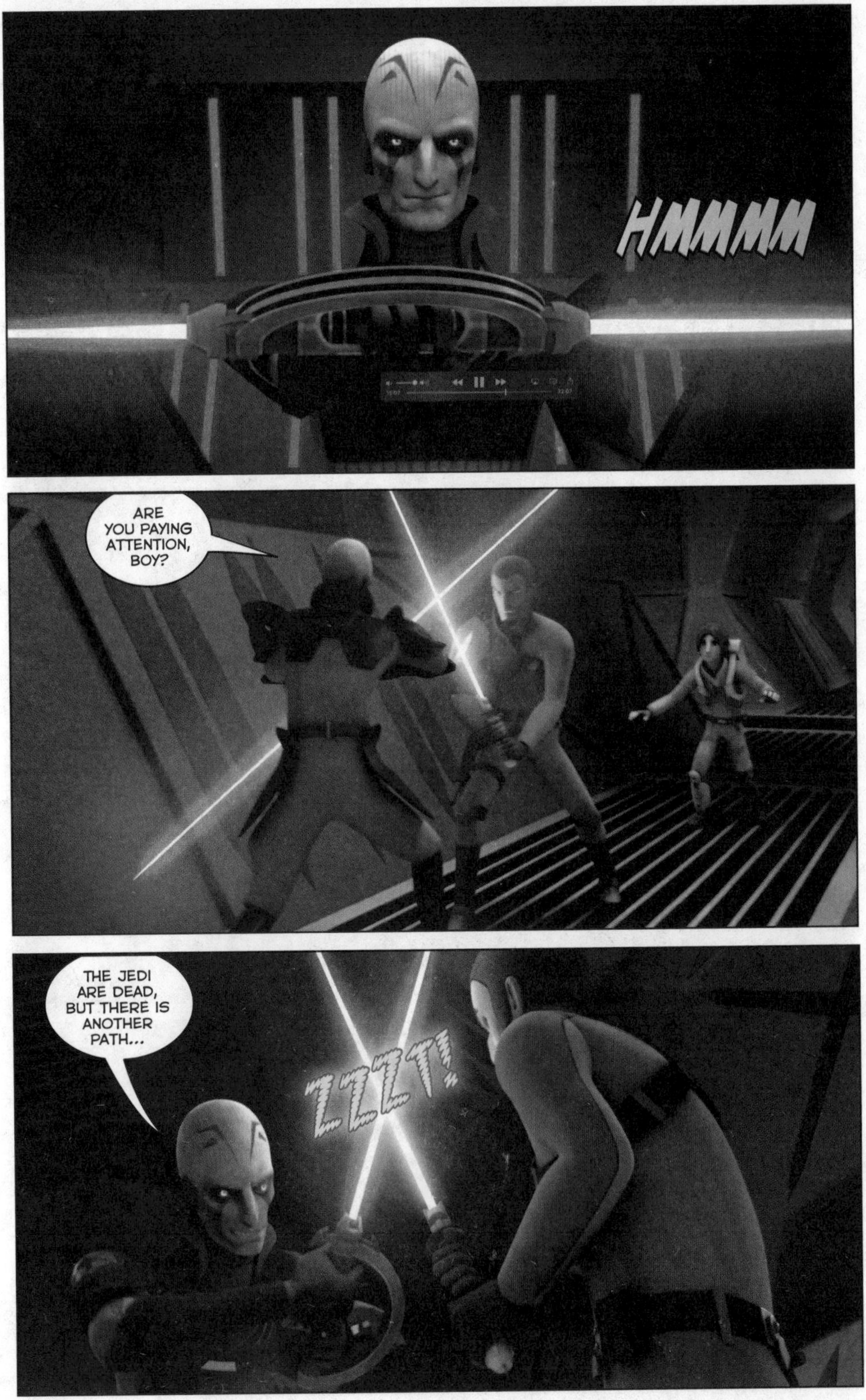
HMMMM
ARE YOU PAYING ATTENTION, BOY?
THE JEDI ARE DEAD, BUT THERE IS ANOTHER PATH...
ZZZT!

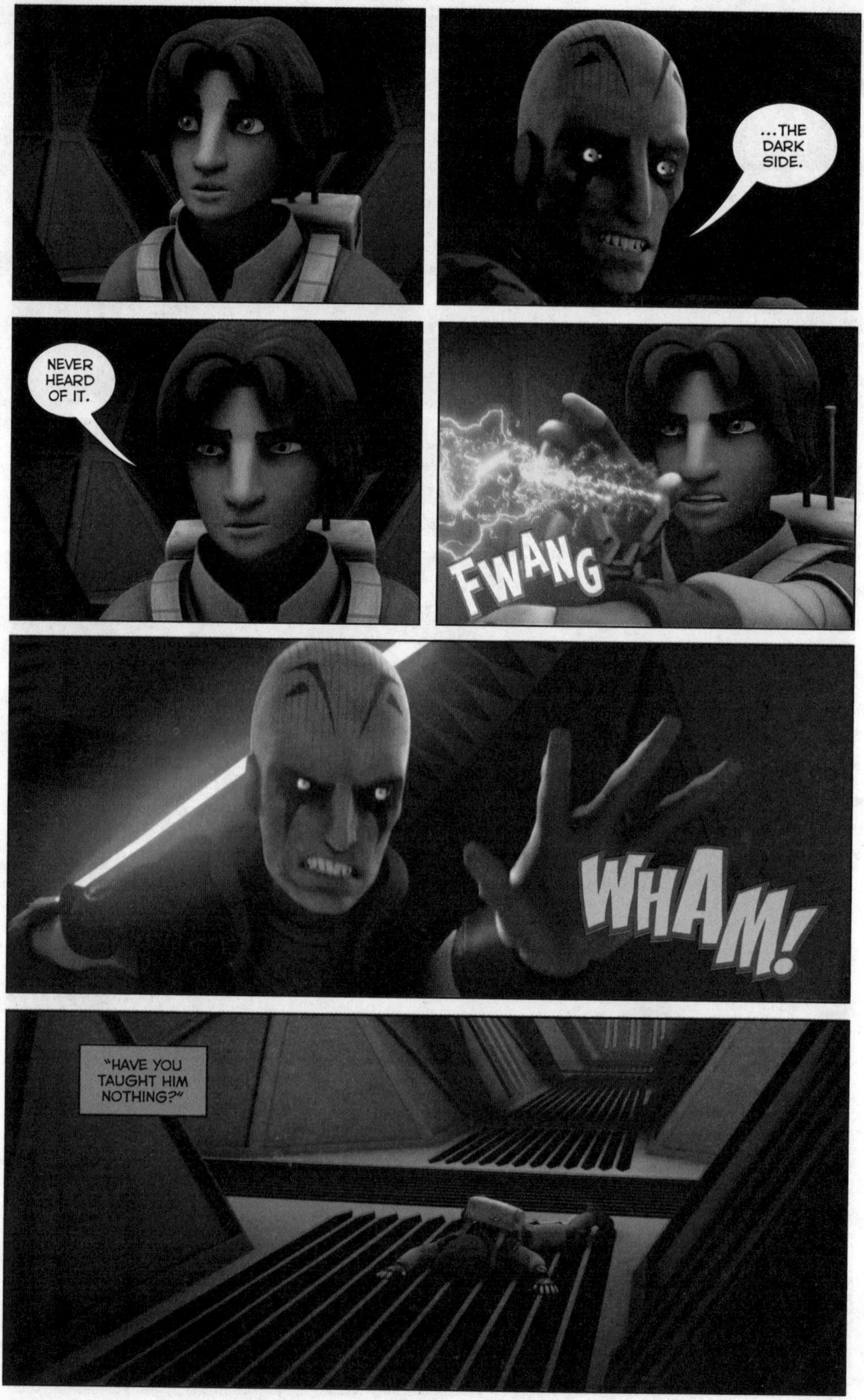

...THE DARK SIDE.
NEVER HEARD OF IT.
FWANG
WHAM!
"HAVE YOU TAUGHT HIM NOTHING?"

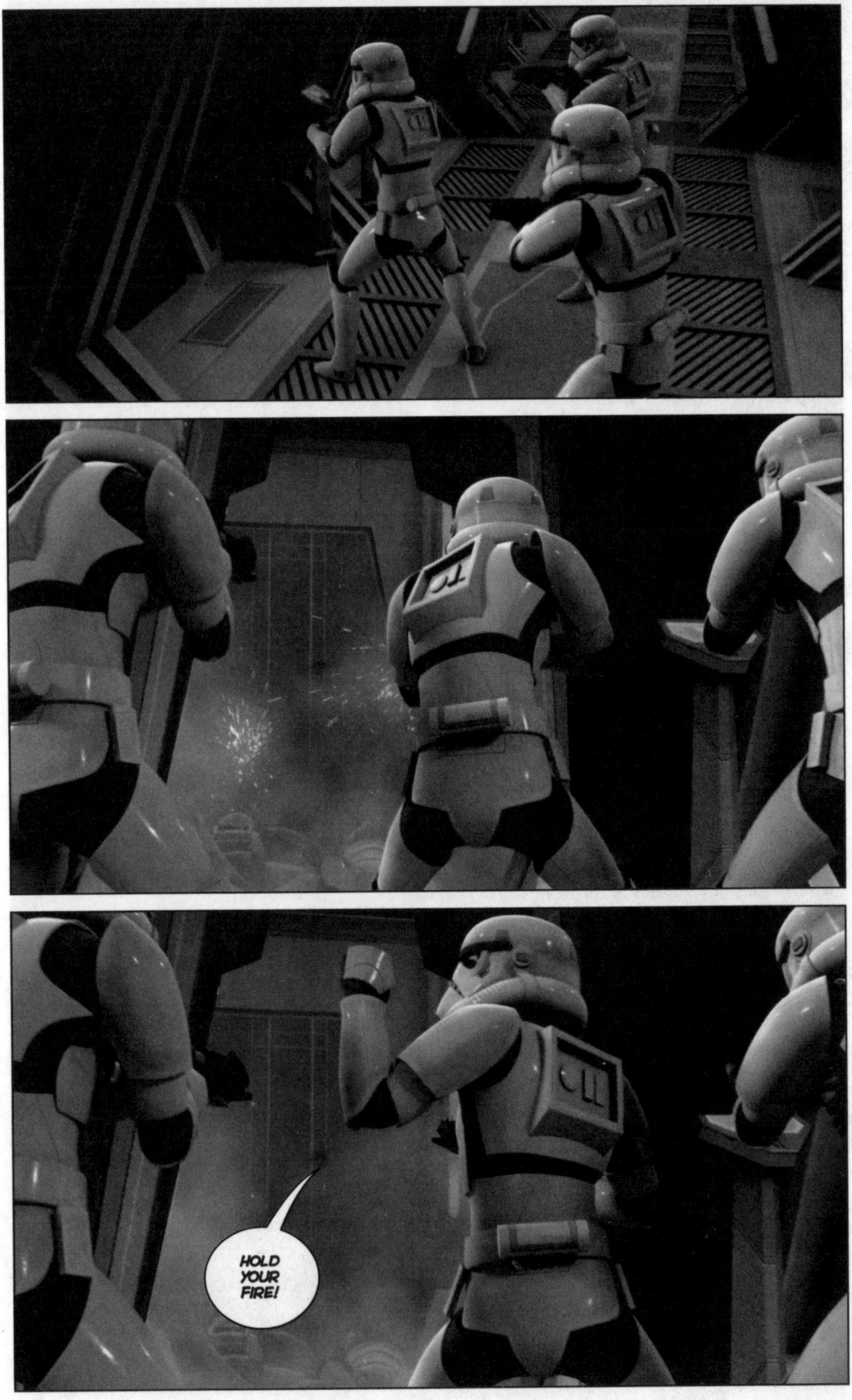
HOLD YOUR FIRE!

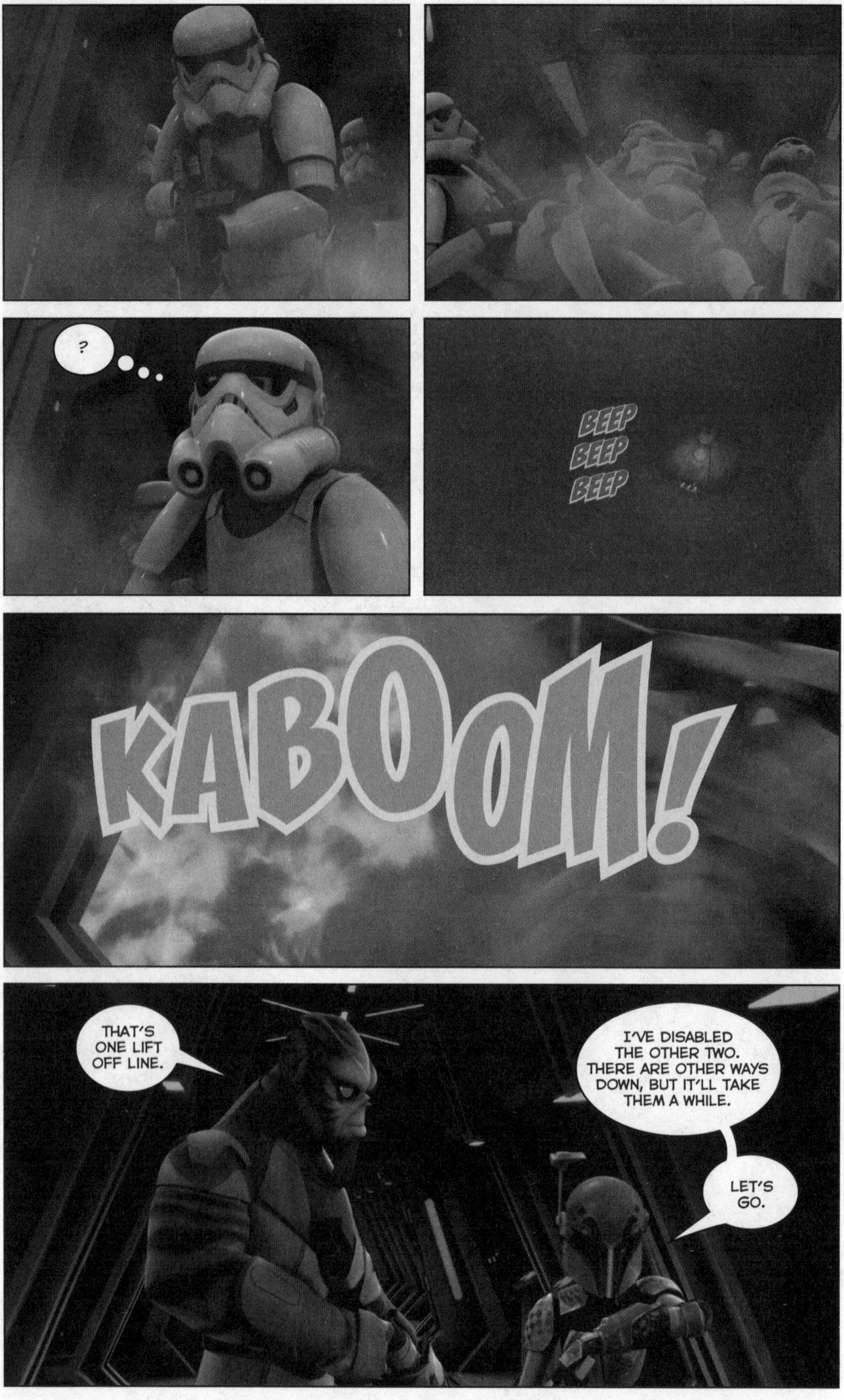
?
BEEP
BEEP
BEEP
KABOOM!
THAT'S ONE LIFT OFF LINE.
I'VE DISABLED THE OTHER TWO. THERE ARE OTHER WAYS DOWN, BUT IT'LL TAKE THEM A WHILE.
LET'S GO.

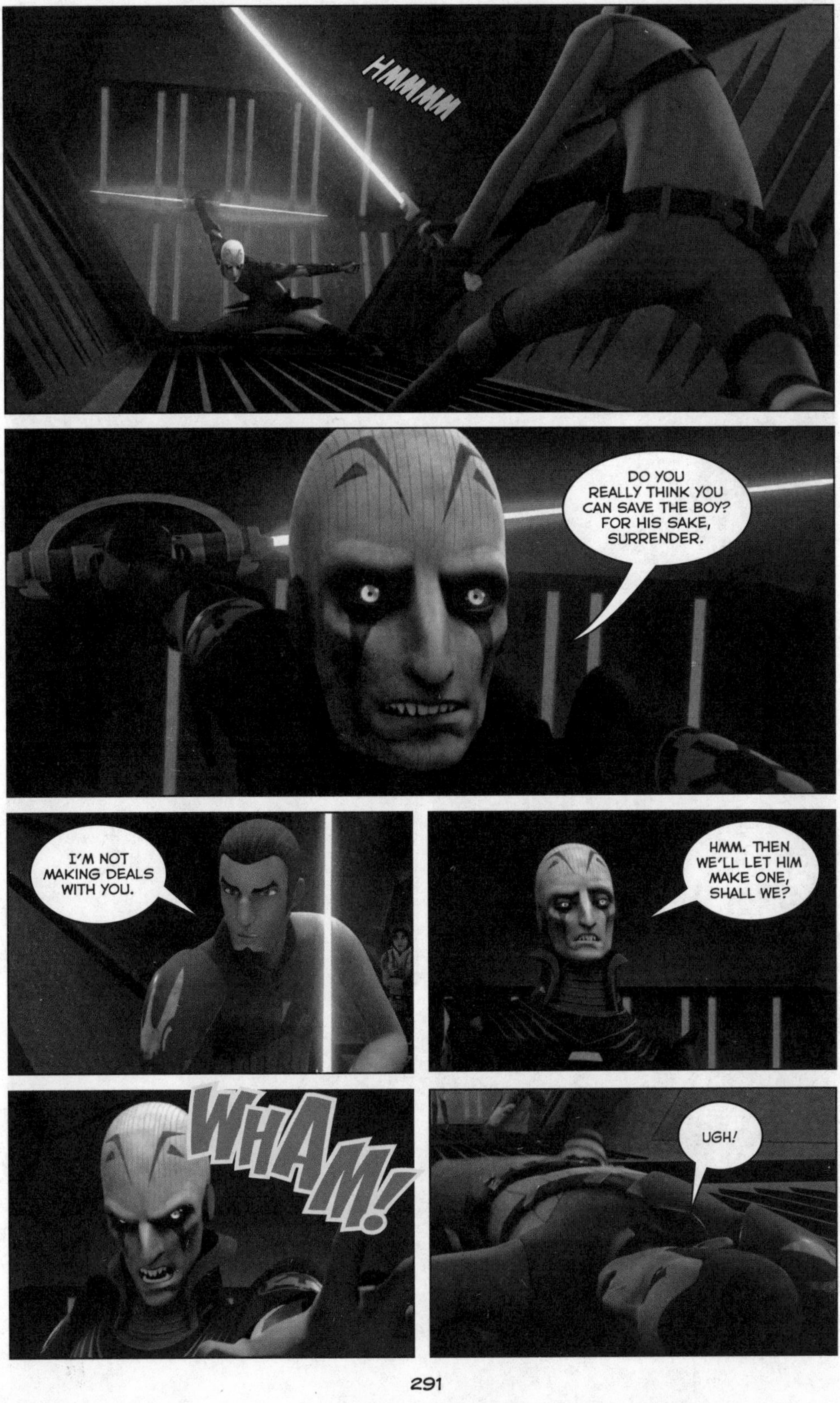
HMMMM
DO YOU REALLY THINK YOU CAN SAVE THE BOY? FOR HIS SAKE, SURRENDER.
I'M NOT MAKING DEALS WITH YOU.
HMM. THEN WE'LL LET HIM MAKE ONE, SHALL WE?
WHAM!
UGH!

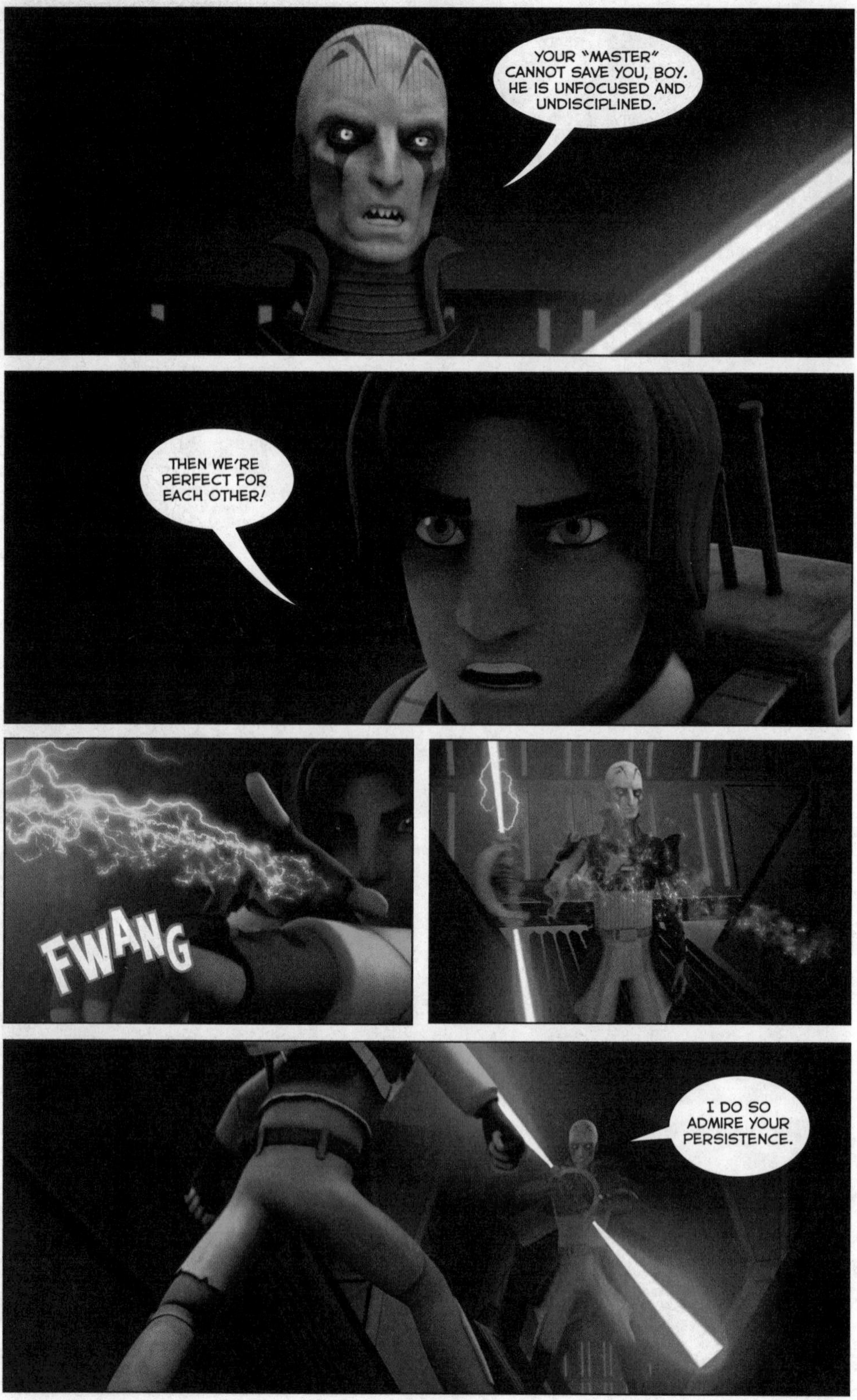
YOUR "MASTER" CANNOT SAVE YOU, BOY. HE IS UNFOCUSED AND UNDISCIPLINED.
THEN WE'RE PERFECT FOR EACH OTHER!
FWANG
I DO SO ADMIRE YOUR PERSISTENCE.

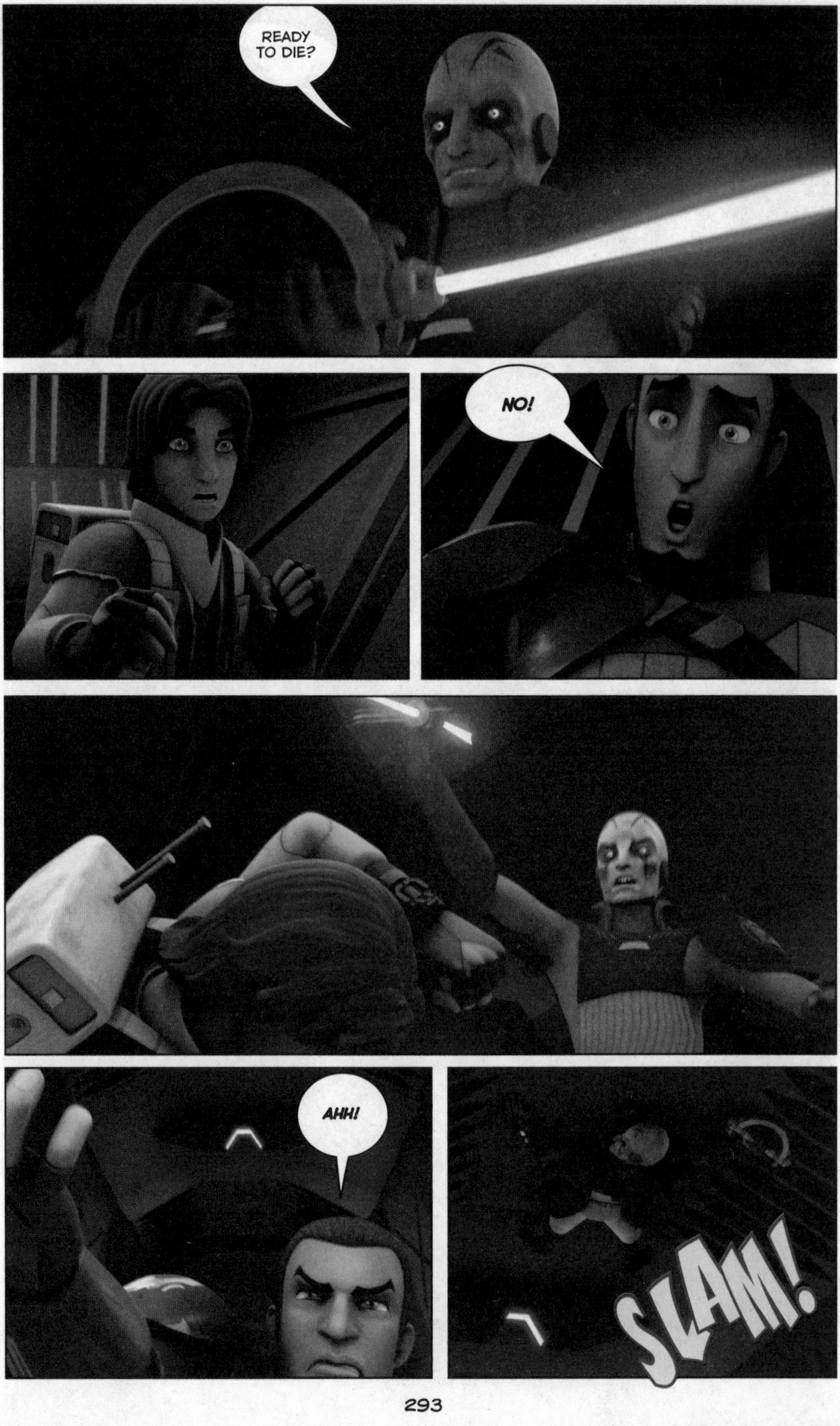
READY TO DIE?
NO!
AHH!
SLAM!

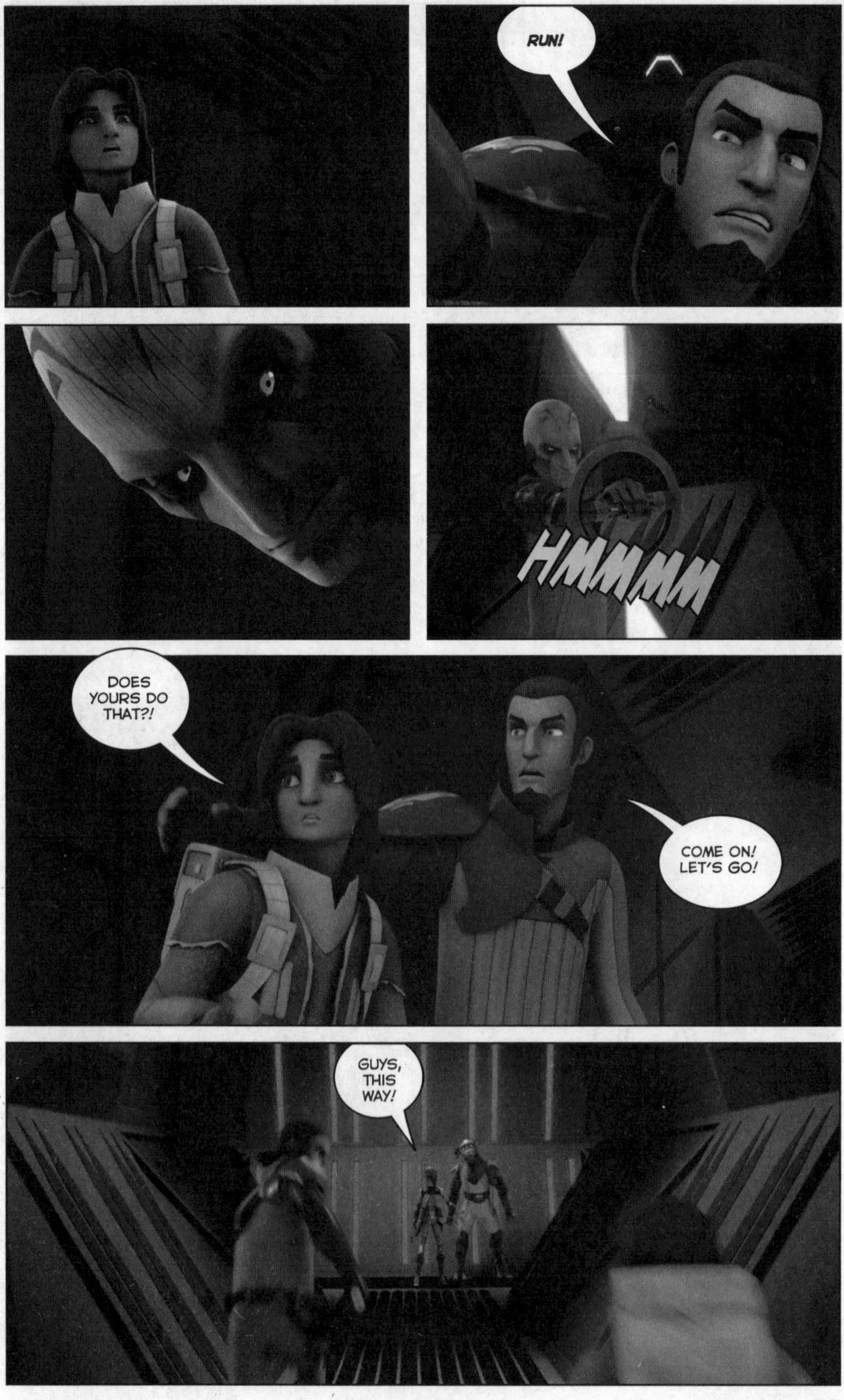
RUN!
HMMMMM
DOES YOURS DO THAT?!
COME ON! LET'S GO!
GUYS, THIS WAY!

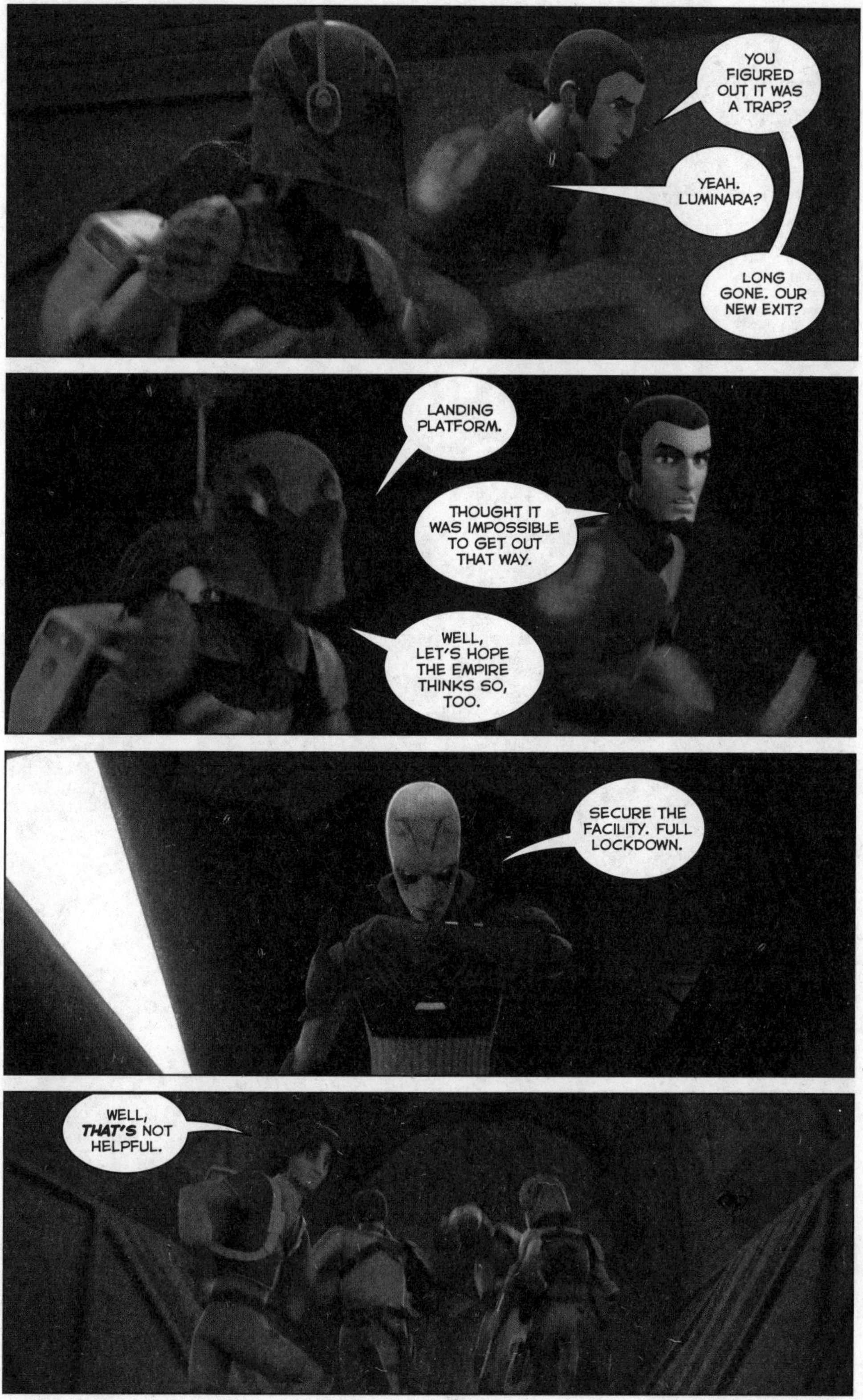
YOU FIGURED OUT IT WAS A TRAP?
YEAH. LUMINARA?
LONG GONE. OUR NEW EXIT?
LANDING PLATFORM.
THOUGHT IT WAS IMPOSSIBLE TO GET OUT THAT WAY.
WELL, LET'S HOPE THE EMPIRE THINKS SO, TOO.
SECURE THE FACILITY. FULL LOCKDOWN.
WELL, ***THAT'S*** NOT HELPFUL.

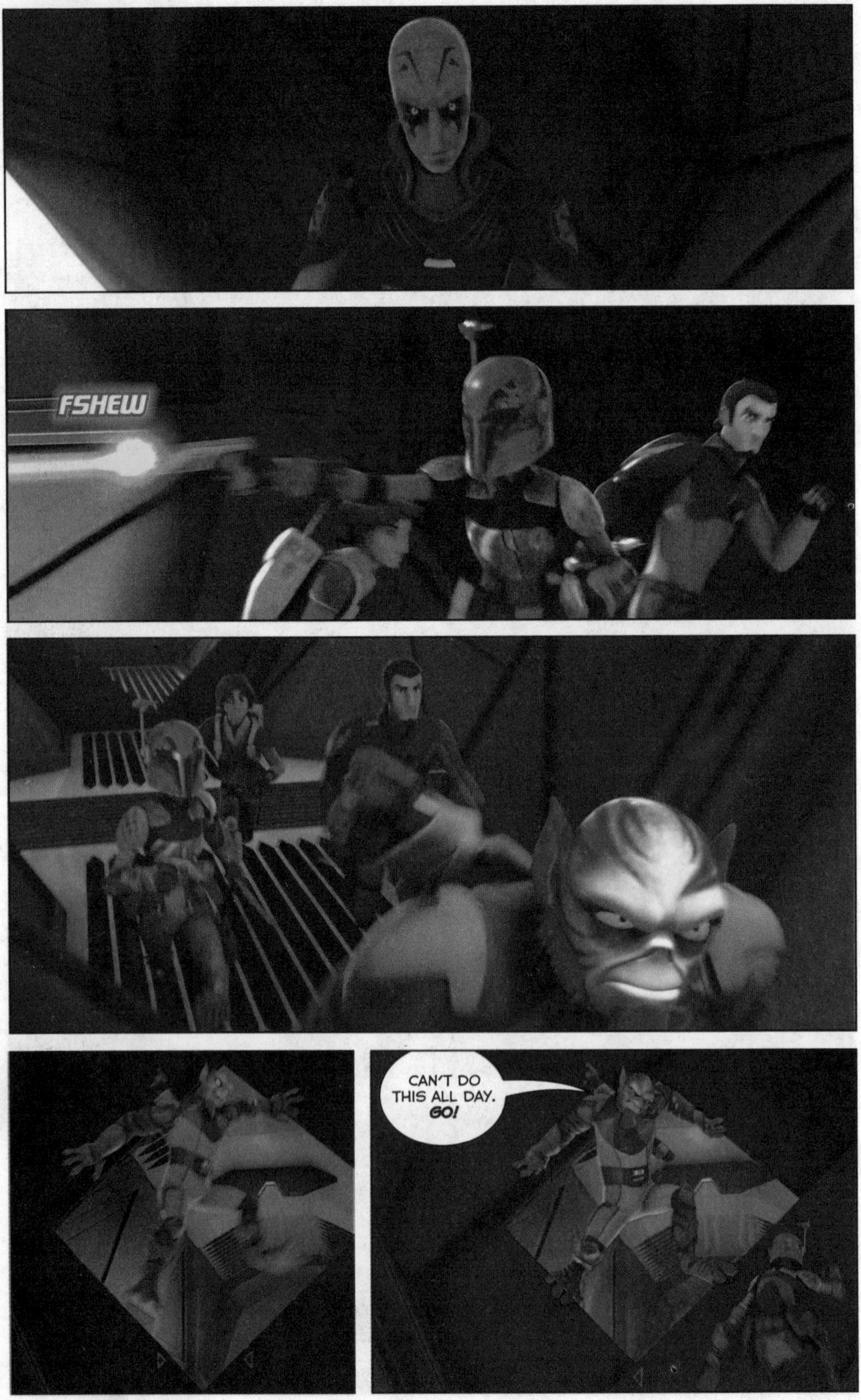
FSHEW
CAN'T DO THIS ALL DAY. GO!

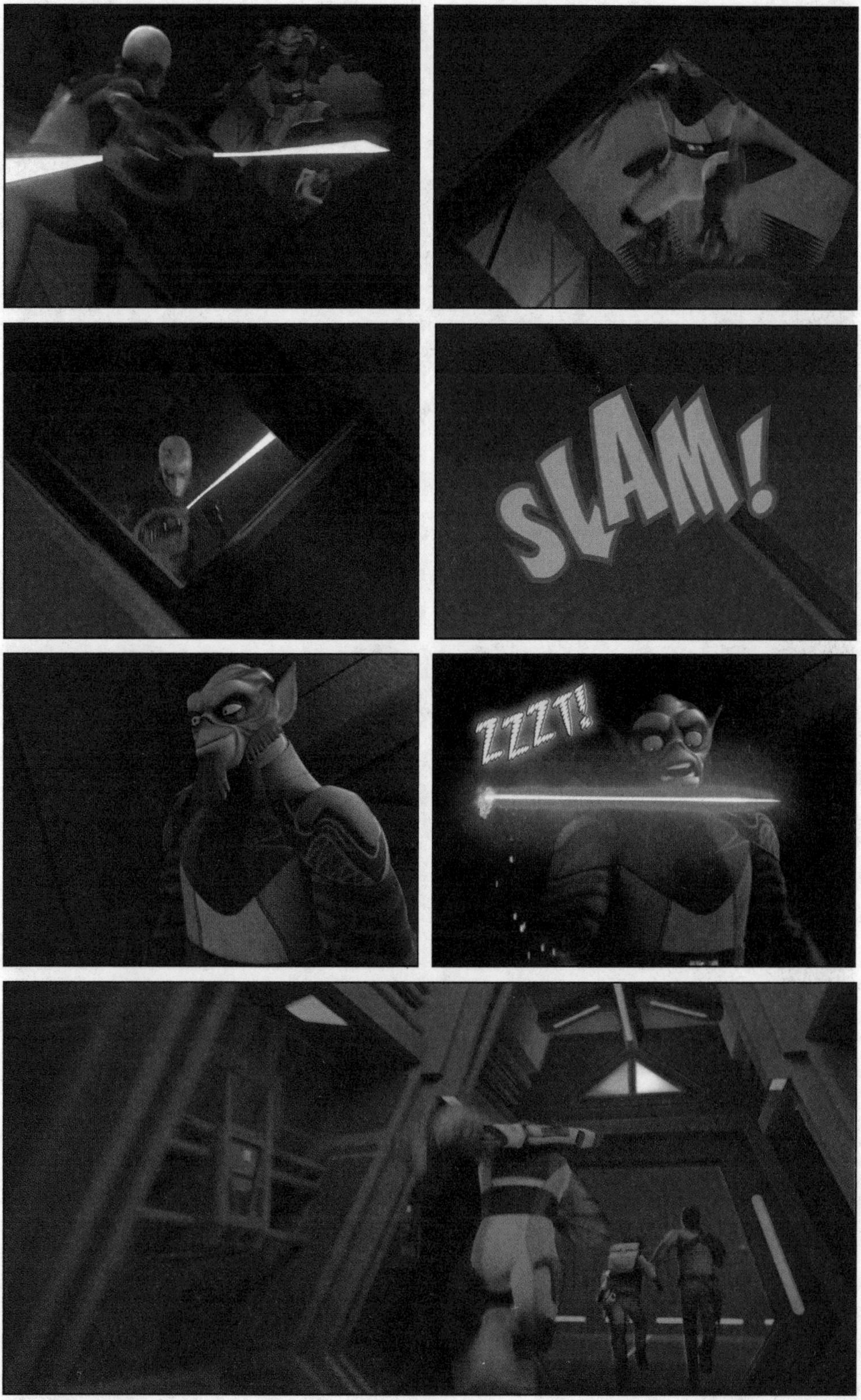
SLAM!
ZZZT!

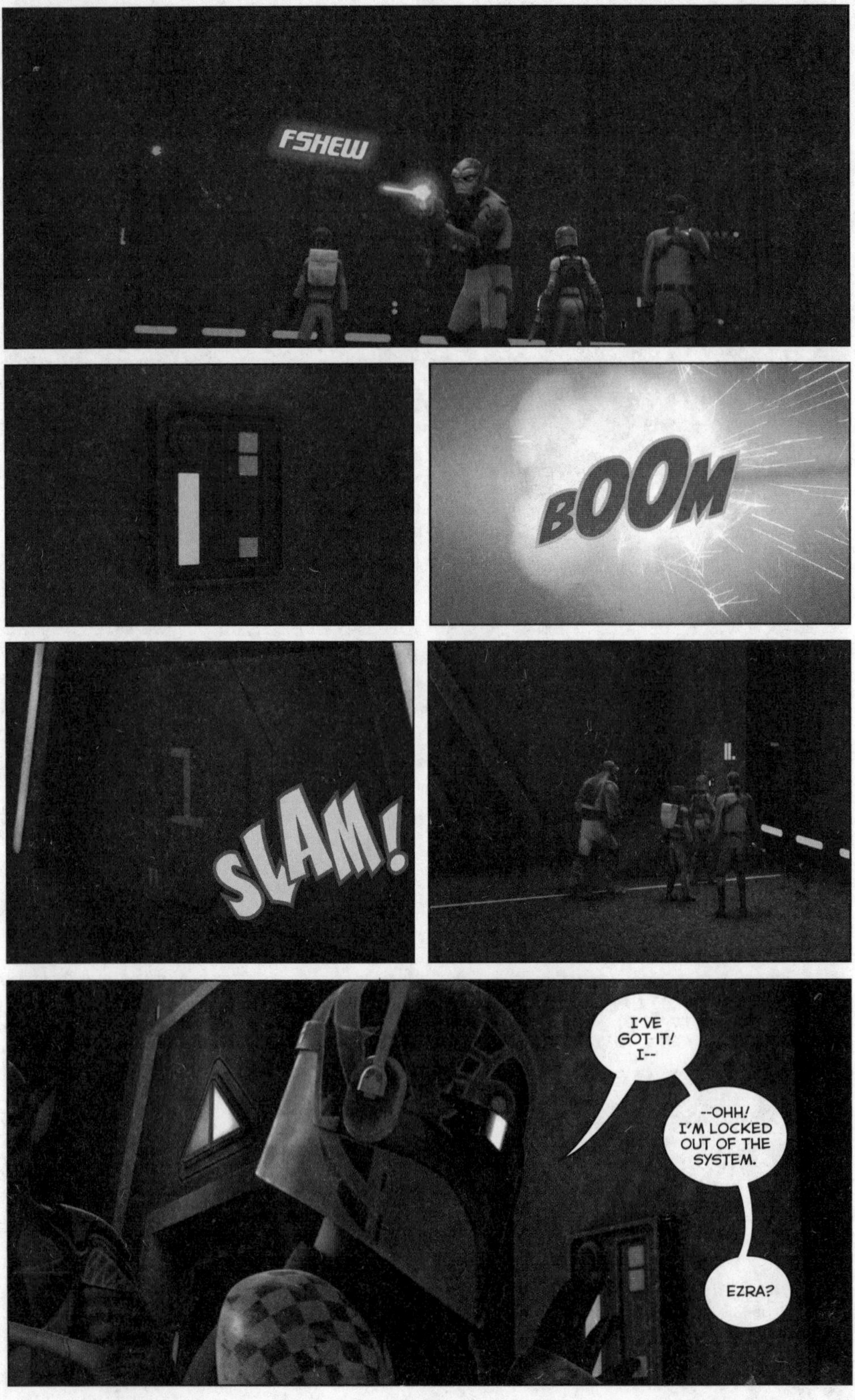
FSHEW
BOOM
SLAM!
I'VE GOT IT! I--
--OHH! I'M LOCKED OUT OF THE SYSTEM.
EZRA?

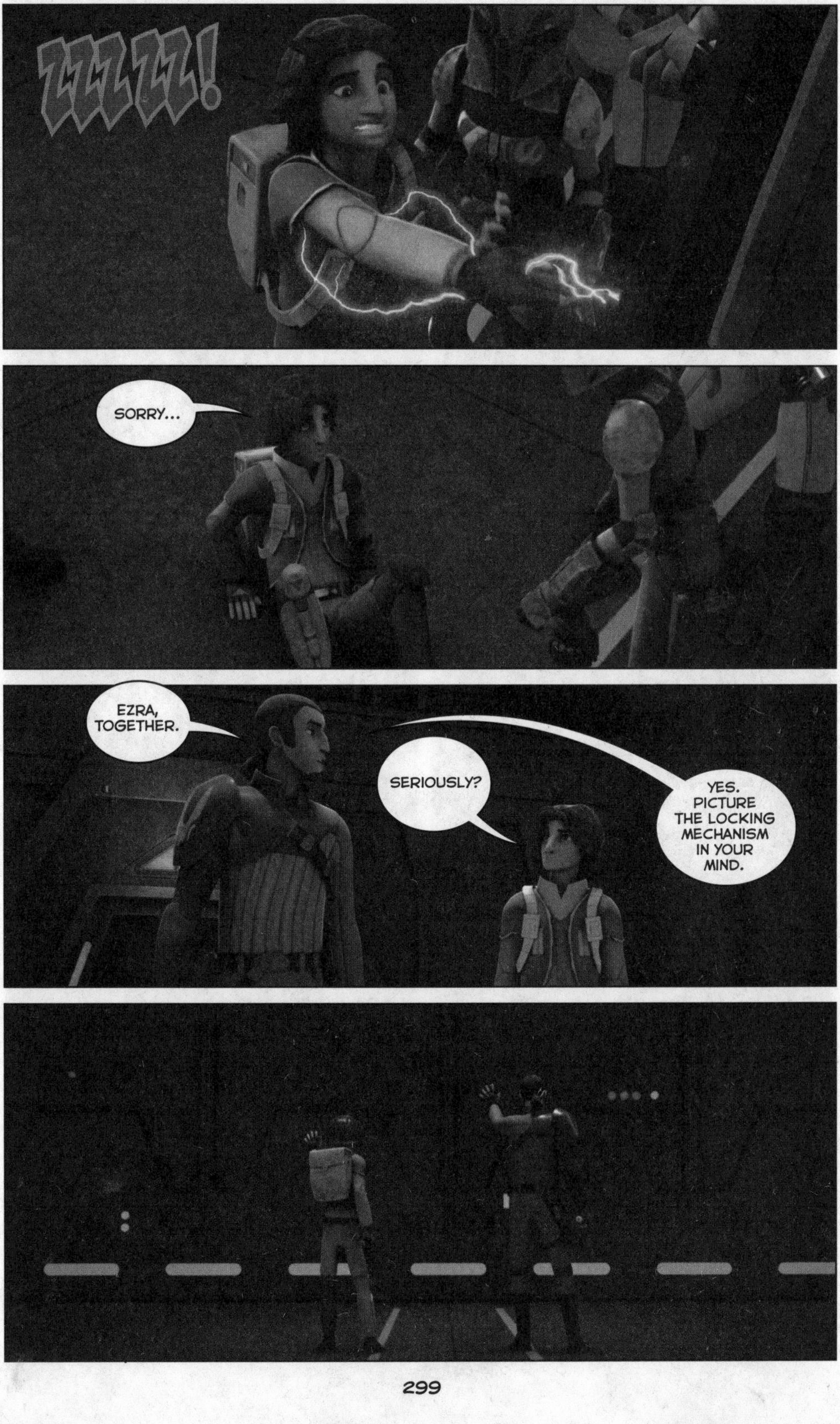
ZZZZZZ!
SORRY...
EZRA, TOGETHER.
SERIOUSLY?
YES. PICTURE THE LOCKING MECHANISM IN YOUR MIND.

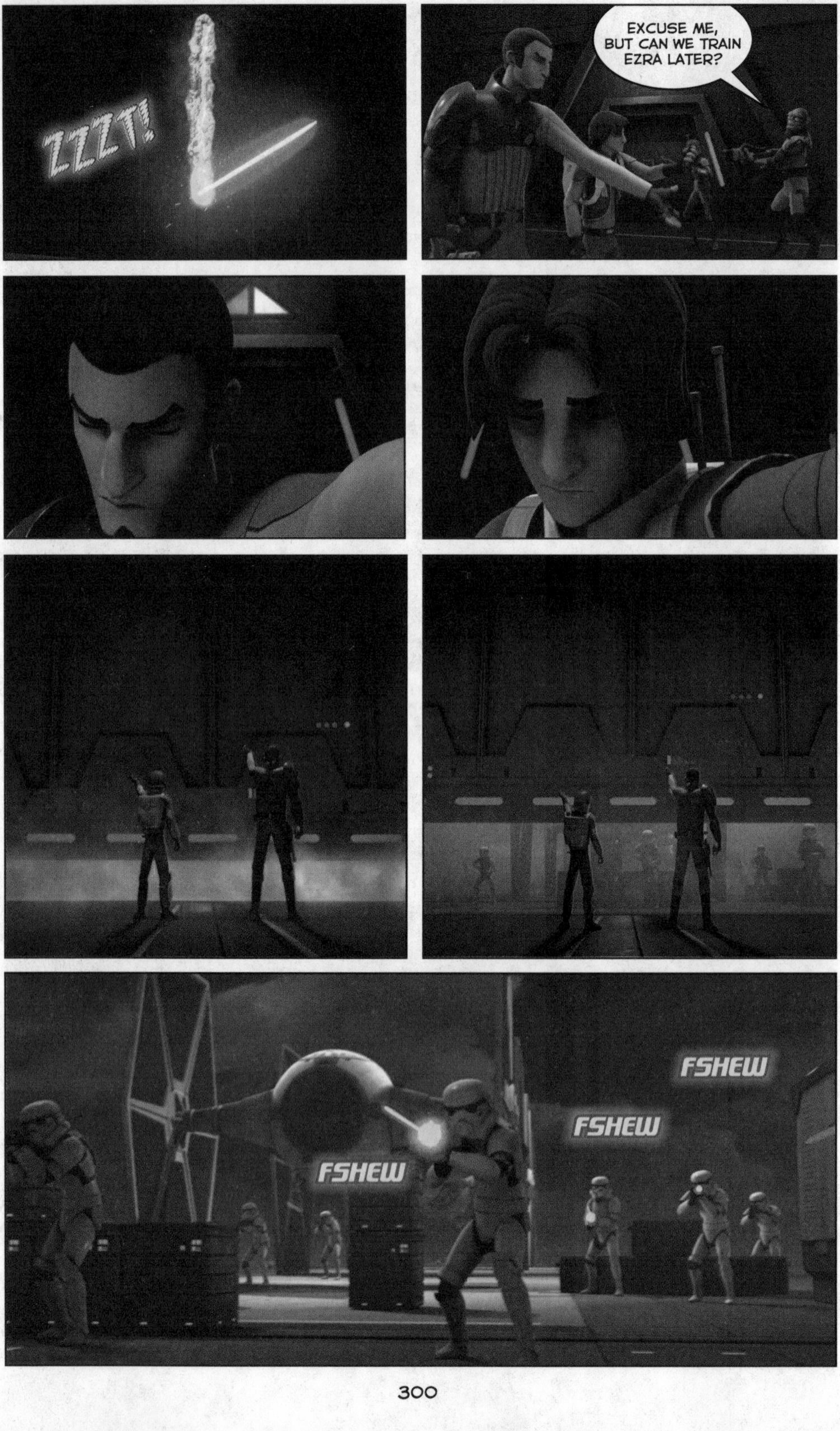
ZZZT!
EXCUSE ME, BUT CAN WE TRAIN EZRA LATER?
FSHEW
FSHEW
FSHEW

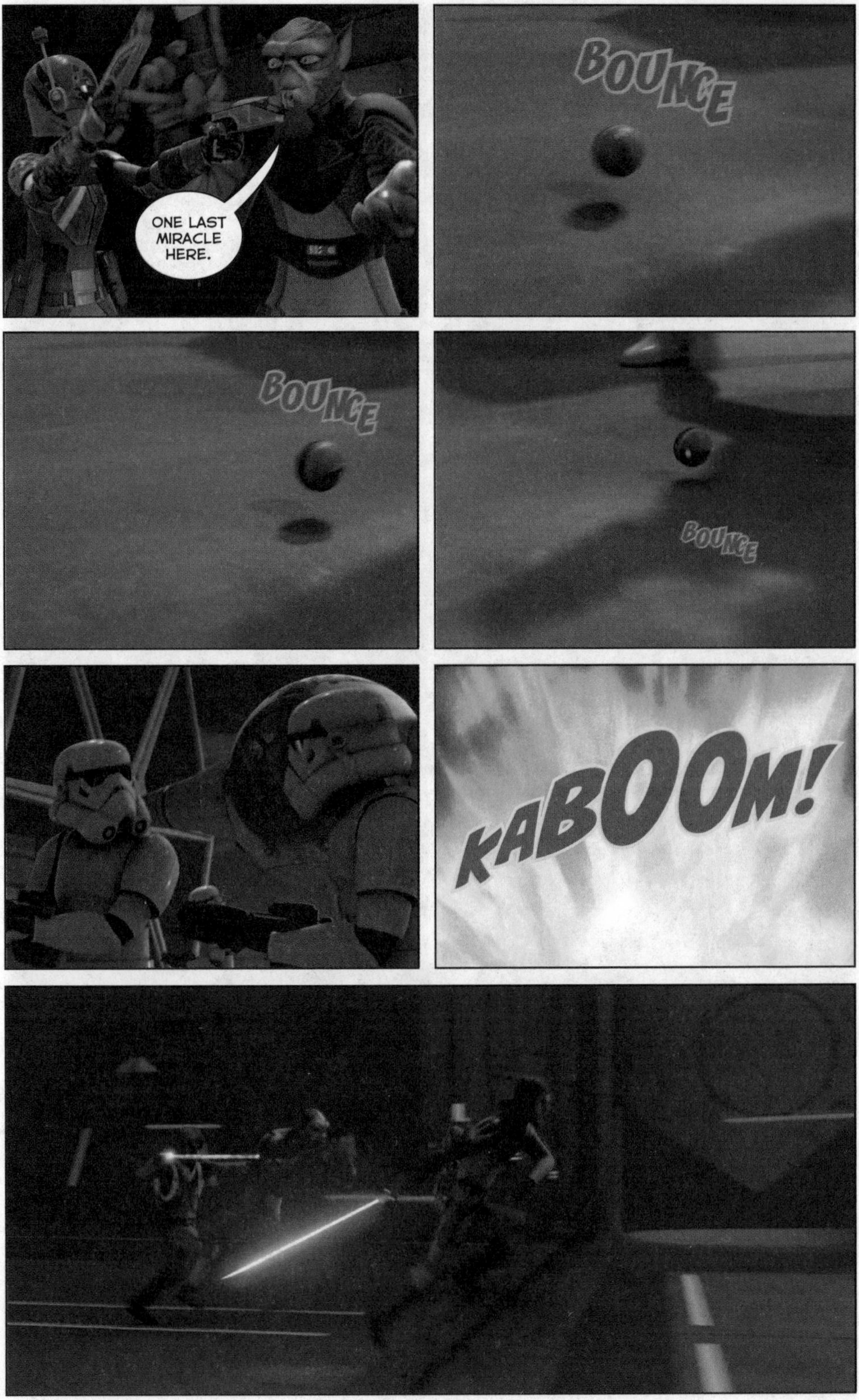
ONE LAST MIRACLE HERE.
BOUNCE
BOUNCE
BOUNCE
KABOOM!

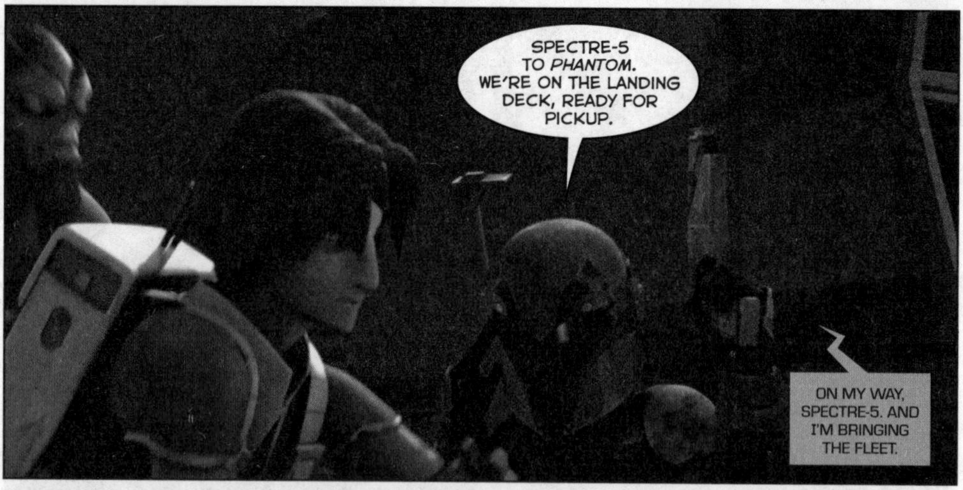
SPECTRE-5 TO *PHANTOM*. WE'RE ON THE LANDING DECK, READY FOR PICKUP.
ON MY WAY, SPECTRE-5. AND I'M BRINGING THE FLEET.

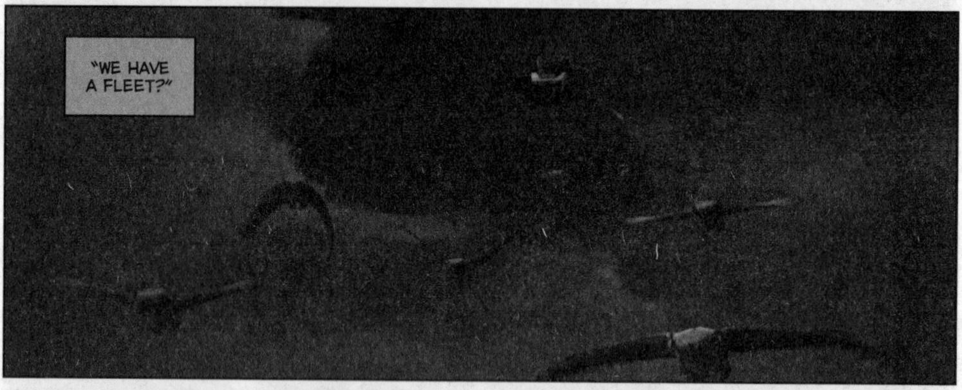
"WE HAVE A FLEET?"

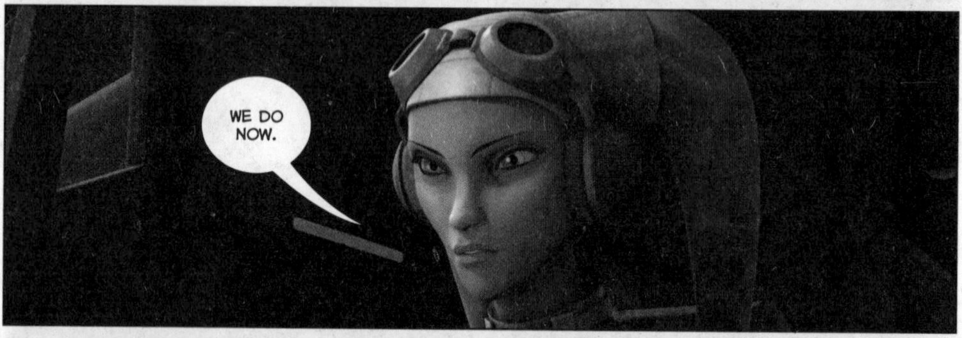
WE DO NOW.

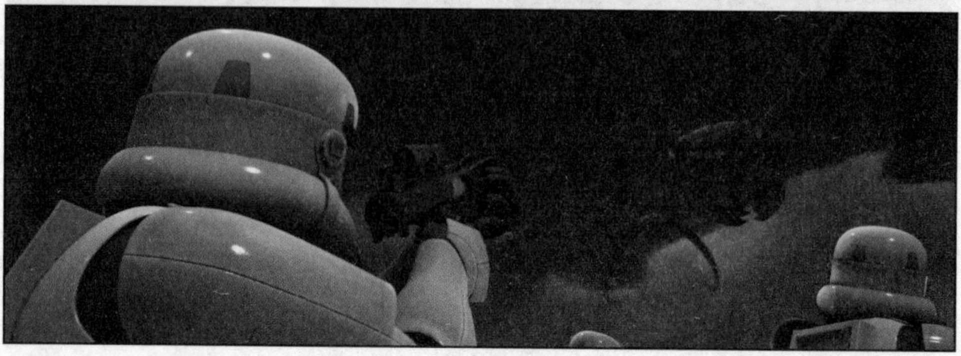

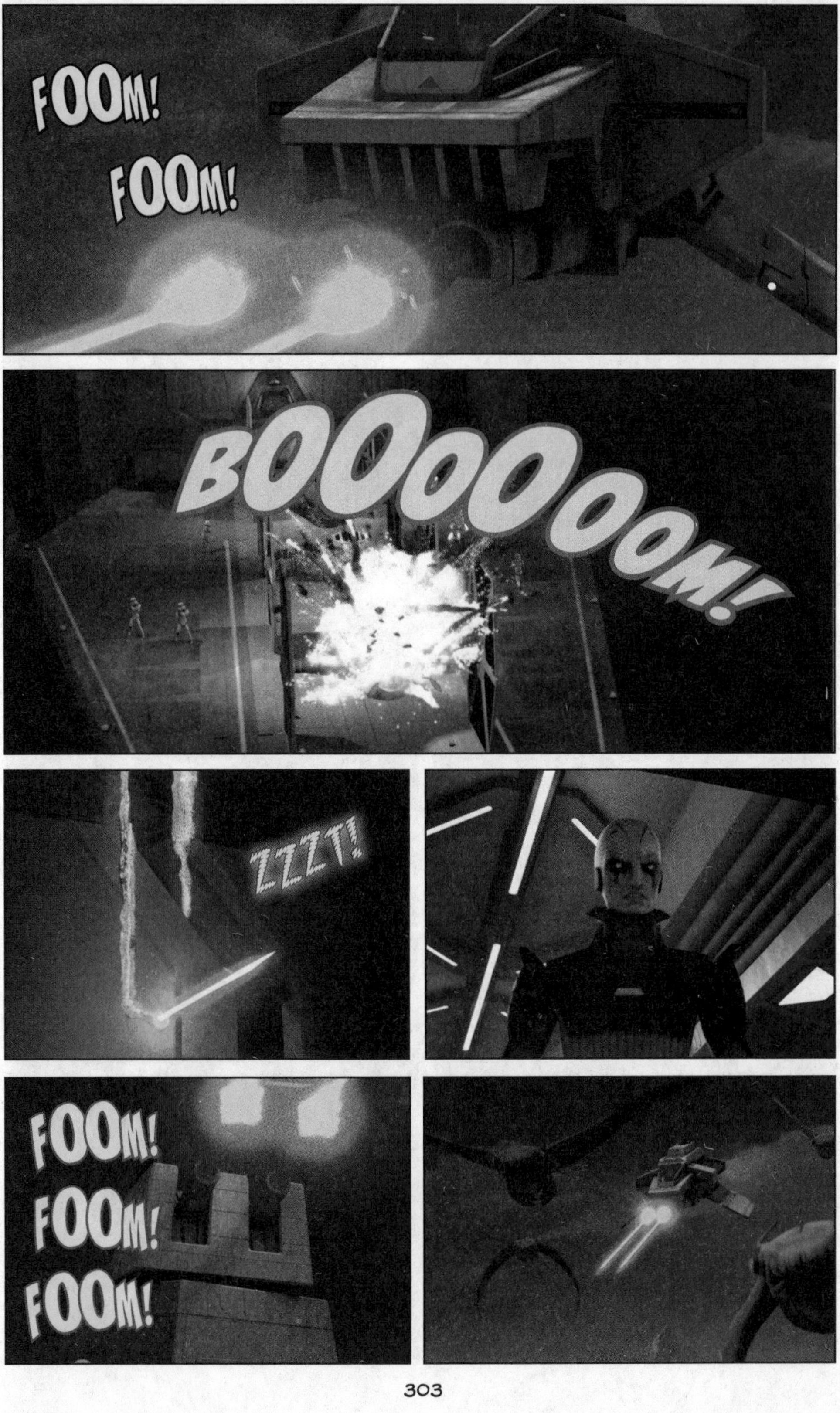
FOOM!
FOOM!
BOOOOOOOM!
ZZZT!
FOOM!
FOOM!
FOOM!

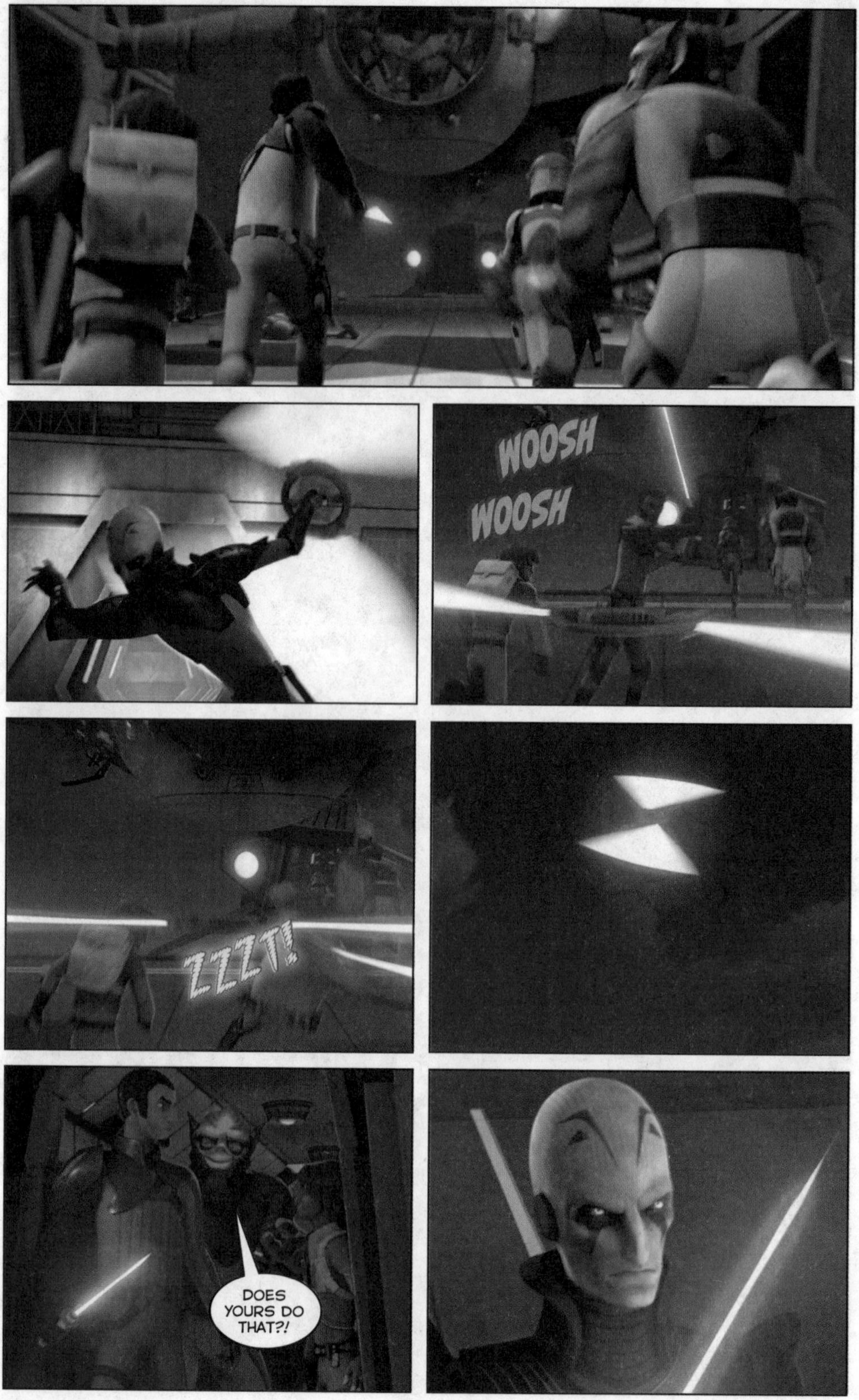
WOOSH
WOOSH
ZZZT!
DOES YOURS DO THAT?!

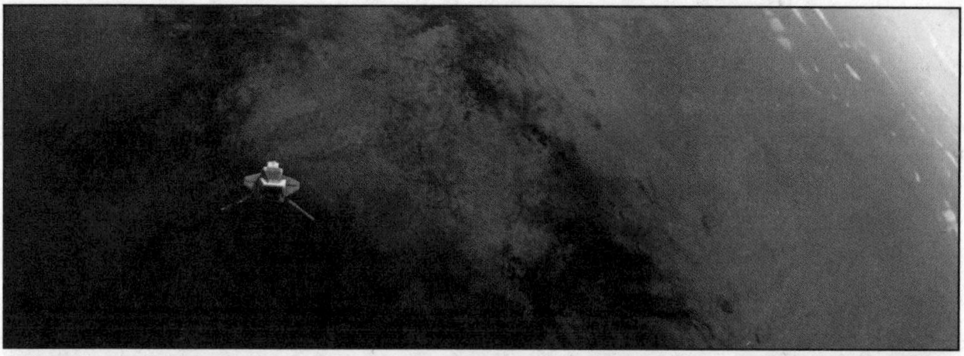

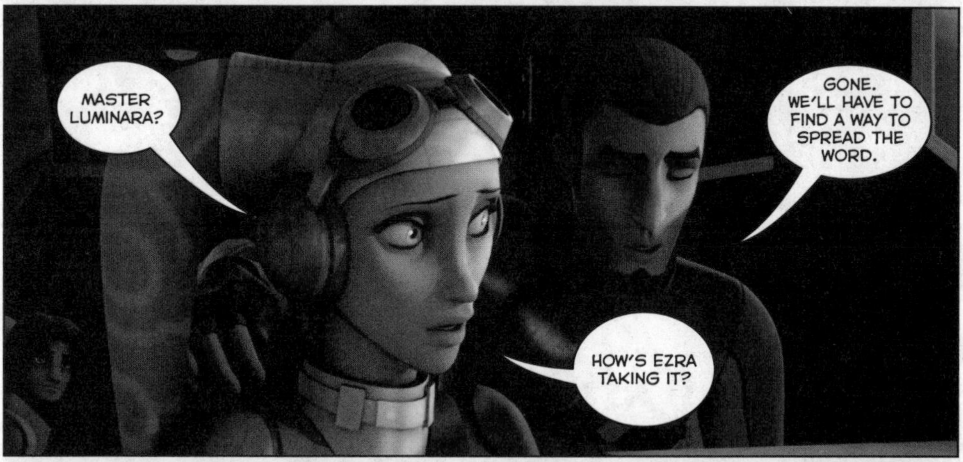
MASTER LUMINARA?
GONE. WE'LL HAVE TO FIND A WAY TO SPREAD THE WORD.
HOW'S EZRA TAKING IT?

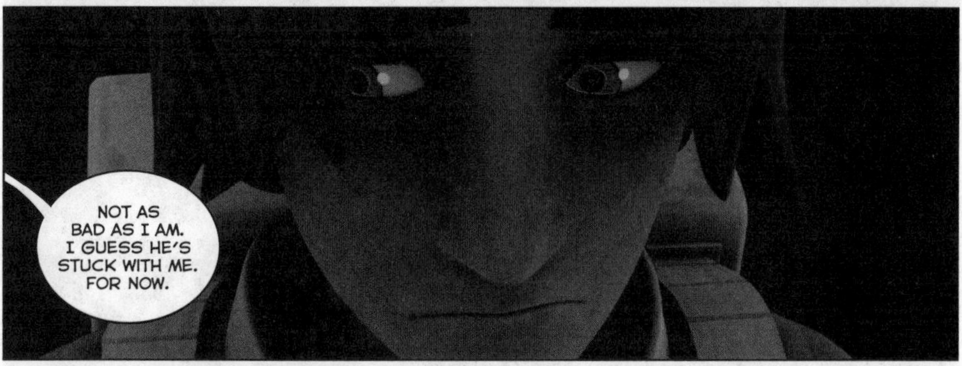
NOT AS BAD AS I AM. I GUESS HE'S STUCK WITH ME. FOR NOW.

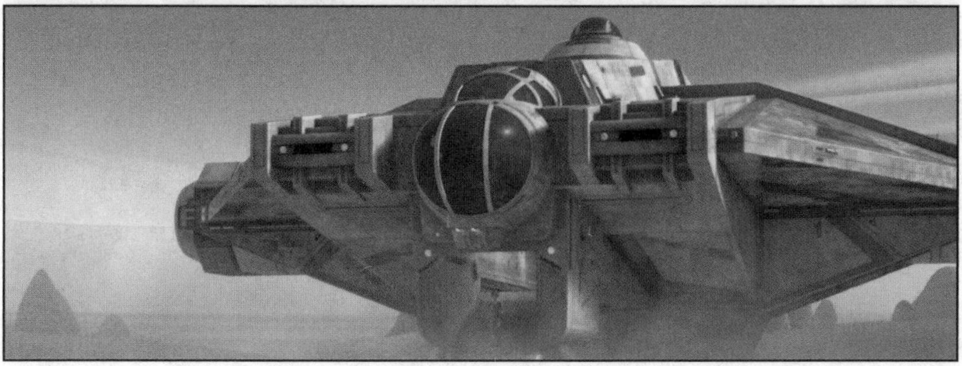

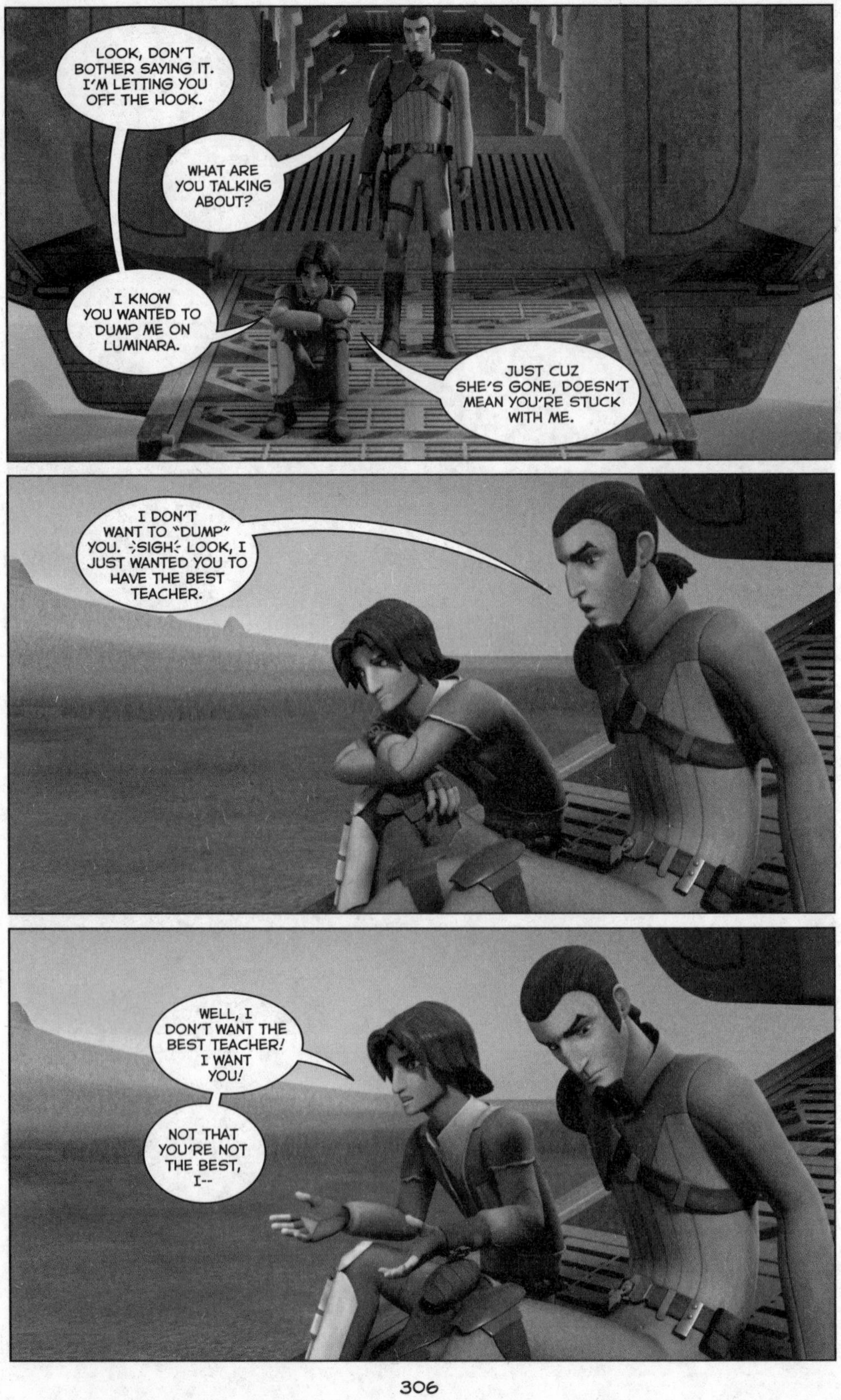
LOOK, DON'T BOTHER SAYING IT. I'M LETTING YOU OFF THE HOOK.
WHAT ARE YOU TALKING ABOUT?
I KNOW YOU WANTED TO DUMP ME ON LUMINARA.
JUST CUZ SHE'S GONE, DOESN'T MEAN YOU'RE STUCK WITH ME.
I DON'T WANT TO "DUMP" YOU. *SIGH* LOOK, I JUST WANTED YOU TO HAVE THE BEST TEACHER.
WELL, I DON'T WANT THE BEST TEACHER! I WANT YOU!
NOT THAT YOU'RE NOT THE BEST, I--

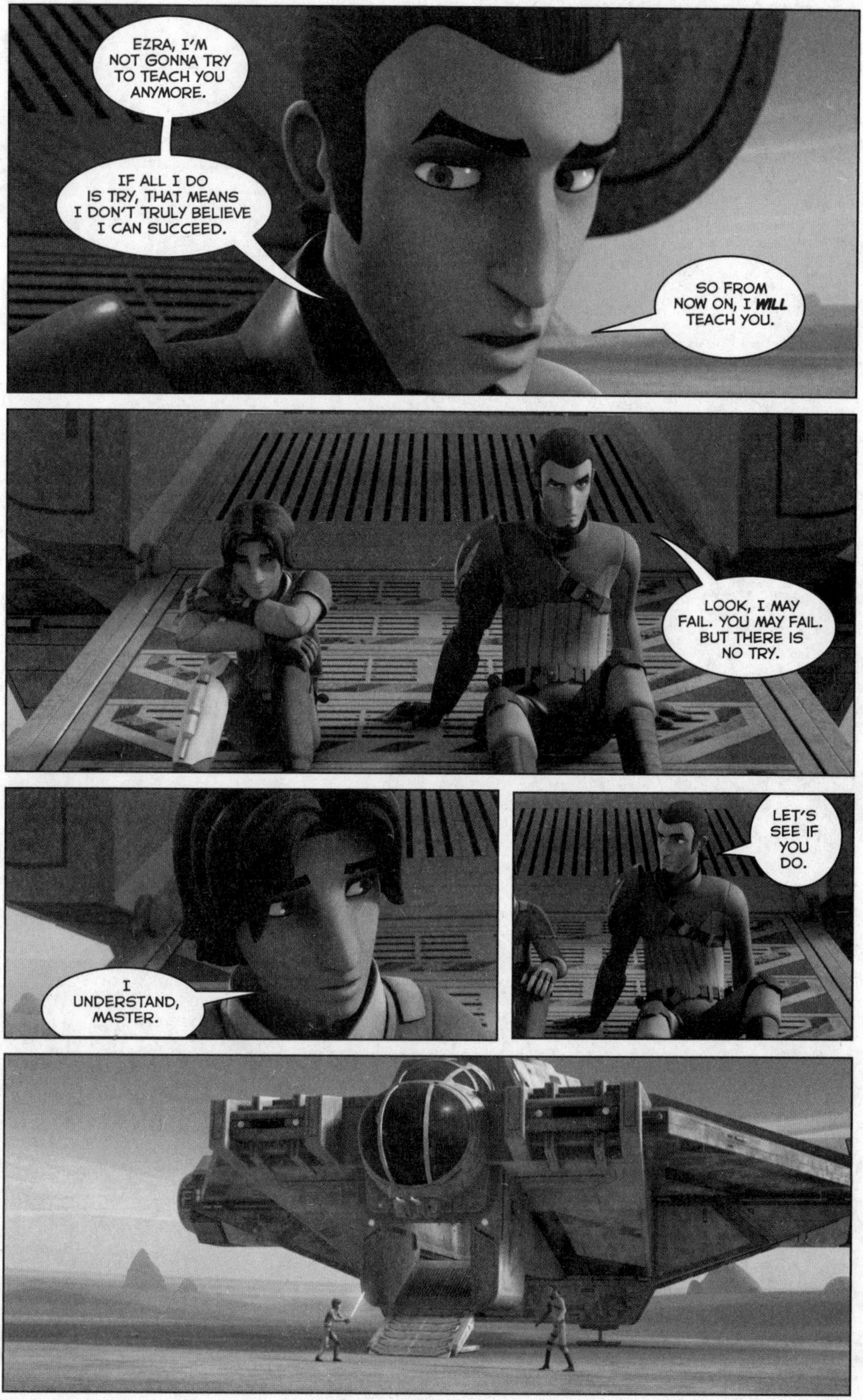
EZRA, I'M NOT GONNA TRY TO TEACH YOU ANYMORE.
IF ALL I DO IS TRY, THAT MEANS I DON'T TRULY BELIEVE I CAN SUCCEED.
SO FROM NOW ON, I **WILL** TEACH YOU.
LOOK, I MAY FAIL. YOU MAY FAIL. BUT THERE IS NO TRY.
I UNDERSTAND, MASTER.
LET'S SEE IF YOU DO.

STAR WARS REBELS™

BREAKING RANKS

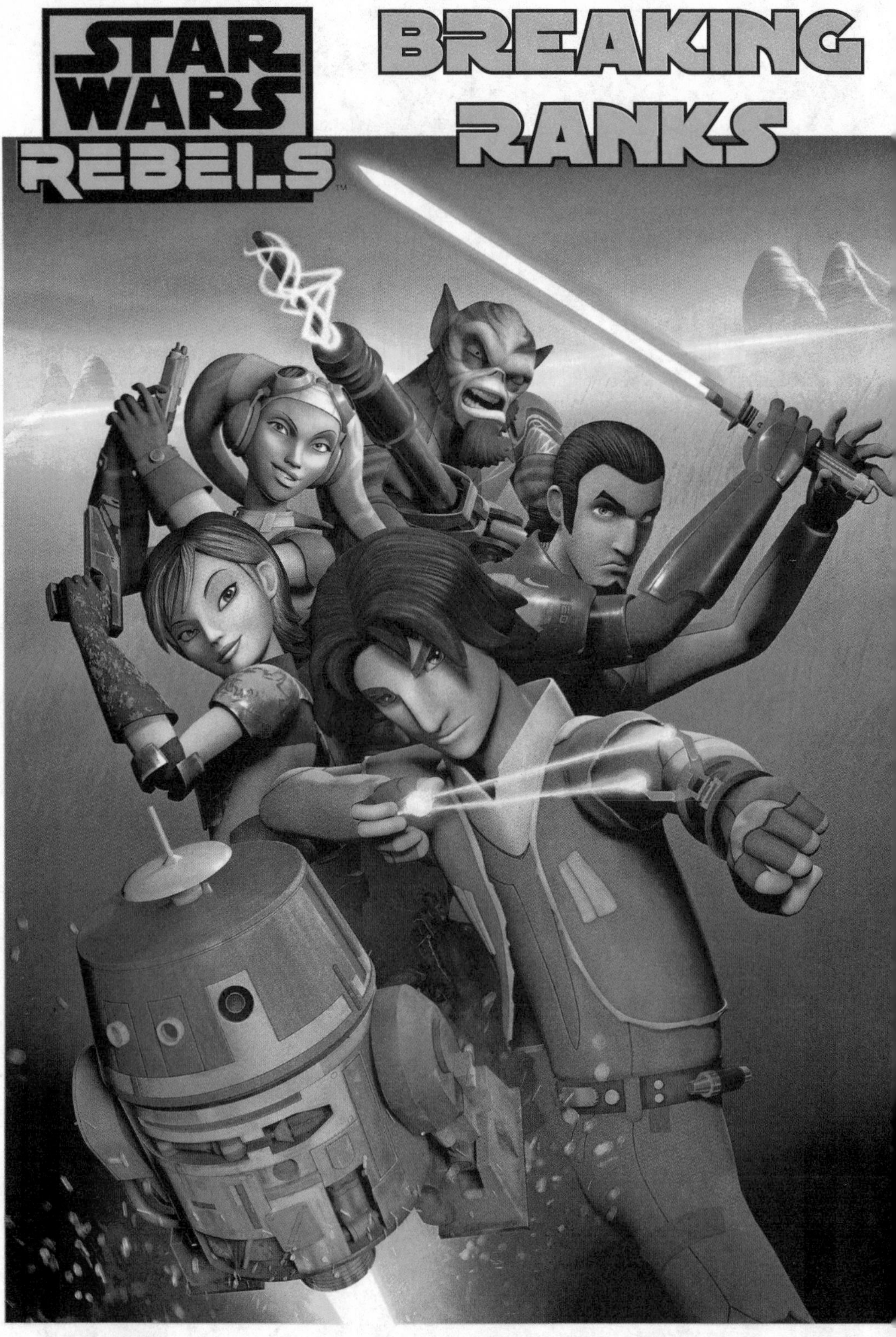

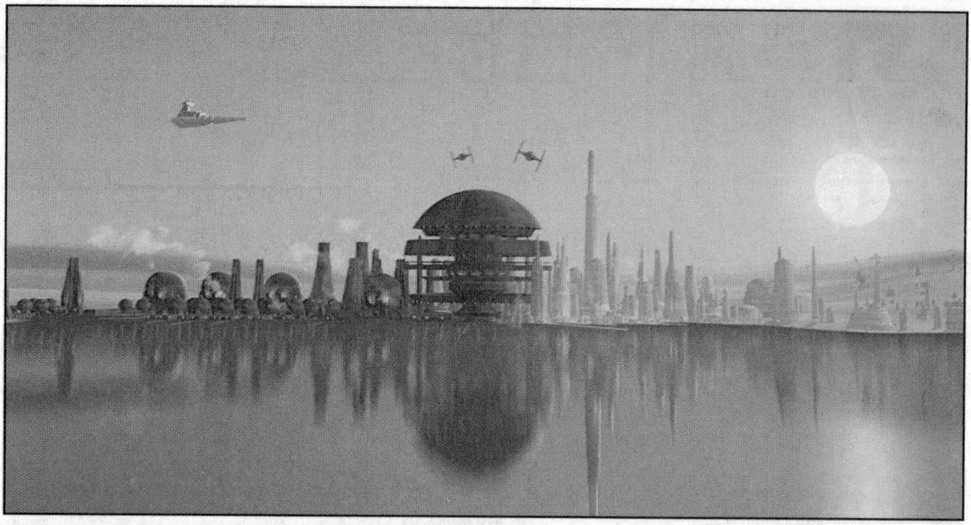

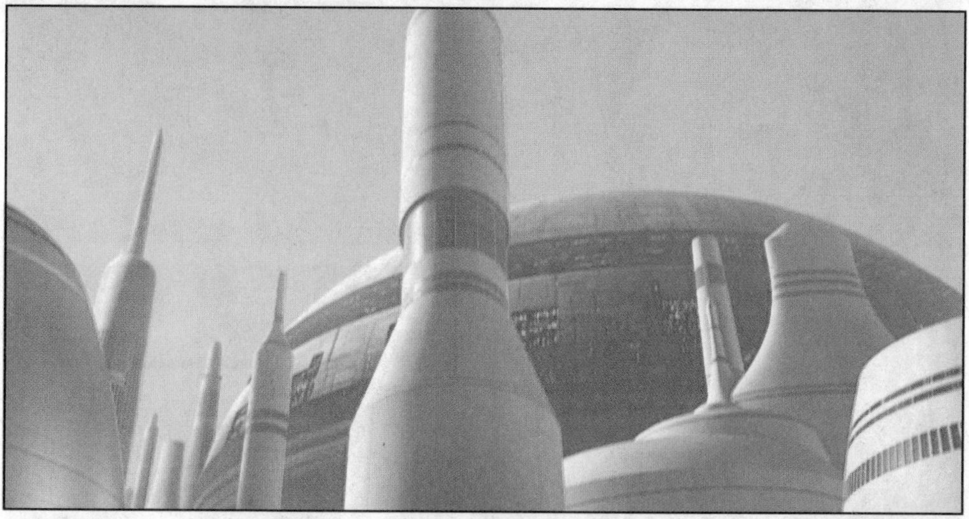

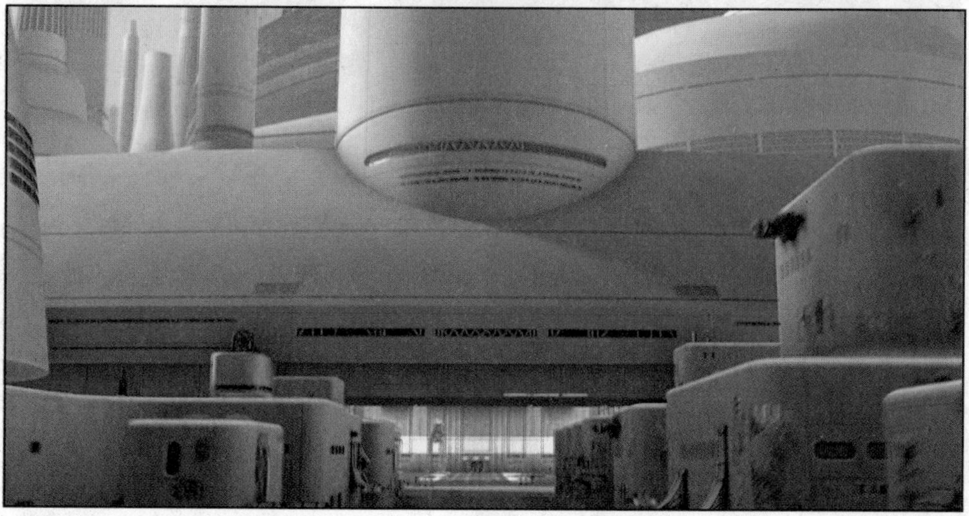

AND HALT!

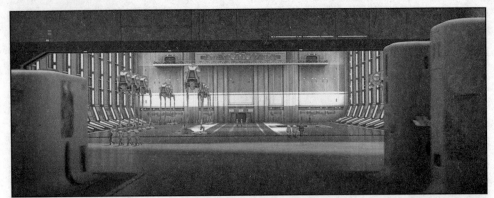

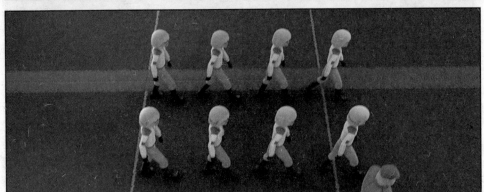

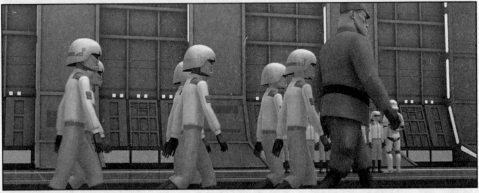

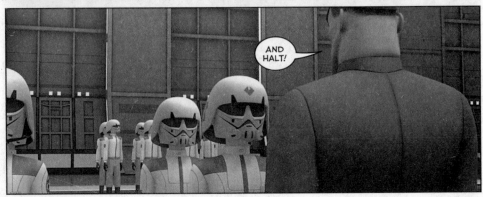

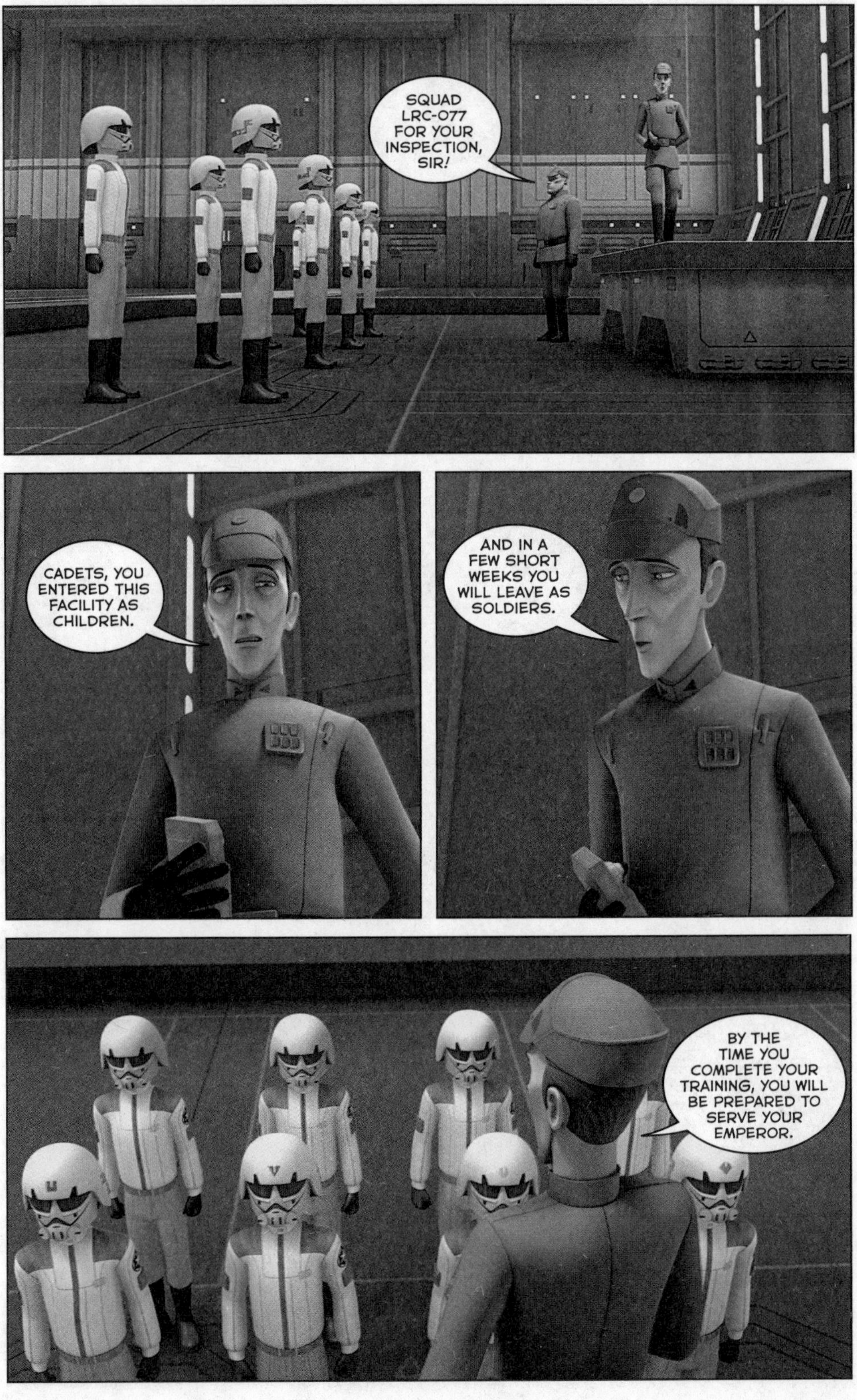
SQUAD LRC-077 FOR YOUR INSPECTION, SIR!
CADETS, YOU ENTERED THIS FACILITY AS CHILDREN.
AND IN A FEW SHORT WEEKS YOU WILL LEAVE AS SOLDIERS.
BY THE TIME YOU COMPLETE YOUR TRAINING, YOU WILL BE PREPARED TO SERVE YOUR EMPEROR.

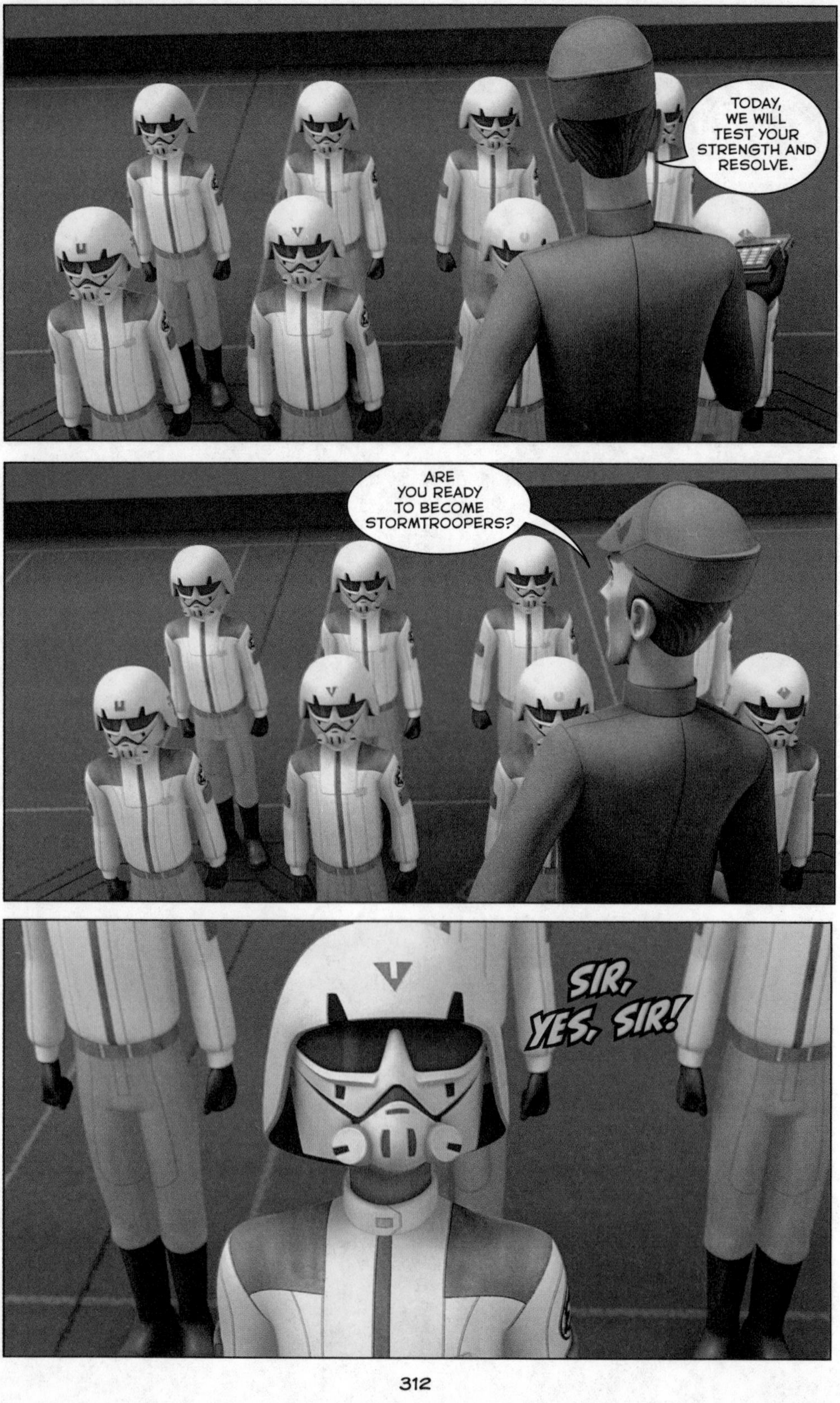
TODAY, WE WILL TEST YOUR STRENGTH AND RESOLVE.
ARE YOU READY TO BECOME STORMTROOPERS?
SIR, YES, SIR!

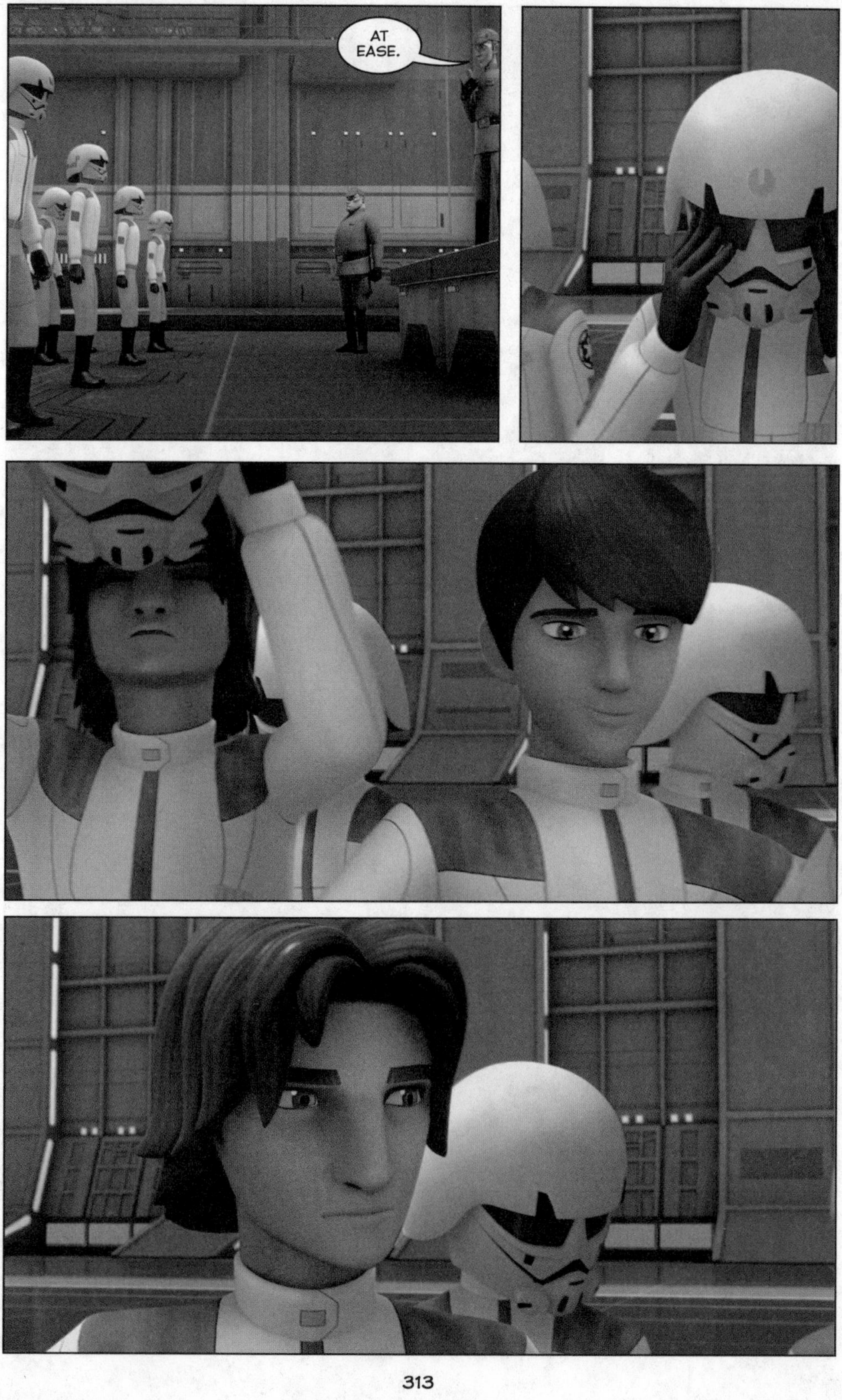
AT EASE.

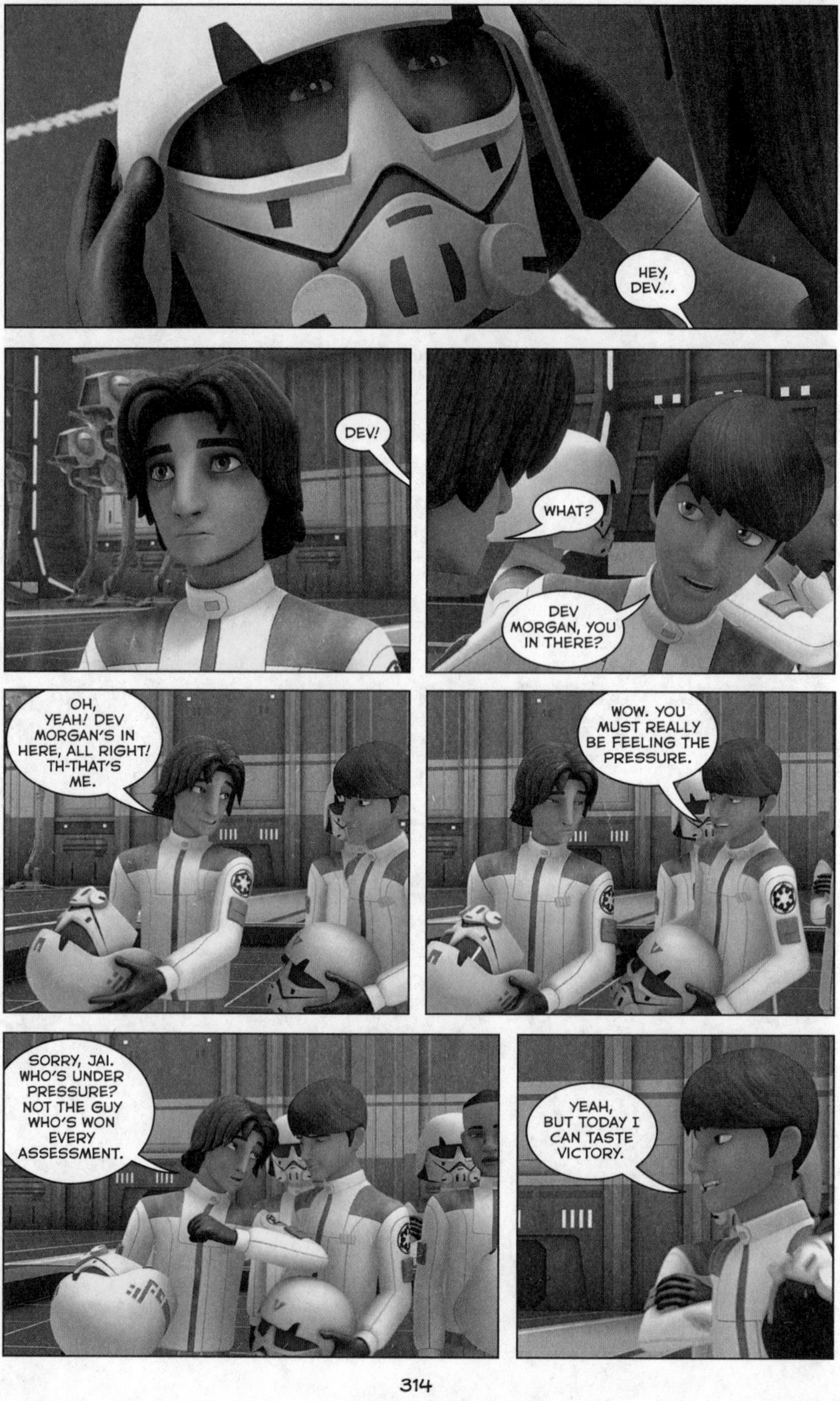
HEY, DEV...
DEV!
WHAT?
DEV MORGAN, YOU IN THERE?
OH, YEAH! DEV MORGAN'S IN HERE, ALL RIGHT! TH-THAT'S ME.
WOW. YOU MUST REALLY BE FEELING THE PRESSURE.
SORRY, JAI. WHO'S UNDER PRESSURE? NOT THE GUY WHO'S WON EVERY ASSESSMENT.
YEAH, BUT TODAY I CAN TASTE VICTORY.

YOU SAID THAT YESTERDAY.

AND WENT HUNGRY.

HA! HA, HA!

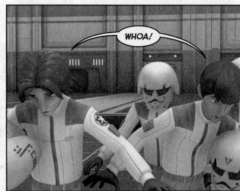

WHOA!

CADETS...

...YOU ARE DESCENDING INTO "THE WELL"...

...AND MUST CLIMB OUT...

...WITH ALL DELIBERATE SPEED.

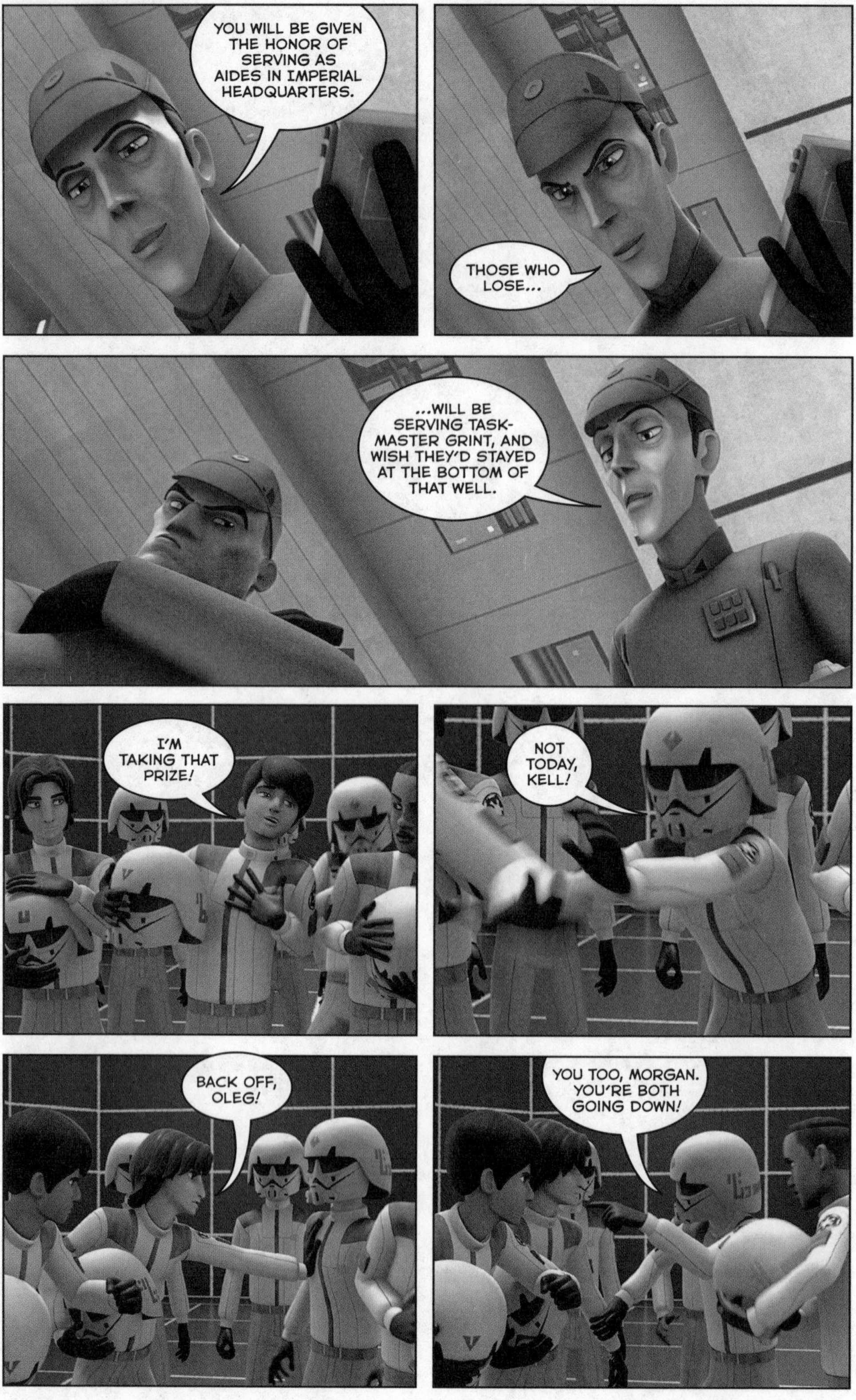
YOU WILL BE GIVEN THE HONOR OF SERVING AS AIDES IN IMPERIAL HEADQUARTERS.
THOSE WHO LOSE...
...WILL BE SERVING TASK-MASTER GRINT, AND WISH THEY'D STAYED AT THE BOTTOM OF THAT WELL.
I'M TAKING THAT PRIZE!
NOT TODAY, KELL!
BACK OFF, OLEG!
YOU TOO, MORGAN. YOU'RE BOTH GOING DOWN!

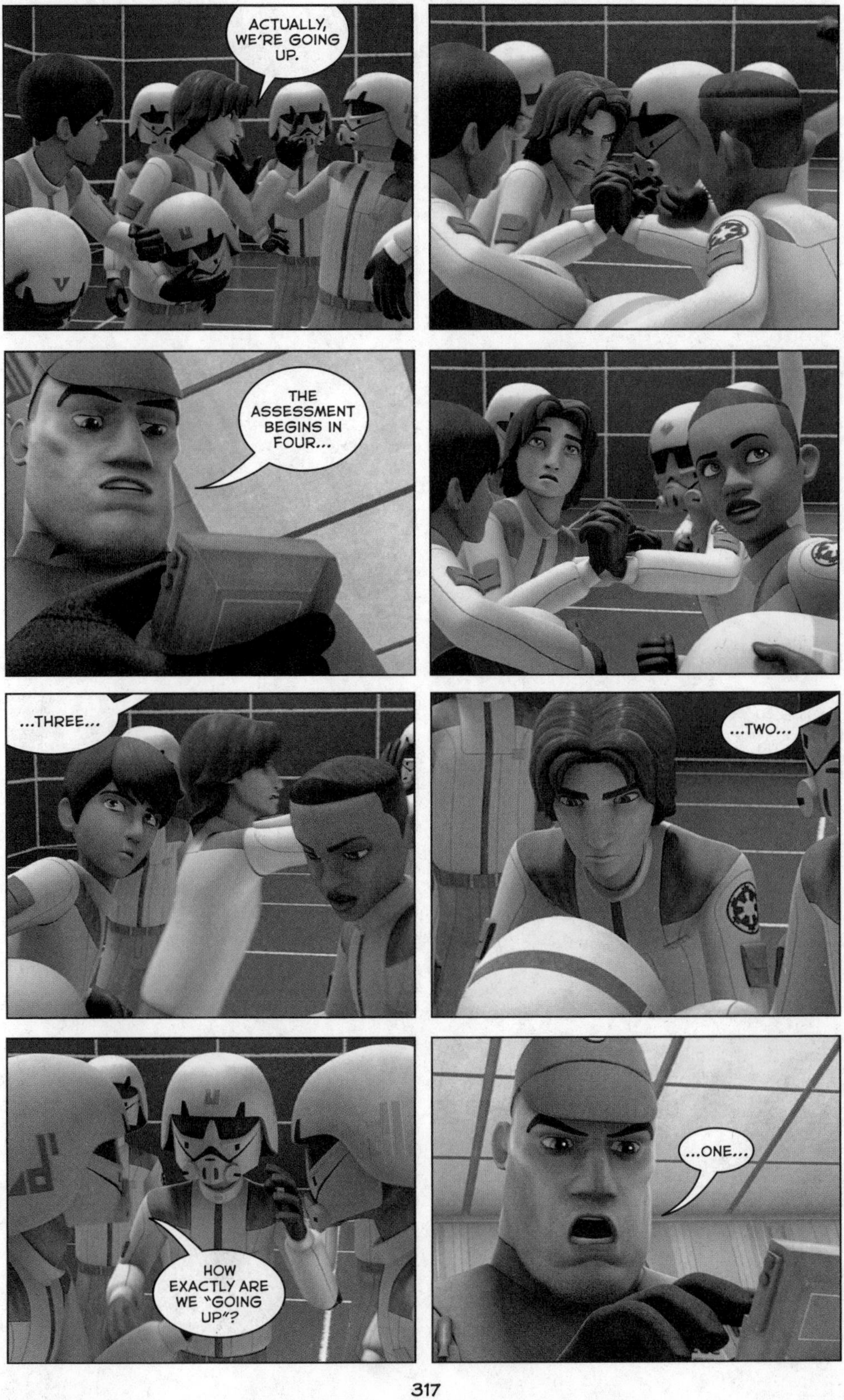
ACTUALLY, WE'RE GOING UP.
THE ASSESSMENT BEGINS IN FOUR...
...THREE...
...TWO...
HOW EXACTLY ARE WE "GOING UP"?
...ONE...

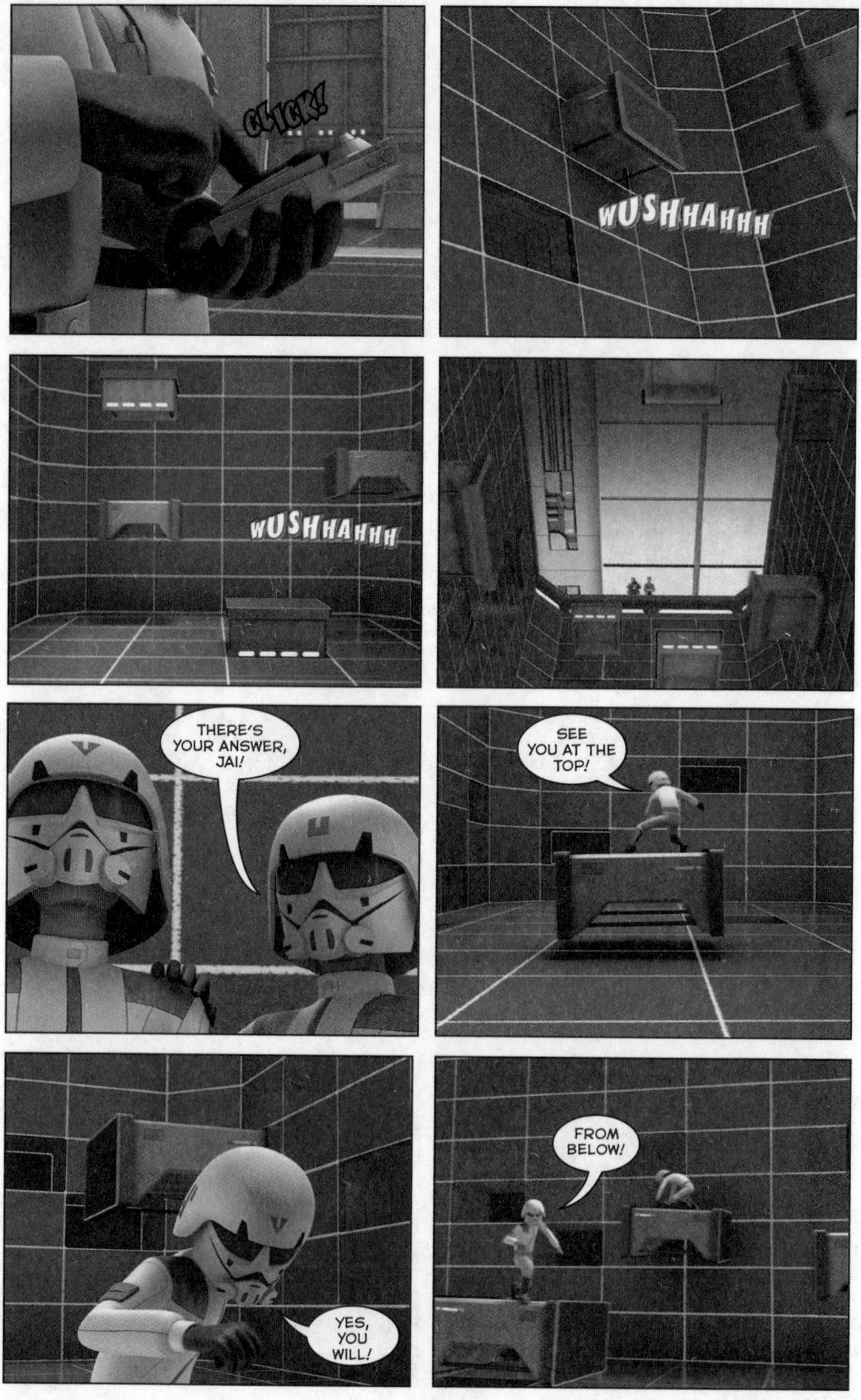
CLICK!
WUSHHAHHH
WUSHHAHHH
THERE'S YOUR ANSWER, JAI!
SEE YOU AT THE TOP!
YES, YOU WILL!
FROM BELOW!

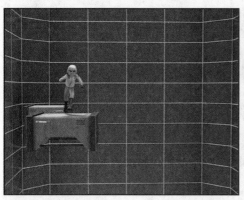

FAILURE IS NOT ACCEPTABLE!

THIS EMPIRE HAS NO USE FOR WEAKNESS!

CLICK!

ZZZT!

ZZZT!

WHOA!

ZZZZ

ZZZT!

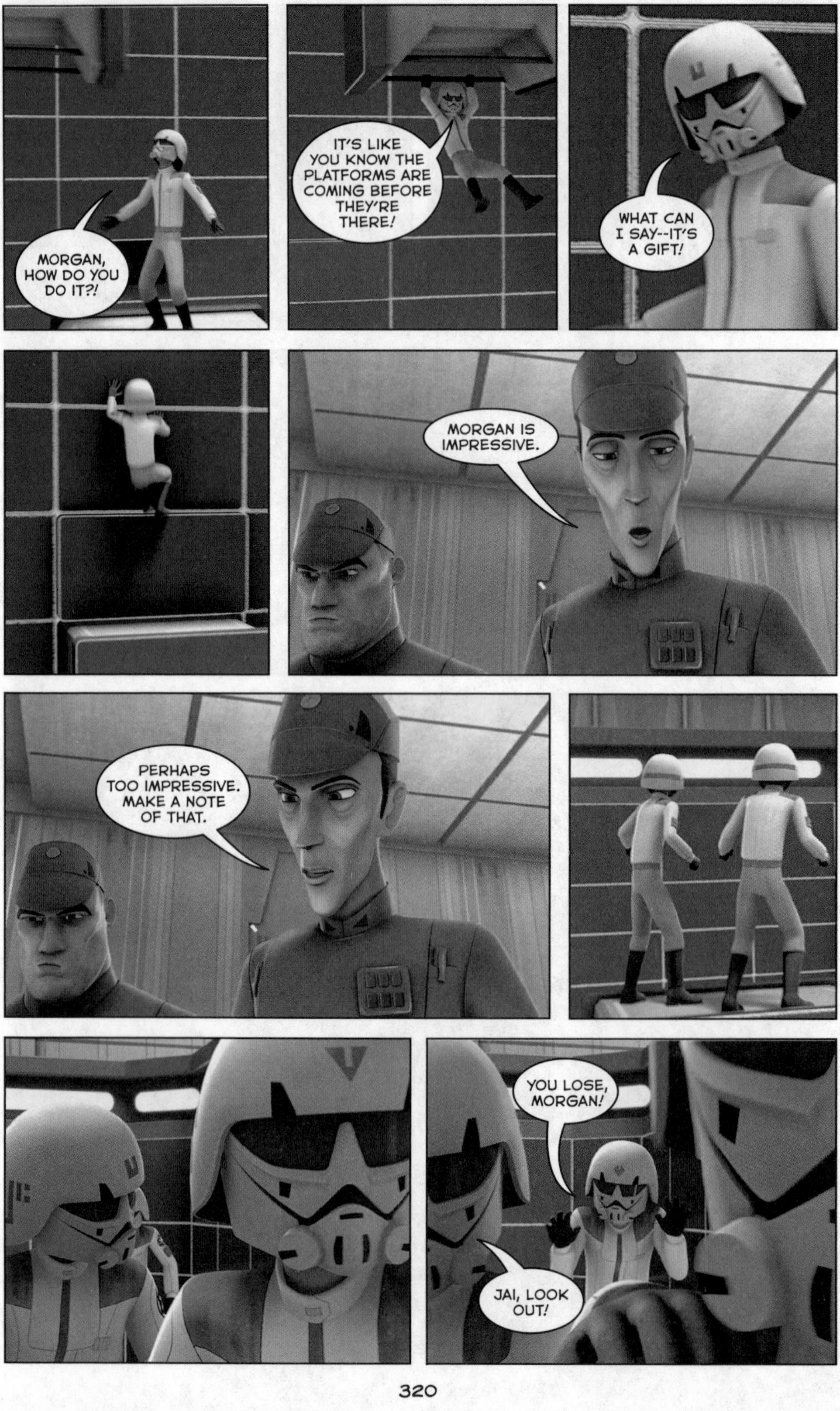
MORGAN, HOW DO YOU DO IT?!
IT'S LIKE YOU KNOW THE PLATFORMS ARE COMING BEFORE THEY'RE THERE!
WHAT CAN I SAY--IT'S A GIFT!
MORGAN IS IMPRESSIVE.
PERHAPS TOO IMPRESSIVE. MAKE A NOTE OF THAT.
YOU LOSE, MORGAN!
JAI, LOOK OUT!

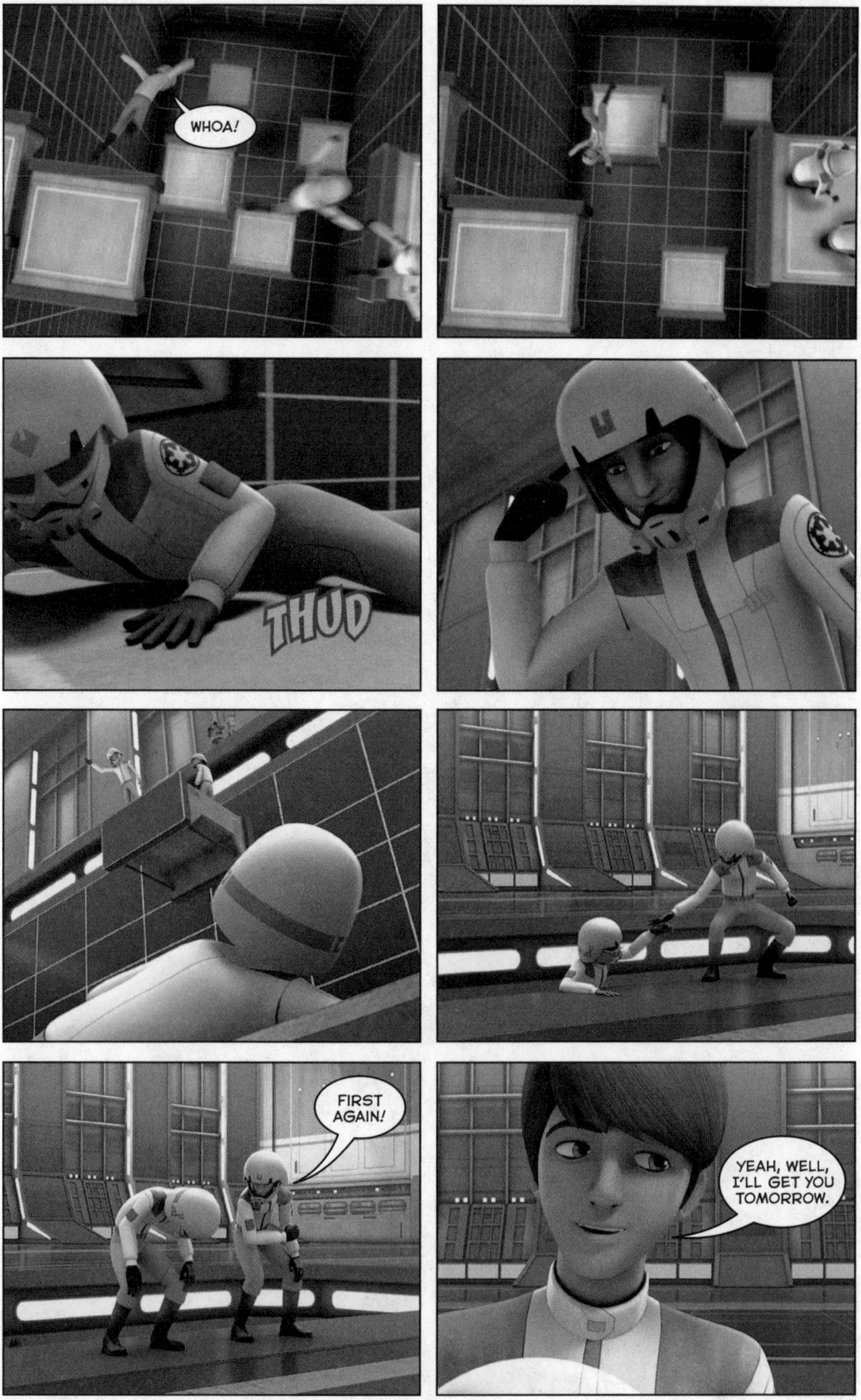
WHOA!
THUD
FIRST AGAIN!
YEAH, WELL, I'LL GET YOU TOMORROW.

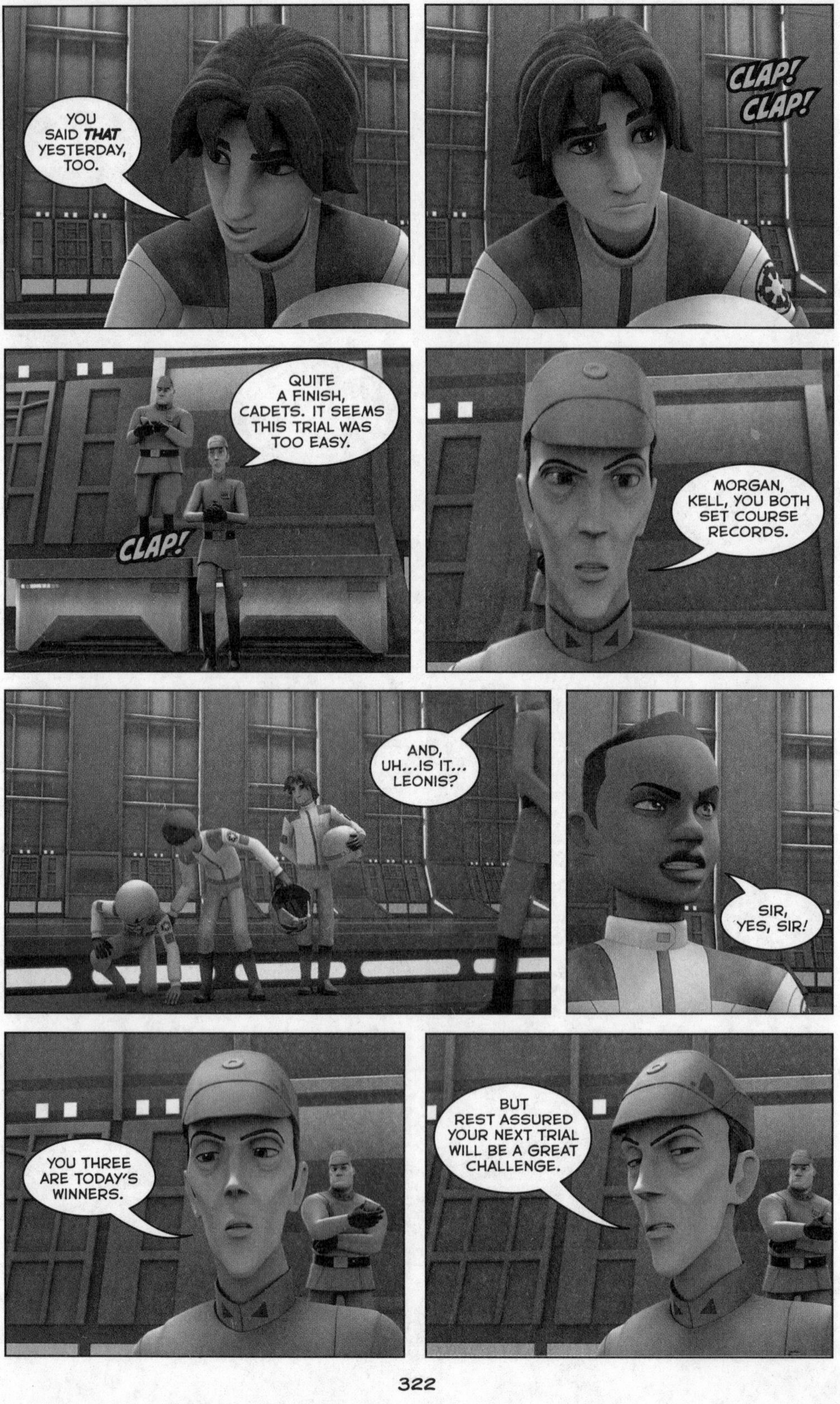
YOU SAID THAT YESTERDAY, TOO.
CLAP! CLAP!
QUITE A FINISH, CADETS. IT SEEMS THIS TRIAL WAS TOO EASY.
CLAP!
MORGAN, KELL, YOU BOTH SET COURSE RECORDS.
AND, UH...IS IT... LEONIS?
SIR, YES, SIR!
YOU THREE ARE TODAY'S WINNERS.
BUT REST ASSURED YOUR NEXT TRIAL WILL BE A GREAT CHALLENGE.

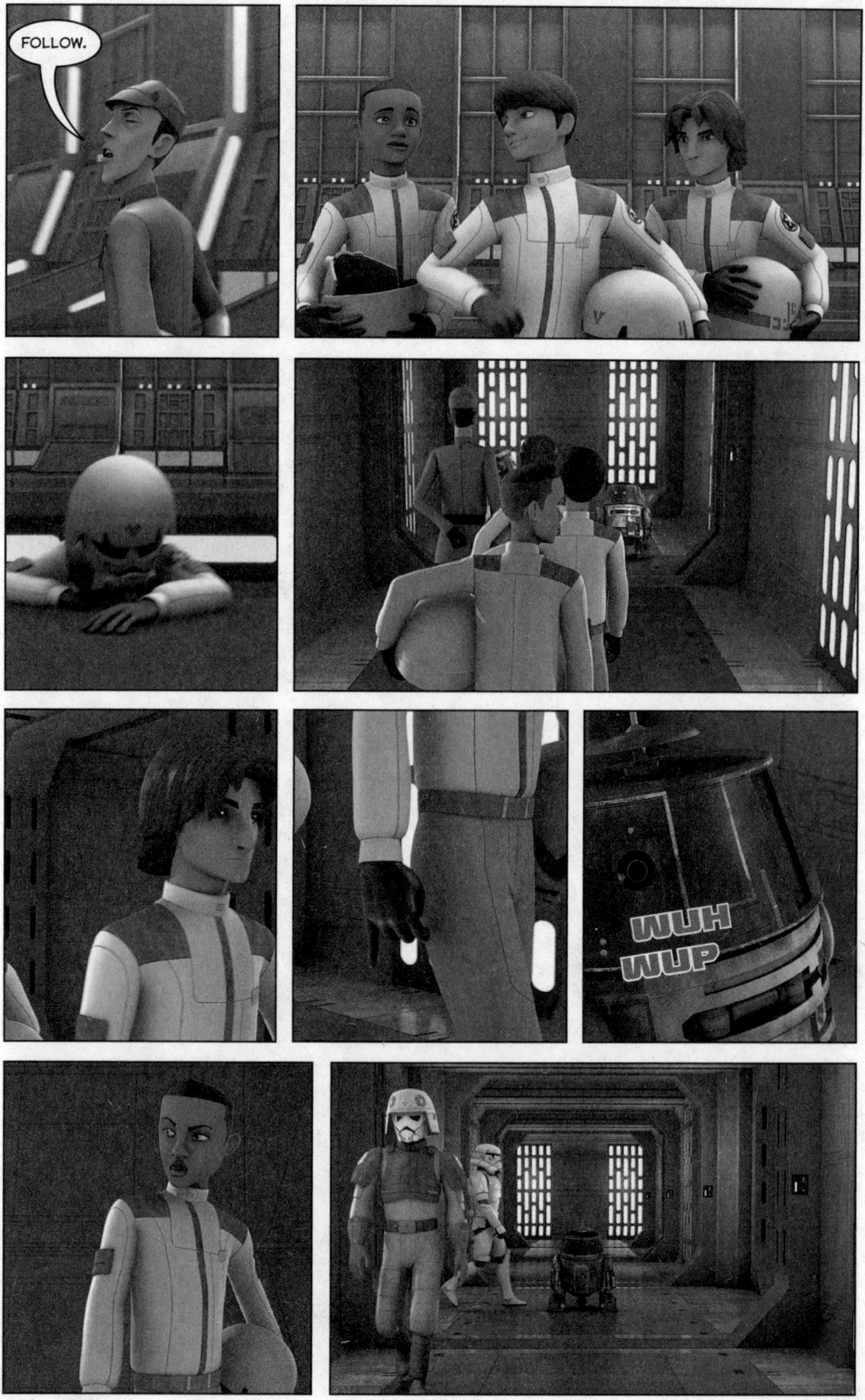
FOLLOW.
WUH
WUP

BLINK
BLINK

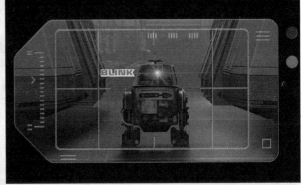

BLINK

SPECTRE-5 TO *GHOST.* LOOKS LIKE THE KID PASSED THE FIRST TEST.

HE'S INSIDE IMPERIAL H.Q.

ROGER, SPECTRE-5. *GHOST* STANDING BY.

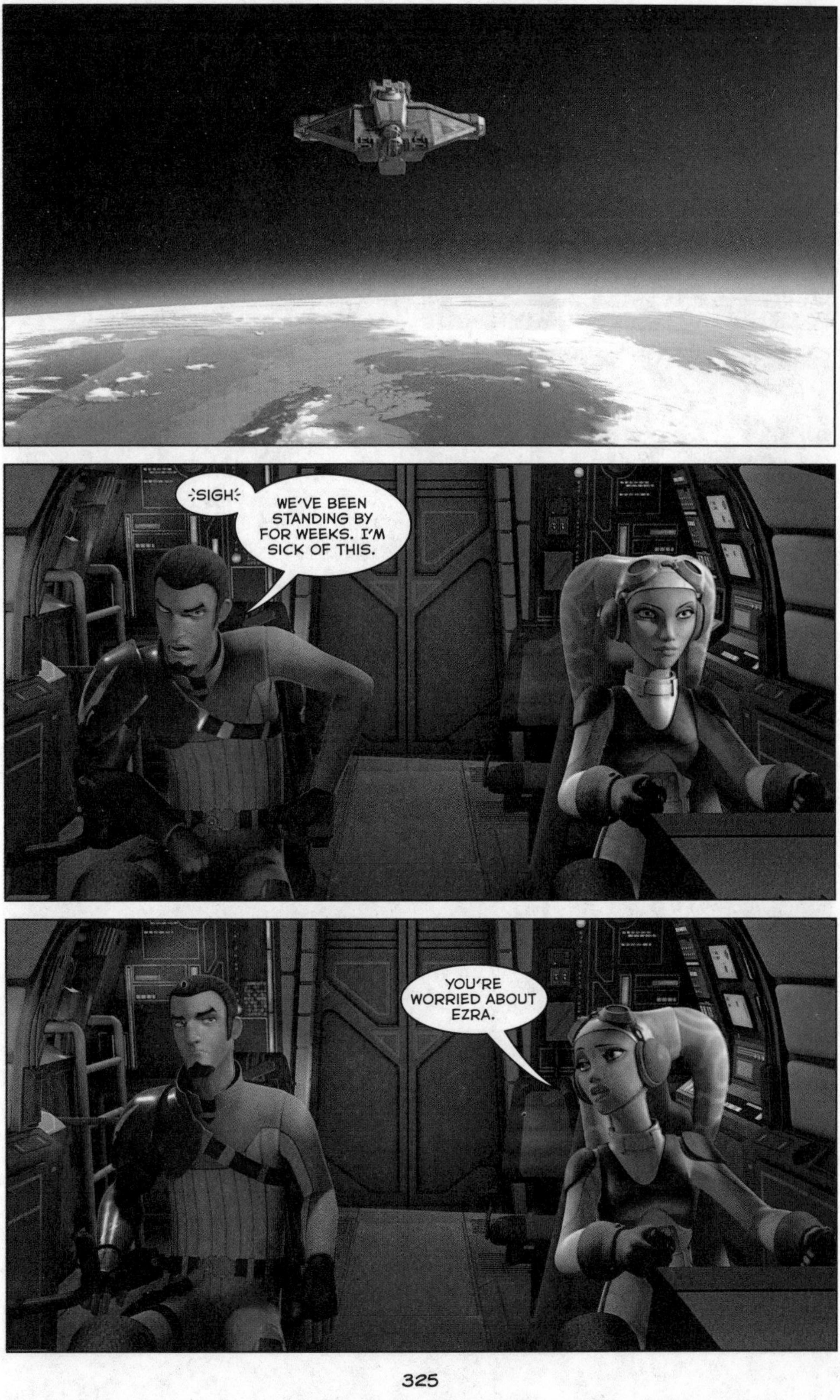

SIGH
WE'VE BEEN STANDING BY FOR WEEKS. I'M SICK OF THIS.
YOU'RE WORRIED ABOUT EZRA.

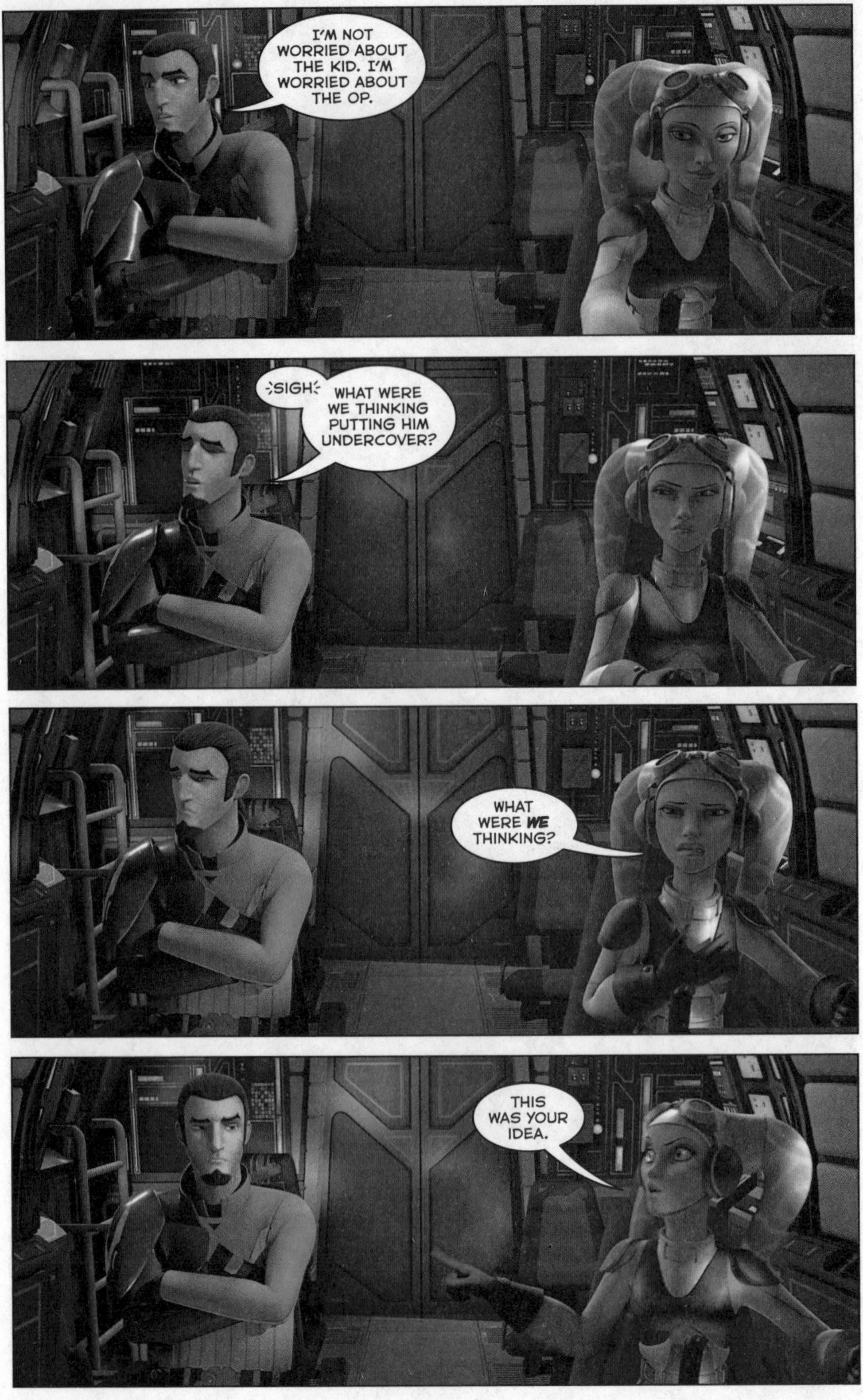
I'M NOT WORRIED ABOUT THE KID. I'M WORRIED ABOUT THE OP.
SIGH
WHAT WERE WE THINKING PUTTING HIM UNDERCOVER?
WHAT WERE **WE** THINKING?
THIS WAS YOUR IDEA.

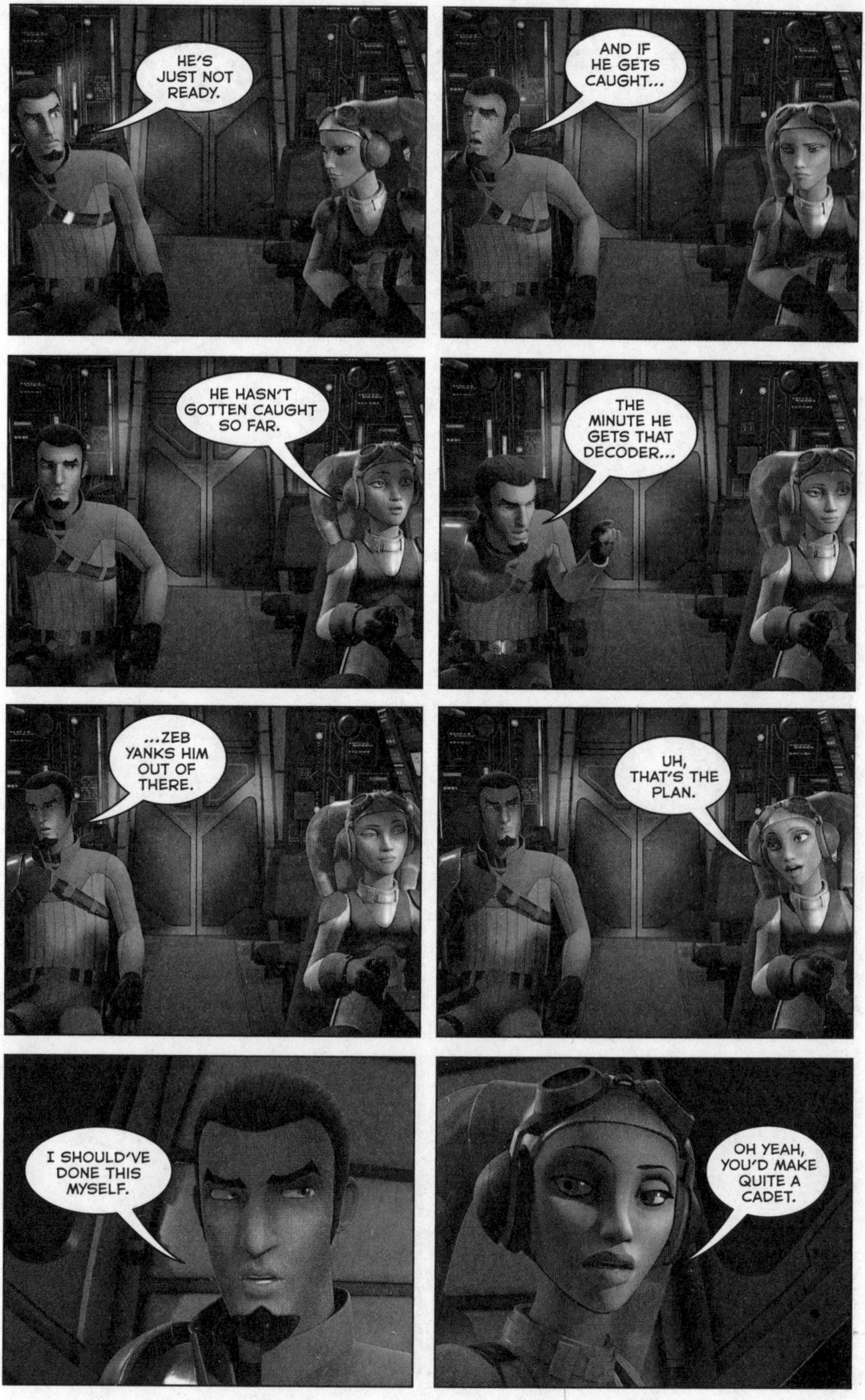
HE'S JUST NOT READY.
AND IF HE GETS CAUGHT...
HE HASN'T GOTTEN CAUGHT SO FAR.
THE MINUTE HE GETS THAT DECODER...
...ZEB YANKS HIM OUT OF THERE.
UH, THAT'S THE PLAN.
I SHOULD'VE DONE THIS MYSELF.
OH YEAH, YOU'D MAKE QUITE A CADET.

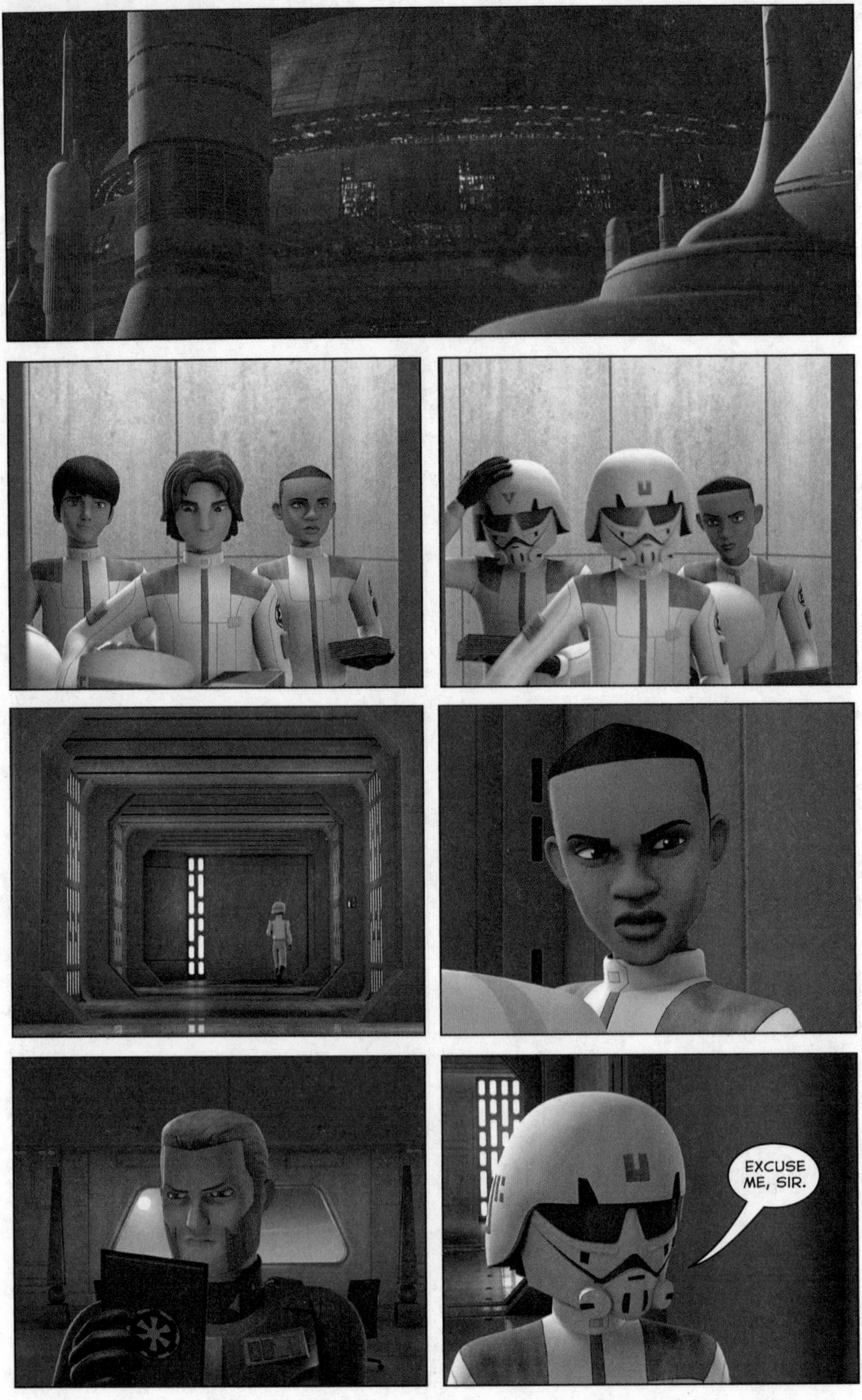
EXCUSE ME, SIR.

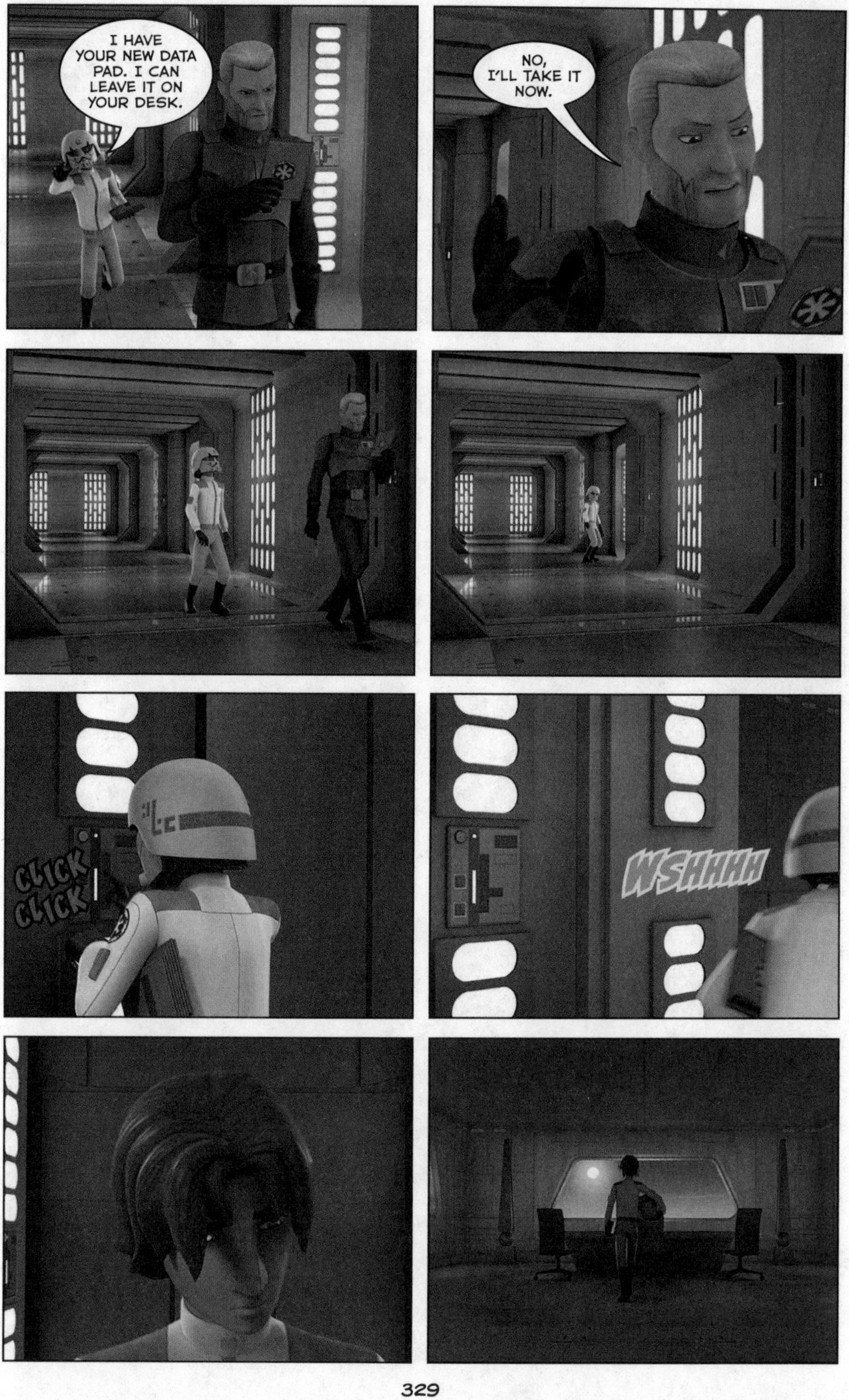
I HAVE YOUR NEW DATA PAD. I CAN LEAVE IT ON YOUR DESK.
NO, I'LL TAKE IT NOW.
CLICK CLICK
WSHHHH

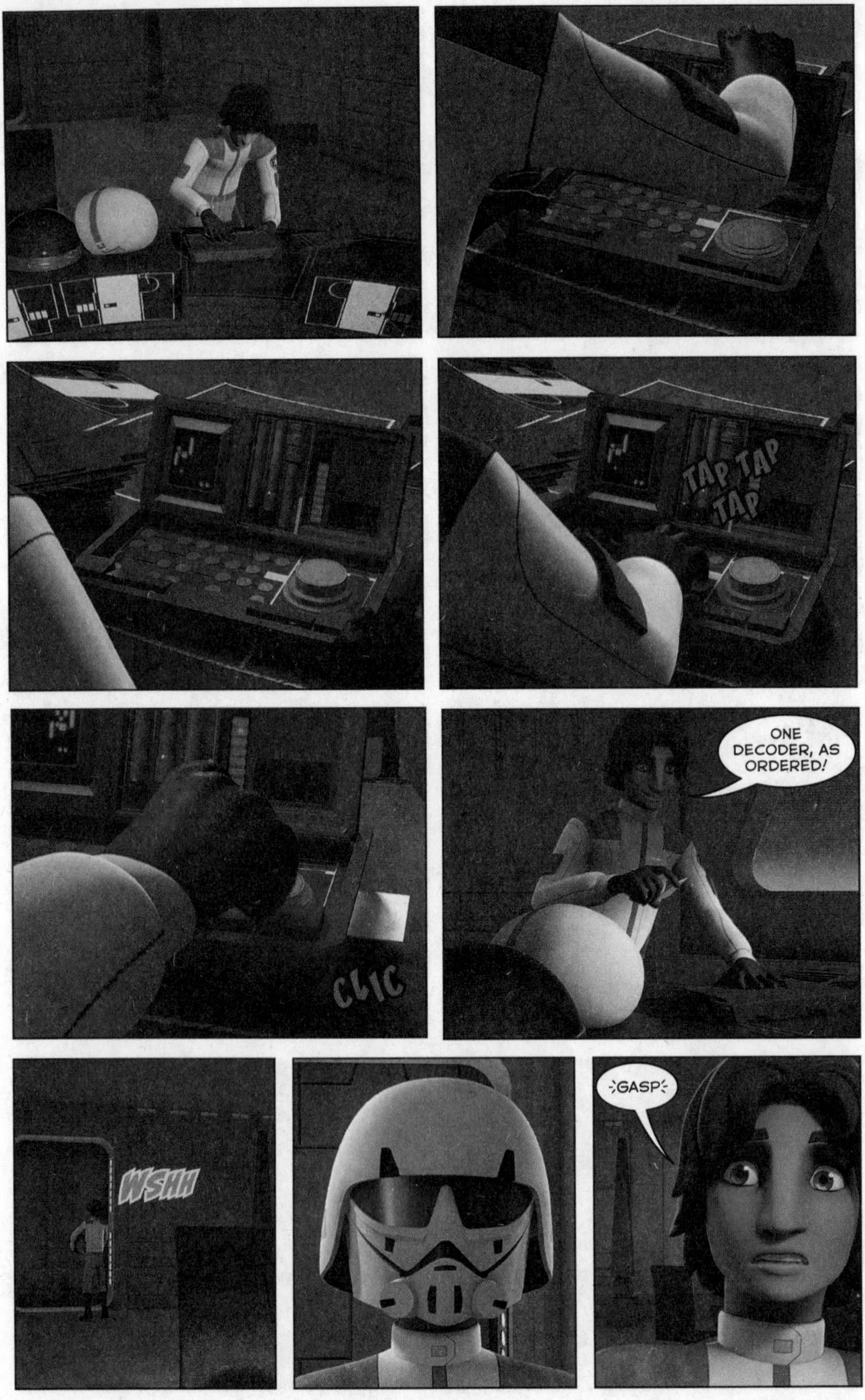
TAP TAP TAP
CLIC
ONE DECODER, AS ORDERED!
WSHH
GASP

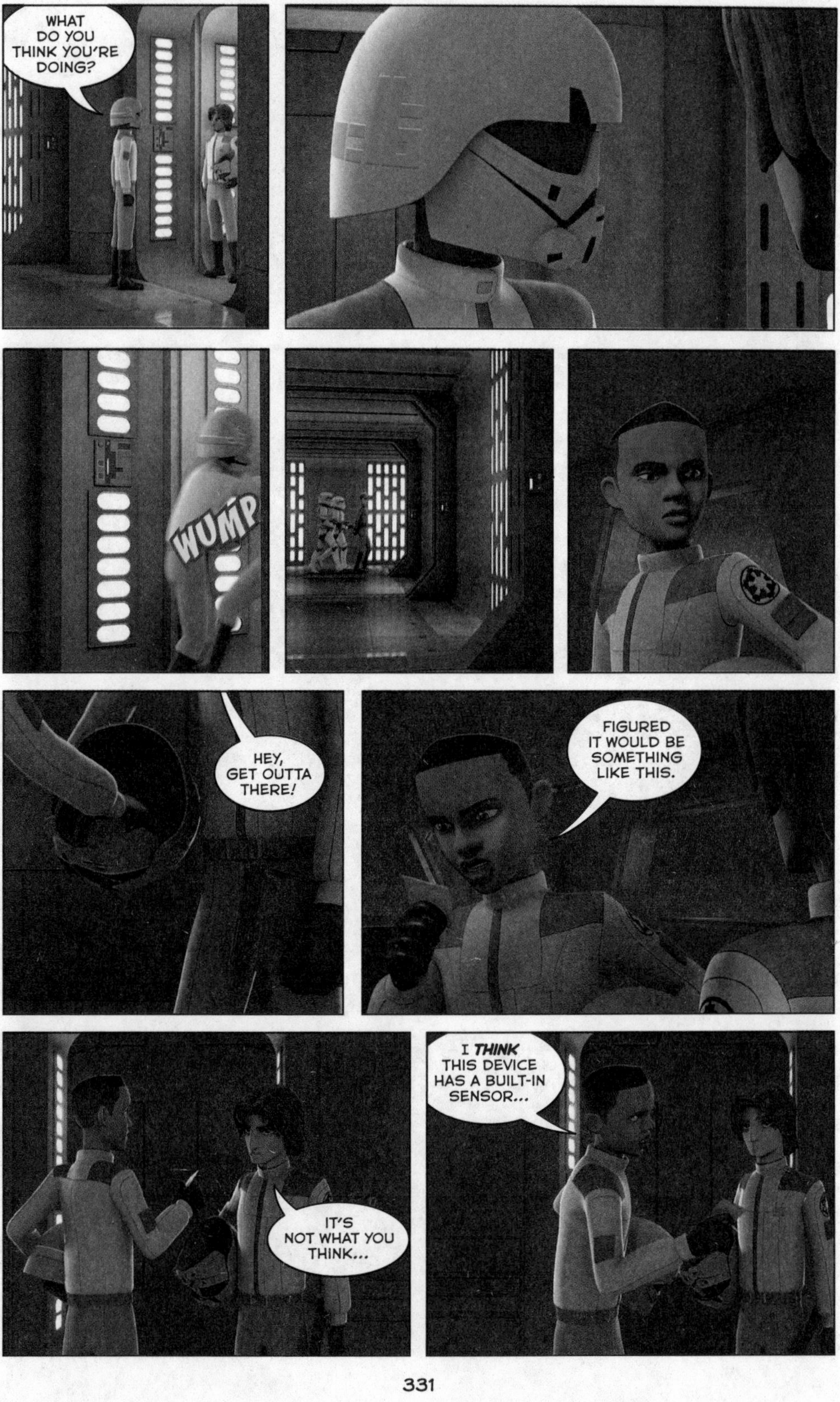
WHAT DO YOU THINK YOU'RE DOING?
WUMP
HEY, GET OUTTA THERE!
FIGURED IT WOULD BE SOMETHING LIKE THIS.
IT'S NOT WHAT YOU THINK...
I *THINK* THIS DEVICE HAS A BUILT-IN SENSOR...

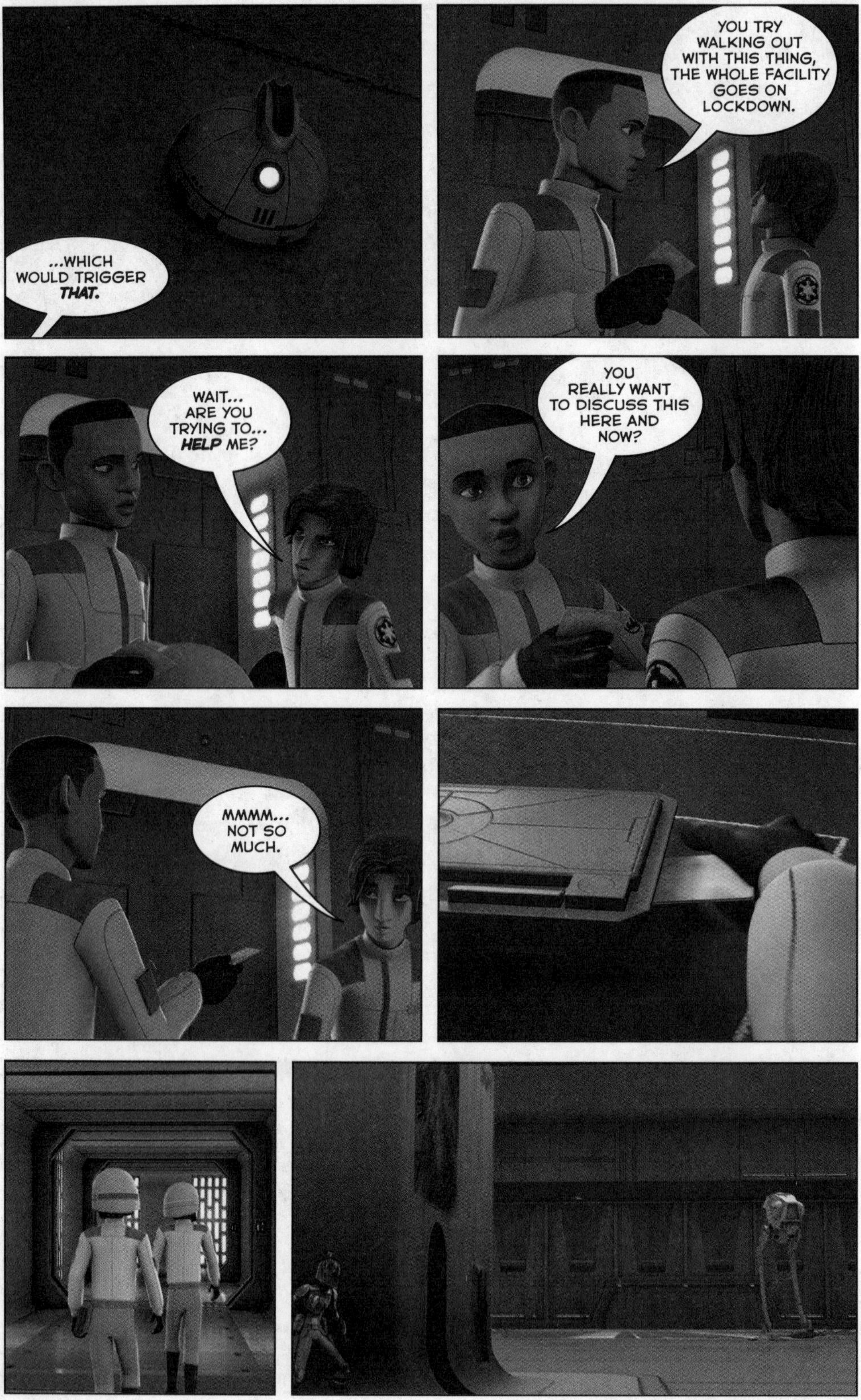
...WHICH WOULD TRIGGER THAT.
YOU TRY WALKING OUT WITH THIS THING, THE WHOLE FACILITY GOES ON LOCKDOWN.
WAIT... ARE YOU TRYING TO... HELP ME?
YOU REALLY WANT TO DISCUSS THIS HERE AND NOW?
MMMM... NOT SO MUCH.

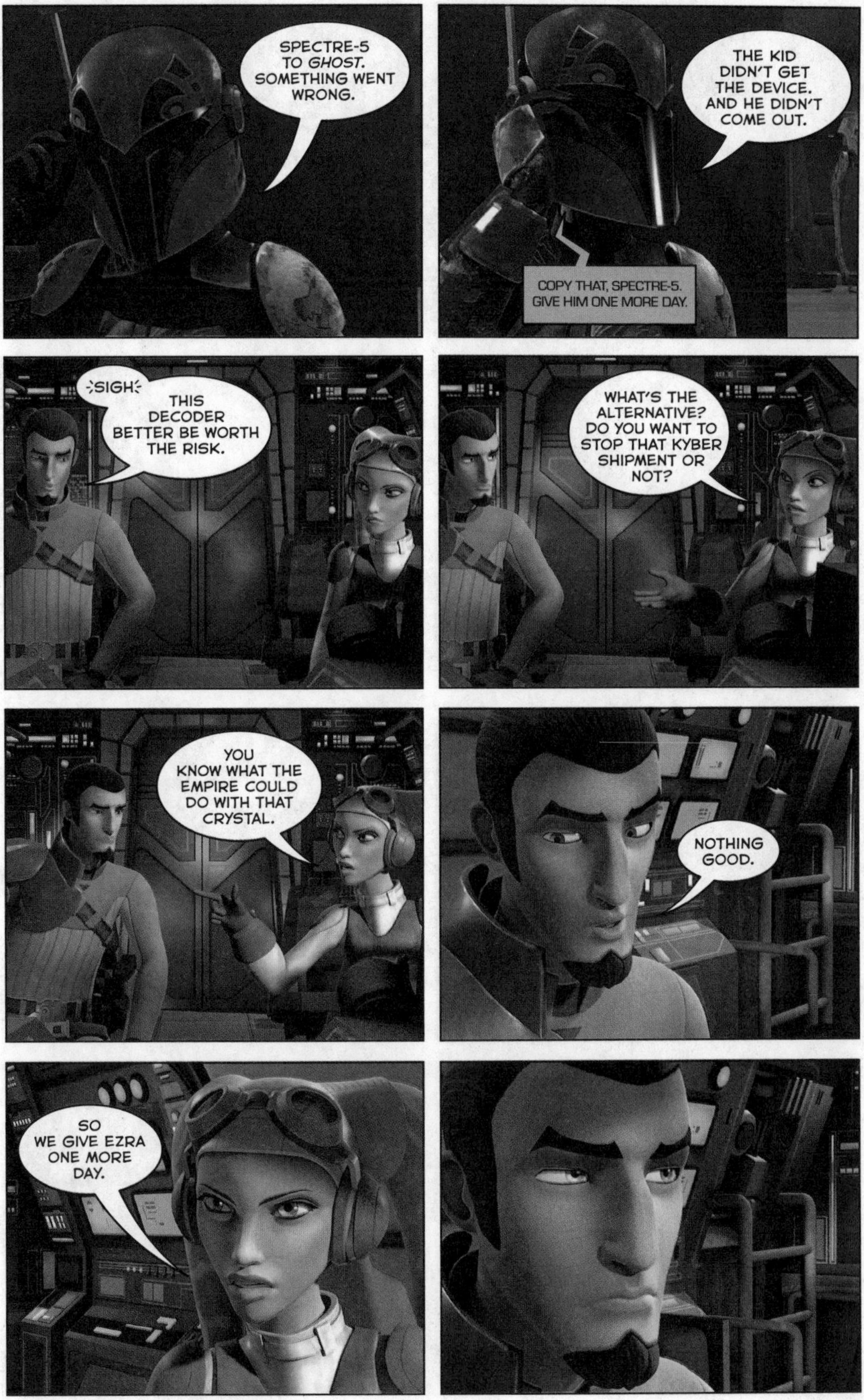
SPECTRE-5 TO *GHOST*. SOMETHING WENT WRONG.
THE KID DIDN'T GET THE DEVICE. AND HE DIDN'T COME OUT.
COPY THAT, SPECTRE-5. GIVE HIM ONE MORE DAY.
SIGH
THIS DECODER BETTER BE WORTH THE RISK.
WHAT'S THE ALTERNATIVE? DO YOU WANT TO STOP THAT KYBER SHIPMENT OR NOT?
YOU KNOW WHAT THE EMPIRE COULD DO WITH THAT CRYSTAL.
NOTHING GOOD.
SO WE GIVE EZRA ONE MORE DAY.

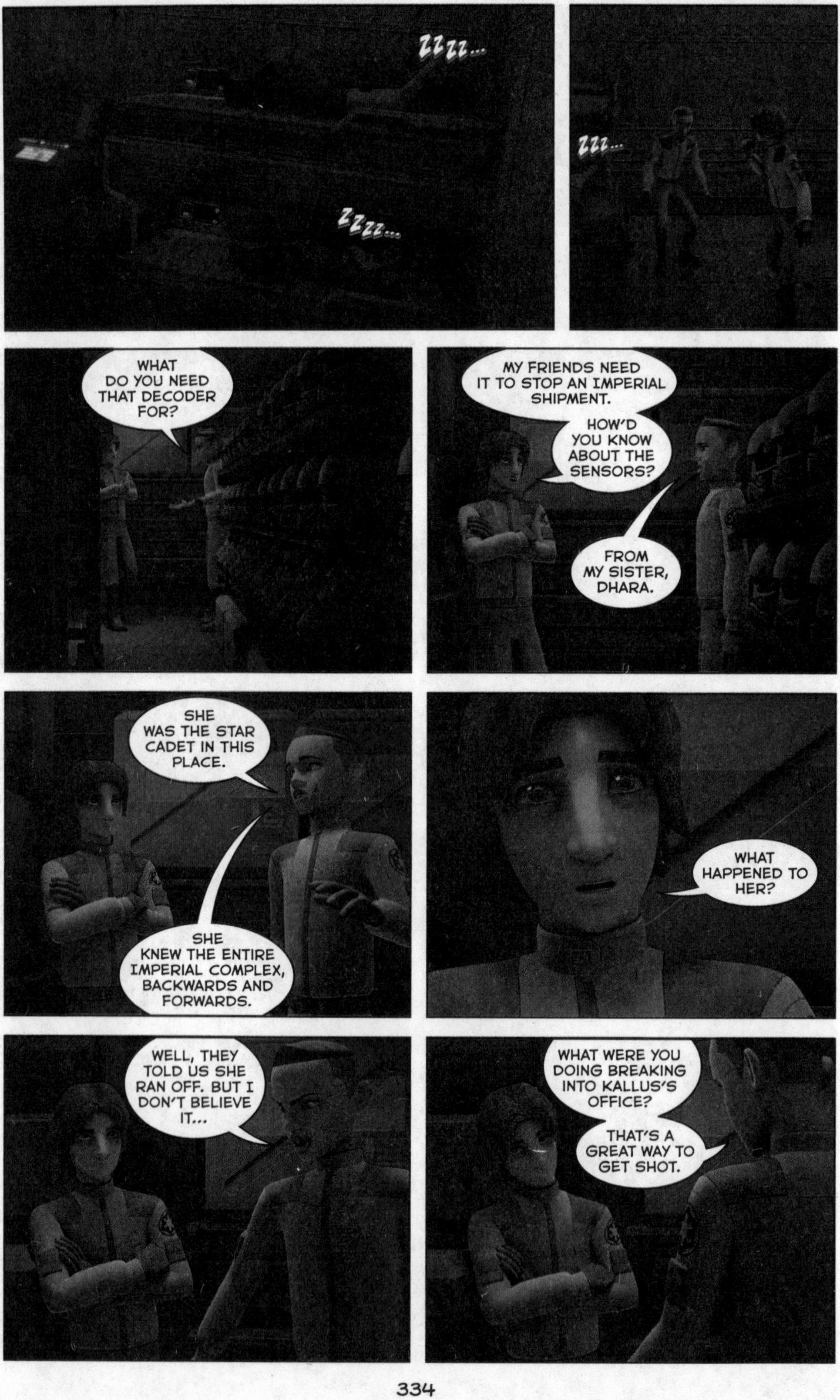
ZZZZ...
ZZZZ...
ZZZ...
WHAT DO YOU NEED THAT DECODER FOR?
MY FRIENDS NEED IT TO STOP AN IMPERIAL SHIPMENT.
HOW'D YOU KNOW ABOUT THE SENSORS?
FROM MY SISTER, DHARA.
SHE WAS THE STAR CADET IN THIS PLACE.
SHE KNEW THE ENTIRE IMPERIAL COMPLEX, BACKWARDS AND FORWARDS.
WHAT HAPPENED TO HER?
WELL, THEY TOLD US SHE RAN OFF. BUT I DON'T BELIEVE IT...
WHAT WERE YOU DOING BREAKING INTO KALLUS'S OFFICE?
THAT'S A GREAT WAY TO GET SHOT.

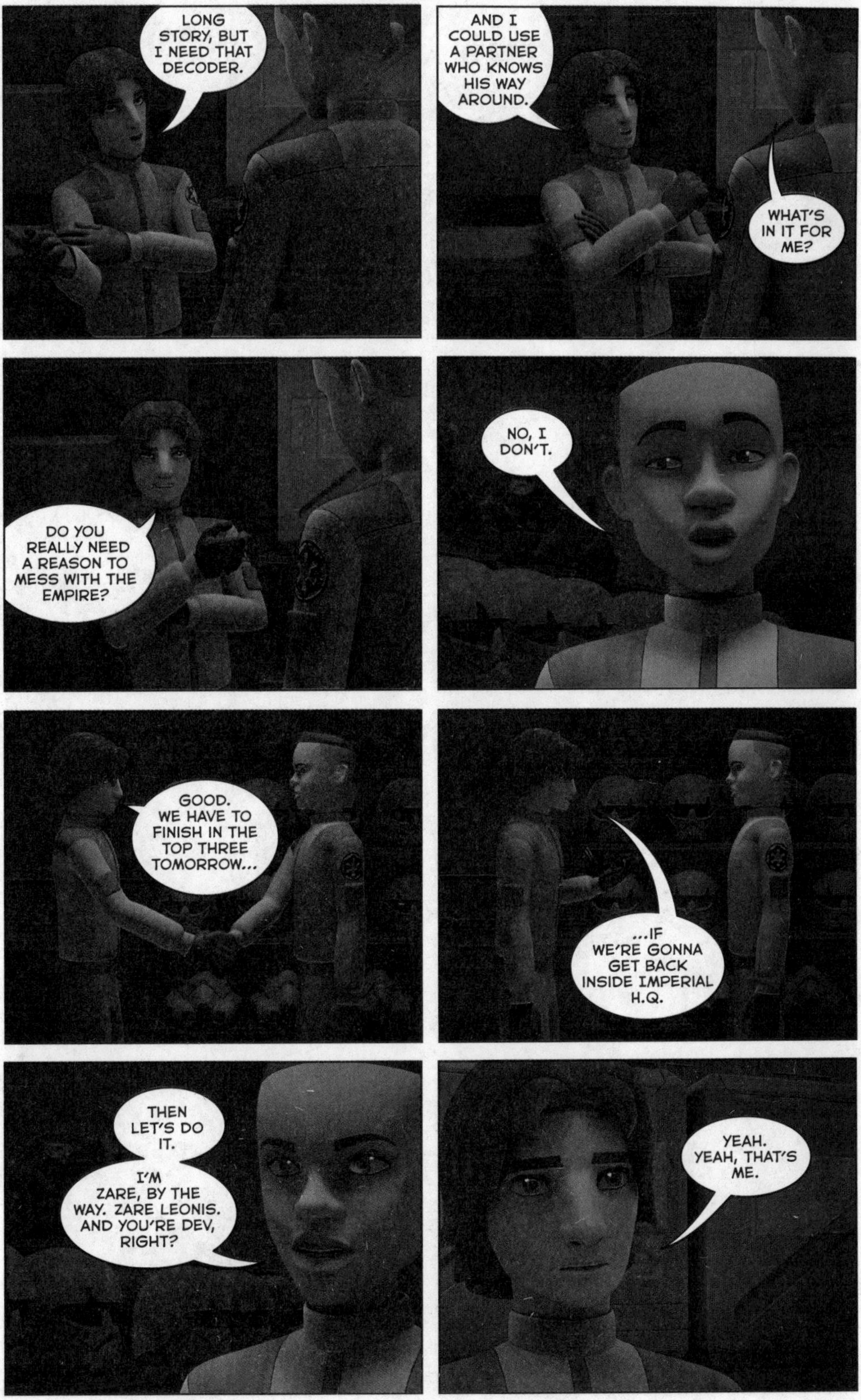
LONG STORY, BUT I NEED THAT DECODER.
AND I COULD USE A PARTNER WHO KNOWS HIS WAY AROUND.
WHAT'S IN IT FOR ME?
DO YOU REALLY NEED A REASON TO MESS WITH THE EMPIRE?
NO, I DON'T.
GOOD. WE HAVE TO FINISH IN THE TOP THREE TOMORROW...
...IF WE'RE GONNA GET BACK INSIDE IMPERIAL H.Q.
THEN LET'S DO IT.
I'M ZARE, BY THE WAY. ZARE LEONIS. AND YOU'RE DEV, RIGHT?
YEAH. YEAH, THAT'S ME.

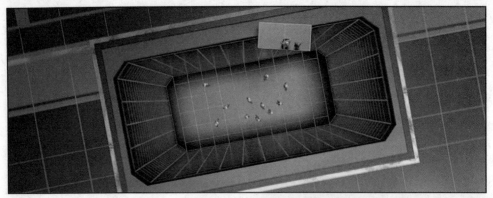

TODAY'S ASSESSMENT WILL BE A LITTLE MORE CHALLENGING...

YOU WILL NEED TO SHOOT THE TARGETS...

...TO ACTIVATE THE PANELS NECESSARY TO CLIMB OUT.

"THREE. TWO. ONE."

FSHEW

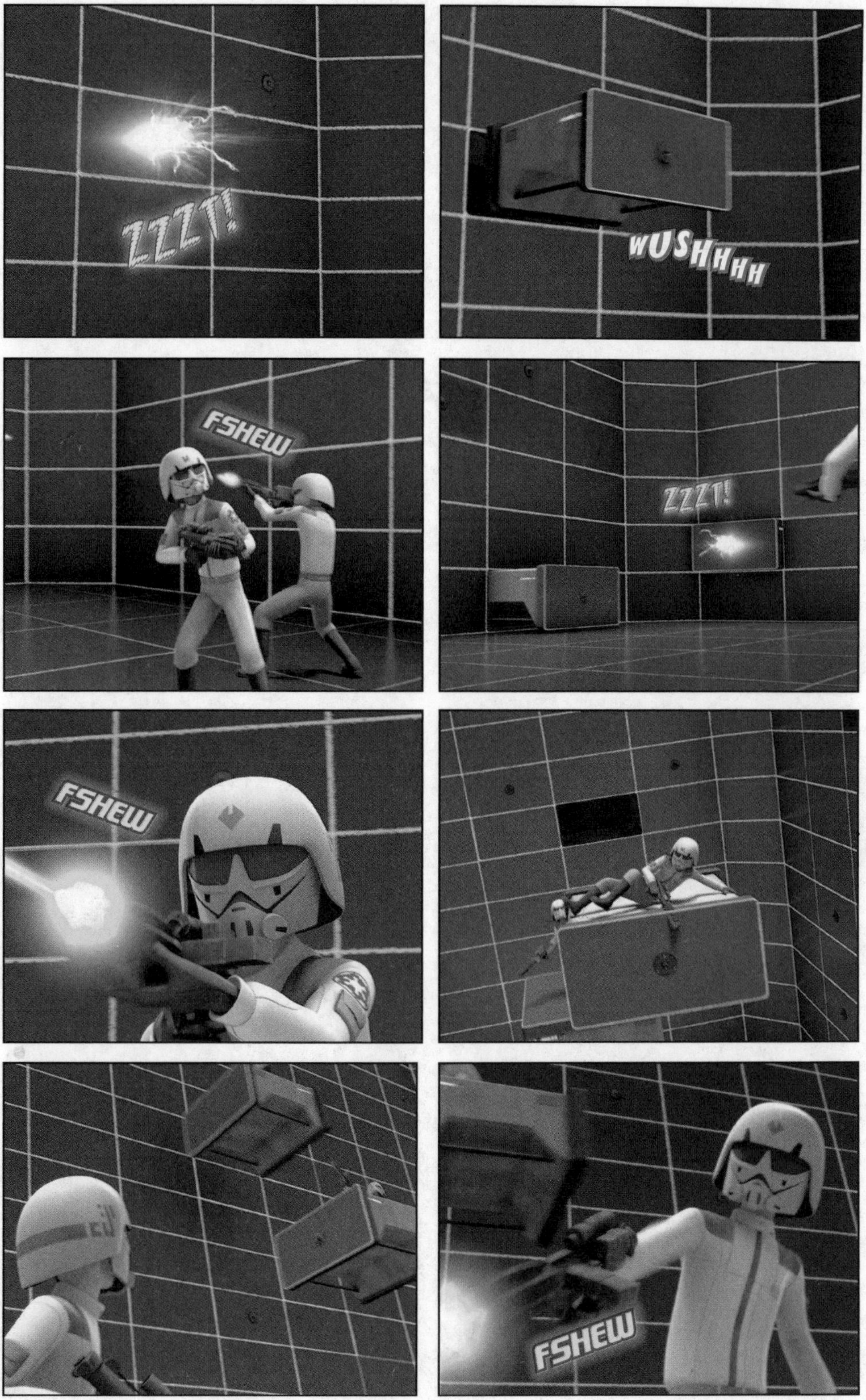
ZZZT!
WUSHHHH
FSHEW
ZZZT!
FSHEW
FSHEW

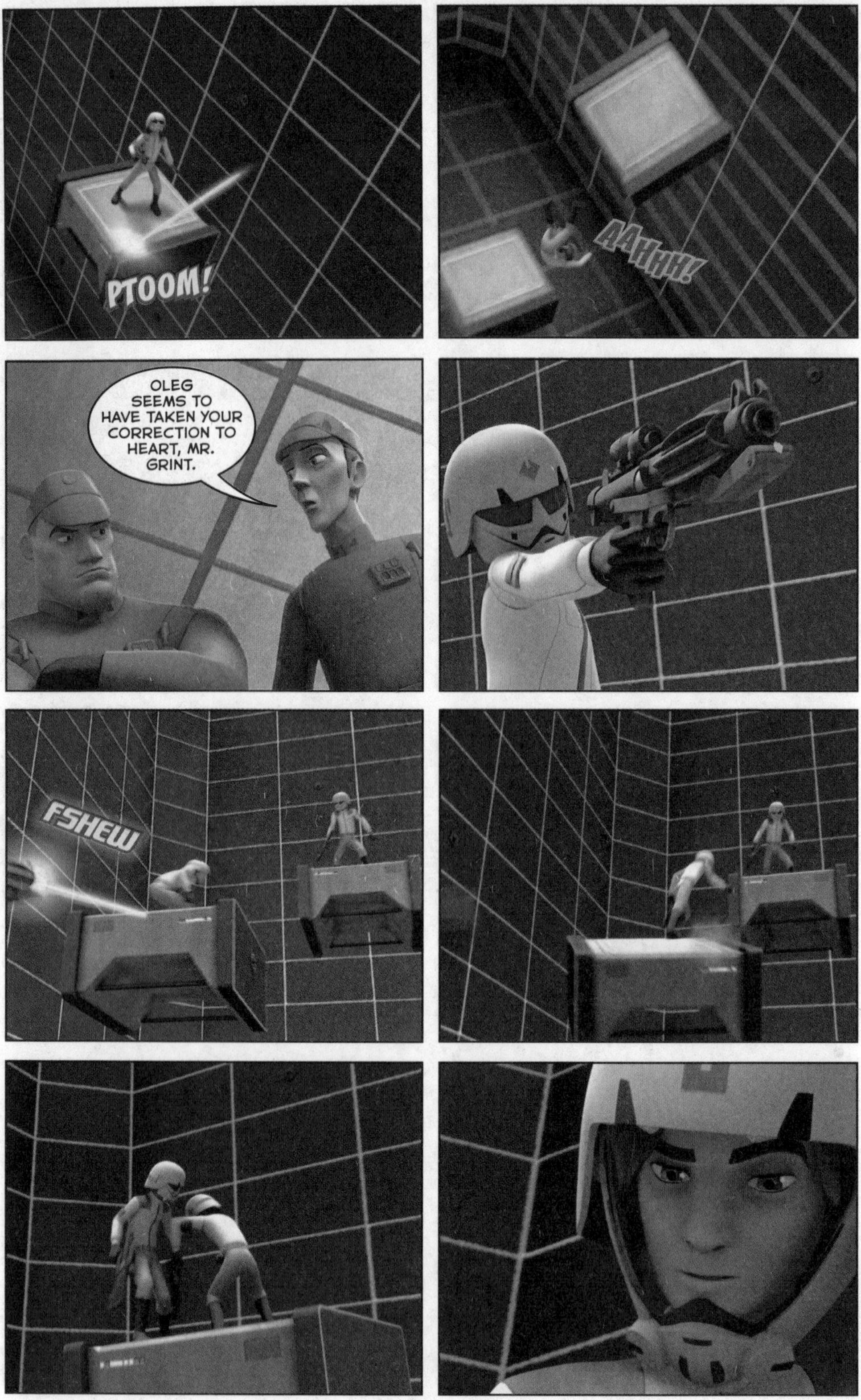
PTOOM!
AAHHH!
OLEG SEEMS TO HAVE TAKEN YOUR CORRECTION TO HEART, MR. GRINT.
FSHEW

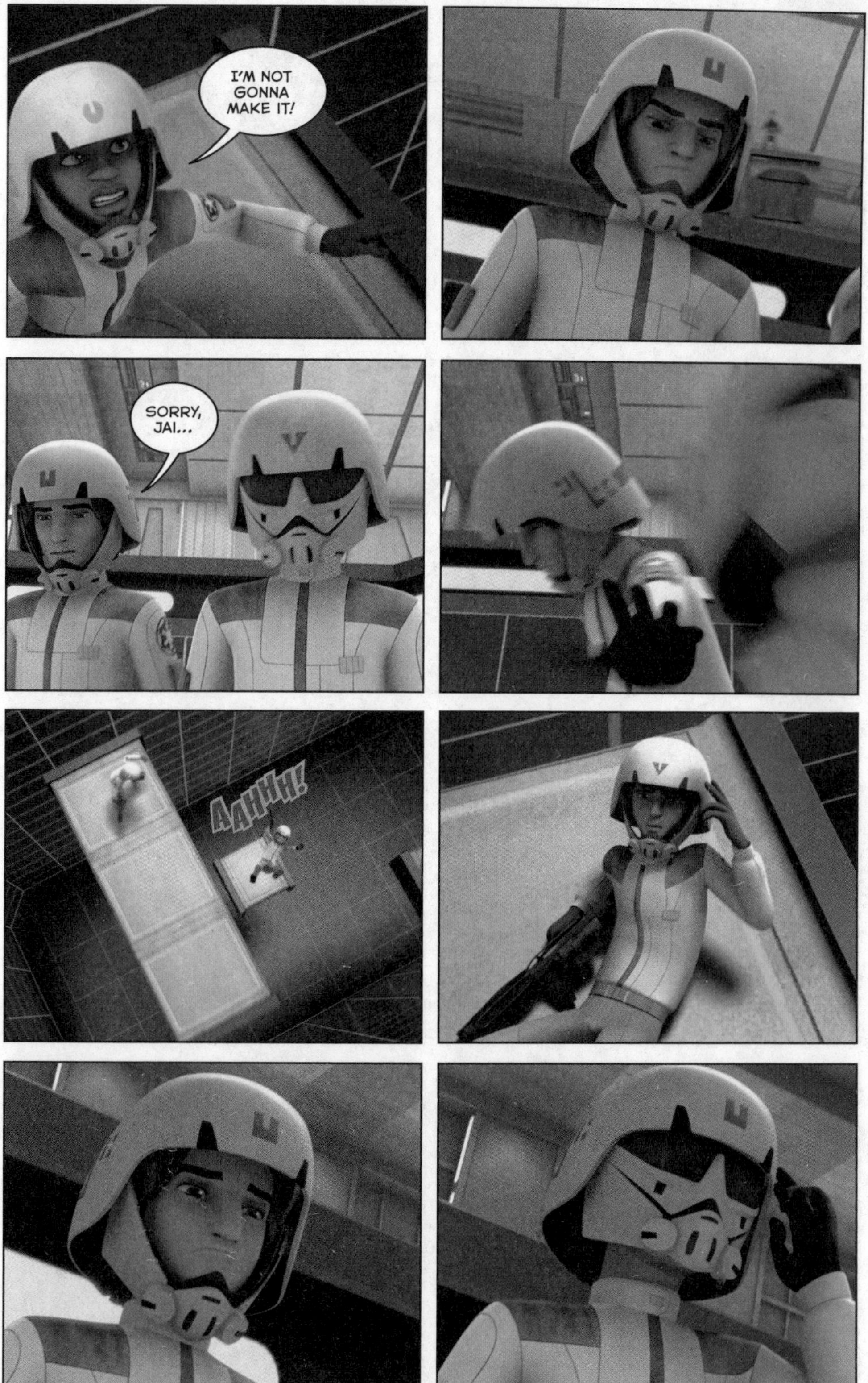

I'M NOT GONNA MAKE IT!
SORRY, JAI...
AAHHH!

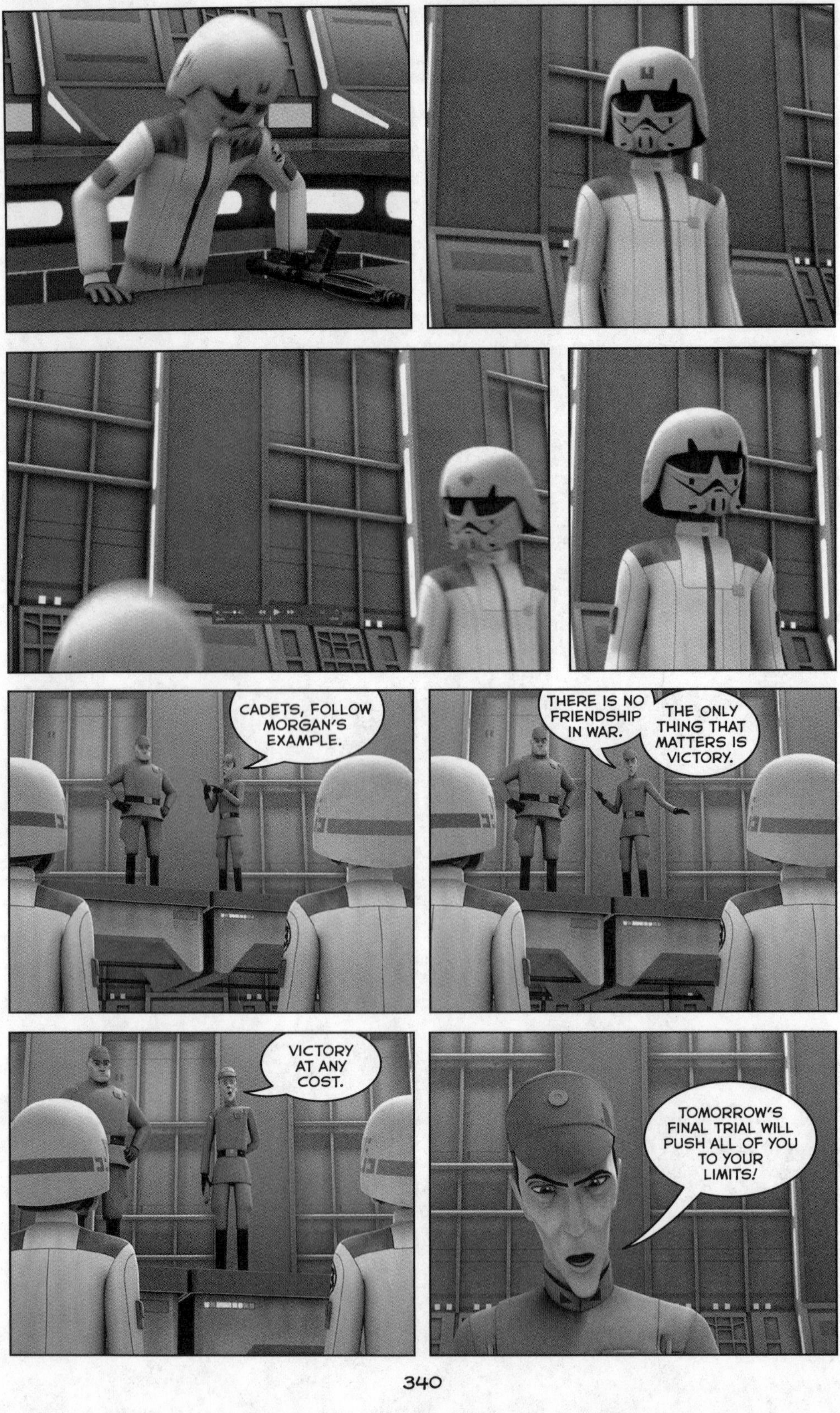
CADETS, FOLLOW MORGAN'S EXAMPLE.
THERE IS NO FRIENDSHIP IN WAR.
THE ONLY THING THAT MATTERS IS VICTORY.
VICTORY AT ANY COST.
TOMORROW'S FINAL TRIAL WILL PUSH ALL OF YOU TO YOUR LIMITS!

THE REWARD FOR SUCCESS WILL BE A TRAINING SESSION ABOARD AN IMPERIAL WALKER!

DEV, YOU SABOTAGED ME!

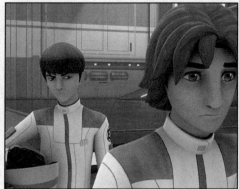

I DID WHAT I HAD TO DO.

GOOD TO KNOW.

HOW ARE YOU GONNA REACH ANYTHING FROM UP THERE?

DON'T WORRY, I'VE BEEN TRAINING TO BE A JEDI.

YEAH, RIGHT, WHO ISN'T?

YOU'LL SEE.

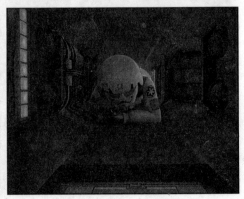

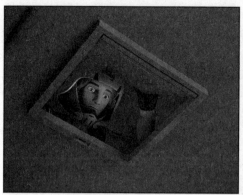

BEEP!

COME.

SIR, YOUR PODRACER PARTS HAVE BEEN DELIVERED.

IF YOU'LL JUST SIGN OFF HERE, I'LL BRING THEM UP...

OBVIOUSLY THERE'S BEEN A MISTAKE.

WHAT WOULD I WANT WITH PODRACER PARTS?

NO MISTAKE, SIR, IT SAYS RIGHT HERE...

343

...TWO CRATES OF SECOND-HAND PODRACER PARTS...

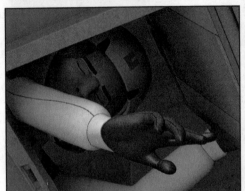

...FOR AGENT KALLUS AND...THAT'S YOU...

NOW, I ENJOY A GOOD PODRACE, MYSELF, SIR.

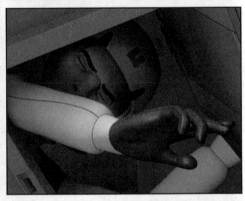

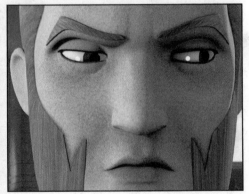

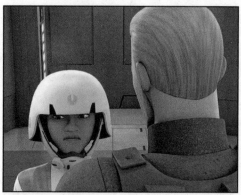

SO...
WERE YOU
GONNA SIGN
IT?

CADET,
ARE YOU
IGNORANT?
I SAID THIS IS A
MISTAKE!

SIR,
YES, SIR!
SORRY,
SIR!

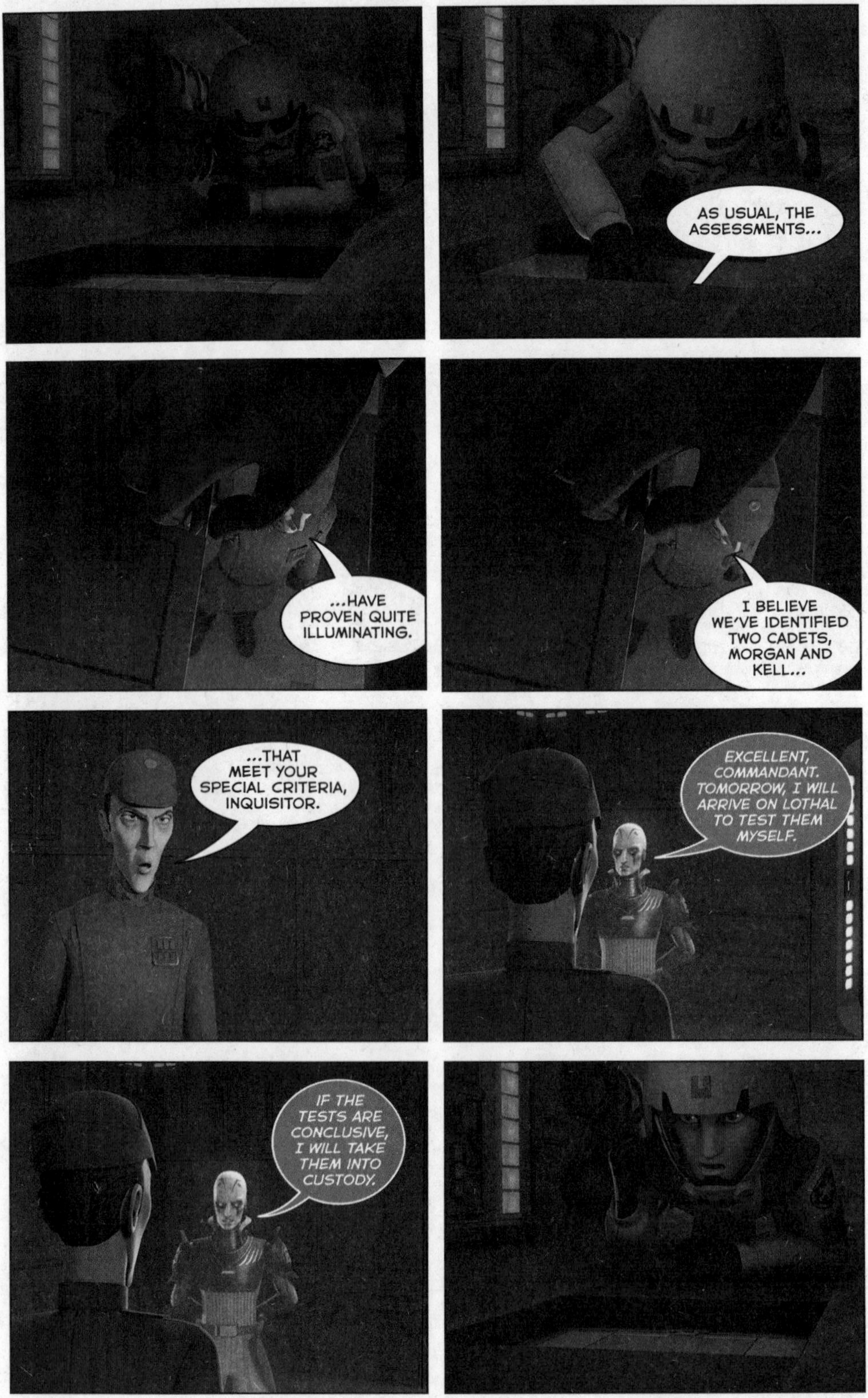
AS USUAL, THE ASSESSMENTS...
...HAVE PROVEN QUITE ILLUMINATING.
I BELIEVE WE'VE IDENTIFIED TWO CADETS, MORGAN AND KELL...
...THAT MEET YOUR SPECIAL CRITERIA, INQUISITOR.
EXCELLENT, COMMANDANT. TOMORROW, I WILL ARRIVE ON LOTHAL TO TEST THEM MYSELF.
IF THE TESTS ARE CONCLUSIVE, I WILL TAKE THEM INTO CUSTODY.

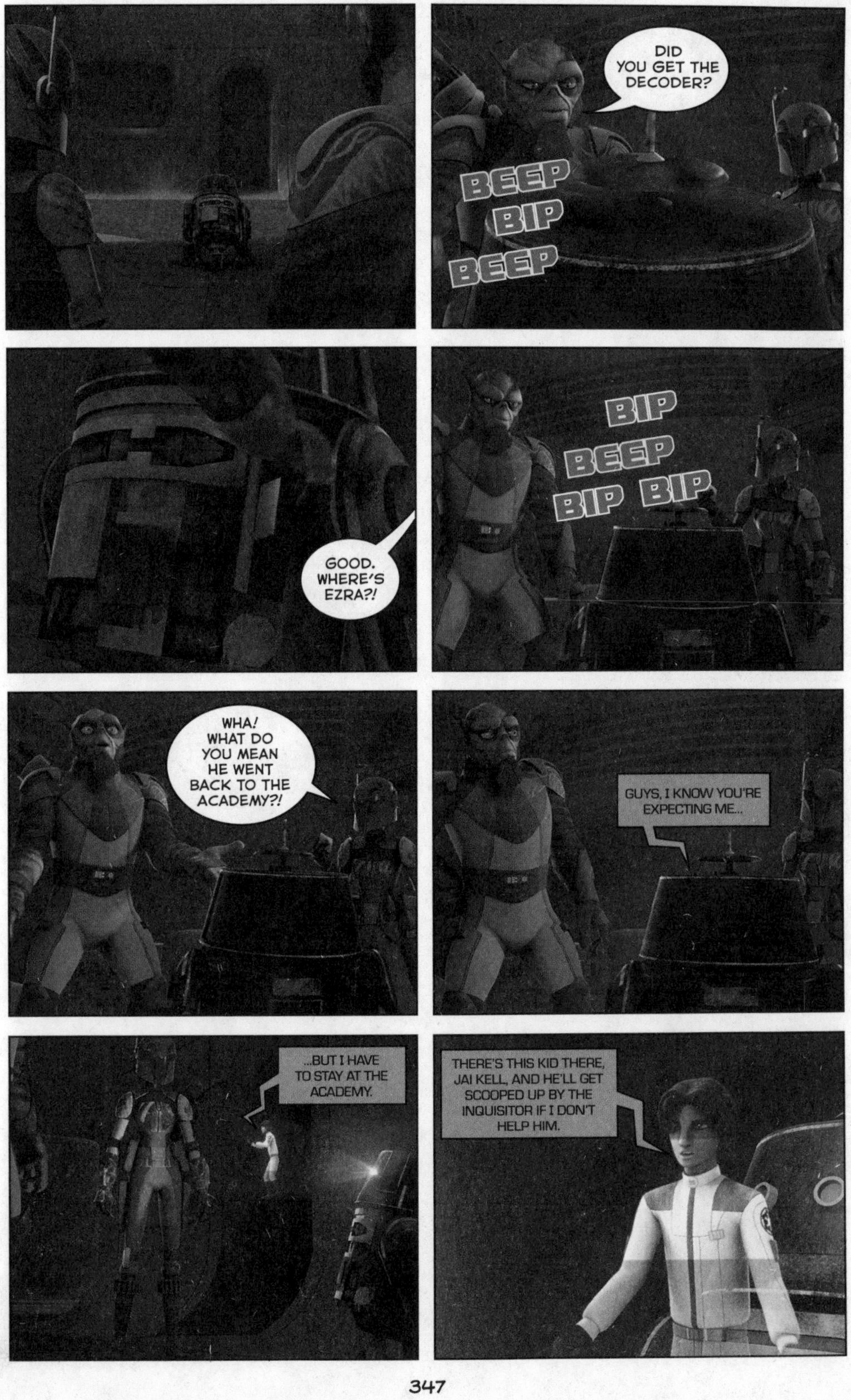
DID YOU GET THE DECODER?
BEEP BIP BEEP
GOOD. WHERE'S EZRA?!
BIP BEEP BIP BIP
WHA! WHAT DO YOU MEAN HE WENT BACK TO THE ACADEMY?!
GUYS, I KNOW YOU'RE EXPECTING ME...
...BUT I HAVE TO STAY AT THE ACADEMY.
THERE'S THIS KID THERE, JAI KELL, AND HE'LL GET SCOOPED UP BY THE INQUISITOR IF I DON'T HELP HIM.

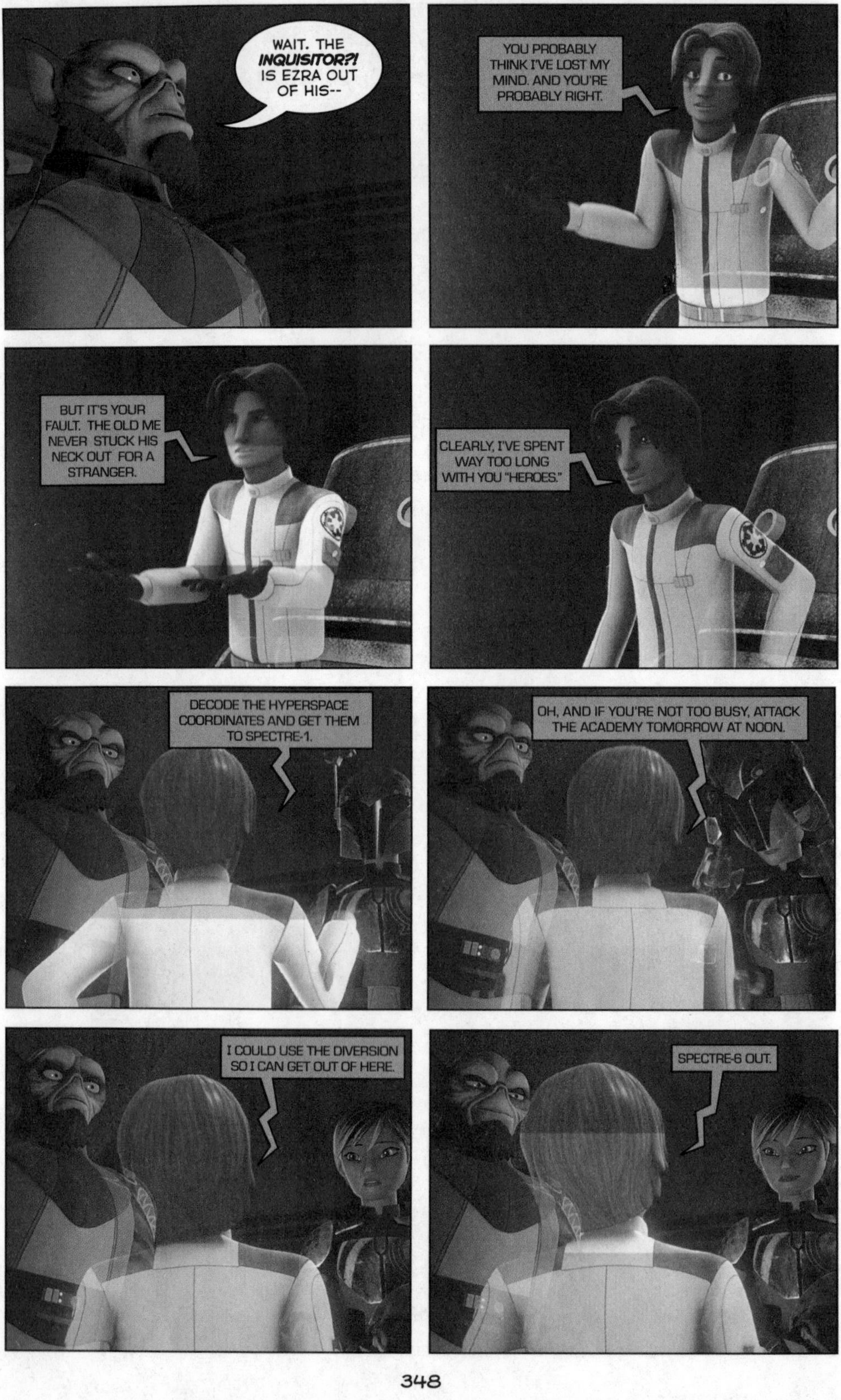
WAIT. THE *INQUISITOR?!* IS EZRA OUT OF HIS--
YOU PROBABLY THINK I'VE LOST MY MIND. AND YOU'RE PROBABLY RIGHT.
BUT IT'S YOUR FAULT. THE OLD ME NEVER STUCK HIS NECK OUT FOR A STRANGER.
CLEARLY, I'VE SPENT WAY TOO LONG WITH YOU "HEROES."
DECODE THE HYPERSPACE COORDINATES AND GET THEM TO SPECTRE-1.
OH, AND IF YOU'RE NOT TOO BUSY, ATTACK THE ACADEMY TOMORROW AT NOON.
I COULD USE THE DIVERSION SO I CAN GET OUT OF HERE.
SPECTRE-6 OUT.

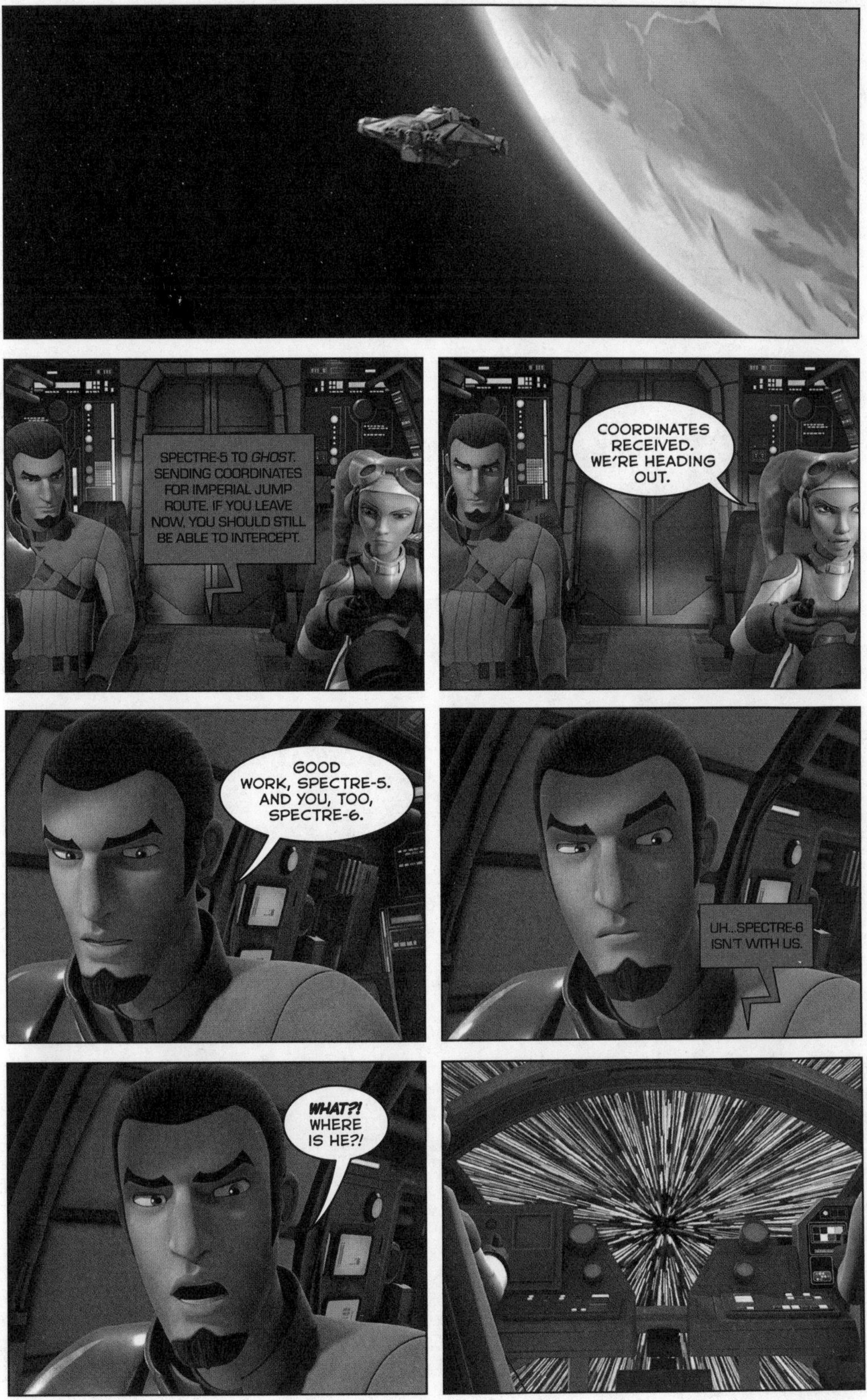
SPECTRE-5 TO *GHOST*. SENDING COORDINATES FOR IMPERIAL JUMP ROUTE. IF YOU LEAVE NOW, YOU SHOULD STILL BE ABLE TO INTERCEPT.
COORDINATES RECEIVED. WE'RE HEADING OUT.
GOOD WORK, SPECTRE-5. AND YOU, TOO, SPECTRE-6.
UH...SPECTRE-6 ISN'T WITH US.
WHAT?! WHERE IS HE?!

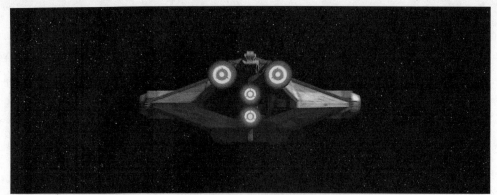

SPECTRE-5, REPEAT! WHERE'S SPECTRE-6?

KANAN, WE'RE OUT OF RANGE.

ALL WE CAN DO NOW IS COMPLETE THE MISSION...

...AND GET BACK AS SOON AS POSSIBLE.

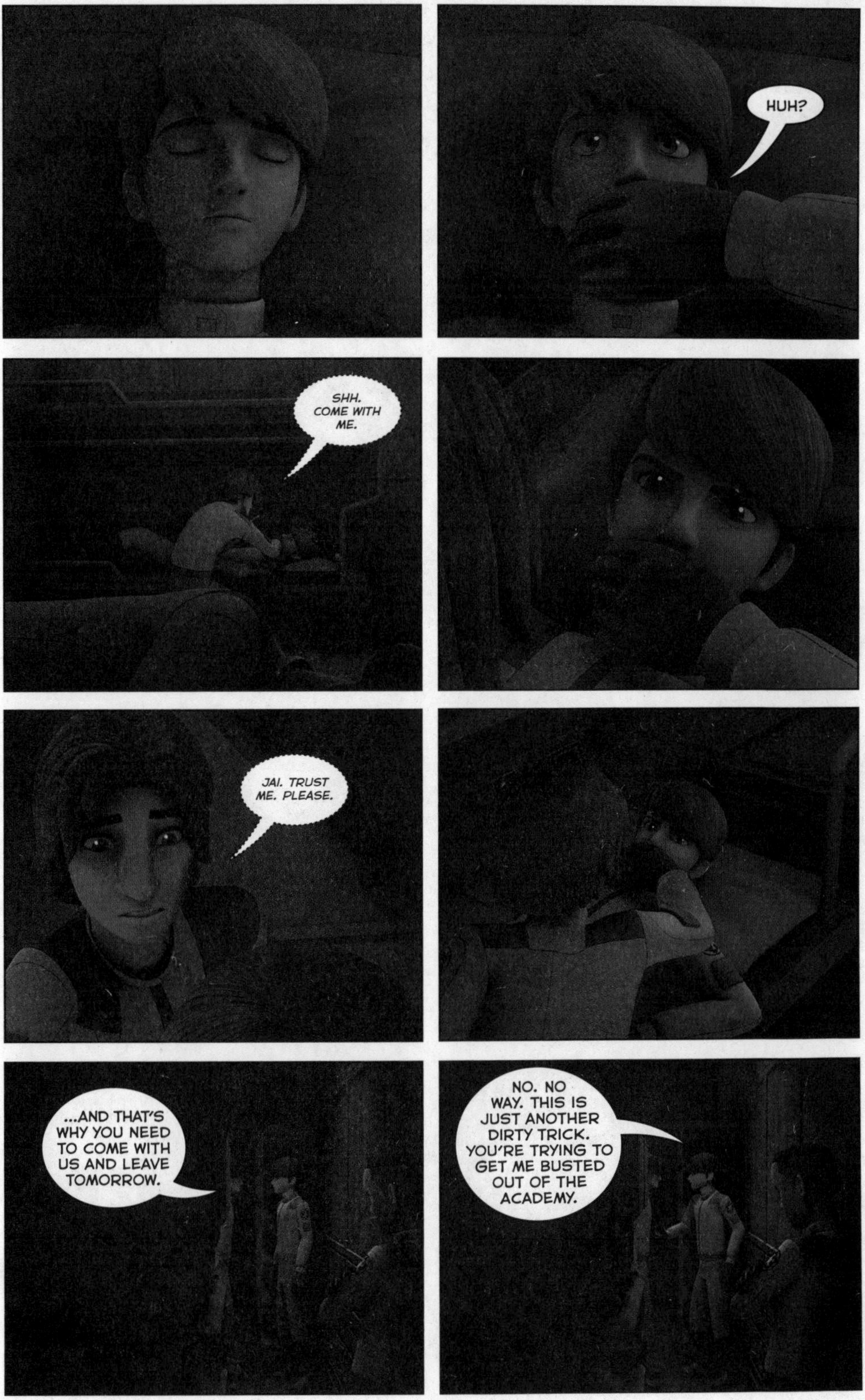
HUH?
SHH. COME WITH ME.
JAI. TRUST ME. PLEASE.
...AND THAT'S WHY YOU NEED TO COME WITH US AND LEAVE TOMORROW.
NO. NO WAY. THIS IS JUST ANOTHER DIRTY TRICK. YOU'RE TRYING TO GET ME BUSTED OUT OF THE ACADEMY.

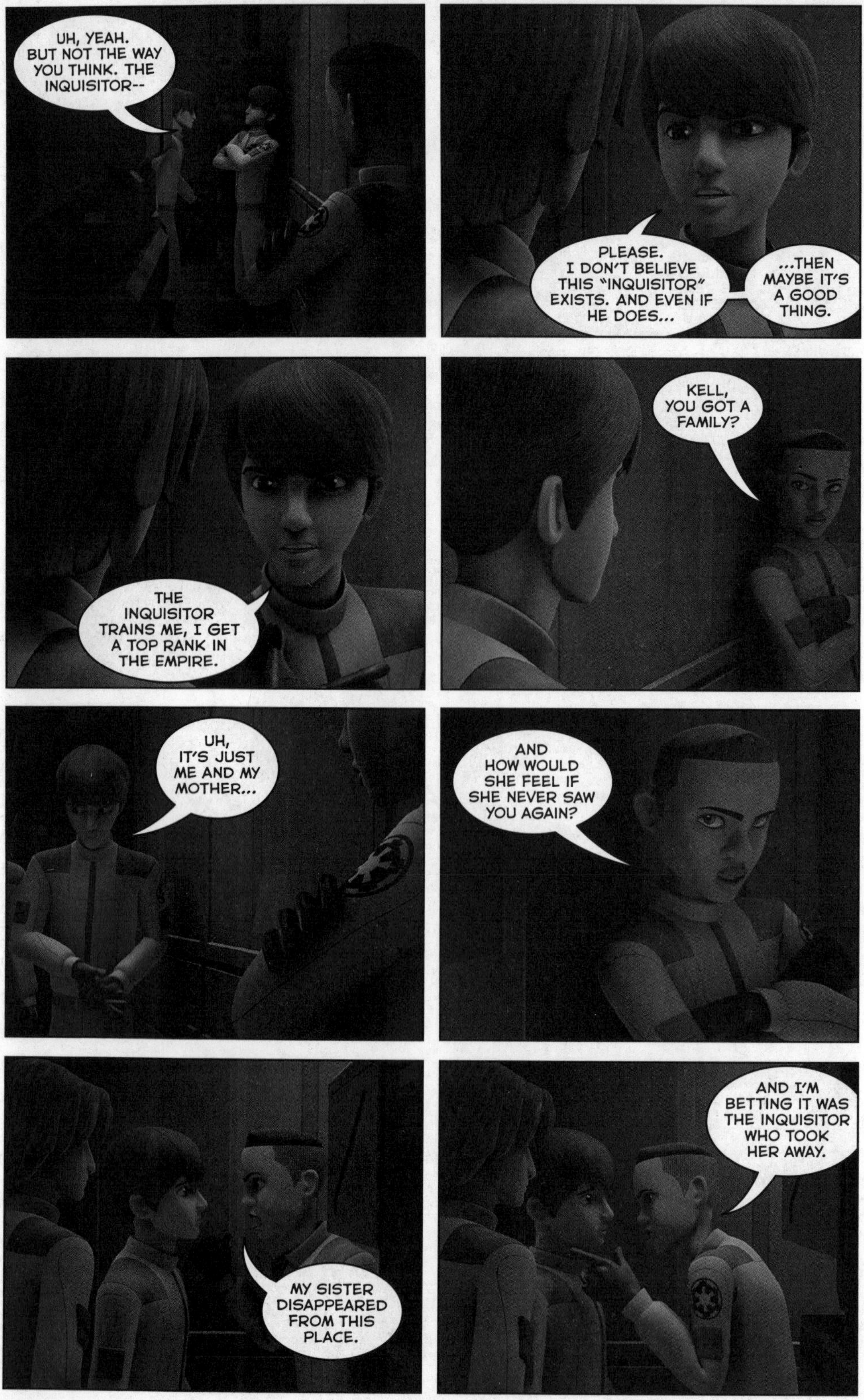
UH, YEAH. BUT NOT THE WAY YOU THINK. THE INQUISITOR--
PLEASE. I DON'T BELIEVE THIS "INQUISITOR" EXISTS. AND EVEN IF HE DOES...
...THEN MAYBE IT'S A GOOD THING.
THE INQUISITOR TRAINS ME, I GET A TOP RANK IN THE EMPIRE.
KELL, YOU GOT A FAMILY?
UH, IT'S JUST ME AND MY MOTHER...
AND HOW WOULD SHE FEEL IF SHE NEVER SAW YOU AGAIN?
MY SISTER DISAPPEARED FROM THIS PLACE.
AND I'M BETTING IT WAS THE INQUISITOR WHO TOOK HER AWAY.

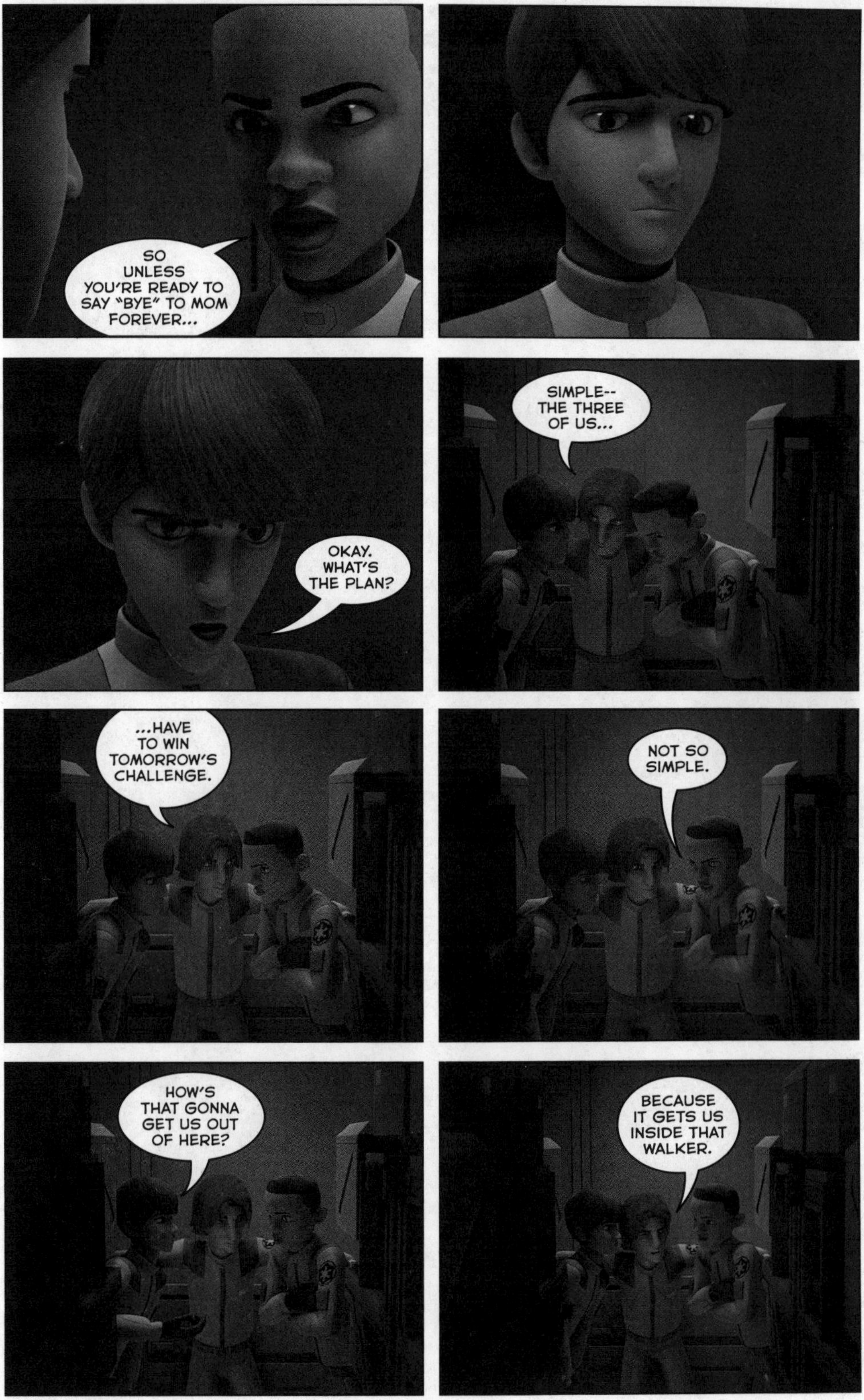
SO UNLESS YOU'RE READY TO SAY "BYE" TO MOM FOREVER...
OKAY. WHAT'S THE PLAN?
SIMPLE-- THE THREE OF US...
...HAVE TO WIN TOMORROW'S CHALLENGE.
NOT SO SIMPLE.
HOW'S THAT GONNA GET US OUT OF HERE?
BECAUSE IT GETS US INSIDE THAT WALKER.

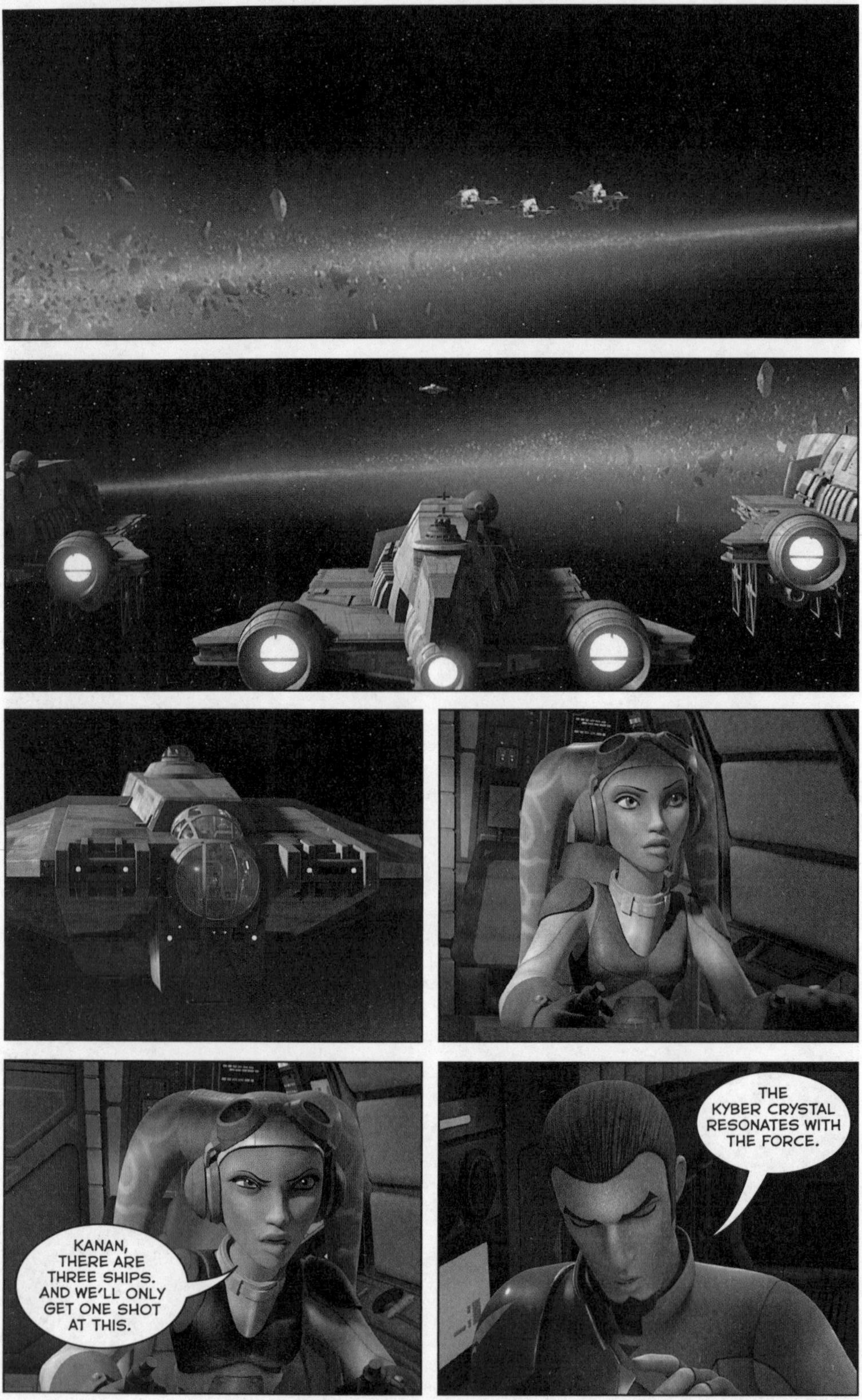
KANAN, THERE ARE THREE SHIPS. AND WE'LL ONLY GET ONE SHOT AT THIS.
THE KYBER CRYSTAL RESONATES WITH THE FORCE.

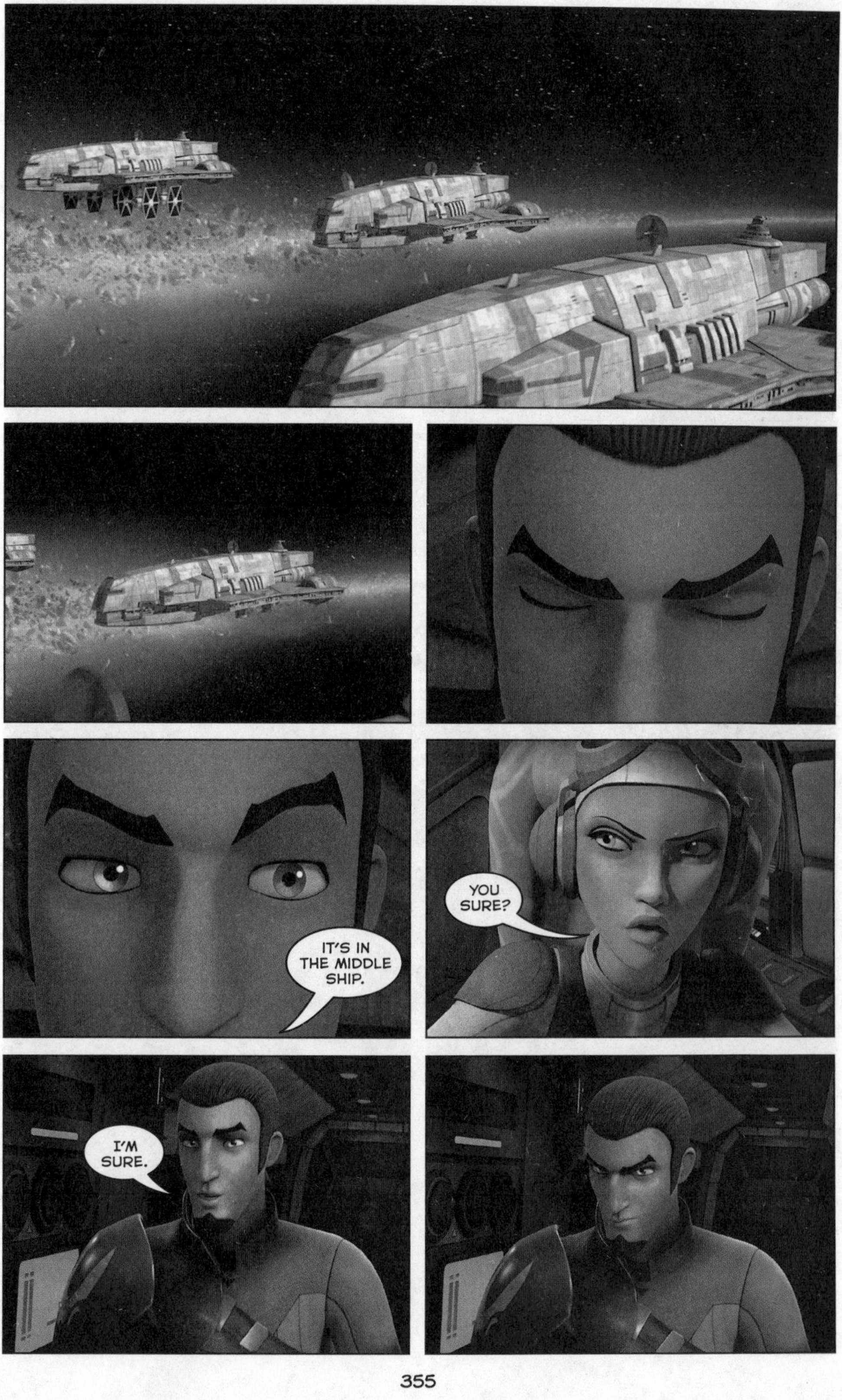
IT'S IN THE MIDDLE SHIP.
YOU SURE?
I'M SURE.

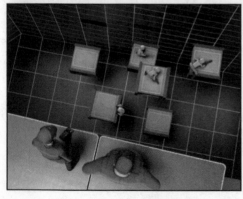

COME ON, KEEP UP!

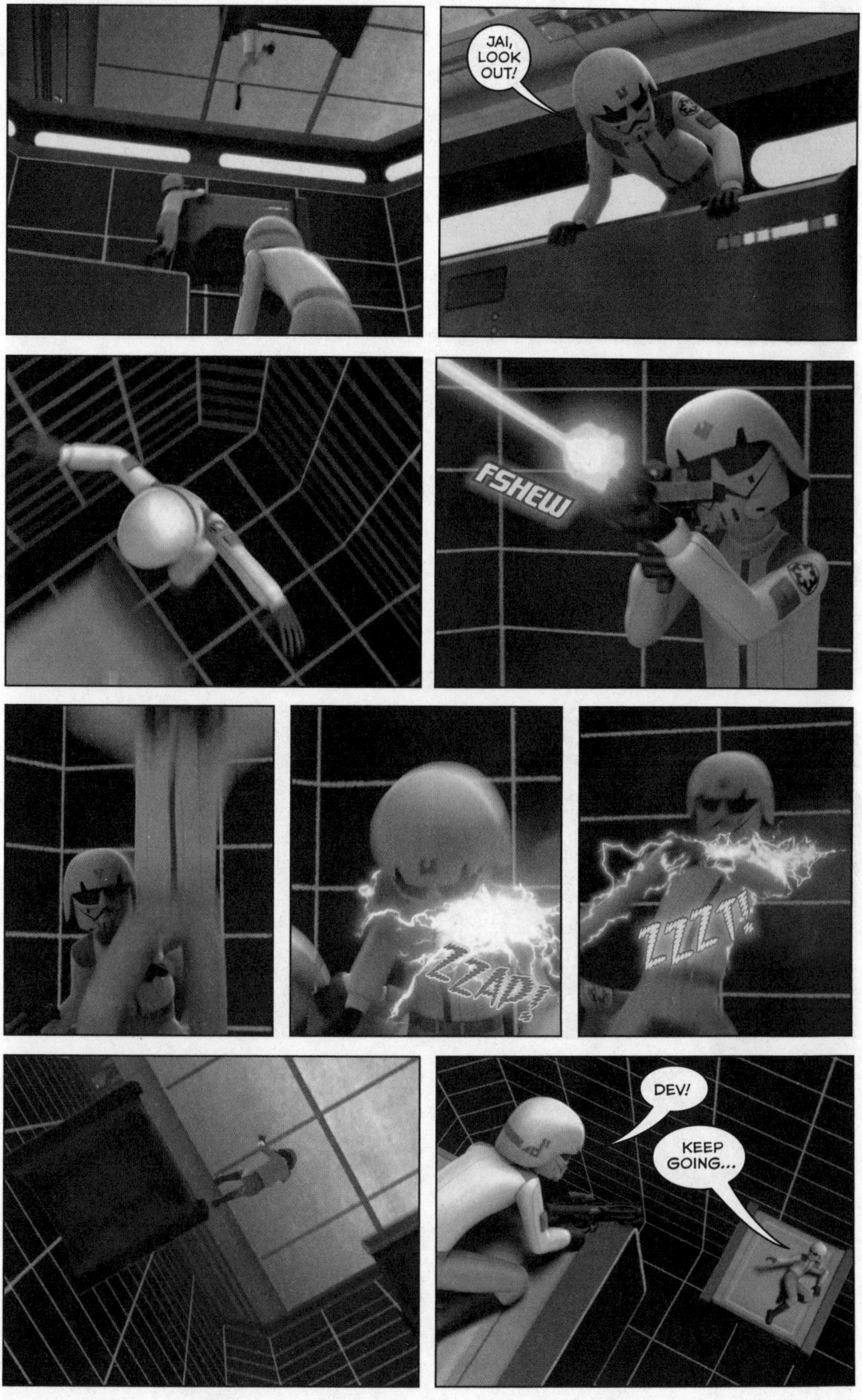

JAI, LOOK OUT!
FSHEW
ZZAP!
ZZZT!
DEV!
KEEP GOING...

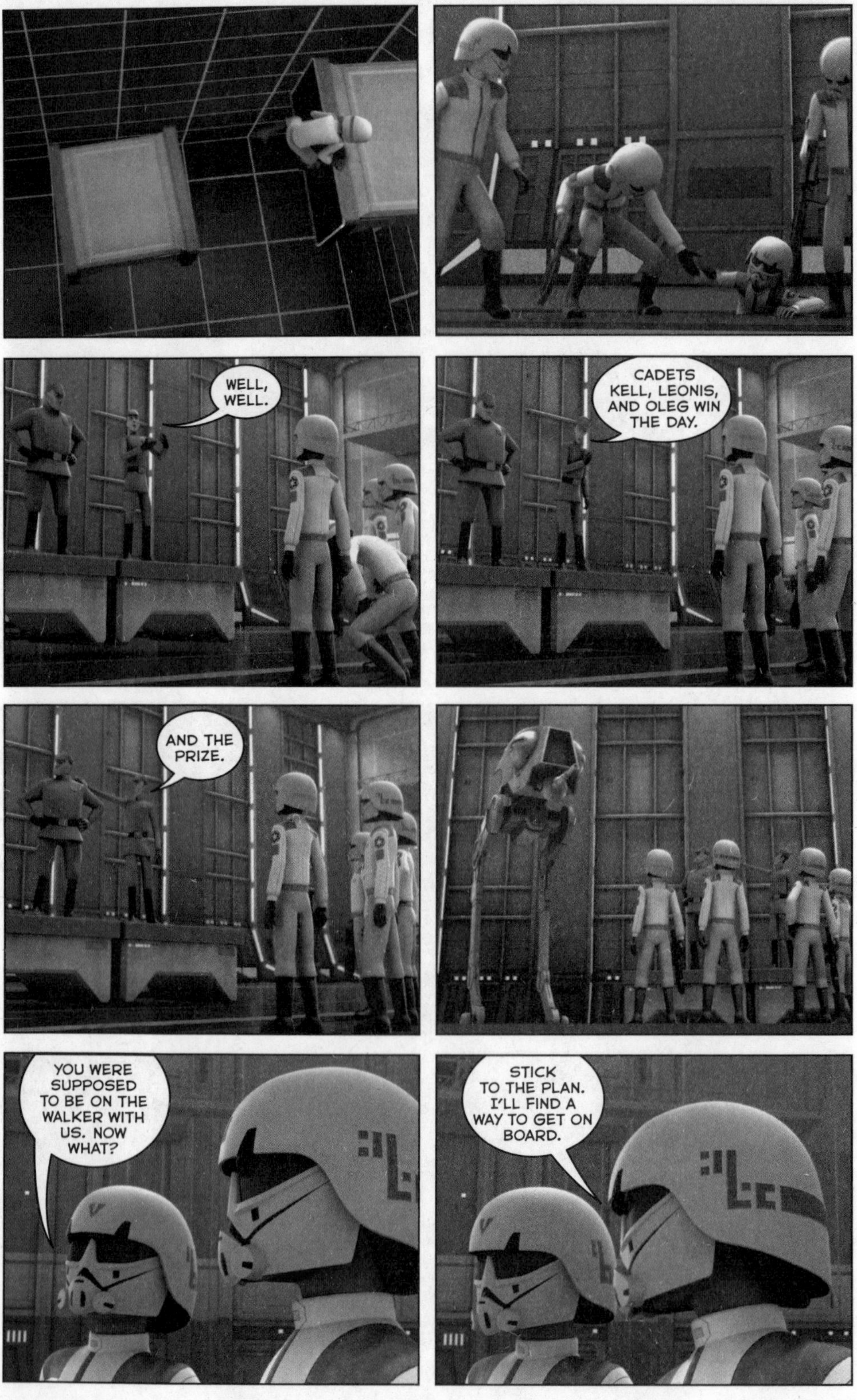
WELL, WELL.
CADETS KELL, LEONIS, AND OLEG WIN THE DAY.
AND THE PRIZE.
YOU WERE SUPPOSED TO BE ON THE WALKER WITH US. NOW WHAT?
STICK TO THE PLAN. I'LL FIND A WAY TO GET ON BOARD.

BOOM!

COME ON, BOYS, TAKE THE BAIT.

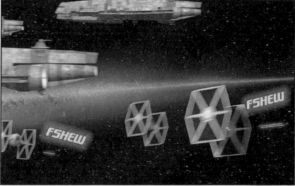
FSHEW

FSHEW

HERA, YOU'RE GOOD TO GO.

COPY THAT.

FSHEW

FSHEW

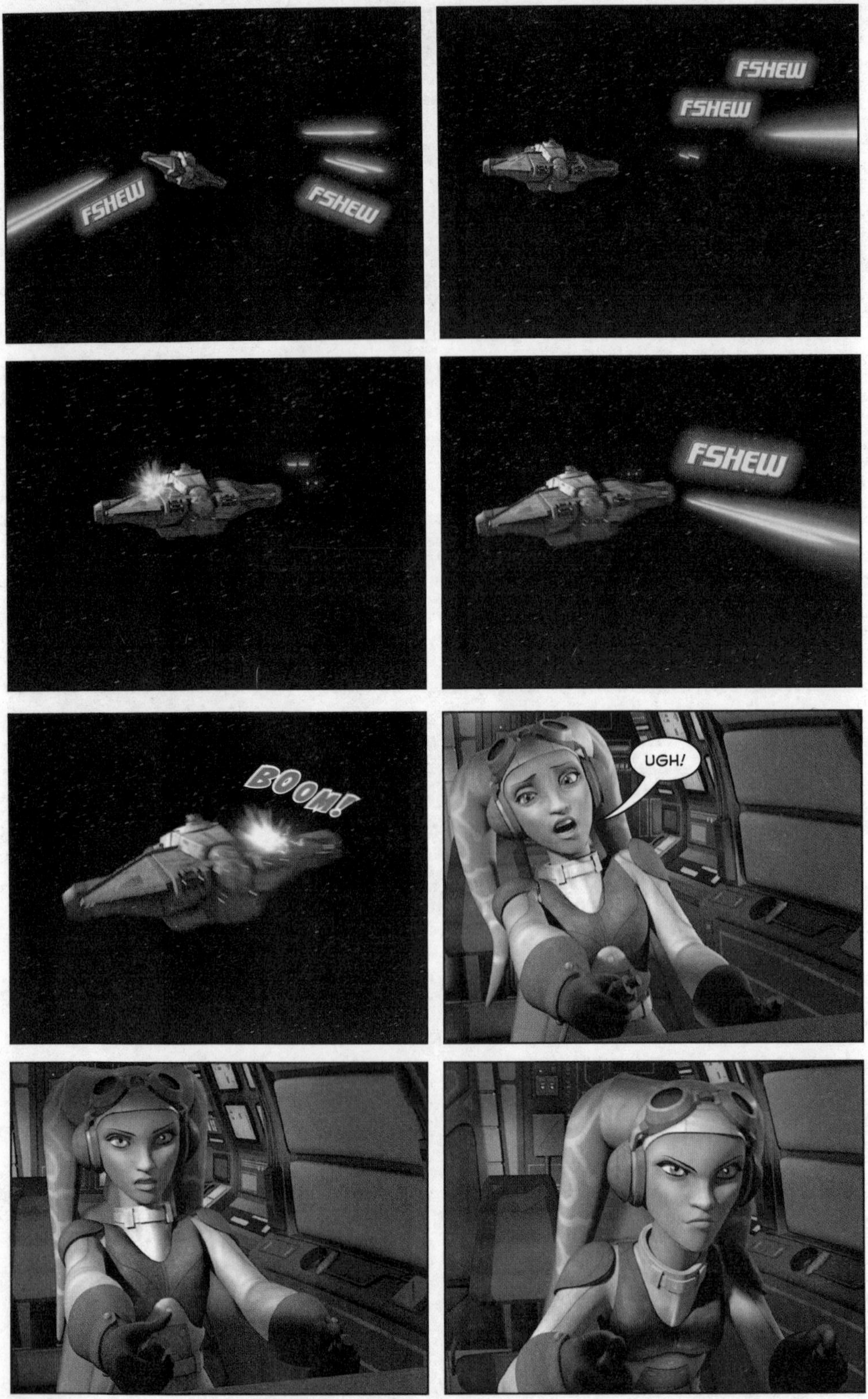
FSHEW
FSHEW
FSHEW
FSHEW
FSHEW
BOOM!
UGH!

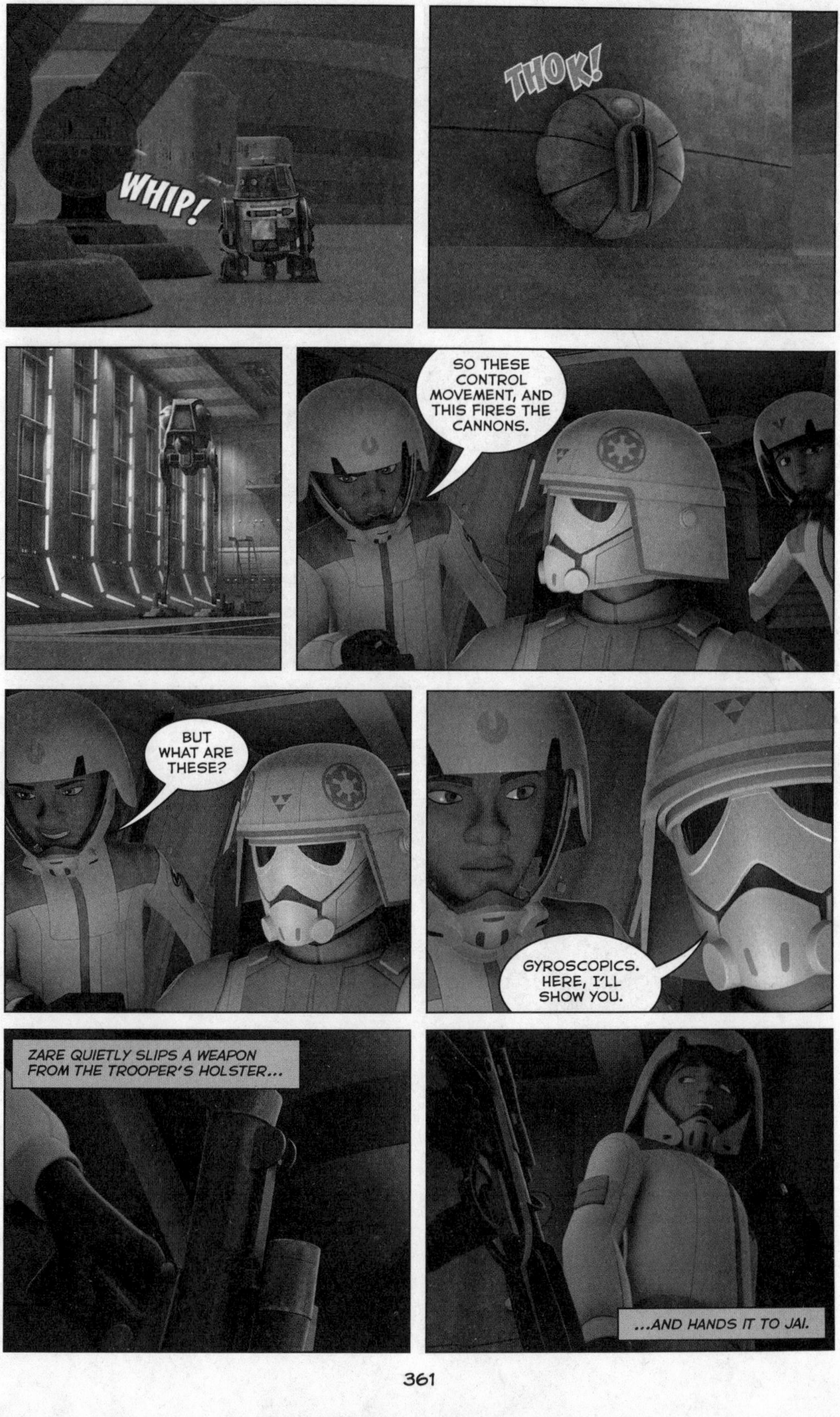

WHIP!
THOK!
SO THESE CONTROL MOVEMENT, AND THIS FIRES THE CANNONS.
BUT WHAT ARE THESE?
GYROSCOPICS. HERE, I'LL SHOW YOU.
ZARE QUIETLY SLIPS A WEAPON FROM THE TROOPER'S HOLSTER...
...AND HANDS IT TO JAI.

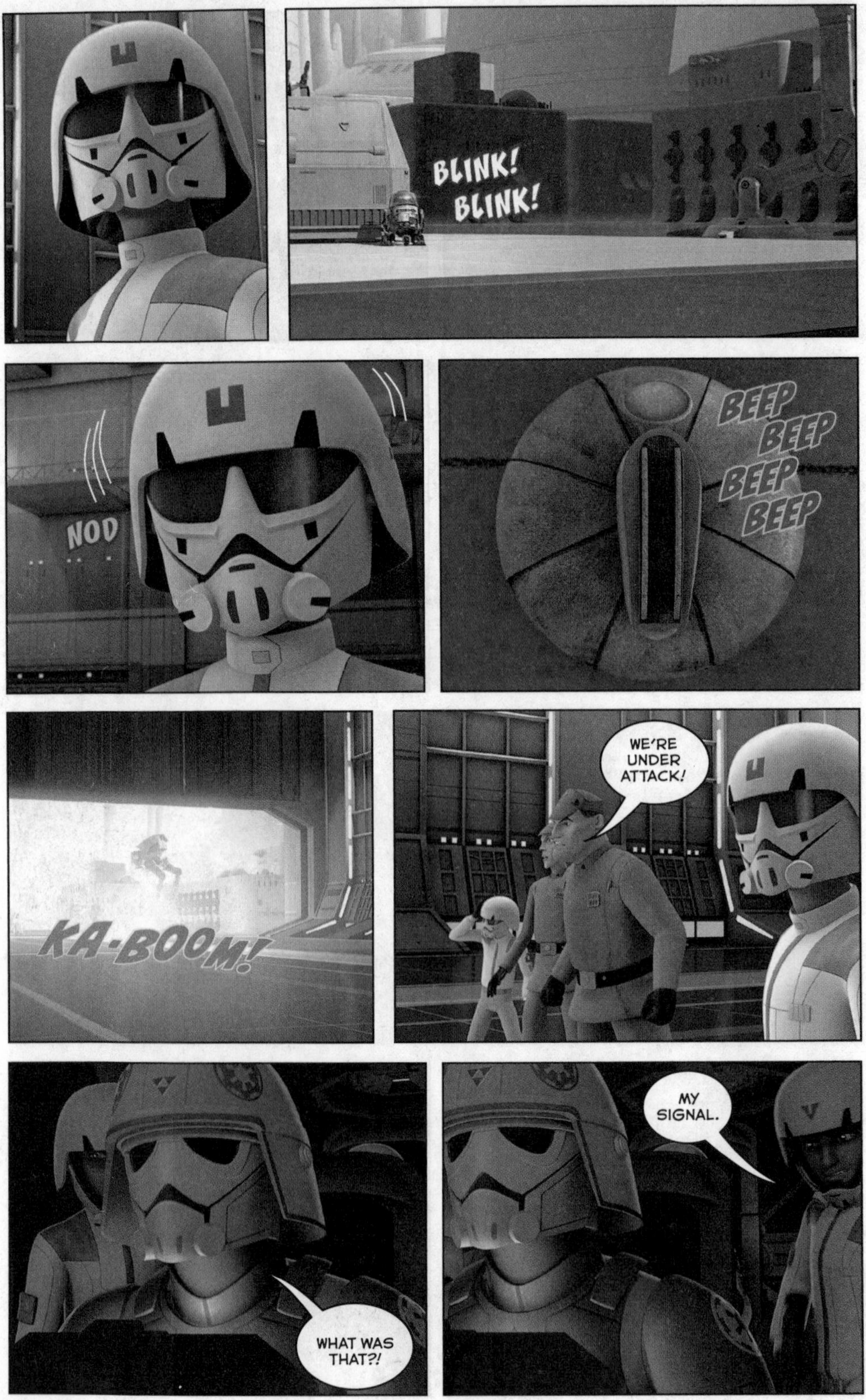
BLINK! BLINK!
NOD
BEEP BEEP BEEP BEEP
KA-BOOM!
WE'RE UNDER ATTACK!
WHAT WAS THAT?!
MY SIGNAL.

AAGH!

PZZAP!

THUD

WHAT ARE YOU DOING?!

PZZAP!

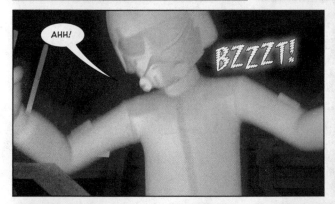

AHH!

BZZZT!

GUESS THERE'S NO TURNING BACK NOW...

NO.

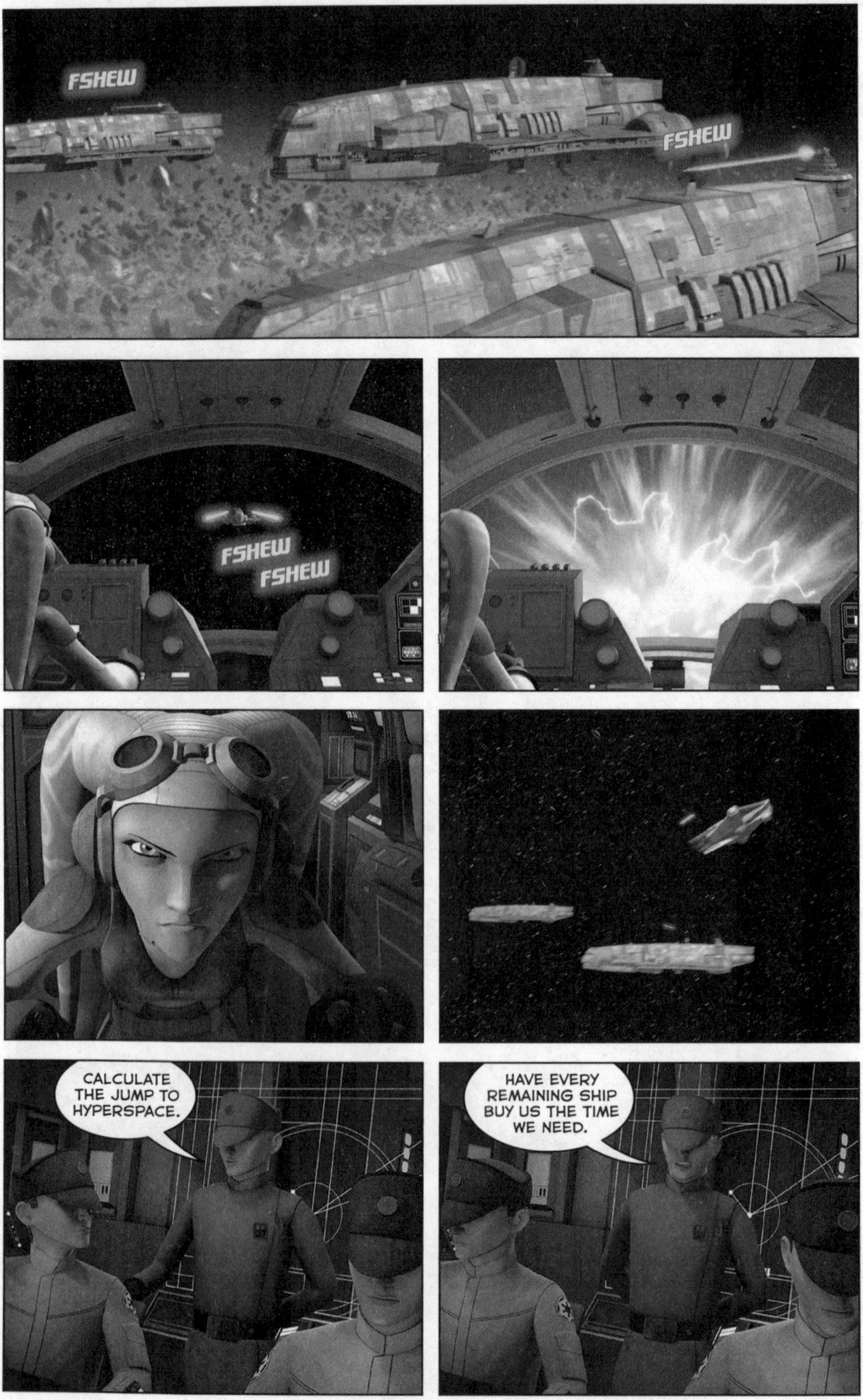
FSHEW
FSHEW
FSHEW
FSHEW
CALCULATE THE JUMP TO HYPERSPACE.
HAVE EVERY REMAINING SHIP BUY US THE TIME WE NEED.

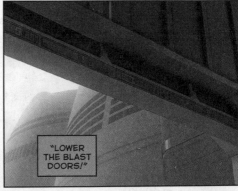

WE ARE UNDER ATTACK, REPEAT, UNDER ATTACK.

"LOWER THE BLAST DOORS!"

LOOK! DO SOMETHING!

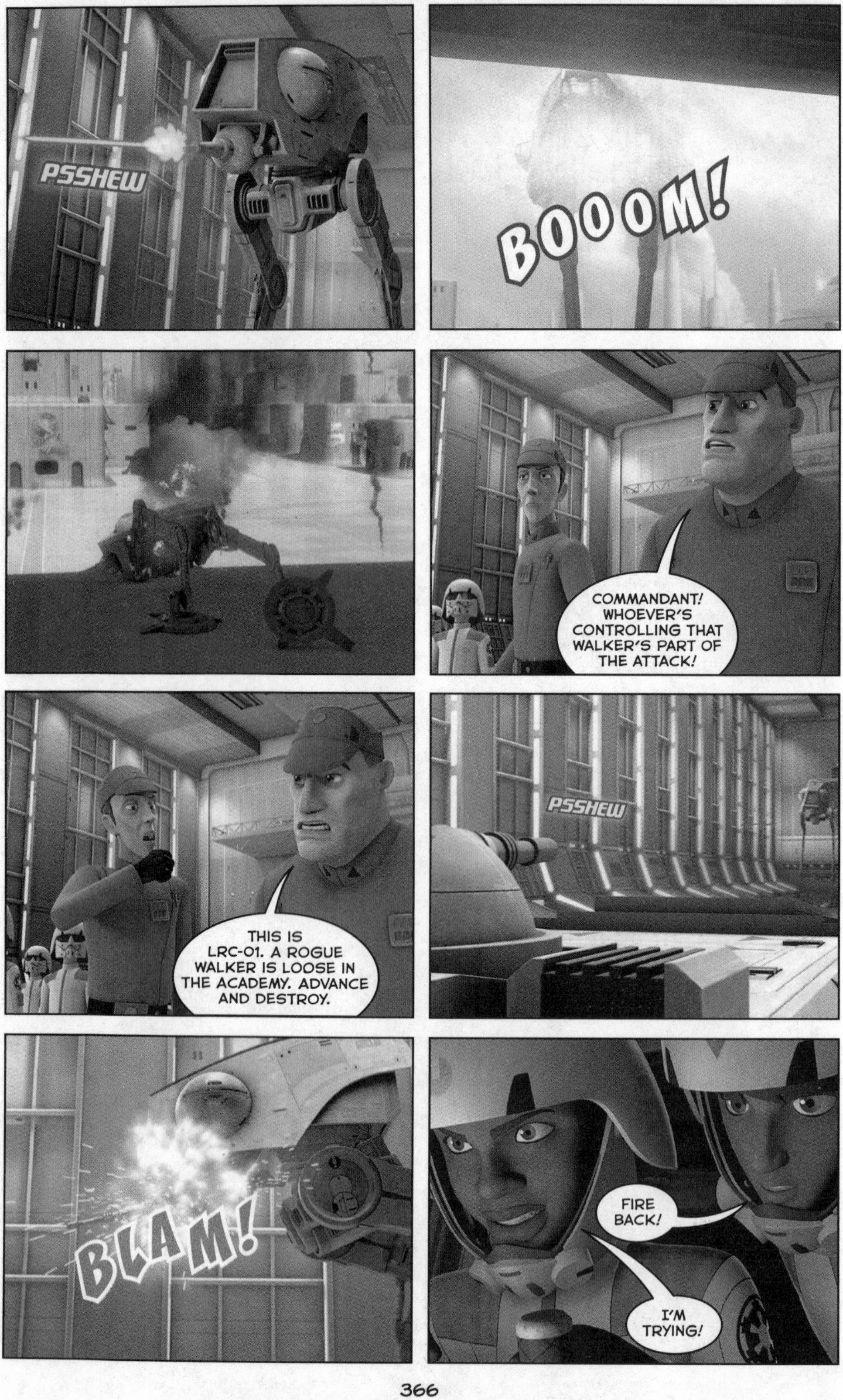
PSSHEW
BOOOM!
COMMANDANT! WHOEVER'S CONTROLLING THAT WALKER'S PART OF THE ATTACK!
THIS IS LRC-01. A ROGUE WALKER IS LOOSE IN THE ACADEMY. ADVANCE AND DESTROY.
PSSHEW
BLAM!
FIRE BACK!
I'M TRYING!

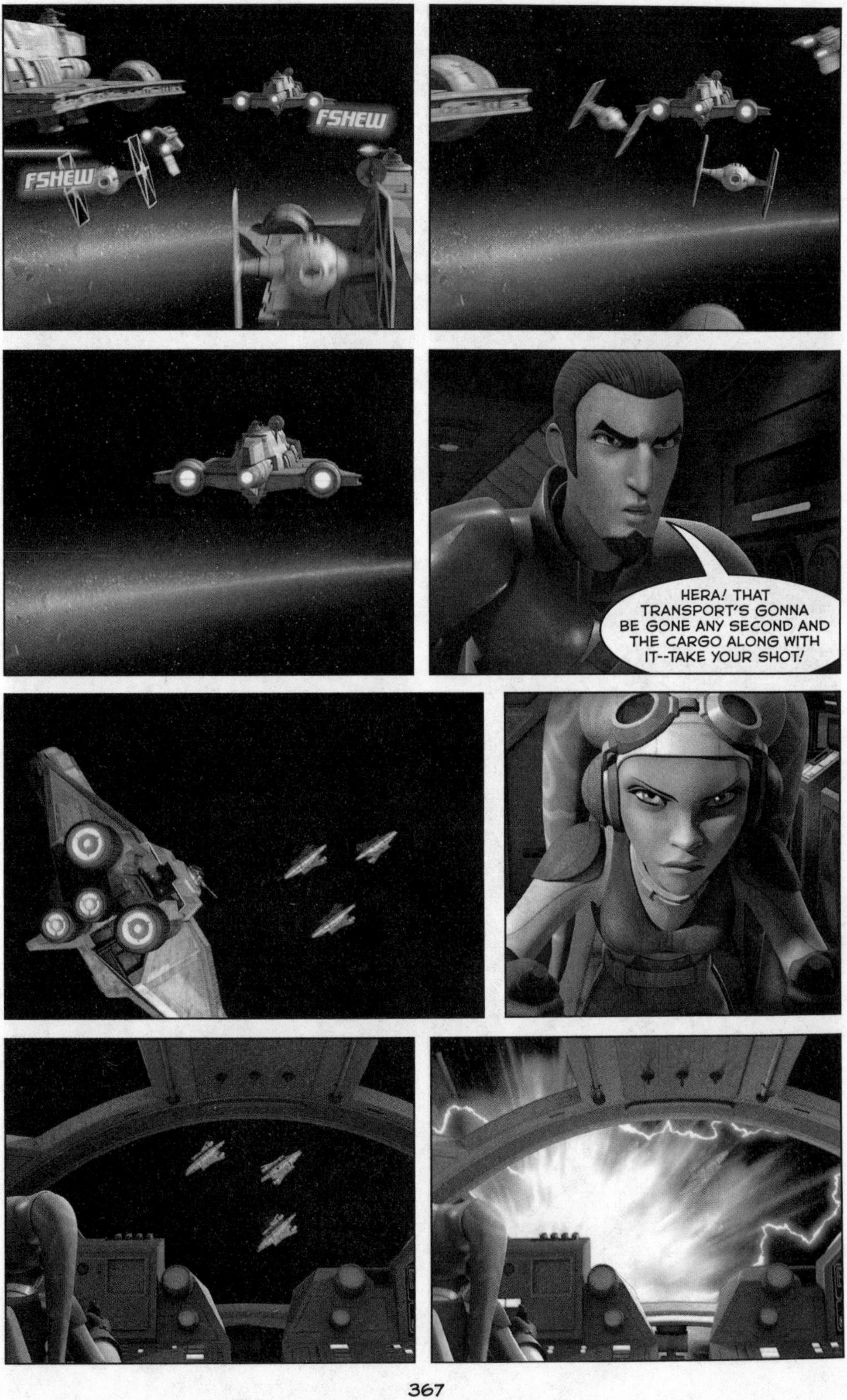
FSHEW
FSHEW
HERA! THAT TRANSPORT'S GONNA BE GONE ANY SECOND AND THE CARGO ALONG WITH IT--TAKE YOUR SHOT!

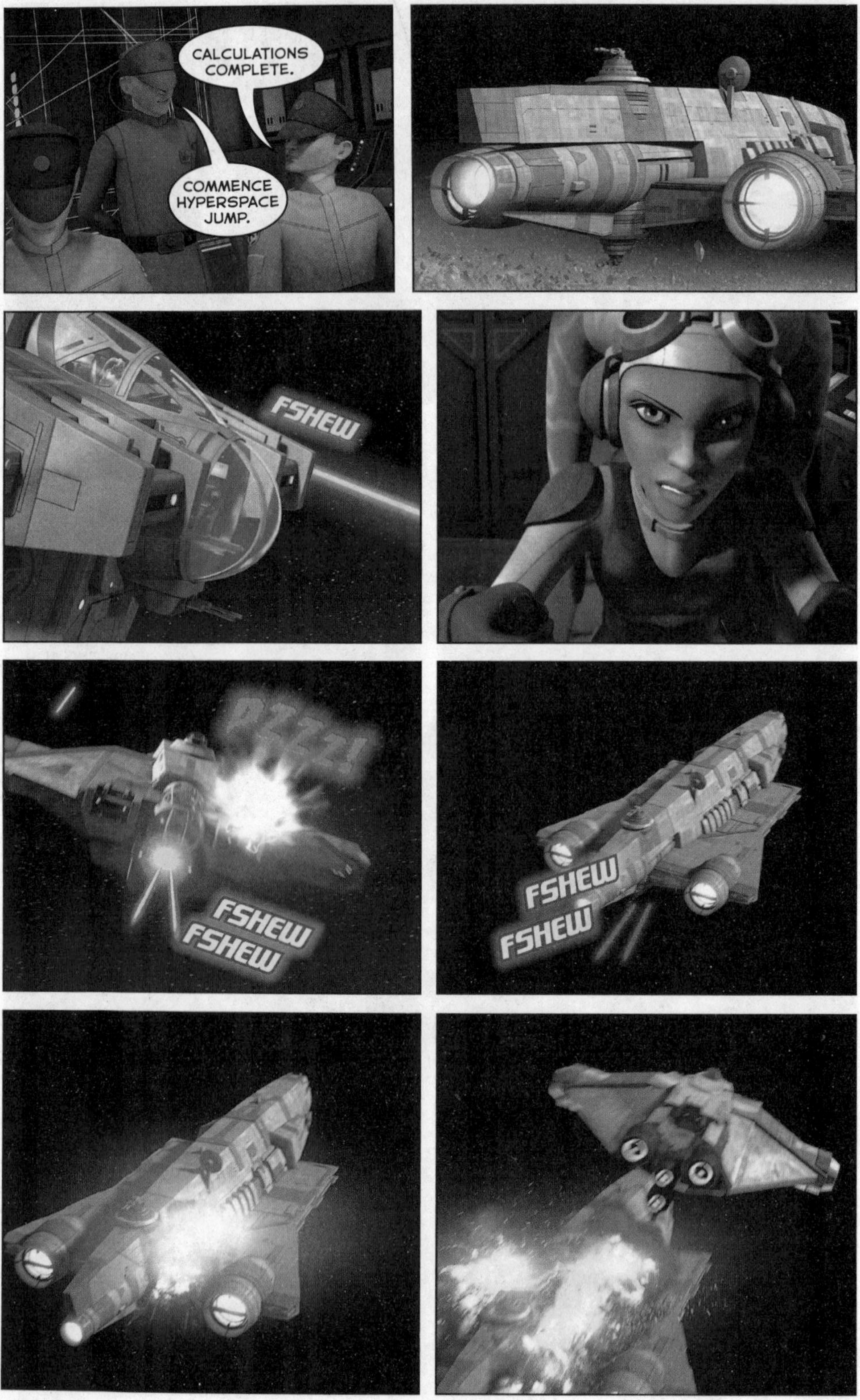
CALCULATIONS COMPLETE.
COMMENCE HYPERSPACE JUMP.
FSHEW
FSHEW
FSHEW
FSHEW
FSHEW

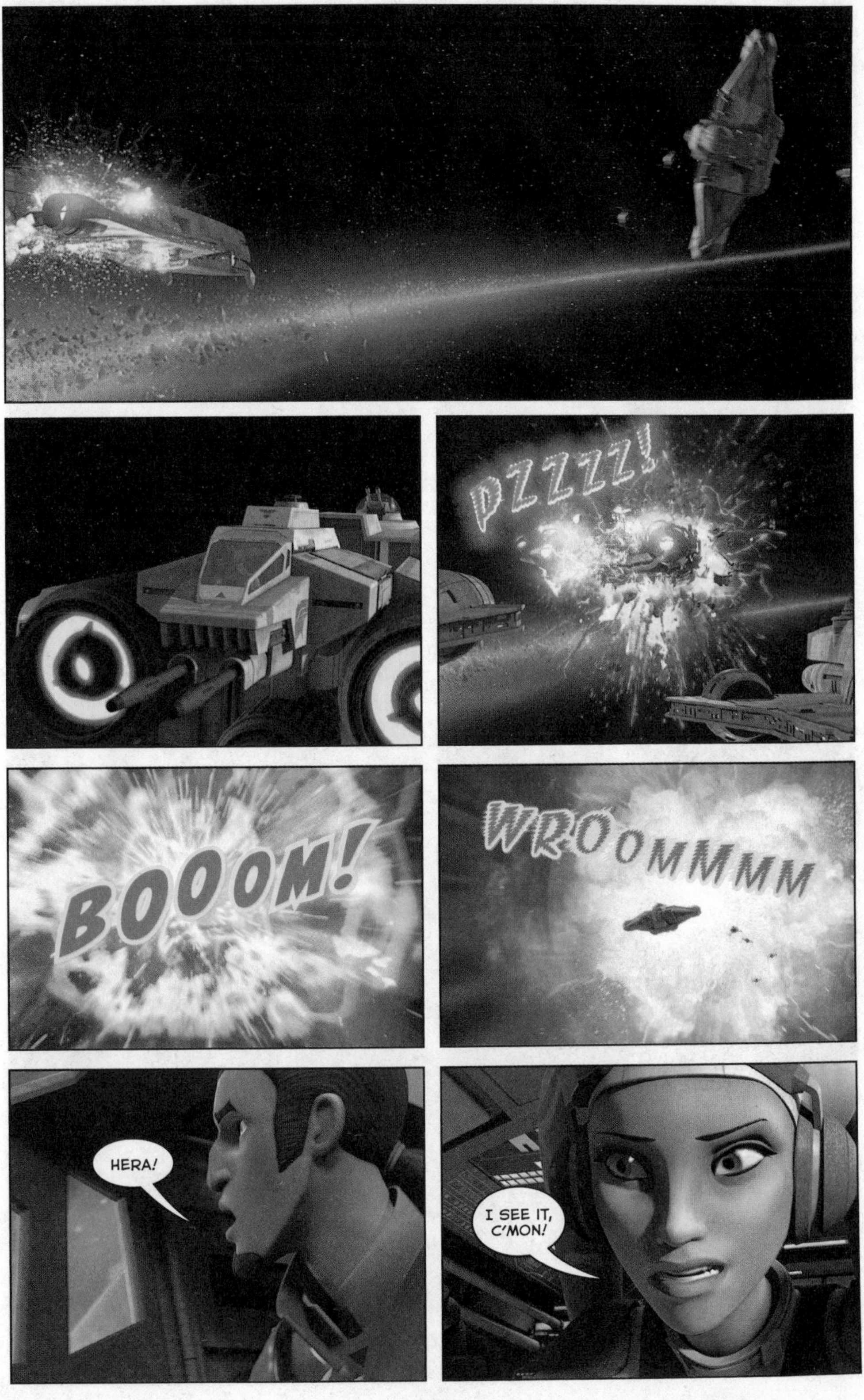
PZZZZ!
BOOOM!
WROOMMMM
HERA!
I SEE IT, C'MON!

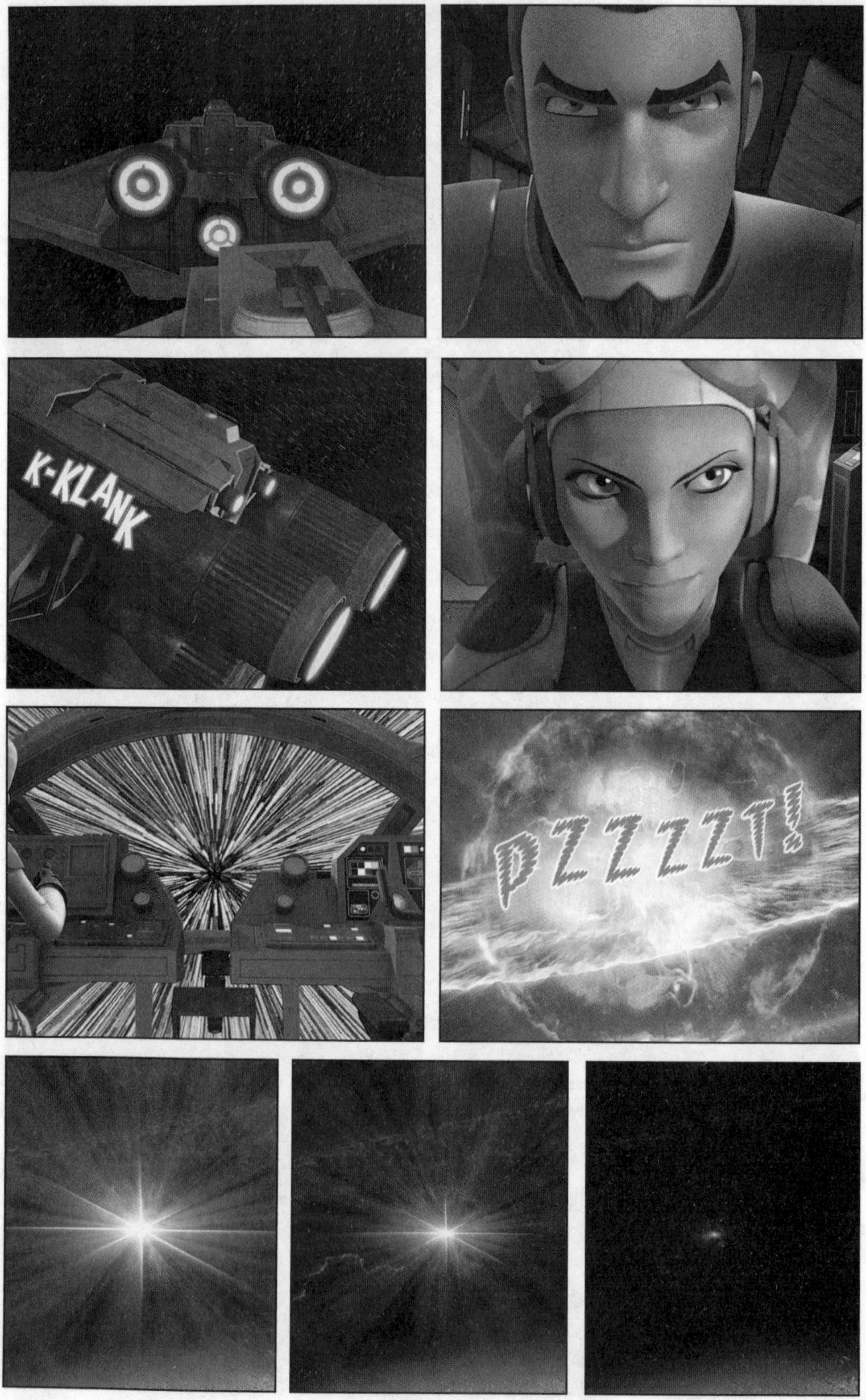
K-KLANK
PZZZZT!

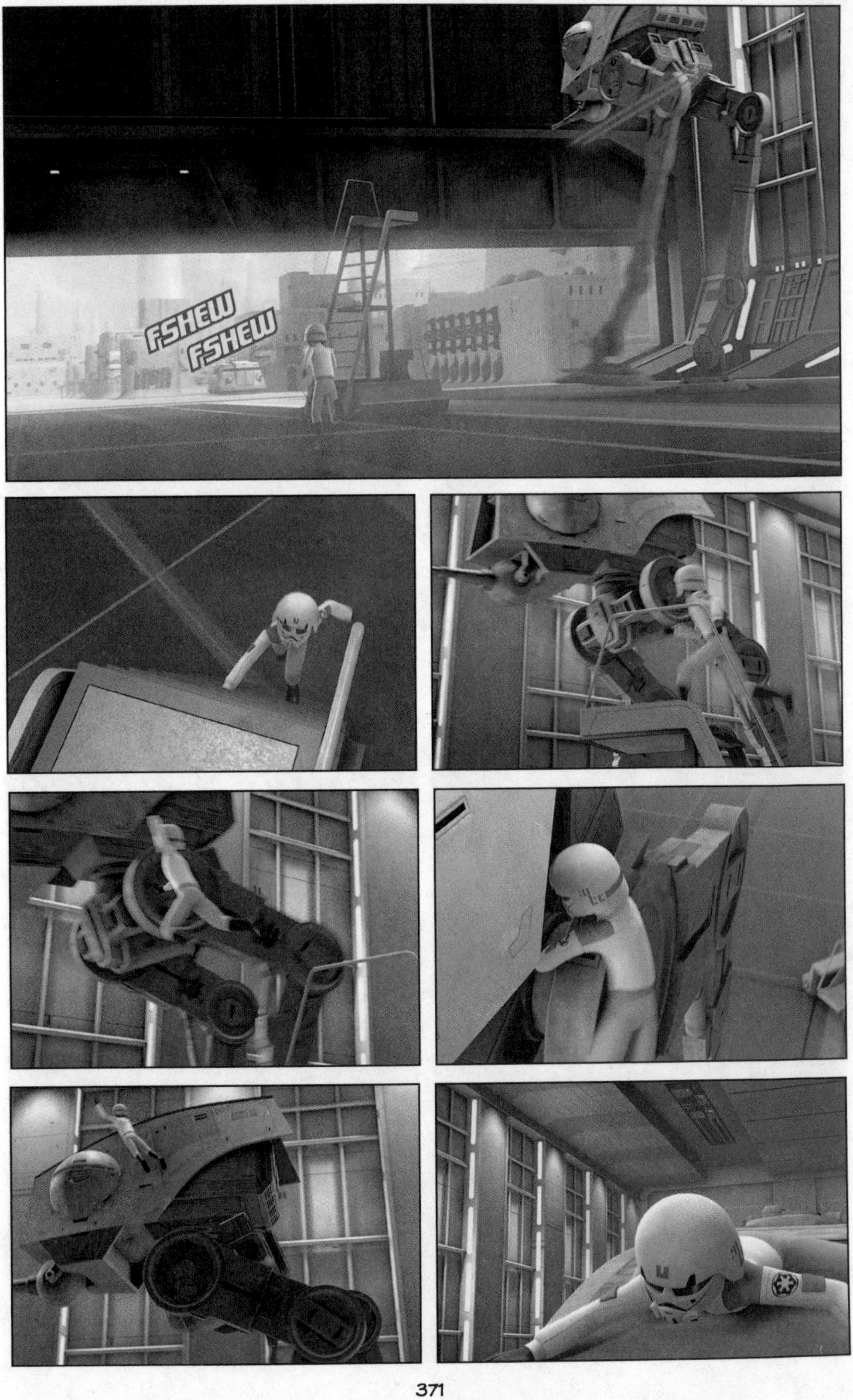
FSHEW
FSHEW

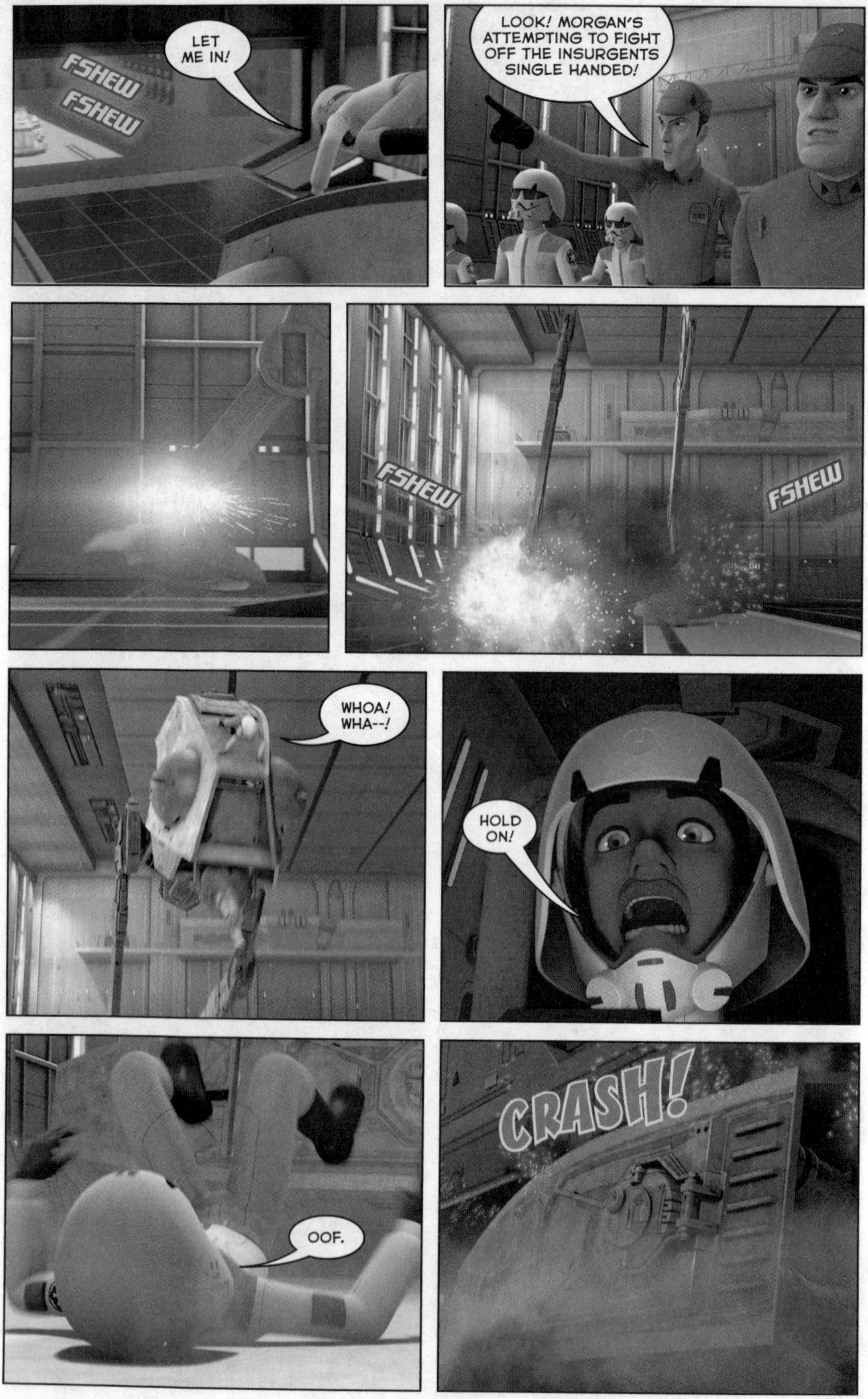
LET ME IN!
FSHEW
FSHEW
LOOK! MORGAN'S ATTEMPTING TO FIGHT OFF THE INSURGENTS SINGLE HANDED!
FSHEW
FSHEW
WHOA! WHA--!
HOLD ON!
OOF.
CRASH!

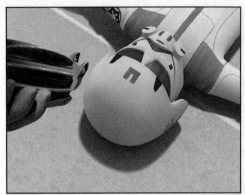

FSHEW

FSHEW

PSSHEW

THANKS.

DON'T MENTION IT.

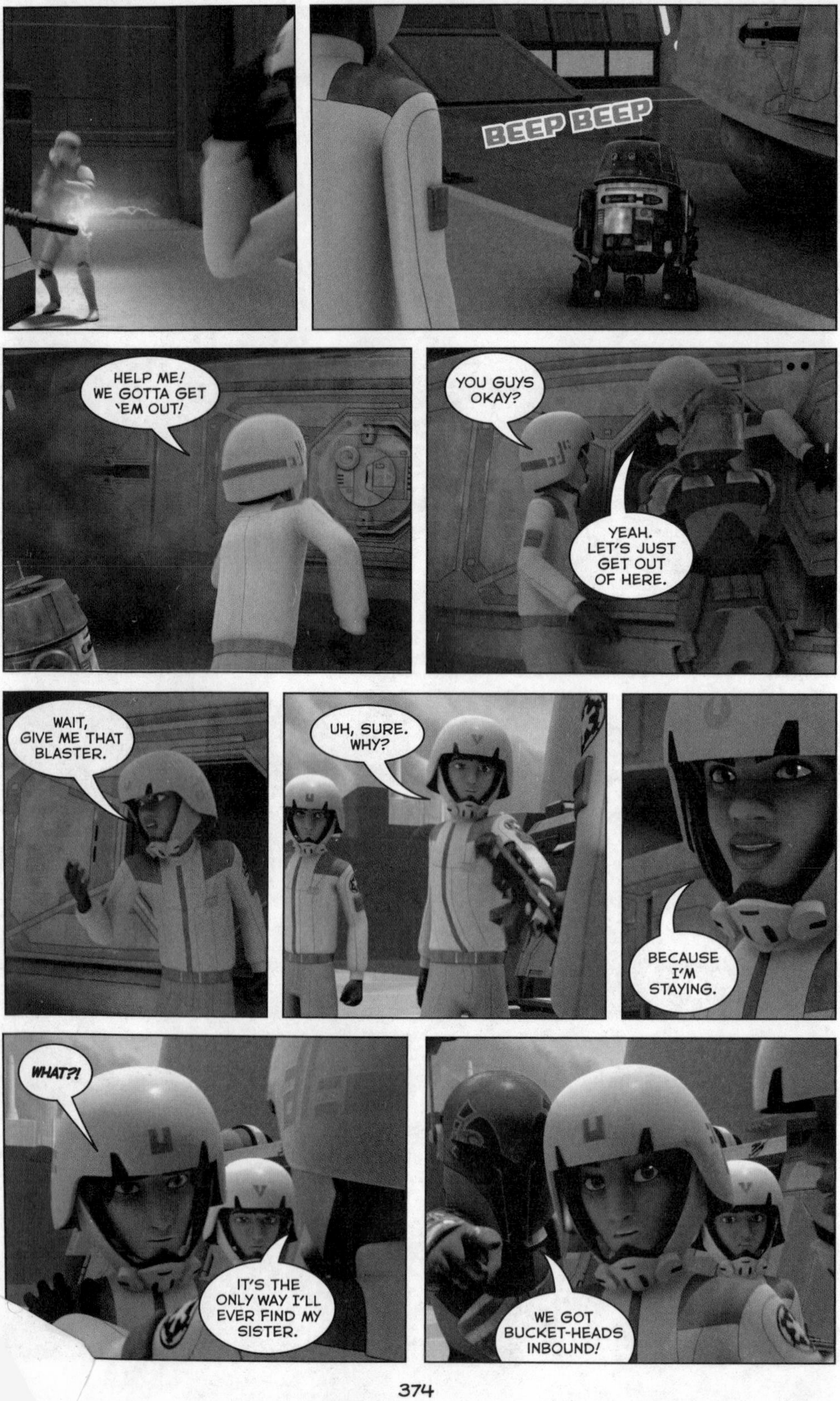
BEEP BEEP
HELP ME! WE GOTTA GET 'EM OUT!
YOU GUYS OKAY?
YEAH. LET'S JUST GET OUT OF HERE.
WAIT, GIVE ME THAT BLASTER.
UH, SURE. WHY?
BECAUSE I'M STAYING.
WHAT?!
IT'S THE ONLY WAY I'LL EVER FIND MY SISTER.
WE GOT BUCKET-HEADS INBOUND!

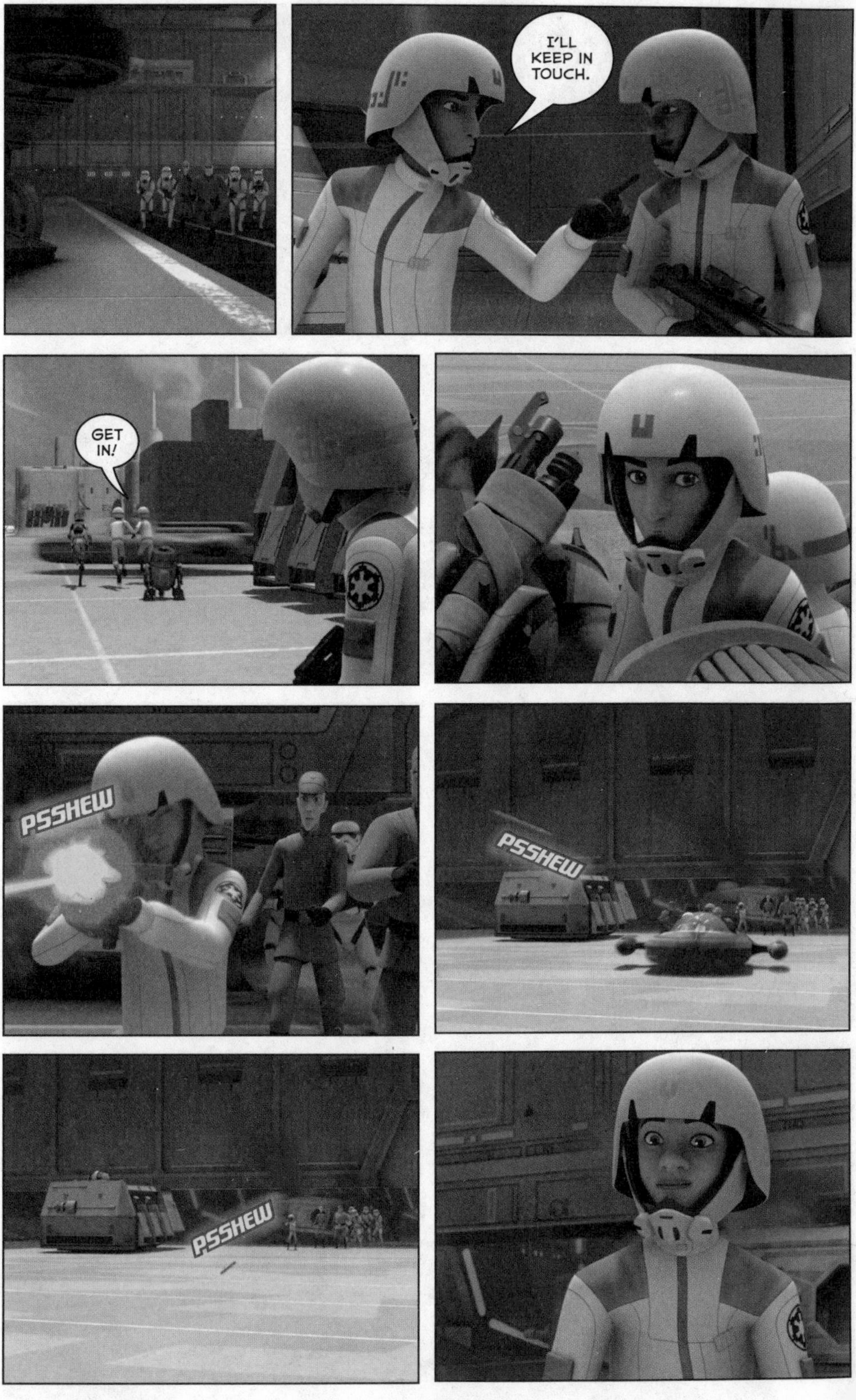
I'LL KEEP IN TOUCH.
GET IN!
PSSHEW
PSSHEW
PSSHEW

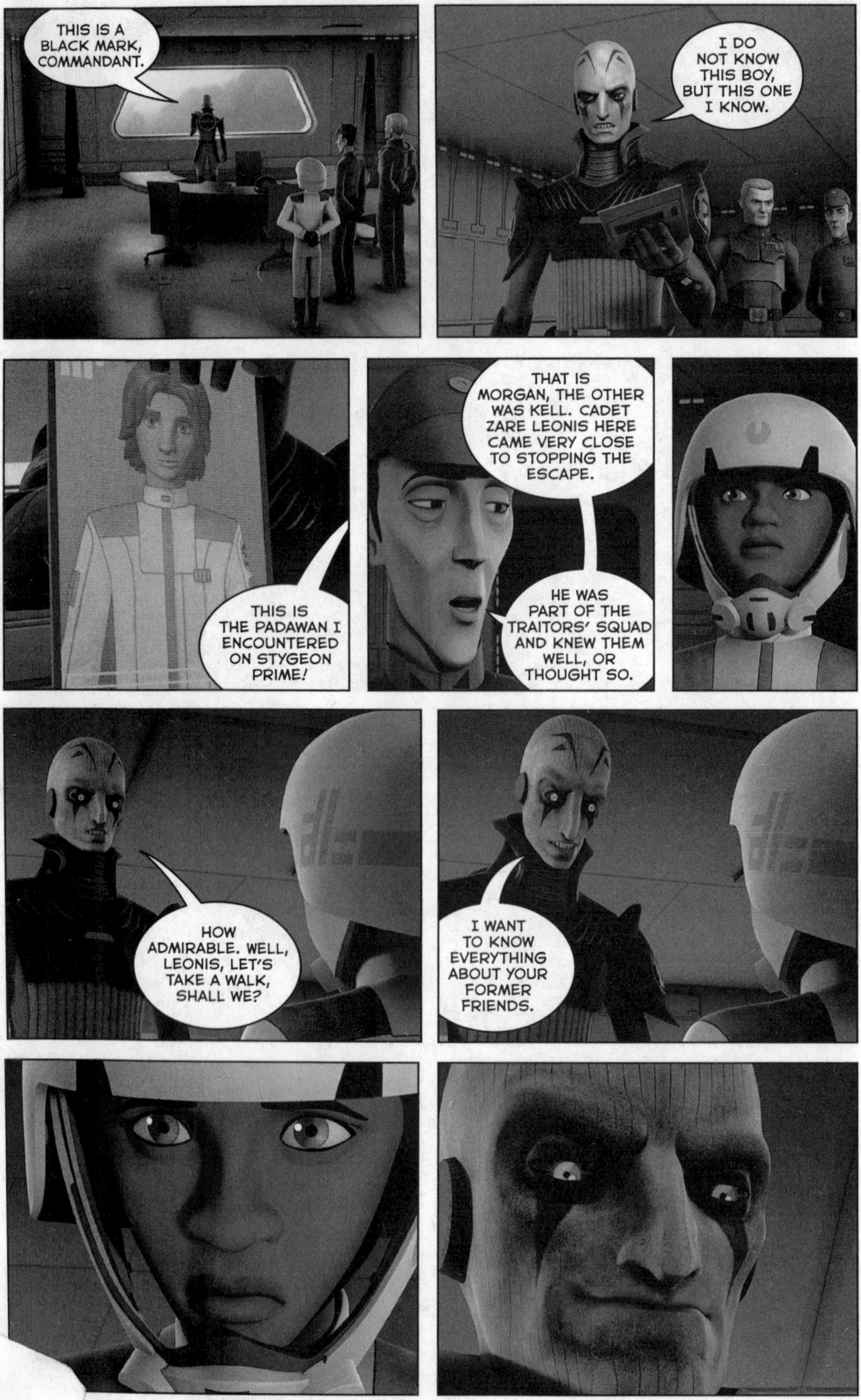
THIS IS A BLACK MARK, COMMANDANT.
I DO NOT KNOW THIS BOY, BUT THIS ONE I KNOW.
THIS IS THE PADAWAN I ENCOUNTERED ON STYGEON PRIME!
THAT IS MORGAN, THE OTHER WAS KELL. CADET ZARE LEONIS HERE CAME VERY CLOSE TO STOPPING THE ESCAPE.
HE WAS PART OF THE TRAITORS' SQUAD AND KNEW THEM WELL, OR THOUGHT SO.
HOW ADMIRABLE. WELL, LEONIS, LET'S TAKE A WALK, SHALL WE?
I WANT TO KNOW EVERYTHING ABOUT YOUR FORMER FRIENDS.

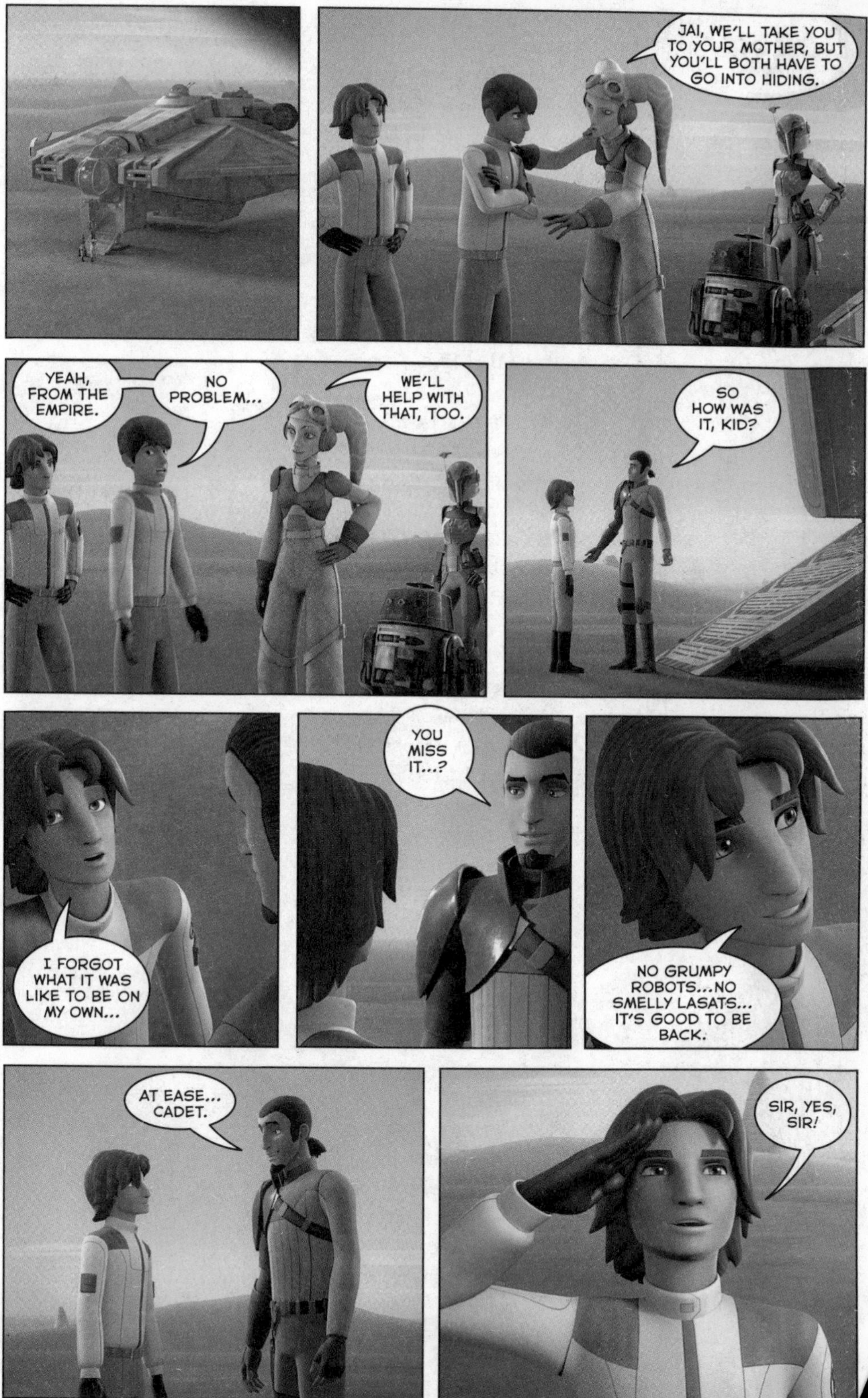
JAI, WE'LL TAKE YOU TO YOUR MOTHER, BUT YOU'LL BOTH HAVE TO GO INTO HIDING.
YEAH, FROM THE EMPIRE.
NO PROBLEM...
WE'LL HELP WITH THAT, TOO.
SO HOW WAS IT, KID?
I FORGOT WHAT IT WAS LIKE TO BE ON MY OWN...
YOU MISS IT...?
NO GRUMPY ROBOTS...NO SMELLY LASATS... IT'S GOOD TO BE BACK.
AT EASE... CADET.
SIR, YES, SIR!

CREDITS

Spark of Rebellion
Supervising Director: Dave Filoni
Directors: Steward Lee, Steven G. Lee
Producer: Kiri Hart
Associate Producer: Carrie Beck
Produced by: Athena Yvette Portillo
Written by: Dave Filoni, Simon Kinberg

Droids in Distress
Supervising Director: Dave Filoni
Director: Steward Lee
Producer: Kiri Hart
Associate Producer: Carrie Beck
Produced by: Athena Yvette Portillo
Written by: Dave Filoni, Greg Weisman

Fighter Flight
Supervising Director: Dave Filoni
Director: Steven G. Lee
Producer: Kiri Hart
Associate Producer: Carrie Beck
Produced by: Athena Yvette Portillo
Written by: Dave Filoni, Kevin Hopps

Rise of the Old Masters
Supervising Director: Dave Filoni
Director: Steward Lee
Producer: Kiri Hart
Associate Producer: Carrie Beck
Produced by: Athena Yvette Portillo
Written by: Henry Gilroy

Breaking Ranks
Supervising Director: Dave Filoni
Director: Steven G. Lee
Producer: Kiri Hart
Associate Producer: Carrie Beck
Produced by: Athena Yvette Portillo
Written by: Greg Weisman